THE DISCOVERER

JAN KJÆRSTAD is one of Norway's most acclaimed writers. His trilogy *The Seducer*, *The Conqueror* and *The Discoverer* (Arcadia) has achieved huge international success and won him the prestigious Nordic Council Prize, Scandinavia's highest literary honour.

BARBARA J. HAVELAND has translated works by several leading Danish and Norwegian authors incuding Peter Høeg, Linn Ullmann and Leif Davidsen.

THE DISCOVERER

Jan Kjærstad

Translated from the Norwegian by Barbara J. Haveland

Arcadia Books Ltd
15–16 Nassau Street
London w1w 7ab

www.arcadiabooks.co.uk

First published in the United Kingdom in 2009
Originally published H. Aschehoug & Co., Oslo as *Oppdageren* 1999

ISBN 978-1-905147-36-6

Typeset in Jenson by MacGuru Ltd
Printed in Finland by WS Bookwell

Arcadia Books Ltd gratefully acknowledges the financial support of Norla, Oslo
towards the translation costs of this book.

Arcadia Books supports English PEN, the fellowship of writers who work together to promote
literature and its understanding. English PEN upholds writers' freedoms in Britain and around
the world, challenging political and cultural limits on free expression. To find out more, visit www.
englishpen.org or contact
English PEN, 6-8 Amwell Street, London ECIR IUQ

Arcadia Books distributors are as follows:

in the UK and elsewhere in Europe:
Turnaround Publishers Services
Unit 3, Olympia Trading Estate
Coburg Road
London N22 6TZ

in the US and Canada:
Independent Publishers Group
814 N. Franklin Street
Chicago, IL 60610

in Australia:
Tower Books
PO Box 213
Brookvale, NSW 2100

in New Zealand:
Addenda
PO Box 78224
Grey Lynn
Auckland

in South Africa:
Quartet Sales and Marketing
PO Box 1218
Northcliffe
Johannesburg 2115

Arcadia Books is the *Sunday Times* Small Publisher of the Year

For Martin

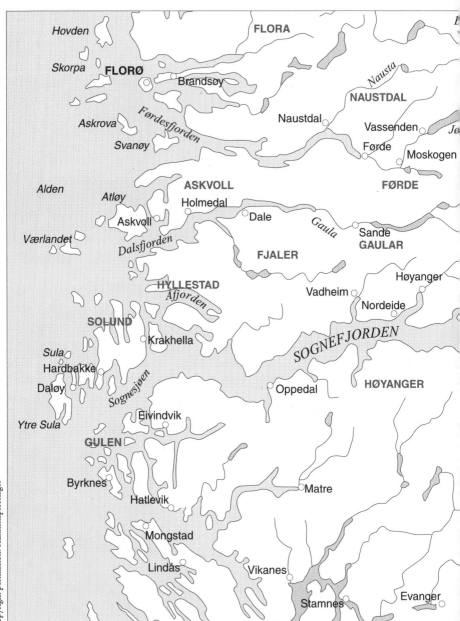

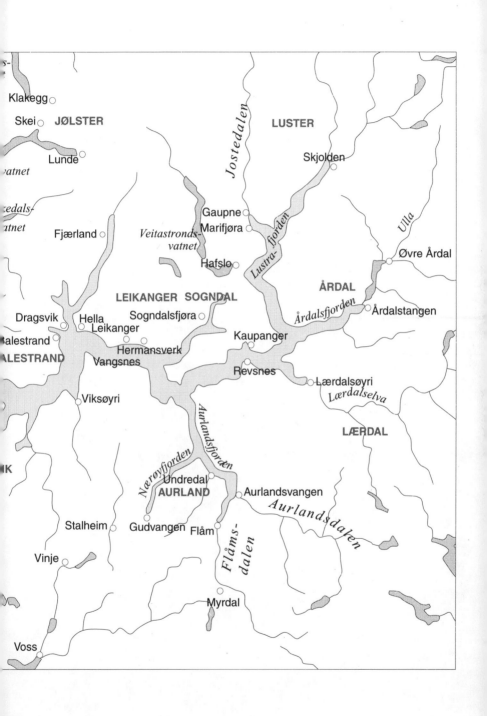

Jupiter

Behold this man. Behold this man, as he feels three tugs on the rope and slowly, after smiling uncertainly, proceeds to traverse, to edge out onto those dauntingly airy galleries. Behold this man as he inches across the rock face; see how with the caution of the novice he feels his way forward using all of his limbs, his whole body in fact, before shifting his weight from one foot to the other. I can sense how frightened, how truly terrified he is, and yet how full of the determination to do this, to see it through, make it to the top. And then, suddenly, as if something has ground to a halt, he freezes. He shuts his eyes. He looks as though he is listening to the wind, while at the same time concentrating hard, trying to place the scent emanating from the rock against which he is pressed. The bright sunlight glitters off the cliff face, sparkles in the runnels of meltwater. As far as I can see he is holding his breath. I have known it all along. This is the moment of truth. On a ledge, with a drop of hundreds of metres into the abyss only a step away. Here you live, or you die.

This is a second I shall remember.

Then he does the one thing I have begged him not to do. He half turns, while apparently hanging on tight with both hands. He looks out. Looks down. As if intent on defying something. Proving something. For a moment he seems to be completely dazzled by the Slingsby glacier far below. Or no, not dazzled, but stunned, panic-stricken. Psyched out, as they say. I refuse to believe it. That this man could be afraid of anything, a man who brought thousands of cars to a halt on Oslo's Town Hall Square and who, by his mere presence, drew a cyclone to himself; a man who has been with three fair maids at once and who would not hesitate to dive to a depth of fifteen metres without an oxygen tank. Yet he hangs there, rigid. Still holding his breath. Or am I wrong? Does he bend down ever so slightly? I think – I know it sounds strange, but I almost believe he is trying to kneel.

One hand fumbles with the knot, as if he means to undo himself from the rope. 'Sit!' I call sharply. 'Don't look down.' But he goes on staring, seeming more mesmerised than frightened now. Or infuriated perhaps, contemptuous. As if this were a set-to with Norway itself, a confrontation for which he has waited years – to stand on the edge of an abyss, without a safety net. I can see temptation written large on his face. He could let himself fall. He could realise the cliché which will forever be attached to his story: that of his downfall. The final, glorious headline.

'You're perfectly safe,' I shout. 'It's all in your head.' I'm jittery too now, I check that the coil of rope is securely fixed around the sharp rock next to me. I know I can trust Martin, who has led the way, hammering in pitons at regular intervals, and is now out of sight behind some large boulders, a short rope-length from the bottom of the chimney. Martin has climbed everything from the Bonatti pillar to Ama Dablam. But never with such a partner, a man who – according to the newspapers – lost his head and shot a woman straight through the heart. I am uneasy. The uncertainty of the figure huddled against the rock face radiates towards me. I may have miscalculated. Perhaps I should have said no after all. Then he turns to me. His face is calm. I can see that he is breathing, drawing the cool mountain air deep into his lungs, hungrily. He smiles, even raises his hand in a wave, traverses onwards.

Behold this man. Behold this man, the bearer of a mystery.

The rest of the climb went well, remarkably well. Down by the stone cottage at Bandet earlier that day I had been worried. A couple of times on the way up the ridge, on the toughest, most exposed stretch, I had considered turning back. I could see that he was gasping for breath, he looked a little lightheaded. The air was keen and thin. Over one stretch we secured our passage with a length of rope – mainly for his sake – and when we started climbing again he dislodged a rock which went clattering down the mountainside, leaving a whiff of gunpowder behind it. An omen. His fleece clothes and the harness made him look like a child – truly, in this situation, like a helpless child. And, funnily enough, *I* felt responsible for *him*.

'Aren't you a little afraid of heights?' I had asked him when we set out from Turtagrø that morning.

'I used to be. I'm a different person now,' he said.

We reached Hjørnet – the Corner, slipped off our rucksacks. It was early in the season, and there was more snow than I was used to. Wetter and dirtier. We wouldn't be able to switch to climbing shoes. It went fine, though, with no great problems – even over the few metres of real climbing up the Heftyes Renne, transformed now into a chill, slippery, icy chimney.

We reached the top around midday. I shall never forget the look of triumph on his face, the way he stretched his arms up and out. To the spring sky. All those years inside. Down. And now, only a couple of years after that first intoxicating taste of freedom: on the roof of Norway. Right at the very top. Everything below us seemed much lower, markedly so. I heard him murmur, partly to us, partly to himself: 'I never thought I would make it.' And a moment later: 'But I knew I had it in me.'

We sat down beside the little cairn. He studied the commemorative plaque fixed to the stone as if expecting to find his name inscribed there. There too. I took the landscape shots I needed. He said not a word, just sat there looking at the view, could not seem to get enough of this, the most spectacular panorama in Norway. The massive Jostedal Glacier, Galdhøpiggen and Glittertind and all the other peaks of Jotunheimen. Alpine forms with peaks and crests, carved and gouged out by the ice. 'Organ pipes,' he muttered suddenly. 'This has to be the world's biggest organ, listen to the wind!' From the massif on which we sat, two jagged ridges wound off like petrified vertebrae. 'What are they?' he asked. 'Kjerringa og Mannen,' I said – the Woman and the Man – and instantly regretted it. A strange look came over his face.

Behold this man.

We prepared for the downward journey. Just as I was wondering how he was going to cope with the abseiling, he turned the wrong way, towards the sheer drop to Skagadalen. I was about to call out, but the cry stuck in my throat. He stretched his arms out to the sides, as if about to do a swallow dive.

Why did he do it?

One has to start somewhere, and a good, not to say almost perfect, departure point – or even, to stick with the climbing motif: viewpoint – from which to examine Jonas Wergeland's life would be another stony edifice, another gallery, a hallowed hall, a room with walls of granite, and an autumn day in the 1980s – an autumn day which would bring with it deep sorrow and wistful joy, as well as a strange mystery, an incident bordering on the scandalous. Nor is it entirely inappropriate that Jonas should be at the organ, an instrument befitting his history and the power which for so long he had exerted over the minds, not to say the souls, of the Norwegian people. Jonas Wergeland is playing the organ, framed by its gleaming, monumental face, making the whole church tremble with his playing, making the very stone, the bedrock of Norway, sing. He is not an organist, but he handles the instrument almost like a professional musician; he is an organist by nature, he might have been made for this part, this pose. No wonder he once replied when asked, in Samarkand, what he did for a living: 'I am an organist.'

Scarcely an hour earlier, after collecting a pile of sheet music, he had closed the gate of the house he would soon be moving into and which people would dub Villa Wergeland, and set off down the road he had walked every day of his childhood. Wherever he turned his eye he risked becoming lost in memories: a life-threatening bonfire, the windows Ivan broke, the wallet in the ditch which brought him a heaven-sent fifty *krone*-reward, the magnetic, nipple-shaped doorbell on the front door of Anne Beate Corneliussen's building. He sauntered along, wishing to prolong the poignant aspect of the moment. There was a strange mood in the air too. It felt as though there was no longer anyone living in the houses he passed. Even the shops looked deserted. It was an exceptionally dull day. Damp. The last leaves had fallen from the trees. The ground was covered with an indeterminate gunge, as if after an incredibly drunken party. The blocks of flats and the shopping centre reminded him of Eastern Europe, the Soviet Union. The whole of life seemed suddenly drab and dreary. And yet – in spite of all this – he felt hopeful. As if he knew that behind all the greyness lay something else, something surprising. Something is about to happen, he told himself.

As his eye was drawn to a couple of solitary clusters of rowan berries, two rosy, bright spots in all the greyness, he found himself thinking of another grey day in his life. The year before, off his own bat, he had gone to Moscow with a friend and colleague from the NRK purchasing department who was attending a television conference there. They had stayed at the Hotel Ukraine, one of Stalin's seven so-called 'wedding-cake' buildings from the fifties, all of which looked like squat, bulky versions of the Empire State Building. One morning he had crossed the grey River Moscow, meaning to walk to the Kremlin. Ahead of him lay Kalinina Avenue, broad and surprisingly empty-looking, despite the cars. The weather was clear, but a haze still managed to leach everything of colour. The distances seemed enormous, and almost in order to escape from those vast, empty spaces thick with the fumes from low-octane petrol, he took a right turn which led him into some narrower streets. Here he found more people. Women in headscarves, carrying baskets. And there *were* queues. Two in one short stretch. For eggs, perhaps, he thought. Or toilet paper? To these people, even the magazines he had bought at Fornebu airport, with their glossy adverts, would be objects as rare as rocks from the moon. He walked along, looking and looking, trying to take in the dreariness around him. Brown, grey, black. Hulking, homogenous buildings. Everything covered in a thin layer of grime. He fancied that he was wandering through a sort of populated desert. Always, when he came to a new place, he went exploring. As a small boy he had transformed every house he visited into an unknown continent. He was a Columbus, stepping ashore. The threshold was a beach. The hallway a jungle, the stairs a mountain, every cupboard a cave. But Moscow: so gloomy, so dispiritingly vast. This was obviously not a city one simply strolled through. Best be getting back, he thought, before I am engulfed by all this greyness.

The problem was, however, that he no longer knew where he was. And as if that weren't enough, he desperately needed to go to the toilet. He cursed his bad habit of drinking too much coffee at lunchtime, while casting about in hopes of finding some building that was open to the public. He fell in with a stream of people who seemed to have been caught by a current and were being swept towards a façade with a large M over the doors. He had always liked the letter M, took this to be a good omen. He was not prepared, however, for the sight which met his eyes, for the way the stony desert gave way to a shimmering oasis.

In his mind he was in Moscow, in reality he was approaching Grorud shopping centre, casting a nostalgic glance in the direction of Wolfgang Michaelsen's garden where every autumn as boys they had gone scrumping for glossy, green apples so juicy and so sweet that they even merited running the risk of the Michaelsens' Rottweiler getting loose. There was a slight haze in the air, the sort of autumn mist that quickens the senses and which, rather than concealing things, seemed to bring them closer, even things that were a long way off. Chet Baker weather, he thought to himself. He felt nervous. Before him lay a sight which triggered memories of childhood theatricals, packed gym halls. The fluttering in his stomach might otherwise have been attributed to his own misgivings, a dawning sense of having come to a dead end. In his life. The problem had to do with his work at NRK TV. He was an announcer, and popular. And yet he wasn't happy. He did not understand it. At some point in his life he had abandoned all of the goals he had set for himself as a youth. He had thrown in the towel halfway through a course in architecture, having previously dropped out of a course in astrophysics. By chance – and not really caring one way or the other – he had allowed himself to be led into a tiny television studio. For many years he had been more than happy with his good fortune, with having found a job where he could do so little, and yet, it appeared, mean so much to so many. But now it seemed that an old ambition was once more stirring. Something he had forgotten. Wanted to forget. His conscience still pricked him. He caught himself looking for a loophole, a way out, a way forward. Which may have been why now, on this day especially, despite his sense of confusion, he suddenly felt optimistic. He had a strong feeling that something awaited him. That it was only minutes away. That something, a curtain, would be pulled back and something else, he did not know what, would be revealed.

As in Moscow. Because, when he penetrated beyond the grey façade with the steel M over the doors it was like stepping into the foyer of a theatre. As though someone up in the flies had dropped a richly hued stage set into place right before his very eyes. He walked along broad, brightly lit corridors, gazing round about him in disbelief; found a toilet without any problem. He had always set a lot of store by mazes and the possibilities these presented. You set out to sail to India, and wind up instead on an unknown continent. You go looking for a toilet and stumble upon a metro station, a veritable treasure house. He seized his chance, followed the crowd, popped a five *kopek* coin in the slot and passed through the barrier. Moments later he was being transported down into the bowels of the earth on the steepest, longest escalator he had ever ridden, a wooden one, at that; then he found himself in a vast, glittering white chamber hung with magnificent chandeliers. A sunken palace. He was Alice in Wonderland, the victim of a supernatural occurrence. He took the hall in which he found himself for a glittering ballroom until a train came rushing in and stopped right in front of him.

Out of sheer curiosity he hopped on, only to alight at the next station – Plostsjad Revoljutsii, he later learned: Revolution Square. It was like entering a museum. The station concourse was full of bronze sculptures. As far as he could tell, they represented the different trades. He was about to take a closer look at a statue of a sailor when he almost bumped into a shabby-looking character sweeping the floor. The man stopped, leaned on his brush and examined Jonas. The look he gave him contrasted sharply with his down-at-heel appearance. Keen eyes studied the small Norwegian flag which Jonas was wearing in his lapel while in Moscow, a badge intended to serve much the same purpose as the tag on a dog collar: indicating which embassy to contact were he to collapse in the street. The cleaner stood for a while staring into space, as if deep in thought. Then: 'Gustav Vigeland,' he said at length, extending his arms to the statues round about them. Jonas nodded. There were certain similarities. 'Gustav Vigeland,' he responded. These two words pretty much said it all. Forged a bond between them. Encapsulated a whole story. Or so Jonas thought, until the Russian leaned towards him: 'Fascism!' he hissed, pointing eloquently at the sculptures. Jonas smiled uncertainly, tried to nod politely before continuing his tour. This man could easily be a professor of art, he thought, but now here he is, sweeping railway platforms for holding certain incorrect opinions on art.

Jonas was right underneath Red Square, but he was not interested in taking the escalator up, out. Why see Lenin's tomb when he could see this? He wanted to stay down here in this brilliantly illuminated secret. Here, in Moscow, they had built their sculpture parks underground. Jonas wandered on and off trains for hours, endeavouring to see as many stations as possible. A subterranean grand tour, he thought to himself. Proof that man had evolved beyond the caveman stage. He strolled through halls faced with every sort of polished stone, a genuine geological museum. Everything was spotlessly clean. Jonas walked upon gleaming tiles, down colonnades, amid copper and steel, surveying all manner of ornamentation: mosaics, reliefs, stained glass, statues of pilots and scientists. All of this decoration sprang from the ideal of bringing art to the people. He thought of his brother's favourite writer, Agnar Mykle: 'Socialism is clean bodies and classical music in the factories.' And art in the metro stations, Jonas might have added. During his visit, Jonas came across nothing that told him more about the Soviet state and, not least, its part in the last war. He had seen something like this before: the Town Hall in Oslo. He went on walking and thinking, considering. What, today, was the greatest public space? Might it not be television, the box, the square common to all. In other words: wasn't that the place for art – in palaces of a sort, beamed into people's living rooms?

After a while he began to discover crossover points between lines, eventually he even found one line that ran in a circle. He would have liked to stay down there for days, becoming part of the network, until he realised that he had reached Kievskaja station, a short step from his hotel. Later he would study the patterns on the onion domes of St Basil's Cathedral and visit the Kremlin with all its undreamt-of treasures; he would see monasteries and churches with incandescent icons and glittering domes, but for Jonas Wergeland nothing could compare with what he had experienced, the sights he had seen, in the underground: a maze of sunken palaces. 'In Moscow,' he would later say, 'I learned that sometimes you have to go down into the depths in order to see the light.'

As he left Grorud station behind him, something told him that the Moscow experience was about to repeat itself, that something which had until now lain hidden awaited him. His current job with NRK was also the happy outcome of a story about going astray. In many ways it was the tale of needing the loo and making, therefore, a bit of a detour only, when all but sitting on the toilet, to be offered the chance to fill a vacancy. Now, though, he suspected that there was a sequel to this story, that his job as an announcer was merely the first – possibly dull – stage along a path that might almost have been said to lead to sunken palaces.

This suspicion was confirmed a moment later when he pushed open the main door of the church and that lofty room lay before him, suddenly much warmer, much brighter, much richer in scents and sensations than before. Myrrh, the thought flashed through his mind. Like a child in Sunday school, sticking goldfish onto a drawing of a fishing net in a book. Like Christmas Eve, he thought, in the days when the church was still a place filled with anticipation, with swelling organ music and coloured light from stained-glass windows. In the days before anyone told you there was no God.

Jonas Wergeland was playing the organ. Or rather: not playing, but weaving, playing Johann Sebastian Bach, causing transparent worlds to pour from the organ casing, causing a succession of veils to drop down over the lofty room. His thoughts flew in all directions. Forward in time. Back in time. Often, on his way home from school or from piano lessons he had popped into the church, where his father was the organist. On a couple of occasions

– during serious crises in his life – he had lain on the red carpet in front of the altar, feeling as though he were dead. Then his father had played, usually fugues, and he had walked out again like a soul resurrected. To Jonas it seemed that his father played life into him. Blew life into a dead thing. 'This is a control centre,' his father had said, pointing to the instrument's complicated keyboard. Jonas was more inclined to call it a rescue centre. He did not think of his father as an organist, but as a lifesaver. Maybe that was why, at an early age, he decided that this was what he, too, would be.

Jonas Wergeland sat on the organ bench in the church of his childhood, playing, weaving music into being, weaving thoughts into being, smiling as he pictured his mother's horrified face, the look that met him when, as a boy, he shot up from the bottom of the bath gulping for air. She never spotted Daniel – a reassuring element – until it was too late. His brother would be perched on the toilet seat in the corner with the stopwatch they used when they went skating or lay in front of the radio listening to broadcasts of various sporting championships, as if they did not trust the lap times and final results quoted by the commentators.

'Blast!' Daniel always exclaimed, in dismay and delight – heedless of his mother's stricken expression. 'He flippin' well did it again. A minute and a half.'

'You owe me five *krone*,' Jonas would gasp, his face tinged with blue, not altogether unlike the image of Krishna in Indian paintings.

Åse Hansen, normally the most even-tempered member of the family, remarkable for her stoic composure even when Rakel did not come home from parties or some ill-mannered relative ruined a Christmas dinner, was for a long time worried sick every time Jonas sneaked off to the bathroom and she heard the water start to run. It played merry hell with her nerves to know that if she peeked round the door she would see her son lying at the bottom of a full bathtub, holding his breath until his lungs screamed for oxygen. One day, when she could no longer turn a blind eye, she flung open the door just as Jonas's head burst to the surface, with him coughing and spluttering from all the water he had swallowed. She gave him a telling off, asked him why on earth he was doing this.

'I'm practising,' he wheezed.

'For what?'

'To save lives.'

Well, there was really no arguing with that. His mother sniffed some remark or other and closed the door, not knowing whether to laugh or cry. But Jonas was in deadly earnest. Ahead of him lay a summer during which he would establish his goal in life. He practised with all the perseverance of the perfectionist. And he became very good.

Some people go through life without sparing the most profound existential questions more than an occasional heavy sigh. They want simply to live. Not to live for anything. For them it is enough just to scrape some money together, to seduce someone. And if that doesn't do it, you can always go parachuting. To what extent such people are fortunate is not something we will go into here, because Jonas Wergeland belonged to another branch of humanity, to that group who from a very early age, possibly a little too early, begin to reflect on the purpose and the meaning of life. Jonas found this question as obscure as it was, for Daniel, crystal-clear: as far as his older brother was concerned the whole point of life was to be the best. At everything, no matter what. Daniel belonged to that category of Norwegian who from the moment they were born seemed intent on dedicating their lives to proving the truth of Gro Harlem Brundtland's later assertion that 'it is typically Norwegian to be good'. For Daniel, the whole point was to be able to ascend the winner's rostrum, be it a high one like Mount Everest or a low-lying one like a woman's mount of Venus.

Jonas, on the other hand, had come to the conclusion that the purpose of life was to make a name for oneself – the reason for this need be nothing more mysterious than that he was distantly related to the people in the Book of Genesis. Although, it could of course also have had something to do with the fact that he liked to walk around town looking at all the shop signs: Ingwald Nielsen, Thv. L. Holm. At night some names, such as that of Ferner Jacobsen, were even written in neon. He could stand for ages on Egertorg, staring at the jeweller's where Aunt Laura had begun her career, admiring the lettering proclaiming DAVID ANDERSEN. More than fame itself, Jonas longed to see his name in lights. The world would read his name and know that it stood for something of great worth, right up there alongside silver, gold and precious stones.

Jonas considered many different options. For some weeks – apropos this business with the names – he was quite convinced that the whole purpose of life was to have a dish called after one. He had long been used to hearing people refer to such culinary delights as Janson's Temptation or beef à la Lindström: names which might not conjure up images of silver or gold, but which certainly made the mouth water. His mother was surprised by the interest displayed by her younger son in the kitchen. But after several unsuccessful, scorched attempts at what he called a Jonas cake: a concoction involving bananas, cardamom and liquorice gums which had Daniel, his guinea pig, hanging over the toilet, throwing up – he started to think bigger.

How could anyone have missed it? All those books, a whole sea of articles and reports on Jonas Wergeland – and no one has mentioned the real prime motive behind everything he did. Because the fact is that Jonas made up his mind in the spring of the year when he turned ten. As he saw it, the answer to the question of the fundamental reason for living obviously had to be related to life itself: it was, quite simply, to save lives. Jonas made the sort of secret, solemn decision of which only a child is capable. One day, he vowed, he would save someone's life. Most children do not give much thought to what they will be when they grow up. Even when coming out with the expected 'A policeman!' or 'A ship's captain!' they are really not that interested. It is too abstract a concept. But Jonas meant it with all his heart when, in response to the grown-ups' questions, he declared: 'I'm going to be a lifesaver.'

From the very start he knew it would have to do with water. With drowning. He could not picture himself reaching out a hand to stop a runaway pram from careering downhill onto the electrified rails of the new subway line, all but stifling a yawn as he did so, or nonchalantly sticking out a foot to prevent some brat on a sledge from sliding into the path of a big truck. No, it would have to be something more spectacular. A real act of heroism. Preferably with masses of spectators. Grandstands full. He toyed for a while with fire as an alternative; in his mind he saw himself rescuing a woman from the licking flames in a burning building; pictured himself dashing out, coughing, his eyebrows singed, with the woman in his arms, just as the fire engines drove up with blue lights flashing and sirens blaring and the whole edifice collapsed in a deadly inferno behind him. In his imagination, the woman was always wearing lacy underwear and had her arms wrapped tightly around him, a reward greater than seeing his name – inscribed in letters of fire, so to speak – on any 'Norwegian Fire Protection Diploma of Honour'.

But training for such an eventuality was not easy, and Jonas realised that it would have to be water – even though this was several decades before television series about lifeguards would become such a hit. For Jonas, this conviction went hand in hand with the knowledge that he was in possession of an extraordinary gift: it could not be for nothing that he had been endowed with his almost uncanny ability to hold his breath. Some day, possibly a cold winter's day, in front of a stunned crowd, he would have to dive off a quayside to save a child that had fallen in and was lying many metres below the surface. There might even be ice, and he would have to find his way back to a little hole in it, like a seal. Shouts and cheers. Banner headlines. His name in shining letters. 'Boy risks his own life'. The classic life-saving exploit. The sort of thing for which people were awarded the Carnegie Medal. Some day the call would come and he had to be ready. In his daydreams the child was usually a girl, a lass with wet hair and lacklustre eyes which, nonetheless, were turned up to him in a look of eternal gratitude.

Jonas trained with single-minded determination. Held his breath on the walk to school, held his breath in the classroom, held his breath before he went to sleep. He thought the hour of his great deed lay far in the future, that he would have to be patient. And then, only a year after he has made up his mind to be a lifesaver, with his basic training barely completed, it is upon him. The accident occurs on a day when he is totally unprepared for it, a day when he has almost forgotten about it or is, at any rate, thinking about something else. A day when the aim is not to save a life, but to see as many naked women as possible.

Jonas Wergeland sat on the organ bench. Remembered a dream he had put out of his mind, rejected as being far too naïve. Of being a lifesaver. The first time his father had taken him behind the organ and shown him the fan and the bellows it had reminded him of breathing, of being able to control your breath. Jonas thought, wove, his playing suddenly more inspired, as if he really could save lives, breathe life, spirit, into something that was dead; manipulated the stops as if he were Dr Frankenstein in his laboratory. There, in Grorud Church, he played Bach, the exquisite 'little' Prelude in E minor, a piece which starts out sounding like an improvisation, a playful exercise in runs and harmonies, but gradually slips into a more definite pattern, following a more distinct theme. Jonas had spent a long time practising to get it right, but now he simply sat there, weaving, or leaving it to Bach, the great weaver of the Baroque. Every musician knows that sometimes – on mysteriously blessed days – one can exceed one's own musical and, not least, technical skills. For Jonas, this was one of those days. It felt good to play. There was something special about the contact between his fingers and the keys, an unusual sureness to his touch, even his feet seemed to dance of their own accord.

Jonas did not know that a woman clad in bright orange was about to enter the church beneath him and, indirectly, change his life. He was playing the organ, and because he happened to be playing Bach on the organ, a piece of music resembling a network within which everything was connected in a comforting and meaningful fashion, his thoughts kept revolving around his father. His father and him. Always these two, Haakon and Jonas. He knew he was the apple of his father's eye, thought it might have something to do with a talent they shared, that his father saw something in Jonas which he recognised. He had the feeling that his father was trying to shield him from something, though he never knew what.

As a small boy, Jonas could have appeared on *Double Your Money*, answering questions on his father. He knew his every wrinkle, every scent, every story. He could describe the way his father ate grapefruit, or his virtual addiction to the *National Geographic*; he could detail his father's method of cutting his toenails or repeat word for word the minutes-long spiels he recited every morning in bed as he stretched his limbs until they cracked. Jonas was the only one, so he believed, who knew of the great pleasure Haakon Hansen took in being able to paddle, edge, his kayak in and out of the little islets around Hvaler. And then there were his father's breakfasts: bacon and egg every morning when there was no school. Instead of bawling out the stand-ard 'come-and-get-it' refrain their father would sit down at the ivories of the piano in the living room and wake them with a rendition of Bach's Goldberg variation no. 6, a piece which is only thirty seconds long, but which Jonas felt was the closest one came to the perfect work for the piano. His father played that same piece every Saturday and Sunday morning, year in year out; the pleasure of it stayed with Jonas for ever, that of waking to Bach's Goldberg variation no. 6 and the smell of his father's breakfast. 'What more does a man need than Bach and a bit of bacon?' as Haakon Hansen would say, thereby making his contribution to the great debate on the meaning of life. It was a weekend in itself: Bach and bacon. And bacon, mark you, that was as crisp as the music of Bach.

Jonas would be well up in years before he understood that even though you knew someone, you might not know them at all.

One day in April they went for a drive in his father's Opel Caravan, these two, always just these two, Haakon and Jonas. A journey of discovery his father called it. Jonas had been given the day off school; he thought they were going to Gjøvik, but they had carried on past it and taken a road away from Lake Mjøsa, running inland. Jonas stared out of the window as they drove through a valley, feeling rather disappointed. Nothing but farms, a few scat-tered houses. Could anything be discovered here, in such a lonely spot? Just at that moment his father pulled up in front of a large, yellow-painted building at the head of the valley. On a sign on the façade tall, white letters gleamed in a rainbow arc: The Norwegian Organ and Harmonium Works. Jonas found it hard to believe that something as thrilling as this could be hidden away deep in the forest. A man greeted Haakon Hansen courteously when he stepped out of the car, as if he were a visiting prince. 'Welcome to Snertingdal,' the man said. Snertingdal – to Jonas it sounded as full of promise as Samarkand.

First they were ushered into the workshop where the pipes were bored. Jonas knew a fair bit about organs, but nothing about how they were made. He was so taken with the carpentry skills of a man working on a console with a manual keyboard that he had to be dragged away to the drawing office, from which they also had a grand view of the valley and the mill next door. To the accompaniment of a droning saw his father pored over the drawings for the new organ for Grorud Church – since that was, of course, why they were here; his father had been informed that work on the instrument would soon be finished. Enormous charts on a tilted drawing board showed the organ from different angles. His father nodded and smiled, traced lines with his fingers and enquired about details which meant nothing to Jonas. To him it looked like a cathedral, or the designs for some fantastical machine.

They were shown round the rest of the factory, saw the storage room and the cabinetmaker's workshop in the basement where the great machines were housed and the façades, wind chests and wooden pipes were made. 'See this, Jonas, cherry wood. And over there: ebony! This is a far cry from whittling willow flutes, eh?' They proceeded to the first floor, to the pipe store and the tuning room where the pipes were given their first rough tuning. His father's face lit up, he picked up pipes and blew into them. Each pipe had a life of its own, was an instrument in itself. Haakon Hansen was looking more and more happy, chatting incessantly to their companion about matters which went way over Jonas's head, about the Principal and the Octave Bass, about the importance of the choir organ to the tonal quality of the instrument. Jonas watched as a man made a notch in a pipe with a knife and rolled back a tongue of metal with a pair of pliers, much as Jonas would have opened the lid on a sardine tin. He wished his mother could have been there, she would have loved this, working as she did at the Grorud Ironmonger's. Jonas always got a great kick out of places which combined ironmongery with music, uniting his mother's and his father's work – in such situations he could well understand why two such different individuals came to be married to one another. He heard his father and the strange man talking about the German factory which had supplied the stops. Jonas loved all the secrecy surrounding the metal alloys for the pipes, it smacked of alchemy. I'm not in an organ factory, he thought. I'm on a visit to a wizard's cave.

Then, to crown it all – a well-orchestrated surprise – their guide flung open the doors of the assembly hall, a room the size of a medium-sized church, and there, standing against one wall, all ready for playing, was Grorud's new organ. A shimmering palace. Jonas's father bounded over to the organ, looked back at the others, his arms outstretched to the gleaming façade, like a child unable to believe its eyes, while people stood there nodding, as if to say: 'Yes, it's yours, you can have it.' Haakon Hansen switched it on, set the stops and began to play. He played the only fitting piece of music: Johann Sebastian Bach, Prelude in E-flat major, *pro organo pleno*, he played so resoundingly that he all but raised the roof. And as his father played, Jonas tried to grasp how everything he had seen, all those separate elements in so many different rooms – thousands of pipes, that alone – could conjoin to form such a palatial instrument, one capable of producing such glorious, polyphonous music – a whole that was so much more than the individual parts which he had seen. A sound which caused the body to swell. It was true, it *was* alchemy, gold was made here, but it was gold in the form of music.

Jonas knew, of course, that with this visit his father was trying to tell him something important, and on the way home Haakon did indeed say something, although it was no more than a single sentence: 'Remember, that was just an organ.' That was all. His father did not say another word on the drive home. Haakon Hansen never said too much. But in his mind Jonas could hear the rest: 'So just imagine how everything in life fits together.'

And that was why you had to save lives. In his mind's eye, Jonas sometimes pictured people as being like walking organs. The first time he saw a dying child on television he realised what a tragedy this was, because what he beheld was a mighty organ into which no air, no spirit, no life was being breathed, one which, in all its senseless and ghastly complexity, was breaking down into its individual parts.

Jonas Wergeland sat in Grorud Church, playing an organ which he had, so to speak, seen unveiled; he was playing Bach, the fugue which accompanied the prelude in E-flat major, marvelling at an invention which enabled him, with just ten fingers and two feet, to produce music so splendid, so powerful, that it penetrated right down into the foundations of the building. Perhaps, when his life was over, this is what would be cited as his greatest achievement: that he had, at one felicitous moment, succeeded in playing Bach's prelude and fugue in E-flat major. He felt the tears falling, realised that he was crying, as if the music had also penetrated to his foundations. He did not know whether he was weeping out of grief or at the thought of an experience shared with his father or because of the beauty of the music, a beauty which reminded him of having his head inside a crystal chandelier sparkling with light and shot with rainbows.

The fugue came to an end. Jonas Wergeland altered the stops, struck up the hymn 'Lead kindly light', and how he played: played joyfully, played wistfully, played as if he were a lifesaver, someone capable of breathing life into people. And from the church beneath him the song swelled up, the singing truly hit the roof, with a force unlike anything Jonas had ever heard before. Because he was not alone. The church was full. He had got there in good time, but the church was already packed when he arrived. That was why Grorud had seemed so deserted. Everyone was here. Well over a thousand people. It had come as a surprise to him. Who was his father? Were all of these people really here to honour Haakon Hansen, to pay him their respects?

Jonas played. Down below, in front of the altar rail, lay his father. Not *as if* dead, but dead. Haakon Hansen had died 'on the job', as they say. Jonas was playing at his own father's funeral, a funeral which some would describe as scandalous, others as baffling, while his mother, who had more right than anyone to speak on the subject, simply said: 'No one would understand anyway.'

Jonas played 'Lead kindly light', Purday's lovely melody, he had the urge to improvise, introduce some provocative chords, produce innovative modulations while moaning and humming along like Glenn Gould or Keith Jarrett. His father would have liked that. Jonas was always nervous when playing for his father. Now too. Even though Haakon Hansen could not hear him. He lay in his coffin, dead. Yet Jonas played as if he could bring his father to life, was amazed to find that he still possessed it: the longing to be a lifesaver.

He had trained so hard, so resolutely. Particularly during the year when he turned ten it seemed to him that he was more in the water than out of it. At Frogner Baths, at Torggata Baths, out at Hvaler, this was his main pursuit: practising staying underwater for as long as possible. Building up his lung capacity. He could swim underwater for longer than any of his chums, had no difficulty in swimming across Badedammen or the length of the Torggata pool. At Frogner Baths, where you could look into the upstairs pool through round windows, he scared the wits out of spectators by diving down and goggling out at them as inquisitively as they were peering in, rather like a seal in an aquarium – except that he stayed there for so long, on the other side of the window, that people began to shout and bang on the glass in alarm. These daredevil dives did not escape the attention of the lifeguards either: 'Any more of your tomfoolery and you're out on your ear,' they bawled at him from their high stools.

But it wasn't tomfoolery, it was conscientious training. Jonas Wergeland was preparing for his great undertaking: that of saving a life.

During this most intensive phase of his life-saving career, he also practised the technique of getting a half-drowned person back onto dry land. Daniel, who reluctantly consented to act as guinea pig, played the lifeless drownee with impressive realism and did his utmost to show just how difficult such a manoeuvre could be, with the result that Jonas sometimes became a mite over-enthusiastic. 'You're not supposed to strangle me, dummy! You're supposed to save me!' Daniel would gasp when they finally reached the shallows.

Even more important, though, were the various methods of artificial respiration. On several occasions Jonas almost cracked Daniel's spine when practising the Holger Nielsen method on his brother – equally uncanny in his simulation of unconsciousness. Daniel drew the line, however, at mouth-to-mouth resuscitation. This last, as it happens, was a story in itself. In the autumn when Jonas was in fifth grade – in biology class, as was only right and proper – the whole class had the chance to practice giving mouth-to-mouth resuscitation to a dummy, or rather: the top half of a female by the name of Anna – a clean-living version, if you like, of the more notorious Blow-up Barbara – over whose mouth they placed a strip of plastic, for fear, perhaps, of being smitten with unmentionable diseases. If they tilted the head back and blew properly Anna's chest would rise. Jonas was praised by the teacher for his attempt. Anna's breasts jutted upwards like two pyramids under her blue tracksuit top. In his imagination Jonas saw how she must have tripped and fallen into the water while out jogging and how he had saved her from drowning with his life-giving breath.

One day when he returned home from Frogner Baths his mother sat herself down right across from him and looked at him long and hard, as if she were wondering whether his alarmingly red eyes were attributable to chlorine or to lunacy. 'Why are you doing all this?' she asked.

'Because I have a talent,' he said. 'I can hold my breath.' What he may perhaps have been trying to say was: I have a duty.

She was still looking him in the eye, but she could not help smiling: 'I'm not sure,' she said, 'but I think it's okay to take life a little less seriously than you do.'

As an adult Jonas would remember these words whenever he had the feeling that he was making too big a deal of things. That is my curse, he told himself. I take life too seriously.

But just then all Jonas could think about was the day, sometime far in the future, when he would be put to the test. His life would culminate in this, the moment when he actually saved a life; his presence on earth would be justified by one sensational exploit, broadcast live, as it were, on prime-time television. Everything was to be a preparation for this. Daniel had a calendar with a metal plate on the back and a red metal ring. Most people moved the ring from one day to the next, but Daniel set it only around important dates. Jonas knew that the moment for his dazzling deed awaited him on one of those magnetic, red-circle days.

Then, one Saturday morning when they awoke to the Goldberg variation no. 6 and the smell of frying bacon, Jonas noticed that the red ring on Daniel's calendar was circling that very day. For a second he construed this as an ominous sign. But his brother lay grinning in his bed. 'Today you're going to see so many naked women that you'll never be the same again,' Daniel said. Jonas breathed a sigh of relief, not knowing that this was also the day when he was to be put to the test.

Now though, for all the basic training of his boyhood, he was powerless.

Down below in the church a father lay dead. Holding his breath would do no good. Artificial respiration would do no good. The day before, Jonas had stood by the open coffin, regarding his father's body. Haakon Hansen looked as though he were alive. Intact. All that was missing, so it seemed, was a little cog. A glowing spot behind his ribs, that glow which wove the network of tiny links between his organs. As Jonas stood there beside the coffin an old question presented itself: What should you take with you? What makes life life? What *gives* life life?

Jonas Wergeland sat at the organ manuals, terraces of keys, putting everything he had into the playing: fingers, feet, his whole body. This was a day with a heavy red ring around it, a red-letter day for Grorud, one which would always be remembered – not least on account of the unforeseen intermezzo occasioned by an uninvited guest, a personage who showed up dressed in orange even though black was the order of the day, a jungle flower in a dim Norwegian pine forest. 'Haakon Hansen was a Buddhist,' was just one of the rumours which would circulate later. 'For over thirty years we've had a Buddhist for an organist in Grorud Church.' Jonas sat up in the organ loft, accompanying a packed church in 'Lead kindly light, amid th'encircling gloom'. And they could have used the light, because it was an exceptionally grey autumn day outside. But the congregation sang fit to make the stained glass glow and the eye of God in the triangle at the top of the large fresco behind the altar look down with gladness upon them.

Before the service began, before making his way up to the organ loft, Jonas had stayed downstairs for a while. He had run an eye over the packed pews, listened to the murmur of voices, inhaled the scent of mingled perfumes. The mood was buoyant, not unlike the first minutes at a big party where the guests have not seen each other in ages. Before him, Jonas saw a cross-section of his own life, his life encapsulated in a church. Here were girls, now women, who had protested when he pawed their breasts; here were mothers, now elderly ladies, who had complained when he played the Stones's 'The Last Time' too loud at Badedammen; here were old men, now ancients, who had shaken their fists at him when he knocked off their hats with snowballs. All tenderly smiling. This was a time for peace and reconciliation. Jonas spotted people he had not seen in years, folk from the housing estate; he nodded to Five-Times Nilsen and his lady wife, nodded to Bastesen the caretaker, who had actually shaved for the occasion, then he was tapped gently on the shoulder by Karen Mohr, the Grey Eminence herself: 'Your father, he would have been worthy,' was all she said. And Jonas knew: 'No greater compliment could any man receive.'

People were still trickling in, even though the church was jam-packed.

Every face shone with that same special radiance, a sort of deep joy born of solemn purpose. Many of the mourners nodded quietly to him. Some of them strangers. Jonas was, after all, something of a celebrity, his face seen on television all the time. He exchanged nods with old teachers from elementary school and sales assistants from the shopping centre, from shops where he had bought his first football, his first blue blazer, his first pencil case. The whole of Grorud had turned out. Jonas spotted Tango-Thorvaldsen, who owned the shoe shop; he spied the dreaded barber and the drunken chemist, and wasn't that the postman – an old, old man now – who had delivered the longed-for letter from Margrete? Jonas remembered, suddenly he remembered so much, and stranger still: he also seemed to remember, or to see, things which were to come, things which had not yet happened in his life, as if he were in the middle of an overture.

Up in the organ loft Jonas Wergeland was playing 'Lead kindly light', and as he played he was able to keep track in the 'gossip mirror' of what was happening at the head of the nave. The choir was like a florist's shop, billowing with bouquets and beribboned wreaths like belated laurels. This, and all the people, brought home to him something which had never really occurred to him, and which he had possibly never completely understood until now; something which for some reason, given the situation, was a great lesson to him: his father had been a much loved man. Maybe that was the whole point of life: to be loved? Jonas's eyes went to his family and relatives in the front pews. His mother was sitting next to Benjamin, his little brother, who had Down's syndrome and who had stared uncomprehendingly at Jonas when told by him that unfortunately he could not begin the service with Abba's 'Ring Ring'. Maybe that was why he had refused to leave his new bow and arrow in the porch and now sat there happily drawing a bead on the angel on the altarpiece.

On his mother's other side was Rakel, she too dressed in black. Though there was nothing unusual in that, she had always worn black. Big sister and rebel. Cheekbones like Katherine Hepburn's. The pride and waywardness of an Irish actor. A true revolutionary her whole life through. A pioneer in what was arguably one of the most male-dominated of all occupations, a samaritan, a Sister – not only to him, Jonas, but to many, to thousands, of others. It was a privilege to have such a sister. In Jonas's earliest memories she was no more than a face buried in a book, a collection of tales, the *Arabian Nights*; costumes and scents gliding through the rooms and turning the flat into a weird and wonderful place for him and Daniel, kids that they were. There they would be, taking life for granted, and Rakel would sweep into the living room, say something or do something, and all of a sudden they were not sure of anything. He remembered her as a perpetually wry, reproving smile. And then she was gone, or at least reduced to collecting the scalps of a string of boyfriends, to leather jackets reeking of cigarette smoke and the roar of a 1000 cc: a black-clad whirlwind that popped in every now and again. Eventually, though, she settled down, made some choices, got married and moved far away; later, she would often live even further away, for years at a time, with just the odd letter from foreign parts to let them know that she was alive and well. She was the only truly sterling individual Jonas knew. She was the one person he admired most in all the world.

Nonetheless, he toyed with the thought that Rakel could have had a very different life, had their father not been a musician. That, when you came right down to it, it was their father who had kick-started her remarkable career. Because, if Haakon had not been an organist and Bach lover he would never have taken Rakel to Oslo's Trinity Church on a late-autumn day in the mid-fifties. What happened on that day in Trinity Church? On that day Rakel met a lifesaver. A real lifesaver.

Rakel would tell the story of this event any chance she got. She had been seven at the time, and the mere fact of being taken into town by her father, to attend what she understood to be a very grand gathering, was wonderful. The sight of the building alone was enough for her. She was almost living in the *Arabian Nights* at the time, so the broad copper dome put her in mind of a magnificent mosque – all that was missing were the minarets. But more was to come, because no sooner had they entered the church and climbed up to the organ loft, where her father shook hands with the few other invited guests, most of them organists, than the guest of honour arrived, a man who, despite being almost eighty, was still strong and spry, with a good head of hair. 'I thought he was so handsome,' Rakel always said. 'I thought it was the Caliph Haroun al-Rashid in disguise.'

This gentleman was no less a person than Albert Schweitzer, in Oslo to be presented with the Nobel Peace Prize which he had been awarded the year before. As far away as Africa he had heard tell of Eivind Groven's curiously pure-tuned organ and he had expressed a wish to play it. Now he was actually here, in Trinity Church in Oslo. He seated himself at the simple organ and played a little – not much, just a little – because his eye had been caught by the old church organ and everyone could see that the world-renowned musician's fingers were itching to try it too. So of course he had to sit down at that fine Romantic organ – built in Norway, as it happens, by Claus Jensen – and after only a few bars he nodded his head vigorously in appreciation of the instrument's tone. He played Bach; it may not have been the perfect organ on which to play Bach, but Albert Schweitzer clearly enjoyed what he was hearing. To Rakel, who was of course familiar with the piece he was playing, Schweitzer seemed to render that marvellous warp and weft of voices quite transparent, and more: the very bricks of the church suddenly appeared translucent. Everything expanded, but at the same time everything was connected. Rakel felt that she had learned a bit more about the breadth of a man. That one could care as much about church organs as about the black people in Africa. She knew instinctively, by observing the ease with which Schweitzer handled all the different manuals and pedals, that this was a man capable of doing several things at once. It came as no surprise to her, later, to discover that he could write high-flown works on the history of New Testament research, that he had the ability to cure such appalling diseases as malaria and dysentery, sleeping sickness and leprosy, or that he could edit Bach's collected organ works. This was a man with respect for life at all levels, who had therefore taught himself to use instruments as diverse as the organ, the pen and the scalpel. 'He was a juggler,' she said. Not until Jonas met Bo Wang Lee did he understand what she meant.

Afterwards Rakel was introduced to Albert Schweitzer; he bent down and stroked her cheek. 'It was Bach who provided me with the first funds for my hospital in Africa,' he said in German, but Rakel understood him anyway. What she liked best about him was his rather bushy white moustache. 'And he had kind eyes,' she always said. 'The boy I marry will have to have eyes as kind as his.'

Although she was only seven years old, and did not understand exactly who Albert Schweitzer was, all the things he had done and everything he did while he was in Oslo, she had been greatly struck by the fire in those eyes, the warmth of that brief handshake, the music that poured out into the church. Unbeknown to anyone else in the family, over the years she garnered various scraps of information about Schweitzer. Then one day, when she was fifteen and had long been a teenage rebel, there it was on her bedroom wall – causing her parents to shake their heads in disbelief: a picture of Albert Schweitzer, hanging between Elvis Presley and Marlon Brando. A curious trinity. 'Some day I'll find my Lambaréné,' she said. And in a way she did.

At the age of twenty, in curlers and a headscarf, she was to be seen reading Schweitzer's autobiography, *Out of My Life and Thought*, the book that would finally persuade her to leave the world of the *Arabian Nights* – if, that is, since she thought the great doctor bore some resemblance to Haroun al-Rashid, it should not be seen as a natural follow-on from it, one tale, or perhaps one should say one form of rebellion, running into another. Be that as it may, it was at this point that she decided what she was going to do with her life. It came to her as suddenly and clearly as the phrase 'reverence for life' by which

Schweitzer was struck on a river in Africa, one evening at sunset as he sat absent-mindedly on board a steamboat butting its way through a herd of hippopotami.

Like Jonas, Rakel wanted to be a lifesaver, but she took a much more serious approach to this than him. Rakel always took things seriously. She decided what her Lambaréné would be. It had to be mobile. She acquired a heavy goods vehicle license and trained as a nurse, in that order; she learned how to reverse a truck and trailer into a garage with a proficiency that put paid to any jokes about women drivers, learned to administer injections in a way that made life flare up. Thereafter, she and her husband, Hans Christian – who could actually have given Albert Schweitzer a run for his money where kind eyes were concerned – drove trucks for just about every humanitarian organisation in the world, always going where the suffering and the danger was greatest. 'I drive caravans through deserts of need,' she was wont to say, as if the vocabulary of the *Arabian Nights* still lived within her. Rakel was a leather-jacketed, 400 horse power Mother Theresa transporting food and medicines across front lines in war-torn zones. With – so it was rumoured – Bach's organ music pouring from a cassette player on the passenger seat. Rakel was the sort of woman who proved that ethics and aesthetics can go hand in hand. Her windscreen was forever being pierced by bullets, but it is said that only once did she get upset: when a piece of shrapnel shattered her cassette player. But just as the Paris Bach Society had presented Schweitzer with a piano with organ pedals, specially built for the tropics, so Rakel, after this incident, was presented by her fellow aid workers with a special, armour-plated cassette player. Rakel had no children, but – and this is not just an empty platitude – she and her husband had thousands of children. Jonas once asked her why she had taken up such a hazardous occupation – whether it was because, at the time, she had felt that there was no rhyme nor reason to life, or because she had felt guilty or whatever? She had stared at him as blankly as Benjamin was wont to do when Jonas said something which he, Jonas, believed to be laudably reasonable: 'I did it because it's a fantastic story,' she said. 'It's the best book I've ever read.'

Rakel represented Jonas's first encounter with a race which he would never understand: the bookworms of this world. Jonas simply could not comprehend how a book, a book with a title as innocuous as *Out of My Life and Thought*, could have such a powerful impact. Throughout her formative years Rakel had been an avid reader, the sort of child who had her nose buried in a library book even on the warmest of summer days. The light was invariably still burning on her side of the room when he went to sleep. She was quite capable of turning away boys at the door, when that time came. Then one day she simply got up, as if she had had enough of fiction, and went out into the real world. For good. Jonas could not rid himself – no matter how hard he tried – of a suspicion that the highly moral life she led was a natural consequence of all that reading; it would not have been possible without the ballast of thousands of tales.

Whatever the case: if any Norwegian can be said to have done their bit to save lives, to relieve want, then it has to be Rakel W. Hansen: a woman deserving of any peace prize you could name. Jonas was downright proud of his sister. She was the most upright – the happiest – person he knew. Every time he looked at her he saw a face that said: I am life that wants to live, in the midst of life that wants to live. So simple, so true. And hence so hard to accept. Jonas did his best, year after year, not to think about it, even when he arrived at the church and saw her mud-spattered black semi-trailer, an alien element – an almost extra-terrestrial object – among the parked cars. But in his heart of hearts he knew: she was the living, provocative proof that happiness lay in helping others.

Jonas Wergeland sat in the organ loft in Grorud Church, playing the organ, feeling almost as if he were in the cab of Rakel's colossus of a truck. He had the same lofty overview. Was in similar contact with tremendous power. He launched into the last verse of 'Lead kindly light', having first closed the swell box and pulled out the Oboe 8 and Gedact Principal 16 to produce an even warmer, richer sound. A comforting sound. He did not know that a bolt of orange lightning was about to strike, an event as unexpected and as inflammatory as him pulling out an unknown stop and suddenly introducing an incredibly dangerous and bewildering voice into the organ's peal.

The hymn came to an end. Daniel stepped up to the lectern, alongside the coffin. Jonas was struck by the symmetry of this arrangement. Two sons. The one playing the organ, the other officiating. One at the front and one at the back. Jonas had often asked himself how Daniel, that sex-obsessed Casanova, that rabble-rouser par excellence, could have ended up as a man of the cloth. Jonas recalled one Christmas in the early seventies when Daniel had stolen up to the organ during the sermon and pressed the button which set the church bells chiming. His father had been back in the vestry, reading a copy of the *National Geographic*. There was an awful row. 'Why did you do it?' the vicar had asked. 'Because I wanted to protest against the American bombing of Vietnam!' But now Daniel was himself a vicar, and did not expect to be interrupted. For once he did not spout a load of rubbish either. Jonas listened, deeply moved, to what his brother said about their father. A lot of people had asked if they might say a few words about Haakon Hansen, but their mother had said no to all of them. Daniel alone was to speak.

In the mirror Jonas could see Daniel's wife in one of the front pews, pregnant yet again and with three sons aged one, two and three crawling around her feet. Daniel must have been reared on ginseng. Or powdered rhinoceros horn. Jonas listened to his brother's solemn eulogy, then all at once he smiled. A memory had come to him as he glanced to his right, at the point where the organ loft curved round. On that spot, for a number of years in his childhood, Daniel had stood with the Bermuda Triangle, the three ladies who led the congregation in the hymn-singing. Which was why, on a Saturday early in the summer between fifth and sixth grades, when they were on their way to Ingierstrand, he had been humming a snatch of a hymn – oddly enough it happened to be 'Vain world, now farewell'. But this was not just any day, this was the day marked with a magnetic red ring on Daniel's calendar. Not until they were on the bus was Jonas solemnly informed of the true objective of this expedition, as if they were commandos and the purpose of their mission could only now be revealed. They were headed for a bay on the other side of Ingierstrand. To a – pause for effect – nudist beach. Daniel gazed at Jonas with round, lustful eyes. Jonas never knew how his brother got wind of such things. He had even brought binoculars; he elbowed Jonas impatiently in the ribs when they got to their stop.

As they walked, or more like tiptoed, through the grove of trees which lay between the road and the water, Daniel began to hum a snatch from another hymn, again one totally at odds with the situation: 'Tread softly, o soul, and guard thy step'. He always hummed hymn tunes when he was thinking about girls, when he was feeling randy. There was a reason for this. He had once been told by a real hardliner of a vicar that the soul lay in the seed. This was, of course, something this clergyman of the old school said in order to persuade boys to control their urge to masturbate; he may not even have meant it literally. Daniel had, however, taken his words to heart. Some may laugh, forgetting, however, that many faiths take a far more complex view of the human seed than that held by the Lutheran school of sex education. In other words, Daniel had a problem, because he was probably the one person in the world least able to keep his hands to himself. If husbanding one's semen was equivalent to husbanding one's soul, possibly even in the sense of life, then Daniel W. Hansen was on very thin ice. The best diagnosis he could hope for was 'permanently impaired spiritual faculties'.

In other words, Daniel had an insatiable need for soul and as luck would have it, this was the very year when he discovered soul music. So whenever Jonas heard the vibrant, emotionally charged songs of artists such as Ray Charles, Sam Cooke or James Brown ringing out of the loudspeakers in Daniel's room he knew that his brother had 'sinned'. Daniel actually believed that he could recharge his batteries, replace lost spiritual energy by listening to soul music. Sometimes, when Jonas came home from school and the two of them were alone in the house, he had the feeling that the air in there was positively seething, the door almost seemed to be bulging. Things were to get even worse, or better, a couple of years later when Aretha Franklin broke onto the scene. In her, Daniel found his saving grace, a woman who really knew how to pour out her soul, to give of her abundance. Jonas found it a bit spooky, his brother's fascination with the First Lady of soul's energetic, insistent and, not least, slyly sensual, nigh on orgiastic, music. Daniel bought every one of Aretha Franklin's records. And when her live double album of gospel songs came out – an indisputable milestone in rock history, incidentally – there seemed to be only one thing for him to do: capitulate, start studying theology. He was fulfilled. His search, his hunger, for soul had led him to the ministry. Jonas always believed that soul music was the moving force behind Daniel's subsequent fiery sermons and charismatic public performances, his ability to improvise and to wail ecstatically while repeating variations on the same words and phrases over and over again. Not for nothing was he famed for his way of 'ministering to the soul'. It was said that women in particular flocked to him to discuss their most personal problems.

Due to his newly awakened interest, or his need, for soul, Daniel had also begun – long before this – to sing with the three so-called lead singers, three women who stood up in the gallery alongside the organ and led the congregation in song. When Daniel and Jonas were little, their father had had to put up with three quavery elderly ladies whom Daniel dubbed The Syrups, because they did all they could, in their farcically shrill vibratos, to slow down the tempo of every hymn their father played; they were always a couple of beats behind the organ. Then one day, in their stead, three buxom young women showed up to lead the congregation in song; and there was nothing wrong with their timing; Daniel thought they really swung – they sang with soul – just like the gospel-inspired backing singers he could hear on certain soul records. He had to get in on the act, found an excuse to join them, to be up there among them, singing with them, even though his voice was not all that great. Basically Daniel just stood there mumbling as if in a trance, encircled by three heaving bosoms. He confessed to Jonas that it was an elevating experience; he called these three busty ladies the Bermuda Triangle, a name which had nothing to do with the Holy Triangle, but with triangles of a quite different nature, and of such a calibre that he felt he was about to be engulfed by them. Thus it came about that Daniel, probably quite unwittingly, took to humming fragments of hymn tunes from his career as a choirboy in the Bermuda Triangle – or comical, hybrid soul versions of them

– at the prospect of erotic encounters. It occurred to Jonas that one really ought not to laugh at this: one *should* have a sense of ceremony, break into a hymn each time one made advances towards a woman.

They had reached their destination. They lay on the hillside right on the edge of the nudist beach, looking down on what was, at this time, years before the opening of a naturist beach at Huk on the island of Bygdøy, the closest secret retreat for those who, for some strange reason, found it liberating to strut about in the altogether even though they knew they made the perfect sideshow for passers-by and other prying eyes. It left Jonas cold. There was nothing particularly arousing about all those naked bodies. Daniel, however, was of a different opinion.

A bunch of kids were playing in the shallows, not far from shore. At one point, when Daniel went off in search of a kiosk or a shop, Jonas was looking through the binoculars when he saw a toddler – he couldn't have been more than two – disappearing beneath the surface. The child was in the middle of the group of children, but nobody noticed him go under. To begin with Jonas thought that he couldn't be in any real danger. And yet time slowed down. He was suddenly aware of everything around him, the bark of the fir trees, a fly, a boat far out in the fjord. The hum of voices on the beach seemed disturbingly loud, as if someone had turned up the volume button. The toddler resurfaced. Jonas relaxed, a great weight seemed to have been lifted from his shoulders. His eyes ached from staring so hard. But then the boy vanished from view again. Jonas fumed with irritation. Not least at the hopelessly apathetic mothers who could sit there chatting, scratching their not very sexy boobs and indulging in tittle-tattle while their kids were quietly drowning. He forced himself to lie still. Surely somebody must have noticed. The drone of the flies reverberated like a pneumatic drill. The ground smelled like a chemist's shop. Jonas surveyed the other adults lying round about, intent solely on exposing as much skin as possible to the sun. Into his head came pictures of basking sea lions. It dawned on him that of all the people nearby he was the only one – thanks, perhaps, to his binoculars – to have seen the boy go under. He knew he had to do something, but some form of acute modesty or shyness held him back. He did not like the idea of having to run through those ranks of shamelessly naked people, betraying the fact that he had been peeping at them on the sly. And what if his eyes had deceived him? He saw himself diving into the water, creating unnecessary panic, pictured everybody pointing, standing there, stark naked, laughing at him. Besides: this was not what he had been training for.

At that moment Jonas learned something: it takes courage to realise your goals in life. You have to act, without fear of the consequences. He tossed the binoculars aside, leapt up. He ran for all he was worth: all those tedious boring 60-metre dashes in PE finally justified. He sprinted between two clusters of naked people, took the few metres into the shallows at a bound and plunged his hand into the water. It instantly made contact with a body, he hauled the child out. As he did so he noticed a bit of a stir on the shore: a woman, a naked woman, who had clearly only just begun to sense that something was wrong. How was that possible? was the thought that flashed through Jonas's mind, but such things *were* possible, they happened all the time. He waded out of the water with a child in his arms. The child had been unconscious, but he started coughing and spluttering even before Jonas reached the shore: a thump on the back – administered by Jonas almost as an afterthought – was all it took. It was as far from giving mouth-to-mouth resuscitation to a beautiful woman as he could get. This was not what he had been training for when he all but strangled Daniel and made Anna the dummy's breasts jut upwards like two pyramids.

It was swelteringly hot, even in just shorts and a T-shirt the sweat was running off him. All eyes were on him. Jonas handed the crying child to the woman, trying hard not to look down at her breasts. Or at the dark, somehow menacing, triangle further down. He interpreted the look she gave him as a question: what the hell was he doing here, on a nudist beach, fully clothed? Although he may have misunderstood. 'Thank you,' she said. 'Thank you.'

Jonas had known, of course, that he was shy. But only now, with all these eyes on him, did he realise *how* shy. He had always dreamed of having an audience, but he had never given any thought to his own reaction when confronted with a crowd of people, especially not such a collection of eyewitnesses. He felt as if he were caught in a Bermuda triangle of sorts, on the point of disappearing. Later he was to wonder whether he had actually *grown* shy, really shy, been struck, as it were, by stage fright, at that moment. Or by that moment. Often, afterwards, when he found himself on a stage, he would picture the people in the audience without any clothes on. 'How come you're so shy?' a girl once asked him. He had not replied, although he had felt like saying: 'Because I once had to save a life.'

Jonas walked off. Not another word had been said. People may not have thought there was any real danger. But Jonas knew that child would have drowned had not he, Jonas, been there just then. Did he feel proud, pleased? No. There had been something devastatingly unheroic about the whole deed. The setting for his act of heroism had been as wrong as it could possibly be. What bothered Jonas most of all was the fact of how easy it had been. How light the child had felt when he picked him up. As if he had overestimated the task, the weightiness of life. 'What's the matter, you're shaking like a leaf?'

Daniel said when he got back, and handed his brother an ice cream. 'I saved a child's life,' Jonas said with a sheepish grin. 'Great,' Daniel said, thinking it was a joke. 'Come on, let's go over to Ingierstrand instead. I passed a couple of real dolls just up the road.' He started fervently humming a hymn. As far as Jonas could tell it was a mangled soul rendering of 'All Things Bright and Beautiful'.

Jonas went through the rest of that day feeling hollow inside. It took him a while to sort out how exactly he felt. What was it that was wrong? He knew, though: he was eleven years old and he had attained his goal. Where do you go once you've reached the mountain top? He had nothing left to live for. What was he supposed to do for the next eighty years? What an anticlimax: all that swimming and diving practice – and all you have to do is to wade out knee-deep and stick a hand into the water. He remembered an incident involving his mother. She had been sitting at the coffee table, doing the most difficult game of patience, one she must have played thousands of times before without getting it to work out. And suddenly it came out right. As Jonas recalled, his mother had seemed not happy, but sad. That was how he felt after that day at Ingierstrand. Eleven years old, he thought; eleven years old and my life is over.

Jonas Wergeland sat high in a hallowed hall, in an organ loft which also offered a wonderfully clear prospect of the past. Daniel, that erstwhile soul freak, stood at the front of the church. Jonas listened to him praying, listened to him reading texts from the Bible, about vanity, but also about hope. Jonas kept one eye on his brother in the mirror as he reflected once again on his own reaction to his life-saving exploit. He felt some of that same hollowness now, though for a different reason. He had a vague sense of being dead. Felt as though he had actually been dead for years. That he was present, not at his father's funeral, but at his own. He was dead because he had lost sight of a gift, lost sight of a goal in life. He was not yet thirty, but he had given up, or settled for second best. Second worst. Had he been asleep? Or was this simply a result of the shyness with which he had, for the first time, been over-come on that beach, faced with all those naked people? Because even though he may have maintained, unconsciously at least, a desire to 'make a name for himself', this shyness had long stifled any urge to expose himself to view. As an announcer he had, however, found himself a little cubbyhole where no one could see him and yet everyone could see him. He was alone with a camera lens, while at the same time entering a million living rooms. It was not unlike being an organist: he could stay out of sight while at the same time making the church tremble with his playing, making everyone quiver with emotion.

Sitting there on the organ bench in the church of his childhood, Jonas Wergeland saw that what he had taken for contentment was, in fact, a state of torpor. For a surprisingly long time he had managed to ignore the question of whether he was making the best use of his talents. He was recognised on the street, he was forever seeing his own name – if not in lights, then certainly in newsprint – but that day, at his father's funeral, he realised that his life was a huge anticlimax.

Jonas looked in the mirror. He saw his brother glance up at the gallery and launched into the opening chords of 'Thine is the Glory'. Daniel had suggested 'Abide with me' but their mother wanted no hymns about eventide, insisted, instead, on 'Thine is the Glory', a song of praise. And Jonas had agreed, not least because it gave him the chance to play the wonderful melody from Handel's *Judas Maccabaeus*.

The man at the centre of it all, his father, lying in his coffin, had died on the job. It had happened late one afternoon. Someone had been walking past the church and heard a great roar coming from it – the building had been positively shaking: it had sounded as though an enormous engine was running at full power in there. This seemed so odd that the vicar was called. He opened the door to be met by an ear-splitting din. It was coming from the organ. In the gallery they found Haakon Hansen, dead. Heart attack. He had slipped off the bench and under the console and lay across the pedal board as if he were asleep. Not that anyone could have slept with such a racket going on. The cluster chord of bass notes produced by the pressure of his father's body on the row of pedals shook the whole church to its foundations, like an earthquake almost. 'He looked as though he was hovering, like a fakir on a bed of notes,' the vicar told Jonas. It was a fitting end. That was how a musician ought to die, Jonas thought. With the organ playing full blast. Everyone should exit this life – all those who had loved it, at any rate – to the accompaniment of just such a resounding peal of protest. If, that is, it ought not to be construed as a fanfare, bidding death welcome. Haakon Hansen had involuntarily composed his own requiem.

Jonas's father had always said he would die at the organ. Most people do reflect, from time to time, on where and how they would like to die. As far as Jonas Wergeland was concerned one thing was for sure: he did not want to meet his end as he had once been certain he would: far out to sea, with no chance of rescuing himself, for all his life-saving practice.

It had started out well enough. Despite a bit of a breeze it had been a perfect afternoon in Krukehavn, over on Hvasser. Jonas was down on the jetty where the pilot boats were moored, he was sitting reading about Venus, and although he was not looking up his eye was caught by a green object – the light made it shine like a precious gem – drifting towards him, bobbing up and down. Even at a distance he spotted the piece of paper inside it and instantly fell to daydreaming about dramatic missives from far-off lands, about the possible, subsequent headlines: 'Message in a bottle from the Falklands', or better still: 'Young man receives gift of a million from Argentinian cattle baron'. That, too, would be a way of making a name for oneself. By sheer luck, pure coincidence.

He clambered down to the water, fished out the bottle. The cork was only half-in, so there was little chance of it having come from Buenos Aires. 'Bound for World's End' it said on the piece of paper he pulled out. Nothing else. In a neat hand. He turned to look back – towards the southern tip of the island, known as World's End – only to be blinded by sunlight. Someone was bouncing it off a mirror at him. He could see nothing except this tiny, dazzling sun dancing in the hand of a person on a jetty a little way off. Then the light went out. Through the binoculars which had, the previous autumn, enabled him to see the moons of Jupiter for the first time he spied a figure, a girl, waving to him. He picked up his book, strolled ashore and along to her jetty. Why did I do it? he would ask himself later. Because I let myself be dazzled?

By the time he reached the girl he had managed to get a pretty good look at her: T-shirt, shorts, bare feet – the only unusual touch was her hat, a white cap with a black skip like the ones worn by naval officers. She was laughing. 'Nice one,' he said, nodding at the mirror she still held in her hand. 'I usually let people know when I want them to give me the sun. So, what was that note about?'

'I heard you were looking for a berth.'

'I'm going further than World's End,' he said.

'I like a boy with ambition,' she said, pointing at the binoculars round his neck. 'I'll take you wherever you want to go.'

'Across the fjord?'

'I'll be getting under way in a minute.'

'Now?' he said. 'But it'll be night soon.' He couldn't take his eyes off her navel. Her T-shirt stopped shy of the waistband of her shorts, exposing her belly button: a small, mesmerisingly black hollow in her midriff, but one which was, nonetheless big enough for Jonas to feel that he could get lost in there. It struck him that he was more attracted to this hollow than to her. He gazed and gazed at it as if he had just discovered an unknown planet, here on Earth. He felt as if he was swirling round and round, as if everything – his eyes, his reason – was being drawn into a deliciously prurient vortex.

'Don't tell me you're scared,' she said. To Jonas it sounded like downright ventriloquism. Her words issued straight from her navel.

'It's too windy,' he said.

'Who's afraid of a bit of a blow,' she said.

'It's blowing pretty hard, I'd say,' he replied. He knew he shouldn't have said this. She smiled, lowered her eyes to his crotch. He was a little embarrassed by her directness. He looked up at the pennants smacking against their flagpoles. These and the swaying trees further up the beach gave plenty of cause for concern.

'What have you brought with you?' she asked.

'I own no more than I can carry, I am a nomad.' He jabbed a thumb at the rucksack slung over one shoulder, then realised that might not be what she meant. That this could be an existential question. That she was actually asking: 'Who are you? Show me something from your civilisation.' He handed her the book he was carrying, a textbook on the planetary system; he was reading up in preparation for the new term and course A 106 at the Institute of Theoretical Astrophysics. She riffled through it briefly. 'Okay,' she said. 'There's no knowing when this sort of thing might come in handy at sea.' She shot a glance skywards. 'You'll see stars tonight, alright.' Everything she said still seemed to him to have a double meaning.

Beside them lay a Knarr, a thirty-foot wooden boat, sturdy and reassuring, but at the same time slender and graceful. It stood out, it had a regal, a noble, air about it, as did she. 'São Gabriel,' Jonas read. She saw him start. 'Didn't you pay attention in school? Vasco da Gama's flagship?' she said.

But he was beyond paying attention now; he had been bewitched by a belly button, tossed into a whirlpool. They left Hvasser behind so quickly that he scarcely realised what was happening. Half an hour later it was all he could do just to hang on tight, they were moving too fast for his liking, the waves were too high, there was altogether too much foaming and frothing and surging and sighing going on round about him. Not only that, but it would be dark soon. Instinctively he held his breath, as if he were already under water. He knew that he had embarked upon an undertaking which he might well regret, or might never have the chance to regret, since he was in fact going to die, out here, in the middle of a storm-tossed sea.

'Death is simple,' his father had once told him. 'You breathe out. You don't breathe in. That's all there is to it.' After a while he had added: 'Do you know why organ music is so beautiful? Because it's a sustained act of dying, pure expiration.'

Jonas had noticed the piece which his father had been rehearsing when he died. Johann Sebastian Bach, Prelude in A minor. It seemed so apt: to be playing a prelude at the moment of your death, an overture as postlude.

Bo Wang Lee was the first to ask the question which Jonas Wergeland would later consider to represent the very crux of existence: what should you take with you. It was a question which could be applied at all levels. What, for example, should one take to one's death? The day before the funeral, Jonas had lingered by his father's open casket long after the rest of the family had gone. There his father lay, in a dark suit, as if he were taking a nap before a party, or prior to some important engagement. A journey. What should he take with him? Somewhere in Africa, so Jonas had heard, coffins were designed as tributes to the deceased. A fisherman was given a coffin shaped like a blue tuna fish, a chief was laid to rest in a golden eagle. Haakon Hansen deserved more than a neutral white coffin. A kayak, perhaps. Jonas placed his father's worn organ-playing shoes in the coffin, along with a book containing Bach's six trio sonatas. A volume of the *National Geographic* also found favour in Jonas's eyes.

What should you take with you? What was life?

The last notes of 'Thine be the Glory' faded away. The woman in orange had yet to make her appearance. Daniel began his address to the bereaved. Jonas crept over to the corner of the gallery from which, as a child, he had so often dropped bits of paper onto people's heads. His eye went to the front pew, to his mother who seemed remarkably small all of a sudden, shrunken. Jonas had three decades of living behind him, but only now did he see it. He had got it all wrong. He had always regarded his mother as the more active of the two; she was the one who saw to the social side of things, who invited people over, organised parties, while his father was the quiet, reserved one, with few friends. Not for nothing had Jonas at a certain point in his life taken his mother's maiden name, Wergeland. His mother was high days and holidays, his father was the bedrock and the humdrum. Jonas had the impression that his father would have liked to be alone, that he longed to lead a monastic life. He was, at any rate, an out-and-out individualist, a man who wanted to be his own symphony orchestra. Now and again it had even crossed Jonas's mind that his father was, to some extent, a loser. Secretly, Jonas felt sorry for him. Which was also why he loved his father so much. But now. All these people. Over a thousand of them. This day showed that he might have been totally mistaken about his parents and their respective roles.

And then, as his thoughts drift off down their own path, his eye is drawn to something, a hub, something inescapable, which he does not at first see, then suddenly spies: Margrete. A large M on a black wall. He starts, amazed that her magnetic attraction should be so strong even when he is seeing her from behind. She is sitting right below the pulpit with Kristin, their daughter. Margrete was wearing one of her strings of pearls. 'I think your father would like it,' she had said when Jonas had wrinkled up his nose at the gleaming white necklace. At first he couldn't think why he had started at the sight of his wife. He looked at the nape of Margrete's neck, noting how clearly it testified to this woman's uncommonly upright carriage. But at the same time he noticed something else, so plainly that he would never be able to dismiss it. He saw how vulnerable it looked. More vulnerable when viewed from here than at close quarters. All at once he understood why he had been so startled: if he knew so little about his father, how much did he really know about Margrete? Later, it would seem to Jonas that things had been arranged thus for just this purpose: that he should be up in the organ loft and catch sight of Margrete's long neck, adorned with pearls; as if he would never have discovered it, that tremendous vulnerability, had he not been observing her from so far away, and on such an occasion, with his father lying in his coffin, dead. Jonas was struck by a feeling – which he promptly fended off – that it all came down to her, even this funeral; that the centre lay here, at the nape of her neck, not up at the altar, not at his father's coffin.

Why did he do it?

Jonas looked away, forced his thoughts to run along different lines, rested his eyes on Karen Mohr's grey coat. Despite his brother's solemn words to the family he was growing restless, as he had so often done as a boy, sitting up here in the gallery, practising his arithmetic by adding up the numbers of the hymns displayed on the wall. When, that is, he was not trying to break an imaginary code, to come up with the magic words that would cause the wall of the church to split open, the vicar to take a header out of the pulpit as the entire, topless Lido chorus hove into view behind him. Such was the osmotic effect of his erotic imaginings. They occupied a spacious chamber at the back of his mind and were forever percolating through, anytime, anywhere, even in church.

Or in a boat, even when he was in deadly peril. He had felt the first stirrings even before they set out, that time on Hvasser. 'Isn't he beautiful?' she said as they hopped on board. It took a few seconds for it to dawn on him who 'he' was. People usually referred to boats as 'she'. 'Oak,' she said, running a hand over one of the timbers. 'Mahogany where you're sitting, fir deck, hull of Oregon pine, spruce mast. I won the Færder Race in him. D'you know anything about boats?' He nodded and shook his head at the same time. Despite all his holidays by the sea he knew very little about sailing. 'Okay, you can start by emptying the bilges,' she said, pointing to the hand pump. He pumped out the bilge water, heard the gurgling as it drained away, was not sure whether it was this or the sight of her, her navel, her brown thighs, which caused a ripple of excitement to run through him.

It was blowing harder now. The gulls seemed to be having trouble staying aloft. The halyards slapped against the mast and the wind sang in the shrouds.

She invited him into a rather untidy cabin for chocolate and biscuits, poured tea from a thermos. Jonas felt quite happy in the cabin despite the mess he liked the smell of it, the atmosphere, the feeling of being so close to the sea, closer here than outside. As if there were only a layer of skin between them and the waves. And yet it felt strangely safe. He found himself thinking of accordion music and Evert Taube's songs of the sea. Her name was Julie W. and she came from Tonsberg. She was studying in Switzerland. Her father was a big man in shipping. Right, thought Jonas, so she's a spoiled rich man's daughter. She was bound to become a force to be reckoned with in sailing circles. He could tell by the Royal Norwegian Yacht Club badge on her cap. She asked him, not too pointedly, to turn his back while she changed. Jonas could not help catching a glimpse of her. A more than alluring glimpse. She tossed him some clothes: oilskins, sea boots, a life-jacket. The waves smashed against the side, filling the little room with burblings and gurglings. Little creaks and groans formed a titillating accompaniment to Jonas's memory of her naked body.

Then they were under way, and he was too busy being amazed by the way she moved, almost dancing as she set the sails, heaved on ropes, cast off moorings, manoeuvred out of harbour, all without engine power – engines were for cissies, she said. 'Wind the foresheet round the winch a couple of times, pull it tight and make it fast to the belaying cleat,' she shouted at him, giving him some idea of how tough this was going to be, with commands in a language that was Greek to him. 'Amateur,' she sighed, coming over to do it herself. The only thing he could just about manage was to hold the tiller. They sailed with the wind, headed north up the lee side of Sandøya then bore east. Before too long, as they drew clear of Store Færder – having rounded a cape, so to speak – the swell hit them in earnest. Sitting there on board the *São Gabriel*, Jonas realised that he was heading into unknown territory, but was not at all sure that he wanted to discover it.

The boat sped across the waves, its sails turned to wings which looked as if they could take flight. 'This is great,' she yelled over the roar of the water, 'we've got a broad reach the whole way there!' He did not know what she was talking about, nor did he have any idea why she suddenly became so busy adjusting here and tightening there, until she explained that she was trimming the sails. 'Feel how well he rides the waves,' she cried once she was satisfied. Her face shone with what looked like pure joy. Jonas made out Færder lighthouse to starboard: an exclamation, a 'Turn back!' sign. To Jonas the boat seemed to skim over the waves, as if they were travelling into another element. 'You'll have to start bailing,' she said, pulling her cap lower down over her brow. It suited her. He was conscious, despite a growing sense of panic, of a feeling of expectancy, as if the knowledge that his life was in danger were acting as an aphrodisiac, inspiring the notion that she was also liable to run a hand over him, every part of him, while saying, whispering, something about oak, mahogany, Oregon pine.

'Shift over to the windward side.' She more or less hauled him over and plonked him down to the right and a little in front of her when he took too long about it. They were sitting very close. She studied a sea chart, keeping her left hand on the tiller. The August sky was taking on the same hues as the insides of the conch shells his grandfather had left behind at the house on Hvaler. They were surrounded by seething water, in a constant swirl. What had become of Evert Taube, the sea songs, the accordion music? We're sitting too close together, this can't possibly go well, Jonas thought to himself, while at the same time fancying that there was some correspondence between the way she handled the boat, her expert manoeuvring, and what she might possibly do to him.

The wind was coming from abaft; he could no longer have said how hard it was blowing. Sometimes, when they were sailing so fast that they overtook a wave – great billows towering over them like ravening monsters three and four metres high – Jonas was certain that they were done for, that the bow would drag the boat under when it surged into the wall of the wave. Yet each time, as if witnessing a miracle, he saw the bow rear up again. Other times, when they were moving more slowly and were hit from behind by foaming breakers – in what seemed like horrible, insidious ambushes – he was equally convinced that the *stern* would be engulfed, only then to see how elegantly it lifted again – he sent a silent thank you to the boat's brilliant designer – so that the waters slid away underneath them and buoyed them up, sent them scudding forwards, surfing, hanging for seconds at a time on the crest of a wave, as if they were flying through the darkness; as if they were not on their way from Hvasser to Hvaler, but were somewhere out in space, between Venus and Mercury.

She beckoned him over. He thought she was going to give him an order, but instead she kissed him, kissed him as if it were the most natural thing in the world, a succulent, provocative kiss, a kiss which, panic-stricken though he was, with the sea frothing menacingly along the lip of the well, left him wondering what it would be like to kiss her belly button, stick his tongue into that glorious little dot and roll it around in there. Might that not give him the feeling of disappearing, of being sucked under by a whirlpool; waking up in another galaxy? Wasn't this – at long last – the woman he had been looking for?

They scudded over the waves. He could see that she was concentrating, keeping an eye on the sails, noting the slightest flap, reading signs that he could not see, following every move of the boat as if it was a living creature; he noticed how firmly she gripped the tiller, yet how gently she moved it from side to side, as if she were not steering, but caressing the waves, leaving the boat to find its own way. He imagined her holding him, his penis, just that way, firmly but gently. 'Haul in the foresheet a bit!' she yelled, as if she had heard his thoughts and meant to give him something else to think about. She had brought them back into a broad reach. He was putting everything he had into it, but he kept ballsing up. 'God, what a clumsy clod!' she snapped, clearly annoyed by his ignorance of sailing terms. As far as Jonas was concerned this merely confirmed what he already knew: that girls had a language all their own. Nonetheless it seemed pretty obvious that something was going on between them, in the midst of the storm; that this sail was bound to culminate in, to carry on into, a race between two bodies, because this was only the foreplay, that much he understood, that much he could tell from the look in her eyes, the fury and the lust he saw glinting in them through the salty spray with which they were drenched every now and again.

The sea grew rougher and rougher the farther east they sailed. Then, dead abeam, Jonas spotted a ship. A massive vessel strung with tiny lights. A starship in space. It looked as though Julie, out of sheer bloody-mindedness, meant to cut straight across its bow. They were done for, he was sure of it. 'Ease up!' he screamed. 'For God's sake, can't you see we're going to ram right into it!'

Up in the organ gallery, surveying the church below, Jonas Wergeland thought to himself that this too was a sea voyage of sorts – or a cruise, perhaps, what with everyone being so primped and perfumed. Against his will his eyes lingered again on the nape of Margrete's neck – that enigmatic vulnerability – until he managed to pull them away and ran them over the rows of pews. He recognised more and more faces and once again it struck him what a springboard for memories this was. Although many years were to pass before Jonas realised that it was during this funeral service that the seeds had been sown of what was possibly his most famous programme, the one on Henrik Ibsen. It had something to do with the sight of a church wherein everything was condensed, to form a mesh, a net, in which the whole of one's life had been caught. If, that is, it had not been inspired by hearing the powerful words from the Bible, by being confronted with the deepest solemnity. For what was the biggest challenge where Henrik Ibsen was concerned? It was to discover what actually occurred at the greatest moment in Norwegian literature. And this too involved a church.

In the spring of 1864, at the age of thirty-six, Henrik Ibsen began his twenty-seven years in exile by travelling to Italy. It was a far from successful writer who left his native land, left Norway – in political terms a Swedish province, in cultural terms a Danish one. He was plagued by money troubles and had not yet written any work of real consequence, or at least not anything that could be described as world-class. It is not much of an overstatement to say that his life was – figuratively speaking – on the rocks.

For a long time Jonas considered centring the programme around Ibsen's arrival in 'the Beautiful South', Ibsen himself having so often described what a revelation it had been to come down from the Alps: 'from the mists, through a tunnel and out into the sunlight'; a dark curtain had been pulled back and suddenly he found himself bathed in the most wonderful bright light. In his mind Jonas saw images of the countryside, an evocative montage of contrasting scenes; was tempted, but eventually dropped the idea.

Because the moment of truth does not occur until the following year, on a summer's day in 1865. The Ibsens are staying in the Alban Hills, at Ariccia, twenty kilometres from the Italian capital. Ibsen is working on *Brand*, but getting nowhere with it. But then, on a brief visit to Rome, things fall into place for him. The incident is described in a letter to Bjørnstjerne Bjørnson: 'Then one day I visited St Peter's Basilica [...] and all at once I found a strong and clear Form for what I had to say.' What can we take from this vague statement? What was it that Henrik Ibsen discovered in St Peter's. Whatever it was, back at Ariccia he completely rewrote *Brand*, working as if in a trance. What had been a monologue became a dialogue. He turned an epic poem into a drama – and reaped the plaudits at home in Scandinavia. This was followed by his masterpiece *Peer Gynt*, and thereafter, almost singlehandedly, Henrik Ibsen created modern drama. Not only that: he also did much to influence, possibly even *change*, the whole tenor of contemporary thought. On that day in St Peter's, something happened which was to put Norwegian literature on the map.

Jonas Wergeland's theory concerning Ibsen's experience in the Basilica bore little resemblance to anyone else's. Because the way he saw it, and presented it in pictures and sound, not until he stepped into the gloom of St Peter's was the outer light which Ibsen had encountered in Italy transformed into an inner light. And even though this provocative assertion found form in a key scene which was strongly criticised for its audacity and its speculative cast, many people regarded this programme on Ibsen as the lynchpin in a series which did for Norwegian television what Ibsen had done for the country's literature. Thanks to Jonas Wergeland, NRK's reputation not only reached formidable heights outside of Norway; his work led also – and far more importantly – to a renewed interest in Norwegian culture in general.

Wergeland did not, therefore, succumb to the temptation to start the programme with a train rushing out of a black tunnel, out into the light of the Mediterranean countryside; instead it opened with an allegorical scene prompting associations with life-saving. You had the impression of rising, along with the camera, after a long dive into the deep; ascending from the darkness towards a bright, shimmering surface, and as you broke through you heard the sound of heavy breathing and saw a bewildered Henrik Ibsen stumbling, wading almost, from the recesses of St Peter's into the sunlit summer's day. It was, in short, a programme about a man who not only came close to foundering, but who was actually drowning, until – quite unexpectedly, perhaps even undeservedly – he saved himself.

Another event which might have sparked the idea for the Ibsen programme, was the mysterious, as yet unexplained, incident which took place towards the close of Haakon Hansen's funeral service, after the congregation had mumbled their way through The Lord's Prayer, after Daniel had sprinkled the symbolic handful of soil on the coffin and given the blessing and everyone had sat down again; just as Jonas struck up the choral prelude to the final hymn, 'Love divine all love excelling'. Jonas did not see the whole thing himself, but he heard about it later, in a wide variety of conflicting versions. Suddenly a woman had come walking up the centre aisle, a woman clad in a bright orange coat, like a flame, a foretaste of the cremation to come. Some people got quite a fright, the singing petered out. She had an intent look on her face, this woman. She looked dangerous, some said. She strode slowly up to the coffin as the singing swelled again, as if with 'Love divine all love excelling' the congregation meant to shield Haakon Hansen from the figure now making her way towards him; a note of discord in this harmonious ceremony. A disgrace, some whispered afterwards. Interesting, said others. Who was she, everyone asked.

No one needed to tell Jonas Wergeland that women were unpredictable, dangerous. Because once, late one night, he had been out in a sail boat in the middle of Oslo fjord, in a storm, along with a girl who seemed ready to risk being sunk rather than give way to a huge passenger ferry. But he need not have worried, they passed astern of it, with plenty of room to spare. She shot him a glance, smiled – or no, she didn't smile: she smirked. He felt such an idiot. He was on the point of collapse. She, on the other hand, still had her captain's cap firmly on her head and was in complete command of the situation; she loved this, Jonas could tell, enjoyed having control over tremendous forces, *exploiting* tremendous forces, the air, the water, because she was not sailing the boat, she was sailing the wind and the waves. Just as she was sailing his thoughts.

If, that was, she wasn't stark, raving mad. Because things were moving far too fast; he was scared, truly terrified. She was the sort of woman who was quite liable to live her life according to that old chestnut from Ibsen: 'And what if I did run my ship aground; oh, still it was splendid to sail it!' The sea was black, dark edged in white. It had been a big mistake coming out with her. She looked as if she was quite capable of hoisting the spinnaker. And more: Jonas had the impression that she was planning to make love to him as resolutely and passionately as she sailed her boat through the storm. The water seethed, the storm thundered all around him. From time to time he heard a crack from the sail, it made him jump, he thought disaster had struck. He was sure his heart leapt into his mouth each time the boat slammed down into the trough of a wave, its joints creaking and rigging groaning; he had never been quite so literally caught between wind and water.

Despite being so afraid he could not rid himself of the thought that there was something epic, something mythic, about this voyage. He had the feeling that he was on a quest, that there was something he had to do, something he had to bring back: a golden fleece, a vital ice sample from one of the rings of Saturn. Or that this odyssey was a kind of training, a tempering process. And when he was most terrified, just when he had told himself: that's it, we're sunk, she would lean forward and kiss him, a hard, wet, salty kiss, more of a suck than a kiss, while at the same time, outwith the kiss, as it were, keeping an eye on the waves. And always with a sly grin hovering around her lips, as if this gruelling crossing was no more than a harebrained bit of teasing.

It should be said, though, that even Julie's face eventually began to show signs of worry. The wind must have grown even stronger. 'We'll have to shorten sail!' she suddenly yelled, as if their lives depended on it. She bent down to Jonas, put her lips close to his ear and told him what to do, so clearly and precisely that he realised this was a very risky manoeuvre. 'Slacken the main sail halyard when I turn into the eye of the wind,' she shrieked, giving him a nudge which bordered on being a kick. He was scared out of his wits, more or less crawled across the deck to the mast, praying to God. The water churned around his feet. She turned into the wind. 'Move it, dummy! Loosen the line round the starboard cleat! And watch out for the corner of the jib!' she yelled as he fumbled about. The sails were flapping wildly, cracking like whips, frightening him so badly that he was almost shitting himself. At last, though, he managed to carry out her order. 'Make fast the luff cringle. Christ, you're slow!' He could hardly hear what she was saying. He spotted the eyelets on the sail, grasped what she wanted him to do, slipped the eyelet over the hook. Even this simple action sent his mind off down another track entirely, so much so that, terrified though he was, he could not help wondering what might happen later, if they survived. She would make him flap and crack just like those sails. Or no: she would sail him until his timbers rent. 'Come here!' she bellowed as she tightened the reef line on the after end of the boom. He managed to scramble back down into the well, totally done in, ripe for a rest home. 'What's wrong with you?' she said. 'You look as though you'd seen Old Neptune himself.'

The sail was well set, she bore onto the right course. 'Good boy,' she said with affected heartiness, slapping his thigh, blatantly, only a hair's-breadth from his groin. 'No reason to spoil the stars with a flare,' she said. 'But take a quick turn on the pump just to be on the safe side.'

The reefing did not seem to have slowed them down at all. He was trembling as badly as ever. What worried him most of all was the sight of the mountainous waves which came from behind, you could see them a long way off: black walls of water barrelling relentlessly closer. He tried to keep his eyes front, but was constantly having to glance over his shoulder at the giant rollers steaming down on them, the surging foam, the sea trying to lap him up like a thousand-mouthed beast of prey. That swelling roar reminded him – of all things – of organ music. 'Right Jonas, time to set full sail,' his father always said when he played *organo pleno*. But this roar had a sorrowful note to it, like the music for a funeral. Still Julie never faltered. Her set face shone with concentration and what might have been pleasure. More and more, Jonas was wondering what was going to happen when – *if* – they reached harbour, he fell to day-dreaming about this, he did not know why, but he sat there, terrified out of his wits, like a condemned man with a hard-on, fantasising about how she would rip off his clothes, demand that he take her from behind, like a mountainous billow, wash over and under her, lift her up, again and again. 'If you don't sit still I'll have to put a safety harness on you,' she yelled, again with that knowing smirk on her face, as he dodged the spray from a huge rogue wave.

It was getting late. She was taking her bearings from the lighthouses. For a long time he had kept his eye fixed on the Tresteinene light. It was so beautiful, quite unearthly. Mawkishly he thought to himself that his life had begun to flicker, like a light bulb just before it goes out, but the light did not go out, it went on flashing at its set intervals as they sailed passed it and Julie cut across the white sector towards Homlungen light, her eyes darting from side to side. She was keeping a sharp look out for spar buoys, barely visible in the gloom. Jonas held his breath until they had slipped past the lighthouse on its headland and he could see the lights of Skjærhalden.

He knew what would happen next. She would ride him like she had ridden her boat across the waves, there would be no reefing where he was concerned, she would not allow him any slack. She would screw him rigid, on and on until she drained his bilges, making him gurgle from top to toe, pumping him utterly dry. And yet it was not her, the woman, he feared, but himself, the forces he felt stirring within him. As if she had set all his sails, generating a potency he had not known he possessed, a desire that rendered him willing to drown if only he could poke his tongue into that navel; an urge so strong that he would not have been surprised to discover that he was actually still on dry land, on Hvasser, staring at Julie's belly; to find, in other words, that this whole, crazy boat trip had taken place inside her navel.

As they glided in to the docks and he noted with relief that it really was Skjærhalden, and not Hvasser, he felt compelled to make a decision. Was his objective – was she, Julie – what he thought, what he hoped, she was? Or was he suffering from another attack of Melankton's syndrome?

They were safe in harbour, securely tied up. Just when it looked as though she was about to drag him into the cabin – she had already tossed her cap through the hatch, in what seemed like the first move in a striptease act – he said: 'Hang on, I need to feel solid ground under my feet first.' And as she went aft to check the anchor line, he seized the chance to grab his rucksack and climb ashore. He strode off briskly to the bus stop, where the last bus for Fredrikstad was preparing to leave.

Jonas Wergeland sat at the organ in Grorud Church, playing 'Love divine all love excelling'. Over the years he had expended a lot of energy on eluding women. Riding out storms. Had his father experienced something similar? Who was this woman walking up the aisle, stepping out like a bride, someone said, as if hearing in her head, not 'Love divine all love excelling', but Purcell's Wedding March. Someone from whom he could no longer escape? Jonas had long suspected that there was a lot he did not know about his father. As a youth, almost grown, he had stumbled upon a scrapbook on his father's desk. To Jonas this was as unlikely a discovery in the familiar surroundings of the family flat as a mineral from another planet. All the cuttings related to one question: whether there was life elsewhere in the universe. No one had known anything about Haakon Hansen's interest in this subject. Could it be that his father had regarded his organ music as radio transmissions of some sort? Could it be that, whenever he played, his father was wondering: is there life out there?

Later still, Jonas was to learn that something else had occurred on that day when Rakel and his father met Albert Schweitzer in Trinity Church. Perhaps it was because the celebrated guest saw the look of appreciation on Haakon Hansen's face – or discerned something else there – that he asked Jonas's father if he would also play something. The latter had hesitated. Haakon

Hansen was not known for showing off. Whenever Jonas was with his father and people asked what he did for a living, Haakon always replied: 'I'm an organ-grinder.' But the others persuaded him to play. So Haakon sat down at the fine old organ. He also played Bach, a trio sonata. Albert Schweitzer was thrilled, he spent a long time talking to Jonas's father afterwards, about their mutual passion for organ playing, the architectonics of the music and, of course, the works of the cantor of St Thomas's Church in Leipzig. Albert Schweitzer was particularly flattered to learn that Haakon Hansen had read his book on Bach, all 800 pages of it – this seemed to please him more than having won the Peace Prize – and he laughed heartily when the Grorud organist made so bold as to say: 'I think it's even better than your book on the mysticism of Paul the Apostle.' Their conversation was so lively and went on for so long that it put the rest of the day's schedule behind time. Schweitzer's entourage more or less had to tear him away from Haakon Hansen, in the middle of a discussion about the incomparable timbre of Cavaillé-Coll's organ in Saint Sulpice in Paris. 'And wouldn't you agree,' Albert Schweitzer called back finally over his shoulder as he was dragged away, 'that people play Bach too fast these days?'

Only a few years later, Jonas met another organist who had been present at this meeting and who told Jonas that Schweitzer had been full of praise for Haakon Hansen. 'You are a world-class organist,' he had told Jonas's father. 'What are you doing tucked away in a small church in a Norwegian suburb?' And it was at that point that Haakon had made the legendary remark – one which was to become a comforting motto in Norwegian organ circles: 'We all have our own Lambaréné.'

These fragments of a story conflicted with the hints their father himself had given the family about his early years. This new information seemed to speak of a possible career which was never pursued, of a light hidden under a bushel. 'People still talk about his debut concert,' one old organist told Jonas. His father had been on the threshold of a dazzling career as a musician when suddenly, for reasons that were never explained, he gave it all up in favour of a humble post as a church organist.

Was this a sacrifice of some sort, or simply a move prompted by shyness, a shyness which Jonas felt he must have inherited? Had his father's choice of career been a waste of talent – or had this decision actually been the saving of him? Perhaps it had to do with finding a balance in life. Between ambition and reality. Between conscience and opportunity. Whichever way Jonas looked at it, he had to admit – especially when he saw the pleasure his father took in keeping a kayak on an even keel – that Haakon Hansen appeared to be a harmonious, not to say contented individual.

Jonas played 'Love divine all love excelling', all but dancing over the organ bench, balancing on his backside while his fingers flew over the manuals and his feet heeled and toed it over the pedals. Now he, too, could see the woman in orange. She took the last few steps up to the dais in front of the altar on which the coffin sat, to his father who lay there dead. In his Lambaréné. A Schweitzer to the people of Grorud. Jonas could not believe his eyes. A woman in orange. Like a member of another religion, another culture, he thought. And behind that thought another, of which he only caught the tail end: or someone from another dimension. A world beyond this one, running parallel to it. Once, when Jonas was small, his father had lifted him onto his lap and played a D major triad, D-F major-A, and explained to him that a piano did not have the capacity to bring out the almost imperceptible difference between an F major and a G flat the way a good violinist could. 'There's a blind spot there, between F major and G flat,' his father told him. As usual that was all he said, but Jonas could finish it for himself: it was the same with life. Maybe this woman hailed from just such a spot. One that lay between the F major and G flat of life. For a moment, a few tenths of a second which also grew in depth like a complex chord, it occurred to Jonas that he might actually owe his life to this woman; that here, in the gossip mirror attached to the side of the organ, he beheld the root cause of his existence. She stood quite still before his father's coffin, as if she were alone in the church. The hymn came to an end. Jonas laid his hands on the console and drew his feet back to rest under the bench, observing, as he did so, how the woman turned ever so slightly, for a second, and met his mother's eye, saw her give an almost imperceptible little nod, saw his mother do the same. Then: the unknown woman went down on her knees. At that same moment a ripple of movement passed through the two angels in the painting on the wall behind the altar. Jonas could have sworn to it, did not think anyone had noticed but him. A stirring of their wings. And the coffin hovered. For a few seconds it hovered in mid-air.

Not until years later, did Jonas realise that it was at that moment that he came up with the idea – in a flash, you might say – for his programme on Henrik Ibsen, one of the twenty-odd episodes of *Thinking Big*, a splendid television series in which each individual programme was as carefully arranged in relation to the others as the pipes in an organ. When that time came, he could not have said where he had got it from – he called it inspiration – but the image stemmed, of course, from this incident: with a woman kneeling in a church. And a possible miracle.

Jonas Wergeland's programme on Henrik Ibsen did not touch on the less sympathetic sides of the writer's character: his arrogance and pomposity, his ruthless ambition and, at the same time, his pathological shyness, his pedantry and penchant for the formalities, not to mention all the shameless arselicking he did in order to obtain honours, his infatuations with very young girls, his drinking, his sexual inhibitions. Nonetheless: seldom has a programme been so roundly condemned. Ibsen researchers and other members of the literati were particularly outraged, describing it as libellous. Because Wergeland's story about Norway's national bard – a fictional drama in the spirit of *Brand* and *Peer Gynt* – dealt with a man on his knees, a man who, in the course of a few minutes, underwent a total transformation.

The key scene opened with Ibsen – in Rome on business – sitting disconsolately outside an osteria in the magnificent Piazza Navona, drinking wine. He was turning over several projects in his mind, but it was the text of *Brand* which was giving him the most trouble. He was getting nowhere. Like Duke Skule in *The Pretenders* he was beginning to have doubts about himself, about his calling. He was afraid that the disparity between the absolute demands and the realities of the situation, between his aims and his abilities, was too great. He sipped his white wine, gazing at the fountain in the centre of the square, at Bernini's evocative figures and the water splashing into the basin, the four jets meant to symbolise the world's four great rivers and, hence, the four corners of the globe; tumbling water, a cascade which – as it was presented on television – reminded him of the waterfalls at home in Norway, the wild landscape of western Norway, the darkness of the water, dangerous forces, the magical powers of the water nixie, the risk of drowning: thoughts which moved him to drink more white wine, get even drunker. And in Jonas Wergeland's rendering it was here, while looking at this fountain, that Ibsen conceived his 'A verse' – not printed until years later – which was recited as the screen darkened: 'To live is – to do battle with trolls / in the vaults of the heart and the mind. / To write is – to sit in judgement on oneself.'

Henrik Ibsen got to his feet, a mite unsteadily, and wove off into the shadows as the sound of bubbling water intensified. The next shot showed the writer standing in a massive doorway, the next again in some dark place, a cave – a studio set conjured into existence by NRK's best carpenters and designers. To the viewers it looked as though Ibsen had stepped inside his own brain or the vaults of his heart, and truly did have to do battle in there with trolls and dwarfs. They saw the writer being hunted, tormented, saw Ibsen's innermost worries swarming around him in the form of ghosts: 'You're not Knud Ibsen's son!' snorted a gnome. 'Why do you deny me?' asked a father. Elves danced around Ibsen, chanting that he was bankrupt, bankrupt. A girl waved a poem at him, crying that he had broken their engagement; a policeman appeared to arrest him and take him off to do hard labour at Akershus Fort. 'You have lost your faith in God,' hissed a troll. The most distinct and most oft-recurring figures were, however, a woman and her son, a child whom one understood to be Ibsen's own, the boy he had, at the age of eighteen, fathered on a serving maid in Grimstad ten years his senior. Henrik Ibsen sat in judgement on himself. His face bore the marks of pride and a passionate will, and of guilt, shame, pain and sorrow. His lips moved. Jonas Wergeland inserted a quote from *Brand*, the play on which Ibsen was then working: 'O, endless the atonement here. – / In such confused and tangled state, the thousand twisted strands of fate', and ended with Brand's cry at the end of the third act: 'Give me light!'

And as Henrik Ibsen raised his head, the whole scene opened out. In a stunning dissolve, Jonas Wergeland had the surroundings change from the hall of the Mountain King to the interior of a church, St Peter's Basilica itself. Through Ibsen's eyes one gazed straight up at Michelangelo's breathtakingly high dome. A ray of light streamed down on him, and to viewers at home it seemed that the light alone brought the writer to his knees.

Jonas Wergeland held this shot for a long time, an eternity in viewers' memories: Henrik Ibsen, the greatest of all Norwegian writers, on his knees under that vast dome, that prodigiously ambitious span, on his knees before the papal altar, under Bernini's bronze canopy, right next to the steps leading down to the tomb of St Peter, the rock on which the whole Christian church was founded, while all around him the light grew stronger and stronger. It was a provocative image, an image which, for many, accorded badly with the Ibsen they knew: a stubborn, antagonistic character who could not write unless bristling with resentment. But to Jonas Wergeland, this was where all of Ibsen's future masterpieces had their beginnings: with him kneeling, humbly, under a cupola, in a church.

According to the programme's version of events, Henrik Ibsen was, at this point, a disheartened man, plagued by thoughts of betrayal in his life and his art; a man who, in sitting in judgement on himself, was bound to find himself guilty. But on his knees under the dome of St Peter's, under the image of the Almighty himself, he met with compassion, or rather: he was *granted* – like a gift for which he had not asked – forgiveness; he was set free. *Brand* was in all ways a reflection of this experience. Just as Ibsen had sacrificed a woman, Else Sophie from Grimstad, and the child he had with her, so too Brand sacrificed, ruthlessly, tragically, his wife and his son, and yet Ibsen concludes the play with a last line proclaiming: 'He is *deus caritatis!*' He is the God of love.

In St Peter's, Ibsen found a light, a relief and a release which also rendered him receptive to the inspiration and, hence, the creativity which great art can bestow. The barbarians came to Ancient Rome and were civilised. So, too with Henrik Ibsen. *Brand* – the new, revised, visionary play, that is – was in many ways a response to the works of art in St Peter's. Most of all to the dome. Michelangelo's mighty vault gave Ibsen courage, the courage to give his imagination wing. To go out on a limb. The courage to go against the accepted taste, the courage to do something crazy. To say: On the contrary. All or nothing. The works of art in that church, and everywhere else in Rome, did not merely provide him with a new yardstick, they also prompted him to ask himself another question: what is a man. It was here, in St Peter's Basilica, that Ibsen made up his mind to be a person who asked questions rather than one who answered them. It was here that he began to perceive the possibility of depicting people as no one before him had done.

Through Ibsen's eyes, television viewers saw him discover the key to his future works. Looking up, he caught sight of the four large mosaic medallions at the four corners of the dome: the four evangelists, four writers, each of whom had presented his version of one man's life. Ibsen may also have been reminded of the four rivers represented in Bernini's fountain on the Piazza Navona. He had a vision: he was standing at the intersection point of four powerful spotlight beams, could feel their influence flowing through him, his mind could run in four directions at once. And at that very moment – so Jonas Wergeland postulated – it came to him, the idea of writing four different versions, four stories about the same man, only he would give him four different names: Skule, whom he had already portrayed, Brand, Peer and Julian. Four characters. And yet one. Presenting, when seen together, a picture of Mankind, its depth and its breadth.

Beneath that boundary-breaking cupola in Rome, Henrik Ibsen was liberated from his stunted self. He was free to become someone else, also as a writer. Henrik Ibsen had been transformed. He had blundered into St Peter's as a troll, enough in himself, and walked out a man.

Jonas Wergeland was, as it happens, firmly convinced that Ibsen's latterly so renowned sphinx-like countenance, his aloof demeanour was a mask he assumed to save revealing anything of his Caritas moment.

A number of people have pointed out that this programme rests on a somewhat objectionable assumption: that Ibsen died and was restored to life, became a new man. Became more than he had been. What people did not know was that Jonas had made this assumption on the basis of personal experience. In one discussion he did, however, claim that in *Peer Gynt* Ibsen himself had hinted at something similar. In several scenes, Peer appears to die, and yet goes on living – on the high moors, in the hall of the Mountain King, in the Asylum, on the boat home. As for Henrik Ibsen, from that summer on, more than one person observed a sudden and marked difference in his manner. He became more impulsive, for a long time he read nothing but the Bible and he changed his whole style of dress. This new sense of freedom boosted his self-confidence. The following year, in his ambitious application for a poet's pension he wrote – in a hand which had also undergone an abrupt transformation – the words which Jonas Wergeland used as the title of his television series: Ibsen would, as he said, fight 'to arouse the Nation and encourage it to think big'.

Jonas Wergeland, still merely an announcer with NRK television, sat in a church, at an organ, and he too saw a light of sorts: a woman clad in brilliant orange, on her knees before his father's coffin. The final strains of 'Love divine all love excelling' still hung in the air. Jonas did not know whether this occurrence, the woman down by the altar, was going to bring everything to a halt, make time stand still, but he got ready, anyway, to play the postlude while the coffin was carried out to the hearse which waited to take it to the crematorium. Time went on. The strange woman got to her feet and met the eyes trained on her from the packed pews. The precious stones in her earrings flashed. What an amazing figure, Jonas thought to himself. In her orange coat, in such a gathering, she looked like a butterfly on a winter's day, a peacock butterfly caught in a snowstorm. A creature who lifted the lid off this funeral scene to reveal that it was all about something else, something more. No one knew – no one ever discovered – who she was or why she did it. Whether she belonged to a past time or, as Jonas was inclined to believe, to a parallel time. As she walked – no, strode – up the aisle she seemed, wordlessly, to be saying: 'You are wrong, this is not a church, it is a palace; that is not an organist in that coffin, but a king.'

Then she was gone. A glowing ember leaving behind it only ashes, dead and black.

Jonas, however, was left with the feeling that she had lit a spark within him. Or that she had blown more life into the tiny flame which he had become aware of earlier when his eye lighted on the nape of Margrete's neck. He focused on his music, prepared to play the postlude, which was in fact a prelude. The same piece that his father had been playing when he died, Bach's prelude in A minor. As if picking up where his father had left off. A triumph. Jonas raised his hands and, as he did so, in a flash he saw how the most disparate threads of life intertwined in this room, at this moment; how seemingly parallel, unconnected events suddenly came together to form harmonies, music, a prelude which showed him that his own life had not even begun yet. Did it always take a death to render complex matters simple?

Jonas played the first few bars, with the A note held as a pedal point, like a prolonged insistence on new beginnings, on life. Jonas threw himself into this work which, strictly speaking, he was in no way qualified to play, but which he managed to play nonetheless, played it so that the whole church shook. And the longer he played, the greater became the feeling of something of colossal importance welling up inside him, something which had long lain buried, and as he neared the end of the piece, as he caught himself holding his breath, one thought outweighed all others, the thought of taking his talent seriously, because he had the opposite problem from Ibsen: he had the ability, but he lacked the will. Jonas made the air vibrate with his playing, and perhaps because he had long since been imbued with the geometric beauty of this moment, and because the music felt like a crystalline net in which every fragment reflected all of the others, and because he was sitting in a small church, building a cathedral out of music, he found that he had already made up his mind: he longed to have more wind in his sails. He would approach his bosses at NRK and ask to be allowed to make programmes. And some day – again he was reminded of those metro stations in Moscow – some day he might create a series presenting the bright spots, the underground stations, in the collective life of Norway, a series of programmes which would encourage the whole nation to think big. Maybe, the thought struck him as the echo of the final chord died away and a hush fell in the church, such a series could even be regarded as life-saving.

Io

On the way down to Turtagrø he turned back several times to look up at the three peaks behind us. 'They remind me of the pyramids at Giza,' he said. Late in the afternoon, down by the car, he stood for a moment regarding Store Skagastølstind, the mountain we had climbed. As if considering something. Then: 'I've seen the Great Pyramid at Cheops,' he murmured at length, 'but this is greater.' To me it sounded as if he were saying: I was dead, but now I am risen.

'Why did you go so close to the edge ?' I asked.

'I thought I could fly,' he said. 'I thought I had sprouted wings.'

We reached Skjolden that evening. The village lay in shadow, but the sun was still shining on the slopes high on the east side of Lustrafjord and on the snow atop Molden, the peak which formed the cornerstone of a chamber in which the shining water constituted the floor and the mountains the walls. The blossom on the apple trees we drove past seemed luminous. The beauty of it was almost too much.

The *Voyager* was lying waiting for us at the Norsk Hydro wharf, below the old Eide farmstead; Hanna and Carl had sailed up the day before. We got ourselves settled in the old lifeboat, a genuine Colin Archer, built over a hundred years ago. For the next few weeks it would be our home. A boat that had saved the lives of hundreds of people in distress. A stormy petrel. A vessel designed to put to sea when others were making for harbour. The perfect mobile base.

Martin promptly disappeared into the galley, I heard chinking sounds coming from his tiny, but discriminatingly stocked drinks cabinet. 'Here you are,' he said, as he came up again with a glass for our guest. 'A Talisker from the Isle of Skye, laced with the tang of the ocean. The perfect whisky for drinking at sea. Welcome aboard.'

'Cheers,' said our guest. 'Here's to a boat fit for an old lifesaver.'

We had to make the most of our days at Skjolden. Carl had been allotted the most important task: the stave church at Urnes. Martin would be concentrating on the natural wonders of the area, particularly the Feigumfossen waterfall and Fortunsdalen. Hanna would be visiting places like Munthehuset at Kroken, where so many painters had stayed. And I was to chart the philosopher Ludwig Wittgenstein's movements in and around Skjolden. In the course of this work I found myself one afternoon on the hill above Eidsvatnet, sitting by the foundations of his cottage, 'Østerrike'. As I leafed through the fragmentary writings in *Philosophische Untersuchungen*, I was suddenly struck by the similarity between the project on which we were engaged and Wittgenstein's efforts to eschew the traditional limitations of the book form, where 'b' inevitably follows 'a'. This made me wish that we could insert a 'link' to a small display – I envisaged a graphic image inspired by Wittgenstein's clarinet – illustrating the connection between the fjord as form, as a network of branches, and the composition of his book.

We had been lucky with the weather. In the evening we were able to sit up on deck, exchanging findings and ideas while the sunlight slowly loosened its grip on the top of Bolstadnosi, behind Skjolden. Was there, for example, any correlation between Wittgenstein's theories and the carvings in Urnes stave church? This was the sort of question we meant to encourage people to ask. Already we had some inkling of what our main challenge would be: of all the information we gathered – what should we take with us?

I think, though, that I spent just as much time observing our passenger, a man who had once had the whole nation in the palm of his hand and almost succeeded in steering it onto a different course, before he was sent to prison for the murder of his wife. Who was this man? I had taken it upon myself to uncover unknown aspects of his life. I had already written a long and elaborate rough draft which I was continually turning over in my mind, in parallel, so to speak, with my actual assignment.

I asked myself who I thought I was, to be undertaking such a task. I was neither a god nor a devil. I was a human being. I was a conjecturing individual. My style – even where my account sounded pretty dogmatic – could not help but be tentative, hypothetical. Full of eventualities and qualifications and reservations. Although I never actually said it, never revealed my scruples, my doubts and my unquestionable shortcomings, not even in parentheses, the whole thing was pervaded by an implicit 'it *may* be that …', or 'as I see it …'. And yet sometimes, even when I was sitting up on deck, making more notes, I felt like a spirit drifting over the water, an omniscient spirit, a spirit with the power to create light, to separate sea from sky. It was easy to become enamoured of this illusion. I *knew* a lot, a nuisance of a lot, about the man sitting on a deck chest across from me. And I considered my youth an advantage. I was not interested in adding anything or tearing anything down. I simply wanted to understand: why did he do it?

I studied him surreptitiously. It was a rare privilege to be able to spend some days with one's subject. Although he looked different after his time behind bars, after his first years of freedom – his hair was grey now, his face thinner, his skin oddly darker somehow – I was surprised to find that he could stroll around Skjolden, check out the goings-on at the Fjordstova community centre – the climbing wall, the library – without being recognised. As far as I could tell, this did not bother him at all. Looked at objectively, though, this was quite something, in fact it was almost unbelievable: his visage had been erased, so to speak, from people's memories. As if someone had pressed a huge 'delete' button.

His slide into oblivion had been a gradual thing, of course: long after he had exchanged the spotlit pedestal of television celebrity for the dim solitude of the prison cell he had remained the object of an interest bordering on mass hysteria. All the newspapers printed special supplements about him, detailing the high points of his career. Both the press and television behaved as if they were suffering from bulimia. They could not get enough of him. It was said that a number of women had tried to kill themselves, that they had been found clutching photographs of Jonas Wergeland. He had been an incandescent, edifying icon to the people of Norway, exalted and inviolable. Many people, I'm sure, can still recall how shocking it was, back in the infancy of television, when a newsreader got a fit of the giggles and thus revealed that he or she was only an ordinary mortal. But the wave of disbelief that swept the country when Jonas Wergeland, a national emblem, the nearest thing to a demi-god, was convicted of murder, was of another order entirely.

Even the most sensational scandals do not last for ever, though. After remarkably few years Jonas Wergeland was no more than a distant legend associated with the best of television broadcasting, He had been reduced to a word, a concept. If his name did crop up it was not uncommonly in the form of a superlative: 'Wergelandian'. His television series – and other programmes made by him – had, however, a life of their own. The repeats had been running for years. The videos of *Thinking Big* also sold steadily. The reaction – an almost religious collective response – to the first showing could obviously never be repeated, but for that very reason perhaps, the artistic merits of the programmes came more into their own. Despite the ephemeral, soon to be outdated nature of the medium, Jonas Wergeland's television series was an indisputable masterpiece. I am not alone in thinking this. A well-known English television critic wrote in his column in *The Sunday Times* that these programmes possessed the same undeniable quality and brilliance as the paintings of Rembrandt or Matisse. Nonetheless, these works of art had taken on a life of their own, independent of Wergeland's person. There was no longer any connection between the name and the face. He could wander, unremarked, around a small Norwegian town, even pass the time of day with people without anyone recognising the features which they had idolised ten years previously.

One evening he was standing outside the old Klingenberg family home, where Wittgenstein had stayed during his first winter in Skjolden, when an elderly man happened along. They got talking. After a while I heard the other man say: 'I hope you don't mind me asking, but what do you do for a living?'

'I'm ...' Wergeland began, then stopped, as if he were trying to say something for which there were no words. 'I am a secretary.'

Which was true. He was now working as a secretary. And he was clearly proud of it.

On our third and final day in Skjolden harbour, he asked me if I would act as driver for him; he wanted to show me something. When we got to Luster he instructed me to turn down a narrow road immediately after Dale Church. We zigzagged up the steep hillside and eventually emerged on a plateau to be met by the unreal sight of a huge, white crescent-shaped building, four storeys tall. 'Welcome to Hotel Norway,' he said. It wasn't as bad as it sounded. I learned later that the place was up for sale, and that a lot of interest was being shown by the travel industry.

This ghostly establishment was Harastølen, an old sanatorium from the turn of the century. The fresh air and the surrounding pine forests had made it a perfect spot for the treatment of tuberculosis; there were still some signs, like the low-ceilinged 'cure porches' set into the embankment skirting the front of the main building, suggestive of a world of deckchairs and blankets – like that described by Thomas Mann in his novel *The Magic Mountain*. Later on, the premises had been used as a hospital for long-stay psychiatric patients.

I don't know whether anyone remembers now, it is already so long ago, but it was here in the early nineties that the Bosnian refugees whom the Red Cross succeeded in having released from Serbian concentration camps and who then came to Norway by way of Croatia were interned. There were around 340 of them all told, counting their families. Many of them were severely traumatised; they had been subjected to what psychiatrists term 'catastrophic stress', they had witnessed the most appalling violence – ethnic cleansing – and were in a very vulnerable condition, one which could easily escalate into acute crisis. The Norwegian authorities meant well, I'm sure – they called it a transit centre – but it does not take much imagination to see that it was not good for people suffering from this sort of syndrome to live in such isolation – halfway up a mountain, deep inside a Norwegian fjord – for over a year. Things became so bad that the inmates staged a hunger strike. But not until over half of the refugees had applied to return to Bosnia – they actually preferred that war-torn region to Harastølen – did the baffled Norwegian immigration authorities realise just how embarrassing the whole situation was. The refugees received a promise that they would be resettled in the surrounding community.

We stood with our backs to the old sanatorium, a brick colossus honeycombed with long corridors and little rooms. Most of the Bosnians had had to stay at Harastølen for a year and a half, some of them for almost two years. I shot a glance at Jonas Wergeland. I could see that he was moved. He knew what it was like to live in isolation, in degrading conditions. He had no trouble imagining how it would feel to have to live here for any length of time. The refugees' Norwegian hosts did not, however, have the benefit of this experience or such insight. Here, in what had once been a treatment centre for TB sufferers and the insane, a desolate spot five hundred metres up a mountainside, these poor people had been stashed away, as if they were either dangerously infectious or crazy. As one of them so neatly put it: 'I feel I have gone from one prison camp to another.'

We stood outside Harastølen, next to the remains of what had once been a cable railway, just the sort to run up to an 'eagle's nest', and gazed across the fjord to the mountains on the other side. In the distance we could hear the sound of sheep bells, like the ones Norwegian supporters ring when cheering their skiers on to more gold-medal victories. Jonas was very quiet. Then, as I was making to leave he said: 'Is it possible, do you think, to understand everything about Norway from such a marginal position as this, in the grounds of a disused asylum?'

And then he began to talk, to talk eagerly and at great length. It was years since I had heard him speak with such commitment. He spoke of how incredibly lucky he had been to grow up in an age marked by the greatest economic, social and cultural changes since the Stone Age. And in that era of unbelievable prosperity he had also had the good fortune to be living in the most privileged and sheltered corner of the globe. But that was also, he said, why he felt so ashamed.

Readers will, I hope, bear with me here, if I slip in a few thoughts on modern Norway plucked from that monologue, that confused blend of praise and blame, delivered by Jonas Wergeland at Harastølen, near Luster. Because, he said, standing here outside this old TB hospital, this erstwhile mental home and, briefly, refugee centre, he felt compelled to consider the growth of modern Norway. And the conclusion he had reached was that it had all happened too fast. That was why we had become so unsympathetic, so intolerant, so callous and forbidding, all affected by a collective, almost panic-stricken case of tunnel vision which permitted us to see only what we wanted to see and which, in our misguided struggle to safeguard what belonged to us, caused us to lose sight of the need for human solidarity and common decency. He simply could not get his head round the fact that little more than a century ago Norway had been a country so poor, so doomed to scrimp and save, that the few gas lamps in the streets of its towns were not lighted on moonlit nights. Would he ever be able to understand this nation which, in the regatta of history, started out hopelessly far behind at the beginning of the twentieth century as a rot-ridden longboat with moth-eaten sails, and rounded the millennium buoy, suddenly in the lead, as a luxury yacht in a class by itself, all gassed up and bristling with electronic equipment – all of this almost without having to lift a finger, and with no one knowing quite how it had happened. Anyone would think a good fairy had flown over us and with a wave of her wand transformed a draughty log cabin into a chalet-style villa with ten rooms and underfloor heating in the bathroom. What had happened to us? Or rather: was it any wonder we didn't know how to deal with our wealth? 'We're like a nation of stunned lottery winners,' Jonas Wergeland said. 'When people get rich too quickly they almost always lose their perspective. In this case a whole society was hit.'

So what did we do? That's right, we cut ourselves off. Suddenly we had become so stinking rich that we could afford to shut out the rest of the world. For although the Harastølen story is not all black and white – things *had* had to be organised at very short notice and so many people had arrived at one time – Jonas Wergeland found it a disgraceful and highly symbolic tale. 'Think about it,' he said to me. 'It took over fifty years for Norway to take in as many refugees as we ourselves produced – Norwegians who fled to Sweden – during the five years of the Second World War. What's happened to our memories? What's happened to our capacity for fellow-feeling? Why didn't we so much as blush when the UN's high commissioner felt obliged to point out that it was more difficult to gain asylum in Norway, the birthplace of Fridtjof Nansen, than in most other countries in Europe.'

Jonas scanned the deserted hillsides on the other side of Lustrafjord as he pointed to the most paradoxical thing about Norway: such wide-open spaces and such closed hearts. We could, it is true – had they been Europeans, and had their sufferings been given enough television exposure – have taken in thousands in almost no time at all. It was the least we could do. If we were to divide the country up among us every Norwegian would have 70,000 square metres of land all to himself. And yet deep down inside we wanted to keep ourselves to ourselves. Stay a rich man's reserve. The accumulated value of our national costumes alone, complete with all their silver ornaments, would exceed the gross national product of many a Third World country. The way Jonas Wergeland saw it, modern Norway was suffering from the King Midas syndrome. Everything we touched turned to gold. But we could no

longer embrace our fellow men. We kept our mouths shut and walled ourselves in, applauding the government's efforts to build a Great Wall around
our borders, constructed out of what were – by its lights – unassailable legal
niceties. To Jonas it was a sad fact: what Adolf Hitler could not do, we had
managed for ourselves. We had built our own *Festung Norwegen*.

Bearing in mind what happened at the tail end of the millennium, when
the Norwegian people were given the chance to respond spontaneously and
unselfishly to the new stream of refugees from the devastation of the Balkans
at least, I have thought a lot about the impassioned monologue which Jonas
Wergeland delivered at Luster. Because even though he was right in what he
said about Norwegians and their long-standing mistrust of asylum seekers,
I have the suspicion that in talking about this he was, in fact, talking about
something else. The Norwegian government's unfortunate consignment of
Bosnian refugees to Harastølen was effected during Jonas's first months in
prison, which is to say at a time when he was taking a harder look at his
own life than ever before. Although I cannot express this very clearly, I am
convinced that in his monologue at Harastølen – his condemnation of such
isolationism – Jonas Wergeland was actually talking about himself.

I started walking towards the car and when he did not follow, I looked
back. I turned just in time to see him kneeling on the steps leading up to the
building, outside what he had described as a monument to our brutish attitude towards everything that was not Norwegian. I was instantly reminded
of the German chancellor, Willy Brandt, going down on his knees on behalf
of the German people before the monument to those who died in the Warsaw
ghetto in the Jewish uprising of 1943. I believe Jonas Wergeland felt the need
to do something similar here, albeit on a smaller scale: to beg forgiveness for
his nation's foolishness, for its eagerness to turn Norway into an impregnable
fortress. Although, when you get right down to it, it could be that this, too,
was done for personal reasons.

Jonas had first encountered this mistrust of strangers when just a little
boy. In elementary school he had had a very strict, very proper, headmaster
who, due to the fact that his initials were HRH, was simply referred to as His
Royal Highness. He was a distinguished-looking gentleman with an aquiline
nose and eyebrows like canopies, who walked with chest out and chin up. He
was notorious for reciting never-ending poems at the drop of a hat, poems
that no one could understand a word of, or at least none of the pupils on
whom he kept such a strict eye and whom he punished so zealously for the
slightest misdemeanour.

One Friday evening, not all that late on, it so happened that Jonas was
making his way from the Grønland district of Oslo to Tøyen with his aunt

– his aunt Laura. And who should he see come staggering out of the Olympus restaurant – something of a drinking den and not exactly known as the haunt of deities – but his dear headmaster, His Royal Highness himself. And not only that, but the headmaster was merrily carolling a popular hit of the day. It was not a pretty sight, or at least: it may have been pretty, but it was hardly designed to induce respect – to see one's school's moral guardian, an elderly man with eyebrows like canopies, rolling down the road burbling: 'Let me be young, yeah-yeah-yeah-yeah yeah!' He did not notice Jonas, he did not look as if he was aware of his surroundings at all. He probably thought he was safe, so far away from his realm.

Such 'revelations', or whatever you want to call them, never made any impression on Jonas. In the case of his headmaster, it seemed that only after this did Jonas begin to feel some sympathy for him and actually acknowledge him as an authority. There was something about this phenomenon, perhaps the very negativity of this way of thinking, this conviction that behind every beautiful façade there lay something rotten, that left him cold. Because that was the rule. Slash through a rich tapestry and you would find a rat's nest. All through his life, Jonas Wergeland was more interested in the exceptions, in the other side of the coin.

Solhaug, the housing estate where Jonas grew up and which, in all essentials, contained a genuine cross-section of the Norwegian population, also had its share of eccentric individuals. Take, for example, Mr Iversen, a timid, nigh on invisible father of four who lived for just one thing: to fire off thousands of *krones'* worth of rockets every New Year's Eve. Once a year he would appear, out of nowhere almost, with a cigar between his teeth and his arms full of fireworks, and for a few moments he was everybody's hero. Then it was as if he went back to earth, not to be seen again until the following New Year. Another was Myhren at number 17, who would not have hurt a fly, but who, when he heard that Jonny Nilsson had beaten Knut Johannesen to set a new world record in the 5,000 metres at the World Speedskating Championships in Japan, had chucked every Swedish product the family owned out of the window: an Electrolux vacuum cleaner, a Stiga ice-hockey game and the collected works of Selma Lagerlöf. When Jonas was growing up, the test of one's manhood was to creep up to Myhren's door and yell 'Jonny Nilsson!' through the letterbox.

But this is the story of a certain lady. She had lived at Solhaug for years, but not even Mrs Five-Times Nilsen knew much about her. Usually you could form quite a good picture of people's characters, gain a peek into the deepest recesses of their souls by keeping the removal van under observation – 'Did you *see* that wall lamp? Talk about hideous!' – but this woman must have moved in one evening, all unnoticed; no one could remember seeing so much as a rag rug. Her skin had a dusky tint to it which gave her an alarmingly exotic appearance, the look of someone of foreign origin. 'She may have nice skin,' declared Mrs Agdestein, the first person in Grorud to own a sun lamp, which she used twice a day, sitting in front of the mirror, in order to look like Jacqueline Kennedy, 'but I've never seen such a frumpy little mouse. She might at least treat herself to a visit to the hairdresser.'

Naturally, all sorts of rumours circulated about what lay hidden within this white patch on the housing estate's carefully mapped-out world. Nilla, who actually lived in the same building, firmly maintained that her flat was full of snakes and lizards and that she got food for them from an acquaintance who worked as a rat catcher. Others swore they had seen a blue light shimmering behind her curtains at night, and took this as a sign that she held seances in there. She also smelled funny. Of spices. Or alcohol. 'Poor little soul, she's a secret drinker,' Mrs Agdestein whispered at the sewing bee. But most people simply thought she could not be very well off – judging, at least, by the drab, grey outfits she always wore, and the glimpses she occasionally vouchsafed of an exceptionally spartan hallway. Her sunbronzed skin notwithstanding, she was nicknamed the Grey Eminence. Jonas had always felt that the greyness was necessary camouflage, that this woman dealt in something secret and dangerous. He knew what it was too: precious gems. 'It's the sparkle from all those jewels that gives her skin that healthy glow,' he whispered to Daniel.

There was one thing, however, on which several of Solhaug's mothers had remarked. On one Saturday in the month, the Grey Eminence left the block dressed up and made up beyond all recognition and took the bus into town. More than one had, from behind their curtains, seen her come home at an indecently late hour. This behaviour gave rise to the categorical assertion that she had 'a bit on the side', an expression which to Jonas's ears sounded as mysterious as 'hocus-pocus', with the same magical associations.

There came a day in early December when Jonas found himself standing outside her front door. He was out selling raffle tickets, having lost a bet with Daniel. Jonas could usually guess how generous people were likely to be just by doing a quick scan of their nameplates – what they were made of, the lettering – before ringing the doorbell. As he eyed up the Grey Eminence's anonymous sign: clear plastic with 'Karen Mohr' in a blue script, he suddenly realised that he was less interested in whether she would buy a raffle ticket than in whether he would get a peek inside her flat. He stood at the entrance to King Solomon's Mines. Inside – he could feel it in his bones – lay mounds of glittering sapphires and rubies.

Jonas barely heard the doorbell ring, it might almost have been muffled, or waking from age-long slumber. But she immediately answered the door, opened it a little way. He glimpsed the corner of a small, grey-carpeted hall. Proper grey. With not a single thing on the walls, not even a three-year-old calendar. But he could smell something. Something unusual, something good. 'Will you support Grorud scout troop by buying a ticket for the Christmas raffle? First prize is a side of pork.'

She frowned, possibly at the thought of having to carve up a side of pork on her kitchen table, all the mess, all the packing, the bother of having to rent a freezer down at the Centre. Then the unexpected happened. Instead of saying yes or no, she invited him in. The thought of Hansel and Gretel flashed through Jonas's mind, but he did not hesitate for a moment, he understood that he was being shown a rare trust. Once he was inside the grey hallway she smiled. 'I like your eyes,' she said. 'They're so big. And so brown. You remind me of someone. Are you a good observer? Do you draw?' She stood for a while simply considering him, even ran a finger over the scar on his forehead, as if trying to guess at the story behind it.

This close to her Jonas could see that she was good-looking, very good-looking. Not only her skin, but her face as well. Her features. She had a face which – what was it about it, he wondered – yes, in that face were many faces. He should perhaps have been on his guard, but it was a pleasure to be admired by Karen Mohr. To be the object of her regard. He liked the fact that she saw something which no one else could see.

All people are special, but Jonas knew that he was more than special. He was unique. He was an exception. From the day when he had learned to tie his shoelaces – not that there is necessarily any connection – every now and again he had been aware of a hidden power welling up inside him. He could not have said what it was. Only that something, something of sterling worth lay pulsating in there. Some rare gift. When the American Marvel comics appeared on newsstands in Norway, Jonas instantly identified with several of their superhero characters, although obviously he did not possess any of their powers. No, it was the certainty that there was more to him. Jonas had no trouble believing that a person could walk up walls, have X-ray vision or fly fast as lightning: all of these were really just variations on, or a slight exaggeration of, this thing he felt slumbering inside him. What it was he was soon to discover.

Years later, when he was working on his programme on Svend Foyn, a colleague happened to notice Jonas Wergeland late one night alone in a conference room at Television House in Marienlyst. There was nothing so surprising about that, apart from the fact that Wergeland was skipping, and that he was doing it in the dark. 'It was actually quite spooky,' his colleague had said. 'He wasn't jumping so much as flying. Anyone would have thought he had supernatural powers.'

The woman who uttered these words was working with Jonas on the *Thinking Big* series. She knew that as far as Svend Foyn was concerned he was stuck, well and truly stuck. After all, how were they supposed to produce a programme, a heroic epic, saluting a man who so strongly personified a whaling industry which by then had almost virtually destroyed Norway's international reputation. Whaling had once given rise to the first oil age, an industrial adventure which had filled the Norwegian people with confidence; now it was an extremely embarrassing business altogether. For various reasons, some more logical than others, many people felt that killing a whale was somehow different from killing a pig or a cow – or a cod, come to that. It was like shooting a brother, a distant relative. Some regarded the whale as the one creature on earth best able to communicate with possible extra-terrestrial beings. Svend Foyn had long since been demoted from national hero to national villain. No one wanted to be confronted with all that gory documentary footage of the flaying and cutting up of a whale carcase, no one wanted to be told that the growing prosperity experienced by Norway at the end of the nineteenth century was founded on a mindless slaughter which almost wiped out an entire species. No one wished to be reminded that their Stressless armchairs were covered, so to speak, in whaleskin.

Jonas Wergeland refused, however, to duck the issue; he wanted, he said, to make a programme in which the killing of a whale formed the key scene. But how to do it?

Much has been said and written about the television series *Thinking Big*. Younger generations may find it difficult to imagine that anyone could have taken a television programme so seriously, that it could have gained such control over people's minds, taken up so many column inches in the press. And yet all those articles and critiques went only a small way towards explaining the exceptional nature of the phenomenon that was Jonas Wergeland. Take, for example, the reasons for his remarkable viewing appeal – Jonas Wergeland himself was a standard feature, the presenter, of every programme. Not one expert had wit enough to see that his inimitable, charismatic screen presence was actually born of shyness. Simply by always appearing so wary and diffident, Wergeland excited as much attention and interest as a stranger in a place where everybody knows everybody else.

And despite all that was said about Wergeland's innovative style, no one saw fit to mention the most amazing thing of all: here was a television series that came close to transcending its own boundaries. The best thing Jonas

Wergeland ever did was to realise, very early on, what an inadequate medium television was, that its days were numbered, that he was working with an outmoded and hopelessly limited art form. In his programmes he clearly endeavoured to discover or to anticipate new – possibly even hybrid – forms. There was, for instance, something about the camera-work in the Foyn programme, the filming, the composition of the shots, the different, but evenly balanced aspects which prompted people to use the term 'virtual reality' in connection with television for the first time – even though anybody could turn round and say that the screen itself was still only two-dimensional. In juggling so radically with opposing elements, Jonas Wergeland was working towards another medium. And in point of fact this had nothing to do with technique, it had to do with a new way of looking at things, or better: of *thinking* about things, a different form of awareness.

The woman who accidentally witnessed Jonas Wergeland's weird skipping session became so intrigued, or so worried rather, that she returned to the conference room almost an hour later and through the open door saw Jonas still skipping in the dark, barely visible in the faint light falling through the windows from the street outside, skipping at breakneck speed, this woman reported. 'I'm almost sure he was hovering in mid-air,' she declared. 'And there was a kind of aura about him.'

Then he had suddenly stopped and raced out of the room. His colleague had observed him later, in his office, engrossed in a mass of papers, with different coloured felt-tips in either hand. It was on this night that the programme on Svend Foyn was conceived, a programme in which apparently unrelated elements were united within the framework of an explosive and deadly cannon shot.

Skipping was a method which Jonas Wergeland had sworn by for years, although what really mattered was not the skipping itself, but what it sparked off. You see, at a certain point in his boyhood, Jonas had discovered what his hidden talent was: a much more important gift than that of being able to hold one's breath: the ability to think. And again one has to ask: how could anyone have failed to see it? Hundreds of individuals have commented on Jonas Wergeland's story, but not one of them has ever mentioned his attitude towards the most elementary of all things: the relationship of one thought to the next. And to a third. And a fourth.

This may sound surprising, but there are not many people who can really think, who are conscious of the process of thinking, and certainly not in the way that Jonas Wergeland could. He wasn't all that good at it at first either, he had a particularly poor mastery of the mental discipline which involved imagining what lay behind closed doors. When, for example, he was invited into

Karen Mohr's flat, he felt sure – since he had already been there lots of times in his thoughts – that he was soon to behold her well-guarded and brilliantly camouflaged secret: her diamond-cutting workshop. But when she opened the living-room door he realised how wrong he had been. He stepped into another world. A world within the world, he was later to think. Although it was snowing outside and quite dark, he felt as if suddenly it was summer, in fact he almost caught a distant whiff of salt water, the sound of waves washing the shore. It was as if he had been looking at a map of the Sahara and someone had pulled it up to reveal a map of the French Riviera underneath. Here, in the middle of Grorud, deep in the suburban desert of Grorud, he had stepped into Provence.

The living room had a warm, an intimate, a – yes, that was it – a *French* feel to it. The floor was tiled in black and white, like a café. On the white walls hung a couple of plants with bright red blossoms, some photographs in woven raffia frames and an unusual and very striking picture. All along one wall, under the window, grew tall, green plants, miniature palm trees. After a while he thought he heard sounds coming from this jungle and when he looked more closely – wonder of wonders – what did he find but a little fountain. On the stippled glass top of the coffee table stood a vase of fresh flowers and, next to it: an elegant glass containing a milky-white liquid. On either side of the French windows onto the veranda hung blue, slatted wooden shutters which – Jonas later learned – could be pulled across the windows to shut out the realities of Norway. There was a faint odour of what might have been liquorice in the room. For this he soon received an explanation: 'Every evening, after work and before dinner, I have a glass of Pernod,' Karen Mohr told him. 'Here, have a sniff, doesn't it smell wonderful?'

Who would ever have guessed that in the heart of the estate, in the midst of all those square, solid blocks of flats through whose doors filtered the smells of stewed lamb with cabbage and fish balls in white sauce, there was a room like this – Pernod-scented, and with shutters on the insides of the windows? If I look out of the window, Jonas thought, in the distance I will see, not Trondheimsveien, but the Mediterranean.

Considered from a broader perspective, however, maybe all of this was not so strange after all. You have to remember that this was in the days when lots of flats were being radically transformed: fashions were changing, people were better off. Suddenly they were chucking out all their old junk and opting instead for living rooms decorated with Japanese minimalism; either that or they were turning doorways into white Spanish arches and converting spare corners into Costa del Sol-type bars with seating for ten. Especially where wallpaper was concerned, your average Norwegian lost all inhibition; some covered their walls with designs that gave you the impression of being surrounded on all sides by rough-hewn logs, others went the whole hog and transformed their walls into gigantic landscape scenes which made you feel as if you were living in a tent, right out in the wilds.

'Would you like a bite to eat,' Karen Mohr asked. 'I was just about to make an omelette, it won't take a minute.'

Jonas took a seat. The living-room furniture was of light, bright rattan with floral cushions. In one corner was a large cage containing two white doves. Jonas never told anyone about this visit or his subsequent visits. As far as he could tell, no one else knew what the inside of Karen Mohr's flat looked like. He came to think of this as a secret discovery; he had found a source – not of the Nile, but of a spate of rumours. But it was also something of a mystery: after all, how could this woman have such a living room without anyone in the sixty other flats knowing a thing about it? Or, to put it another way: how could so many people be so wrong?

The plate on which his omelette came was a memorable experience in itself, with a pattern of vine leaves running round the rim. This was the first time Jonas had ever tasted an omelette, eggs folded into a surprise package. It was also softer and creamier than any omelette he would be served later in life. If the truth be told, Karen Mohr set a standard for omelettes to which no future omelette could hope to aspire. 'Did you enjoy that?' she asked, raising her wine glass. 'Could you tell that I had added a dash of nutmeg and cardamom?' Along with it they had a baguette: a long, thin loaf of bread which she had baked herself. She took a chunk from the basket: 'You simply break off a piece, like this,' she said brightly.

Behind all this there was, of course, a story – and not just any story; a story which Jonas was soon to hear, becoming, as he did, a regular visitor to Karen Mohr's flat, especially over that first winter. But long before she told it to him, Jonas's mind had been occupied with trying to guess what sort of story it might be. And even he, child that he was, knew that it had to be a love story. Whenever she disappeared into the kitchen to make omelettes and he was left sipping a glass of real lemonade and fingering the bamboo of a rattan chair, he would try to spin his own stories, inspired, for example, by the ceramic figurines on the bookshelf or the full-length mirror which dominated the wall opposite the window, the kind of mirror which opened onto another, dimmer, room – a mirror which might even have been capable of making time stand still. At such moments, when that mirror also opened his mind, Jonas used to wish that it would be a while yet before his omelette was served.

That winter he made a big discovery of his own, again concerning a mirror.

It happened at home, in Rakel's corner of the bedroom, one day when she had gone to the cinema. A strong smell of hair lacquer hung around her dressing table. Jonas sat down in front of the oval mirror and examined his face in it. Rakel claimed this was a magic mirror, like the one the queen in *Snow White* had. His eye went first to the strange scar, or more correctly: two scars on his forehead, just above his eyebrow, which sometimes seemed to form a cross. Making him look like a marked man. Marked out. Gradually, though, he became more aware of something else; he noticed how flat his face looked. Flat, that is, in that his whole face seemed like a mask covering something totally unknown. Not another face, but something indescribable, something beyond thought.

He could not remember when he had first latched onto his disquieting discovery: the world was flat. Not in the sense that the earth was flat – although Jonas had to admit he had a weakness for the notion that if you dug down deep enough you would end up in China. *Everything* was flat. Objects were flat, people were flat. The first time he was taken to the theatre – to see 'The Wind in the Willows' – not for one moment did it cross his mind that the marvellous characters on the stage were just an act. To him they were every bit as real and true as everything else round about him. He took the play to be a faithful reflection of reality. To Jonas, more than anything else the word 'flat' meant 'simple', a little *too* simple. A lack of depth. The fact that he had once saved a child's life merely by sticking an arm underwater had taught him a bit about the shallowness of existence. The flatness of it. He never dared say this to anyone, partly because he thought he was the only one who knew: we had barely touched the world, we had scarcely begun to scratch the surface of it. The world might be round, but life was still flat.

To begin with, this did not really bother Jonas, but as time went on he felt a powerful urge to break through, to reach *beyond* the flatness. To discover something round. Something deep. Or no, not deep: he wanted to get at something else entirely. In his mind he called it 'Samarkand'. Occasionally he caught himself stamping the ground hard, on impulse, as if convinced that a thin film would shatter, just like the first fragile coating of ice in the autumn. A similar thought occurred to him when he looked into Rakel's mirror. Again he had a strong sense that there was something more, a certain potential, behind him, within him, which eluded his eye, his comprehension. I am quite different from how I appear in the mirror, he thought to himself. Afterwards, he would blame it on the fumes from the hair lacquer. He rammed his fist into the mirror with a force and a vehemence that surprised even him. He maintained that he had seen a glimmer of orange, of something enticing, in there behind the glass. He had lashed out quick as a flash, as if hoping, by dint of a surprise attack, to catch a glimpse of whatever it was that lay behind, as the mirror shattered, so to speak.

What this incident – and, not least, his badly cut knuckles – taught him was that using his fists would not help him to come to terms with the flatness of the world. It was, however, becoming increasingly clear to him that he was blessed with a gift which might enable him to penetrate beneath the surface, of objects and of people.

Jonas had always been a great one for fantasising – and by that I do not mean the sort of daydreaming in which many people indulge. For a boy of his age Jonas had an exceptional aptitude for thinking. He had detected the first signs of this ability – though he knew right away that it ought to be regarded as a gift – in his Aunt Laura's flat in Tøyen, in that world of Oriental rugs and brocade, precious metals and Lebanese cooking. Aunt Laura looked like an actress, or a diva, but she was a goldsmith, highly skilled and sought after, who had her workshop – a veritable Eldorado to a child – set up in a corner of her living room. One day when, for the umpteenth time, Jonas had begged her to tell him something about the 'greatest journey' she had ever made as a rug collector, her trip to Samarkand, she said, in order to distract him: 'Why don't I teach you to play chess instead.' The discovery he was about to make did not, however, have anything to do with the game of chess, or with anecdotes about famous matches, it concerned the pieces. 'I played chess, silver against gold. No wonder I never became a master,' he said later.

As a young woman Aunt Laura had made a chess set, with gold and silver plated miniatures of famous sculptures for the pieces. For the bishop she had chosen the Ancient Greek statue of the discus thrower, for the knight, Marcus Aurelius on horseback; Brancusi's slender *Bird* was the rook, Michelangelo's *David* the pawn and to Henry Moore's *Reclining Woman* fell the honour of being the queen. Jonas learned a bit about art history along with the rules of the game. So for him chess was not so much a game as a story consisting of criss-crossing tales; tales, what is more, which dated from different times, since the pieces reflected the styles of a wide variety of eras. Not even the fact that his aunt wore a silk dressing gown which made her appear more naked than if she had been wearing nothing at all could divert Jonas's attention from all those different sculptures. Brancusi's bird was particularly intriguing. The artist seemed almost to have caught what lay *behind* the bird's flight.

But the main point here is this: the first time Jonas laid eyes on Aunt Laura's king, namely August Rodin's *The Thinker*, he lapsed into reverie. That's me, a voice inside him cried; that's mankind, that's how we are. Aunt Laura would always mean a great deal to Jonas, but above all else he loved her for making *The Thinker* the king. From that day in his aunt's flat at Tøyen he was sure: his talent had, in some way, to be related to thinking. Jonas would promptly have applauded René Descartes, had he known of that gentleman's attempt to establish one thing for certain, with his celebrated statement concerning the relationship between thinking and being.

Nobel prize-winners are often to be heard describing how as children they took old radios apart or built little laboratories in which they carried out chemical experiments. Jonas made do with his own thoughts. His mind was all the laboratory he needed. He took to meditating. In the most literal sense: he sat himself down and proceeded, quite resolutely, to reflect on things, letting observations run into one another while at the same time endeavouring to be aware of what he was doing, to map out where his thoughts were taking him. The average human being is said to have fifty thousand thoughts a day and it was as if Jonas meant to scrutinise every one of his – make a record of them, just as he would sit by the roadside, noting down car registrations. After a while he discovered that, oddly enough, his thoughts flowed best when he assumed the same position as Rodin's figure: with his chin resting on his fist, his elbow propped on his thigh. From this point onwards his teachers and his chums would automatically resort to the same words to describe Jonas: 'He's a *thoughtful* character.'

Of all the many aspects of contemplation, the one at which Jonas really excelled was make-believe. Before too long he had become a master of pretence. He had the ability to create whole worlds inside his head, experience them with all his senses. Before leaving elementary school he had visited some of the most exotic countries on earth, really thought himself there with the aid of odd bits of information he had heard or had gleaned from school books. He had even visited Io, one of the moons of Jupiter. All you needed was a little piece of something and your imagination would do the rest, like Sherlock Holmes finding a scrap of clothing. Thanks to his powers of imagination Jonas had been a lion and a flower, not to mention a pencil and the gas helium. As for women: he had kissed Cleopatra – she had smelled of milk – before he had his first kiss. By the age of eleven, Jonas Wergeland was afraid that the world had been used up. He suspected, in other words, that he had reached a dead end where the possibilities of thought were concerned. He was also well aware that he was quite alone in appreciating his gift. At the start of a new school term, when the teacher asked where they had spent their holidays, Jonas had replied: 'In the Kalahari desert. With the pygmies.' Everybody had laughed. They had fallen about. They did not see that a fabrication could be as real as reality could be fabricated. Or, to put it another way: that the fiction could be less flat than the real thing.

So it took Jonas a while to get to the stage where he wanted, or dared, to properly acknowledge his almost unnerving talent for thinking. But this new sense of self-awareness triggered a chain reaction: he discovered that he was also gifted in other areas; discovered also how alarmingly simple it is to distinguish oneself, how easy to score cheap points.

Like most children, Jonas liked kicking a football around. At Solhaug, they played on the grass or on small, rough patches of waste ground. Any car park could be Ullevål stadium, or Wembley. They had next to no interest in tactics, or formations, 'line-ups' as they are now called. It was basically a big free-for-all, with everybody going for the ball at the same time, and everybody taking a shot at goal as soon as they got it. It was as much like wrestling or rugby as it was football.

Jonas did not take football too seriously: it was a game, a way of killing the odd half-hour until dinner was ready. And although he clearly had a way with the ball and was quick on his feet, he did not take up the game seriously until quite late on. It was Jonas's best friend, Leonard Knutzen – Leo for short, later to be better known by his professional name, Leonardo – who persuaded him to overcome his shyness and join the Grorud under-15s team. And here I should perhaps say that schoolboy football in the sixties was not such a serious and competitive business as it is today; nor was there any great fight for places on the team. So, since they were short of a forward on the left side of the field and since Jonas was equally good with both feet this was the position he was given. Back then it was called the 'left wing' – which sounded as if you were in the air force – or 'outside left'. Jonas immediately felt at home there.

Two things surprised Jonas once he started playing football more seriously. The first had to do with the fact that he was now playing on a proper pitch. The new pitch at Grorud sports ground had only just been laid; it looked so beautiful and, more importantly, it was absolutely *massive*. To Jonas, used to the narrow mazes around the garages and blocks of flats, this was undreamt-of freedom. Here you could really kick up your heels. He was all the more astonished to find, therefore, that even at this level players had a tendency to crowd together in the centre of the field. And it did not take Jonas long to discover – speaking of wings – that he had a whole runway to himself on the left-hand side.

Nonetheless, he played it canny. He held back, as if knowing intuitively that this discovery – like all significant discoveries – could have fateful consequences. He started with a few trial runs, as if to check whether it was *true* – had the other team really not realised that from here he could stroll unhindered all the way up to their goal line? No, it was right enough. Again and again he was able to sprint in lone majesty up to the visitors' corner flag.

He took more and more delight in this: dribbling the ball, kicking it up the touchline, sometimes all the way to the goal line. It had a demoralising effect on the other team. Jonas felt as though he had discovered an unknown side of football. Sometimes he wished he could have gone even further, tried running off the pitch, along the strip between the chalked line and the gravel; transcended the possibilities of the game.

Even though Jonas Wergeland's cheeky raids on the left wing cannot be compared to the so-called 'Flo pass' used so much by the Norwegian national team in the 1990s – a long lob from Jostein Flo's own half of the pitch to one of the forwards, who would then knock the ball on with his head – these two phenomena had one thing in common: both were examples of bold strategies, staggeringly simple moves which produced good results.

Jonas grew more and more daring and Leo, who had caught on quickly, spotted that Jonas was alone out there on the left wing, sent the sweetest crossballs flying straight to his toes. Jonas would charge up the touchline, all the way to the other team's goal line, then chip the ball neatly into the box – where, not infrequently Leo ran in to put the ball in the net.

If, that is, he did not score himself. Because the other discovery he had made also had to do with the scale of things. With the goal. At home in Solhaug they had played with narrow goalmouths and no keepers: two bricks a metre apart or two jerseys for posts, possibly with one of the little kids standing between them as an excuse for a goalkeeper. But here he had a proper goal. A huge cage. Designed for giants, so it seemed. A huge expanse of sky between the ground and the bar. A barn wall between the posts. Jonas did not get it: how could you not score, at least if you were inside the sixteen metre line and not actually unconscious at the time? Later in life – and knowing what he knew – he could hardly stand to watch a football match, to see so-called professional players who were being paid millions, sending the ball flying over the bar from only five metres outside an open goal. They were obsessed with the need to impress. They couldn't just score, they had to make the back of the net bulge. So they shot too hard, or were so intent on doing something spectacular that they miskicked completely. Jonas found it painful to watch, proof as it was of the male's eternal problem: lack of control.

As a boy, Jonas discovered that you could get away with a remarkably soft shot, as long as it was well placed. If you were ten metres away from the goal and aimed to place the ball just inside the post it would get past most keepers. While the other boys were busy practising juggling with the ball, Jonas came up with a new training exercise for himself. Following the example of tennis player Bjørn Borg, he hit the ball up against a wall or a garage door at home. He worked on his marksmanship, shooting at the same spot again and again.

And although he had a lot of different shots at his disposal he tended mainly to practise the simplest and the safest: a chip off the inside, the broad side, of the foot. Sometimes he used a tennis ball, to make it more difficult. And it paid off. Grorud's under-15s began to move up the league. And Jonas was their top scorer. Jonas was not your typical Norwegian. He was best with a ball.

He was careful, though, not to make too big an impression. Tried not to score more than two goals in any match, preferably none at all if he could see that Grorud was going to win anyway. Because there was something else to which he had soon become alive: the hostility of the opposing team. Their rancour if humiliated more than was necessary. Jonas did not like rough play, hard tackling – especially since in those days hardly anyone wore shin guards, certainly not Jonas. He was, both on and off the pitch, an extremely peaceable character. Only once did he ever hit anyone: when some guy declared that the Beatles' *Rubber Soul* was a rotten album. This unsuspecting individual was knocked flat; Jonas was so mad that it was all Leo could do to calm him down. Aside from this one incident, though, Jonas was never involved in any trouble in his teens.

But then came the day of their home game against Lyn – the Lyn under-15s team, top of the league and a team which boasted some very good players, lads who might well make it onto the Lyn first division team, maybe even the national squad. Lightning by name and lightning by nature, that was Lyn; a club from the middle-class west side of Oslo, from the Outside Right, you might say. Grorud versus Lyn – talk about a class war. Before the match, Jonas spent hours honing his dribbling technique on the green at home. Watch out, he told himself; this is going to be a helluva battle, a momentous match.

In the years prior to this Jonas had been more given to dribbling thoughts. The more intricate the contemplative pattern the better. While other people tried to put their thoughts in order, Jonas attempted to do the opposite. He did not shy away from the really big questions in life, deliberations worthy of Immanuel Kant himself: 'What can I know? What should I do? What can I hope for?', but would also throw himself, with just as great a will, into the consideration of lesser, but just as pressing questions, such as why the yellow chewing gum in the Kip pack tasted better than the pink or the pale-green. It was not unknown for him to speculate until his head spun. The way Jonas saw it, there was only one valid reason for passing out: because you had over-taxed your mind.

Even before he started playing football – possibly in consequence of his life-saving fiasco – Jonas knew that he was not destined to imitate any of the standard, archetypal success stories: winning an Olympic gold for skiing, becoming a company director, opening the finest restaurant in Norway. Others might lock themselves away in their rooms with guitars for years, to then emerge as stars. Somehow Jonas felt that this was too simple. He was cut out for other things. He wanted to be thinking's answer to soccer-great Roald Jensen. His talent lay in his grey matter. Which made it the perfect endowment for a rather reserved young man. He would be free to perform his deeds, break new ground, without being surrounded by crowds of people.

Jonas grew more and more inclined to regard the mental raids he carried out and the networks he formed inside his head as being real. It occurred to him that the most dramatic, the most significant event in his life could be a thought. As a small boy he had often dreamt of making a name for himself by discovering something – an unknown mineral, an unknown flower or, best of all, an unknown land – and having it called after him. It made him sad to hear the grown-ups say that there were no white patches left on the map of the world. Now, however, he realised that he *could* discover a new continent, but that it would lie within him.

His visits to Karen Mohr in her herb-scented Provençal flat confirmed this belief. You could actually *live* inside a thought. For quite some time Jonas had had the notion that she had taken an idea and furnished it, turned it into a home, a suspicion which was only reinforced when she eventually got round to telling him, in her quiet way, the story behind her extraordinary living room.

At the age of twenty, after completing her schooling, Karen Mohr had set out to travel around Europe. This was in the years just before the Second World War. One summer day in the south of France she came to a small place called Mougins, a few kilometres outside of Cannes, that town later to become so famous for its film festival. And it was here, while sitting all unsuspecting in a café, that the incident occurred which would change – Jonas did not know whether to say open up or lock down – her life.

She had been eating an ice-cream cone when she sensed that she was being watched, keenly observed, although she could not have explained what gave her this impression – not until a striking looking man approached her table. He must have been about fifty, balding and short of stature. He asked most politely if he might sit down. She was not sure, but after looking into the big, dark eyes fixed on her own, she nodded. 'I'll never forget those eyes,' she told Jonas. 'I know what they spoke of. You see it in children's eyes. The light of imagination. Irrepressible curiosity and irrepressible creativity.'

He was a painter, he said. She had an extremely distinctive face. Would she allow him to paint her? Would she come back to his studio with him? Karen Mohr found this quite funny: artists like him probably said the same thing to all the ladies. And yet – she was tempted. There was something about this man which told her he was not just another artist. That he was more than that. That what she was being offered here was not the chance to visit his studio, to pose as a model, but a turning point in her life. She sat for a while, thinking it over as she licked her ice cream. He played with a couple of *croissants* from a basket on the table, stuck them on either side of his head, pretended he was a bull about to ravish her. He made a lovely sailboat out of a fork and a napkin; he looked as if he had trouble sitting still, always had to be doing something. But from time to time he would stop and just look at her with the blackest pupils into which she had ever gazed.

She indicated that she was in a quandary. He asked where she was from, asked if she was enjoying her visit to this part of France, asked if she had been to any art exhibitions, whether she was fond of animals, whether – this was important – she had tasted lavender honey. She was filled with a sense of tranquillity. Of gravity. Of light. Felt that she was being lit from within. Suffused with life. 'I grew as he watched me. I felt as though I was being lifted up, that I sprouted wings,' she told Jonas. 'My head was perfectly clear. All of a sudden I could see *through* everything. See how everything was connected.'

That's how it should be, Jonas was ever afterwards to believe. But just at that moment he was growing impatient: 'What did you say?'

She had paused, deliberately taking her time, because she wanted the moment to last, wished she could sit there, under that probing gaze, and be discovered, be *beheld* with this same intensity, for all eternity. She felt as though, with those eyes, those senses, he discerned a multiplicity, saw things in her that no other man had ever perceived. He saw, she felt, her hidden beauty, all her potential for love. 'The feeling of it was stronger than any kiss, if you know what I mean,' she told Jonas. 'I'm sure that not even ... you know what, could compare with it.'

Jonas felt his heart pounding, though he could not have said why. 'So what did you do?' he asked.

'I thanked him, but declined. Politely.'

She could tell that the man was disappointed, genuinely disappointed. Sad, even. He asked if it would be alright for him to draw her portrait as she sat there in the café. She nodded. He pulled out pencils and some sheets of paper, sat facing her, totally absorbed; covered a couple of blank sheets with black strokes. 'I drew you before you were born,' he murmured. She stayed perfectly still. Again she wished that time could be suspended. That she could sit like this and be studied, drawn, by this enigmatic, this dynamic man, for ever. 'I felt as though he was unveiling me,' she told Jonas, 'really unveiling me, stripping away veil after veil.'

'Until you were naked?' Jonas flinched at the boldness of his own remark. 'More than naked.'

When the stranger was finished, he stood up and handed her one of the sheets of paper. 'Would you like me to sign it?' he asked. She instinctively knew that this was more than the offer of an autograph; that it was meant as a gift, something which she could possibly trade in for a lot of money. 'No, you don't need to do that,' she said, not even glancing at the sketch. He made ready to leave. 'Would you come to the beach with me tomorrow?' he asked. 'If it is too hot for you, I can hold a parasol over your head while we walk along the shore.' She shook her head. Although she was not really there, her body shook her head without her being aware of it. He walked away, stopped in the doorway and sent her one last searching, almost mirthful look.

Not until later, in her room, did she take out the sketch and examine it. She saw her own face. It definitely looked like her, that she could see, but it was a likeness that went far deeper than any photograph, although it was a very simple drawing, more like something a child would do. And he seemed to have drawn her face three times, as if he had been viewing her from three different angles at once. She sensed that, simply by being in his company for those minutes – and perhaps by being drawn by him – she had been given fresh eyes. He had transfigured her purely by observing her. She had been blind and his regard had been like a healing hand. She walked over to the window and opened the shutters. The countryside, the light, the people – everything had looked different. She had met a man, and the world was as new.

Jonas thought, but did not say out loud: that place, Mougins, was Karen Mohr's Samarkand.

'That's it there,' she said to Jonas, pointing to a framed drawing on the wall, next to one of the plants with the scarlet blossoms. Jonas went over to have a look at it. He had never seen anything like it. It was the sort of picture which, once seen, is never forgotten. A drawing that gave off sparks. Jonas remembered every line of it for the rest of his life. It could easily have been Egyptian, he thought to himself. Face on and side on at the same time. Although maybe he had seen something similar before, in real life: triplets.

Triplets were a rare sight in the fifties. But only months after Jonas came into the world, at the same hospital, three girls, identical triplets were born – a sensation which was duly reported in the press; in fact some papers actually gave more space to this than to the climbing of Mount Everest – an order of priority at which no one should wrinkle their nose, since the feat performed by every woman during childbirth is every bit as awesome as the conquest of the highest mountain in the world; you only have to look at print-outs from the latest CTG machines, the patterns of contractions like the silhouetted peaks of the Himalayas.

Jonas remembered the first time he had ever laid eyes on them; he must have been about four or five and he was in the grocer's shop with his mother. No one had told him about the triplets. He just stood there staring at them, exactly as one is always told not to gawp at people who have something wrong with them. They were standing next to the crates of fruit and to Jonas they seemed as exotic as the bananas from Fyffes – a name which you always ended up spraying rather than saying. They stood in a huddle, staring back and sticking out their tongues at him in such perfect sync that he was sure there had to be only one girl, that he had been dazzled, was seeing double, triple. He had to shut his eyes several times before coming to the stunned conclusion that there actually were three of them.

These triplets grew up in Grorud, they lived at the bottom of Trond-heimsveien, but he seldom saw them and on those occasions when he did run into them he tended to regard them more as bringing a touch of carnival to the neighbourhood, like some sort of freak show, or like April, May and June, Daisy's three nieces in the Donald Duck comics. Seeing them swimming and diving together at Badedammen was tantamount to a preview of the synchro-nised swimming which Jonas was to see on television years later.

It wasn't until school, though, that he really *discovered* them, more specifi-cally in fifth grade, when suddenly it was okay to look at girls – when, indeed, this had become the boys' favourite pastime. Jonas was tempted to don a pair of those special glasses he had seen people wearing in the cinema, with one red lens and one green, to see if the three of them would merge into one mind-bogglingly three-dimensional girl. He started taking more and more notice of them, to the point where he realised that he was in love – in love with all three of them at once. He was faced, in other words, with an appar-ently insoluble problem: which one should he choose? Or, as Bo Wang Lee would have said: 'What should you take with you?'

Actually, it was thanks to the triplets that Jonas – so he believed, at any rate – made his big breakthrough in terms of his gift, his powers of thought. He knew, as I have said, that this talent of his had its own inherent potential, that there was more to it than merely being able to make believe, to pretend that he was an anaconda, or that he had crossed the Gobi desert with Sven Hedin. The problem was, how was he supposed to invoke it, how to find the password that would allow him access to the treasure.

Along with the triplets, a rope played an important part. In later years this would, for Jonas, acquire an air of mystery, rather like the one in the Indian rope trick. It belonged, naturally, to Wolfgang Michaelsen, but Jonas was often given the honour of carrying it to school, slung over one shoulder and across his chest, as if he were the leader of an expedition to the top of Tirich Mir. A comparison which is not as far off the mark as it might seem, since this, too, was a case of an epoch-making drive forward in life.

It was springtime, the high season for skipping games in the playground. It was still permissible to play with the girls, even though those days were gone when one child would skip while the rest of the gang chanted 'Teddy bear, Teddy bear, touch the ground' and other such instructions to perform bizarre, and occasionally comical, actions while jumping the rope. The only possible option when boys and girls played together was 'joining in', as they called it. 'Join in, three and nine,' the caller would shout, which meant that the next person in line had to jump in after the first person had jumped three times. And since the first person had to jump nine times before running out, this meant that three kids were jumping at the same time. It could be a lot of fun, and the more kids you had skipping in time, the more fun it was: a whole tribe of leaping Masai warriors.

Such a game required a certain sense for *timing*. You soon heard about it if you muffed it and hit the rope on your way in or out. The aim was to build up a smooth, steady stream of jumpers in constant vertical and horizontal motion. The rope was long and thick and called for plenty of muscle power on the part of the kids holding the ends and doing the turning; it smacked hard against the tarmac at every turn, emitting a deadly whiplash crack. Now and again someone would take a nasty tumble and end up with badly skinned knees, having come in too late and had their feet knocked from under them by the rope.

A few of the kids had been known to try somewhat more advanced moves, executing intricate interlacing patterns, coming in from opposite sides, jumping in from the wrong side or, harder still: jumping two shorter ropes swung in opposite directions. There weren't many who could manage this last, it could easily give you the claustrophobic feeling of being whipped up by a giant egg whisk. The simplest version, the one everyone could join in, was also the most popular: jumping in one after another, while the rope formed a beautiful, elongated ellipse around them. The usual order was boy, girl, boy, girl all the way down the line. It just worked out that way. It was great to jump up and down in a cracking circle of rope with a girl to front and back, the crisp ting-a-ling of bicycle bells in your ears, the sight of coltsfoot growing on the grassy banks and the scent of freshly lit bonfires in your nostrils. It released a tension in them. Or whipped them up, to puberty.

On the day of this particular incident, the caller shouted 'Join in, four and ten', which is to say: four people jumping together in the loop at any given time. And on this occasion, just as he jumped in, Jonas was unwittingly struck by a powerful thought. It had been triggered a split-second earlier by something he had seen out of the corner of his eye: the teacher on playground duty, wandering around with his hands behind his back; or at least, what had actually caught Jonas's eye was the big bunch of keys dangling from the teacher's finger. And as he was jumping, and gradually working his way towards the other end, a new thought occurred to him, one which involved a group of little girls from second grade who were chalking out a hopscotch grid over by the bike shed, and not only that, but he realised that he could hold onto that first reflection, the one about the teacher and the bunch of keys on which, not least, the sight of the whistle that was blown whenever anyone got into a fight, spurred on his imagination while he carried on considering the other thought, the one concerning the little girls and their game of hopscotch and the numbers they were chalking inside the squares; he could hold them both in the air at once, as it were. Now Jonas, like all children, had, of course, already had some small taste of this same phenomenon, this knack of being able to do several things at once: read a book, listen to music, maybe even watch TV with the sound turned down, but taking everything in, and on top of all that, at the back of all that, responding to some question from his mother – that same mother who, by the way, regularly palmed the boys off with a: 'Don't bother me right now, I can only think of one thing at a time!' But this phenomenon, these thoughts he carried with him into the rope, were different, much stronger; his mind could be said to have been totally focused on both images; he could enter into them completely, be in two places at once, he could see every single key on the teacher's keyring, as if they were keys which would open an endless succession of rooms, while at the same time dwelling on, really giving thought to the little girls' hopscotch grid over by the bike shed, contemplating a pattern of squares which led to thoughts of a plane, or of marble, which in turn transported him to Athens and the Acropolis.

One of the triplets had jumped into the rope in front of him. Behind him he had another triplet. At one point he was skipping in the loop flanked by two almost identical individuals. Jonas detected a touch of the supernatural in this. He was quite certain that the two triplets had had something to do with the way his thoughts had split in two, and towards the end, before the accident, he had the feeling that he was on the verge of unearthing a third, parallel, image, one relating to the teacher on playground duty, who also taught handwork – a subject which triggered a whole host of thoughts with its sharp knives and stupefying glue fumes. So intrigued did Jonas become with this phenomenon, this possibility, this pleasure, that he went on skipping, even after he had skipped his forty times and was supposed to jump out. Kids were piling up behind him, among them the third triplet; there was some muttering, shouts for him to get out of there, but Jonas went on skipping in his own two-fold, and soon – if the others would just leave him alone – three-fold world, because he instinctively knew, or thought, that skipping, and possibly this whole complex of people, including two triplets, jumping up and down inside the ellipse formed by the smacking rope, was what was needed in order for him to keep two, close to three, thoughts in the air at one time. And sure enough: when an impatient Hjørdis or Helga or Herborg or whoever went so far as to shove him out of the rope, he lost not just one, but both, all of his thoughts. They burst like bubbles. He went rolling across the tarmac as if he had been hurled out of a massive centrifuge. He hurt himself quite badly, he was bleeding from a cut to his brow, where it had rammed into a sharp stone. But it had been worth it. And in a way it seemed only reasonable that such a discovery should send you flying flat on your face. He walked home from school that day with an ugly scab forming on his forehead where he would bear a scar for the rest of his life, feeling as though he had been ennobled, or that he had found the badge of mankind's nobility: the potential to think more than one thought at the same time. The rope, which was once again slung over his shoulder and across his chest was no longer a rope, but the sash of a noble order.

He never tried to repeat this exploit, partly because he didn't want to annoy the others, and partly because he realised that this was something he could experiment with on his own. He may also have been afraid that the faculty of which he had caught the merest glimpse might disappear. That great care would have to be taken with any further experiments. Oddly enough, Jonas made his new discovery around the time of Esso's first major advertising campaign, when everywhere you went you saw the slogan 'Put a tiger in your tank'. Jonas had done just that, put a tiger in his think-tank. That, at least, is how it felt, and with the same hint of danger. His prospective gift might just as easily bring him bad luck as good, something far worse than a cut brow.

He was to make this same discovery again and again: if you did not keep your exceptional talent to yourself, you had a much greater chance of being laughed at, or even penalised, than of being applauded. It was the same with football. But when his team's fiercest rivals for the top position in the league, the west-side team Lyn, came to Grorud, hubris got the better of Jonas; he could not contain himself. The whole Grorud team was more than usually keyed-up, balefully eyeing the fancy cars which pulled up outside the club-house, bringing the Lyn players and their trainers. 'We're going to hammer you lot black and blue,' one slick-haired Lyn player remarked blithely as he hopped out; referring, with this dig, to the colours of the Grorud strips.

'Bloody snobs,' Leo hissed through his teeth as he stood there with Jonas, glowering at these boys who seemed to come from another stratosphere, who dressed differently, who had different haircuts, who seemed, in short, more grown-up than them, as if the whole bunch could, at any minute, turn round and become lawyers, company directors and stockbrokers. Lyn supporters will have to excuse this mythologising of their team, this is simply a description of the way in which Jonas Wergeland and his teammates saw it.

For a long time during this crucial match, too, Jonas was able to charge more or less unhindered up the left wing, but unlike the other teams they had come up against that season, Lyn had a trainer who spotted Jonas's uncommon ability and shouted some instructions to his defence, mainly to one of the right-backs who looked, to Jonas, a bit like King Kong. Jonas became the brunt of some really dirty tackling. During one such foul he must have cracked a rib; the pain was almost unbearable, but he played on. He should have known. He should have stopped, kept his talent hidden. But at that moment he just couldn't. He got too carried away. There was something about Lyn, Lyn on Grorud's home ground, something historic, symbolic. It was the Right against the Left.

Jonas scored two goals, even with his chest hurting like mad he scored two very simple, but very sweet goals with little chip shots off the side of the foot, one into either side of the net, well out of reach of the Lyn keeper, he was so taken aback he didn't even have a chance to make a dive for the ball. The Lyn defenders were clearly rankled by the utter prosaicness of these goals, their cheeky nonchalance. Jonas saw the dirty looks they sent him. A curving shot skimming under the crossbar from twenty metres out, that they could have stomached, a superb lob or a lethal half-volley shot, but these soft, ruthless shots to the foot of the post were just too demeaning. This was socialism in practice: painfully simple.

The score was 3–3, with five minutes of the game to go. Jonas was alone out on the left flank, received a pass from Leo in their own half, ran up the wing, wincing at the pain in his ribs, but crossing the halfway line nonetheless, no one in his way; all the players were starting to flag, Jonas had a free run up that side of the pitch, and on he ran, hugging the touchline and registering, out of the corner of his eye, Leo running parallel with him, like a neighbouring idea in his mind: two thoughts, utterly dissimilar, but with a common goal. And it may have been at that very moment that he made up his mind to stay out here for the rest of his life, on the left wing. Because, despite his short-lived career in football, from that day onwards Jonas saw himself as belonging to the 'outside left'. No matter what cause he was fighting for, he would always try to find an outsider position, a sideline along which he could dribble the ball while everybody else clustered together in the centre, and although where Jonas was concerned, it was more a psychological than a political appellation, he would have had nothing against being a founding member of a new party, to be called the Outside Left.

This also sheds some light on his later attempt to expose the opposite wing for what it was. As an adult – not least in prison – Jonas Wergeland spent a lot of time trying to analyze the most disturbing watershed in the history of modern Norway, a sort of collective fall from grace. 1973 is fixed in the global consciousness as the year when the oil crisis gave a serious indication of the state the world was in, and of its grave economic problems. In Norway, however, where they had only started pumping out their black gold a couple of years earlier, the situation in 1973 was almost the very opposite: in Norway they were having trouble coping with their nascent wealth. This fact manifested itself most clearly, if indirectly, at a public meeting in the Saga cinema in Oslo in April of that year. The choice of venue was most apt, since it would be quite true to say that a new saga had its beginnings here. A saga of the grimmer sort. On the stage stood a seasoned public speaker: an eccentric dog lover in a suit and a bow tie, with a bottle of egg liqueur to oil his vocal chords. Anders Sigurd Lange was his name, and he made a speech which was interrupted by bursts of applause over a hundred times. This meeting led to the founding of a political party which initially went by the curious name of 'Anders Lange's party for the drastic reduction of taxes, duties and state intervention'. Later it acquired another and possibly even more curious appellation: *Fremskrittspartiet* – the Progress Party.

Much has been said about that strange organisation, the Norwegian Maoist Party – the AKP in its Norwegian abbreviation – which ran rampant in Norway in the seventies. But as far as Jonas Wergeland was concerned, the most significant political movement of the day, in the long run at any rate, was not the AKP, but the ALP. Anders Lange was not, in himself, a bad man; Jonas did not have the slightest interest in him as a person, what fascinated him was the society which had raised an individual like Anders Lange to prominence, which is to say: Norway. Lange was a symbol, the carrier of alarming symptoms, in the same way as Harastølen, the refugee centre at Luster. He was, among other things, one of the first examples of a growing trend among politicians to become solo performers. And proof that they could get away with this, not to mention actually build up a following, even when they were little short of utter buffoons. Everything hinged on the individual concerned. It was no longer a matter of a political party, but of a skilled demagogue, surrounded by a crowd of whingeing Norwegians who could, what is more, be replaced at regular intervals.

None of this would have been possible, however, had it not been for certain requisite factors, the most important of these being the media and, not least, the television broadcasting service of which Jonas Wergeland himself would one day become a part. With Anders Lange's Party – not the man, but the phenomenon: the combination of rapacious media and one figure as catalyst, began the decline of civilised politics. Within just a few months a handful of individuals succeeded, with the help of the media, in totally vulgarising the Norwegian political scene. It did not take long for every politician to realise that presentation was more important than substance, that one might as well master the rhetoric of advertising right at the start. The politicians, press and TV entered into a symbiosis of sorts: each ensuring the other of publicity, however short-lived, and whatever the cost.

Anders Lange himself declared that they had reached a turning point in Norwegian history, and he was to be proved right. In the election held in the autumn of 1973, in a Norway in which, for three decades, everyone had pulled together to build up the country, marching shoulder to shoulder behind the banner of solidarity, more than 100,000 Norwegians voted for Anders Lange's Party. Its founder and three other members won seats in parliament. Jonas Wergeland saw this as the beginning of a period in which the proud, time-honoured tradition of May 1st soon gave way to the egocentric celebration of Me 1st.

With Anders Lange, populism came to Norway for good and all. The responsible, ideological, considered style of politics had had its day. Opinions, votes, were no longer founded on vision, but on discontent, not least with an overly high rate of income tax. Anders Lange – an indefatigable writer of letters to the press, had a nose for the mood which lay dormant in many Norwegians, a mood which can best be compared to the sulkiness of spoiled adolescents. This may well be the least sympathetic and most incomprehensible aspect of modern Norway: the fact that the wealthier the country became, the more it was possible to play on this feeling of discontent, this collective 'gimme more' frame of mind. From the mid-seventies onwards Norway rode towards the millennium on the wave generated by its new ideology of Self: self-righteousness, self-centredness and self-sufficiency. For decades, the most prevalent catchword in Norway was 'self-determination'. And there *is*, in fact, a shadowy and little recognised connection between that meeting in the Saga cinema in 1973 and Norway's vote against joining the EEC the previous year. Where the initial focus had been on general political self-determination, the demands were now to be extended to cover the right to individual and – worst of all – ethnic autonomy, with all decisions being made independent of the international community.

And here, in this worrying development, we have the crux of Jonas Wergeland's monologue at Harastølen: xenophobia. The most ominous aspect of the new populistic movement founded in the Saga cinema was its latent racist tendencies. Anders Lange could hardly be accused of being a racist, despite a bunch of somewhat dubious remarks and an unconcealed fondness for South Africa. But many of his supporters were, and contempt for people of a different skin colour has always dogged this party like a shadow. Even before the election in 1973, that ignominious year, one of the party's members openly expressed a sentiment which had not been voiced in decades: Norway for the Norwegians. The future leader of the party, Carl Ivar Hagen gradually gained a lot of ground by ingeniously, discreetly and, not least, impunibly fuelling the flames of people's intolerance and their antipathy to foreigners. To Jonas Wergeland, the ban on immigration which was introduced only two years after the meeting in the Saga cinema simply seemed to be the logical next step. Thanks to the far-right Progress Party and the knock-on effect its success had on the political scene in general, the whole of Norway was transformed into another Lyn: a privileged and pampered team, desperately on the defensive. Or, as Kamala Varma so neatly put it during one heated discussion: 'Modern Norway is a society founded on the seven deadly sins.' It was the Progress Party which propagated the notion that has taken root in far too many Norwegians: that every person who comes to Norway seeking asylum is only here for the money and is merely out to defraud the Norwegian welfare state. For Jonas, this had always been the most notable feature of the Outside Right: its prejudice against foreigners, its lack of solidarity with people outside the chalked line marking the geographical bounds of Norway.

But now, to use an expression from the football broadcasts: over to Grorud sports ground, because out there on the pitch, the Grorud under-15s are playing at home to Lyn and Jonas Wergeland is running unhindered up his beloved left wing. To anyone who had been following the Lyn team all season it must have been agony to watch these normally excellent players, known for their lightning attacks, having to adopt what was for them an unwonted defensive strategy, putting their name and their reputation to shame; they now looked as if they would be very happy to settle for a draw, the whole team had pulled back into their own half, suddenly the very embodiment of the Outside Right, displaying a dogged defensiveness which refused to accept that anyone could be as good as them; in fact they were boiling mad, ready to break the legs of anybody who tried to get through their wall, especially anyone sly enough to try a shot from the wing. Jonas ought to have sensed the change in atmosphere, but he was too caught up, and a bit groggy from the pain in his ribs; he was almost level with the box, cut across towards the

Lyn goal, heading for the corner of the sixteen metre line, and as the afore-mentioned King Kong from the Lyn backs charged at him, a gorilla in red and white, Jonas passed the ball smoothly to Leo and received it back from him as he jinked round the big back and crossed the sixteen metre line. But Lyn's colossus of a defender had had enough, he dashed off in murderous pursuit, mainly because he realised that a goal was in the offing; he could see Jonas considering into which corner of the net he should place the ball, softly, but in the net nonetheless, as sure as death, so he rammed the toe of his boot into Jonas's calf with all his might, from behind – Jonas felt as though his leg had been knocked from under him by a leaden skipping rope: the Lyn back had lashed out at him partly in desperation, partly out of pure malice; he didn't even try to go for the ball, he went for Jonas's leg, with the result that the casualty department had to deal with a broken fibula which the doctor on call described as one of the nastiest he had seen in a long time – a fracture which, by the way, also paved the way for Jonas Wergeland's subsequent career as an angry young man in the Red Room, but that is another story. Jonas crashed to the ground with a howl, just had time to register the scent of grass, earth, to observe that the world was flat, too simple; you thought you had a clear run, only then to slam straight into an invisible barrier, a wall of thick glass. Everything went red, then white and finally blue. He passed out.

It could not be anything but a penalty. As Jonas was coming round, a few metres outside his beloved left touchline, as his mangled leg was being exam-ined, through a haze of pain he saw Leo deposit the ball neatly in the corner of the net.

He had learned how easy it was to achieve his aims. And yet: was it worth the cost? They had beaten Lyn. Nonetheless, this experience had taught Jonas a lesson: he ought to have concealed his gifts. Although he could not have put it into words, Jonas was beginning to understand why his father preferred an anonymous existence on the organ bench at Grorud Church.

Although his painful encounter with Lyn lay in the future, as early as fifth grade Jonas knew that it was best to keep his thought experiments to himself. He did not tempt fate by causing more chaos in the skipping games. But he did still believe that skipping was an absolute prerequisite. He toyed with the term 'mental gymnastics', envisaged skipping as a way of building up his thinking muscles. He purchased a good, professional skipping rope, a Lons-dale with ridged hand-grips weighted to give it the right whip and speed. He found a suitable, unfrequented spot in the basement of the block of flats and started skipping all on his own. He liked to switch off the light, skip in the dark, caught inside the invisible bubble formed by the arc of the rope. He had watched the girls skipping, knew that there were lots of different steps. You could skip forwards or backwards, or on one leg, then the other; you could sling the rope out to the side at set intervals, skip with your arms crossed, or a whole host of combinations. But what Jonas liked best was double skips or simply 'doubles'. His thoughts flowed best of all with those. Maybe it was the swish of the rope that did it, but skipping doubles gave him a feeling of hovering in mid-air, of no longer being subject to natural laws or the laws of causality. And his reflections altered character, becoming more like the mode of thought he experienced when he dove down deep. When he skipped in the dark, he felt as though everything round about him began to glow, that he was like a dynamo, that he created energy, a force field. He was not simply doing mental gymnastics, he was practising for a great battle. He recalled pictures of boxers – fighters like Ingemar Johansson: massive characters, skipping as light as you like. As if they were training for something other than boxing.

Gradually his efforts began to pay off. He became capable of considering more than two thoughts at the same time. He managed to keep first three, then four parallel thoughts in the air. It was an intoxicating feeling. Like being on board a sailing ship with sail upon sail being run up mast after mast and everything moving faster and faster. Sometimes the basement smelled like the air after a violent thunderstorm. Soon, however, he also found that the more widely diverging his thoughts were in subject matter, the more exciting it became. It was like keeping an eye on several separate cogs in the workings of a clock at one time or, more correctly perhaps, several different sets of clock workings in different places in the room. It also seemed to him that time stood still, or went more slowly, the more simultaneous thoughts he managed to set in train. Jonas would not have been surprised had someone told him that he appeared to be skipping in slow motion. And now and again – he could have sworn it – he thought in a way that caused him to see his name written in lights in the darkness before him.

It can surely have been no coincidence that he should at this time have had a crush on the aforementioned triplets, Helga, Herborg and Hjørdis. Although he did not know it, he was also on the brink of one of the great milestones in the life of any individual: the moment when you press your cheek against the cheek of the one you love. For Jonas this would prove to be an even more powerful experience than his first kiss, simply because it came first. If it were possible to talk about a 'close encounter of the third kind' in Jonas Wergeland's life, then it was one which involved skin rather than mucous membranes.

It can hardly have been because their father was a big man in the labour movement that the triplets exhibited such an uncommon degree of mutual solidarity that one could have been forgiven for thinking they lived by the motto 'All for one, and one for all'. It would, however, have been misleading to call them The Three Musketeers, since they were absolutely identical, at least to anyone who did not know them well. They all looked like troll dolls, or like the Icelandic singer of a future era, Björk Gudmundsdottir. Like the Beagle Boys from the Donald Duck comics they needed placards on their chests to differentiate them from one another. And since Jonas did not make up his mind until late in the autumn that was more or less how he managed to tell them apart – by the different coloured scarves they wore: red, blue and yellow. For Jonas those scarves were a tricolour waving over the land of love. But that still left him faced with a not inconsiderable dilemma: which one should he choose? There was something about the sight of them which made him think of a box of chocolates, the stunning prospect of all that confection-ary, a golden tray full of delights, all equally tempting: 'Eeeny, meeny, miney, mo.'

After the summer holidays he had watched them on the sly when they were hula hooping in the playground, a circus turn that quite took his breath away: three identical girls with their hips gyrating in perfect synchrony. He also had a passport-size photograph of each of them, the sort everybody had to have taken at one of those machines if they wanted to be part of the status-giving and rather frenetic swapping game they played at that age, where the main point was not to have as many photos as possible, but to have the right photos – much in the same way as cards are exchanged in the business world and in diplomatic circles. A few of the girls' photos had a high exchange value; you could, for example, get both Britt and Kari, maybe even Gerd into the bargain, for one Anne Beate. Jonas studied the pictures of Helga, Herborg and Hjørdis through a magnifying glass as if faced here with the equivalent of those seemingly identical cartoons in weekly magazines in which you have to spot the differences; but he really could not perceive any dissimilarity between them. They were *absolutely* identical. Jonas was struck by an outra-geous thought: what if he were able to go out with all three of them at once? What an unbelievably intense experience that would have to be?

But by the winter he had come to the conclusion – although he could not have said why – that he liked the triplet with the yellow scarf best, and the one with the yellow scarf was Hjørdis. By following the standard ritual of using middlemen to gauge the other party's interest before making tentative overtures – a procedure which suited a shy boy like Jonas perfectly – before too long Hjørdis L. was officially his girlfriend. And only days later, when they had barely got to the stage of daring to hold hands, with gloves on, Jonas was to make contact, for the first time, with a girl's skin.

He had on his skating cap, or Hjallis cap as they called it, after their speed-skating hero Hjallis Andersen. He was standing with a bunch of kids from his class in the cul-de-sac next to their building when Hjørdis came out wearing just an open anorak over her blouse, and her scarf wrapped loosely around her neck. She said she was home alone. Everybody knew what that meant. Jonas's chums slapped him blokeishly on the back, egging him on; they were all but shouting 'Go for it, Jonas!', as if this were a speed-skating race – 'two insides and leave 'im standing', 'silver is failure' and all that. He went up to their flat with her, discovered that the sisters' rooms lay side by side down a corridor; he would have liked to have taken a peep into each of them, just to see if they were all decorated identically, but Hjørdis quickly pulled him through her door, into her room, which smelled faintly of Yaxa deodorant and had a bookshelf containing a fair selection of Gyldendal's Girls' Classics; a perfectly ordinary girl's room, apart from the tennis racket in the corner and a large glossy poster of the American group The Supremes, also triplets of a sort, who had just had their first big hit. They sat next to one another on the bed-settee and proceeded to flick through a copy of *New* magazine – appropriately enough, since all of this was new to Jonas. She edged imperceptibly closer to him and he felt the warmth from her shoulder and her arm spreading through his body. A breathtaking scent emanated from her. She read out something from an agony column and laughed, he hadn't heard a thing, but he laughed anyway to be on the safe side, it must have been funny; he laughed as he took in her fingers, her bare forearm, the pale skin with its fine bloom of golden hair. They went on leafing through the magazine, he turned the pages too, kept brushing against her hand. It felt as though someone was whipping a rope around them, generating a magnetic field. Suddenly she looked straight at him. Her eyes had a dewy look to them, the expression 'eyes to drown in' flashed into his mind. Or perhaps it was the actual thought of drowning, that this had to do with life-saving. Purely on instinct he laid his cheek against hers, gently. The touch immediately sent shivers running through him. It was such a surprise. The softness. And the warmth even more so. Added to which there was the smell, a girl smell which was even stronger at such close quarters and induced an uncontrollable tightening of his throat. He steadfastly maintained later that his first chemistry lesson began here, sitting cheek to cheek with a girl. She was still holding the magazine. He saw the golden hairs on her arm rise up, stand on end, as if electrified. The magazine slid to the floor. Her hands found his body, felt their way around him. They sat with their arms round one another, cheek to cheek, for a long, long time. Held each other and hugged. There were lots of variations on a hug, gentle or firm, quiet or energetic. Even the quiet hugs left them breathless and flushed. Jonas liked it best when his cheek barely grazed hers. He wished he could maintain this contact with her skin for ever, sitting like this with his nose close to the nape of Hjørdis's fragrant neck. She pulled away, her eyes glassy, muttered something about homework, saw him out. The others were still hanging around in the cul-de-sac, like spectators waiting for an athlete to cross the finishing line. He gave them the thumbs-up, a victory sign, making sure that he could not be seen from the window.

He had not even had a chance to answer the other kids' eager questions when Hjørdis also came out. But she only stayed for a moment before slinging the yellow scarf round her neck and pulling him back inside. His chums whooped and whistled, impressed by Jonas's way with the girls. 'She can't keep her hands off you, you lucky dog!' Once more, Hjørdis led him to her room. 'What about your homework?' he asked. She just had to have one more hug, she said with eyes one could drown in and pressed her cheek to his. Jonas seemed almost to have forgotten already how shockingly soft and warm it felt. Again the touch of her skin sent an electric charge running through him and the scent of her left him breathless. She managed to push him away just before he lost control.

As he was making his way back downstairs to his mates – who were still waiting impatiently for his report – Hjørdis came running after him, as if she had had second – or third – thoughts; she grabbed him by the arm and dragged him, laughing, back up to the flat. His chums' shouts sounded more envious than acclamatory now. Jonas was proud of having such an effect on her. He followed her inside yet again; this time they simply stood hugging in the hall, but this was, if possible, even more exciting; he just could not get over the wonderful softness of it, the warmth. These hugs gave rise to the same ecstatic thrill inside him, and the scent of her took his breath away. She managed to prise herself loose the second before he lost his head and started pawing at the more forbidden parts of her anatomy. Jonas stood there, feeling this glorious sensation coursing through him. Did he think of Melankton? It was good, no matter what. It was like being a child and never tiring of hearing the same story over and over again.

Minutes later, as he was making his way across to the gang, to finally take his bow, so to speak, all three triplets appeared on their balcony. They were almost faint from suppressed giggling. The other two had been home all the time. Helga and Herborg had simply borrowed Hjørdis's yellow scarf. Jonas's chums were in stitches, they were almost rolling on the ground with laughter, they called him a bigamist and worse. As I said, the triplets might seem to have adopted the Musketeers' motto: 'One for all and all for one'. They shared everything, even boyfriends. Or maybe they had been trying to make him accept a package deal. Jonas hardly dared show his face at school the next day.

But deep down he was really quite chuffed. When it came to the archetypal story of 'My First Hug', he won hands down with his 'My First Three Hugs'. And he had, in fact, come close to realising his impossible dream: of being with them all at once. Jonas, in his skating cap, felt as though he had won gold, silver and bronze in the same race.

He was still puzzled, though, especially by the fact that every hug had felt equally good to him. Was it, then, something about himself he had discovered, rather than something about girls? He had thought the fact of being in love was an infallible Geiger counter, when maybe it was nothing but an animal response, a simple reflex, a bio-zoological process which had blithely picked out three different girls, each with equal certainty, to be the one for him. The more he thought about it, the more sure he was that they had not each given him their own passport photo, they had given him three pictures of Hjørdis. He felt a vague twinge of fear. It was almost as if he had unintentionally discovered that there was no difference between one girl and another, they could all fill you with the same delight, were distinguishable only by the colour of their scarves. He had a mental picture of his future: a succession of women wearing different scarves, but otherwise absolutely identical. This led him, in turn, to imagine how impossible it would be to find what *New* magazine called 'Miss Right'. If love endowed you, as Karen Mohr had implied, with fresh eyes, then he was definitely on the wrong track. She, Hjørdis, or the three of them, had shown him, rather, that love is blind. He shuddered. He thought of Melankton. Thanks to the triplets, Jonas was beginning to believe that it was not only the world and people which were flat, but possibly love, too. Was there such a thing as round love?

This was Jonas Wergeland's first experience of the female sex. Right at the start he was made aware of how unpredictable they were, how different. The next day, Hjørdis came up to him in the playground to say she was sorry. Jonas shrugged it off as if it was no big deal. Actually, he had lost interest, he 'broke it off' shortly afterwards. And even if he was not exactly mad at her, this may have been an instinctive rejection of girls who did not take love seriously. Who did not consider it absolutely central. The fact is, though, that Jonas himself did not know whether he had been moved by pride or fear. After all, if she could fool him with a hug, who could say where it might end.

Jonas often thought of Helga, Herborg and Hjørdis, three girls so alike that you could take them for one. The funny thing was that in the years to come they began to branch out in different directions – became so unlike one another that they were known to some as The Good, the Bad and the Ugly. More than anyone, it was the triplets who taught Jonas that nature and nurture did not necessarily say everything there was to know about a person.

And although all three were passionate climbers, possibly because their births had coincided with the conquest of Mount Everest, it can be revealed that only one of them became a public figure, an eminent diplomat and expert on the Middle East. In interviews she always said the same thing: 'As one of triplets you have to be a good mediator.'

It seems only reasonable that Jonas should have been torn between three girls at a time when he was also something of a mental bigamist – in making, that is, his first clumsy attempts to pursue several streams of consciousness at the same time. For months it became a regular routine with him to go down to the basement where, in the darkness, with the aid of the skipping rope he conducted his exhausting, but felicitous mental workouts. After a while, however, a new challenge presented itself: what was he to do with it, this discovery that he was capable of thinking multiple thoughts? So far it had simply been something beautiful, like sparkling crystals, like walking on air – a kick in itself. His dream of becoming a lifesaver, his first serious undertaking, having ended in a miserable anticlimax, he had become more and more convinced that the power of thought might hold the key to a worthy alternative, a possible new goal in life.

Could these parallel reflections save him from the flatness? Skipping gave him a reassuring sense of being inside a sphere, thanks to the arc of the rope. His observations, the layers of ramifying thoughts, could perhaps help him to get to the *other side* of things. What if he could plumb his own true depths through thought? Prove that reality was round. Even if the world was flat. If he was to be a discoverer, he would have to be the type who made discoveries with the mind, not with the eyes.

Or rather: Jonas suspected that his powers of imagination would make him good at a game such as chess, possibly very good, but then people would think he was a run-of-the-mill genius and he did not want to be a run-of-the-mill genius, he wanted to be an extraordinary human being. There were plenty of minor geniuses around, but few exceptional individuals. He aimed to be an exception.

Karen Mohr was clearly an exception. The more visits Jonas paid to her, the more he talked to her in that Provençal-style living room in the middle of an otherwise drab Norwegian housing estate, the more sympathy he had for this woman who believed that a moment could constitute a whole life. The way Jonas saw it, the reason she maintained her glowing complexion was that she lived under a mental sun lamp. He had the feeling that Karen Mohr also skipped, that she had succeeded in doing something which he had unconsciously been striving to do for some while: she had stopped time, she hung suspended in a permanent double skip.

'I thought you worked with precious stones,' Jonas said on one occasion as he stifled a contented belch, having just consumed one of her superb omelettes, a golden half-moon with a filling which was a delight to the palate.

That was not such a bad guess at that, she said, stroking one of the shells on the shelf. She probably could be regarded as a diamond-cutter of sorts. She was in the process of cutting a very big diamond, endeavouring to bring out the light in it. 'I have spent years, many, many years on extracting every ounce from that day,' she said. Jonas suddenly felt that he could discern different facets to her countenance, or that he was observing her from three sides at once, just as in the sketch on the wall. One thing, at least, was for sure: Karen Mohr did not have 'a bit on the side', what she had lay in the centre.

During his visits Jonas often noticed Karen Mohr run her fingers over a ceramic figurine or a smooth, round pebble on the shelf, with an absent-minded smile. Or she might pause beside the green plant which Jonas liked best because its leaves looked as though someone had taken the scissors to them – a *mónstera*, she told him later. Sometimes she would fall to fingering those elaborate leaves as if, through them, she was suddenly transported into reminiscences in which she relived certain inexhaustible seconds.

'Did you leave right away?' Jonas asked.

'I stayed for some weeks,' she said. 'But I never saw him again, if that's what you're wondering.' She poured herself a glass of Pernod. Jonas loved to watch the clear liquid turn greyish and semen-like when she added water. He had conceived the notion that this might be what fertilised her imagination.

Jonas's eyes also lingered on the objects in her living room, as if he were understanding more and more of what he was seeing. At first he had thought that she was sad, hurting somehow, but he soon realised that she was happy; she was one of the most contented people he would ever meet. Karen Mohr taught Jonas that happiness could be something other than he had imagined.

'It may be that we only *live* once during the years when we walk the earth,' she said, as if reading his thoughts. 'In which case we really have to cherish this time.' She cleared the table. 'I was lucky. I had those weeks by the Mediterranean. Some people, a great many, I think, have never experienced life – raw, vibrant life – in such a way.'

A lot of folk would, nonetheless, automatically have construed that eccentric living room of hers as being an escape from something. Jonas – possibly because he was a child – never thought of it that way. He understood, although he could not have put it into words, that even though Karen Mohr might retreat into a parallel world from time to time, she never lost sight of the 'normal' world. It was more as if that other world, her memories of Provence, was forever filtering through to enrich her life in Oslo. She said it herself: 'I don't live in another world. I live in two worlds. Compared to most other people, who inhabit just the one, I am twice as happy.' It would be no exaggeration to say that Karen Mohr was one of the greatest teachers Jonas Wergeland ever had. A true educator. Someone who brought out the best in him. Broadened his mind. Raised his consciousness. She taught him that it was possible to live in two places at once.

In due course, Jonas received an explanation for her mysterious outings on that one evening each month. One Saturday afternoon when he happened to be there, she suddenly said: 'It's time you were going. I have to get changed. I'm going into town.' It turned out that she was going to a restaurant at the bottom of Bygdøy Allé by the name of Bagatelle, commonly known as Jaquet's Bagatelle, after the owner Edmond Jaquet – although actually by this time it was being run by his son Georges. The Bagatelle was still a colourful and popular restaurant when Jonas was at university, not least because Georges Jaquet kept his food and wine prices low enough that even Jonas and his friends could afford to eat there. And since they were studying astrophysics, they gave Georges Jaquet many more stars than the latter-day Bagatelle could ever boast.

On one Saturday evening in the month, Karen Mohr dressed in her best and dined alone at Bagatelle on Bygdøy Allé. She described to Jonas what a pleasure it was to be welcomed by the unfailingly charming Georges in his dark suit and be seated at a white-clothed table under a drawing by Le Corbusier himself, who also happened to be a cousin of Edmond Jaquet's. Jonas's mouth watered when she told him what a treat it was to read the menu – different every day and written in both French and Norwegian; the thrill of running an eye over such tempting offerings as *turbot au vin blanc* and *riz de veau grand duc*. And she always had a word with the head chef or the sous-chefs, often in French. Georges set great store by regular patrons like Karen Mohr; she could even take the liberty of nodding discreetly to journalist Arne Hestenes or Robert Levin the pianist. Jonas never asked her why she frequented Bagatelle, but he fancied that he knew the reason. She went there to contemplate her life. To consider the fact that she had turned down one of the greatest painters of the twentieth century. Perhaps the name of the place helped her to reduce the whole episode to a mere bagatelle. Or maybe she was actually *celebrating* it. Whatever the case, it was not a nostalgia trip, but a salute to a moment. Jonas imagined her having snails as a starter, to check the speed of her reminiscences, ensure that they slid through her very slowly.

On another occasion in her flat, when Jonas was enjoying freshly baked *croissants* and Karen was drinking what she called *café au lait*, not from a cup but from a bowl, Jonas had asked her why she had turned down that painter, because he understood that she had rejected him, had said no to more than just having her portrait painted. Karen had thought for a moment, most likely because she was not sure whether Jonas would understand. Then she had said: 'Even though I had only met him minutes before I knew that he was, how shall I put it, too simple. I could tell that he was a genius, and yet – perhaps for that very reason – he was too simple. Most men are too simple.' To Jonas it sounded as if she were saying: too *flat*. Karen Mohr raised her bowl to her lips and took a sip. Jonas suspected that she was concealing a smile.

The worst of it was that she had no regrets, she said. Despite the intensity of the moment, those few charged seconds, the pleasure of being the object of his searching gaze, and despite the fact that she may well have been saying no to living with him, to sharing the luxury of his fame. And she had made the right decision.

'Even though you could have made a name for yourself?' Jonas asked.

She looked at him as if she did not understand the question, then went on talking about something else – if, that is, it was not the same thing: 'I did not deem him ... worthy,' she said. That word 'worthy' was to become a catchword in Jonas's life.

'Did you ever find someone who was worthy?' he asked, doing his best to pronounce the word with the same gravity as Karen Mohr, stretching the vowels and rolling the 'r'.

'No, I never did.' And then, anticipating Jonas's next question. 'But I have never reproached myself.'

Jonas could not know that many times in the future his eyes would fill with tears at the memory of her face as she spoke of this. She had provided him with a mainstay, one that would stand within him forever; she taught him something about the uncompromising nature of love, the solemnity of it – a solemnity which made him feel a little uneasy, gave him a sense of the heavy responsibility which rested on his shoulders whenever he was faced with a woman. Karen Mohr had received an offer from a man admired by half the world, but had not deemed him worthy. Love is no mere bagatelle, that's for sure, was Jonas's first thought.

The memory of Karen Mohr would come into his mind in the oddest places, such as the time, decades later, when he found himself confronted by a desert of sorts, and saw thousands of warriors marching towards him, soldiers in full battle gear, rank upon rank. For a few seconds he had thought that they were coming to get him, to punish him; that this vast army had been mobilised because he, Jonas Wergeland, had been unfaithful in love, had shown himself *unworthy*.

For several terrible weeks Jonas had laboured under the delusion, as night-marishly vivid as only the mind of a jealous man could produce, that his wife was having an affair with one of his closest friends. It is tempting to recount all his suppositions and mental agonies, his occasionally churlish behaviour and pathetic accusations, but while the whole notion of being a cuckolded husband is not nearly as old hat as many would have it – the sort of thing that only befalls the Strindbergs of this world – these aspects must take second place to the account of how the other party, Margrete that is, dealt with the situation and, not least, with her husband's need for a bulwark of promises and assurances, in short: his desperate longing for security. And when one considers what Jonas himself had created in the way of problems some years earlier – with his fateful escapade in Lisbon – it is hard to see how Margrete managed to muster the patience she displayed; it says a lot about originality and forgiveness, about a woman who in so many ways had no equal.

For months Jonas inhabited two worlds, one of which – the delusional one – gradually gained the upper hand. In his imagination, he was constantly witness to every detail of Margrete's infidelity, her rendezvous and sexual gymnastics with a man whom, till then, he had counted his friend. And every night in bed when, shamefully but nonetheless belligerently, he confronted her with accusations based on his delusions, lengthy tirades which always ended with him asking how else she could explain why she was no longer interested in him, sexually, she would hear him out, then repeat what she had said the night before, and the night before that: 'It doesn't matter what I say, you won't listen anyway.'

Then one December day she came home from work and asked him to take the following week off from his job at NRK. 'Why?' he asked. 'Just do it,' she said. 'Make some excuse about illness in the family,' she said. 'But why?' he said again. 'Because I want to show you a world as unreal as the one you're living in right now,' she said. Later Jonas was to think that what she had actually been saying was: 'Because you are dead. Because I want to bring you back to life.'

A week later they were at the airport. Jonas wanted to ask where they were going, but some foolish sense of pride prevented him from doing so. Margrete did not say anything either, not about their destination anyway, otherwise she was quite chatty, making comments about the other passengers, relating funny incidents from her many travels as a girl. Not until they were in the transit hall at Copenhagen's Kastrup Airport, when Margrete indicated to him that their flight was now boarding, did Jonas see the name of their destination on the display: Beijing! Beijing, China. Margrete slept through most of the long flight, but Jonas was so agitated that he was not even capable of enjoying the deluxe in-flight service. But when they landed, she said, as if referring to his recent uncivilised behaviour: 'Here, in these people's eyes, we are both barbarians, here – on neutral ground – we might be able to talk to one another.'

As it turned out, though, Beijing was merely a stopover point, they still had a bit to go. Once again Jonas was amazed by what a woman of the world Margrete proved to be in such situations. She obviously knew a smattering of essential Chinese words and phrases – she could certainly make herself understood – and while they were waiting for their domestic flight, she managed to get hold of some sort of fast food: bulky, white polystyrene boxes whose contents Jonas dared do little more than pick at, but which she, Margrete, gobbled down with every sign of genuine relish, aided by chopsticks which she plied as if they were natural extensions of her fingers. With her faintly oriental features one could have been forgiven for thinking that these were her natural surroundings.

Throughout the flight, on board a domestic aircraft which reminded him of a run-down flat, reeking of grease and stale cooking smells, Jonas sat stiff with fright. Most of the passengers were soldiers, all clad in heavy overcoats which they kept on and which gave off an odour of sun-warmed rubbish bins. Jonas kept an anxious eye on the emergency exits – he could feel a distinct draught from the one closest to him. In all the confusion he had not caught the name of their destination, so he swallowed his pride and asked Margrete. 'Wait and see,' she said. 'Why can you never just enjoy a surprise?'

But when they landed, late in the afternoon, Jonas still had no idea where they were. There was no snow, but it was bitterly cold and it was getting dark. They were met by a driver and a man who was obviously some sort of guide. Margrete had arranged everything in advance, more as a matter of form than out of necessity. It very quickly became plain to Jonas that she was every bit as well-informed as their guide. They drove through a broad, monotonous landscape. Jonas recalled a film he had once seen, *Yellow Earth* by Chen Kaige. 'Excuse me, but can you tell me where we are?' Jonas asked the guide. The man turned to look at him in some surprise: 'Welcome to Xi'an, one of the oldest cities in China,' he said with a smile.

At the hotel, a showy but characterless modern building right next to the old clock tower in the heart of Xi'an, they ate a silent supper in the restaurant. Their guide, a middle-aged man whom Margrete had invited to join them, sensed that something was up and in an effort to lighten the mood, as they were finishing their meal he went over to an ancient, out-of-tune piano and began to play a piece which at first – and mainly because that was what he was expecting – Jonas took to be a traditional Chinese melody, some old chestnut, a worn-out tune, but suddenly he recognised it. It was not very well played, but it was, nonetheless, 'Morning' by Edvard Grieg. The other diners applauded enthusiastically. The guide was all smiles when he returned to Jonas and Margrete. Jonas knew he ought to say something, that he owed it to the guide to ask how he came to know that tune, since the answer would no doubt reveal a lot about the man and his background, his life, but Jonas had been poisoned by his own thoughts, his own worries, by the underworld which at all times existed alongside the one he inhabited: a phosphorescent green stalactite cave in which Margrete committed the most obscene acts with another man, one of Jonas's friends, at that; an ice-cold basement which, by means of some sort of osmosis, had seeped into his Xi'an world. He was so bewildered that he proceeded once again, in the hotel room, as if it were the only thing of which he was capable, to ask Margrete what the other man was like in bed, whether he took her from in front or behind? He knew he ought to be feeling more enthusiastic, show some interest in the place and the sights they would be seeing there, but his mind was clouded, as they say. The thought of Margrete's supposed affair bulked larger for him than the whole amazing existence of China. Margrete did not answer him. But she talked, chatted about other things, reassured him indirectly, as it were. And at night she snuggled up to him, she did not get mad; at no time over the past six months had she avoided him, not even when he had hurled the most appalling accusations at her, even though it was possible – he did not dare to pursue this thought to its conclusion – that she had problems of her own; every night she lay down behind him, snuggled in close to his back, as if to warm him. Or as if he were a child, a little creature that did not know what was best for it, that had to be protected from itself. It was bitterly cold in Xi'an that December: 'I'm freezing,' he said.

'I'm here,' she whispered behind him, in his ear. He felt her warm breath against his skin.

Somewhere, deep down in his subconscious, Jonas suspected that these fancies were nothing but red herrings, meant to distract his mind from something possibly more troubling: the fear that he was not worthy. 'Worthy' pronounced with stretched vowels and a rolled 'r'. From the moment when he had run into Margrete again he had known that she was a more intelligent person than he. Better equipped, in all ways. He had thought – as if he were living in the age of chivalry – that he had to bring her something, as proof that he was, despite all the signs to the contrary, good enough. That he quite simply had to do some great deed. And although he eventually abandoned such notions, he was occasionally inclined to believe that this was why he had never really settled into his cushy announcer job, and was indeed what had moved him to make the whole *Thinking Big* series. Nevertheless, here he was, in Xi'an, and he was so afraid. Afraid that even that great work was not enough. Afraid that in some way it was too simple. So afraid that he had had to seek refuge in another, more plausible reason for his fear; a non-existent lover. Part of him cosseted the thoughts that raged inside his head, part of him was ashamed of them, of the details which he magnified to the point of unrecognisability, as though he were on the track of a crime far more serious than adultery.

The first thing Margrete did the next morning was to take him to a clothes market down a side street where, for next to nothing, she bought him a green quilted military greatcoat with gold buttons and an imitation fur collar. They climbed into the car and drove for half an hour through Shaanxi province, past bare fields and gardens full of leafless trees, to the district of Lintong, where they pulled up outside what looked like a huge hangar surrounded by smaller buildings and a busy souvenir shop. Margrete knew exactly where to go, she bought tickets then made a beeline for the largest building and led Jonas up a stairway flanked by urns adorned with dragons. Then suddenly, after passing through a dimly-lit vestibule lined with sales booths, they came face to face with what Margrete had brought him halfway round the world to see. And actually this said all there was to say about Margrete Boeck, this was her in a nutshell: you accused her of something and instead of answering you she took you to China.

And so it was here, as they stood at the pale-green railing on a platform overlooking a piece of ground the size of a football pitch, a sort of enormous sandpit, that Jonas, clad in a military greatcoat, discovered himself, or rather: an army of replicas, semblances of himself. Thousands of petrified human forms. He felt himself to be every bit as dead as them. He felt as if he had been baked, burned, by love.

It was the strangest sight. Jonas stood there like a general inspecting his troops of fired clay, terracotta, who looked as though they were marching up out of the ground, ready to do battle. There had to be a couple of thousand soldiers there, row upon row of them, all life-size, and behind them thousands of others, still hidden in the earth and waiting for the archaeologists to dig them out. The whole thing seemed oddly familiar, he must have read about it somewhere or other. Either that, or he had had this feeling inside him for a long time. The feeling that something, an entire world, would rise up out of the ground itself. Ever since that summer with Bo Wang Lee. And he understood, or thought he understood, what Margrete's purpose had been in bringing him here to see this wonder.

While he leaned on the railing, as if on a boat, gazing at an ocean, Margrete told him about the Emperor Qin Shi Huangdi, tyrant and reformer, who built with one hand and pulled down with the other; the emperor who was responsible both for the Great Wall and the decree ordering the burning of all scrolls. Less well-known were his paranoid endeavours to safeguard his life even after death. Archaeologists had not yet ventured to explore the burial mound, the mausoleum itself, which lay some kilometres from there, and which Jonas would see on the way back.

Jonas listened, and the more Margrete told him, the more this story seemed to find an echo in his own ambition, his urge to make a name for himself, not least when he thought of the television series into which he had invested such an inhuman amount of work and which he had only recently presented to over a million Norwegians – a Great Wall of images, if you like.

Jonas surveyed the thousand-odd soldiers so far unearthed. He thought he could also descry, like something lying *behind* them, the over six thousand figures waiting under the ground. They were all part of Emperor Qin's vast kingdom of the dead. The terracotta army was there to defend his tomb, ensure him of eternal life. Margrete concluded her tale. Jonas looked at her, saying nothing, but with a wordless question on his face: Why are you telling me all this? And at that same moment it dawned on him that in talking about Emperor Qin she was actually talking about him, Jonas; she regarded them, Qin and him, as parallel characters, though not in the way he had first imagined – the real similarity between them had little to do with their ambitious undertakings.

'Extreme security calls for extreme brutality,' she said.

Jonas knew what she meant. He stood there inside a huge hangar, as far away from home as he could possibly be, on Earth at any rate, stood there clad in a quilted military greatcoat, like a living, breathing terracotta soldier, and he knew.

She caught and held his eye. 'Jonas,' she said. He met the gaze of those dark-brown eyes which did not see through him, but into him, seeming to embrace his whole being. 'You can never feel secure,' she said. Or did not say. He read it in her eyes.

They spent some days in Xi'an, in that windy, dusty city which seemed to Jonas to mark a new beginning for Margrete and him, or at any rate a fresh chance. It was also the starting point of the Silk Road, Marco Polo's Chang'an, once the greatest city in the world. Jonas had spent a whole day walking about on his own amid the fumes of coal fires and baked yams, trailed up and down Xi'an's four main streets, which ran to the four points of the compass: symbolic, so it seemed, of four alternative paths. His marriage, which had been pretty rocky for some time, suddenly seemed full of possibility again, there was no knowing where it might end. He wandered the streets in his heavy greatcoat like a terracotta soldier resurrected; roamed around Xi'an, his head buzzing with thoughts – and it came to him. No matter what *he* did – built a wall around her, built a wall *for* her – he could never feel secure, there was no guarantee that she would find him worthy. All he could do was to trust her. He had been like a lump of clay, set hard, but he had been brought back to life. And he knew why. She had breathed life into him.

He woke up, became a new man. Margrete took him by the arm and showed him around, needed no guide. In an almost tourist-free Xi'an, under a clear, cold blue sky, they visited the Big Wild Goose Pagoda and the Green Dragon Temple and the Provincial Museum of History which, as it happened, was also a mosque. Something about her passion for candied plums, which they bought threaded onto a stick, and the way she ordered the taxi drivers about, told him that she had been here before. With amazing assurance she tracked down the best herbalists and silk merchants, as well as the most out-of-the-way restaurants, hidden down backstreets, in gardens where carp and mandarin fish swam in glass tanks and snakes coiled in cages with reassuring stones on their lids. Margrete, too, seemed different now, somehow relieved, or hopeful; she came out with all sorts of information about China, smiled and pointed at little children with knitted Gagarin helmets on their heads, but bare bottoms showing through the slits in the backs of their trousers even in the biting cold. At night she lay and looked at him, reminded him of things they had done when they were going out together in sixth grade. Of the weighing machines at the Eastern station that dispensed wise sayings along with a note of their weight. Of the time when Jonas won a ski race because the weather suddenly changed and all the other competitors' skis got clogged up. They laughed. Laughed together as they had not done in ages. Her eyes were golden, deep and smouldering. And like gold they only really came into their own in the twilight.

One night, in the moonlight, she took Jonas by the hand and led him up onto the city wall beside the north gate. And here, as if it were the most natural thing in the world, she produced a kite she had bought and flew it from the top of the wall in the winter night, steered it expertly, making it swoop low then soar again, a sight which reminded Jonas of something he had seen before, in another life so it seemed. 'Here, you try,' she said, standing behind him and helping him, guiding him. 'Well done,' she said, as if talking to a child. Jonas stood there, wrapped in his thick, quilted coat, and flew a kite so high that it was just a black dot in the moonlight. It was all about control. About relaxing. Letting things run.

Margrete said not a word. Jonas Wergeland stood atop a city wall in China, flying a kite in the moonlight and he understood.

So why did he do it?

At the airport, on the day of their departure, Jonas took their guide aside. 'That was so nice, that piece by Grieg you played. Thank you.' The man was gratified by this, he could see.

'Yes, Grieg was a great hit-maker,' the guide said. 'I know several tunes by him. Next time you come to Xi'an I will play them for you.'

Again that night in the hotel in Beijing Margrete snuggled in to his back, as if wanting not only to warm him, but also to defend him against attack from behind. She lay there, breathing on him. He was dead, a mere form; he had not yet discovered his true potential. He might have created the most famous Norwegian television series of all time, a worldwide success, and be arguably the biggest celebrity in the whole country, but he had not found his way in life.

The rows and rows of terracotta warriors had also given him a sense of déja vu. They reminded him of his youthful endeavours back home in the base-ment at Solhaug: the skipping, the rope, the thoughts that were unearthed, in serried ranks. Maybe his basement had been just such a subterranean realm, a place where he had tried to do much the same as Emperor Qin: to make time stand still, win eternal life. Build a world of his own, which no one could invade, where he would be safe.

But during that secret basement period of his life, on his journeys of dis-covery into the world's most beautiful hemisphere: the brain – to the extent that this is the seat of thought – his objective kept shifting. At one stage all his efforts were focused on mastering a triple skip, what he called a triplet. Gradually, however, he became more and more obsessed with punching a hole in something, breaking down a sort of wall of thoughts, of reaching *beyond*. He took it into his head that if he could just get enough thoughts turning in his mind simultaneously, something would burst open, all those different reflections would latch onto one another, their united weight rip the surface and they would sink down to illuminate something in the depths, like a bathysphere exploring some hitherto unplumbed fissure in the seabed. Or perhaps the 'other place' thus revealed would turn out to be what, in his mind, he called Samarkand. Many a time when he was skipping like a soul possessed in the dark basement, with the rope whirring round him as he did doubles, he felt as if he were caught in a whirl, as if he were a dervish of the skipping world. More and more often, once he had mastered the knack of following four trains of thought simultaneously, he had the impression that he was on the point of making some great find – that something massive, something colossal, was lying in wait, that it could break through at any minute. This reminded Jonas of the thrill of anticipation he experienced with a well-composed pop song the second before the chorus kicked in, or the feeling inside him when his father reached the final chord in a choral prelude and the hymn proper was about to thunder out. But even then, hovering inside the arc of the rope with four thoughts held suspended in the air, that was as far as it went. It was like working his way up to an orgasm, a liberating climax, which then subsided. The world which he sensed was there, remained hidden behind an unopened door, so to speak. It was as if he could hear it knocking, but could not open the door to it.

And speaking of unopened doors, for a long time Jonas had no idea what Karen Mohr did – for a living that is. But she was a great reader, that much he knew. Jonas had a theory that it was tales from warmer climes which had endowed her skin with such a dusky tint – if, that is, it was not her perpetual and powerful memory of the Riviera. Frequently, especially after a glass of Pernod, she would find occasion to quote thoughts on love to him, primarily reflections she had come across in French literature. One Saturday afternoon, one of those Saturdays when she was not due to dine at Bagatelle in Bygdøy allé, she told him about a writer by the name of Stendahl. He had written a whole book solely about love. 'Would you mind nipping into the bedroom and getting it?' she asked him. 'It's called *De l'Amour* and it's just on your left, at eye-level, as you go in.'

Jonas was at a complete loss, did not know which way to turn. She pointed to the wall. Still Jonas was none the wiser, he stood there listening to the tinkling of the little fountain in among the plants, as if hoping it might inspire his imagination. Was he supposed to walk through the wall? Then he spied it. A door. He had never seen anything there before but a rug hanging on the wall, but this – he now noticed – exactly covered the door. The door handle had been there all the time, but it was almost invisible. It wasn't unlike the secret doors in films set in old country houses or castles. It had never occurred to Jonas that of course there had to be other rooms in the flat.

'It's odd,' Karen Mohr said when Jonas laughed and pointed at the door. 'We're always so interested in the room we happen to be in. In whether it consists of still smaller rooms, harbours secrets. We open drawers, peep behind the sofa. We are so intent on this that we don't notice the secret doors in the room, which could lead us to great wings containing other rooms entirely. We all live in bigger houses than we imagine.' On a later occasion – as she raised her eyes to her own portrait on the wall, sketched in Mougins before the war – she framed it in other, more personal, terms: 'Our secret chambers lie not within us, but outside of us.' For once her voice was husky with emotion.

As with her living room, he was not prepared for the sight which met his eyes when he walked through her bedroom door. In a way this came as an even greater surprise. Jonas came from a home almost devoid of books, although Rakel did own one work entitled *My Treasury*. This, Karen Mohr's bedroom, truly was a treasury. Three of its walls were completely covered with bookcases which looked, with all their rows and rows of books, like brightly-coloured panels. Jonas had the impression of stepping into a warm, mystical forest. The bed was under the window. 'I sleep well in there,' he heard Karen say in the living room. Jonas could well understand that. This was how a bedroom ought to be: full of stories. Initially he just stood there staring. It immediately struck him that there was a connection between the two rooms, different thought they were. That this bedroom, with all these books, was the roots and the living room was the tree. Or maybe it was the other way round. The bedroom-cum-library was more like an *interpretation* of the living room. Her book collection had grown, blossomed, out of her thirst for understanding.

Or perhaps – it later occurred to him – all those books dealt with the search for someone who was worthy. It was as complex as that.

It took him a while to find Stendahl. On the left. But at *her* eye level. *De l'Amour*. Outside left, Jonas thought to himself. He had to stand on tiptoe to reach it. But it was wedged in tight: the shelf was crammed with volumes. He tugged and tugged, trying to pry the book free – only to end up working the whole shelf loose and bringing the entire row of books tumbling down on his head like a flock of wrathful birds. The ensuing din brought Karen Mohr rushing in, but she merely laughed when she saw what had happened. 'Are you alright?' she asked, still laughing. He gave his head a shake, dazed. The shelf must have been loose, she told him. There was something wrong with the screws that held the shelves in place. She should have had those bookcases fixed long ago.

'I'm really sorry, but I had to reach up on tiptoe,' he said.

'Silly boy,' she said. 'You *always* have to reach up on tiptoe to get at the right books.' She glanced cheerfully at the volumes that had crashed to the floor as he tried to pull out Stendahl's *De l'Amour*. 'But let this be a lesson to you,' she said. 'When you reach out for love you will soon discover that it is bound up with everything else.'

Jonas, on the other hand, was thinking to himself: I'd bet anything there's a secret chamber behind these bookshelves too. And there was. A veritable palace. One day Karen Mohr would take him there.

'Come on, we can sort this out later,' she said, pointing to the mess on the floor. She could tell from his face that he had had enough for one day. 'It's time for a ham omelette.'

Karen Mohr's bedroom, her secret forest, reinforced Jonas's belief that beyond this world another one lay waiting for him. That the world was not flat. He was still skipping regularly in the basement, in the dark, spinning thought after thought, layers of thoughts, above and below, behind and in front of one another, pursuing, or trying to pursue as many as possible at one time. He skipped and he skipped, but he had still not made any kind of a *breakthrough*. He had a suspicion that this would only happen if he were to succeed in weaving all of those simultaneous thoughts, at all those different levels, together in his mind, if he could get them to intercommunicate even though, in terms of content and substance, they were all very different. Because that was the really fascinating part: discovering the links between reflections which were worlds apart, which apparently had nothing in common. Was it possible to get these thoughts to chime in unison, like on an organ where the manuals and the stops gave you command, as it were, over several smaller and very different organs, each with its own individual character and unique tone. Jonas had seen how, when his father played, he coupled the Principal to the pedals and the Swell – deep in the background, so to speak – with the Choir to the fore; had heard how, in so doing, he produced the most wonderful sound, in which all the minor parts, all the voices from so many different directions, blended together to produce the most divine music. It might be that his trains of thought could also be regarded as strings of notes, as melodies which he had to weave into concords. Occasionally, if he was lucky, Jonas would hear his thoughts singing inside him, like a choir, exquisite wordless harmonies. And sometimes, if he went on doing doubles for long enough, until he was almost hovering in the darkness of the basement, he felt as though his whole body had turned into an organ.

It was also largely thanks to this sort of approach that, as a grown man, having taken up skipping again, he was able to resolve the problems surrounding his programme on Svend Foyn. Many of the episodes in the *Thinking Big* series had something of the character of a discovery about them, but with the programme on Foyn one felt more like an inventor, or rather: felt as though one had a front-row seat inside the mind of an inventor. Jonas Wergeland made a programme about Svend Foyn's moment of revelation, a few seconds which, on television, lasted for forty-five minutes. When viewers got up, their armpits damp from excitement, and looked at the clock, they could not believe the time.

The programme opened with a shot being fired from a cannon in the bows of a whaler and it ended with a bomb-tipped harpoon slamming into the side of a whale – hardly anyone spotted that the latter scene had been filmed on an underwater set. And presented between the shot and the strike were Svend Foyn's thoughts, his speculations on how to catch a whale, with Wergeland switching every now and again from this to a brief flash of the harpoon – the spearhead of his thoughts, as it were – flying through the air towards the back of the whale in the sea, in much the same way as, in more recent films, we can follow the flight of missiles or Robin Hood's arrows. By using trick photography Wergeland made it look as though the camera was fixed to the projectile, an illusion so effective that viewers felt almost as though they were being sucked into the picture.

But as I say, what really made the programme was not the special effects, but the way in which Jonas Wergeland succeeded in reflecting a thought process, one which actually continued, with much trial and error, for some years, but which Wergeland condensed into one compact burst of effort. As the outer framework to this one had Svend Foyn – actor Normann Vaage received a great many compliments for his snowy mane and magnificent white beard – slumped pensively in a deckchair on a deserted beach, gazing out to sea. To either side of him were other deckchairs, all empty. The wind made their fabric billow out like sails.

Jonas Wergeland started with images, which is to say with the line of thought which illustrated the first part of what was a multifaceted problem: the question of whether the whale was a good commercial prospect; in other words: Foyn's reflections on contracts and markets, on how a new industry of this nature should be organised and which products were likely to be the most attractive – oil, for example, and whalebone. The other question which had to be considered, was that of the boat – huge, fast-swimming whales could not be caught from rowboats. This train of thought gave rise to a series of shots, concluding with a scene showing Foyn's introduction of the steam engine to whaling; he had figured out that what he needed was a small, powerful steamship with good manoeuvrability – the prototype was christened *Spes & Fides*. This was followed by another reflection, a fresh problem, with Jonas Wergeland continually cutting to shots from the first two lines of thought. The third problem, the trickiest of them all, concerned the harpoon itself, since there was no way, either, that such massive and immensely strong creatures could ever be caught with hand-held harpoons. In this lay the programme's greatest challenge – to depict the experiments which led to Foyn's greatest invention, the bomb harpoon: the development of the right sort of explosives and detonators for the right harpoons; the discovery that explosive device and harpoon would need to be combined in the same projectile. And finally, or more correctly, interwoven with the three other visual threads, came the scenes in which television viewers were at long last introduced to the target: the whales, colossi such as the humpback whale, the fin whale and the blue whale, as yet unconquered by man, creatures which did not die easy, but which, when they did, sank. Svend Foyn had spent a lot of time sailing the Arctic Ocean and had invaluable experience of the nature and behaviour of the whale. This made, as one might expect, for some captivating scenes, footage which had been bought-in – there is nothing quite like the sight of a whale, that exotic creature, swimming in the ocean, surfacing, spouting. And then there was the soundtrack, recordings of so-called whale-song played in the background throughout the programme, communicating non-stop with the subconscious. Once or twice, when a number of whales sang out at the same time, Jonas raised their singing into the foreground, this euphonious, enigmatic music forming an accompaniment to Foyn's branching lines of thought. And apropos this last: as a child, crawling into the organ casing and seeing all the pipes that surrounded him, Jonas had often made believe that he was inside the belly of a whale.

Jonas Wergeland presented the progression of these four main thought processes by showing Svend Foyn sitting in more and more deckchairs until at last – just before all of his thoughts intertwined to give one solution – there were four Svend Foyns, or Foyn quadruplets, sitting side by side on the beach looking out to sea and the waves rolling to shore. Foyn, or the Foyn quads, thought of the whale's progress through the sea, the whale's speed and power, the whale's need to breathe, considered how long the whale stayed on the surface each time it came up; Foyn wrestled with financial forecasts, pondered the question of whale oil and all the uses to be found for whalebone, from corset stays to fishing rods, contemplated the matter of oil residue, and wondered whether the guano could be used as fertiliser; Foyn thought about the boat, about the size of the boat, its manoeuvrability, its crew; and above all Foyn applied his mind to the subject of the whaling tackle: what the line should be like, how many barbs the harpoon should have, how the bomb tip should be constructed, whether it ought to explode when it hit the target or seconds later; he considered the blending of the gunpowder, the fuse, his work with Esmark, the country parson and gifted chemist and the lessons he had learned from previous, unsuccessful, attempts by others: all of them had come up with a piece of the puzzle, but only he, Foyn, would succeed in fitting all the pieces together in his head.

The invention of the bomb harpoon, the absolute *sine qua non* of the modern whaling industry and cornerstone of Norway's first oil age, represented the culmination of all these thoughts on the whale as raw material, on the vessel's construction, on the animal's behaviour in the sea, on the properties of the harpoon; the result of these thoughts being considered at one and the same time, in concord, inside Svend Foyn's head. In the last scene but one, at the moment when the solution dawned on Foyn, actually in the form of a series of inventions springing to mind at the same moment, Jonas Wergeland showed him – which is to say all four Foyn quads – jumping up and shouting in unison: 'I have it!' From there Wergeland cut quickly to the final scene in which, like an echo of that cry, the harpoon hit the whale and exploded inside its body with a muffled, yet mighty boom – a fanfare, almost; and that this strike should have been regarded by viewers as a great victory, a climactic shout of triumph, at a time when whaling was so unpopular, proves just what a masterpiece this programme was. The viewers did not see the whale's death as something bad or traumatic, but as something symbolic: it was not a whale that had been caught, but a difficult and complex concept, a leviathan of the imagination. The passage of the harpoon through the air represented the flight of thought, and the impact with the whale signified the explosive moment of insight.

With a little good will Jonas Wergeland could be said to have laid the foundations of this programme when he was just a boy, in a basement – in the darkness of the deep, you might even say – at the time when his skipping fever was at its height. Before too long, however – he could not have said exactly when, but possibly during the transition from boy to youth – he discovered that he could make his thoughts branch out even *without* skipping, although it still worked best – and would, in fact do so for the rest of his life – when he had a rope whirling through the air around him, as if this gave him a particularly good charge. Whatever the case: by dint of thought Jonas was forever trying – with or without a rope – to become like a tree, to branch out. Most people strive to become pure and upright, to become pillars, poles, the sort of thing from which to fly a flag. Jonas wanted to be a tree. He often wandered around inspecting the different trees of Norway. When he was at the height of his fame he considered, not altogether in jest, writing his autobiography and calling it *My Life As An Oak*.

Although Jonas believed that he was really on to something, there came a point in his teens when he put his skipping, or rather: his thought experiments, on ice. He was, if the truth be told, a little alarmed by what he had discovered. On the one hand he felt his gift was a problem. He was afraid that he would never have the chance to use it. That he possessed abilities which would never do anything but confuse him. On the other hand, he hoped that it was only a matter of becoming more mature, gaining more experience. Then he would be able to resume his experiments. In any case, one thing was slowly borne in upon him, the longer he lived: there were possibilities, powers, within the realms of thought greater than anyone could imagine. Sometimes when he was contemplating, ruminating, he was conscious of a kind of mental 'lift off', a feeling of acceleration not unlike the 'boost' you get in the small of your back in a plane just before it takes off, as it approaches the end of the runway and suddenly picks up speed. In the long process of mankind's evolution, Jonas knew, we had not got beyond the very beginning. So far, man had only raised his body upright, not his mind. We had no right to our species name. We were *Homo erectus* and *Homo sapiens* on the outside, but not on the inside. It was one thing to walk upright, quite another to think upright. To be upstanding in one's mental life. When it came to awareness, man was still crawling ignorantly around on all fours.

But this line of reasoning was a thing of the future. For many years of his childhood skipping was one of Jonas's favourite pastimes. He skipped and skipped, as if unconsciously reaching out for something more, reaching upwards. He built shell after shell, layer upon layer around himself with the rope, and one day when he was skipping in the dark in the basement, in the midst of a heart-stopping, minutes-long stint of doubles, just as he felt that something was about to rip wide open, a veil be swept aside, as four or five thoughts which he was pursuing simultaneously began to converge, like the numbers in a combination lock which would suddenly click together to open a set of great, heavy doors – when he was just about there, only an arm's length away, he passed out.

Jonas came round when his sister switched on the light – having come down to fetch a jar of blueberry jam for pancakes. His forehead hurt, and when he put his fingers up to it they came away with blood on them. He must have struck the brick jamb of the storeroom door as he fell. He would be left with a scar, a pale line intersecting that other scar, his souvenir from the playground skipping game. I'm a marked man, he would think from then on, whenever he looked in the mirror. Although he did not know whether this meant he was damned or that he was to be saved. 'If you ask me, I think you should do a bit less skipping and eat a few more pancakes,' Rakel said when she saw her brother's ashen face and the blood trickling over his brow.

On the way up the stairs, with the aroma of freshly made pancakes making his stomach rumble, Jonas could not help wondering whether there might not be some connection between the two ventures to which he had so far dedicated his life; that there could, in fact, be a link between his ability to hold his breath and his talent for thinking parallel thoughts. Might it be possible to think so well that one could save lives.

Saturn

Is there anybody going to listen to my story ... I sing to myself. Humming it as an intro to what may prove to be my own story. Or an attempt at it, at any rate. I have been inspired by the unlikely fact that once more I find myself here, on board the *Voyager*, surrounded by stories, layer upon layer of scents, the switches to huge mechanisms in my memory. I kept my mouth shut when Hanna said that the boat had once belonged to 'a legendary actor'. She was well aware, of course, that I had known Gabriel Sand. Much has changed, though. For one thing, they have installed a four-cylinder Volvo Penta diesel engine. A wise move. Here, among such high mountains, the winds can be everything from insidiously capricious to absolutely non-existent. *Voyager* is also a grander name than the old one, the *Norge*. It befits a boat which, by their way of it, is going on a voyage of discovery. Into a new millennium. The *Norge* was more apt for a vessel which lies safe in harbour and never sets sail.

I had a strange experience out at the point north of Mannheller. I was on deck, sitting on the hatch of the forepeak, taking in the view all around me. I felt a surge of excitement. I could see into three or four fjords at the same time: into Lustrafjord, into Årdalsfjord, into the mouth of Lærdalsfjord and down Sognefjord itself. It was an awesome sight. And yet strangely familiar. I came to the conclusion that I must have come here as a small boy, on the ferry that used to run between Revsnes and Naddvik. That time when we drove all the way to Årdal, a real safari. I realised that this sight must have stayed with me, left its imprint on me. Like the belief that it was possible to look down several channels of possibility at once. I have been to Tokyo, I have visited Timbuktu, I have – speaking of safaris – scratched the backs of rhinos and held crocodiles in my hands, and yet – this short trip up a Norwegian fjord must have made a greater impression. Deeper. It had branched out into me.

While we were moored at Skjolden I had the chance to take a run down to Urnes with Carl. We drove along the narrow road past Feigumfossen and Kroken, out to the bare green hilltop on which the stave church sits. It was morning and the light slanted down from the sun hanging over Tausasva. The wooden walls of the church had recently been oiled, it smelled of boats. We strolled round to the north wall and studied the most famous wood carvings in Norway, one of the reasons why Urnes church is on the UNESCO list of those buildings in the world most worthy of protection and preservation.

'That is pretty much what we have in mind,' Carl said. '*That* is what I call software.' I stared for some time at the sinuous figures. '*That*,' I said, 'is what I call a fjord.' Carl eyed me quizzically: 'So what's the difference?'

I have to laugh – they are so keen. They hare about, talking to all and sundry, trying to track down people with access to archives, hunt up local contacts. Not surprisingly, here in Lærdal they are mainly regaled with stories about salmon, tales of the English salmon lords of the nineteenth century, the best 'pools', the fierce competition for fishing rights, the problem of parasites and the poison tipped into the river to combat them, thus putting the river out of action for years. None of them know much about salmon – apart from Martin possibly – but a visit to the Wild Salmon Centre has left them a lot wiser. They have already decided that fly fishing has to form one of the cornerstones in their presentation of the place. They buy books, collect brochures, take photographs, shoot video film. They delve and probe. They look, to me, as though they are investigating a serious crime, trying to unravel the threads of a massive conspiracy. They inspect the houses that have been preserved in the old part of Lærdal. They drive up to Borgund Stave Church. I go with them. I spend most of my time on the boat, but occasionally I go with them. I am, by profession, a secretary, I am used to tagging along. We walk the age-old, overgrown paths: Sverrestigen, Vindhellavegen. They are constantly discussing things. Making notes. Doing sketches. Drawing up charts, diagrams of which I cannot make head nor tail: they look like trees. Or fjords with lots of arms. They hear rumours of a French painter who is a regular visitor to Lærdal and usually stays at the home of a wealthy Norwegian family. Someone shows them reproductions of his work, abstract paintings inspired by the fjord, the mountains. Or by the colours and the patterns of salmon flies. They are familiar with the much-loved piece of music said to have been conceived at Lærdal. They pore over the plaque fixed to the rock face next to the jetty where we are moored, on it the first four bars of 'The Ballad of Giants' and the composer's signature: Harald Sæverud. They have a tape with them, play the first bars of this protest against the occupation as they take in their surroundings. On the hillside on the other side of the lake they can just make out the ruins of a German bunker. They listen, they think. It seems so comical and yet so serious. But I have to admire their get-up-and-go. It is not enough for them simply to collect facts, catalogue information. They also need to come up with an outer framework, a story to bind the whole lot together.

She has chosen her team carefully. Hanna was born in Korea. Carl has an American mother, a Norwegian father. Between them, like two wings, they extend Norway to east and west. Martin provides the local credibility: he hails from Nordkjosbotn – 'a crossroads in Troms,' as he said. With pride. I remember what Kamala, who was seriously discriminated against until she became famous, said in one television debate: 'Civilised society consists not of fortresses, but of crossroads.' Martin is cook, ruling over the galley down below according to the principles of 'enlightened absolutism', dishing up everything from couscous to sushi. I have no idea how he came by such skills. He is the type to have long since drunk snake's blood, with the snake's beating heart and all. Himself, he claims to have picked it all up in Nordkjosbotn: 'What did I tell you – it's a crossroads.'

She has called her company the OAK Quartet. The OAK stands for Oslo Art Kitchen. They have shown me their website, laid out like an inviting kitchen – an appetising work of art in itself. I can see why people would spend time there, avail themselves of their services. This tempting cyberspace reminds me, of all things, of Aunt Laura's seductive, limitless flat.

They often play string quartets on the CD player in the saloon, as if wishing to learn, to be stimulated. The music is pure and powerful, it is easy to hear how everything has been pared to the bone. The four young people on board truly *are* like a quartet. They each have their own strength, their own 'instrument'. They are like one of those pop groups in which no individual member stands out, but where the combined effect is mind-blowing.

I sit on deck, scanning the sheer cliff face on the opposite side of the fjord. At its foot, where the land begins, is a little beach. It is growing chilly. Martin came up just a moment ago with some piping hot soup, a bowl of *soba*, Japanese noodles, and some chopsticks. 'You slurp it down,' he told me. The clouds are hanging low today. Rays of sunlight break through here and there, dancing like spotlight beams over the landscape. I cannot get enough of this sight, the play of light and shade on the mountainsides. I was in China once, in Xi'an, with Margrete, and simply by showing me a few sights she made me well, cured me of my all-consuming jealousy. I have sometimes thought that she stuck tiny, imperceptible needles into me, treated me to a sort of mental acupuncture. In the watchtower at the north gate in the old city wall we found a shop selling prints, those long, rectangular pictures that can be rolled up. I was particularly taken with these paintings, with their depictions of tiny, solitary individuals in the wilds of the countryside, and their complete lack of any fixed focal point – the perspective altering every time you moved your eye. These were living, breathing pictures, in which the emptiness, the unpainted areas, formed an indispensable part of the composition. Margrete bought one for me. 'Every time you look at it, think of me,' she said.

I misunderstood. Did not see what she meant until it was too late. I had it hanging in my cell. I looked at it often. I travelled around in that picture often, a little person in a vast, rugged landscape containing any number of focal points. I have something of the same feeling here, in a narrow fjord running between plunging cliffs. When I see Sognefjord on the map, it looks to me like a dragon winding its way into the country. A dragon as they are drawn in China, long and sinuous. This too is a journey through a dragon.

I had been wrestling for ages with a big project. I was always wrestling with some big project. I kept having to redefine it, and almost as often had to rename it. Not until late on, *too* late on, did I see what my real project in life should have been.

One time on Hvaler – I must have been seven or eight – I found a cork bobbing about in the sea. I was out in my grandfather's smallest rowboat, a craft which even I could handle. As the boat drifted past the cork curiosity got the better of me. I backed the oars. Pulled them in. I leaned out and fished it up. I noticed that there was a rope attached to it. This made me even more curious. I started to haul on the rope, pulling it into the boat. It turned out, of course, that I had got my hands on a net; although – it should be said in my defence – it was of an unusual make, and with an illegally fine mesh. No one could see me from the shore. Very carefully I pulled it in. Some flounders were caught in the top of the net, but I spotted something intriguing glinting further down. I pulled harder. I saw the pale, gleaming surface turn into something huge – and hideous, like a great maw lunging up at me. I got a fright. Dropped the lot. I do not know what it was, possibly a small Greenland shark or the underbelly of a giant crab. I have thought about it a lot since then. That experience reminds me of Margrete. You're sailing through life when you spy a cork in the sea, you lift it out and there is this huge net, a skein full of things of which you could never have dreamed. You know, impossible though it is, that if you went on pulling long enough, if you put your back into it, kept at it, you would eventually haul the whole world up into the boat, including yourself and the boat.

Why did she do it?

I do not know when I first understood it. Or no, now I'm being coy – I never did understand it. But very early on in our relationship, something occurred, an incident which I made light of at the time, but which gradually came to seem important. Like a choice. It was one of those moments when I was able to look into several arms of a fjord at one time.

It was a normal afternoon. We were still living in her parents' museum of a flat in Ullevål Garden City. Margrete was a doctor, doing her specialist training in dermato-venereology at the University Hospital. I was in the process of putting my architecture studies, which is to say Project X, behind me. We were both head over heels in love, by which I mean that we were still at the stage in a love affair when you have been caught up in a warm wave and are just letting yourself be swept along. We showed face at all the timeless places, at Herregårdskroa where the service was so appalling, Frognerseteren with its overrated apple cake, Theatercafeen, where we were so wrapped up in one another that we did not even hear how badly off-key the old dinner orchestra was. We went to the cinema merely in order to sit with our eyes closed and hold hands; we went to the theatre solely so that we could smooch openly at the bar during the interval; we went to exhibitions for the sole purpose of gazing adoringly at one another amid the crowds of art-goers. We rediscovered the city: the shrimp boats, the chestnut trees, the glove shops, seeing everything for the first time, because we were together. But above all else: we made love, for hours at a time; laid each other down and sailed over and around each other's bodies; we were Captain Cook circumnavigating the globe, or Bartholomeo Diaz bound for the Cape of Good Hope. We might start by exploring one another's toes or foreheads, eventually to reach the middle where she always ended up running her ship aground on my lighthouse.

It was a perfectly ordinary afternoon. Margrete was lying in bed. We had made love. We had made long and glorious love. So it cannot have been that. The bedroom was white. Even the pine floorboards had a whitish sheen in the bright afternoon light which streamed through the fine veil of the curtains now that the blinds had been pulled up. The only objects in the room were a double bed with white bed linen and a brass headrail, and a gleaming gold statuette from the East. It was just how a bedroom, a place for lovemaking, should look. Love was, and always will be, a white patch, an undiscovered continent, watched over by an alien god with half-shut eyes.

This room and the kitchen were the ones I liked best in that otherwise unreal flat. The other apartments were chock-full of all manner of souvenirs from the Boeck family's hectic diplomatic life in distant lands. Buddhas of jade and stone, Japanese garden lanterns of cast-iron, floral patterned china plates, camphor-wood chests, marble torsos, bronze temple lions. They may have been mementoes, but they did nothing for me. At times I had the feeling that I was wandering around inside other people's memories. At others I thought: the first time I set foot in this house I knew that marriage would be the greatest journey of my life.

Buenos Aires, the white, stucco-like façades on the Avenido de Mayo. Moscow, the dull gold of the domes on the Kremlin. The Victoria Falls, the glistening black of the snake that crossed my path. Shanghai, the noxious brown river. Samarkand, the sweet, yellow melons. Margrete, the blue veins at her temples, a tiny fjord with a multiplicity of arms.

She was lying in bed in the bedroom. Or rather: I thought she was lying in bed. I had gone out to fetch a jug of iced tea from the fridge – iced tea was a habit, or a vice, she had acquired in other climes. When I walked into the white bedroom, which still smelled of sex, she was kneeling on the bed, on the pillow, banging her head against the wall. Not all that hard, perhaps, but it was a brick wall. She was naked. She was quite oblivious to me. I stood there holding the jug. Two slices of lemon twirled slowly round, two small, unconnected wheels. She went on beating her head against the wall with trance-like regularity. I noticed the way the light refracted and formed a rainbow around her. I heard a sound like the tinkling of wind-chimes, possibly from the empty glasses on the floor. Or from her brittle skull. I remembered the first time I saw her. Through a teardrop.

My maternal grandmother, Jørgine Wergeland, was not like other grandparents, or any other old people for that matter. Granny's house did not smell of Pan Drops or 4711 eau-de-cologne, instead there was a pronounced aroma of cigars. She can best be described as an activator: she made things happen wherever she went. I always looked forward to visiting her flat in Oscars gate, behind the Palace. The memory of one occasion in particular has stayed with me. 'You'd better come over,' she said on the phone, in a voice befitting her statesmanlike countenance. 'It's time to dismantle the Crystal Palace.'

This is a story about seeing the love of one's life. Not about the first meeting, but about *seeing* one's beloved. Afterwards I said to her: 'Now I've really seen you. Seen you as you are.' I did not know how true that was.

The Crystal Palace was not a place in England. It was a huge, rare and precious crystal chandelier which hung over the dining table in Granny's sitting room, a room lofty enough to accommodate it. Once a year, usually on a day like this, a bright, sunny Saturday in August, Granny and I would lift the big mahogany table out of the way and set up the stepladder preparatory to cleaning the chandelier, removing dust and dirt and, not least, the film of nicotine from Granny's cigars which had built up in the holes bored in the crystals. It was a big job, a combination of chemistry and physics lessons, of window-cleaning and jigsaw puzzle. I had the task of climbing the stepladder and 'tearing down the castle in the air' as Granny put it. The chandelier had been restored and altered slightly. So the spikes on the base, hundreds of them, were no longer fixed to the rings, but had to be unhooked, one by one. The festoons, the chains of prisms running from the top to the hoop were easier to remove.

I carefully detached each piece and handed it to Granny. They were then dipped in basins filled with warm water and soft soap and rinsed, dipped in soapy water again and rinsed, then laid on soft cotton cloths by Granny to dry. It was a job which called for patience. And precision. Just as I had reached the stage of building complicated Lego constructions without having to follow the accompanying, step-by-step instructions, so my grandmother knew the position of every piece by heart, even though there must have been over a thousand of them. Fortunately, many of them were joined together. She sorted through them, separated them into groups. I could spend ages just marvelling at the assurance with which she arranged crystals of different shapes and sizes on the cloths. When I saw all those prisms glittering and twinkling on the dining table I felt like Aladdin in the cave, surrounded by clusters of precious gems.

At a certain point we changed places. Granny mounted the stepladder – not unlike a young seaman on the *Christian Radich* – and cleaned the gilded bronze stem and light sockets while I dried all the crystals with a dishcloth, polishing them until they shone. It was a solemn undertaking. I remember every detail of it to this day. The feel of sharp edges against my fingers. The sunlight streaming through the windows. The smell of soft soap. The sound of tinkling glass, like sleigh bells. Old crystal is not white, there is a touch of grey in it, of pink and violet, and when I turned the prisms to check that they were clean, patterns of light danced across the walls. It was quite a spectacle: tiny, vibrant spectrums at every turn. That is how I remember Granny: encircled by rainbows.

On the day she came, the day on which I was to see my beloved, I was up the stepladder, taking the single prisms and the chains handed to me by Granny and hooking them back into place. It was all going very smoothly. Crystals hung thicker and thicker on the chandelier. Only once did Granny have to give me instructions: 'No, no, that Empire spike should go further out!' I was glad to see her in such good form. For over six months, according to my mother, she had done nothing but lie in the bath, smoking cigars and listening to the BBC World Service. She had been suffering from depression following the death in January of her idol Winston Churchill, in bed with his cat beside him.

Reassembling the chandelier took time, but the end result was commensurate with the work involved. The chandelier had a spiked base, an inverted pyramid consisting of three circles of long, slender prisms. I could get almost the whole of my head inside that cone of glass before hanging the nethermost pendants on their hooks. As far as I was concerned there was nothing quite as wonderful as being encircled by a close-knit network of crystals. To stand amid those glittering prisms and hear them chinking against one another. For many years, the lighting of those sixteen candles was, for me, the very definition of beauty. Not even Mr Iversen's extravagant New Year's Eve firework display could come close.

It had not always been so easy. I remembered the first time. I was seven. I was to be staying at Oscars gate for a couple of days. Without any warning, Granny had started carrying one cardboard box after another into the sitting room, finishing up with what, although I did not know it, were the stem, rings and arms of a chandelier. 'The spoils of war,' she remarked mysteriously.

She proceeded to unpack the boxes. I thought at first they were full of bits of cloth and tissue paper, but concealed inside the cloth and the paper were diamonds, prisms of Bohemian crystal. It seemed to me as though Granny were *unravelling* an enormous crystal chandelier from paper, from a pile of small boxes. She spread the whole lot out on the dining table. It was years since she had packed it away; she tried to remember what bit went where. The whole scenario reminded me of a Christmas Eve when I was given a jigsaw puzzle with over a thousand pieces.

We spent the whole weekend figuring it out. And when, after much trial and error, the freshly washed chandelier was finally mounted and hanging from the ceiling over the mahogany table – sixteen tiny flames multiplied into a starry firmament – Granny put a record of Strauss waltzes on the gramophone, elbowed me in the ribs and announced proudly: 'Welcome to the Queen's Chambers!' Which was not that far from the truth. Because there was a story attached to that chandelier.

I have been dogged all my life by my association with those hand-ground pieces of glass. Nothing could ever beat the sensations I experienced, the air of festivity with which I was filled, under that crinoline of crystals, bathed in a light which was both absorbed and emitted. The first time I heard of a network formed by computers I immediately thought of Granny's chandelier. I had actually had a prism of my own since I was very young. I used to play with it a lot, regarded it as something lovely and perfect in itself. Not until my grandmother brought out her chandelier did I see that my prism was part of a greater whole. It would not surprise me if this realisation lay at the root of my Project X, the idea that all but broke me.

I had almost finished re-hanging all the droplets when it happened. I had my head stuck half inside the chandelier, was running my eyes over crystal after crystal, as if in a trance. It was not true what the grown-ups said: that they only reflected partial, splintered images. Here, inside the chandelier, I could see the whole picture, all the different sides of it at once.

I was standing inside a circle of light when it happened. Sometimes, in order to hang a crystal on another part of the chandelier I turned it round. All at once I found myself at the centre of a carousel of tinkling diamonds. I saw everything so clearly. Correlations, associations. The only right thing was, of course, to play, not Strauss, but Johann Sebastian Bach. Again, as always: Bach.

So there I was, with my head inside a shimmering wheel, when it happened. Suddenly, beyond the light, I discerned a figure in the doorway. It was Margrete. Or maybe I could tell from her voice: 'Jonas?' I did not see her, saw only the reflections, scintillating light. Often, since then, I have found myself wondering: was that why I fell so madly in love. Was it those prisms, that golden glow, which bound me to her for always?

How does a man meet his wife? I met mine several times. I met her for the first time – was quite literally bowled over by her in sixth grade, just before the summer holidays. We crashed into one another on our bikes right outside the school gate. I remember nothing from that collision except her eyes, her eyes staring at me. And not so much her eyes, as her pupils: it was the first time I had ever remarked on only the pupils of a pair of eyes; I had never seen anything so black, so – what's the word – bottomless. That collision was like hearing that abrupt, resounding G7sus4th chord at the very beginning of 'A Hard Day's Night': a false start, if you like, before things really got under way. Like a build-up of tension waiting for release.

It did not really come to anything, though, until later in the year, just after we started in seventh grade. One day after school I went swimming with Leo. A lot had happened over the summer holidays, we were older and maybe that is why we did not bike out to Badedammen, where we had always frolicked in the past – beginning our swimming careers there under the careful eyes of anxious mothers – but to Svarttjern, the Black Tarn, a very different class of swimming hole, and more of a challenge in terms of location, lying as it did right out in the wilds, as it were. Badedammen was for little kids. Svarttjern was for strong, experienced swimmers. We had to park our bikes at the foot of Ravnkollen and walk quite a way into the forest to get to the bewitching little tarn ringed by fir trees. Strange to think that today this isolated lake, or what is left of it, is hemmed in by the tower blocks of Romsås, one of the biggest satellite towns in Norway. Although maybe this was simply bound to happen: this was a tarn which had to be civilised, tamed. Rumour had it that many people had drowned there, and that it was the perfect pool for suicides who did not wish to be found. Let me put it this way: Svartjern was not a lake you swam in alone at night. Sometimes, on the way there, I would find myself thinking that anything could happen at Svarttjern.

I spotted her right away. How could anyone not notice her? She was gold among silver. She was much browner than the other girls. I did not know whether this was because she already had a good base tan from Thailand where she had been living before, owing to her father's work with the Ministry of Foreign Affairs, or whether she was just blessed with such fabulous skin. And yet it was possibly not her looks that impressed me so much as her bearing, her movements. The way she dried herself, the way she walked, almost danced over to the rock when she was going in for a swim. There are no words to describe the unique quality of Margrete's beauty, but in my mind I called it 'Persian'. She wore an orange bikini which accentuated the golden effect. And her figure, I might add, because she had the body of an eighth grader, a body which had just begun to reveal something of how it was going to look in four or five years' time. I had to force myself not to stare, not to be caught with my eyes glued to that sexy bikini top.

Even when she was lying still, apparently deep in thought, Margrete was the centre of attraction. Everything revolved around her. I observed her out of the corner of my eye. I caught the flash of a bracelet. She took something from her rucksack and handed it round, it obviously was not a pack of Marie biscuits; judging by the exclamations from the others it had to be something fantastic – Chinese fortune cookies or suchlike.

Breakfasts with Margrete. Every one an occasion. Her face. The things she could come out with. Her body language. Her way of being quiet. Her expression when she was thinking. Her habits from an itinerant life abroad. Always linen napkins. Always fresh flowers on the table. Always toast. Always a particular brand of English marmalade. Always freshly ground coffee beans, her own blend. Always orange juice which she pressed herself.

We lay not far from one another. There was really only one spot where you could lie at Svarttjern, a couple of hillocks on the west side. It was also a good place to dive from, or rather: try to impress the girls with your latest, well-rehearsed dives. Margrete was not impressed by that sort of thing though, she never so much as glanced in the direction of the daredevil divers and their antics. I peeped at her on the sly. Peeped is the word. I felt like a Peeping Tom. It got to the point where I was staring quite blatantly. I couldn't help it. I felt my heart swell with love. It had possibly been lying dormant during the summer holidays, but now it flared up. I thought of my grandfather lighting the primus stove in the outhouse, the moment when the flame turned blue. I knew it, I was a goner. This may sound a mite high-flown, but I lay there thinking of one of the words which Karen Mohr often used: fate. I am quite certain that the thought of marrying Margrete Boeck crossed my mind there, on the banks of Svarttjern, on an August day when we were in seventh grade. But how was I to catch her attention? Catch her? Or, more correctly: how was I to get her to *discover* me?

Why are salmon more given to biting at certain flies? Or is it only that we think they have a greater tendency to bite at certain patterns? It is a mystery. The salmon is not looking for food when it swims up river. As the spawning season approaches it reduces its food intake. In theory, it should not bite at a fly. And yet it does. Is it that it feels annoyed? Is it trying to defend its preserves? Might it simply be that the fly, this elaborately tied lure, is so irresistibly beautiful? Why do we fall in love? You are faced with three girls. Triplets. As good as identical. And yet you choose one of them. The one with the yellow scarf. You bump into a girl at the school gates and you lose your temper, you snap at her. Only afterwards do you realise that you are hooked. Why did I 'bite' at Margrete – like a salmon going for a Blue Charm?

There were many obstacles in the way. To begin with the most obvious one: she was lying next to Georg. It was so bloody predictable. You only had to say that there was a new girl starting at the school, from Bangkok, that she was like this and or like that and everybody would stick their hands in the air and say she was sure to end up going out with Georg. He was in the year above us and had always been the first at everything: the first to own a Phantom ring, the first with speedway handlebars and cross-country tyres, the first to wear a reefer jacket, the one whose voice broke first. He always had a match clenched between his lips, as if he were terrified that somebody might ruin his perfect teeth, his flawless looks.

I hated it. Looking at Georg was like staring at a poster that said 'Forget it!' I tried to tell myself that I was not in love. It was one thing to wrest Margrete out of another boy's embrace. It was quite another to try to compete with Georg – Georg, who could blow three smoke-rings and get them to hang in the air while he stuck a finger through them, Georg who documented every new conquest with pictures of him French kissing the girl in question in the photo booth at Eastern station. They might not be going out together yet, but there were depressing rumours to the effect that Margrete 'fancied' him. I watched them out of the corner of my eye, in agony, noticing the way they were giggling together, suffering even greater agonies when Georg – all solicitude, so it seemed – straightened one of her straps at the back.

Something had to give. I lay there with a blue flame burning inside me, my hopes rising when the girls went in for a swim. I believe I prayed to God that something would happen, that I would be given a chance. Now. This minute. And not the way it happens in the movies, where the hero usually has to wait until the wedding, until only seconds before the bride says 'I do', before he can steal her out of the other man's arms.

I have been thinking: there was something about Margrete's glossy black hair, which was cut quite short, that reminded me of Bo Wang Lee. Was that why I fell for her the way I did?

My chance presented itself. Leo and I were sharing a bag of monkey nuts, absent-mindedly snapping shell after shell. The girls were in the water. Suddenly Margrete screamed so loudly that everybody turned to look. I thought she must have got her foot caught in one of the tree trunks which could be seen floating, like water nixies, just under the surface and which, if you were unlucky, you could get caught on, or even be dragged under by. Then I heard it: 'I've lost my bracelet,' Margrete cried. She was so upset that she switched to English, as if she was still at the International School in Bangkok. I managed to grasp, nonetheless, that it was her mother's bracelet, that she had borrowed it, that it was of gold and a bit big for her, which is why it must have slipped off without her being aware of it. Who but a girl from Thailand would wear a gold bracelet when she went swimming? She was broken-hearted, sobbing loudly. Some of the girls tried to comfort her.

Georg and the others leapt into the tarn. Shouts and yells filled the air as the water was transformed into a churning mass of flailing bodies. It occurred to me that this was how it must look when natives dived for coins thrown by tourists. Eventually they gave up, one by one.

Margrete glanced up at the hillock on which I was lying, snapping peanut shells in two. I thought I saw a question in that look. Or was it an entreaty? With her streaming wet hair, her forlorn expression, she seemed more bedraggled. More attainable. Georg looked almost sheepish, the match between his teeth was gone.

'Let me have a go,' I said, getting to my feet amid the sort of dramatic hush that falls when someone steps forward and volunteers for an impossible mission. Aunt Laura had told me the story of how van Gogh cut off a piece of his ear to impress a woman. This might not have been quite so original, but still – it was something. I would happily have dived until I cramped up.

'You?' Georg said. 'Can you swim?' I saw the confusion in his eyes, a desire not to lose face, a suppressed fury. I faced up to him. A sergeant taking command from a colonel. He was blocking the way to the water. He could have punched me. Or, he could have tried to punch me. But he must have guessed that just at that moment nothing could touch me. That inside me there dwelt a miracle. He took a step to the side, like a crab. I walked, no: I strode down to the edge of the rock and with all eyes upon me I dived in; it was in all probability the best dive of my life, with little or no splash. I came up to the surface and flicked my hair back with a practised toss of the head. 'Whereabouts?' I shouted, heard it echoing in the silence around the tarn. Margrete had come down to the water's edge. She pointed. She seemed to be pointing at me. 'There,' she said.

I dived. To begin with the others stood and watched. I heard the odd gasp of admiration at the length of time I stayed under. I dived. Surfaced, filled my lungs with air and dived again. The comments petered out. There was a deathly hush every time I surfaced. People began to leave. The shadows were also lengthening over the lake. Georg had his match stuck between his teeth again. 'Good luck,' he said when he walked off, as if he could afford to show a degree of magnanimity. He shot a glance at Margrete. She did not meet his gaze, sat where she was. Sat there in all her Persian beauty, looking at me. She looked at me as though she were asking: Who are you?

Many years later, when I met her again and we started living together, I would wake up in the middle of the night to find that she had switched on the light above the bed and was lying there considering me, as if trying to uncover a secret: 'Who are you?' she would whisper then. On more than one night I was woken in this way. It was as though she were studying me, thought she could discover more about me when I was asleep than when I was awake. 'You look about seven years old,' she told me. 'I *am* seven years old,' I said.

Now and then she would ask me about a dream I had just had. She might ask me why I had shot wide of the goal. And I would actually have been dreaming about football. She could read my dreams, or was so interested in me that she could guess what I was likely to be dreaming about. Or – this thought has occurred to me – maybe she gave me them, put these dreams into my head by lying there looking at me, considering me.

Even at night when we were making love, I would occasionally feel her fingers running over my face in the dark, as if my features were in Braille and she was trying to read me.

Her curiosity about me. And not the other way round.

Soon we were alone. Even Leo had left, pointedly, as though washing his hands of the whole business. I dived again. It was dark down there, the water was turbid. The bracelet could have fallen off at a spot so deep that I would not be able to reach it, even with all the training I had done – out at Hvaler, too, where I had made several dives to a depth of ten metres with flippers. Her black pupils followed me, stayed fixed on me, as if she were not only asking: Who are you?, but also: Where are you when you dive?

I would not give up, took another deep breath before gliding down into the depths. The pressure was getting to me. My ears were starting to hurt despite the fact that I pinched my nose shut with one hand. I *could* not give up. I felt the pressure, as much from within as from without. This was a situation which would work a change in me.

The pressure. And this might be a good point – here, with me in a submerged position before an expectant Margrete – at which to allude to what lay at the core of my image of myself, a view so complex – or so simple – that I am afraid it goes beyond words: in my life it has not so much been a case of developing as in growing, but rather of evolving.

When I went to my grandfather's outdoor privy on Hvaler I always left the door wide open so I could gaze out to sea, at the boats sailing past. There was nothing quite like it. The quiet. The spider in the corner. The green moss outside. The smell of the beach, the sea. My eyes had often been drawn to a piece of cloth which had been rolled into a ball and wedged into the hole in the door jamb where once there had been a lock. One day, on impulse, or because I had a hunch about it, I winkled the bit of cloth out. And when I gently began to pull on the ends, opening out the clump of fabric which, over the years, had become almost totally gummed up, it proved to be an old tablecloth. Some scorch marks explained why it had been discarded. Printed on the cloth was a map of the world. And filthy though the fabric was, I could see how nice it was. The names of lots of countries were quite legible. I never forgot this experience. That I could unfold a disgusting-looking clump of fabric and reveal a hidden world.

I probably ought to keep quiet about this – especially considering the lowly part I now play – but there is something I have to confess, although I never dared to say it out loud: I was a child wonder. Or, no: that is not quite right. I was a wonder. As a very small boy I was sure that I could speak seven foreign languages and jump ten metres in the air, all I had to do was to figure out how. Sometimes I felt, with such swelling conviction that it scared me, that I could make objects shatter just by staring at them very hard, that I only needed to clench my fist in order to set great wheels in motion – if not within my own immediately perceptible surroundings then somewhere far out in space. At times I felt a pressure, almost a pain, inside my skull, often throughout my whole body, as if something was trying to unfold itself. As if I carried within me a seed containing a mighty tree.

One Sunday the whole family went for a drive after church. We stopped out on Ekeberg moor where some gypsies had made camp. They were something of an attraction. For ten *øre* some of the gypsy children would sing, one girl danced. But – and this was far more thrilling – you could also have your fortune told. Some curious onlookers stood in a semi-circle around a young woman seated on a chair outside a caravan. 'Heavens to Murgatroyd, what a stunner,' Daniel hissed, and then he shoved me through the circle of people and gave the woman a *krone*. 'Now you can find out whether you're going to end up dumping sewage or washing bodies,' he muttered out of the corner of his mouth. 'Or whether you'll get off with Anne Beate Corneliussen.' The woman smiled invitingly. She really was a stunner. Dark. Genuinely mysterious. She took my hand. She tilted it slightly. I felt her stiffen, almost jerking backwards in her seat. She raised her eyes and looked at me. I do not know how to describe it. As if she were afraid? Overwhelmed? She waved me away, said nothing, simply gave Daniel his *krone* back. She motioned to me to leave, as if she did not understand, had not been able to see anything.

I was a child. And yet. We have tens of billions of nerve cells in our brains and each of them capable of connecting with hundreds of thousands of other nerve cells. From time to time some expert can be heard to state that we are not even close to utilising the brain's full capacity. A large proportion of our genetic material is also said to be a mystery: we have no idea what purpose it serves. What if I had detected talents which were in some way associated with those white patches in our knowledge, I would think at heady, almost uneasy moments when I was older. Should I regard this as a blessing or a curse?

I cannot deny it, however. For long periods this was my driving force, my strength and, at the same time, the source of the deepest misgivings: I felt *unfinished* as a human being. Which is not to say that I was unhappy with myself, with the person I was. But I knew – and this rankled me – that I harboured untapped potential. It lay coiled up inside me. Or packed away in little boxes, like Granny's chandelier. I was, in other words, less interested in what I was than in what I could *be*. So one minute I was on the lookout for situations which would help this unknown quality to uncoil, enable me to excel myself. Or, more precisely: become the real me. The next minute I was filled with the need to hide, the wish that these latent gifts might leave me be. Sometimes, I confess, I even hoped they would never come to anything.

In my life, unlike many people, I have never been all that concerned about traumas or evil inclinations, all the things that drag me down. I have been more interested in whatever it is that lifts me up. I have *felt* something lifting me up. Of all the questions I have had to address, this is the one I hold to be the most crucial: is mankind descended, metaphorically speaking, from the animals or the angels? Or perhaps this is merely a variation on another question: should we let ourselves be ruled by the past or the future? By who we are or who we will become?

It was during a visit to Aunt Laura that I first received some intimation of how radical my potential was. Or at least, I believed that I was given a sign. I must have been about seven. My aunt was a goldsmith, specialising in avant-garde jewellery. In her flat in Tøyen all the walls of the living room and the rooms adjoining it were covered in rugs she had bought on her amazing and, as she told it, not entirely risk-free, travels in the Middle East and Central Asia. This home represented, for me, a source of stimulation that cannot be overrated. And although the name Tøyen actually stems from another word entirely, it always made me think of the word 'tøye', meaning to stretch and hence, for me, represented a place where I would be broadened, extended. A feeling which was enhanced by the flat itself; it seemed almost boundless. As if, by some magic, this average-sized dwelling consisted of hundreds of little nooks and chambers.

In the evenings, when my aunt was making dinner, I was allowed to shut the kitchen door and play in the living room. Aunt Laura bound a silk scarf around my head like a turban and lent me a torch. Then I switched off the living-room light and made believe I was a sultan going out in disguise to see how things stood in my realm – just like the Caliph Haroun al-Rashid in the *Arabian Nights*. I was especially fond of pretending that I was walking around the bazaar, where I envisaged the most arcane occurrences taking place. The platter of oranges on the table was transformed with ease into a cornucopian fruit stall, the bowl of little pistachio cakes turned into an aromatic pastry shop and the coils of silver wire on the workbench in the corner became glimpses of palaces in a distant city. My imagination was given added wing by the delicious smells issuing from the kitchen, often from my aunt's speciality: Lebanese dishes, including my favourite, *machawi*, small chunks of meat threaded onto a skewer and grilled – the skewer was a treat in itself. When I shone the torch on the many different oriental rugs they altered character. As with the one in Karen Mohr's home they, too, concealed doors of a sort leading to new and exciting chambers. Their labyrinthine patterns took on a fascinating depth and revealed an assortment of tableaux; took me on journeys of discovery to cities such as Baghdad and Basra and, if I was lucky: to far-off Samarkand.

One evening, when Aunt Laura spent longer than usual in the kitchen, I fell asleep among the soft cushions on the sofa. I was woken by my aunt shaking me gently. Other children might wake with a start and imagine that they had just grown in their sleep. I tended, instead, to wake with a shudder. As an adult it struck me that this was not unlike the spasms of an orgasm. On this occasion, too, that deep tremor ran through me from top to toe, as if all the molecules in my body were swapping places. I looked around me. Everything was different. The same, but altered. When I had switched out the light there had been a platter of oranges on the table. Now the dish was piled high with lemons, inflamingly yellow and with that little tip which, later in life, always made me think of a girl's breast. When I had last seen Aunt Laura in the kitchen, she had been wearing a gold sea-horse on a chain around her neck, a piece of jewellery she claimed was made from the wedding rings of men with whom she had slept. But now a dolphin dangled before my eyes.

I said nothing. Not because I was not sure, but because I was scared. The Jonas I had now become had more to him than the Jonas who had fallen asleep – whatever had happened. There was much to suggest that whatever I had, until then, taken to be myself was only a fragment of a much larger whole. Amid all my fear and confusion, however, I also detected another, conflicting emotion: one of wild excitement.

It is tempting to dismiss all of this as no more than a fanciful childish or youthful daydream. Nevertheless, for years it coloured my life; I have no wish to deny it. The same went for my suspicion that the pressure I occasionally felt, that sense of being unfolded, was connected to something else. For, while my brother Daniel had a constant fixation with soul, I let myself be seduced, possibly as a protest, by a rival concept within those same hazy and exalted spheres. Spirit. I would not be surprised if that was why we ended up in such different walks of life, despite having one lowest common denominator: the Queen of Soul, Aretha Franklin's impassioned rendering of 'Spirit in the Dark', more especially the live version, sung with Ray Charles – Aretha's ecstatic scream of 'Don't do it to me!' left us both with goosebumps on our inner thighs. This was soul and spirit in perfect harmony.

I automatically pricked up my ears at any mention of the phenomenon. I cherished words such as 'spirited' and 'inspirit'. I understood that life and spirit were inextricably bound up with one another. Always, without thinking about it, I would say inspire rather than inhale. I felt the same about breathing as other people did about the heart or the pulse. Even as a small child

I would find myself taking big, deep breaths, in and out, as if performing an exercise of some sort; as if I instinctively knew that I had not mastered this vital function, nay, this art. Whenever I saw pictures of the lungs they reminded me of sails, two spinnakers designed to speed us along. I would eventually come to have great respect for the wise men of other cultures who called attention to the link between breathing and thinking, between breathing and our potential for reaching unknown areas of the mind.

One thing became clear to me very early on: in order to unfold as a person, I had to have spirit. Once, when I was in elementary school, I went into town with my father. We were strolling along the dockside at Pipervika – we had just bought a bag of shrimps from one of the boats tied up there – when we were witness to a demonstration down by Hønnørbrygga of a new type of life-raft. At first I could make nothing of it. The raft was just a small white egg, a glass-fibre pod with two halves to it. But when the container was thrown into the water and a man tugged on a cord a raft proceeded to swell out of the egg, truly to unfold, black and orange, like a brightly hued bird emerging from a conjuror's hand. It must have been very closely packed, because it was big. Our curiosity aroused, we moved closer and heard a man saying that there was a gas cylinder inside the pod. The cord was attached to a trigger which punctured a membrane inside the cylinder, thus releasing air into the raft and inflating it. 'Do we have a cylinder like that inside us,' I asked my father. I think there was a hopeful note in my voice.

In ancient languages such as Hebrew and Greek, the word for spirit and wind is the same. I have the feeling that this may explain my weakness for the organ, an instrument which so perfectly combines these two words, converting wind into spirit. My father often said to me: 'Playing the organ, Jonas, that's truly inspired work.'

Not until long after my father's funeral did my mother tell us what she had done when she got the urn back from the crematorium. She took some of the ashes and put them into five separate, airtight envelopes which she addressed to five organists in different parts of Norway, all of them good colleagues and friends of Haakon Hansen who had agreed to carry out the Grorud organist's wishes and his plan. These five went to their respective organs and poured the ashes down into one of the large pipes producing the deepest pedal notes, and at a prearranged moment they began, simultaneously, to play the same Bach prelude. 'That was your father's real funeral,' my mother told me. I saw it more as a resurrection. He had been assured of a kind of eternal life. The thought appealed to me: my father lying there in different parts of Norway, vibrating in the air from his favourite chords, hovering on that exquisite music. As spirit.

The aim was not, of course, to become spirit. The aim was to become more of a person. I often thought of that incident when I saved a little child from drowning and how, afterwards, completely disillusioned, I had felt that my mission in life had been accomplished, that my life had, as it were, been fulfilled. It took a while for me to realise that this, all the practising, had simply been a preparation, training for a more difficult task: that of being filled with spirit. In order to expand and grow. All of the diving, those many minutes under water, had simply been an excuse for learning to control my respiration. My diving was a testimony to my powerful lust for life.

I had this same feeling as I swam down into the depths of Svarttjern, frantically diving after Margrete's gold bracelet. My ability to hold my breath was finally to come into its own. *This* was what I had been training for. I had been training to win Margrete. I had been training to save my own life.

Every time I surfaced her eyes met mine, questioningly. Even from a distance I saw those eyes only as pupils – like deep, black pools. I had the feeling that I was as much diving in them, after the gold in them; that this was also my first attempt to get to the bottom of her. Of Margrete's 'Persian beauty'. She sat perfectly still, said not a word, and yet, with her eyes she was saying: How long can you hold your breath for me?

I took a rest then dived again, determined to beat every record going. I slipped down into the darkness, pinched my nose and blew through my mouth, equalising the pressure. Five metres down the water was noticeably cooler. I could not see a thing. But it was as if I was being given a warning: this is what life with her will be like, a long dive into the darkness, hunting for gold.

I noticed that my thoughts ran along different lines when I was underwater. It may have had something to do with the pressure, the buoyancy, the lack of oxygen. I acquired second sight. Down in the darkness I saw images from a whole future drift past my eyes, as if the water was developing fluid. I saw a golden elephant, a long-playing record, a dangerous swim, two adults in soft spring rain, a doctor's white coat, a flat full of things from all over the world, a woman banging her head against a wall, a child, a television studio. And finally I saw a gun.

I had to hunt for the bracelet with the hand that was not holding my nose. I felt about in the most likely spot, directly below the knoll she had jumped off several times. Despite the darkness I swam with my eyes open, as if I thought it must be possible to discern a smouldering glimmer of gold. A glimmer of love, I thought feverishly. I could not see a thing. I was reduced to groping with my fingers. My lungs were starting to ache. My ears hurt. I thought of van Gogh. I thought I saw tropical fish glide by, like the ones in the television Interlude. I would not be able to take it much longer. A shiver ran through me. What if she had taken off the bracelet on purpose? What if she had wanted to test the boys, find out which of them was most deserving of her. Which one was *worthy*. Was she liable to do something like that? Would she be willing to sacrifice her mother's expensive bracelet even if she received no answer.

I ran my hands over the bottom, centimetre by centimetre. I thought of the tales from the *Arabian Nights* which Rakel had read aloud to Daniel and I when we were small, particularly of those stories in which a character came across a ring embedded in the ground; and when he lifted the ring he raised a trapdoor, revealing stairs leading down into another world. Was it something like this I was searching for, without knowing it?

I have asked myself: what is the greatest driving force in my life? I think I know. It is the desire to work in depth. To invent something simple which would, nevertheless, have major consequences. Something along the lines of the wheel, the rudder, the stirrup. A new alphabet. To work at the most fundamental level. Like a power station deep inside a mountain. Lighting up cities far away. Being a spring which suddenly wells up and renders a desert fertile. Or being someone who shakes things up. Shakes up the classifications. Shakes the foundations. Like Samson toppling those pillars and bringing a whole heathen temple tumbling down. Being someone who splits open the shell we have built up around mankind.

I think that was why I loved diving. Diving down into the depths as I was doing now. I understood, somewhere in my subconscious, that this was not merely a search for a piece of jewellery, this was an undertaking which could lead to my making a fundamental discovery.

Even so, when I rose to the surface after one particularly gruelling dive, I was ready to give up. I ached all over. But as I gasped for breath I seemed to take in something else, something more: spirit. One more dive, I told myself. And as soon as my hand reached the bottom my fingers lighted on the circlet. I did not touch gold. I felt I was touching the future.

Later she presented me with a book. We were at her place, alone, in the villa down the road from the school. She wanted to give me something, the finest thing she could think of, as a thank-you for finding her bracelet. It was *Victoria* by Knut Hamsun. 'It's a love story,' she said with a look which implied that *that* said it all. She gave me her own dog-eared copy. I liked the title, liked the association with victory. Too late I discovered that I ought to have perused more than the title of that novel. A lot of people have had their own personal experience of *Victoria* by Knut Hamsun, I'm sure, but none has been anything like mine.

She had pressed fresh orange juice and this she poured into two elegant wine glasses. We drank as one. I felt strange, as if she had stirred a magic powder into the drink. Then she kissed me for the first time. I felt even stranger. Filled with light. *Filled.* I could have drawn this conclusion at that moment, but I did not: it might be that what I called spirit was just another word for love.

Afterwards we sat in the garden, on a green lawn. I was feeling so light-headed that I had to lie with my head in her lap. There was a sprinkler on the go. Opera music drifted from the house next door. I lay with my head in her lap. I could have lain there for the rest of my life. I looked down on myself from high in the air, saw myself lying there in a luxuriant garden with my head in a girl's lap; I saw how lovely and how right it was, saw that this might even be what was known as working in depth.

Few triumphs in my life can compare with the moment when, with swelling heart, I clambered ashore and handed her the bracelet. We were alone at Svarttjern. We stood on the only rock still in the sun. Neither of us said anything. First she slipped the bracelet onto her wrist. The metal glowed against her skin. She gazed into my eyes and then she wrapped her arms around me. I stood there inside a circlet of gold. I looked up at the sky. I noticed that the clouds were moving faster, that something was happening to the weather, the whole atmosphere. The water was perfectly still, reflecting the dense, shadowy forest all around. For me Svarttjern would always be a sacred lake. She held me for a long time. No more than that. Just held me. I experienced some of the same pressure that I felt underwater, when I dived. She held me and I unfolded; I stood still, inside a circle of skin, and I was transformed. Being held by Margrete. If God gave me the chance to relive one thing in my life I would choose this: to be held by Margrete. Held, tight, long.

I was to make the acquaintance of this pressure in an embrace again, on a later occasion. That too began with a dive, but into a different body of water, a lagoon just off a small private beach on a tropical island. I was fraught with presentiment, fraught with expectancy; I had been staying at the home of a certain woman for three days and so far nothing had happened, I had hardly seen her. I whiled away the time by swimming, diving, holding my breath under water, still pursuing that old hobby. On the morning of the fourth day – I thought she had gone to work – I went snorkelling out on the coral reef.

I was following a dense shoal of small fish along the reef when she suddenly came gliding towards me through the mint-green water, she too wearing a mask, as if I were a fish she wished to take a closer look at. Her hair streamed out behind her as she swam straight towards me, her breasts, barely contained by her low-cut bathing suit, looking heavy and commanding. I became rather shamefully aware of the way my eyes were being drawn to the cleft between them, while at the same time conscious of an unbearable pressure building up in my body, even though I was only a metre below the surface.

What is love? My escapades, though few, have been thought-provoking. One day, out of the blue, I received a letter bearing some strange and intriguing stamps. It was from Anna Ulrika Eyde, a girl I had known all through school, but with whom I had lost touch when she moved to England to study engineering. She was currently working on a bridge project on an island in the Indian Ocean and was actually inviting me to come and visit her. And stay at her place.

Anna Ulrika, or Ulla, was what you would call ugly, extraordinarily ugly, in fact. Although I would be more inclined to say: fascinatingly ugly. Her hideousness teetered on the brink of incomparable beauty. To be honest I think I was always a little besotted with her. We had dubbed her the Iron Woman, both because she was so unattractive and because as a little girl, unusually for her sex, she had had a Meccano set from which she created the most intricate – not to mention extremely impressive – constructions out of gleaming, perforated miniature girders. But the woman who came to meet me, years later, at Plaisance airport was surprisingly good-looking. Or, the word came to me right away: 'striking' – beautiful as only rather ugly girls can be; the sort who often become famous models. She seemed to have opened up a wing in her person that no one had known was there. She laughed at me; laughed at my evident surprise. The backsweep of her lips, in particular, was hard to ignore; she was so unexpectedly attractive that it made me uncomfortable.

For the first few days I was left to my own devices. Ulla worked for the contractors responsible for the building of a new bridge on the west side of the island. I took a break from diving in the lagoon to visit the island capital, saw the sights, strolled around the central market: you could buy absolutely everything there, from dried squid and herbs for treating asthma or a bad heart to models of pirate ships made out of tortoiseshell and objects for sacrificing to the gods. The most amazing item I came across, however, was a tattered old poster of Sonja Henie in the midst of a soaring split jump against a backdrop of snow-covered Alps. 'Want to buy?' the Hindu who owned the stall asked. 'Very popular. American star. Danced like Shiva on the ice.' I had to smile at this find. I was struck by the unreality of it, not least because of the cultural and geographical divide: a picture of skates and ice, here, in the middle of the tropics, where books rotted in the heat and humidity and I spent my afternoons lazing on the beach below the bougainvillea-framed bungalow which Ulla had rented close to the beautiful Grand Baie beach.

Then, on the morning of the fourth day, she suddenly showed up in the water, or rather: under the water. Buxom and smiling. She had the day off, she explained as we floated on the surface. Might she be permitted to give me the grand tour?

We drove in her car through a landscape so green that all Norwegian notions of the concept 'green' seemed to fall short; the old Peugeot bowled along through Gauguin-hued mountains which took on new and fanciful forms with every turn of the road. Ulla showed me round a recently opened aquarium full of fish which made me think of all the women in brightly coloured saris whom we had passed along the way; knowing that I had just started studying architecture she took me to see some of the island's bold new, ultra-modern hotels. We climbed the many steps up to a small candy-coloured Tamil temple set high on a ridge overlooking Quatre Bornes, one of the island's main towns. And at all times: that involuntary sense of attraction, the pull of her lips.

Late in the afternoon, after several stops at places and buildings which struck me as being nothing so much as a series of contrasts, reflections of the country's numerous ethnic groups and cultures, we came to a lake in the south of the island, Grand Bassin, a mirror-image of the sky amid all the greenery, a sacred lake, site of one of the annual Hindu festivals. Someone was in the process of planting fruit trees. Gradually, possibly due to the look in her eye, her eagerness, it dawned on me that it was not the country, the island, she was showing off to me, but herself. With everything she pointed out to me – boys selling ice cream from big cool boxes on the backs of bicycles, the falling blossom from the flame trees which in many places carpeted the road with red – and all the things she raved about, she was saying: just so, just as diverse, as multi-faceted, am I. And you never knew. She too, Anna Ulrika Eyde, the Iron Woman, was a tropical island in a foreign ocean, one which I had to dive after, *discover*. In taking me around the island she was also inviting me to uncover the unsuspected mountain formations and impenetrable plantations within her – her temples, her beaches, her reefs.

I stood wreathed in incense fumes, scanning the mirrored surface of the lake while, heedless of my presence, she took out a lipstick and ran it over those enticing lips, laying it on extra thick, as if inspired by the gaudy idols in the little, open-sided temples perched on stilts in the rolling countryside around the lake.

We drove on through fields full of sugar beet. She had suddenly gone quiet. I felt as though we were making our way through something sweet. On our way *to* something sweet. The green beet plants grew shoulder to shoulder, soon they would be as tall as the drifts at the sides of the roads on the mountain passes in Norway in the winter. But then the countryside opened out and the road wound uphill, into wild country. We pulled in at a lookout point, a lay-by with benches and tables.

From a paper bag she produced small, deep-fried chilli balls and a pineapple which, to my surprise, she proceeded to pare, cleanly and proficiently, slicing away the skin in a neat spiral with a knife that was almost as big as a machete. Before I could take in how she did it the fruit lay before me like a finely carved work of art, fresh and tangy, ready to eat. 'I learned that from an old man on the beach,' she informed me solemnly. I liked it: the contrast between the spicy bite of the little meatballs and the luscious fruit. I liked the way she handled that big knife. I liked the pressure she exerted. I liked the jolts of excitement that were running through me.

I admit it: there are few things I know less of than love. Sometimes I think about my sister, who went out with loads of boys. One of them was called Hans Christian. Rakel liked him a lot. But he wasn't the only boy she fancied. Hans Christian was a truck driver; he had just bought a magnificent new trailer of which he was very proud. One evening he learned that Rakel was at the home of one of her other admirers – she had not yet decided which one to choose. He was so mad that he drove his new sixteen-ton trailer-truck into the garden of his rival and straight through the wall of the extension containing the bedroom. Although it has to be said that he had first checked that Rakel and the others were in the living room, watching TV. The bedroom extension and the double bed were completely wrecked, as was the truck. Rakel was so impressed by such red-hot determination that she married Hans Christian. 'Believe it or not, but he has eyes as kind as Albert Schweitzer's,' she said. To me, however, his conduct in this matter was clear proof of the folly of love. Or its unfathomability.

What is love? Due to an unexpected letter I found myself, as if by magic, among rugged, sculptural mountains on a tropical island with Anna Ulrika Eyde. I savoured the taste of chilli and pineapple, my eyes fixed on her red lips. We were standing by the railing on the edge of a sheer drop into a deep gorge. We were so high up that we could look down on a kestrel swooping over the chasm. To our right a waterfall plunged into a narrow crevasse. 'There's nothing lovelier than falling water,' she said. At the bottom, far below, a river meandered through billowing green jungle, on its way to the ocean. The sky was a clear blue. Again my eyes went to those red lips of hers, the half open blouse, the cleavage between her breasts, every bit as wild and precipitous as the chasm at our feet. Without warning, my body underwent a chemical change; it was as if a powerful pill had suddenly begun to take effect. At that same moment she turned and met my gaze. Her face was unrecognisable, swollen somehow. The next minute we were kissing. I had no chance to register what happened between the look and the kiss, it was explosive. We kissed, almost doing battle with our tongues. It tasted strong and sweet. We kissed as if our lives depended on it, body hard against body. I felt a tremendous pressure in my chest. I could have driven a truck through a wall. She smelled faintly, arousingly, of sweat, tasted of salt water, chilli and pineapple. I do not know how long we stood there kissing. It may have been a good while. I looked up and noticed dark clouds building up, as if the attraction we felt for one another had given echo in the weather. As if a storm had been lying out at sea and we, with our bodies, had drawn it towards land. If, that is, it was not simply a projection of the charged atmosphere between us. The palm leaves scraped against one another in the wind, emitting a hollow, plastic rustle. We had only just emerged from something akin to a maelstrom, gasping for breath, when the first raindrops fell, slowly, far apart: large, glittering, like a crystalline net. For a split-second I had the impression that I could see the whole island, the whole world, including her and me, in every drop.

She took me by the hand and ran laughing towards the car, opened the door to the back seat. We fell upon one another, groping blindly, found each other's mouths again, kissed, licked, bit, kissed, literally took leave of our senses. I pawed at her breasts like a teenager while her hand felt hungrily for my crotch. It was a bit like what as boys we had called petting, heavy petting. I have ridden in similar old Peugeots since then, mainly in a number of Third World countries, and I have never been able to sit there on those rather lumpy, plastic-covered seats, or look at the rickety chrome door-handles – those that aren't actually missing – the ashtrays, the distinctive dashboard, without thinking of Ulla and petting.

Something was happening outside, in line, as it were, with what we were up to in the car, or rather: the weather appeared always to be one step behind us, mimicking our ardour. In between all the kissing and feeling up I managed to take in the fact that the wind had risen dangerously and the palms were taking on the form of inside-out umbrellas. She tore off her blouse and bra, amid much loud and impatient moaning, wriggled out of her skirt, then her panties, tossed these garments into the air as large leaves began to swirl past outside; she arched her back with excitement, thrusting her pelvis into my face, offering herself like a piece of peeled fruit, the flesh glistening. The rain outside increased to a torrential downpour. Through the window I caught an occasional glimpse of the surrounding countryside, which now had the look of an underwater scene, as if we were inside a bubble that had been lowered into the ocean – I almost expected to see fish swimming past; and what I saw between her legs had also acquired something of a marine cast, reminiscent of sea anemones, coral reefs. I felt – there, inside the car – the same heavy pressure as when I went diving. I had the weird notion that this must have summoned up a depression, that all of this was my fault. It was the very end of the cyclone season, no warnings had been issued, and yet this, the tumult outside, had all the makings of a cyclone, the sort of cyclone which, at its height, could cut the sugar harvest in half. Rain streamed down the windows, making it impossible for us to see out, it was like being in a car-wash. Side by side with, or underlying, her desire, Ulla seemed to have a fascination with the power of the rainstorm, as if she drew energy, an even greater sexual charge, from the water pelting down, striking the car roof with a sound like the drumming of small, galloping hooves. I am not certain, but it may even have been here that she had the crucial flash of inspiration which, some years later, would find artistic expression. Ulla turned to making fountains, monumental works; she became an internationally renowned and much sought-after fountain designer, an artist who married the soft with the hard, moisture with steel, water with stone, the softly purling with the rigidly erect. She was intrigued with the possibilities of building such fountains in deserts and received commissions to do just that, primarily from wealthy Arabs, people with a reverence for water. Ulla made a fortune from water, from her ability to work on the borderline between engineering and art, her knowledge of the power and the beauty of falling water.

She must have been sunbathing in her swimming costume; her body was completely white, while her limbs and face were brown; she appeared to be lifting a torso up to me, or at least, I remember thinking of armour, that this, the white section of her body was an impenetrable carapace, something of which I knew nothing, even though I was well into my twenties. She spread her legs. I had the impression of something swollen and inflamed, as though she had applied lipstick there too. I had never done this before, she helped me by putting her hands at the back of my neck and drawing my head down to her fragrant and moistly glistening vulva. I licked those lips, poked my tongue inside, the rain poured down, drummed on the roof, a stray branch hit the bonnet with a bang, she hardly noticed, I too was in a daze, only half aware of what was going on. But when the lightning began to fork across the sky and the thunder made the ground shake – the car was basically sent flying, it hovered in mid-air – I started to worry, as though I were half expecting us to collide, partly because at that moment her body began to writhe uncontrollably. She came – she came to the accompaniment of a rending bolt of lightning and a piercing scream which passed over into a stream of incomprehensible babble, then she burst into floods of tears, all while we were on the point of being engulfed by water and shaken to bits by thunderclaps. 'Where are you?' she sobbed, grabbing at me, trying to pull me down, pull me inside her. And just as I was thinking: I've waited long enough, I've waited a damn sight more than long enough – which is to say, just before I gave in, lifted her up onto my lap, slid her down over me – I realised, with another part of myself that we would be wiped out by a natural disaster if I were to fulfil my intent, that only restraint on my part could prevent the cyclone from sweeping full force across the island, and I pulled away from her with a grunt of disappointment, coupled with a sense of truly having saved our lives.

Why did I hesitate back then? It certainly was not because – to use a Freudian cliché – I wished to sublimate my lust. I think I may have had some inkling, in the grip of desire though I was, that it was really supposed to be different. That even sex, for all the indescribable pleasure it gave, ought to be different. Better. Even better. I was about to say: higher. In the same way as I wrestled with thoughts concerning suppressed sides of my nature, so I knew, or suspected, that not even in the sexual sphere could we realise our true potential, stand upright, as it were. What if human sexuality was still at the reptile stage? Because there was no denying: despite five thousand years of civilisation, sex did not seem to have moved on at all. Of all the arts, the sexual act was the least evolved. While painting had had its Rembrandt, its Monet, the art of love was still stuck in the Stone Age. For a long time I did not know what to think about it, this restraint I displayed in the final instance with women. I do not believe it did me any harm, though. Not until I met Margrete when I was a grown man, did I see everything – including this – with fresh eyes.

Only seconds later the rain stopped, leaving behind it the same sense of release as when a drum roll, like a crescendo in the subconscious, suddenly ceases. The wind subsided. We – she also – came to our senses with the same air of bewilderment as people woken by a hypnotist. We stared at one another, or quickly looked away from one another, shyly almost, before opening the doors and clambering, all but tumbling, out of the car, out into the sunlight which streamed unexpectedly and with added intensity down over a strangely sodden landscape, anyone would have thought the whole countryside had had an orgasm. The air was searingly fresh, it reminded me of my childhood and the smell of Granny's tube of Mentholatum.

I never did find out what had actually happened. Nor could the newspapers provide any explanation for the sudden storm. That was sex with a woman for you, I told myself. A tropical island in a foreign ocean. A clip round the ear from a cyclone. Forces over which we had no control, would never have control. I glanced round about, feeling as though I ought to be happy to have survived. Not the cyclone, but the amatory eruption.

I eyed her up and down. Her face seemed distorted, her mascara had run, her lipstick was smeared. I was glad I could not see myself. I was sure that more powerful forces had been at work inside the car than out – and that despite the fact that I could see the devastation all around me, the sturdy broken branches strewn on the ground, as if a giant had wandered past.

On the plane home, perhaps because I was seeing the topography of the island from high above, I could not help wondering about the energy I had discerned in her orgasm. That glimpse of something exceedingly powerful. And somehow circular, like a cyclone. Since then I have come to the conclusion that my own very best orgasms could also be described in terms of a circle, if not quite in the same way. I think of Granny's crystal chandelier, that starry firmament in miniature; I think of the times when I stood almost right inside it. For me this is the only experience that comes anywhere close to reflecting the shattering beauty and luminescence, not to mention the wealth of imagery, inherent in an orgasm. Although this could also have something to do with the fact that I was surrounded on all sides by those glittering crystals the first time I saw Margrete. Saw her properly.

As a child, standing on the stepladder in Granny's flat, with my head stuck inside the chandelier, I often had a sense of being strangely powerful, invincible. That I *was* what I sometimes suspected myself to be: a wonder. I sensed that the rays of light issuing from all those crystals had a focal point of sorts at the very spot from which my thoughts sprang. This had an effect on my brain. Associations shot out in all directions. The prisms appeared to refract my thoughts in the same way that they refracted the light. A thought would occur to me and in next to no time it would have split into seven, and each of these seven would be split by another crystal, and so on. I wished that I could take the chandelier to school, that I could stick my head inside it every time I had to answer a difficult question. 'Jonas, what do we mean by democracy?' 'Wait a minute, miss. Let me just slip on my crystal crown.' It would turn me into a wise man. I wondered whether people, scientists or whoever, were aware of this: that they might find answers to all their problems if they stuck their heads inside just such a chandelier.

The August day when I saw my love, really *saw* Margrete for the first time, I was standing on the stepladder under the crystal tree. We had finished giving it its annual clean. The sitting room smelled of soft soap and the walls were patterned with light. I only had a couple of the nethermost rings on the spiked base left to fill. And Granny had found one crystal droplet which we had forgotten, it was cut like a precious gem. I was too busy figuring out where to hang it to hear anyone knocking or ringing the bell. I was standing with my head stuck way up inside the chandelier, searching for the eyelet through which to thread the hook. I did not notice her going into the hall to answer the door. I gave a start when I became aware of the sitting-room door opening and heard someone say: 'Jonas?'

I saw nothing but a shower of sparks, a myriad rainbows, reflected light. And in the midst of all this, a figure. I moved down a step, treading halfway out of the chandelier. And, maybe because I was shy, or speechless with confusion, I held the crystal droplet up to my eye, as if wishing to hide behind it, use it as a mask. I saw everything through it. I saw the sitting room and the open door. And I saw her. Except that there was not one figure but seven. I could see them quite distinctly when I held the droplet right up close to my eye, like a monocle. Seven people, one in the middle and six in a circle round about it. I saw who it was. It was Margrete. A princess.

This thought was not simply plucked out of thin air. Whenever we washed the prisms, Granny had to recount the fascinating history of the chandelier. Because it had hung in the Royal Palace, the very building that I passed on my way to Oscars gate. I was not surprised. The chandelier was so magnificent that it could only have come from there. A lot of the crystals, purchased in Berlin, were removed and sold at auction at the turn of the century, when the Palace switched to electric lighting. 'And this,' Granny said, pointing, 'I came by in a roundabout way. Spoils of war.'

I gathered that it had belonged to her husband. And *that* subject, I mean that of the man who came into her life during the war, after Grandpa's death, was one on which I never touched, because then I would simply have to listen to her ranting on about Churchill for hours. 'It hung in the Queen's Chambers, in the Yellow Cabinet,' Granny said, always with a melodramatic widening of her eyes. Those terms, the Queen's Chambers and the Yellow Cabinet made me tingle all over. I could imagine nothing finer, except perhaps for it to have hung in the Queen's Bedchamber. Because I often sat staring up at the chandelier. If I stared hard enough I could convince myself that I saw pictures in those small glass pendants, especially when Granny played Strauss waltzes on the gramophone; scenes which had been stored up inside them and now presented themselves to me, images of royal personages and their guests amidst furniture made from jacaranda wood and walls covered in yellow silk damask. If I tried really hard, peered for long enough into the biggest crystals, I could even see pictures of the balls at the Palace.

And now here was Margrete, standing on the threshold of the Queen's Chambers as if this was her natural and rightful place. I was surprised. I had never thought she would come. Two days earlier I had dived into Svarttjern and she had put her arms around me. And yet I had hardly dared speak to her when we walked out of the school gates the day before. I had said I was going to see my grandmother the next day. She had asked where she lived. I mentioned the address, Oscars gate. 'Why don't you come over,' I had said, knowing that that would never happen. 'What if I did come,' she had said. 'Come,' I had said. 'Won't you come?'

And she had come. Found me in my hideaway. Suddenly she was just there, filling the doorway, filling the crystal droplet in front of my eye. Standing there alone, or all together.

To view one's beloved through a crystal. I wish everyone could have that same experience. It was so luminous, so scintillating, so magical, and as such it was a true reflection of the emotions roiling inside me. I told myself that it was probably the lead in the crystal that lent this image such weight, made it so unforgettable. And often in the weeks ahead – not because of any prisms, but because I was in love – I would find myself seeing her in this same way, even when she was simply standing, say, in the playground: surrounded by a rainbowed aura.

'Margrete,' was all I said, the word barely audible. I knocked into some crystals. They tinkled like tiny bells.

'Jonas,' she said again and laughed. 'You look like a king with the world's biggest crown!'

'Who's this?' my grandmother whispered to me.

'I'm his girlfriend,' Margrete said.

I had not asked her. But now it was official. We were boyfriend and girlfriend. That was always her way. She cut through all the chit-chat and formalities. You saw ghosts and she took you to China. She walked through a door and said things straight out.

Up on the stepladder I felt the chandelier lose a little of its lustre, as if it had at long last met its match. I realised what it was that this wondrous object lacked: humanity. Life. Margrete could be said to have invaded my brittle world of glass and light, my blessed symmetry. With Margrete came disorder.

'Aren't you going to say something?' she laughed.

But I just went on standing, dumbstruck, under the chandelier, looking at her. In the silence all that could be heard was the faintest tinkling of the glass pendants. I held a crystal droplet up in front of my face, a large teardrop and endeavoured to take her in with my eyes. I did not know it, but I was also looking into the future.

It has occurred to me that I ought to have been looking at her through tears many years later, in Ullevål Garden City, when she was kneeling on the bed, steadily banging her head against the wall. Naked, heart-rendingly exposed somehow. But I merely stood there watching, still clutching the handle of a stupid mug of iced tea. I stood there quietly, I too naked, but with all my wits about me, with no excuse, and watched Margrete Boeck, my wife-to-be, banging her head against a wall. I stood there looking at her, as dumbstruck, as nonplussed, as I had been that time in Granny's sitting room. In my head I heard what might have been the tinkling of the crystals on a chandelier. What she was banging off the wall was every bit as fragile. But I knew that this was infinitely more complicated. So inconceivably much more precious and beautiful.

Why did she do it?

This was not like Margrete. The Margrete I had come to know after we met up again was, in fact, really quite the opposite. I often caught myself marvelling at her conscious presence in the moment, her appetite for life. She would wander about in the mornings with almost unashamed content-ment written all over her. As if it was enough simply to draw breath. That was her. Euphoric, delighted just to be alive. I could stand, lost in wonder, in the evening or as night drew on, watching her as she sat on the terrace, with or without a glass of wine, surveying the apple trees in the garden; envi-ously I would contemplate her blissful features, the way she shut her eyes and savoured the moment. I felt that I was witnessing sheer, unadulterated, incomprehensible joy.

She was strong too. From the moment I met her in elementary school I had viewed her as being much stronger than me. She also possessed what I would call a jade-like quality: in a dim light that partly translucent, partly impenetrable side of her shone through. At such times her eyes had an even richer golden glow to them. You had a sense of her depth, of that rare inner strength. I always felt that she was the sort of person who would survive in a concentration camp.

And so, when I found her kneeling on the bed, banging her head off the wall, I thought she was larking about; I thought it was some sort of a joke, some symbolic act which I was supposed to interpret – a bit like playing cha-rades, when you have to mime a song title and your team has to guess what it is. If I could just say the magic words she would stop. I stood in a bedroom in a house in Ullevål Garden City and watched a woman – a woman whom, what is more, I loved – pounding her head against the wall, with a thud that was more soft than hard. I glanced down, as if looking for help, into the mug of iced tea, to where the wheels of the two lemon slices twirled each in their own direction. 'Margrete?' I said. No response. She simply persisted in that mesmerising action, as regular as a pendulum. 'Margrete, what's wrong?' I said. 'Stop it, please.'

I have a wise daughter. She has set up her own company, inspired by the belief that we keep coming up with more and more ingenious methods of communication, but with less idea than ever before of what to say, what to communicate.

Margrete went on pounding her head against the wall. The thought flashed through my mind that this meant trouble. That I was going to become embroiled in some immensely complicated situation. And this was not a good time. In fact it was, to put it mildly, a very bad time. I had worries enough of my own. For weeks I had been agonising over whether to abandon Project X. This sight that I beheld, Margrete's soft skull striking the wall again and again was like hearing a knock at the door when you absolutely do not wish to be disturbed.

And beneath all this: why was I surprised? After all, from the moment I saw her through my crystal monocle I had known that she was many. Or greater. She reminded me of Aunt Laura's flat: viewed from the outside it consisted of four rooms, but when you stepped inside it seemed to go on forever. To begin with, just after we met one another again, every time we went out for a meal or had a drink in one of the innumerable new bars that opened up around that time, I felt as though I had to ditch my previous impression of her and start from scratch. She kept displaying different facets of herself. I had merely been spared seeing this side of her till now.

Or at least, there had been an incident, earlier on. It may have been a warning. We had been sitting at the piano, playing a Mozart sonata four-handed. Is that something which should give me pause for thought, I wonder: that she liked Mozart best, while I liked Bach? Then, all of a sudden, she slid off the bench and burst into tears. No ordinary crying fit, this, but an abrupt, loud and totally despairing fit of weeping. She crumpled up on the floor in the same position that Muslims adopt when they pray, rocking backwards and forwards. I felt shaken and helpless. It was the most harrowing sight. But when I cautiously knelt down, put my arm around her and asked her what was the matter, all she said, through her sobs, was: 'I love you so much.' I assumed, therefore, that she had been moved by the Mozart piece we had been playing, that sparkling sonata. And I left it at that. It was so typical of her, to burst into tears at the thought of us, two sweethearts, sitting side by side and managing with our four hands to produce that carefree music. It occurred to me that she must have seen it as a harmonious foretaste, a sign of how happy we would be together.

But this was something else, this was worse, this went deeper: to bang your precious head off a wall, as if intent on smashing it or ridding yourself of something that was eating away at you in there. 'Margrete?' I said. No response. She seemed somehow heavy. It crossed my mind that Margrete was also trying to drive a truck through a wall. That she was doing this out of love for me. It was, nonetheless, madness. In my eyes. Something from which I backed away. I had no wish to be confronted with this kind of love. It scared me. I stayed where I was, losing patience now, watching her, watching her beat her head against the wall, slowly, but with uncanny steadiness. 'Margrete?' I said again. More sharply. No response. I felt as if I was standing a long way off. As if an impassable gulf stretched between me in the middle of the room and her on the bed. I, an erstwhile lifesaver, stood there and watched a person drowning, unable to lift a finger to help.

I cannot go on. I have to stop. I need to dwell on this contrast, this old lifeboat lying at the quayside in this quiet fjord. She walks past on the deck, smiles, hands me a cup of coffee, pretends not to see the notebook, the pen. Who is she? I have a feeling that she carries a dark burden of her own. After what she has experienced. Which goes beyond just about anything that is usually likely to befall a young person. Certainly, in the past – when she came to visit me – I occasionally used to pick up worrying signals. I keep catching myself studying her. I know that she also studies me. We have a tacit understanding. She always wears a black beret, prompting associations with guerrilla warfare and with art. It has become her trademark; thanks to her, more young Norwegians than ever now sport such headgear. I never tire of looking at her. She has a little flaw, a relatively big gap between her two front teeth, one which she has deliberately done nothing about. 'In some African countries it would give me enormous cachet,' she remarked on one occasion. It simply serves to render her appearance even more intriguing. She is, as one journalist put it, 'made for television'.

She cannot take one step off the boat without people stopping to stare, whisper. She has lived only a couple of decades, but already she is an idol. For a long time I thought she would be a writer. You sometimes hear of kids reading *Anna Karenina* at the age of thirteen. Kristin tried to write *Anna Karenina* when she was thirteen. One time, just before she died, Margrete came across something that Kristin had written. 'She's so good it's uncanny,' Margrete said to me. 'It almost scares me. She's barely in her teens, but she writes like an adult.'

I knew she was special. As a little girl she happily lumped together alphabet blocks, Barbie dolls, old Matchbox cars, train sets and bits from Airfix construction kits. The way she saw it, they were all part of the same world, so there was no reason why they could not be used in combination, rather than separately. She was already practising what would later be referred to as 'sampling'. One winter night when we were gazing up at the stars and I had dusted off my old knowledge of astronomy, on the spur of the moment she dubbed Orion 'the Hourglass' and changed Leo's name, right then and there, to 'the Question Mark'. She had a head like a pinball machine. Her thoughts were forever zooming this way and that; you could positively hear them go *ping*, see the lights flashing behind her brow.

I sit on the mizzen shroud, as if wishing to be close to the lifebuoy. The coffee is exceptionally good, it reminds me of Margrete's, although Martin bemoaned its quality. 'Not exactly what you'd get at Caffè Sant'Eustachio in Rome, where they roast their beans in a wood-burning stove,' as he said. Martin hails from Nordkjosbotn in the far north, but with his rawboned, weatherbeaten features he might just as easily have come from Marrakesh. He also tends to wear stripy, loose-fitting clothes, not unlike the sort of thing worn in North Africa.

As far as I can gather, the OAK Quartet has been commissioned to devise a product, a good or a service which I find impossible to define – the term 'multimedia' seems too tame, already old hat. Nor do I understand the language they use, all those words flying through the air: 'information architecture', 'navigation design', 'hierarchy of levels'. What I do understand, however, is that this is a large-scale undertaking with solid financial backing from the most diverse institutions, not least from the business sector. This trip is just a first foray, a kind of reconnaissance mission; I am not certain who their target group are, whether the product will be geared towards the travel industry or is also designed for educational or entertainment purposes. Nor am I clear on whether the end-result will be sold in CD form or put out on the Internet – or be presented in one of the many other media spawned by the digital revolution. The OAK Quartet are forever discussing the question of what's next for television. Everything changes so fast these days. Their main concern appears to be that the actual concept, its sum and substance, the thinking behind it, should be applicable to lots of forms, including some yet to come. And they must remember to allow for the possibility for continual updating. 'We have to try to envisage all sorts of media, forms of communication of which we haven't even begun to dream,' Hanna said one evening. Hanna is almost thirty and the eldest of the group. Her Asian looks sometimes put me in mind of a geisha – not due to any promiscuous tendencies on her part, but because of her air of refinement. Hanna is in charge of finance and marketing, she works out plans of action with clients, acts as producer and coordinator. She is also the vessel's skipper, keeps the logbook, coils ropes east to west and can put out a spring line and make fast in a way that would make Colin Archer proud of her.

Who are these young people, I have asked myself. Are there such things as short cuts to getting to know a person? One day I was talking to Carl. He is the OAK Quartet's graphic designer as well as being something of a film buff, an expert on dramaturgy and cinematography. I have already had one argument with him about Orson Welles's masterpiece, *The Magnificent Ambersons*. Possibly because Carl, with his close-cropped head and his tall, broad build, reminds me of a nightclub bouncer or a bodyguard, I was surprised when he told me that I only needed to know one thing in order to understand everything about him: 'In my pocket I have a little brass figure,' he said. 'It represents Ganesh, an Indian god with the head of an elephant. I've carried it in my pocket for the past fifteen years.' Was it really true? Could one detail reveal almost everything there was to know about a person? I pondered this nugget of information about Carl the webmaster and the figure of Ganesh in his pocket. It certainly fired the imagination, made me think of a giant with a mouse as a pet.

Which detail would say most about me? It would have to be the fact that there is nothing I do not know about the Beatles' *Rubber Soul* album. I could tell you that Ringo played finger cymbals on 'Norwegian Wood'; that 'I'm Looking Through You' was inspired by Paul McCartney's girlfriend Jane Asher; that John Lennon stole a line from an Elvis song for 'Run For Your Life'; that the lyrics to 'The Word' were written in coloured pencils; that what one heard on 'In My Life' was not a cembalo solo but a speeded up recording of George Martin on electric piano.

I think Carl is right. Such a detail would say just about everything about me.

After some years in a cell, for the first time in my life – if I discount my work on 'the golden notebook' – I felt the need to write. I got it into my head that I could survive by trying to tell my own story. All sorrows can be borne if you put them into a story, as someone once said. But which story? That was the problem.

To begin with I just wrote, without any thought for what the end product would be, who would read it. I wrote with a pleasure which surprised me, I wrote with a delight at finally understanding Margrete's mania for writing. And I make no secret of the fact that I also had in mind the offers made to me by a number of publishers. 'Now we'll have Marco Polo himself putting pen to paper, not his cellmate Rustichello,' as one editor put it to me cajolingly. I toyed with various titles: *Twenty-three Fragments From a Killer's Hand, Eight Planets I have Visited* and the like. For a long time I was tempted to call it *The Confession of a Fool*, not knowing that that title had already been taken.

Rumours that I was writing were reported in the press. I think people were looking for a public confession or something of the sort. But the more I wrote, the less interested I became in the idea of others reading what I wrote. People were expecting The Truth. Either that or some sort of act of revenge. An exposé of everything and everybody, not least of life inside NRK, the escapades of the celebrities, who was sleeping with whom. But the content of the piece changed character. For a while it seemed to me that this was something between me and a higher power. In the end, though, I came to regard it as an honest-to-goodness Book of the Dead, equivalent to the papyrus scrolls buried with the dead in Ancient Egypt. It was a pile of paper, a scroll which I would take with me to the grave, so to speak. A password, a token I could present, so that I, or my spirit, could gain admission to the hereafter.

It was a confusing manuscript. It developed into a long, incoherent narrative. All the nouns seemed to be there, but none of the verbs. I could see only one solution: I destroyed it. For one very simple reason: no one – with one or two exceptions – would have been able to make head or tail of it. I burned my 'confession' with a light heart. Despite the fabulous sums offered to me, during those first years of my imprisonment at least, by a lot of publishers.

It is a relief to be on board the *Voyager*, to be with the members of the OAK Quartet. It is not that I believe them to have fewer worrying traits than previous generations of young people, but they seem different. Broader. They are just as interested in each single person as they are in society as a whole. They aspire to stronger individuals and a greater spirit of community. And none of them feels bound to stick only to their own specialist area. Martin, with his Marrakesh-style appearance, is a typical computer freak, a whole college on his own when it comes to his technological know-how, but I have long suspected him of being able to turn his hand to just about anything – and not only exotic cookery and mountain climbing. The other day, as we were round-ing the point at Fornes he picked up his guitar and sang 'In My Life' with such feeling – I have never heard anything like it. The other three gradually joined in, singing in harmony, and it seemed only natural that they should know all the words. I had to take a walk around the deck to save anyone seeing the tears in my eyes. In any case, they could never know what a ridiculously sen-timental appeal that song holds for me.

It is amazing, really, that Kristin should have wound up in such company, on board an old lifeboat. When she was offered the chance to work in televi-sion I strongly advised her to turn it down. She went against my wishes – it may be that in this particular instance she *had* to go against me. Kristin, this young girl, was given the job of hosting a prime-time, Friday evening pro-gramme, a talk show on which it did not really matter who the guests were: it was the presenter who was the star. And she was a star. Pert and saucy and smart in a way that Norway was ready for. As the papers said, she had star quality. Amid all the hullabaloo surrounding her my name rarely came up, and then only as a by-the-way, and only at the start.

Then, when she was right at the top, she bowed out. After a couple of interim stages – high-profile pursuits – she set up her own company, one that in many ways involved all the things with which she had worked: music, software development, television, advertising, journalism. Her business card gives her occupation as 'association artist'. According to Hanna she is a genius when it comes to spotting, forging, connections, inserting 'links' as they say. She has become something of a guru within IT circles. At an age when I had barely begun to figure out what my first project should be, she already has a whole lifetime behind her.

When I asked her about this one evening – Martin had served margue-ritas up on deck – about all the things she had done and whether there was any common denominator between them, she had looked at me in surprise, glared almost. 'I'm a storyteller,' she said. 'Isn't it obvious? The future belongs to the storytellers. I've always known that. And that's the challenge with what we're doing here. To find the underlying story.'

I sit here in a fjord, surrounded by steep hillsides, and think of fly tying. The questions are always more important than the answers. In Lærdal the salmon flies are the question and the fish is the answer. I am fascinated by the craftsmanship involved. Many salmon flies are real works of art. The pat-terns, and the poetry of the names, make me think of cocktails, or butter-flies. Golden Butterfly, Yellow Eagle, Evening Star, Jock Scott. A Victorian salmon fly might consist of more than forty materials, some of them taken from exotic birds and animals; they looked like magical ornaments. If I were part of the OAK Quartet I would weave in lots of information on salmon flies. They keep talking about 'teasers', items designed to catch the browser's interest. Could not the whole story of Lærdal be encapsulated within those flies? They are the perfect bait for the eye.

In the evenings I tend to sit off to one side and listen to them discussing things in the warm light of the paraffin lamp in the saloon. The conversation is fast and furious, almost as if they were bouncing rubber balls to one another, or playing a variation on 'My ship is loaded with ...'. A thought which is not so far out, at that. The *Voyager* is a cargo ship. They are loading it with information.

Most of their talk has to do with the task in hand, here in Sognefjord, but they keep straying onto other subjects. They may start out talking about Lærdal fly tier Olaf Olsen, and from there the conversation will turn to Loki, who took the shape of a salmon, before winding up with a discussion of all the Hollywood films they have seen in which fishing plays a key part – particularly those in which someone spends their whole life trying to catch the king salmon itself, only to let it go again when they finally succeed. The other day they spent over an hour debating Martin's assertion that Sisyphus was the happiest man in the world. Hanna maintained that only Job – poor, tormented Job, mark you – was happier. In the middle of all this Carl proceeded to hold forth on his fascination with those blue pellets or cubes that used to be found in urinals. As far as I could gather, he believed these could be employed as a form of narcotic. The OAK Quartet have an almost shocking ability to hop, for example, from the question of whether jam should be put on cornflakes before or after the milk, to thoughts on the undulating lines of Alvar Aalto's architecture, and finish up with an exchange on whether or not Mother Teresa was an egoist – as if all of these issues were of equal importance. It reminds me of the talk show which Kristin presented, *Container* it was called: it was in many ways epoch-making television, a real lucky dip of a programme filled with all sorts of rubbish out of which she forged meaning. She had people talking about empty trivia one minute and deeply serious matters the next. So too on board the *Voyager*. They take the same burning interest in Wittgenstein's philosophy of language as they do in the design of a complex motorway intersection or the lyrics of the Swedish Hoola Bandoola Band's protest songs from the seventies. I have also remarked that they keep branching off into stories. Maybe it's the boat that inspires them, maybe that is what comes of sitting in the glow of an old paraffin lamp.

I am instilled with their sense for detail. I understand how fraught with meaning ostensibly dry, neutral objects can be. What bearing has the old, black Bakelite telephone had on my life. All of the different watch-straps I have owned, the appearance and feel of which I can recall with a clarity that astonishes me?

Is there some detail which could explain why she did it?

I have been given the whole of the for'ard cabin to myself – Hanna and Carl occupy the bunks in the saloon, Kristin and Martin share the big bunk in the aft corridor. Every evening I lie here thinking. The creaking of the rigging, the smell of paraffin and tar conjure up memories not only of an old actor, but also of Margrete. Before I go to sleep, my thoughts often go to those two other *Voyager* ships, small vessels sailing along, way out there in space, beyond the rings of Saturn, packed to the gunnels with answers to Bo Wang Lee's question: What should we take with us?

I am writing again, something which comes almost as a surprise to me. Not that I don't do a lot of writing now anyway, I *am* a secretary. What I mean is: writing about myself. I have been stimulated. By her. I know she is writing something. She has always been a great one for writing. I think she means to have it published. I have nothing against that.

My motives in writing are somewhat different this time around. I feel as if I am suffering from amnesia. I want to try to remember. And more than anything I want to try to remember the middle part.

In Grorud, when I was a boy, there were some old stonemasons who were real hard drinkers. We did not know what to make of them: these drunks – grown men lying senseless on the edge of the wood in the middle of the day – never moved us to feel critical of society or of our home town. But we were not scared of them either. They wouldn't have hurt a fly. On one occasion we crept up on one of them to pinch the empty bottles that lay scattered around him on the grass. Suddenly the old drunk came to and started telling us a story, as if we were a longed-for audience. He stank of beer and piss, his crotch area was all wet and disgusting. We stayed and listened for a while; I thought it was very interesting, it was all about the cutting of the stone, about the huge, unwieldy blocks, but the others were itching to get away, to cash in the empties, buy gumballs from the new vending machine from which a lucky turn of the handle might deliver a ring as well. I went back later. The drunk man was still sprawled on the grass and I was able to catch the end of the story; and a pretty powerful ending it was, something to do with meeting a nursing sister, a future wife, in a hospital – not even the stench of beer and piss could spoil it. I ventured, from a safe distance, to ask why he had told this story. The drunk answered that it was a good story. He just *had* to tell it, even if no one was listening. This taught me something about stories.

About telling stories to no one. Even more importantly, though, I was filled with curiosity. I had heard the beginning and the end, but not the middle bit. And what I wondered was: what had occurred between what I knew of the beginning, the part about the stone cutting, and the wonderful ending? An accident?

A tale told by a drunken man. I think of what I wrote in my cell, the lengthy manuscript which I destroyed. I know a lot about my childhood and youth and I know a lot about the time since I went to prison. But what happened in between? What is the midpoint of my life?

Margrete.

And at the centre of this story?

Margrete on her knees on the bed, banging her head against the wall. Margrete in a white bedroom, in the light streaming through gauzy curtains. And me looking at her, standing there paralyzed, watching.

In retrospect it is alarming – and vexing – to think how clear it was to me that this would be the most significant moment of my life. In personal terms, as moments go this was the equivalent of the Big Bang, the mystery of what happened during those first seconds in the history of the universe. If I could understand what was going on here I would understand everything. I stood at a crucial fork in the road.

So why hang back so?

It was Margrete who made me see that I was not only a wonder. I was also a fool.

At first I did not believe it possible; no one could be engulfed by darkness in such a bright room, certainly not after such incandescent lovemaking. It was as if she had drawn down a black blind inside herself. And a blind between us. It crossed my mind that she must have remembered something terribly sad. This was, as I say, at the time when she was doing her specialist training in skin disorders, including venereal diseases. She came across enough distressing cases, heard lots of disillusioning stories. For one crazy, almost grimly comic, moment I wondered whether she might be trying to test how much her skin could withstand. Or how thick-skinned she was.

One night, in the dark, she told me what had made her decide to become a doctor. She had actually had her heart set on becoming an actress. While living in Paris she was part of a travelling theatre group which staged dramatisations of episodes from *The Mahabharata* – Margrete often entertained me in bed with little stories from the Indian epic; I really enjoyed them, particularly the adventures of the hero Arjuna who was conceived through the offices of the god Indra. Then one of her girlfriends suddenly became seriously ill and died in terrible pain. The helplessness she had felt then, at her friend's sickbed, made her decide to study medicine. To help people. Ease suffering. Margrete had a tendency to take things upon herself.

I did not know her. I had a suspicion that her past had been one long search for the next adrenalin rush. My lack of ardour was a constant source of annoyance to her. As was the fact that I was so reserved. 'You're not shy, you're spineless,' she said. I had been the baffled witness to her occasional need to scream from a mountaintop – quite literally, I mean: she would actually climb to the top of a mountain and *scream* for all she was worth. That was why I did not react right away to the head-banging. I was prepared to regard it as some necessary, harmless exercise.

She was a tireless advocate of the wisdom of feelings. 'I feel sorry for you; you're not in touch with your feelings,' she often said to me. One evening I found her lying blubbering for no apparent reason, when I came to bed. I asked what was wrong, but received no answer. 'Get a grip!' I cried when she kept on sobbing. 'Why should I?' she asked, suddenly angry.

At such moments it was as if words failed her. 'If something's worrying you, won't you please tell me what it is?' I said on one of the few occasions when I found her like this. 'There are no words to describe it,' she had said. She had had this helpless, sorrowful look on her face. 'It's like it goes deeper than thought,' she said. I could not understand it – this intelligent woman, a brilliant doctor in the making, all that reading – that she should be lost for words. But when I looked into her eyes, nor could my own thought penetrate the black depths of her pupils.

I stood there naked, holding a mug, watching her bang her head against the brick wall. I had the desire to translate this sight into something rational. But behind it all I knew: this was a scream. A scream for help disguised as a senseless action.

It is easy to say that I should have stopped her, that I should have done something, slipped a pillow, a fender, between the wall and her forehead, grabbed hold of her and pulled her away from there by force. But just at that moment that monotonous, destructive action seemed to have a paralyzing effect on me. Something about the unexpectedness of it – we had made love, I had only gone out to fetch a mug of iced tea – made me feel as though I had fallen into an ambush. I got it into my head that I had to stay perfectly still, to save anything even more awful from happening.

Or at least, that is not the whole truth. I know, I remember, that I had the rather cruel, almost delirious, thought that if I stopped her right now, if I threw myself between her and the wall, I would miss this chance of seeing her reveal a side of herself of which, until now I had known absolutely nothing. Just a few minutes ago I had asked her whether she was content. 'Content?' she had replied. 'Not just content – happy.' What if there was no contradiction between the fact of being happy and the act of beating one's head against the wall as I had at first thought. What if, in her world, this was an expression of a deeper, logical deduction. As if she were saying: 'I am happy and I slam my head against the wall.' Or: 'We all have our ways of generating ideas. You skip. I beat my head off the wall.'

Egoism disguised as impotence. I felt my thoughts shooting off in lots of directions at once, as if the sight of her had provoked an amazing shift in consciousness, so powerful that for a while I forgot about her and instead stood there with all of my attention focused inwards as I attempted to pursue as many as possible of the countless lines of thought which were branching outwards at breathtaking speed and which might, if I could only mobilise all of my powers, lead me to some unique flash of insight which would justify the fact that I did not intervene. She went on beating her brow against the white wall, as if trying to break through a barrier, using her head as a battering ram. I stayed where I was, mug in hand, staring at her and pursuing my own thoughts while, with another part of my brain – in a third corner of my mind I could not help admiring this facility – every now and again, mainly to salve my own conscience perhaps, saying her name: 'Margrete'. It came out almost as a question, as if I was afraid of waking her. Something about the golden statuette in the room moved me to imagine, just for a second, that this might be some sort of religious ritual, much like making one's devotions to a god in a temple. One which, in this case, would have to be akin to Kali, the goddess of destruction.

Oh yes, she knew how to destroy. I was only twelve years old when she all but broke me. I have always felt that that was why I was afraid of love. That that was why I did not dare to try again for such a long time. Or never dared. After all, how was it possible? How could anyone be so broken up inside, so miserable, simply for the want of a slender hand to hold, a mouth to which to press one's lips, a body to put one's arms around? The most powerful force on earth, so they say, is that created between two particles in an atom. I would venture to suggest, however, that no force on earth is greater than the love between an adolescent boy and girl.

Is there anything I remember more clearly than that day in seventh grade, the day she told me it was over? There had been an incident the week before when we were out skating. Since then she had acted differently towards me, seemed to be seeing me with fresh eyes. I hoped. I hoped, while waiting only for those awful words to fall.

They were uttered one afternoon. In the rain, an unseasonal downpour of the sort that all children hate because it ruins ski trails, snowmen, ski-jump hills, and the ice for skating, all of the best things about winter. It also ruined everything for me.

Through her most odious henchwoman – that in itself an ominous sign – I had received word that she wanted to meet me outside the Golden Elephant, the posh new restaurant in the shopping centre. In one final attack of wishful thinking I took her choice of meeting place as a sign that she wanted to make up. Well, why there of all places? The Golden Elephant was a new and exotic addition to Grorud; the lovely miniature elephants gave the illusion of a little piece of Asia in the middle of our little suburb. I even had the crazy idea that her father, a genteel diplomat, was going to take us out to dinner. But I was also afraid that the name, the Elephant, would remind Margrete of Thailand, Bangkok, a world of which I knew nothing, a standard I could never meet.

On top of everything else, she was late. She was never on time. Not as an adult either. At that particular moment it was sheer torture. To have to hang about waiting. But when she appeared, a quarter of an hour late, in all her 'Persian' beauty – her skin golden even at that time of year, late in the winter – I was not annoyed, only relieved. Or again: hopeful. Desperately hopeful. I feasted my eyes on the lithe body which I had seen turning cartwheels in the summer. And at the same time, through my mind flashed the thought: I don't know her. I've been going out with her for almost a year and a half and I don't know her, I have no idea what she is liable to do, or say. And even at a distance I could see that withdrawn look in her eyes.

I was to observe that same look on another occasion, as a grown man, at Villa Wergeland. One autumn. At night. She didn't see me. I stood in the living-room doorway and regarded her where she sat, in a chair by the unlit hearth, lighting matches one after the other, a whole box of them; letting each match burn all the way down and not turning so much as a hair when it scorched her fingers, then tossing them, burnt out, into the fireplace. A totally dark room. Her eyes turned inward. Match after match. As if she were trying to light something inside herself.

I stood outside the Golden Elephant and watched her walking towards me. Should I have known, from seeing those seven figures in Granny's crystal prism? That there was also a ruthless, a pitiless, a – why not say it – cruel Margrete?

But I knew nothing, I was simply terrified, trying to hold on to hope, but terrified. Shivering. Shaking. The way I did when I was really dreading something. A performance. A vaccination. The school dentist. Dr Mengele. Most of us have been there. And we all know the agony of it. To stand there and watch a girl walking towards you, a girl who embodies all of your adolescent yearnings, the sum of your tender, supremely vulnerable sensibilities. And then she stands in front of you, and then she looks at you, and then you swallow, and you try to say something, and not one word will come and then she says it, straight out, before you can open your mouth, with no beating about the bush: 'It's over. I'm breaking it off.' She did not even glance away, she looked straight at me, straight into me with those remarkable eyes of hers, pupils floating in irises of gold. It seemed such a contradiction for two eyes as warm as those to belong to the utterer of such cold, such harsh words. She gave me a look that expunged all trace of doubt from my soul. It was over.

I was left with a question on my lips which I never got to ask, but which, standing in the rain outside the Golden Elephant, I formulated in my mind for the first time: Why did she do it? It is here that this whole story, everything I have written so far, has its start. Margrete must have known: in India, Ganesh, the elephant-headed god, is the god of storytelling.

I believe, all things considered, that this was the hardest blow I have ever been dealt. I believe, if I am honest, that not even the shock of finding her dead on the living-room floor many years later, was as bad. And the pain was of another order, much more all-embracing than it was that time when I broke my leg, when I lay writhing on the grass after being injured by a spiteful Lyn player. I, a past-master at holding my breath, found myself fighting for air. I knew what was happening: I was quite simply having problems with my respiration. I was losing my vital spark.

I stared at her black hair, her woolly hat. With eerie clarity I discerned every strand of hair, every drop of rain on the wool. I tried to think, tried to hold onto one thread, but it was all such a tangled mess, just one big agonising, indissoluble backlash.

And then she walked away. From me. The back of her jacket retreated out of the shopping centre, and was gone. I had been dumped. I was not worthy. This was in the days when everybody wore ridiculously long scarves; even wrapped twice round the neck they still hung to the hips. Once she was out of sight I pulled mine off as if it were a boa constrictor.

I was gasping for breath. The lungs, not the heart, are the seat of love. If I had not known it before I knew it now. I almost fainted, I was so horribly short of breath that I almost fainted. I thought I was going to die. And maybe I did. I died even though I was on my feet. I died as I watched Margrete's back retreating.

I must touch, once again, on this mystery in my life. I would like to make it clear that it has nothing to do with megalomania; I write this in all humility, in sorrow almost, since I have understood so little of it. To be honest I have never dared try to get to the bottom of these thoughts and incidents.

I did my best to forget that time at Aunt Laura's when I woke up to find that the oranges had been replaced by lemons. Or rather: I *wished* to forget. Not least because such an experience, ability, or whatever I ought to call it, seemed so utterly useless. But then a couple of years later, one summer, I had an even more curious experience. It was a Sunday morning, very early. I was playing by myself while I waited for some of the others to appear. I climbed a hill on the outskirts of the estate, one with lots of steep, rocky outcrops. It had rained during the night and the rock was slippy. I ventured beyond the fence skirting a drop which our parents deemed dangerous. And as I was standing there, feeling pretty pleased with myself and a bit miffed that there was no one there to marvel at my daredevil climbing feat, I lost my balance, fell over the edge and died. I say this without a qualm. I am convinced that I killed myself on that Sunday morning early when I was nine; I can even remember being aware, in a flash, in the hundredth of a second as my head struck the tarmac at the foot of the cliff, of embracing death. But when I opened my eyes I felt no pain. I put my hand to my head. I could detect no wound, no blood. I pulled myself to my feet and ran an eye over myself. I was wearing shorts and a short-sleeved shirt. Not a scratch. Not a mark on my clothes even though the ground was damp and muddy. No one had seen me fall. Everybody was either sleeping or having breakfast. I squinted up at the cliff, it had to be a drop of at least eight or nine metres. I simply could not have survived such a fall.

There were times, later, when I felt that the same thing had happened to me again, although never under quite such dramatic circumstances. More often it was a case of waking up filled with the absolute certainty that I had been dead. And inseparable from this: the certainty that I was a different person from the one I had been before. I was the same, but with more to me. As if my original self had been expanded. All of my senses seemed to be fresher. Sharper. I do not know how to describe this sensation, the word death seems to be the only one that covers it.

Sometimes I did not even recognise the room in which I woke up, and it would take me some seconds to realise that I was in my own bedroom. The smell was different. As was the way the light fell on the wall. One morning I actually jumped when I walked into the kitchen. No one noticed anything. But it took me a while to figure out who these people were, that they were Mum and Dad, Rakel and Daniel.

Once, as if she had suddenly thought of it, my mother told me something, just a little story, which I tucked away in my memory. When she was in Akershus Hospital, riding out the last contractions, only seconds before I was born, the Oslo region was shaken by an earthquake. It was, by Norwegian standards, a big quake. Everyone who happened to be indoors at the time felt it. My mother told me this story almost as a joke. And she said no more about it. Nonetheless, I brooded over this piece of information. I even went so far as to check whether it was true. It was. I wondered, yearnfully almost – or fearfully – whether this shaking of the earth's crust might have given rise to a loop in my genetic material, equipping me with some sort of attribute which few, if any, other people possessed. I imagined, feared, that I might be the first of a new – I will not call it mutant – branch of human development, that I had stumbled almost by accident upon a clue to the future nature of mankind. And although I fought against it, for many years I was visited by an all-pervading sense of a pressure inside me, of being unfolded, slowly. And yet I was unable to identify this possible new addition to my person or put it to use. In later years I would take comfort from the words of my old elementary school headmaster: 'Four thousand years of civilisation and we still know next to nothing about human nature.' I never told anyone about this feeling. No one would have understood me anyway.

I know that many people saw me as being a shy man. But I was not so much bashful as self-effacing. I wanted to stay out of sight. I did not want to run the risk of anyone discovering my secret. My confusion over an experience which I did not understand and my uncertainty as to where it might lead. I made myself as inconspicuous as possible. At school I raised my hand as seldom as I could in response to the teacher's questions, and never if I was the only one who knew the answer. It may sound silly, but sometimes I had the urge to wear a wig in order to distract people's attention. They would say: We've found you out. You wear a wig! And I could pretend to be suitably embarrassed. But I would have prevented them from exposing the *real* wig: the fact that I was not who I appeared to be – a possible wonder. I concealed my true identity in the same way as a Red Indian on an enemy tribe's territory would cover up the tattoo which revealed him to be the son of a chief. I had to hide myself away, prepare myself, await my opportunity, wait for the time to be ripe, as they say. I just had to hope that at the end of this frustrating process, once I was fully evolved, a project would present itself. And it would seem so obvious: a unique opportunity, tailor-made, so to speak, for me, to allow me to work in depth.

It should come as no surprise to learn that hide-and-seek was my favourite game. I remember the glee of discovering a really good hiding place. But

I also enjoyed being found. In the autumn, when we played hide-and-seek in the dark, my heart would pound with delight every time someone shone a torch beam on my face among the bushes and shouted: 'I've found Jonas!' There was nothing to beat it. I think I felt as if someone was saving me from myself.

I had the same feeling that day when Margrete showed up in Granny's sitting room: that she had shone a torch beam on me, found me in one of my favourite hiding places. Saved me from – how can I put it – a false existence, delusions which, although I did not know it, could have been harmful to me. With Margrete, too, came something new. Till then I had believed that in order to unfold as a human being you had to have spirit. Now, thanks to Margrete, I realised that spirit was possibly just another word for love. I could feel it when she kissed me. Margrete could positively paper me with kisses. She could kiss my lips a hundred times and never tire of it. It was as if she were practising life-saving. Mouth-to-mouth resuscitation. This was how love was supposed to be, I thought to myself. Close together. Face to face. Mouth to mouth. And each time she put her arms around me, kissed me, I felt a pull, a pressure, as though something lying tightly coiled inside me was starting to stir, to unfurl. Margrete helped me to see how the two main threads from my youth – my longing to be a lifesaver and my dream of becoming a discoverer – ran, or were woven, together. Because I discovered new life. Not new life in the universe, but on Earth. I found new life inside myself. I discovered that we human beings contain *more* life than we think.

So when Margrete walked out on me and I was left alone outside the Golden Elephant with my lungs aching, I was filled with a woeful certainty that great prospects were slipping away from me, that my *vital spirit* itself was forsaking me. I felt utterly dispirited. It is not, in fact, entirely unthinkable that I really did die.

I had one ray of hope. Faint, but still – a hope. 'You'll get a letter,' she said as she turned to leave. A letter. Never have I looked forward so much to a letter. Because she had to tell me why she had done it. Give me a reason. Unless of course it was – oh, hope – a letter to say that she was sorry.

Waiting. Have I ever waited like that? I have never waited like that. For two weeks, waiting for a letter became a full-time occupation for me. During that time I would have had no trouble answering the question as to the meaning of life. The meaning of life was to wait. I do not recall whether I ate, or went to school, or did my homework, or slept; I remember only that I waited, that I *was* the waiting. I trembled at the thought of it, I dreaded it, longed for it, pictured words, expressions, phrases – even her handwriting, her distinctive 'a's – I saw them all so clearly. And underneath it all: the hope.

At long last a letter arrived. Or rather: a parcel. I received the collection slip from the post office on the same day that I was given the awful news – again by one of those ghastly friends of hers, a stuck-up bitch with buck teeth – that she had moved away, that she had left Norway again, gone off with her parents to a country so far away that I had scarcely heard of it, a country where her father, the bloody kidnapper, was to take up a post at the Norwegian embassy. The knowledge that there was a parcel at Grorud post office, waiting to be collected, made it easier for me to cope with the grief of her leaving. At least I would be enlightened as to what had happened, what had been going through her mind. And maybe she would have said something about coming back soon. About – oh, hope – missing me.

I collected the parcel. It was square in shape. And flat. It was an LP. I hunted through the wrappings again and again. No sheet of paper, no distinctive 'a's. Just that record. A parting gift, I thought. Only later did it dawn on me that it *was* a letter.

All I had managed to stammer out when we were standing outside The Golden Elephant was the start of the question that was on my lips: 'But why ... Why ... Why ...'

She had looked at me for a long time. 'Idiot', she said. I realised that this was an answer. That one word. Idiot. It was a key. For me it has always been a key. I looked it up. It means an ignorant person.

The LP was *Rubber Soul* by the Beatles. I played it nonstop for a year. That record was like a chandelier, each song an arm, each verse a crystal droplet, each line a different colour. I would stand like – yes, an idiot, for hour after hour, watching the record spin round and round, hypnotised by the rainbow defining the radius of the black disc. Even today my eyes are liable to fill with tears, to the consternation and mystification of everyone around me, whenever I hear one of the songs from that album. All it takes is the intro to that played-to-death golden oldie 'Michelle', or the bouzouki-style guitar on 'Girl', and I have to sit down to save being laid flat out by all the emotions, the memories, that come tumbling over me.

I can safely say that I have never listened to any record, any bunch of songs, as closely as I did to that one. I attributed deeper meaning to those in many ways hopelessly banal lyrics than to, say, *The Cantos* by Ezra Pound. I looked for signs, messages, codes in each note, each instrument, each word, in between the words. Later, when I heard of people who tried to pick up hidden messages by playing *Sergeant Pepper* backwards with their fingers, not to mention those who pored over the cover and lyrics, searching for clues to the effect that Paul is dead, I was not the slightest bit surprised: I had long been familiar with such overheated modes of interpretation.

I am quite certain that no one in Norway knows as much about this particular record as I do. *Rubber Soul* may well be the only subject I have ever known anything at all about. For months, one of my chief pastimes involved learning absolutely everything I could, every little detail about this record. Such as the fact that Ringo played the Hammond organ on 'I'm Looking Through You'; that 'Norwegian Wood' is a song about infidelity, not drugs; that Paul was given some help with the French words in 'Michelle' by Jan Vaughan, the wife of one of his friends. All the effort put into unearthing this information was part of an unconscious defence mechanism, a way of distracting myself, leaving me less time for pining. It reached the stage where I could have appeared on *Double Your Money* to answer questions on *Rubber Soul*. There was nothing I did not know: about the fuzz box attached to Paul's bass for 'Think For Yourself', George Martin playing the mouth organ on 'The Word', the cowbell on 'Drive My Car' or the jazz chord on 'Michelle'.

From a more objective point of view, it seems only fitting that my break-up with Margrete should be bound up with this music. Because as I began to get things into a broader perspective I realised that the Beatles had left a more indelible stamp on the sixties than all the assassinations and political debacles, or phenomena such as Woodstock and the rise of the Black Panthers. I venture to make this assertion on the grounds that neither the story of the group nor their music has ever lost its grip on people. The Beatles pervaded the consciousness of a whole generation. The Beatles *were* the sixties. The Beatles stand as the most powerful story of that decade. Their music was, still and all, the worthiest accompaniment I could have had to my grief, my anguish, my despair.

I am not sure, but I doubt if I have ever hurt as badly as I did during those first months after Margrete left me. This was also my earliest experience of a psychosomatic disorder, of being ill, feeling pain even when the doctor can find nothing wrong with you. I suddenly realised that it was possible: you could die of a broken heart. Strictly speaking, considering all I had learned about my own body, all its irrational responses, I really ought to have been better equipped to comprehend the anguish which Margrete suffered. The thought has also occurred to me – a dreadful thought, but I cannot rid myself of it: was my later blindness simply a form of revenge?

Broken-hearted as I was, I listened to the fourteen tracks on *Rubber Soul* with an intensity, a sensitivity, which might even have surprised Lennon and McCartney. To this day any one of those songs – 'You Won't See Me', for instance – can still knock me off my feet. Not only my soul, my legs too turn to rubber. If I'm driving along in my car and the radio starts playing the ambiguous lyrics to 'Drive My Car' I have to pull into the side and stop. I'm almost ashamed to admit it, but I feel like curling up in the foetal position and dissolving into fits of sentimental sobbing. The beautiful vocal harmonies on 'Nowhere Man' hit all of my senses smack in the solar plexus. And every time I hear 'Norwegian Wood' the sitar playing sends me into a sort of trance, the real world seems somehow to dissolve, to melt into a succession of veils. It's odd. I can listen, say, to Sibelius's violin concerto, that intense, impassioned and in many ways stirring music, without so much as a twitch of an eyebrow. But those simple melodies: 'Wait', or 'If I Needed Someone', with their even simpler lyrics, can just about do for me, they are almost more than I can bear.

I have been thinking about what I wrote concerning the incident outside the restaurant, about losing my spirit. I have since come up with another explanation. She left me because I *lacked* spirit. Because I was incapable of communicating, did not speak her language. I deserved to be called an idiot. Well, it was obvious really: spirit also entailed being able to understand, having the gift of empathy. At any rate if my ever growing suspicion was correct; if, that is, spirit and love belonged to the same family of words.

In religious instruction classes at elementary school I was much taken with the description of the Holy Spirit. It was a real treat to hear our teacher relate, as only she could, the events of the Pentecost, when the disciples were endowed with the Holy Spirit and tongues of flame descended upon their heads. All at once they were able to speak and understand every language. I studied the illustration by Gustav Doré in the Family Bible. I could do better than that, I thought. I drew that same picture again and again: people with huge fires blazing on their heads. The teacher could not help laughing, but for me this was something to aim for, a sudden longing. How was I to acquit myself, how to utilise my gift, such that I too would be crowned with flame, become a torch. Be understood by all. Or, more importantly: understand others.

Maybe that was why I went into television: to be able to work with such a bright, such a far-reaching light – with fire, you might say. With communication. Spirit. I remember my father and what he said when he converted air into music at the organ. Now I could say the same thing myself: 'My work has to do with true inspiration.'

Much has been said about the television series *Thinking Big*. Much has also gone unsaid. In 1989 the walls came tumbling down all across Europe. Even in the grey, dreary Soviet Union which I had once visited the colours began to peep through, those that had been lying dormant, in the underground at least. But that year also saw the fall – one almost as momentous – of a wall of sorts in Norway, in *Festung Norwegen*. The *Thinking Big* series made the country open up, if only for a very short while. People pointed this out, almost incredulously, in newspapers, discussed it on television. One comment from that year stuck in my mind, one of the greatest compliments I have ever received, as it happens: 'These programmes have engendered a new mood of tolerance in Norway, they have led to a new mode of communication with the world around us. Only a truly inspired work could have such an effect.'

How paradoxical. So why all this difficulty in getting through to a person whom I only needed to put out my hand in order to touch.

I had been looking forward to working on Lars Skrefsrud, the thief and jailbird who became Norway's most famous missionary. Not even the religious aspect of the subject could put me off. Television was the perfect medium for this. At the sight of satellite receivers – we see them everywhere we go here in the Sogn area too – I always find myself thinking that television is the religion of our times, that these dishes are the private domes under which people worship their new god. In more misanthropical moments I am inclined to feel that the TV room has become the poor man's Nirvana, a place in which we can empty our heads of all thought, step into the Void, switch off completely. If that is so, then it is also the fault – and possibly the boon – of the programmes being shown. The majority of television channels see it as their job to induce people to cut off, and out, completely.

I do not know whether to be sorry or pleased that no one has ever spotted the numerous autobiographical elements which I introduced, unwittingly perhaps, into the *Thinking Big* series. Although some are impossible to detect, since in these instances I had to abandon my original idea. As in the programme on Skrefsrud. From the minute I started on the groundwork for the programme I knew what I wanted to have as its hub: a book. A volume which would perfectly encapsulate the essence of Lars Skrefsrud: a man of spirit, a man who could communicate. Because that is the basis of all missionary work. If you wish to talk to a stranger, to explain your beliefs to him, you have to learn to speak his language. Her language. Skrefsrud's work in India represented a lifelong endeavour to understand other people's beliefs, something which also required him to expose himself to their culture.

Lars Skrefsrud arrived in India in 1863. He had been sent out there by the Gossner Society, but after some years he left the mission station at Purulia along with Hans Peter Børresen from Denmark to go to the village of Benegaria in Santal Parganas, and there, among one of the indigenous tribes of India, they set up their own centre, now known simply as the Santal Mission. They also founded the Ebenezer mission station. Skrefsrud had found his purpose in life. To master the Santals' language.

There are few programmes on which I have spent so much time and effort, and few programmes with which I have been less happy. This was one of those unnerving experiences which gave me to know that I was an idiot, not a wonder. Or more of an idiot than a wonder. In the end I had to construct the programme around the dramatisation of two crucial and telling events in the history of the Santal Mission: contrasting its tentative beginnings, the baptism of the first three Santals, with the consecration twenty-two years later of the new church at Ebenezer, a building capable of accommodating as many as three thousand. By this time, thousands of Santals had become Christians and the mission station resembled a small, well-tended version of Paradise. The television footage was certainly colourful enough – piquant, you might say, as a curry compared to the bland fare of the Norwegian state church – but I was not happy. The Skrefsrud programme was in all ways a stopgap solution. I derived no comfort from the record number of applications to the Missionary College that year. My aim had been to make a programme about a book, about one man's struggle to understand and be understood. I had wanted to depict something which lies deep inside every human being: the dream of speaking the same language.

Lars Olsen from Skrefsrud was a man of words. The first thing he did when he was released from prison, in which he had made up his mind to become a missionary, was to buy French, Greek and Latin grammars. He was already fluent in German and English. At the Gossner Society's school in Berlin he studied several other languages including Hebrew and, not least, Hindi. In India he taught himself to speak Bengali and later went on to learn four other Indian dialects. Although it is unlikely that he spoke more than forty languages, as some would have it, it would be no exaggeration to call him a linguistic genius. His command of foreign tongues extended all the way down to the most difficult part of all, the actual tone of voice.

It is not that long since I read through my notes for this programme, with a good deal of nostalgia. I was amazed to find how well I remembered the original concept, and particularly all the details relating to Skrefsrud's efforts to give the Santals a written language – take, for example the mere fact that before anything else he had to create a system of characters, an alphabet of sorts, using fifty 'letters' to reproduce the various sounds of the language. Having done this, he then wrote a grammar, while at the same time constantly noting down new words. More and more words. Within a very short time he had collected over ten thousand words which he later passed on to another Norwegian missionary who, in due course, included them in a massive five-volume dictionary. Norwegians have accomplished many great deeds; Roald Amundsen was, for instance, the first to reach the South Pole, but as far as I am concerned – you'll have to pardon my subjectivity – there can be no greater deed than that of bestowing a written language upon a people which has none of its own. I like to think of Skrefsrud standing in front of a mirror beside a Santal tribesman, pronouncing words, sounds; I picture him mimicking the Santal, before examining his larynx and vocal chords with a laryngoscope. In my mind's eye I see him roaming the countryside, on horseback, on foot, on his month-long expeditions among the Santals, always with his notebook to hand.

But what intrigued me most was the grammar he wrote. Might this be the most important book written by a Norwegian? I had actually held it in my hands, an exquisite volume with blue covers tooled in gold. I had spent hours leafing through it. *A Grammar of the Santhal Language.* Published in Benares – that alone: Benares – in 1873. It was hard for me to conceive of such a feat. Skrefsrud believed that the uninitiated underestimated the Santals' language. He maintained that it was one of the most complex and philosophical in the world, as sophisticated as Sanskrit. The verbs in particular had such an overwhelming wealth of different forms. I flicked through the pages, shaking my head in disbelief at the thought that any man could wrest the intricacies of a language from it in such a way. I came to the part on the verb tenses – there were no less than twenty-three of them. How could that be? I still remember some of them: the Optative, the General Incomplete Present, the Indecisive Pluperfect, the Inchoative Future, the Preliminary Expostulative, the Continuative Future. I leafed through this book, almost enamoured of it – so much so that I really felt like learning Santali.

Suddenly I was struck by a strong sense of déjà vu. I had actually done something like this myself. Skrefsrud's linguistic interpretations and his attempts to break through the Santals' sound barrier had their parallel in my own life, in my year with *Rubber Soul.* I had received a communication from Margrete about a foreign language and had attempted to translate this album into something comprehensible, edifying even.

Where Skrefsrud succeeded I failed. That language remained a mystery to me.

I did not manage to realise my idea of making a programme about a man and a book. I still have a videotape on which I have preserved some lamentably bad clips from it. From these it is easy to see how difficult, not to say impossible, I found it to produce a memorable programme about a book. My powers of imagination laboured under my – then, dare I say – halting relationship with books. I was not well enough read, it was as simple as that.

Unless of course this fiasco had its roots in my inability or unwillingness to understand. My fatal defect. I possessed none of the patient resolve shown by Skrefsrud. Because Skrefsrud understood the full enormity of the task. In order to understand a man's language you had to understand everything about his society. Her society. Skrefsrud taught himself the Santals' songs. He, a Christian, participated in their rites, danced with them – danced naked some say. He, a missionary eager to communicate, realised how vital it was for him to acquaint himself with their sayings and ideas, their tunes and their customs, their knowledge of medicinal plants, their tales and legends. Consequently, Lars Skrefsrud also took an interest in the Santals as people and pled their cause with the authorities. Lars Skrefsrud was nothing less than one of the most significant figures in the history of the Santals.

I am not sure, but I have always felt that I should have spent more time on Skrefsrud. Had I done so, I might have gained more courage, and not have recoiled in such fear and cowardice when confronted with the greatest foreign culture I would ever know: a woman. I cannot rid myself of the thought: maybe Margrete would have been alive today.

To understand another human being. *A Grammar of the Language of Love.* I stood in a house in Ulleval Garden City and watched Margrete beating her head off the wall and I thought to myself: I don't understand her. This is another culture. With a different god. An unfathomable language. From my viewpoint, in my universe, this was a woman beating her head against a brick wall. In her world, it might be an attempt to shed a skin, emerge from a chrysalis. If, that is, she was not trying to show me something. A chamber of which I knew nothing – of which I was not qualified to know anything. A wordless chamber. One which no words *could* describe. All at once I felt afraid. Or lost heart. The realisation crept over me: even if I were to intervene, or she were to stop, I would never know why she did it.

In prison I gave a lot of thought to the question of how much two people need to have in common in order for a relationship to work, for them to be able to talk to one another and not past one another. How great would the lowest common denominator have to be? The mission service has a similar problem. A missionary has to try to find areas of common ground. After all, how are you supposed to translate concepts such as conscience and absolution into a language which has never heard of such things? You meet a strange woman and you wonder whether she has something, some sort of mechanism, which enables her to understand your words. Do the two of you have – pretty essential, this – the same word for love? As far as the missionary is concerned, there is, for example, the question of whether he can use the tribe's name for god as the name for God. The Santals' highest deity was known as Thakur-Jiu. Elsewhere in India, missionaries used the name Ishwara for God – Ishwara being the Sanskrit word for Lord. Lars Skrefsrud was of the opinion that in Santali God should be called Thakur, but he had to give way on this point: the word finally decided upon was Isor, a Santali version of Ishwara. Could that God ever be the same as Skrefsrud's God?

The night Margrete died, before I called the police, I spent a long time in the office we shared at Villa Wergeland. In among all her medical textbooks and journals I found some books that I had never noticed – although it could be that she had only recently put them there, having brought them from somewhere else. Many of these books were in Sanskrit, and it looked as though she knew the language – going, at least, by all the underlinings and the remarks in her handwriting. I discovered that these were copies of the Vedas, the Hindus' oldest sacred texts. A number of the other works proved to be religio-historical commentaries on the Vedas. Why had she not told me about this? I leafed through a treatise on the *Rig-Veda*. She had made lots of notes in the margins. Particularly in the chapters dealing with the tenth book. I read a little of it. But it was too involved, especially considering my frame of mind. I did, however, absorb the name of one of the hymns with which, to judge by all the underlining, she had been most taken: *Purusasukta*. Now and then, in prison, I would murmur this word to myself, like a mantra.

Those books in Sanskrit – was that her Project X?

This discovery got me thinking. I remembered that during the carnival fever which had gripped a normally so phlegmatic Oslo in the early eighties, when it seemed that everyone had had a sudden urge to transport the Norwegian capital to another, warmer, more temperamental latitude, Margrete always wore saris. She had a number of these. At the age of nineteen she had lived in New Delhi, when her father was the ambassador there. She had looked fabulous in those colourful garments; she could almost have passed for an Asian thanks to her black hair and her 'Persian' beauty. 'You didn't know you'd married a woman from the *ksatriya* caste, did you?' she said.

Oh, the bliss of unwrapping her from those exquisite lengths of fabric when we rolled home drunk from the madcap dancing in the streets. The luminous silks seemed to make her bubble with joie de vivre. 'Come here and I'll show you a position I saw carved into the stone in one of the temples at Khajuraho,' she would say, pulling me down onto the bed.

I thought I understood her. Lars Skrefsrud wrote about missionaries who claimed to be able to speak the Santals' language. One of them lost his temper and warned the Santals that he would give them a hare if they did not listen to him. The Santals told him that they would be happy to take the hare, but not his words. He had meant to say that he would punish them, but instead he said he would give them a hare. Nor were the Santals all that impressed with the Christian God when another missionary announced that: 'God sends his Holy Spirit to laugh at us.' He meant 'to comfort us'.

I was still standing in the middle of the white bedroom in Ullevål Garden City, there was no help to be had from the statuette in the corner, a golden god with half-shut eyes. She was still kneeling on the bed, banging her head against the wall. If I said something – would she construe it as comfort or ridicule? Was she aware of me at all? I sensed a distance akin to that I was to feel when Kristin was born the following year. That through the haze of pain she both knew and did not know that I was there.

The pounding seemed to intensify. She was gripping the rails of the bed-head as if they were the bars of a prison, as if she were locked up and was making a desperate attempt to break out. In any case it was not healthy. That much I could tell from the sight of her brow, from which the relatively rough brick wall had now drawn blood.

And then, without any warning, she stopped. She simply slid down onto the sheet with her eyes shut and pulled the duvet over herself. 'Margrete,' I said again. She had her back to me. She put out a hand to me, that was all – but it was something. I set down the mug of iced tea, lay on the bed, took her hand in mine. I saw, I felt, how small it was.

She fell asleep. I lay there thinking. A new tension had been introduced into my image of Margrete. If I were to describe it I might say that it was similar to the tension between a painting by Vermeer and one by Munch. The tranquil and the hysterical. A combination of *Woman Pouring Milk*, a person absorbed in an everyday chore, and *The Scream*, a person ridden with angst. Two such pictures laid one on top of the other. She was *many*. It was like being with the triplets again, all three at once.

I am no stranger to the thought that this day marked the beginning of my work on the television series *Thinking Big*, even though it would be another seven years before I had the idea for it. As soon as I saw Margrete banging her head against the wall I started looking for an excuse. I had the feeling that I would never be able to cope with her vulnerability, that I needed to have something I could blame, some demanding, all-consuming project, so that at some point – when the accusations started flying – I would be able to say: But I was so busy.

That evening, when we were sitting in the living room, I asked her about it, why had she been beating her head against the wall? 'Nothing,' she said. 'It wasn't anything,' she said. 'Don't give it a thought,' she said.

And I accepted that. I wanted to accept it. To look upon it as an isolated incident. Anyone can lose their balance, even in a flat field. But underneath an immediate sense of relief churned the certainty: I had been sent a clear signal. I could shut my eyes to it, but from that day onwards I bore a responsibility which I would much rather not have had to bear. She was not as strong as I had thought. She might survive a concentration camp, but I realised – or at least, after that incident, I suspected – that the slightest thing could be enough to break her, and I mean forever.

As a boy I had rescued a child. It had been easy – light work, you might say, in more ways than one. I had been almost annoyed by how easy it was to save a life. Sitting in that living room in Ullevål Garden City, surrounded by cast-iron Japanese lanterns and silver crosses from Ethiopia, as Margrete's fingers felt for mine again, clutching at my hand, as it were, I felt an icy pang of fear: I would not be capable of dealing with the real weightiness of life.

Although I do not see the connection I am suddenly reminded of how I met Leo, my best friend when I was in my early teens, my sparring partner in the Red Room. We had actually been in the same class for four years, but this was the first time I had really noticed him, felt like getting to know him. It happened one spring day when two of the bigger boys, a pair of notorious hooligans, had tricked some little kids into setting light to a huge stretch of tinder-dry grass at the bottom end of the estate. When the fire got out of control and began to spread towards the wood the big lads made themselves scarce and the little kids were left standing with their shoe soles scorched, watching and blubbering. Some of the mothers alerted the fire brigade. The fire was put out. One of the firemen – I can still recall those commanding bass tones – asked: 'Who started the fire?' Everybody pointed to a little lad who was still standing numbly with the matchbox clenched in his fist. I could tell just by looking at him that this boy would go under if the grown-ups believed that he was to blame, that this was the event which would change his life for ever. Then up stepped Leonard Knutzen, or maybe he had been there among the group of bystanders for some time; Leo in a spanking new pair of black Beatles boots with pointed toes – murder on the feet, but they won you bags of prestige. 'I did,' he said. One of the mothers was so angry – she had also laddered her stockings – that she promptly gave him a searing clout round the ear. Leo merely shot her a forbearing glance before he was led away by the grown-ups. It had all happened so fast and been so unexpected that none of us who knew what had really happened managed to get a word in. In any case, there was something about Leo, the black boots, his manner, the ghost of a smile on his lips, which prevented anyone from objecting. You could tell that he was tough enough to take it.

I was right in the midst of my life-saving career and felt obliged therefore to give a lot of thought to this incident. This, too, was a form of life-saving. How far would someone go in order to save a life? I found such an idea shocking. To save a life – not by some heroic deed, but by playing the bad guy almost. Or to be made to suffer even when you were innocent.

Once when we were flopped in bed after a strenuous sexual workout, between gasps for breath I told Margrete about my fear that my heart might give out. As my father's and my grandfather's had. 'I need to be careful, I've got a weak heart,' I joked. I thought she would laugh, but instead she said: 'Yes, that's what's wrong with you.'

Maybe she would be alive today if I had not had such a weak heart.

I am on board an old lifeboat once called the *Norway*, now renamed *Voyager*. I have long had the feeling that I am on a journey, making my way out of something. I say this because for so many years I was motionless, shut off. I cannot shake off the memory of Harastølen at Luster, that ludicrous one-time refugee centre halfway up a mountainside. For some days I have had the suspicion that this may also say something about me personally. That this problem: *Festung Norwegen*, the fear, and my own problem, the one which has dogged me all my life, are one and the same: an unwillingness to open oneself to one's full potential. I sometimes think of myself as a fertile egg which has put up an effective barrier against all the spermatozoa that have sought me out, that I have, metaphorically speaking, inserted a coil into the womb of my thoughts. I have been aware of my exceptional gifts, known that I might even be a wonder, but I have baulked at using these gifts. So too with love: I never dared to accept it. Like Norway I suffered from the Midas syndrome. I was a gold-plated celebrity, but I could not embrace other people, I could not return the affections of the woman who loved me.

We are out sailing again. I find myself far up the longest fjord in the world.

Dead ahead looms Haukåsen, covered with a white cape of snow. Gulls hover motionless on the wind, level with the boat, almost as if they were tame.

I feel a bit like an apprentice with the OAK Quartet. I am particularly interested in the way they communicate. Initially I was surprised to find how little of their work involved computers. The boat is of course packed to the gunnels with the latest digital aids – it is like a Noah's Ark for our technological society – but they seem to prefer large notepads and coloured pencils. Either that or they just talk and jot down key words. Dialogue, that is the key. Occasionally, through the skylight, I can observe them down in the saloon, deep in discussion, making obscure squiggles on whiteboards. And yet – much of what they do and say reminds me of my own efforts to simulate, to make believe when I was small. Is this what it all comes down to: rediscovering the realms of imagination, the childhood belief in the impossible?

The smell of *chicken korma* drifts from the galley. A gimballed Primus stove with two burners is no hindrance to Martin. My thoughts turn to Kamala. She will be joining us at Fjærland. I miss her. My meeting Kamala was – how can I put it – an undeserved gift. Kamala saved me. She saved my life, it is as simple as that.

Sometimes I have the notion that I must have acquired a new identity in prison. No one recognises me. I have been forgotten. Not my name, but my appearance. I ought to be pleased, look upon this as cover of a sort. Because in people's minds my name is linked as much with a crime as with my television celebrity. Everyone believes that I killed my wife. It was on the front page of every newspaper, it was proclaimed on the television and radio, and it was established by judge and jury in a court of law.

Why did she do it? I need to write more.

Titan

While there could, of course, be several explanations for Jonas Wergeland's fantastic flair for picture-making, his success in television should come as no surprise to any of those who know that in his youth he associated with such greats as Leonardo and Michelangelo. Many people can boast of having attended the French school in Oslo, but very few have, like Jonas Wergeland, belonged to the Italian school.

Jonas and Leo became chums towards the end of their time at elementary school, but did not become really close friends until both started at the local junior high school, Groruddalen Realskole, only a couple of stone throws from the railway station. Jonas's new road to school took him past the church and down the steep slope of Teppaveien, and in one of the old villas on this road lived Leonard Knutzen. Leonard always stood and waited for Jonas, or rather: sat waiting on the satchel which they used in those days instead of a rucksack and which, in the winter, they would send skimming down the hill like a curling stone. At one point during the eighties, after Leonardo's sensational activities became public knowledge, Jonas received a number of tempting offers from the tabloids to speak out on the subject of their boyhood friendship. He turned them all down. But he could just see the headlines, what a story, full of details which no one could have guessed at.

Leonard's family belonged to the bastion of the district's working-class; for generations they had walked at the head of the local 1st of May parade. Aptly enough, their house rested on a solid granite plinth, as if in tribute to the valley's proud stonemason tradition. Not only that, but they also overlooked the area where the first mills had been built, beside the falls at Alna. Olav Knutzen, Leonard's father was a big, burly, majestic-looking man with a backswept mane not unlike that of the writer and Nobel prize-winner Bjørnstjerne Bjørnson. It was quite obvious to Jonas that Leonard adored him. In the summer, father and son would go off on long walks in the hills together, and in the winter they would sleep out in snow holes. Leonard, too, was tall and well-built, and he had his father's flashing eyes. Leonard liked to joke that he and Jonas were of royal blood, since both their fathers – Haakon and Olav – were called after kings. 'We're both princes,' he declared, thumping Jonas on the back.

Jonas would later think of this time in his life as the Age of Wrath. Because what did they do? They sat in the Knutzens' basement, whipping themselves up into a fury. I yell, therefore I am – that was their watchword. They joined the endless ranks of young men who are filled with pent-up rage in their late teens – a wrath which may simply stem from disgruntlement over the fact that there are no changes taking place in the world around them to match the revolutions that have suddenly broken out in their heads and bodies. But for Jonas there was more to it than that: these furious verbal outbursts also acted as a safety valve, a way of giving vent to his frustration at not being able to turn his parallel thoughts, his feeling of being in possession of exceptional gifts, into something concrete – some extraordinary deed, for example.

In fact, Jonas's anger had actually burst into full flame on the day when he was brought down and hurt so badly by that Lyn player on the football pitch. He made a secret vow to stay way out on the sidelines for the rest of his life. Sometimes it seemed to him that they had founded their own republic, the Republic of the Outside Left, in Leonard's basement. Jonas espied the glimmering of an alternative mission in life: to become the greatest Norwegian outsider of all time. He had not yet abandoned his dream of making a name for himself, but as yet he had come no closer to it than when, in eighth grade, he found himself in the headmaster's office, standing stiffly to attention in front of HRH – His Royal Highness – himself, having to explain why he had committed an act of vandalism by carving his initials into his desk in large capital letters.

So when Leonard announced that they were going to work up an indignation towards society and an aloofness from it which would make the airy-fairy Kristiania Bohemia of another age look like a sweet little kindergarten, Jonas was with him all the way. It was the two of them, Jonas and Leonard, against the rest of the world. Against the rest of the universe. They would spend hours sitting in the basement, that breathing space from their otherwise intolerable and stiflingly inane surroundings, in a world which seemed even flatter than before, pouring curses and gall on the heads of moronic teachers, gormless girls, overrated sporting heroes, brainless television presenters, talentless Norwegian pop groups, the rat-faced hotdog seller at the stall next to the taxi stance; even Kjell Bondevik, the Minister for Church and Education, whom they had never met, nor seen, and about whom they knew very little, came in for his share of abuse. Not even the stupid old moon was safe from them. What was it doing, hanging about up there, enticing rocket-mad men with its cheesy face? In short, they showed no mercy. Towards anything or anybody. The word happiness, which cropped up at every turn, was taboo. 'Get mad!' was their motto. If, during this period, some brave soul had confronted them with the Bo Wang Lee question 'What should you take with you?' they would have had no hesitation in replying: 'Nothing!' Had it been up to them, the Ark could have been torpedoed out of the water any time. In the end, though, the incident on the football pitch was not enough of an explanation; Jonas did not know where all the resentment, the boundless contempt sprang from, or the unstoppable stream of sarcasm. He had heard that colours could affect people's moods and for a long time he wondered whether the walls in the basement might actually have had an effect on their subconscious minds. Because the basement walls were painted bright red. Leonard's father called it the Red Room after the café immortalised in Strindberg's novel of that name, the Bohemian haunt of artists and literati. Whatever the case, since they were now possessed of this fiery temperament, Jonas realised – after a while, at least – that what mattered was to give it direction.

He was in a fortunate position, having for years been able to observe his brother's demonstrations of different possible plans of attack. Daniel – who in Jonas's mind was always not just one, but ten years his senior – had proved very early on to have a talent for playing the outsider. This was made perfectly clear, if it had not been before, one time when he had the mumps. He had come swaggering into the living room, all puffy-cheeked and wearing Rakel's cigarette-fumed biker jacket – the resemblance to a very young Marlon Brando was staggering. 'The wild one,' he growled with feverish relish before staggering back to bed.

Jonas never knew where his brother found his inspiration, where he picked up his knowledge of Marlon Brando, for example, or other 'rebels' who were not particularly well-known at that time, or certainly not to boys of Daniel's age. When asked, usually at large family gatherings, to speak about his plans for the future, he did not get flustered and stammer, as other teenagers might; Daniel would get quietly to his feet, his eyes burning, and commence by intoning: 'I have a dream …' He once went on a hunger strike for several days – he was actually capable of such a thing – in protest against his parents 'strict' ruling that he had to be in by nine o'clock in the evening. He solemnly declared that he was acting in the spirit of Mahatma Ghandi, and Haakon and Åse Hansen, inwardly smiling, were forced to relent. An attempt to mount a demonstration to demand that the whole estate be allowed to pick the apples in Wolfgang Michaelsen's garden came, however, to nothing. Daniel had a failing. Just as Jonas wavered between various projects in life, so Daniel wavered between different rebel role models. One day he was to be found wearing a funny black cap, nasally whining 'A Hard Rain's A-Gonna Fall', the next he would be driving his mother to despair by charging about with a bucket in one hand, splattering paint onto huge sheets of paper spread out on the floor. He simply could not discover what his field of rebellion should be.

Jonas had always been convinced that his brother would end up as a soldier, become a sort of guerrilla leader. As a child, Daniel had loved everything to do with war and fighting and had evinced the most tireless inventiveness when it came to weapons. He very quickly discovered that it was best to load a cap gun with a strip of caps four layers thick, and by making an adjustment to the workings of the battery-driven machine guns which later appeared on the market he could produce a noise that left the little kids stunned. There was something special about the rubber bands and scraps of leather from which Daniel's catapults were constructed that made his stones fly further; he refined peashooters to the point where the other kids feared him as much as an Amazon Indian with a blowpipe and poison darts. He was forever coming up with better materials for his bows, and fixed the lead tips from real bullets to his arrows. If not on the military front then Jonas certainly expected his brother to make a name for himself within the field of weapon technology. Instead Daniel, who also happened to be a hell of a ladies' man, became a man of the cloth. So what happened?

Daniel was what Jonas would have called a tiresomely high achiever. He just kept forging ahead, as if on some endless red carpet, did not know the meaning of the word 'opposition'. It was the same with sport, which also looked like being the one area in which Daniel could give his rebellious tendencies full play. Daniel had always been a fitness fanatic. He had, for example, been Grorud's first proud owner of a Bullworker, a piece of equipment not unlike a telescope or a bazooka for which ads had suddenly started popping up everywhere and which just as quickly became the word on every boy's lips, because it could give you a bull-like physique in no time flat. Jonas could not compress the cylinder by so much as a centimetre. Daniel, on the other hand, pumped it in and out with ease, while at the same time – as if the masturbation-style action automatically led his thoughts in that direction – holding forth on his latest girlish conquest.

It was, however, in athletics that Daniel was expected to do great things. He meant to walk – or rather, run – in the footsteps of the Kvalheim brothers who hailed from the flats down by Grorud station. Jonas had always admired Daniel's alarming gift for self-abuse; it could be snowing buckets and still his brother would be out running; he practised interval and tempo training until he collapsed or threw up. And through it all he remained a rebel. Where Jonas, more by accident than design, had a scar in the shape of a little x above his eyebrow, there came a day when Daniel put a large X after his name. This came in the wake of the summer Olympics in Mexico City. Daniel insisted on being known only as Daniel X and that autumn, at an athletics meet at which he had won every event, he mounted the podium wearing dark sunglasses and a black glove on his right fist which he held demonstratively in the air. It all went so well and was so outrageously provocative until some aggrieved soul asked him what he was protesting against. At first Daniel was lost for an answer. It was one thing to protest against curfews and high garden fences, quite another to stick one's fist in the air, and a black-gloved fist at that. He saved the situation with a watertight reply: 'Everything!'

But in protesting against everything you protested against nothing. And when it came to the crunch Daniel's anger, too, lacked direction. So maybe that was why he put an X after his name, to indicate that he was searching for a particular, but hidden, field which lay there waiting for him and his rebellious urges. To Jonas, the letter X seemed more indicative of a mysterious, unknown side to Daniel's character. This suspicion was soon confirmed. His big brother finally met with opposition: a nerve-wracking experience which brought him down to earth with a bump. Daniel ran, as it were, smack into the gravity of life. And, of course, it involved a girl

Prior to this event and parallel with Daniel's more harmless excesses, Jonas and Leonard conducted their passive protest in the Red Room. They were rebels without a cause. For months at a time, against all good advice, they let the sun go down on their anger. After a while, though, there was not much to be got out of whiling away their time down in the basement, nursing their seething contempt for everything and everyone. It was like sitting next to a pot of boiling water with nothing to put in it. For a time, therefore, their anger looked set to take a socially conscious turn. They decided to follow in the footsteps of Leonard's father. And Leonard's father was not just anybody.

One forenoon on board the *Voyager*, as we were about to bear due south into Aurlandsfjord, I came upon Jonas Wergeland sitting on a bollard. He was writing in a book which he must have bought in Lærdal, a big thick notebook with blank pages and stiff covers. We were just sailing past the Frønningen estate with its fine, white manor-house and the pine forest behind – we already knew that this was the family home of a famous painter, that the place even had its own art gallery. Martin was on the foredeck, on the lookout for killer whales – a school had recently been spotted in the area. The smell of the loaves he was baking in the old wood oven was already drifting up from the galley. Jonas Wergeland made no attempt to conceal the fact that he was writing, he merely looked up, smiled. I noticed that he wrote in a big, neat script. Like a beginner, someone who has not had much experience of writing by hand. It occurred to me that he might have been inspired by the surrounding scenery, by Sognefjord. If, that is, it was not the suspicion, or the knowledge, rather, that I was writing about him.

I had not meant to write anything. I do not know when the idea came to me. Maybe it was when he spoke about his *auto-da-fé*. He had spent several years working on a manuscript. As far as I know I was the only one to have seen it. I thought of Nehru, who wrote a history of the world for his daughter while he was in prison. For some years I regularly received envelopes containing twenty or thirty pages which I, in turn, handed back when I went to visit him – or rather, they had to pass through security control before getting to him. I read it like a serial. He did not ask for my comments. Sometimes I would say something, other times not. Had I known that he would destroy it, I might have made a copy. Although I don't know. It was so – how can I put it – clumsy. Or, at least: there was so much of it, it was such a muddle. As if he was forever trying to get everything down. Even so, now and again he would write a passage which completely bowled me over, something so dazzlingly astute and original. And poignant. I read it with a mixture of confusion and gratitude. He also wrote about people and events that no one else had ever mentioned. About Mr Dehli the schoolmaster, about Bo Wang Lee, about a breathtaking kiss on Karl Johans gate. Nonetheless, I always had the feeling that he was circling around something, a central point which he could not capture in words.

So when he destroyed the whole lot, every last sheet of it, I was struck by a sense of responsibility. I had read it. I remembered a lot of it. Certain details word-perfect even. And I knew that many of these stories deserved to be made public. *Ought* to be made public. I also had something of an advantage. I knew a lot from before. In my more presumptuous moments I actually felt as though I knew everything. I had once drawn pictures with him. I had sat up in a tree with him and asked him why the sky was blue. I had been a child in his arms. And a child sees a great deal. I did not know him from the television, I knew him face to face; I knew him with my fingers and my cheek and my nose. Not only that but, particularly during the years when my brain was at its most malleable, he had been the person to whom I talked the most. I loved him more than anyone in the world. If the young Jonas was right, if the whole point of life was to save lives, then I had a job to do: to save him, metaphorically speaking, from drowning in lies.

What held me back was not my inevitable sympathy for him – I considered this a strength, not a weakness – but the thought of having to write a book, of actually putting words on paper. Because I realised that no other medium would do. If I was to get my message across. If I was to succeed in driving a wedge of doubt into the fossilised myths surrounding him. If I was ever to be able to say something about his genius, the origins of his creativity, the motives behind that peerless work of art *Thinking Big* – arguably Norway's greatest cultural contribution to the world in the twentieth century. I would of course have preferred to use my own form, my own medium, but that was still in its infancy, it was nowhere near being fully developed. And few people understood it. Few people were *willing* to understand it. I had to make a compromise, take up again a tool I had abandoned in favour of something better. I was also forced to resort to a genre, the biography, which was akin to an antiquated, all but obsolete – though still popular – fictional form. It scared me. To have so much to say, to know so much – and to have to employ such an imperfect, passé mode of expression. To risk being dismissed for being too conventional, for sticking to the set rules for how to render characters vivid and believable; notions based on simple, recognisable elements, a set of 'valid' devices born of centuries of literature. I felt as though I was setting to work with a hammer and chisel.

I knew, of course, that in undertaking this task, I was stepping out into a whole industry – or perhaps I should say: onto a battlefield. And the merchandise to be fought over was Jonas Wergeland, his life and reputation. Not least the latter. At the point when I started writing, eleven books about him – not to mention countless news reports and articles – had already been published. Of the eight which appeared after his conviction and imprisonment, six would have to be described as extremely negative, almost derisive, with their hindsightful, moralistic tone. The two exceptions were Kamala Varma's book and the curious biography, penned by another it is true, but at Rakel W. Hansen's behest. I soon realised that my own writing style had been coloured by these two last-named works – possibly because in them I discerned something I could use, an approach which I recognised from my proper work.

The writing of Jonas Wergeland's story should have been a laudable project. He was a figure from a period of change, in many ways the last representative of a bygone age, a television age – dare I say: an uncomplicated age. And yet, despite my good intentions I could not rid myself of an underlying scepticism. Or doubt. As I wrote, as I attempted to recapitulate some of the stories Jonas himself had grappled with in his manuscript, I kept wondering whether it was possible, in this limited and dauntingly simple form, to gain some clue to the one question which occupied me more and more and which rapidly became my deepest motive for writing: Why did he do it?

Throughout the sail down Aurlandsfjord he sat up on deck, making notes quite openly. He kept looking up, looking around him, as if he could not get enough of this landscape, could hardly believe it was real. Now and again he would catch my eye, smile, then drop his gaze as if suddenly feeling shy. Although in truth he *was* shy. I always had the feeling that his eyes were the key. Sometimes they would glow so fiercely that it was almost frightening. It was so ardent, that look; he seemed to have to make a conscious effort to tone it down. I have heard women describe those eyes as 'penetrating'. They felt that he saw all the way in to their innermost recesses. Or *beyond* them, as Kamala said. But it was not that simple. The real reason for the look in his eyes was shyness. The fact of being strong, but embarrassed by his strength. It was, as I have already suggested, this that set him apart from other television personalities. Such a focused gaze, such an intense presence, combined with a sort of bashfulness, as if he really did not want to be there at all. Was constantly questioning, felt uncomfortable with his own part in things. When you saw his face on the TV screen you had the impression that he was doing his best to hide something, some piquant secret. The effect was astonishing. A bit like seeing a good actor underplaying a part. Television viewers could scarcely believe their eyes: here, at last, was someone – a baffling exception to the hordes of exhibitionist, publicity-mad NRK personalities – who held something back, a man who could have ruled the world, but chose to appear on Norwegian television. That was why they loved him.

I was glad that he had hit it off so well with the crew of the *Voyager*, especially with Martin. I could hear them down in the galley, discussing how to make *pasta al burro*. 'Don't argue with me,' Jonas was saying. 'I learned to cook from an Italian chef in Grorud. A chef by the name of Leonardo, no less.' With Hanna he tended to talk mostly about music; he was impressed by the string quartet collection she had brought along with her, although he could not understand how anyone could prefer Bartók to Haydn.

At this point I became aware of a problem. I was finding it more and more difficult to work on two projects at once, even though one of them, the book about him, was simply stewing away at the back of my mind. I realised that I was observing him as much as our surroundings – which ought to have had my complete and undivided attention. While studiously mapping out folk museums, farm museums and galleries in Aurland and Flåm, I was just as busy studying him. I observed him as if seeing him in the flesh could show me whether what I had written, what I was thinking of writing, was correct. True.

I began to suspect that his presence was, to an ever-greater extent, colouring my ideas concerning the OAK Quartet's product, the groundwork for which we were laying on this sail along the fjord. Or that, in my mind, he had taken charge of the project. Or that these two were one and the same. As I wandered around Aurlandsvangen, looking at the shoe factory, the remarkable church – Sogne Cathedral – and the old Abelheim guesthouse, he was constantly in my thoughts. One day when I had gone for a walk on my own to consider whether we ought to link the writer Per Sivle with Flåm or with Stalheim and whether we should include anything at all on humanist

Absalon Pedersøn Beyer – who hailed from Skjerdal, just north of Aurland – I suddenly stopped to look at Jonas Wergeland. He was sitting by the fence surrounding the playing fields alongside the river, up next to the school and the community centre, watching some boys practising the long jump. All at once I remembered why he should be so interested in seeing how far the boys could jump. I got distracted, forgot all about Per Sivle.

In everything he did or said I saw or heard stories, or connections with stories. The evening before we left Lærdal I happened to open a document and read something I had written about his programme on Thor Heyerdahl. He could not have known this, but when we cast off the next morning he said, with a sly glint in his eye: 'This boat is another *Kon-Tiki*. A vessel which will prove whether it is possible to sail from the continent of the past to that of the future. From an old life to a new.' He was talking, of course, about himself, but still.

Deep inside Aurlandsfjord Jonas stood gazing up at the steep slopes and high mountains rising on either side. 'What is Samarkand compared to this?' I heard him murmur. Although, did he actually say that? Or was it only a voice inside my head? At one point, after staring open-mouthed at my first sight of the tiny church at Undredal, the snow-covered peaks rearing up out of the valley beyond, I happened to glance round, to look up at Stigen, the little hill farm perched on its ledge – had people really lived there, and managed to scrape a living from it – and saw Jonas staring at a power line running across the fjord just ahead of us, strung with those spherical orange markers that look like basketballs; I heard later that a Dutch fighter plane had had a near miss there. Jonas stood there, utterly mesmerised, gripping the main shroud and peering up at the high-voltage cable. 'Are you thinking of Lauritz, your uncle?' I asked gently. He nodded, somewhat surprised that I should be able to guess this. I was not alone in seeing stories in the landscape. When Carl arrived with the car – he had driven through the new tunnel and was full of ideas for ways in which we could present the most spectacular stretches of road around the fjord – and we prepared to carry on down to Flåm, to see what we could possibly make of the railway line there, which had already been done to death, Jonas chose instead to go and take a look at a dam built as part of the hydro-electric development in the Aurland region. He ordered a taxi, asked to be taken to Låvisdalen. He wanted to find the spot where Olav Knutzen had taken that famous photograph of Leonard. 'You understand, don't you?' he said to me. I understood.

Leonard's father was, as I have said, not just anybody. Some people may recognise the name Olav Knutzen, since he was at one time a well-known photographer with the working-class press. And if the last part of his surname evokes associations with a Zen master then that is not really so sur-prising, since Leonard's father could almost have scored a bull's eye blindfold. He had such an eye for things, as well as a set of values so solid that he could make a picture of a granite quarry in Grorud seem as fascinating as the rock tombs in Egypt's Valley of Kings.

The basement room in which Jonas and Leonard nursed their youthful wrath was not only painted red – an ideological prerequisite, you might say; the walls were also covered with framed photographs calling to mind the growth and the triumphs of modern Norway. Because Olav Knutzen was a staff photographer with *Aktuell* weekly; he called himself 'a reporter with a camera'. *Aktuell* was the sort of publication in which the pictures were as important as the words. The international flagship of such publications was *Life* magazine. These days, when the full media circus seems to be on hand for every occurrence, it is easy to forget that there was a time when a single photograph could be the cause of an event becoming known worldwide. As Thor Heyerdahl discovered when he sold the photographs from the *Kon-Tiki* expedition to *Life*: pictures which captured the imagination of the people in a way that written reports of the expedition could not do.

It is to be hoped that many do still remember *Aktuell*, that admirable weekly, which had its foundations in the labour movement and its roots in the old ideal of popular education. Younger generations may well find it hard to imagine that such a thing ever existed in Norway. And if anyone should wonder whether we have lost sight in Norway of certain ideals and values, all you have to do is lay some copies of the old *Aktuell* alongside its modern-day equivalent: the tabloid *Se og Hør*. Jonas was, of course, familiar with *Aktuell* before he and Leonard became best friends, not least thanks to the pile of old copies in the attic of his grandfather's house on Hvaler. Jonas never tired of reading those dusty magazines. Which is to say: he looked at the pictures – photographs of reindeer races at Kautokeino, or from a revival meeting in Skien, or from a farm halfway up a mountainside run by two sisters, little old ladies in their eighties, or from Mandal where – Jonas stared in disbelief – Arnardo's elephants could be seen lumbering through the streets. I think it is safe to say that during the first couple of decades after the war this magazine represented the contemporary equivalent of television. Like an earlier day's *Round Norway* it presented the country to the people.

While waiting for Leonard to finish his dinner meatballs Jonas would sit in the Knutzens' red-painted basement, leafing through the back numbers of *Aktuell* ranged proudly on the shelf alongside the Workers' Encyclopedia – as if this were all the learning one needed. He studied picture spreads depicting the building, step-by-step, of a tanker, or the life at the huge steelworks in

Mo i Rana. Some of the street scenes in the older numbers were especially fascinating, not least if the subjects were familiar to him. Had the Eastern station really looked like that? And the bus stop by the gasworks? Such photographs were clear proof of how time flew. Only fifteen years ago, and yet things seemed unrecognisable. For Jonas, *Aktuell* was rather like an Illustrated Classics version of an ideology. Jonas Wergeland never read up on the theoreticians of the labour movement, but he always felt that he had some knowledge of the subject, just as he knew a bit about Joseph Conrad's *Lord Jim* after reading the comic-strip version.

Aktuell presented articles from all over the world, but what Jonas liked best were the features and series on Norway. From the Red Room's somewhat dilapidated sofa he could accompany the fishermen to the fishing fields, lumberjacks into the forest, construction workers into tunnels; *Aktuell* described a day in the life of a checkout lady, it followed the course of rubbish men through the city and depicted the world inhabited by the potato peelers at the Rainbow Restaurant. Below many of his favourite photographs Jonas could read the name of Leonard's father, Olav Knutzen. Sometimes all it said was OK, as if this were a stamp indicating that these pictures or – why not? – the reality they portrayed had been approved. 'In a basement room in Grorud I got to know Norway,' he was to say later. When Jonas Wergeland thought back on the golden age of the Norwegian Labour Party he always thought of *Aktuell* magazine.

What with his father working in the church and his mother at the Grorud Ironmonger's, Jonas was a little envious of Leonard. Both *his* parents worked in the city centre. And not only that, but in buildings on the city's finest square. Because if Oslo had a heart at that time, a real, pulsating heart – as London had its Smithfield Market, Paris had Les Halles and Rome the Campo de' Fiori – then it had to be Youngstorget. Leonard's mother worked in an office at the People's House, headquarters of the National Federation of Trade Unions, and his father was based on the first floor of the People's Theatre building itself, when, that is, he was not out travelling.

In the summer especially, the boys were forever running into town to meet Olav Knutzen on Youngstorget. Leonard always swelled with pride when his father came walking towards them with his Leica or, even better, the two-eyed Rolleiflex dangling over his stomach. There was something so bohemian about his big, burly figure. Apart from the eyes. These Jonas thought of as *sharp*. It was almost as if every now and again the z in the middle of his surname triggered a flash in his eyes, a little bolt of lightning. Olav Knutzen often took pictures of the boys standing among the market stalls on the square, munching plums or pears. In later years Jonas would often look at the copies of these photographs which he had been given, because they documented something he had already forgotten: how that time-honoured square had once been a cornucopian fruit and vegetable basket, possibly even a Red Room, for the whole city.

Leonard was proud of his father, and especially of those keen eyes of his. 'That's what it all comes down to,' he often said when they were sitting in the Knutzens' basement room. 'The eye. The ability to perceive the world.' He believed that he had inherited this gift. Leonard was, in general, uncommonly interested in the attributes passed on from parent to child. And Jonas had to admit that there was something about Leonard's eyes, a quality reminiscent of a finely ground optic, an exceptional system of lenses, of the sort found in a Hasselblad camera. Jonas had been aware of this right from the moment when Leo stepped into his life, in a pair of Beatles boots, after the brushfire: those dark, *alert* eyes which seemed constantly to be on the lookout for things that were hidden from others. 'You have a "da Vinci eye"', Jonas told him. They agreed to train this one sense: their sight. As a beginning. And in so doing they might even find a direction for their anger; discover, throw into relief the one detail which would lift the lid on the whole shebang. And that was exactly what Leonard would, unwittingly, do.

Since there was another reason, besides the colour of its walls, for calling their basement den the Red Room, the most obvious form of training seemed to be to join Olav Knutzen in the darkroom which he had set up in one of the storage rooms in the basement. Jonas was in his element in that dim, orange light, surrounded by the sweetish smell of chemicals; he loved the sense of anticipation as shadows began to form on the white paper in the developing dish, to then consolidate into sharp images in the clear liquid: Jonas and Leonard, grinning, each with their ice cream, and with the police headquarters and Youngstorget arcade in the background; a close-up of Jonas with a plum between his teeth, so sharp and with so much depth to it that the dusty, purplish bloom on the plum was readily discernible even though the print was in black-and-white. Later, when Jonas thought of Olav Knutzen, he would envy the way he could endow a snapshot with an eternal dimension, something which the ephemeral images on the TV screen could never do.

For Jonas, the darkroom with its red ambience and its chemical processes also came to symbolise a space one could inhabit mentally. Soon he was going to fall in love with a girl called Eva. Very much in love. As if his wrath had found its parallel in *desire*. This was in the middle of that stage in life when one is almost always in love, when one suddenly has the ability to blow up the tiniest detail to colossal proportions, not to mention a capacity for developing the most bizarre images in one's mind. This is a time when, as most people seem to intuit, it is only a short stumble from love to stark, staring madness.

Jonas was in the school playground one day, and it would not be too far from the truth to say that an anorak made him see red. He never did figure out how or why it happened, whether it could be attributed to a keen-honed eye or what. He felt as though he was in a darkroom, watching a face come into view on a sheet of white paper, as if out of nowhere. All of a sudden she simply stepped out of the crowd during break at Grorud School and was so obviously the One. She was one of a kind, too. Words such as 'proud' or 'noble' sprang to mind when you looked at her. Eva N. was then, and even more so later, the sort of figure whom male artists would use as a model when illustrating the Norse sagas. First and foremost she was, however, a notorious skier. She wore a red anorak all winter, as if life itself was a high moor, and in the plastic pocket in her wallet she carried a picture, not of Cliff Richard or Mick Jagger, but of cross-country champion Gjermund Eggen. She went skiing as often as she possibly could, it was her passion. Every weekend, Sundays in particular, she would set out from Grorud on long expeditions into Nordmarka. From reliable sources Jonas learned that she almost always stopped in at Sinober, the Skiing Association café at the northern end of Lillomarka, and so he devised a plan whereby he would bump into her there, accidentally on purpose and in such a way that she would take him for an expert skier, a real bouillon and malt-beer-drinking mile-eater who more or less lived on the hills in winter.

In order to understand just what a crack-brained plan this was, one has to bear in mind what an exceptional antipathy to skiing Jonas had. One reason for this was Daniel's excessive keenness for this very sport. Once or twice as a small boy Jonas had attempted to keep up with his brother on the many tough slopes leading up to Lilloseter: an experience which would appear to have satisfied his need for the taste of blood in his mouth and the feel of a string vest sticking to his back as he stood on a senseless finish line gasping for breath, with his whole body pulsating and his lungs feeling way too small.

So it says a lot about his achievement and even more about his red-hot infatuation that for several Sundays in succession he went for long runs along the ski trails of Lillomarka, despite being in very poor skiing form, to say the least of it. He staked all his hopes on running into her on the lot outside the main building at Sinober, possibly while she was engrossed in the inscrutable mysteries of ski waxing. Jonas was so besotted with Eva that he was quite sure luck would be on his side. Although in his frame of mind you did not think in terms of luck. You dealt in imperatives. She *would* be there – waiting almost – at Sinober. And how was he to make his entrance onto the lot? In this lay the very heart of his plan, the cunning detail designed to win her heart: he would come skimming in like a ski racer, or one of the elks of Lillomarka. At full speed and with a rime-coated face as proof of how fast he had been going.

This was a trick he had learned. If it was cold enough, and fortunately on those Sundays it was, he would pull up at the foot of the last slope before the café – having taken it nice and easy up to that point, while constantly looking over his shoulder, just in case *she* happened to be coming up behind him – and puff his breath up onto his face, building up a becoming layer of frost on his eyelashes, eyebrows and the edge of his woolly hat. And bearing this irrefutable evidence of breakneck speed he would sprint over the last rise and come swooshing onto the clearing in front of the café, hawking and spitting and panting just heavily enough.

Sadly, the one thing lacking was the key ingredient: Eva was conspicuous by her absence. That he received approving glances from other skiers every time he swept onto the lot decked with frost like a Lillomarka elk was of little comfort. No red anorak, no noble girl with strong fingers wrapped around a tub of ski wax or a mug of blackcurrant cordial. Sunday after Sunday Jonas stood at the foot of that last slope, breathing frost onto his eyebrows, and even he could see the funny side of it, see himself from the outside – this boy, puffing and blowing like some animals do when mating. But even this laughable bird's eye view of the situation could not stop him; he was convinced that Eva would only deign to bestow her attention, a *glance*, on him, if she could see what a brilliant skier he was.

Sunday after Sunday Jonas went haring off into the forest; it occurred to him that these cross-country treks might be a sublimated form of anger, that here on the ski trail he had actually found a direction for his wrath: love. Sunday after Sunday, by dint of some hefty double poling – over the last stretch at least – he would skim onto the lot at Sinober which, in his mind, had gradually become a symbol of a crazed red haze, an infatuation which he found almost frightening. But Eva always seemed to be somewhere else in Nordmarka. So Jonas ascertained, with equal disbelief, every time; he did not see how she could *not* be there when he had strained every sinew, masked himself so magnificently, rime-encrusted eyelashes and all, and was so bone-wearily lovesick. He stood outside the Sinober lodge café, feeling trapped, possibly because he happened to be staring down at his 'Rat-Trap' ski bindings. But still he held to his belief that he would meet her there. And sometimes he would glance up and, for a split-second, see a mirage, a red anorak, and he would be as sure as ever again: next Sunday she would be there. He could already picture the look on her face: first amazement, then sincere delight and finally: her inevitable, reciprocated love.

In the meantime there was some consolation and distraction to be found in the orange glow of the darkroom, watching Leonard's father forcing, as it were, negatives into something positive. From the very outset of their friendship Jonas had kept telling Leonard: 'You should take up photography, too, you know. If you want to be any good, you need to get started right away.' Jonas felt so strongly about this that on more than one occasion he actually thrust Olav Knutzen's well-worn Rolleiflex at his chum, rather like a relay baton. Leonard never took it. He felt he ought to make it his aim to do something else. It was not enough merely to foster the gifts you had inherited – a pair of penetrating eyes; you also had to improve upon them. 'I know where I'm going to start,' he said one autumn. 'With films. We should always surpass our fathers' achievements.' Leonard did not know how right he would prove to be.

Again: how could anyone fail to see it? When one considers everything that has been written about Jonas Wergeland's ingenious and innovative television programmes, it is a mystery that no one has ever mentioned his passion for the most closely related of art forms.

The next couple of years were pretty hectic. After a little doctoring of their school ID cards – a crime of which not a few were guilty – Jonas Wergeland and Leonard Knutzen became in all probability the youngest ever members of Oslo Film Club. And if anyone got wise to their scam they never let on. Leonard was big for his age anyway, and Jonas masked himself as well as he could – if not with frost then with a moody expression. During the late sixties, every Saturday afternoon without fail they would go along to the Saga cinema, or sometimes the Scala, and take their seats together with people who viewed new Polish or Japanese films in utter silence, or sighed with pleasure at Orson Welles's three-minute long, unbroken opening shot from *Touch of Evil*.

Jonas started going to the cinema more often, on his own too, not knowing that this interest would one day lead him to the foremost university in England. He was very soon convinced: the motion picture had to be the highest form of art created by man. Nothing had ever spoken to him as strongly as this. Through the photographs in *Aktuell* and the many films he would eventually see, he discovered man's weakness for illusion. Because even though, when he took his seat in the cinema and saw with his own two eyes that the stretch of canvas hanging above the stage was flat – as flat as the world, he was struck every time by the unimaginable depths which this two-dimensional panel acquired as soon as the house lights went down and the stream of images was projected onto the screen. He realised that he had underestimated his inherent capacity for embellishing upon the story, investing the magnified pictures on the flat surface in front of him with thoughts and dreams.

This may go some way to explaining why, in the television series *Thinking Big*, he very surprisingly and, in the eyes of some, most provocatively, chose film as the angle from which to address Thor Heyerdahl's achievements and the significance of his work. True, Jonas Wergeland concentrated on the *Kon-Tiki* – but not on the expedition as such. The whole, absolutely all, of the programme on Heyerdahl dealt with *Kon-Tiki* the film.

It is often said that people today do not really believe that something has happened, in real life that is, until they see it on television.

Thor Heyerdahl's stroke of genius lay in the fact that he actually foresaw the advent of this way of thinking only two years after the end of World War II, when he embarked on the *Kon-Tiki* expedition: possibly the most famous of all bold Norwegian expeditions. With him he took not only food and drink, he also had a cine camera. In our own day this has become the first commandment for all journeys of this nature; even solo expeditioners to the North Pole make sure to film themselves while, one is tempted to say, freezing to death or being eaten by polar bears. Jonas Wergeland's programme on Heyerdahl rested on the thesis that the documentary film on the *Kon-Tiki* voyage, and a crudely shot film at that, constituted a greater feat than the voyage itself.

And apropos those two budding rebels in the Red Room, when it came to a keen-honed eye Thor Heyerdahl was the perfect role model for them. When he looked at a map of the world he did not, as others did, see the continents as being separated from one another. Instead, he saw the oceans as linking them to one another. And he saw that the Earth was round, even though the scientific reality was flat. Not least, Heyerdahl understood the importance of the ocean currents, and advanced heretical theories on migrations across the Pacific Ocean. What if the islands of Polynesia had been discovered by voyagers from the east? What if someone in ancient times had managed to sail from Peru to Polynesia? All of the figures in Jonas Wergeland's television series were discoverers: Ibsen with his monocled eye, Foyn with his long telescope, Skrefsrud with his laryngoscope – a linguistic magnifying glass, if you like. And Heyerdahl with his eye for connections. Columbus may have discovered the sea route to America, but it was Heyerdahl who discovered the next stage, as it were, of that sea route, who showed that the world was one continuous realm; that for thousands of years the possibilities had existed for contact between different cultures, despite the great distances between them.

Scornful experts – unwittingly displaying the sort of glaring ignorance so often found among so-called scholars – dismissed any likelihood of a prehistoric voyage from South America. For one thing, they were positive the raft would absorb so much water that it would sink after two weeks. So in order to prove them wrong Heyerdahl set out on just such a journey, on a craft similar to the one which he believed these early seafarers had used. The *Kon-Tiki* expedition was, first and foremost, an undertaking which Heyerdahl felt compelled to carry out in order to make people take his hypotheses seriously. Thor Heyerdal's voyage on those nine balsa logs lashed together was part of an attempt to prove a fact. But instead he gave birth to a piece of fiction. Jonas Wergeland did not know what Heyerdahl himself felt about this paradox, whether he would have regretted having underestimated the way in which such a sail would appeal to people's imaginations, but in Jonas's book it was a far greater achievement to star in a modern-day odyssey than to prove a scientific theory. Heyerdahl could write fat treatises till he was blue in the face. In the mind of the world he would always be the *Kon-Tiki* man. That was why Jonas Wergeland presented the whole programme from the angle of the *Kon-Tiki* film, of Heyerdahl as a film director. In Jonas's eyes, it was the film which had made Heyerdahl who he was.

After just twenty minutes' instruction in a camera shop in Oslo, amateur photographer Thor Heyerdahl used his 16 mm camera for the first time to film the building of the raft at the Callao naval yard outside of Lima. The US government had given them a supply of film, but when they went to collect their equipment at the customs in Peru they found that most of the colour film had been stolen. A lot of film would also be ruined at sea by the dampness and the heat. So there are no interior shots of the raft, no scenes showing Heyerdahl writing in his diary or Bengt Danielsson with his feet up, reading one of the seventy-three sociological and ethnographical works which he had brought with him. But Heyerdahl captured a lot of other stuff on film: flying fish on the deck, huge whales rolling on the surface, the crew hauling dolphins aboard. He filmed members of the expedition cooking, measuring the height of the sun with a sextant, playing guitar, dipping a pen in the ink from an octopus. Shots of the raft taken from a distance – which Heyerdahl obtained by rowing recklessly far out in the little rubber dinghy – turned out particularly well. He went on using the camera until everyone had been picked up from Raroia, the atoll on which they foundered after sailing and drifting 8,000 kilometres across the Pacific Ocean. By which time he had, almost symbolically, shot as many thousand feet of film.

Heyerdahl wanted to try and sell the film, so he had it developed in New York. Useless, said the people from Paramount and RKO after the first showing of the unedited footage, or extracts from it. Besides having been shot at the wrong speed the film was a mass of flashes and flickering, a hodgepodge of images: pelicans taking off, waves washing over the deck, a floundering fish, close-ups of the sail, of a man's legs, a snake mackerel, a face, clouds.

And shark heads from every conceivable angle. Only occasionally were there longer scenes in which something actually happened. Viewing the uncut film, for hour after hour, was a genuinely disheartening experience, even for Thor Heyerdahl; these disjointed fragments were pretty much the very opposite of the great unified whole, the existence of which he was trying to prove.

The one detail above all others which Jonas Wergeland chose to pluck out of Thor Heyerdahl's eventful life, the moment he decided to blow up, was Heyerdahl's decision to cut and edit a 16 mm version of the film himself. In a scientific cliffhanger to rival the search for the structure of the DNA molecule, the programme showed how for days Heyerdahl and his assistants worked round the clock in a hotel room in New York, cutting the hopeless raw footage down to just over an hour of film. In sequences that were as jerky and chaotic as the uncut film, Jonas Wergeland showed Heyerdahl looking and looking, searching for scenes which could be cut out and spliced together. There were close-ups of flickering countdowns, of the splicer, of eyes and frantic fingers. Long, monotonous shots of food being prepared or crew members manning the rudder were cut up into a lot of shorter clips – shots of Lolita the parrot in particular were slotted in at regular intervals; they alternated between wide shots taken from the top of the mast and close-ups, they switched back and forth between depictions of everyday tasks and more dramatic scenes, such as the visit from the whales and yet more shark-fishing, sheer action drama. The scene depicting the expedition's final and most alarming moment – the collision with the deadly coral reef – was little short of a masterpiece, with an effective cut to the telegraph operator, ostensibly sending a last report on their position, though this was in actual fact a shot from a totally different stage of the voyage. This, Jonas Wergeland told the viewers, was Thor Heyerdahl's greatest achievement: a cut-and-paste *Kon-Tiki* expedition; days and nights spent in a hotel room, editing a jumbled, unusable mass of images into a film which captured the interest of the whole world by saying something about what a single, inspired individual could accomplish.

Through this, Wergeland also managed to say something about the importance of the montage technique. Even for a scientist like Thor Heyerdahl. In the hands of a skilled editor uninteresting material can be rendered fascinating. And to some extent that was what Heyerdahl did: wove information together in a new way. The pieces were all there, but no one had ever put them together before. Heyerdahl combined arguments from archaeology and ethnology, folklore and religious research, botany and zoology, linguistics and physical anthropology. But he also took account of the Polynesians' own legends, discoveries from ancient times and natural phenomena such as winds and ocean currents. There was, he said, a need for a new kind of science, with researchers from different fields working together, building, assembling.

The big test, a moment every bit as crucial as that when the raft had to force Raroia's jagged reef, came with the talk and the presentation of the cine film at the Explorers' Club on an autumn day in 1947. This was the *Kon-Tiki* film's real world premiere. Half an hour beforehand Heyerdahl was still gluing the strips of film together. During the showing he received the first sign of what was to come: the fairy-tale ending. Because, just as with a good story the less one embroiders upon it the more likely it is to appeal to the imagination, so too with this simple and technically flawed film. No matter how colourless and wavery the pictures may be, in their minds, people will blow them up. The greyer, the better. The flatter, the deeper. It was a huge success. The audience went wild.

Thanks to a couple of exceptionally committed and technically proficient Swedes, foremost among them Olle Nordemar, it was later possible to re-edit the original film from the lecture at the Explorers' Club to the point where, on 13 January 1950, *Kon-Tiki* could have its cinema premiere in Stockholm. And, although the contribution made by the Swedes – not least in improving on the editing – must not be forgotten, this was, and still is, the proudest day in Norwegian film history. The *Kon-Tiki* went on to crown its voyage by bringing home an Oscar to Norway – the country's first, and for a very long time only, Academy Award. Some might say that Heyerdahl's book has also played its part in fixing the story of the *Kon-Tiki* in the mind of the world, but in doing so they forget that the film, in due course also the televised version, has reached half a billion people. It was a film which had an *effect* on people. Cinemagoers felt as though they were actually on the raft. There are reports of people feeling seasick and having to be helped out by the usherettes. The film even evoked personal associations for Jonas Wergeland when he saw it again while working on the programme. His thoughts went to a traumatic sail across Oslo fjord in a gale.

Thor Heyerdahl presented a bold new theory on the origins of the Polynesians. Here was a Norwegian who truly dared to think big. He set out, quite simply, to rewrite the history of mankind. And, of course, the inevitable happened. The expedition's one hundred and one days out on the Pacific Ocean, the main purpose of which had been to document the validity of a fat treatise, became a thrilling tale of adventure, straight out of the *Arabian Nights*. Heyerdahl was acclaimed as the author of a brilliant manuscript. In Britain the film was compared to the tales of Jules Verne and Joseph Conrad. The Americans cited myths shaped by such novels as *Robinson Crusoe* and *Moby Dick*. Thus – very subtly – Wergeland showed *Kon-Tiki* to be an archetypal

Norwegian film. Its message was that Norwegians were a seafaring people, and that they had always had a tendency to turn science into an adventure, a heroic exploit. Jonas Wergeland could never quite rid himself of the thought that there were certain parallels between Heyerdahl's film and Heyerdahl's theories. That just as he had made an enthralling film out of his poor raw material, so his provocative theories were built upon very shaky foundations.

Be that as it may, Jonas Wergeland found it hard to imagine any greater feat: to win an Oscar, in the USA itself, a country where the competition to attain such dreams is so fierce. In the scene where Jonas himself made his appearance in the Heyerdahl programme, this was the point which he highlighted. When you walked into the Kon-Tiki Museum on the island of Bygdoy, Wergeland said, the first thing one should look at was not the raft, but the glass case containing the Oscar statuette. This was the museum's main attraction. It was this figurine, 33.5 cm in height and four kilos in weight, made from zinc and copper and covered with a layer of ten-carat gold, which spoke of the truly great deed. And it could also be said to symbolise Heyerdahl's life-long dealings with statues great and small.

Through his television series, Jonas Wergeland showed that it was not just in sport that a country like Norway could make its mark in the world, despite what many young Norwegians – like Daniel – had been brought up to believe. You could win gold in the arts. Because Heyerdahl did not win his gold, his Oscar, for a sporting achievement – though some would reduce it to such – but for his vision, his idea. As far as Jonas Wergeland was concerned, that statuette was worth more than all the Olympic and World Championship golds ever won by Norway.

There was also the odd Oscar winner among the films seen by Jonas and Leonard as members of the Oslo Film Club. But primed as they were by their hotheaded sessions in the Red Room, with its library of old *Aktuell* magazines, it took them only a few months to discover their first love. As the son of a 'reporter with a camera' with the working-class press, Leonard felt sure that he was destined to fall for Italian neo-realism, films which – for all their differences one from another – testified to a strong social conscience, and often had a documentary element to them. But even Jonas, who had no real concept of Italy or 'the Eternal City' other than that formed by the garish postcards he had received as a small boy from his Uncle Lauritz the SAS pilot, felt strangely drawn to such films as *The Earth Trembles*, *The Bicycle Thieves* and *Rome, Open City*.

It was only natural that this interest should have an influence on their appetite, their palates suddenly seeming to yearn for flavours to match what they saw on the cinema screen. The basement – which in the Knutzen family's more frugal past had housed a lodger – also contained a makeshift kitchenette with a cooker and a small fridge, and this proved to be all that was needed for Leonard's culinary experiments, his flights into the realms of Italian cuisine.

Leonard was, however, a realist; he confined his endeavours to one dish. They had of course heard of such wonders as *minestrone* soup and *pizza*, but when they dreamt of Italy they thought, first and last, of spaghetti. If one were to compare, as we did earlier, their seething wrathfulness and lack of a cause to sitting empty-handed and devoid of ideas next to a pot of boiling water, then at last they had found something to put into the pot: pasta. It goes without saying, when one considers the time and the place, that they did not go so far as to purchase professional utensils or try their hand at more exacting and fiddly variations such as *ravioli* or *tortellini*. Leonard concentrated solely on the different sauces, and soon confirmed that these were not limited to ketchup and the dry-fried chunks of minced beef which his mother sprinkled over spaghetti on the rare occasions when she happened to make it for dinner. All it took was something as simple as a knob of butter and some toasted poppy seeds for Jonas and Leonard to feel they were partaking of their pasta several hundred miles further south.

Leonard took it very seriously. He could not get his hands on the uncooked herb-based sauce, *pesto*, but he did things in that spartan kitchenette in the Red Room which had never been attempted in Grorud before – not even in the swish Golden Elephant restaurant. It was here, for example, that Jonas first saw someone make a tomato sauce from scratch. Otherwise, just about everything went into Leonard's sauces, not least into his *bolognese*; Jonas never did find out what he threw into the pot, but his friend was a sight to be seen, standing over the simmering stew, sampling it, then promptly grating some nutmeg into it, as a finishing touch which, nonetheless, spelled the difference between lip-smacking success and inedible fiasco. At the peak of his culinary career he actually grew basil on the windowsill. As a grown man, Jonas would dine at critically acclaimed *trattorie* in Florence and Genoa, but he never tasted a pasta sauce as good as the ones which Leonard Knutzen dished up in a modest kitchenette in Grorud.

Leonard received a lot of help from his father. During the long summer season, when Youngstorget abounded in fresh vegetables, Olav brought home the finest fresh produce. There was, however, one problem: a want of parmesan, and even worse, of olive oil – remember, this was Norway in the 1960s, in gastronomic terms a Third World country. Luckily Leonard eventually discovered Oluf Lorentzen's treasure-chest of a shop on Karl Johans gate, where not only did they have that essential piquant cheese, they also had an olive oil which, to his delight, was called Dante. And garlic, of course. Jonas and Leonard were probably the first people in Grorud to smell of this plant. And who knows, this may even have been a stronger indication of their outsider position than an obsession with Italian films. To reek of garlic would have been regarded by lots of people in those days as a more radical sign of wrath than an upraised fist in a black glove.

The food spurred them on to even more enthusiastic discussions of the Italian cinema. It almost seemed as if it was the spaghetti itself which made it so easy to talk vociferously and gesticulate wildly, vehemently brandishing one's fork while yelling pointed remarks at one another. 'I'm telling you, it's the low budget that makes Rossellini's editing so bloody brilliant!' Leonard declared. 'Better a back street in Naples any day, than all of Griffith's phony studio sets and daft cardboard elephants!' cried Jonas. They became more hot-blooded, a strange new temperament awoke within them. One of the things they liked best was to mop up the last of the sauce with chunks of the white bread. At such moments they seemed about to break, quite spontaneously, into Italian.

And then one spring, as if the one thing led quite naturally to the next, they attended a seminar on Italian film held at the Film Institute in the Oslo suburb of Røa. If they had been looking for something to 'believe in' and were expecting it to appear on the silver screen, then this was their epiphany. Their introduction to Michelangelo.

They took their seats in the cinema expecting more neo-realism, instead they were presented with something quite different. On that weekend at Røa they saw four films in all by the Italian director Michelangelo Antonioni: L'Avventura, La Notte, L'Éclisse and The Red Desert. They were shocked, outraged almost. His scenes reminded them of the stupid, stylised illustrated serials in weekly magazines. Was such a thing possible? They saw figures walking in different directions, one in the foreground, one in the background. The pace was so slow that they had to stifle a yawn. The close-up of a face could be held for ages. Occasionally characters would move out of shot, but the shot, the empty scene, would be held, long. Antonioni did not seem to have any intention of telling them a story. His characters did not do anything, they acted no parts. They *looked*. As if none of them could make sense of the world in which they found themselves. Jonas and Leonard understood little of it, and even less of what the thinking behind the films might be. They kept wanting to get up and leave, but they never did. Jonas suddenly realised that he had found a kindred spirit, someone who was out to show them that the world was flat.

On the train back into town they sat staring out of the window. Was it possible? To make a film which ended not with a man and woman meeting as they had arranged, and as everyone expected, but with a seven-minute long sequence in which the audience saw nothing but dull scenes from somewhere in a city. And yet: over the next few days, every now and again either Jonas or Leonard would suddenly exclaim: 'Claudia! Anna!' in that typical, exaggerated Italian accent. Or, with anguished expression: 'Perchè? Perchè? Perchè?' And they knew that they had been sucked into that universe. Or it had taken up residence inside them.

As to the search for some direction for their anger, its future looked precarious. Instead of sneering at the deplorable state of the world, they were more liable to spend an hour discussing Monica Vitti's bone structure and the broad bridge of her nose: part lioness, part porn model. Her lips. The way she made up her eyes. One Saturday at the Grand café, after the Film Club, Leonard announced – apropos the power of the Italian tradition – that all philosophy, all questions, including that of Monica Vitti, boiled down to the subject of Raphael's fresco *The School of Athens*, the contrast between Plato pointing upward and Aristotle pointing forward. One pointing to heaven, the other to the world. 'So which way would you choose?' Jonas asked. Leonard reached a hand into the air, pointing upward. Jonas thought that was his answer. 'Two coffees,' Leonard said when the waiter came over. 'And two marzipan cakes, since there seems to be a shocking want of *tiramisù* around here.'

Things started to become rather hazy. They did not do much except wander around, looking. Without any idea of what they were looking for. When not eating spaghetti with a carbonara sauce, or possibly a processed cheese and walnut sauce, down there in the basement, in that red laboratory, or darkroom, in which they had originally planned, by dint of experimentation, to figure out what to do with their lives, to develop images of possible plans of attack, they sat and vacillated. And not only that: they doubted. For the moment at least, Leonard seemed more interested in wielding the pepper grinder – Jonas would never forget the sound of that utensil – than in getting hold of a camera. But he succeeded in justifying his vacillation. 'I wander around absorbing impressions,' Leonard said, expertly twirling spaghetti round the base of his spoon with his fork. He was gearing up for his career as Norway's greatest film director. He was honing his eye.

And his role model, or honing steel, was Michelangelo – Antonioni, that is. They discussed his films. The flagpoles in *L'Éclisse*, the church bells in *L'Avventura*, the humming radio masts in *The Red Desert*. They marvelled at the way in which Antonioni reduced everything to flat planes, even using a telephoto lens to compress the depth of the image. It surprised them to find how well they could remember whole scenes, seemingly meaningless snippets of dialogue. The long sequence on the island in *L'Avventura* had made a particularly strong impact on them: all those people wandering around on their own, tiny figures cutting this way and that across the deserted landscape, looking for Anna, the lost girl. While Jonas regarded Antonioni as a kindred spirit, mainly because his films seemed to be all thought rather than action, for Leonard he was a mentor. He almost wept with rage when a guy at the Film Club told them that Antonioni had been forced to work in a bank for a while. A bank! Leonard, with a father working for the left-wing press and a mother in the Trade Union building, considered this the most degrading of all occupations. 'A bank! You'd be better working for the Society of the Blind.'

At long last Leonard decided that his eye was sharp enough. From one day to the next he started calling himself Leonardo – since the Christian names of all the great Italian film-makers ended in 'o': Vittorio, Roberto, Federico, Luchino, Pier Paolo, Bernardo. The time had come for him to make his own films, to found 'the Italian school' in Grorud. While other boys received Tandberg tape-recorders or gold watches as confirmation gifts, Leonard was able to show off a fabulous 8 mm cine camera, complete with projector and splicer. And he was hooked. He became as fanatical about his camera as Jimi Hendrix – a fellow outsider – was about his guitar. Word had it that Hendrix slung on his instrument as soon as he got up in the morning; he fried bacon with his guitar hanging at his back and took it to the toilet with him. Likewise, everywhere Leonard went his camera went too. He also started wearing sunglasses, whatever the weather: with black frames, like the ones worn by Marcello Mastroianni in *La dolce vita*. Later, during his years at high school, his style of dress also changed. While Jonas stuck, during the cold months of the year, to his duffle coat, Leonard went around with a heavy coat swinging from his shoulders like a cape and a scarf which he never tied, but simply draped over the coat. No Afghan coat for Leonard. 'There goes an intellectual,' his attire said. Or rather: 'There goes a film director. A Leonardo.'

Jonas was press-ganged into a brief but intense career as an actor in various enigmatic films, or more correctly: disjointed scenes played out in and around Grorud. On one occasion he had to get up at the crack of dawn to sit stock-still in front of the lovely glass rotunda by the ornamental pond in the middle of the shopping centre. Not a soul around. Nothing but an ethereal light. Buildings on three sides. Clear geometric shapes and long shadows. A touch of the Giorgio de Chiricos. 'Look straight up into the air,' Leonard shouted as he circled with the little camera. 'Think of something … deep.' After shooting four rolls of three-minute film he was satisfied. 'Superb,' he said. 'What were you thinking about? You had a face like a dream machine.'

Possibly because he had been sitting facing the Golden Elephant restaurant,

Jonas had been thinking about the one subject that was often in his thoughts, although he was not always conscious of it. Her. Always her. Even when he imagined that he was thinking about other girls. He would experience the same thing again, or a slight variation on it, some years later when he found himself in another almost deserted square, a very long way from Grorud, although here too he was surrounded on three sides by buildings – albeit of a more monumental and very different character. Jonas Wergeland was in that place in the world which had been the goal of his dreams, a shimmering pin-prick inside his skull, for as long as he could remember: Samarkand. To Jonas Wergeland this fact seemed so incredible – and so mind-boggling – that he might as well have been standing on Saturn's moon Titan.

His dreams of Samarkand could be laid, of course, at the door of his Aunt Laura and years of veiled references to a city which, as far as he could gather, was the most important place in her life. 'Tell me who you met in Samarkand,' he urged her time and again as he lay on the sofa, letting himself drift dream-ily into all the rugs on her walls. 'As for Samarkand and what I found there, that I can never tell you,' she would always reply patiently from the corner where she was working at her glittering little goldsmith's bench. 'You will have to go there yourself.'

It was odd, really. He had come here, travelled such a ridiculously long way, all because Aunt Laura would *not* tell him what had happened to her here. It was not a story, but the absence of a story that had led him deep into Central Asia. From the moment when he first heard his aunt pronounce those syl-lables, Sa-mar-kand, he had longed to visit this place. The very word itself fascinated him. For Jonas, Samarkand had become the one place in the world most likely to hold the answer to the riddle of every human being. Sometimes Jonas felt that all that was needed for him to become complete was a tiny cog, and that this last little piece just happened to be in Samarkand. He *had* to go there. Jonas Wergeland's trip to Samarkand was, in the very truest sense, a formative experience or, as it used to be called in the old days: a Grand Tour.

Perhaps that was why getting there proved so difficult. Nowadays, when everybody and their uncle is circling the world on a bike with a video camera and a laptop, or visiting every city in the world beginning with the letter B in the course of a year, it is as easy to get to places as it is hard to discover anything knew, anything semi-original. Of all the journeys Jonas Wergeland made, there was only one which he considered to have been really gruelling, and that was the trip to Samarkand. For a Norwegian in the seventies, it was one of the few places which was completely out of reach. It presented a chal-lenge on a par with crossing Antarctica on crutches. Getting in to Uzbekistan, in that far-flung corner of the Soviet Union, at that time – with no excuse other than an incomprehensible urge to see Samarkand – was an accomplishment, a feat of daring unparalleled in Jonas Wergeland's life. Strictly speaking it could not be done, but Jonas did it. Thanks to the art of persuasion, bluffing, bureaucratic hurdling, charm, patience and amazing luck. And, not least, wrath. Jonas simply got so mad that he won through. For a short while his anger found a direction, a clear purpose.

So the contrast, once he was actually there in Samarkand, was all the greater. Because no one appeared to care any more. It was all very peaceful and undramatic. He may well have been under surveillance, but he was free to go where he pleased, see whatever he liked, alone, ostensibly at any rate, in a city which nestled so beautifully among the snow-covered mountains; where everything, as far as he could tell, revolved around cotton and melons. And silk – a reminder of a time when this city was a bustling hub on the Silk Road. Jonas had the feeling that he knew this place. He found himself thinking, of all things, of Snertingdal. He half expected to see a sign saying 'The Norwegian Organ and Harmonium Works'.

He knew what he wanted to see first: Registan Square, the centre of the city, this too once a marketplace. And when he sank to the ground there, simply sat right down with his legs crossed, he knew that it had been worth all the travails of the preceding days; all the hassle, all the discouragement, all the dirty looks from officials in hilarious big hats. Although Aunt Laura refused to tell him about her own experiences, she had described this place to him again and again, told him that it was far and away the finest public square in the world – the West had nothing to equal it. She had compared it to a square with the most imposing gothic cathedrals on three of its four sides. 'Imagine the Town Hall Square,' she said, 'And then imagine another, almost identical, Town Hall where the Western Station is, and a similar building on the spot where Restaurant Skansen sits. And all of them covered in the most exquisite ceramic tiles. Can you picture it?' Yes, Jonas could picture it. The Town Hall in Oslo was, for many reasons, his favourite building in Norway.

Jonas sat in a sort of lotus position on the edge of the square, soaking up these ornamental riches, now partially restored after years of neglect. The buildings – the Ulug Beg to the west, the Tillya Kari to the north and the Shir Dar to the east – had once been *madrasahs*, Muslim colleges. Minarets flanked the three massive façades, in each of which was a doorway thirty to forty metres tall. The entire complex was faced with glazed tiles in bright colours, a mass of geometric patterns, floral motifs and Kufic calligraphy. An incredible jigsaw puzzle. Jonas lingered over each wall in turn, not worrying about the time, loving the way the slowly shifting light kept revealing new details in the mosaics. He opened up. Tried to make himself open to something which lay within him and was only waiting for him to find a way of drawing it out. He *would* find a missing piece here, a story, or at least a snippet of a story.

He had sensed it the moment he reached the square and sank down onto the ground.

Jonas sat there gazing at the three façades. Like three gigantic oriental rugs. They almost seemed to cancel one another out, to generate a void of sorts, concentrated nothingness. He could lose himself in those walls, in the ornamentation, disappear into them. Get to the back of them, he thought. If he stared at them for long enough he might even be able to step out into Aunt Laura's bazaar of a flat, where he had played as a child, with a torch in the dark.

Samarkand was more than a place. Jonas was conscious of a Samarkand beyond Samarkand, something which was not a city, but a crucial insight. This feeling was confirmed as he sat cross-legged on Registan Square. Because if there was any truth in his suspicion, that the world was flat, then here, in Samarkand, he had found the edge. Samarkand had to be a good place for an outsider. An outside-left position from which one could open up the game, change the rules almost. Not for nothing had Samarkand's greatest ruler invented a variation on chess using twice as many pieces. For an instant, Jonas had a sense of being back in the world as it was before Copernicus, before people knew that the earth was round. Of being able to start afresh. Follow another fork in the road than that which humanity had so far taken.

And then, just as he felt that something vital was about to rise to the surface, that Samarkand beyond Samarkand, much in the way that one feels a sneeze building up, suddenly it slipped away and in its place was another thought, or a cluster of thoughts, as impenetrable and manifest and rich in nuance as one of the glowing façades before him: Margrete. He had come to this place because he thought he would meet Margrete here. Or at least that there was a possibility of meeting her here. If there was the slightest chance of meeting her anywhere in the world it had to be here, in Samarkand. After all, what was Margrete like? Margrete was the sort of person who could easily take it into her head to go to Samarkand. He realised, although he had never come anywhere close to formulating such a thought before, that he was *sure* he would meet Margrete here. It was the same sensation, albeit greatly intensified, which he had occasionally experienced as a lovesick teenager: you would go a long way out of your way, or ski for miles, if there was even the most microscopic chance of running into the girl you loved, as if by pure accident. And Jonas saw that, unconsciously, this was exactly what he had been thinking this time too. If he went to Samarkand, the most unlikely place in the world, he was bound to run into her. It was a simple as that.

And with thoughts of this nature running through his head, he realised how much she had been on his mind all the years since she had left, how much he missed her, what an indelible impression those months with her had made on him. *This* was the story which he had come here to uncover. This was the Samarkand beyond Samarkand. The story of Margrete's absence, the gaping void she had left inside him. Unbeknown to him, the memory of Margrete had bulked larger and larger in his mind. Maybe, he thought to himself, he was more deeply, more devotedly hers here, now, than when they were going out together.

Jonas rested his eyes on the blue dome of the Tillya Karis, let his mind dwell on a blue found nowhere else in the whole world. Wasn't blue the colour of hope?

He felt that he was ready. Ready for something. The world was flat and he was sitting on its edge. He knew that something was going to happen, but he was not prepared for the fact that it was already happening. He was just getting to his feet, and then it happened. He felt a hand being placed lightly on his shoulder. There was someone behind him.

Why did he do it?

During his years with Leonardo, in the epoch of the Italian school and more especially at the height of their Grorud filming fervour, Jonas imagined that he had forgotten Margrete. One might even say that Michelangelo Antonioni helped him, or consoled him, by making films which showed that love today was an extremely tricky, and possibly downright impossible, business. Only once did the thought of Margrete crop up, like a wound, in his mind – when they were hunting for a leading lady. They were looking for a girl who would be as ravishingly beautiful as Jeanne Moreau or Monica Vitti. 'Whatever happened to that Bangkok chick of yours,' Leonard asked. 'Shut up,' Jonas retorted. It was one of the few occasions when he felt like punching his pal.

In the end they picked Pernille, mainly because she was a year older and had a scooter, a Vespa, which was the perfect prop for a film as heavily influenced by the Italians as Leonard's. Jonas could not deny that Pernille was disconcertingly attractive, with a dark and rather sulky beauty reminiscent of Claudia Cardinale; secretly he dreamed of being kissed by her the way Cary Grant was kissed by Ingrid Bergman in *Notorious*: for three whole minutes, the most famous kiss in the history of the cinema, or the most groundbreaking at any rate, in the way it so cunningly got round the censors.

But Leonard wanted them back to back. A good many weird ten-minute tales were shot in open countryside, with a lot of wandering past one another, far apart, a lot of staring into space. 'Look anxious,' Leonard would yell at Jonas, 'look as though you're feeling guilty about something, although you don't know what.' Nothing happened and everything was a mystery. Nonetheless, Jonas was often amazed by the way in which what, to him, was simply a succession of obscure scenes could, when shuffled around and spliced together in the final, grainy short films which Leonard showed on a sheet in the Red Room to the accompaniment of the projector's hum, suddenly appeared to have a vague plot. He once asked his friend what he enjoyed most about film-making and was not at all surprised when Leonard replied: 'The editing.'

Then came the great revolution. Or the great loss. The loss of wrath. If, that is, it had not been lost long before. Jonas and Leonard had missed seeing Antonioni's new film *Blow-Up* at the cinema, having been on their summer holidays at the time, but just over a year later they found themselves in the Oslo Cinematographers' screening room in Stortingsgaten along with the Film Club study group, for a showing of this unforgettable movie, so steeped in the London of the sixties, steeped in the music and design of the sixties and, above all else, steeped in metaphysical overtones. It was about a photographer who had taken some pictures of a couple, eventually just the woman, in a park and when he enlarged the photographs discovered that on film he had also – possibly – caught a crime being committed in the background, in the bushes, a man with a gun and a body on the ground. Amazing, thought Jonas. You take pictures of what you think is a love scene, and it turns out to be connected to a murder. With his heart in his mouth he watched as the main character blew up one section of the photograph, from which he then blew up another section. Jonas and Leonard sat in the dark, eyes glued to the screen, letting themselves be seduced by Antonioni's visual conjuring tricks. Like the photograph they, too, were blown up, enlarged. For a while after this Leonard regretted having chosen film rather than photography. They felt like borrowing Olav Knutzen's Leica and Rolleiflex and taking pictures of every bush they saw. What would they find if they enlarged sections of them? For several weeks they were possessed of an urge to blow up everything.

It so happened that the memory of a personal blow-up was still quite fresh in Jonas's mind. The year before he had been head over heels in love. And blow-up is the word. After all, what is love but one huge exaggeration. And even more so if it hits you during that crazy, mixed-up period known as adolescence. Jonas was constantly aware of how, depending on the circumstances, his eyes would turn into a microscope or a telescope. All of a sudden his ears were as sensitive as the finest microphones; he could readily detect ten different nuances of tone in one 'Hi.' He could smell a girl at two hundred metres, and if a feminine shoulder or arm were to nudge against him, his skin felt as tender as a newborn kitten. Just watching a girl sucking on a lolly pop made him want to run amok. The sight of Anne Beate Corneliussen using his bicycle pump to blow up her tyre could send him into inordinate frenzies of excitement. Jonas felt as though his head was becoming human, while his body was still stuck at the animal stage. And maybe it was this same split which gave rise to the tendency to exaggerate everything – if, that is, it was not a last, desperate attempt to hang on to childhood, a state in which reality and fantasy could exist side by side. Later, on the other side of the border, so to speak, it would occur to Jonas that exaggeration was a toll you had to pay when you passed into the realms of adulthood.

For Jonas Wergeland the summer of 1967 was never the Summer of Love. He would have understood, though, if anyone were to describe the following winter as the Winter of Love. Because those were the months when he saw red, which is to say: when his love for Eva N. burned brightest and he made fruitless forays into Lillomarka on skis every single Sunday, hoping to run into her – quite by chance – at Sinober.

Then, on the eleventh Sunday, an exceptionally cold day in the middle of March, Fortune smiled on Jonas. Having taken Daniel's laughing, but well-meant, advice to apply grip wax to the middle section of his ski soles, he plunged into the forest, where skiing conditions were still decent. He strode out frantically, as if he knew that this was his last chance; conscious, shame-fully almost, of how much fitter he was, and that he was really getting the hang of it now, even managing to exploit the give of the skis in the innumer-able dips. Yet again he stopped at the foot of the last slope before Sinober to blow a coating of rime over his brows and lashes, and yet again an impressive diagonal stride brought him skimming up to the café. Everything was the same as always, apart from a bright flash of red outside the main café build-ing. At first he thought maybe he was seeing spots in front of his eyes, due to his racing pulse, but no, there she was, there was Eva's sturdy figure and, not least, her red anorak.

He pretended not to see her, leaned nonchalantly on his poles, as if resting for a second or two, before wheeling round, voracious mile-eater that he was, and scooting off again. He stopped beside the signpost, at a crossroads with lots of arrows pointing to different lives. In the end she came over to him, with half a slice of bread and goat's cheese cupped in her mittens. She eyed his rime-covered eyebrows curiously. 'Jonas? What are you doing here? I didn't know you liked skiing.' What she did not say was that she fell for him at that very moment.

A month later Jonas asked himself, for several reasons, why a girl like Eva N. should have fallen for him. From a subjective point of view, flushed with love as he was, he had of course been sure that he would win her, but objectively he knew that she was unattainable. He could execute all the best Gjermund Eggen moves and it would make no difference. He could not know that what Eva, like a couple of dozen other women, had fallen for was, quite simply, the look in his eyes. Or an expression which was written large on his face, as clear as the scar over his eyebrow. They immediately perceived that he, Jonas Wergeland – although he did not know it – was restlessly searching for something great, something important, and every one of them believed that they were the key to this great and important thing for which he was searching. Jonas's conscious or unconscious urge to discover things and the indefinable talent from which it derived was as obvious to these women as a set of antlers on his head would have been. In their eyes he was one in a billion. The bearer of different thoughts, a man whose eyes, whose face, testified to the fact that he was obsessed with the desire to achieve a goal, an outer limit, possibly even a backside, with the power to expand reality. And this, they thought – while at the same time thinking that he must sense it too – he could only do through a woman. To them, that handful of women, this was irresistible, more powerful than any aphrodisiac. They were not attracted by good looks or power or money – and most certainly not by skiing skills – but by a curiosity which was focused on an impossibility.

Jonas looked at her from under the crust of rime on his eyelashes, which was now starting to melt. He was about to say something, but his voice cracked, everything cracked. She looked so strong. Invulnerable. She was the sort of person who could withstand anything. Sleep out in temperatures of forty below. Drink urine and eat reindeer moss. But Jonas saw something else too. He saw what was written all over her: Danger. High Voltage.

'Fancy going on a bit further?' she asked, bending down and picking up a fistful of snow, squeezing it, examining it, as if debating whether to rewax. Rewax life, Jonas thought. This was not part of the plan. He had never been further than Sinober. Places such as Varingskollen or Kikut were only vague names. He glanced up at the arrows. The signpost looked like a many-branched tree, it called to mind the ones found at certain tourist attractions, with signs showing the direction and the distance to various capital cities. Here the signs pointed out across the winter landscape, towards Movatn, Nittedal, Snippen, Grefsen, Sørskogen. He could ski like a champion – as long, he hoped, as he didn't have to ski down to Movatn, or to Tømte. Might as well ask: Do you want to take a run down to Hell?

'Fancy a run down to Tømte?' she said.

'Yeah,' he said, quick as a wink. Knowing this was sheer lunacy.

Now Jonas had, for some time before this, associated women with a certain amount of risk. He was well aware that in giving a girl the eye you also laid yourself open to the possibility of losing your head. Jonas was by no means a stranger to the idea that, when you came right down to it, women were dangerous.

All of this had its roots in the first death which Jonas could remember. A death which was, in the words of the grown-ups, 'mysterious' and 'incomprehensible'. Uncle Lauritz, the SAS pilot, had been killed in an accident – not on a scheduled flight, a cataclysmic, catastrophic crash in a Caravelle, but in his little Piper Cub. It so happened that Jonas's mother had to take him with her on the day when she had to go through her brother's things. His grandmother could not face it. The accident had clearly brought back painful memories. When the news was broken to her she had gone to lie in the bath and listen to the BBC. This was always a bad sign. 'He was an excellent pilot,' she murmured, chewing on the butt of a cigar. 'Never have so many owed so much to so few.'

Jonas was glad of the chance to visit the flat. Lauritz had been his hero, although his uncle was hardly ever around. He was like a knight who rode into Jonas's life from time to time and dropped off a toy from Paris or a box of Quality Street from London. Once, when some bigger boys were threatening to beat Jonas up for puncturing their football, a taxi pulled up and Uncle Lauritz got out, dressed in his navy-blue uniform with the four gold stripes on the cuffs. The other boys just stood there, awestruck, outside Jonas's building. At that moment, in Jonas's eyes, his uncle was an angel.

His mother had never been to the flat before. Her brother had never invited her or any other members of the family over. If he asked them out it was always to Restaurant Skansen or the Moorish Salon at the Hotel Bristol. 'Lauritz lived his own life,' she explained apologetically to Jonas. He was seldom home either, what with him being a pilot. Jonas could tell that, grief-stricken though she was, his mother was also a little curious. 'He was actually very shy. Bashful. A bit like you. It must run in the family,' his mother remarked to Jonas. She and Lauritz had not had much to do with one another since their childhood days at Gardemoen. Even as a boy her brother had been obsessed with the desire to get away: 'I want to fly high. And far.'

In the end, though, his flight was short. And low. The general view – and the one also expressed in the coroner's report – was that it was unthinkable for a pilot as experienced as Lauritz to have flown into a high-voltage cable by accident, or certainly not the cable in question, which was a known hazard. It wasn't as if the weather had been bad, nor had it been particularly windy. No one actually came out and said it, but it was there between the lines: suicide. Jonas preferred the words 'mysterious' and 'incomprehensible'. Rakel said the whole thing reminded her of what had happened to a legendary French flier by the name of Saint-Exupéry – Jonas liked the name the moment he heard it – who had disappeared on a mission towards the end of the Second World War. Neither he nor his plane had been found.

Some said he had crashed in the Alps, others that he went down in the Mediterranean. No explanation for the accident was ever forthcoming. Which was just how it should be, Jonas thought. The death of a knight, not to mention an angel, ought to be shrouded in mystery.

'It must have been a woman,' Jonas heard his mother say to his father. His uncle had worn a locket around his neck, the sort with a compartment for a small picture. But when they were preparing for the funeral and his mother opened it, it was empty. Still she stuck to her theory. 'It's the only possible explanation,' she said. 'An unhappy love affair.' Jonas pondered this expression. It was the first time he had heard a negative word used in conjunction with the one word which he held to be the most positive in life. He sampled this pairing: 'unhappy' and 'love'. This was the first intimation Jonas was given of the gravity of love, and different in nature from what he would later derive from Karen's Mohr's story from Provence. This one spoke of the possible consequences of love. Love did not only make you fly high, it could just as easily make you fly low. Too low. Maybe love was not something one should reach out for without thinking. Jonas had the wild idea that all girls ought to wear signs around their necks saying: 'Danger. High voltage.' Love was like electricity. It could give warmth and light, but it could also black out a life, short-circuit it.

'What do you think his flat looks like?' Jonas asked on the way over there.

'I've no idea. He'd only been living there for three or four years. Probably just the same as anyone else's. Perfectly ordinary.'

Jonas guessed that his mother was hoping to find some clue there to her brother's decision to end his life by embracing a high-voltage cable. A solemn declaration on his desk, maybe. A box of passionate love letters. Jonas, on the other hand, was thinking that he was soon going to be entering the flat of one who had loved, a man who had been a victim of love. In short, he was about to see the chamber of love itself. It started out well enough. As far as Jonas was concerned at any rate. A door with three big, burglar-proof locks. No one had keys to it. There had been no keys in his pockets. 'There are no keys to a human being,' his father had said softly from the piano bench, having declined to come with them. His mother had called a locksmith, made an appointment, the man had arrived at the same time as them. 'Lauritz didn't open up to anyone,' his mother muttered when the door was finally breached. Jonas's first thought was that this place must harbour some great – and possibly dark and scandalous – secret. After all, you didn't have three huge locks on your door for nothing.

They stepped inside. Jonas tried to conceal the hope he felt. He remembered the first time Wolfgang Michaelsen had invited him into his room and he walked in to find lots of model warplanes hanging in the air, at least fifty of them, and every one painted in the right colours. It had come as such a shock, it made you start; it was like opening a door and walking straight into the middle of World War II.

More than anything, Jonas was hoping that they would find something valuable. A legacy of some sort. He wished that he had other qualities in common with his uncle, apart from shyness. He saw a secret room. Full of gold ingots. Or unknown paintings by Tidemann and Gude, worth millions. Or at the very least a few volumes of comic books.

But the flat was all bare. And all white. It was like breaking into a massive safe and finding it empty. They wandered through three large rooms. No books, no rugs, nothing on the walls. Nothing in the bathroom, not even a razor or a bottle of aftershave. The kitchen too was empty. The fridge, all the shelves were bare. Maybe he really was an angel, Jonas thought, a being who did not need food, did not need to shave. There was nothing in the bedroom but a bed, perfectly made. In the fitted wardrobe hung a couple of suits and uniforms. Apart from a few spartan pieces of furniture and the requisite electrical appliances they found only one thing of any value: underneath the window sat an imposing, exclusive stereo system, exotic pieces of equipment which gave the living room the look of a large cockpit and, next to them, an orange box full of Duke Ellington records. Jonas was to think later that this was possibly as good as any flight recorder, that if you listened carefully enough to these discs, tried pronouncing their titles, you would find the answer. This thought struck him, of course, only after Margrete had given him *Rubber Soul* as a farewell present. For all they knew, this box of records could have been the equivalent, for Uncle Lauritz, of a box of love letters – worth more than all the gold ingots in the world.

The bare white walls made Jonas feel as though the whole flat was just one big white room. The opposite of a darkroom. A place where not a single picture could be developed. The more he thought about this, the more reasonable – and right – it seemed to him. Everyone needed a place in which they could feel lonely. In his day-to-day life Uncle Lauritz the SAS pilot occupied a room that encompassed the whole world. So vast. So full of everything. One day Cairo, the next Athens. Which was why he needed this inner space that was all his own. Maybe for him it could never be white enough or empty enough.

Just before they left, Jonas spotted something. A small dark square on one of the living-room walls, like a stamp stuck on Antarctis. A sign of life. Jonas went over to it. It was a portrait, smaller than a passport photo, fixed to the wall with a pin. A woman's face. His mother was standing next to him. She said nothing. Jonas knew what she was thinking: this was the picture which had once sat in the locket that Uncle Lauritz wore around his neck. 'I knew it,' his mother said, sounding almost relieved. 'It was a woman.'

And yet for Jonas this altered everything. The flat was no longer empty. It was full of love. Unless, of course, that microscopic portrait betokened a desperate wish to minimise things, a frantic attempt to render the greatest thing in life nigh on invisible. However that may be: the flat did have a secret room. That tiny picture, that face.

Jonas had not yet met Bo Wang Lee; nevertheless it did occur to him that this flat also constituted an answer to the question of what you should take with you. You walked for a while on this Earth. What was worth collecting? He liked Uncle Lauritz's simple answer: the music of Duke Ellington and a face.

On the way home his mother suddenly said, more to herself than to Jonas: 'She wasn't good enough for him. If you ask me she was a tart.'

Jonas pretended not to hear, but this comment confirmed his misgivings – paradoxical though they were, considering those white rooms – concerning the darker aspects of love, and the risk of losing one's head completely.

He was to learn more about what it meant to lose one's head that day at Sinober when he stood under the ski-trail signpost, those arrows pointing in all directions, staring as if bewitched at a gigantic white room covered in snow. He had agreed without a moment's hesitation when Eva asked if he wanted to take a run over to Tømte with her, even though he knew that in order to get there they would first have to ski down to Movatn Lake. And Movatn was the main reason that Jonas had never gone beyond Sinober. The slopes down to the lake were legendary, known for being among the very worst the whole of Nordmarka had to offer in the way of downhill runs. Even Daniel, fanatical skier that he was, referred to them with a faint shudder as the Slopes from Hell. And as if that wasn't enough, there had been a bit of a thaw, then the surface had frozen hard again: the trails were covered in a lethal layer of ice.

Even on the first, not particularly taxing slopes, Jonas knew that he had embarked on a downright dangerous expedition. 'Careful, now,' Eva called over her shoulder a moment later, then the back of her red anorak disappeared over the top of something which looked to Jonas like an endless plunging descent, with steep slopes rising up on either side. The track was narrow and icy, there was no chance of ploughing; Jonas felt like he was on a bob-sleigh run; fir trunks loomed close, tightly packed, braking was impossible, he simply had to go for it, even though he had tears in his eyes and was travelling faster and faster over the glassy surface; and at the bottom there was a sharp turn to the left, one which the experienced skiers knew about, but not Jonas, with the result that he shot straight off into the forest at breakneck speed and crashed, inevitably and sickeningly, into a tree. Although to Jonas it was not a tree, but a high-voltage cable. He had known it was there ever since he fell in love, knew that he was bound to go careering into it sooner or later. For a few seconds everything went black. Or, not black: red.

He came round to find Eva standing over him. Fortunately he had hit the tree with his feet, with the sides of his skis first – there was an ugly gash in the trunk – even so he was battered and bruised and seemed to have broken, or at least sprained his leg, possibly tearing up his old football injury, the very source of his wrath. He could not get up. Then he noticed something which, for a moment, made him forget his pain. Eva was looking at him with a face which was unrecognisable, which pulsed with warmth, as if she were running a high fever. Jonas realised that Eva was in love, although in his dazed condition he thought that this was something which had only happened now, thanks to his accident. His battered state was the whole premise for her falling in love. The fact that he was done for. Down for the count. Not strong at all, no Lillomarka elk, but weak. She bent down to put her arms round him. Jonas caught a faint whiff of goat's cheese, blackcurrant cordial and universal wax. She slipped as she tried to help him up, fell on top of him, almost on purpose, he thought. Jonas was conscious of her lips brushing his cheek, felt her breath on his neck, the smell of her, the softness; that 'hard', fit, muscular girl, and yet this softness. As if the contours of her body were more palpable through anoraks and sweaters and tights than if she had been naked. For a few seconds there, it seemed to Jonas that he could feel every millimetre of that half of her body which was in contact with his.

It was worth it all for that instant of intense closeness. Jonas had the feeling that they did not need to do any more than that. That this brief, electrified moment more than justified all the ski trekking, the months of red-hot expectation, the pictures of her which he had blown-up almost to the point of unrecognisability and caressed in his dreams.

They got to their feet, brushed off the snow. His leg hurt. She turned to run her fingers over the marks his ski binding had made in the tree trunk, as if he had carved their names inside a heart. Although he tried not to, eventually he had to meet her eye and as he held her gaze he saw it all, as in a red haze, a darkroom in which pictures were developed at lightning speed. Up to this point you might say that he had merely loved her with his eyes, and only now did his mind seem to catch up with his vision and compel him to perceive her in another way, forced him to consider whether his eyes might have been wrong. Again he was made aware of what a blessing and a curse it was to be able to extract all he could from a girl at their first meeting, or from the moment when he understood that things could get serious. He was unable to stop the thoughts that flew off into the future, there to branch out in all directions, as if he were standing at a crossroads, covering every possible ski route at the same time – and all in order to determine whether she was the person he hoped she would be. Within a matter of seconds he found himself delving, despite his youth and lack of experience, deep into the exhausted possibilities of wedded life, into the petty arguments of a fifteen-year-old marriage; and not only that, he also explored all of the alternative forks in the road, the various, hypothetical paths in life he encountered at different points along the way. He stood there gazing into her eyes, and in his mind he saw their first kiss, actually saw quite vividly how he caught the taste of raspberry jam, then saw them going to the cinema and, weeks later, how he touched her breasts – from outside a flannel shirt, it's true; how he had dinner at her house, not only that, but that they had grouse, shot by her father, and then how, late one evening, in front of a roaring fire he slipped his hand between her legs; how they got engaged, the mad, passionate lovemaking in a sleeping bag; how they got married, the speech she made at the wedding, their first child, buying a house – log-built – dinners with friends, the general wear and tear, the quarrels over lopsided cheese-cutting. Everyone knows the expression 'to undress her with his eyes'. Jonas carried on where others left off. Not only was Jonas Wergeland capable of simulating an orgasm, he could simulate an entire marriage.

They struggled back up the hillside to Sinober. She kept her body pressed close against his the whole time, acting almost as a crutch. They phoned from the café. Haakon Hansen drove up through Nittedal to collect him. As Jonas shut the car door she stared at him through the window with eyes that made him quake. He was hers, those eyes said, or so Jonas imagined. And she wanted him as he was now, hurt, an invalid of sorts, someone on whom she could take pity, care for, help. Jonas did not know whether he was misinterpreting all this. His mother had once hinted that maybe he took life too seriously. Sometimes Jonas thought that he also took love too seriously. Or was too scared. Scared of being disappointed. Scared of finding that not only the world but love, too, was flat. In other words: scared of catching Melankton's syndrome.

When he returned to school a couple of days later, she came straight over to him at the morning break, wanting to hold his hand, to show that they were going together, although there had been no talk of this between them. He refused, but again she had looked at him with that feverish expression on her face which told him that any rebuff would be lost on her. At every break that day she came running happily up to him and groped eagerly for one of his hands. He kept them in his pocket.

By the last interval of the day the penny had finally dropped. 'I can't go out with you,' he said, barely managing to get the words out before she grabbed him roughly and threw him to the ground, hard, right down into the slush. More in desperation than in anger. Several of the others saw it, whispered. She walked off. She sounded as though she was crying. Jonas could not understand how someone so apparently robust and strong-minded could react in such a way.

Then, one night in March when Jonas was just on his way to bed, the whole family heard someone shouting out on the flag green. They went to the windows. In the centre of the patch of lawn between the blocks of flats stood Eva N. in her red anorak, calling his name. Loudly and clearly. And broken-heartedly. Daniel almost killed himself laughing, but his mother shushed him sternly.

No one would ever forget that night. Eva had brought something with her. It looked like a cartridge-case. She did something to the top before holding the tube straight up above her head. For a moment Jonas was afraid that she was going to set light to herself, like those Buddhist monks in Vietnam. Up shot a rocket, a coruscating streak, hundreds of metres long, accompanied by a whistling sound. It was a distress flare. Jonas remembered that her father had a boat. The flare exploded high in the sky above the flats. People had come out onto their balconies, they stared up at the bright red ball slowly descending on a tiny parachute. Falling gently and gracefully, burning with a strange intensity. The whole of Grorud seemed to be bathed in red light. And in the scant two minutes for which it lasted, the girl on the grass called Jonas's name, just his name, helplessly almost, as if she was crying out to be saved, rather than loved. As if she was saying: 'Look, I am bleeding.'

It was all very embarrassing, of course. That the family, the whole estate, should have been witness to this drama. Mr Iversen was cursing under his breath about people turning a March night into New Year's Eve, robbing him of his once-a-year shot at the limelight. 'It's against the law,' he muttered. 'It's sheer madness.'

At the same time Jonas could not help feeling rather proud. Here was this girl, in the middle of the flag green, and so in love with him that she did not care two hoots whether she was making a fool of herself in front of the whole estate. It was almost as though, standing there on that March night in the red glow from the flare – in a vast darkroom, if you like – she thought that she could develop love. It may well have been madness. But, looked at another way: she had nothing to lose. She was in distress. She did it in order to save herself, Jonas thought to himself. She wanted to maximise the crisis, so to speak, get the heartache over and done with. From that point of view the red light was the saving of her. And who knows, maybe she recalled this episode, in many ways a heroic deed, years later – by which time she was a famous, long-established leader of polar expeditions – when she saved her own life by sending up a similar parachute flare in Antarctis after her kayak was wrecked and she was left drifting on a large ice floe.

But to get back to the red thread of our story: Jonas was well-equipped to identify with *Blow-Up* – a film that revolved around a room suffused with red light in which an individual produced more and more blurred enlargements of smaller and smaller sections of a photograph. It was a film about the mystery of the image, all images. It was a film which quite simply questioned the nature of reality. Do we see what we see? Or, in Jonas Wergeland's version: Are you in love when you are in love?

Somewhat against their will, both Jonas and Leonard were drawn further and further into Michelangelo Antonioni's universe. Something was happening to them. Very gradually. Jonas began to feel unwell. His wrath turned to perplexity. They were looking for answers, but were given nothing but questions. They wanted to train their eye, hone it, but instead found themselves losing confidence in it. Leonard did not know that he was soon to lose confidence in everything, including his own origins.

For them this was a time of confusion. They ate their spaghetti with an ever growing repertoire of sauces: tuna with olives and tomatoes, a cream sauce with ham and leeks, while their discussions became more and more woolly. As their uncertainty and sense of alienation grew, so the Red Room underwent a metamorphosis. Leonard – now simply Leonardo – had started replacing the familiar photographs from *Aktuell*, hung on the walls by his father, with others. He removed from its frame the picture from Norsk Hydro of workers stacking bars of aluminium and in its stead put a still from Fellini's *8½*. A photograph of miners on Svalbard was supplanted by a shot from *The Red Desert* of Monica Vitti in an industrial wasteland. Reality was giving way to fiction. They hardly ever left the basement now; day after day they sat in the Red Room eating pasta and discussing films they had seen, films they had not seen and films which Leonardo envisaged making. Jonas would not emerge from this state of confusion and woolliness until he rediscovered both his wrath and a focus for it through taking part in a spectacular demonstration in the Town Hall Square. By then Leonardo was long gone.

Later, Jonas would think it only natural that their almost parodically artificial existence should explode into pitiless reality. He was spending less time with Leonard by then, having started at Oslo Cathedral School. And there was no way that Leonard, or even a befuddled Leonardo, was going all the way into the city to attend some toffee-nosed school. 'You're a traitor to your class,' he muttered to Jonas, in a brief flashback to their early, neo-realistic glory days in the Red Room. Leonard went on to a high school in the Grorud Valley. Though with a heavy coat swinging from his shoulders like a cape.

Leonard's dreadful discovery was made shortly after his last hike with his father. It was years since they had gone hill-walking together, but it may be that Leonard was making an effort to shake himself awake, thinking that the Norwegian mountains and fresh air would form a counterbalance to the Red Room and the flickering images of individuals incapable of making contact with one another. In the summer of 1970 he and his father went walking in the hills around Aurlandsdalen and it was here that Olav Knutzen took a picture which would eventually find its way into a host of yearbooks and reference works. Because by this time a new trend had long been apparent in the media: they would all – every last news outlet – descend on one spot. Everyone covering the same story. And even though at one time there had been some debate about Aurlandsdalen and the question of inalienable natural heritage versus energy needs, in the press as well as in an uproarious edition of television's *Open to Question* chaired by the Grand Panjandrum himself, Kjell Arnljot Wig, the focus shifted away from Aurlandsdalen with the advent of the Mardøla affair. That summer, the eyes of the nation were on the great falls in the Møre og Romsdal region and a demonstration during which protesters, including professor of philosophy Arne Næss, were gently and politely carted off by the police. Meanwhile, in Aurlandsdalen, the Oslo Electricity Board could quietly get on with the work of damming Viddalsvatn and the waters beyond to form one huge lake, without anyone blocking the broad construction road with so much as a twig. So, with the accuracy of a Zen master, Olav Knutzen took the only photograph from Låvisdalen recording the merest hint of a demonstration, a faint protest, at least, against the development which got under way here in June of the same year as the Mardøla project. It was an important piece of documentary evidence, this picture, which is also why it has been reproduced so often; because in Norway it is Aurlandsdalen, and not Mardøla, which represents a watershed in the history of nature conservation; the Aurlandsdalen controversy was proof that an element of reflection had bored its way into all views on constant progress, heedless growth – something which led, among other things, to the establishment a couple of years later of an environmental protection agency. Olav Knutzen took his snap at the point when work had just begun on a structure of pyramid-like dimensions, a dam 100 metres in height and 370 metres in length and as broad at its base as it was tall. This photograph – in the background of which one can see the building contractor, Furholmen's, massive construction machines at the foot of the dam, as well as some summer steadings which would soon be under water – shows Leonard with a wry little grin on his face – whether of confusion or anger Jonas could never decide. In his hand he holds a placard bearing the legend: 'SAVE THE DALE'. Although perhaps what it should have said, or so Jonas would later think, was 'Save the illusion'.

That same autumn Leonard got in touch with Jonas, and as soon as Jonas entered the basement room he knew that something was badly wrong. The aroma of simmering pasta sauce was noticeably absent. His friend greeted him with a face as deadpan as Buster Keaton's. 'I've made a horrible discovery,' he said. 'I've learned something that has changed my life. I'm not the person I thought I was.'

At the time Jonas had merely laughed at him, but much the same thought was to strike him years later, before his trip to Samarkand. The fact is, you see, that Jonas went all the way to Samarkand, to that blow-up in his mind, because he was in something of a dilemma regarding his future. He felt the need, therefore, to find some place far beyond the real world, a place where he could contemplate himself and his life at the greatest possible remove. And without realising it he fell back on Leonard's choice of words: I am not the person I think I am. In short, Jonas set out on the long journey to Samarkand in order to discover himself.

After having sat for a long time exposing himself, exposing his body to the intricate beauty still discernible in the faded façades on Registan Square, Jonas got to his feet with the vague idea of visiting a nearby museum. It was at this moment that someone placed a hand, very lightly, on his shoulder. Jonas turned round and stared in bewilderment into the face of a man around his own age. He must have been sitting right behind him, in his blind spot, so to speak. The stranger smiled at the way Jonas started. 'Tourist?' he inquired, in pretty good English. 'I did not think I would ever see a tourist here.'

Jonas was in no way prepared for what happened next. Although he ought to have been prepared. He was in a strange state of mind. And he was in Samarkand.

'And you?' Jonas asked.

'I too am a tourist, although I suppose you could say this is my own country,' the young man said.

Jonas was still feeling somewhat shaken by the sight of the other man. His features seemed disconcertingly familiar. Something about him filled Jonas with an uneasy curiosity. 'I am from Leningrad,' the young man said. 'My name is Yuri.' He offered his hand, they shook. Jonas also introduced himself, finished by saying 'Norway'. As if it were a mantra. It never failed. Norway *was* a word which elicited a response from people, no matter where, as if they immediately associated it with something exotic, even those who did not even know that Norway was a country. The thought struck Jonas: there might be people in the world for whom Norway was a Samarkand, a spot so unreal that it acquired a magical, seductive aura.

Not so with Yuri. When he heard where Jonas was from he pulled out a piece of paper and scribbled something down on it with a pencil, so vehemently that the graphite virtually flew in all directions. He handed the slip to Jonas. Then he waited, in evident suspense, as if he had just handed over a passport which would gain him immediate entry into Jonas's world. On the paper was a fractional equation: figures and letters and infinity symbols. Jonas could make neither head nor tail of it. 'Abel,' said Yuri. 'Abel!' he repeated, even more emphatically, pointing at the piece of paper. 'From a proof of convergence criteria.'

Jonas realised that this had to be an extract from one of Niels Henrik Abel's theorems, did not dare to admit that he was completely stumped, even though he had attended the same school as Norway's greatest mathematician. He merely nodded. Affected to nod enthusiastically, knowingly.

'One of my teachers showed me this,' Yuri said. 'He called Abel the Pushkin of mathematics. The poet of algebra.'

Jonas was quite taken aback by the thought of a country where a schoolteacher could be acquainted with such advanced mathematics. Unless, of course, there was talk here of a Russian Mr Dehli. Jonas was intrigued by this: Abel, a Norwegian name and at the same time a word, a fascinating word at that, in a universal language. Abel and Samarkand could have been said to belong to the same word-class.

He considered politely taking his leave. He had been planning to visit a museum and then Timur Lenk's mausoleum. He was constantly reminded by his surroundings of his mongoloid younger brother, Benjamin; Samarkand had been one of the Mongols' cities, first destroyed by Genghis Khan, then designated their capital by the mighty Timur Lenk, or Tamburlaine, one of those restless rulers who had shaken the world.

But when Yuri invited Jonas to accompany him to a nearby *chaikhana*, or tea house, Jonas knew right away that this person was more important than any historic sight, more important, even, than Timur Lenk who had made the whole world tremble. Minutes later they were sitting surrounded by old men wearing turban-like headgear or small embroidered skullcaps, drinking tea under large, retouched photographs of Communist leaders. Yuri told him a little about himself. His father was a musician, a pianist; his mother worked in a shop selling ironmongery. He had an older sister who, when she wasn't driving a truck, did nothing but read novels. 'And I have a brother, a year older than me,' Yuri said with a smile. 'A real tearaway. Best at everything. And an incorrigible womaniser.'

Round about them men were eating *shaslik* or *plov*. Some were playing the mandatory chess or dominoes. Jonas heard what Yuri was saying, but tried to distance himself from it. He was in a ferment. The worst of it was that he knew what was coming. And come it did. 'I also have a little brother with Down's syndrome,' Yuri said. 'Do you know what that is?'

Jonas nodded. Took a sip of his green tea. Glanced round about, glanced out of the window. Dusk was falling. He ought to be getting back to his hotel. He felt dizzy, disoriented. He had been in a kind of trance ever since he had looked deep into the walls of the buildings on Registan Square, gazed into flat surfaces which had suddenly, as a whole, assumed a depth – or no, not depth: many dimensions, more than three.

The young Russian was still talking about his little brother with Down's syndrome. Jonas was dreading the revelation of one particular fact. That, too, was forthcoming. 'It was all my fault,' Yuri said. 'I won't go into detail, but it was because of me that my mother had that baby.'

Jonas sat for a while saying nothing, hardly dared to ask. But: 'What do you do?' he said.

What was he to think if the young man opposite him told him that he was going to university, but that he had still not made up his mind which subject to study.

'I've just been offered a job in television,' his companion said.

Jonas breathed a sigh of relief. Some of his sense of unease left him.

'Television,' he said, laughing out of utter relief. 'What's so exciting about that?'

'It's the future – I thought everybody knew that,' Yuri said, genuinely amazed that anyone should respond in such a way; not only that, but a young man from what could almost be described as an eastern province of the USA. 'I want to make programmes,' Yuri said. 'Programmes that will work a change in people, make them think differently. Without that there is no hope for this bizarre country, these countries. You see – I can say this to you – Communism is already dead.' The way he said this, lowering his voice and glancing wryly at the portraits of Politburo members, allowed Jonas to laugh even more.

It was almost dark when they left the tea house. Yuri pulled Jonas towards a bus. 'I want to show you something that far too few people know about,' he said. They alighted in the north-eastern quarter of the city and walked up a hill. Jonas thought they must have come there for the view, but Yuri headed towards a small building. A man was just locking up. Yuri spoke to him, beckoned to Jonas. They could go in. It transpired that hidden away inside this building, a simple vaulted structure, was something extraordinary: a hollow cut out of the rock face. This was all that was left, Yuri told him, of Ulug Beg's massive observatory; a circular building thirty-five metres high. They were standing next to the remains of a gigantic instrument. Yuri explained that this was part of a narrow meridian arc, two parallel rails covered in polished marble slabs. He pointed to incisions in the stone, marking the degrees. This instrument had been used to make various astronomical observations. Jonas looked at the arc, tried to imagine the rest of it extending towards the heavens. It looked like a ramp.

They were back on the square outside. The weather was clear. The points of light in the darkness above their heads seemed unusually close. 'I am going to use the television camera like a telescope,' Yuri said. 'I mean to find the stars on earth, among my own people.' He said this lightly, but something in his voice spoke of serious intent.

They both stood with their heads tilted back. This place, the remains of the observatory, inspired them to assume this position. 'Did it ever cross your mind that we could give the constellations new names, start from scratch, if you like?' Yuri asked. When Jonas did not reply Yuri went on talking, but his voice began to fade, as if Jonas were being picked up, carried off. Which was only natural. Because, having achieved what was just about the most impossible thing on earth and made it to Samarkand, to the edge of a flat world, there was only one way to go and that was *out*. Samarkand was one big launch pad. With his head tilted back, his eyes fixed on the stars, Jonas realised that he would have to go beyond Samarkand; he had to get out there – out into space – to find the spot for which he was searching.

So, for anyone who still has not grasped it, it was here, on a little hill in Samarkand, that Jonas Wergeland decided to study astrophysics, to take the step, so to speak, from the Silk Road to the Milky Way. Here, in Uzbekistan, possibly due to the limpid blue his eyes beheld on the domes of the mosques, or because of the stars in the mosaic patterns of the Ulug Beg *madrasah* doorway on Registan Square, suddenly, although never before, not for one moment, had he considered such a move, he took the first step into a realm of

red dwarfs and supergiants and black holes and hundreds upon mind-blowing hundreds of billions of galaxies. It struck him that astronomy could be
his Samarkand. A standpoint from which he would be able to see everything,
including the world, from the outside. After all, it goes without saying really:
there is only one reason for taking up astrophysics: a desire to understand the
Earth. Or, to be more precise: a desire to understand oneself.

And Margrete was probably still there at the back of his mind, in the
form of a belief that concealed within science there was alchemy, that there
was, nonetheless, a link between astronomy and astrology. Jonas may have
been hoping, through research, through some grandiose project, to influence
future occurrences, alter predestined chains of events. In other words: if he
could make his name shine, quite literally, all across the sky, maybe she would
see it. Come back.

Later, when Aunt Laura asked him, what he had found in Samarkand,
Jonas answered without a second thought: 'In Samarkand I met myself.'

After his hike around Aurlandsdalen Leonard had made a similar discovery, though of a more down-to-earth nature, more brutal and shocking. And
sitting, battered and bruised, you might say, in a basement no longer redolent with delicious pasta sauces, he told Jonas all about it. Jonas always felt
that the moment of Leonard's revelation should have been illustrated with a
slow-motion sequence like the one at the end of Michelangelo Antonioni's
Zabriskie Point, the climax of the film, when a building blows up and we see
the explosion replayed thirteen times from different angles and distances. To
cut a long story short, Leonard had found out that his father, Olav Knutzen,
was not in fact his father. Leonard had been every bit as blind as the central
character in *Blow-Up*; he had not seen what was going on in the bushes, as
it were.

So who was his father? Leonard met Jonas one Friday afternoon on
Youngstorget – which, by the way, standing as it now does as a monument
to a sacred, bygone ideal, is the closest one comes in Oslo to Samarkand's
Registan Square. They hung around on the corner of the Trade Union building for half an hour. Jonas thought they were waiting for Leonard's mother,
who worked there. Leonard said nothing, just hopped up and down impatiently. Suddenly he pointed to a man coming out of a bank across the street
which was now closed for the day. 'That's him,' Leonard sobbed. 'That's my
father.' Jonas refused to believe it. A smarmy little git, a dark, skinny guy in a
blue suit, with slicked-back black hair. He could actually have passed for an
Italian, maybe even a film director, but he was just about the very opposite
of Olav Knutzen with his weighty, Nobel laureate presence. His name was
Dale and Leonard was one jump ahead of Jonas in himself acknowledging

the irony of the legend on the placard he was holding up in the by then published photograph from that summer: SAVE THE DALE. 'And shall I tell you
what the worst part is?' Leonard said. 'He works in a bank, on the cash desk.'
Jonas remembered Leonard's vituperative, indignant rants against bankers
and banking, prompted by the story of how Antonioni had had to earn his
living early on in his career. From the way Leonard spoke it sounded to Jonas
as though his friend were pronouncing his own death sentence. Leonard had
such a morbid obsession with heredity that one look at that little shrimp, his
biological father, was enough to tell him that those genes offered no hope
whatsoever. Such a man could not possibly sire a prince.

Jonas never did learn how Leonard had found out about it. Whether it
was just that his mother had finally got round to telling him, or whether he
had, quite by accident, caught something going on in the background while
filming the everyday doings on Youngstorget; something which he had blown
up, enlarging it until he could make out a detail – a clue. Or whether it should
simply be put down to a keen-honed eye. What if a young bank clerk had
lodged with the Knutzens when they were just setting up house together,
what if the basement really had been a darkroom, a red-lamped love nest.

Whatever the case, this discovery fairly took the wind out of Leonard's
sails. The way he saw it, he no longer had the letters OK, Olav Knutzen's
initials, stamped on him. And in losing the 'z' in his name, he seemed also to
have lost a vital chromosome – that lightning bolt, that flash – the guarantee
of a good eye. All Leonard's grand, elaborate plans were quashed. That 'z'
now seemed more emblematic of sleep. He dropped out of school, shelved
his cine camera and the outline for a twelve-minute 8 mm film on reduction,
and away he went.

Or at least, before he disappeared he asked Jonas to please meet him
at the Film Institute at Røa. Jonas had duly shown up, fearing the worst.
They were alone. Jonas was ordered to take a seat in the screening room,
and there he sat, surrounded by forty-six other, empty, seats while Leonard
ran the film. Which film? *Blow-Up*. But this was a new version. Leonard had
re-edited it. Jonas sat all alone in the screening room, watching the film. He
was impressed. And intrigued. Because this was a totally different story. Less
confusing. As if the gap between art and reality had been edited out. And as
far as Jonas could tell, the murder was actually solved. The film, or rather:
Leonard's version of it, ended with the central character going to his studio to
photograph, and more or less seduce Verushka, the fabulous fashion model:
a scene which, in the original film, came right at the beginning. It was pretty
close to a happy ending.

Jonas was often to think that the roots of his best and most famous television programmes were to be found here, in a tiny cinema in the Oslo suburb of Røa. He sometimes thought of the *Thinking Big* series as being just one film, cut in different ways.

On the way back to town, Leonard told him that some kind soul at the offices of the film's Norwegian distributor had given him a worn-out copy which was actually due to be scrapped. And a sympathetic person at the Film Institute had let him use the cutting desk there. So? What did Jonas think? There was a note of anxiety in Leonard's voice. What he had done might well seem like sacrilege. To re-edit *Blow-Up* – it was tantamount to re-editing Michelangelo's Sistine Chapel.

Jonas did not know what to say. In time he would come to see that Leonard had possibly been conducting an experiment inspired by genetic engineering. He wanted to prove to Jonas that he could reconstruct himself. That there was hope, despite his little shrimp of a bank teller father. But at the time Jonas could not see anything to suggest that Leonard had succeeded in his venture. All the light seemed to have gone out of his friend's dark eyes. There was not a spark. Only blackness. As if a shutter had dropped down for good and all.

Then Leonard Knutzen disappeared. Someone said that he had gone to India, that he took LSD and had long since blown his mind out completely. Others claimed to have seen him, or someone who looked like him, in the centre of Copenhagen, carrying a sign – or probably a placard – in the shape of a big hand pointing to a dive down a side street, the sort of place where, in the very early seventies, you could see grainy German porn movies.

Jonas thought often of how fragile a life was, how very, very little it took to knock a person off course. Or onto a new course. You bend down to tie your shoelaces and when you straighten up again your life has changed. Jonas himself had been an astonished witness to the moment when Daniel, high on innumerable easy victories, was suddenly brought face to face with the gravity of life. Jonas never really understood his brother, but he would have bet anything in the world that Daniel would never have become anything as outrageously far-fetched as a minister of the church.

That autumn Daniel had little thought for anything but his prospects as a star athlete; he was going through a phase when he was, in many ways, at his most intolerable, a tearaway disguised as a rebel, Daniel X with his black-gloved fist. Almost as if it were a natural extension of stretching his muscles after a tough training session, he started going out with a girl who sang in a Ten Sing choir. When it came to getting into a girl's pants, Daniel was not fussy; it was okay by him even if the girl in question was a member of something as soulless and unmusical as one of those YWCA choirs: spotty teenagers singing off-key, backed by a band with badly tuned guitars – a nigh-on blasphemous set-up, in Daniel's eyes, and about as far from Aretha Franklin's gut-wrenching, wailful ecstasies as you could get.

It took more than the Queen of Soul and her seductive gospel strains to bring Daniel to the scripture, though. Jonas began to notice that Daniel seemed unusually agitated, then one evening he confessed to his little brother: he had knocked up his girlfriend. He was as desperately certain as you can only be when you are sixteen and have finally 'done it', with all the imprudence and raw self-assurance of the first-timer. Jonas could not resist it: 'Maybe you should have put a black glove on your dick as well,' he said. His brother, who would normally have flattened him for that, pretended not to hear, and instead went on cursing his spermatozoa, those microscopic champion swimmers that could make a woman's body swell up like a balloon. He admitted to Jonas that suddenly he was seeing pregnant women all over the place. Wherever he looked there were people with prams and packs of nappies. He was done for. He could already see the headlines: 'Grorud's youngest parents.'

It was in this frame of mind that Daniel attended one of the last athletics meets of the year, and at the Jordal Amfi Arena, more specifically in the long-jump pit, he felt a higher power taking a hand in his life.

Daniel was an unusually gifted athlete and had always been particularly good at the long jump. He loved the combination of sprinting and jumping; he revelled in the challenge of hitting the board just right. So he was not at all happy with his first jump of five metres and twenty-seven centimetres – he was used to jumping around six metres. It could not just have been a case of nerves, a slight loss of concentration at the thought of a Ten Sing girl who was alarmingly 'late'. Something had held him back in the air, he said later. A weight, a heaviness, as if there were some connection between gravidity and gravity. This feeling was even more pronounced on his second jump, when he hit the board perfectly and yet – as if the gravitational force had somehow doubled – jumped a shorter distance than normal. When the measuring crew announced the length – the same as before: 'Daniel: 5.27' – he did not give it too much thought. But when, on his third and last jump – the schedule at this meet only allowed for three tries – he jumped exactly five metres and twenty-seven centimetres yet again, he began to wonder. For the first time in his career, Daniel walked away from the long-jump pit without a medal.

Over the next few days, his mood exacerbated no doubt by growing anxiety over his girlfriend's overdue period, Daniel started to give some serious thought to his weird result in the long-jump: 5.27 three times in a row – that was more than a coincidence. And with his natural propensity for speculation, it was not long before he consulted the old Family Bible, on the principle that a long-jump result was like a grain of manna, a little slip of paper that you picked out of a bowl, like a tombola ticket. Although he had never believed a word of it before, at that particular moment he was sure that the scripture would determine the course of his life. In the Book of Daniel, chapter 5, verse 27, once he had managed to decipher the elaborate Gothic lettering, he slowly read to himself, with eyes as wide, surely, as those of King Belshazzar himself: 'TEKEL; thou art weighed in the balances and art found wanting.' The context, together with Gustav Doré's dramatic illustration, left him in no doubt: the writing was on the wall. Weighed and found wanting.

Daniel knew what this meant. His *soul* was too light. For someone as concerned with the health and well-being of the soul as Daniel was, there could be no harsher verdict. At an early age he had read how certain religions believed that the soul was placed in a scale after death. If it proved too light it was cast into the jaws of a monster which sat next to the seat of judgement waiting to receive it. To Daniel this Bible text could mean only one thing: she *was* pregnant.

Although, there might still be hope. What if this were a final warning from a merciful God? Daniel fell to his knees. Just at that moment Jonas walked in, then pulled up short on the threshold. He could not believe his eyes. Daniel with his back to him, on his knees next to the bed. Daniel the rebel, a pig-headed bugger who had never in his life bowed down to anything. Softly and, if the truth be told, a mite fearfully Jonas retreated. What his brother said, what he prayed for, what he promised – because he must have made some sort of deal – Jonas never discovered. But from that day onwards Daniel W. Hansen was a Christian. You might say that he rotated his X forty-five degrees, turning it into a cross. And I hardly need say: there was no pregnancy. Soon afterwards, Daniel's girlfriend came to see him, all smiles, to tell him that everything was okay. For days afterwards, Jonas could hear Daniel humming to himself when he thought he was alone, and Jonas's hearing was good enough for him to recognise the hymn: 'Hallelujah, my soul is free.'

Daniel kept his promise, though. He remained a Christian. It may be that his time as Daniel X had merely been a harbinger of what was to come, as Jonas had thought – an intimation of an unknown x inside him, a religious chamber. If, that is, he did not believe that he had at last found the field which had been there waiting for his rebellious heart. To Jonas it was nothing short of a miracle. Proof that at any moment a person can suddenly change. So when other, normally peaceable individuals suddenly became raging revolutionaries, Daniel, with his slumbering, inborn talent for rebellion, was holed up indoors with his nose buried in his Bible, as if he had already started studying theology, embarked upon his career in the church. He had found his Samarkand. His life had acquired weight.

Leonard Knutzen, too, gained weight. Or at least his wallet did. Years later, when Jonas rarely ever thought of his old friend, Leonard's name suddenly appeared in the newspapers. Although eventually the headlines spoke simply of Leonardo. In photographs his coat was always slung over his shoulders like a cape, a touch which now seemed elegant rather than affected. And his eyes looked keen again. The first article appeared in conjunction with a much publicised exhibition of works by young Norwegian photographers. Leonard Knutzen had put up the money for the exhibition. A lot of money. Leonard Knutzen was a rich man. Fabulously rich. But no one, not even in media circles had ever come across his name before. He lived abroad. Leonard had quietly made himself a fortune on the stock market. The image of him presented in the press was of a shrewd individual much to be admired, a financial artist; it was them, the media, who nicknamed him Leonardo, without knowing anything of his heroic past as the Italian-inspired director of a good number of twelve-minute 8 mm films full of scooters and people gazing in different directions. Leonard had done it – done what he had shown he could do with *Blow-Up* in that tiny cinema at Røa. He had actually re-cut his own fate. He had used the art of montage to create a new life for himself. Or perhaps one should simply say that he had enlarged himself.

To Jonas, Leonard seemed the very personification of modern Norway – a nation which led the most anonymous, the most discreet, of existences, alongside the other nations of the world, while the money simply poured into the state coffers. Likewise, Leonard sat in his faraway office, pressing buttons, unremarked by anyone in his native country, while the money pumped into his offshore accounts. The press's glowing reports of Leonardo's doings reminded Jonas of a conjuring trick. Leonard was now blowing up money, he could take a *krone* and, by dint of an abstract, magical process, magnify it into ten. Both Leonard and Norway had discovered that you did not need to work – or not, at least, in the old-fashioned physical fashion depicted in *Aktuell* magazine – in order to get rich. Leonard had finally found a use for his keen eye. That was still the key. An eye for where to put one's money. An eye for the perfect stock. In interviews he said, half in jest, that he supposed he might be a Leonardo when it came to spying investment opportunities which no one else believed possible. To Jonas it seemed more as though Leonard had determined to blow the abilities, the genes, of a lousy bank teller into something great. He had produced a happy ending, against all odds, and in spite of the original film.

On the other hand, Jonas also had the definite impression that for Leonard the driving force was still wrath. That Leonard had rediscovered some of the Italian temperament from those evenings in the Red Room, a little of the bite of all those spicy sauces they had spooned over their pasta. The fiery grindings of the pepper mill. Either that or he had accomplished something which only very few ever manage: to preserve some of the indignation which we tend and nurture so carefully in our youth. Jonas could not help thinking that one should possibly take this as a lesson. Maybe everyone should have a little placard stuck to the fridge door of their settled, routine existences, a slip of paper saying: SAVE THE WRATH.

All the write-ups on Leonard Knutzen did, however, also lead Jonas to immerse himself in much more serious reflections. He was reminded of another time. He had, he recalled, not only been mad at the world. Once he had actually tried to open up the world. In junior high he had met a master, a schoolmaster, and before that Bo Wang Lee.

Uranus

In his youth Jonas Wergeland had the ability to follow several lines of thought at once. For long periods of time he also had the feeling that he was living parallel lives. While he may have spent some parts of the day in a basement, seething with rage, for other parts of the day he was, for example, at school – where he came across as a rather shy, polite and, not least, inquisitive young man.

The first time Jonas Wergeland saw the slogan 'The real thing' he thought, not of Coca-Cola, but of *realskolen* – junior high. For him, this truly was 'real school'. It is not the case, as certain influential branches of psychology would have it, that our characters are formed by the time we are around seven. Things are not, I am glad to say, as dire as all that. Like the mighty banyan tree, human beings too can put down roots from branches high above. Jonas Wergeland received his 'upbringing', his most crucial stimuli, at junior high.

If it is true that from the cradle to the grave, from childhood games with stones to the puffing and blowing of old age, man lives out, as it were, the whole history of the species, then junior high was, for Jonas, a Renaissance, a revival of age-old learning, and particularly of the elementary knowledge instilled in him in 'antiquity', those three glorious first years at school. Not because he spent so much time with his chum Leonard, known as Leonardo, but because he came under the wing of a person, a teacher, who fully merited the epithet applied to individuals of exceptionally wide-ranging talent and cultivation: a Renaissance man.

Who was this person? Well it was certainly not the Iron Chancellor, who drummed the litany of German prepositions into their heads, nor was it Dr Jekyll, whom they had for English: on the surface a gentleman to his finger-tips, dressed from top to toe in tweed and corduroy, but capable of exploding into the most pyrotechnical fits of rage, to which the snapping of a pointer was but the mildest prelude. Nor was it their enigmatic maths teacher, Miss Pi, who could stir a boy's blood simply with the circular motions of her arms, or the Weed, their natural history teacher, who swooned at the very mention of the word 'dissect'. And for any favour: forget PE teacher, Tamara Press. At an age when they positively oozed disrespect, only one person slipped through the needle's eye of their tolerance. He was even exempt from the usual fiendish practical jokes, such as balancing the teacher's lectern on the very edge of the dais or breaking off matchsticks in the lock of the classroom door. It is a mark of his standing that he did not even labour under a nickname. He was, quite simply, Mr Dehli. Jonas had him for Norwegian and history. In ancient myths and legends one often hears tell of inspired masters, the sort who teach the hero to fence or shoot with bow and arrow. Mr Dehli was such a master. Although the 'e' in his surname was actually sounded as 'ay' and the 'l' and the 'h' were the wrong way round, Jonas always pronounced it like that of the capital of India – for reasons which will later become apparent. 'We're not going to have Norwegian now,' Jonas would think before his classes, 'we're going to have *Indian*.'

In all the heated debate which constantly rages around education reforms and books and buildings and grades, it is astonishing how people forget what a difference a teacher can make. You snore your way through years of deadly dull history lessons, then you have a reserve teacher for two periods and you're hooked on the Thirty Years War or the books of Marguerite Yourcenar for life. Ask anybody – what they remember from school are the teachers. There is nothing to beat an inspiring teacher. There is no substitute – absolutely none – for the charisma of an enthusiast. And if anyone radiated infectious enthusiasm, it was Mr Dehli. He was never seen in the duster coats worn by some teachers in those days; he always came to school looking spruce and dapper in a white shirt, a jacket and a bow tie which was always hopelessly askew by the end of a zestful lesson, as if he had just been in a fight, or on a wild airplane ride. Jonas Wergeland said more than once that he had had only one real teacher in twelve years of schooling. It was also, and not unimportantly, Mr Dehli who introduced him to Maya.

It sometimes seemed to Jonas that it was not actually people who made him feel embarrassed. He was embarrassed by the world. Or for the world. Because of its alarming flatness. But thanks to Mr Dehli, after only a few months at junior high Jonas again began to discern a suggestion of depth, little glimpses of something *behind* the flatness. Through a fruitful process of repetition Mr Dehli also succeeded in reawakening the round-eyed joy of the first years at school; the delight of drawing a cow's four stomachs, the pride in managing to construct a ninety-degree angle with the aid of compasses, the wonder aroused by a word like 'accusative'. And suddenly Jonas understood the full magnitude of things: the purpose of the meridian concept, the consequences of Caesar's statement when he crossed the Rubicon, the wealth of associations contained within a word like 'stamen'. Mr Dehli got them to write whole stories in the pluperfect, or the past-future-perfect tense.

'What is this?' he asked during their first Norwegian period, writing a large H on the board so emphatically that chalk flew everywhere – Mr Dehli could pull a stick of chalk out of his jacket pocket quicker than any gunslinger.

The whole class looked blank. 'Take a good look,' he said. 'Can't you see that it's a ladder? Every letter in the alphabet is a ladder. Use them well and you'll be able to climb wherever you please.'

Mr Dehli set out to *elevate* his pupils. Provide them with ladders to enable them to reach a higher plane. He never brought a pupil down. Instead, as an educator in the truest sense of that word, he drew out the best in them, drew from them things they did not even know they knew. He was not unlike a personage who would later appear on Norwegian television, the charismatic presenter of the musical quiz programme *Counterpoint*, Sten Broman who, like Mr Dehli, performed his duties dressed to the nines, in suits he designed himself, and had a knack for eliciting the correct answers from teams who, to begin with, seemed totally stumped; he seemed to take pride in bringing out the contestants' subliminal knowledge.

Schoolmaster Dehli employed a number of unorthodox methods. When they were studying Ibsen, he turned up for class with a pocket mirror in one hand and his chest covered in medals. 'It is impossible to understand Ibsen without also taking into account his vanity and his ambition,' Mr Dehli declared. Who could forget something like that?

Often he would turn things on their heads. 'There are any number of possible futures, everybody knows that,' he said during one history class. 'But did it ever occur to you that there also exists a wealth of possible pasts? For tomorrow I want you to write a couple of pages on what the Second World War would have been like for someone from Japan. Don't just sit there gawping. Make a note in your homework books.'

Mr Dehli's main interest lay, however, in impressing upon them the way in which the different subjects were all interconnected, as in an organic system of learning. He showed them how just about everything can be set into a fresh context. He told them about poets in history class and religion in Norwegian classes. It came as a shock to Jonas to hear his teacher say that there was nothing to stop them introducing elements from the Weed's or Miss Pi's domains, from natural history and maths, that is, into their essays. Mr Dehli advocated a viewpoint which would hold sway in the universities a decade later: if you wanted to do something original with your life then you needed to have both feet on the ground, firmly planted in at least two different realms of study. The more remote from one another the better.

Although Mr Dehli could not know it, in his mind Jonas likened this idea to a necklace he had seen as a child. On it hung a disc engraved on both sides with obscure strokes and dashes which, when you spun the disc round, spelled 'I love you'.

Despite his conviction that he was special, despite his gift for thinking, up until now Jonas had not done particularly well at school. Or at least, he had not been interested. With the advent, in fifth grade, of the more soporific, factually oriented lessons, he fell behind. Not even the weird and often funny sentences which their teacher made up to help them remember the names of towns in southern Norway or the fjords of Finnmark could enliven his interest. Particularly when it came to writing Norwegian essays Jonas had a problem: he tended to lose himself in the ramifications of his own mental associations. His essay for the exam in eighth grade was a disaster, rewarded, or punished rather, with a P for Poor.

But here he had found a teacher who did exactly the same thing, the difference being that Mr Dehli turned it into a strength. 'What is the opposite of truth?' he asked on one occasion, and answered before they had time to think: 'Clarity.' Mr Dehli was an expert climber; he would venture out onto the thinnest branches of a line of reasoning, then with a sudden swoop come swinging back to the trunk, possibly on a creeper. This, for Jonas, was more thrilling than the trapeze artists at the circus. Frequently he would sit at his desk, following – heart in mouth, almost – their master's exposition of a complex topic, with one thought leading to another as he scrawled key words and phrases on the board. And just when Jonas was sure that their poor teacher had lost his way completely, when Mr Dehli, with his hair covered in chalk dust and his bow tie woefully askew, was stammering 'and … and … and…', suddenly it would come, that blessed 'but …', and a sigh of relief would run through the classroom, to be followed by the master's closing triple-somersault of an argument, which he delivered while circling some of the key words and drawing a couple of connecting lines that made Jonas gasp with surprised understanding.

'Watch this,' Mr Dehli said in Norwegian class one day, placing a glass beaker of water over a Bunsen burner. 'Today we're going to produce an ester.' He poured equal amounts of ethanol and acetic acid into a test tube and let it sit for a while in the boiling water. 'See? Nothing happens,' he announced, absent-mindedly waving a grammar book in the air. 'In order to instigate a reaction we need something else. Watch carefully now.' Mr Dehli added a few drops of concentrated sulphuric acid to the test tube and put it back into the boiling water. A lovely smell, like fruit or perfume, filled the classroom. What was going on? Jonas wondered. Chemistry in the Norwegian class? 'Imagine that those two liquids are two different thoughts,' Mr Dehli said. 'Put them together and nothing happens. But then imagine that a third thought suddenly comes to me and I think this along with the other two. Abracadabra! A reaction is triggered!' Mr Dehli pointed triumphantly to the test tube containing the sweet-smelling liquid. 'These are the thoughts you have to pursue,' he concluded, thereby making the final link between chemistry and

Norwegian. 'Those which act as *catalysts*.' No one understood what he was getting at better than Jonas, who had for years been whipping up parallel thoughts while skipping doubles and – perhaps even more crucially – had seen the world grow, thanks to a real live 'catalyst'.

It's true, one day the world did grow. Jonas was ten years old, sitting all alone on a rock beside Badedammen – the lake that had been converted into a bathing pond for the residents of Grorud back in the thirties. It was early evening and unusually quiet. No yells from down by the weir, where the boys were given to chucking squealing girls into the water; no shouts, half-fearful, half-gleeful, because Jonas – did he have gills? – was swimming all the way across the pond underwater; no mothers lazing on the grassy slope in distracting bikinis with one anxious eye on the toddlers playing by the water's edge. A brief shower, a warm drizzle, had only just sent the last bathers home for dinner. Now the park-like surroundings were once more drenched in a warm light. The lifeguards, holders of the most coveted of summer jobs – those white uniform caps alone – had quit the scene, having first emptied the elegant wrought-iron litter bins. The shutters were closed on the kiosk and its rich store of ice-poles and ice-cream cones. Jonas sat with the sun on his back next to the diving board where, only days before, Daniel – clad in his new, tiger-striped bathing trunks – had executed a somersault for the very first time; his triumph marred only by the fact that he forgot to look where he was going and ended up ripping the lilo of a lady who, fortunately, managed to roll off it in time. Jonas stared at a dragonfly which was flitting back and forth across the smooth surface of the lake. A dragon from China. He sat there, hoping that something would happen.

Absently he threw a stone into the water, watched the rings spreading out, further and further out, circle upon circle, a huge target. He was bored, he had no one to play with. The summer holidays had begun, his chums were all away. He cursed the disagreement, instigated by an overbearing uncle, which meant that the summer would be half over before Jonas and his family could go to Hvaler.

He picked up another stone, flung it further out, gazed at the rings which began to spread outwards, felt his thoughts, too, flowing in all directions, fanning out from him in a sort of circle. At that same moment something happened to the ripples on the water. They were broken. Or rather: they ran into rings radiating from some other point. He had not heard a splash, the other stone must have been thrown at exactly the same instant as his own. Jonas's eyes lingered on the pretty picture in the water, the pattern formed by the waves colliding, intersecting – a much nicer sight than the solitary set of rings.

And then a boat came sailing towards him; it emerged from some bushes to his left and bore in a gentle arc straight towards the spot where he was sitting. He shut his eyes, opened them again. It might have had something to do with the landscape in the background, the absence of people. The boat grew. The whole pond grew. The perspective twisted. The boat became a real ship, a magnificent liner. The pond became the open sea. And suddenly Jonas recognised the vessel, it was the *MS Bergensfjord* itself, the finest of the American liners. Jonas could not have said how long this vision lasted, an actual ship from the Norwegian American Line on a small lake on the fringes of Lillomarka, but it was dispelled, at any rate, when the model ship rammed into the shore right at his feet. The illusion shattered; his surroundings shrank, reverting once more to the familiar bathing pond.

Jonas fished out the boat: an exact, thirty-centimetre long replica of the splendid Atlantic liner he had more than once seen docked in Oslo harbour. The propeller was battery-driven and you could flick the rudder back and forth. With the ship cradled in his hands he set out along the path leading to the spit of land further up and there, behind the bushes, was another boy of about Jonas's own age. A Chinaman, was Jonas's first thought. And the other boy really did have a Chinese look about him. An impression which was only reinforced later when the boy told him his name: Bo Wang Lee. He seemed very secretive, hastily folded up a map. Jonas only caught a glimpse of a couple of lines clearly forming a cross. They must have been made with the stub of pencil stuck behind the other boy's ear. Underneath the map a yellow notebook came into view. Bo Wang Lee's trademarks: a pencil stub and a little yellow notebook.

'Look,' Bo said, picking something off the ground. It looked rather like a divining rod, one of those forked sticks used to find water. But Bo Wang Lee was never one to content himself with something as simple as finding water. 'This is a detector which can locate secret underground chambers,' he said. The word 'detector' alone was enough to impress Jonas. 'We might be able to discover a treasure vault. Or a whole city even.' Bo spoke Norwegian with a slight accent. Jonas had the feeling that the other boy was trying to divert his attention from the business with the map.

Jonas said he didn't see how you could find a whole city underneath the ground. He handed the model ship back to Bo, then he picked up a small, flat stone, threw it hard and low and got it to bounce six or seven times across the surface of the pond. Bo was not to be put off. His father was an archaeologist. And Bo's father had told him about the mighty Emperor Qin Shi Huangdi in China, who had ordered the building of a massive underground tomb for himself. Even though Bo was spouting all this information, Jonas did not feel that he was showing off. Again Bo brought out his yellow notebook, and proceeded, while apparently consulting it, to paint a vivid picture of how this mausoleum had looked. Just listening to this description almost took Jonas's breath away. The Emperor Qin had designed his tomb in the form of a whole city – or no, more than just a city: a miniature replica of his empire, a place in which to live even after death, with palaces and little streams of mercury, mountains sculpted out of copper and a firmament studded with pearls. The Emperor Qin's obsession with immortality bordered on madness, Bo said. A host of intricate and lethal booby traps were meant to prevent robbers from getting at the wonders within. 700,000 of Qin's subjects were said to have helped build this vast complex. Bo showed Jonas an astonishingly realistic sketch in the yellow notebook, he claimed it was based on the description by an ancient Chinese historian which his father had read aloud to him. 'When I grow up I'm going to go to China and find that tomb,' Bo said with a determined look on his face. 'It's in a place called Xi'an. Will you come with me?' As if in a symbolic attempt to persuade Jonas he started up the *MS Bergensfjord* again and set it in the water.

'I don't see me ever going to China,' Jonas said as he watched Bo flick a stone across the water too. It skiffed an untold number of times, reaching almost all the way to the other side.

Now Bo Wang Lee was obviously not Chinese, but that is how Jonas would always think of him; he had such an inscrutable air about him, as if he really did belong to some distant, exotic and, above all, tremendously wise civilisation – or as if there was a mysterious buried city inside him too. Later, it struck Jonas that he had felt older during those weeks than he did in all the time spent smouldering with wrath in Leonard Knutzen's basement.

As time went on Jonas also came to think of Bo as a prince. With his coal-black hair, cut in an odd pudding-bowl style – later Jonas would associate it with the Beatles' hairdos on the cover of *Rubber Soul* – his friend was almost the spitting image of Prince Valiant, whom Jonas had come across in the only comics which Rakel, his sister, deigned to read; she had a whole pile of them under her bed.

The two boys got so caught up in skiffing stones that they did not notice until it was too late that the *MS Bergensfjord* was on a steady course towards the gap in the weir where the water flowed out. Again Jonas felt the perspective twist, felt that the model boat had turned into a real ship and that this slit represented a rift in existence, that the boat was not headed for America, but into another reality, at the back of this one. He did not have time to follow these thoughts to their conclusion. They took off along the path, past the diving board and down to the car park next to the weir. They got there just in time to see the *MS Bergensfjord* come sailing over the falls on a cascade as thin and bright and clear as a curved glass panel, before being dashed inexorably against the rocks in the shallow stream below. 'Shit, shit, shit!' Bo cried, lifting out the model boat which, luckily, was not too badly damaged. As Bo bent down, Jonas noticed a chain with a little disc attached to it fall out of the neck of his shirt. Later he would have the chance to study this disc more closely. There were marks and dashes engraved on either side. 'It's cuneiform writing,' Bo joked. But when he flicked the disc and it spun round fast, Jonas saw the words: I love you. Jonas found this much more impressive than Daniel's somersault.

Jonas and Bo did not find any treasure under the ground around Bade-dammen that evening, but they did find one another; they found one another with a force that almost made Jonas feel uneasy. He could tell with half an eye that this was someone with whom he would become best friends, that this was the sort of person who would send ripples spreading far into his life. The four weeks which lay ahead of him would seem like one long, breathless journey of discovery, in which simply picking globe-flowers along the banks of the stream became an expedition into the least explored reaches of the Amazonian rainforest, and to sit in Charlie's Chariot, the wreck of an ancient Volkswagen down at the dump, was to be driving in the arduous Paris-Dakar rally with Bo as navigator and multilingual interpreter. Bo Wang Lee was like a tropical butterfly which, for a brief and unforgettable time, fluttered into Jonas's life.

'I'm telling you, we *can* find a whole city,' Bo said, looking like a giant with the sparkling waterfall, a tiny Niagara Falls, behind him and the Atlantic liner under his arm. And as if to prove the truth of his words he pulled out the yellow notebook and waved it in the air. 'Are you coming?'

And Jonas went. It is probably safe to say that he would have followed Bo anywhere. In the course of those weeks they undertook an expedition which would stand forever in Jonas's memory as the most important journey he ever made. They went in search of the Vegans.

After this, Jonas did not hear of Vega again until junior high, when Mr Dehli gave a short, but enthusiastic lecture on the Swedish writer Harry Martinson's *Aniara* – neither in Norwegian nor history class, but during a *lunch break*, right outside the staffroom door with, beyond it, the packed lunch which Mr Dehli never got to eat. Without once having to straighten his bow tie he told them how the spaceship in this poem cycle was bound for the constellation of Lyra, whose brightest star was called Vega. Oddly enough, modern astronomers believed that there might be life in that very area, the schoolmaster said, hinting with a raised eyebrow at the prophetic gifts of the writer. Then the bell rang.

The last period of that same day finished, incidentally, with this tireless mentor of so many young and angry, but enquiring, minds running an uncommonly chalky hand through his hair and making the following announcement: 'Tomorrow I'm going to tell you about Maya. This may change your lives.' Now *that* was how a school day ought to end. Jonas could hardly wait, he imagined that this Maya had to be some really extraordinary girl. But despite Mr Dehli's warning he was in no way prepared for the fact that she truly *would* change his life.

Girls frequently took Jonas by surprise. He was, for example, most definitely not out girl hunting one Saturday morning two years later when he wandered into the National Gallery and heard music playing. He and Leonard Knutzen were there to check whether it might be possible to use the Antiquities Room, a gallery claustrophobically full of sculptures, in one of Leonard's – or rather: Leonardo's – new cine films, a work which, at the manuscript stage, was looking exceptionally promising, wanting only just such an unusual location to make it absolutely superb. Jonas was at high school, the Cath, by this time; he did not see as much of Leonard any more, but he still lent a hand with shooting films when the occasion arose – films which, according to Leonard, would do for Oslo what 'the new wave' had done for Paris and, before that, the 'neo-realists' had for Rome, thanks to his discriminating choice of locations. So now and then Jonas would accompany Leonard on his walks around the Norwegian capital in search of symbolic advertising signs on gable ends, dockland areas populated with particularly grim-looking cranes, decoratively tiled entranceways, statues which looked good in pouring rain, parks lit by lamps with metaphysically dull surfaces, staircases which split into two. According to Leonard, the Antiquities Room at the National Gallery was the perfect place with which to illustrate the weighty legacy of history. But Jonas did not join him among the Greek and Roman statues, because he had caught the strains of beautiful – or sweet – music filtering down from the first floor, and followed the sound. It was coming from the room containing the best-known paintings from the National Romantic period: works by Fearnley and Cappelen, Balke and J.C. Dahl – and back then also Tidemand and Gude.

In the centre of the room was a string orchestra. They were playing Tchaikovsky's 'Serenade in C-major'. But even more captivating, for Jonas, than the music was the sight of a girl sitting in the front row, playing the violin and, in the absence of a conductor, directing the others with nods of her head and raised eyebrows. She was in the parallel class to his at the Cath. She had caught his eye mainly because he had seen her carrying a square guitar case. And if this surprised him, then he had been even more impressed to find that it contained a red and white twelve-string Rickenbacker, identical to the one which George Harrison had played in the first Beatles film. At a meeting of the school debating society she had rigged up an amp and played a couple of instrumental numbers so brilliantly and with such feeling that everyone there had been completely knocked out. He asked around after this, found out a bit about her. Sarah B. was her name and she played in a girl band, one of the few which would, in fact, attract some – well-merited – notice at the time; and in later years she would become even better known as an ambassador for the arts in Norway with her electric twelve-string guitar, a pioneer within what became known as world music, a blend of folk airs, jazz and timeless melodies – an echo perhaps of the house in which she had grown up, designed by an eccentric father: a mansion bristling with spires and turrets and stylistic features drawn from every corner of the globe. Jonas had only ever seen her playing an electric guitar, he was not at all prepared for the sight of her sitting here in a gallery, dressed in a long, elegant dress, rather like a throwback to the previous century, and with a violin in her hands. It would be some years yet before she came down in favour of the guitar as her first instrument.

It was an impressive sight. These young people, in the most fascinating of all the fascinating rooms in the National Gallery; romantic music performed in a gallery full of marble busts and gilded frames, glistening oil paintings of moons half-hidden behind dramatic cloud formations and wrecks being relentlessly beaten against sharp rocks. All the members of the orchestra were elegantly dressed, the boys in dark suits, the girls in long dark-blue frocks of various design, and with their hair up. All were possessed with that elation and ardour only found in young musicians who have just reached the stage where they can master any piece of music. There was an exuberance and a passion in their playing, in the tossing of their heads, the flaring nostrils, the glances they exchanged, that you never saw in an established orchestra consisting of older, experienced musicians. To Jonas they all looked as though they were in love. As though this wholehearted, fiery performance was merely the foreplay to some steamy, feverish lovemaking. He could not tear his eyes away from Sarah. She made a natural focal point with her theatrical, but at the same time natural arm movements. Jonas felt particularly drawn to her hands and fingers; one had the impression that she could have done anything with them, produce sound from a stone. And as he watched, as she kindled and sustained a wonder in him and in the other museumgoers who stopped short then sank down, entranced, onto the chairs set round about, he thought what a rare delight it would be to feel those graceful fingers on the back of his neck, running through his hair.

The paintings gave added resonance to Tchaikovsky's serenade, the music lent a new glow to the canvases on the walls. Balke's pale images of the North Cape and the lighthouse on Vardø positively *shimmered*. Jonas ran his eye over motif after motif, over mountains, glaciers and waterfalls, cog-built farmhouses and milkmaids in traditional costume, menhirs and herds of wild reindeer. It may even have been that Jonas saw the twenty-odd paintings in the room as forming a frieze illustrating Norway itself: an impression so powerful that – yes, why not – he actually began work on his television series *Thinking Big* right here.

And speaking of that mammoth television production: we have already touched on Jonas Wergeland's schooldays, so something ought also to be said about the final and by far the most surprising phase of his education, a brief, but momentous apprenticeship on which he embarked towards the end of his time as an announcer on NRK television.

Having abandoned his original, high-flying plans – behind him lay several disheartening years at university and college – Jonas Wergeland considered himself lucky to have found a job in which his talent did not trouble him, where he could, in fact, in all likelihood, have buried it for good and all. But since he and Margrete had been together – he was inclined to say: because of Margrete – an ambition had begun to stir in him once more. He wanted to make television programmes himself. In the early eighties, Jonas Wergeland made the leap from announcer to programme-maker, moved by a desire to try to dive, as it were, from the surface down into the depths. When the NRK bosses agreed to his request he packed his suitcase, with Margrete's blessing, and left the country. If one did not know better, one might think that he had had second thoughts, that he was running away from his big chance.

Later, all manner of rumours went the rounds – prompted mainly by the acrobatic, televisual feats Wergeland performed – about where he had been and what he had done. Some people affirmed that the original idea discernible behind all of Wergeland's programmes could only be ascribed to his having been inspired by Sufism during a visit to Samarkand – an assertion which also appeared in print in a serious article. Others maintained, with all the confidence of insiders, that he had been sitting at the feet of the celebrated film director Michelangelo Antonioni. There were even a few who, in the wee, small hours in some bar, could be heard to mumble something about a Mexican woman by the name of Maya. None of these more or less mythical accounts came anywhere close to the truth. Over the years, to the question regarding what had led up to his epoch as a programme-maker, Wergeland honed an honest, if cryptic reply which not uncommonly so nonplussed his interlocutor that he or she asked no more questions: 'I got to the top by lying on my back.'

In going abroad, Jonas was making a virtue of necessity. Timewise, his trip fell exactly midway between the two referendums which led to Norway saying no to Europe. Although Jonas Wergeland often viewed his homeland as an unscrupulous *Festung Norwegen*, there were times when he was more inclined to liken the Norwegians' tendency to shut themselves off to a mentality he found reflected in René Goscinny's and Albert Uderzo's hilarious Asterix comics. For while their Gallic neighbours allowed themselves to be conquered by the Romans, Asterix and his kinsmen stood their ground. One small village still held out, as it said at the beginning of each story. The same could have been said of Norway. The way Jonas saw it, the wealthy land of Norway had surprisingly many things in common with Asterix's indomitable community. Norway, too, shielded itself from the world around it, while raising menhirs to its own excellence and having its praises sung by unspeakable bards. Like Asterix's Gauls, the Norwegian people considered themselves invincible, and the oil was their magic potion. Jonas Wergeland did not find it at all hard to envisage Norway as the world's largest village, surrounded, and almost driven into the sea, by the mighty civilisation of the Roman Empire.

But, like Asterix, sometimes one had to journey out – out of the provinces, to the Rome of one's day. And because of his special requirements, Jonas Wergeland was never in any doubt as to what was the Rome of his day: London. Jonas's favourite Asterix story was, as it happens, *Asterix in Britain*. Generally speaking, Jonas felt he had a lot of ties with the British metropolis, from the music of LPs such as *Rubber Soul*, recorded at Abbey Road, to the exterior scenes from films like *Blow-Up*, which had got into his blood.

Jonas booked into a hotel in Harrington Road in South Kensington, only a stone's throw from the tube station. The hotel is under new ownership now, and has a new name. Nonetheless, they ought to hang a plaque on the wall outside, because it was here that Jonas Wergeland laid the foundations of his illustrious career. It was in this part of the city, too, that he would have two encounters which would totally floor him, the one physically, the other mentally.

Jonas Wergeland never took an academic degree in Norway, but if his uncompleted studies in astrophysics and architecture could be said to count as a foundation course of sorts, then his major course of study was conducted in London. Jonas always maintained that he left Norway to study at Britain's foremost university. And by Britain's foremost university he meant neither Oxford nor Cambridge, but British Television. Jonas Wergeland travelled to London quite simply to watch television. So he had only two requirements in choosing a hotel: the television in his room and the accompanying remote control had to be in good working order, and the bed had to meet a satisfactory standard. I should perhaps also say that this was in the days before satellite dishes made it possible for NRK – or anyone else, for that matter – to receive virtually any channel you could wish for. Although Jonas would probably have gone anyway: he preferred to conduct these studies in secret.

Having got himself installed, he strolled eagerly down to Exhibition Road and a shop selling art materials. Here he purchased a large notebook with blank pages and marbled covers together with a couple of good pens. For once, Jonas Wergeland was planning to write, and to his mind this was such a momentous decision that he thought of his new acquisition as a copybook, much like the ones in which he had written his first 'a's, or 'H's, ladders up which to climb. In a newsagent's next to the tube station he bought the *TV Times* and the *Radio Times*, which between them provided information on the week's programmes on all four channels. And the rest, you might say, is history. Jonas pulled out a pen, opened the notebook at the first blank page, switched on the TV and settled back on the bed, and there he stayed. In one month he got through four thick notebooks with different coloured marbled covers, filling them with terse notes in tiny writing, as well as lots of little diagrams and sketches. In later years he would refer to these four volumes as 'the golden notebook'.

It's odd really. Norway's most influential television personality of all time was for a long while very sceptical of television. A scepticism which quickened one late August afternoon towards the end of the sixties when he and a couple of chums went home with one of their classmates to complete a tricky homework exercise set by Mr Dehli. Instead, they all ended up with their eyes glued to the television screen. And what were they watching, these otherwise so rebellious, angry young men, who should perhaps have been more concerned with what was going on in the newly invaded Czechoslovakia? They sat totally transfixed, watching the wedding of the Crown Prince of Norway to Miss Sonja Haraldsen. They were dazzled by how brilliantly NRK controlled the eighteen cameras in operation for the occasion: five inside the cathedral and thirteen along the procession route. Norway had taken the definitive step into the television age and the era of the mass media, a time when the world once more became flat and small, a time when people seemed to imagine that a screen could represent reality.

Jonas Wergeland's negative attitude towards television changed, however, over the next decade, thanks in large part to the passion for films which he indulged along with Leonard. He also understood that he would have to take television seriously for the simple fact that people around him would spend something like ten years of their waking lives as Homo zappiens, stuck in front of the TV screen. And that this box would therefore act as the fount from which they would obtain almost all of their knowledge, their humour and their moral values. People would no longer read, they would *watch*. Jonas Wergeland was one of the first to comprehend that the NRK building in Marienlyst far outweighed the Parliament when it came to influencing people, to shaping the attitudes and opinions of the Norwegian people.

Nevertheless, he continued to be extremely selective in his viewing, and his scepticism remained intact. What bothered him most was that, as a medium, television did not exploit its own inherent potential to the full. On top of which, he had observed that television almost always rendered intelligent individuals dumb. Or perhaps he should have said 'flat'. He first witnessed a demonstration of this on an *Open to Question* programme in which the Aurlandsdalen question came up for discussion and one of Norway's most knowledgeable botanists was laughed out of court, made to look like a complete fool and treated as such by the programme's chairman – the first, by the way, in a long succession of television presenters who would be applauded and admired for making fun of clever people.

It did, however, take Jonas some time to find the common denominator in his favourite programmes, productions which made an indelible impression on him, almost in spite of himself: all were British. Over the years Jonas would come to have something approaching a love affair with the BBC, as well as ITV – the collective name for such independent television companies as Granada, Anglia, Thames and Yorkshire Television. Jonas's heart instinctively lifted whenever one of their logos appeared on the screen: Thames Television's reflected image of St Paul's Cathedral, Anglia's revolving knight.

So what did Jonas watch? First and foremost, through NRK's Television Theatre he was introduced to examples of superb British television drama, plays by such strong and controversial figures as Peter Watkins and Ken Loach and lengthy, top-quality series like *The Brontes of Haworth* and *David Copperfield*. NRK's own clued-up drama department had screened marathon productions such as *The Forsyte Saga*, *Upstairs, Downstairs*, *The Onedin Line* and *I, Claudius* – every one of them so good as to be unforgettable. And thanks to the NRK documentary department – or the Swedish channels, for those who could receive them – the people of Norway were able to enjoy mammoth ventures along the lines of *Life on Earth* and *Civilization*, in which the programmes' respective presenters, David Attenborough and Kenneth Clark, popped up here, there and everywhere as if it were the most natural thing in the world, to inform, to *enlighten* viewers on the mysteries of Nature and mankind's tortuous cultural development. Jonas realised early on that some of these television programmes would leave their mark on an entire generation, not only in Norway, but throughout the world; that they would be employed as rock-solid points of reference in life.

All credit to NRK. Other than Denmark, Norway was the only country in the seventies to import more programmes from Great Britain than from the United States. Not much is known about Jonas Wergeland's political views, beyond his adherence to an obdurate Outside Left line, but it is safe to say that he regarded the Americanisation of Europe with something resembling serious concern. It was one thing to be dependent on the United States where matters of security policy were concerned, quite another to be reliant on the US when it came to making sense of the world. There was, for some years, an ongoing debate as to whether America should be allowed to deploy missiles in Norway, but what everyone forgot was that it had already deployed something far more important there: its television programmes. So when Jonas Wergeland elected to go to England to gain inspiration for television projects – and not to America, as so many other people in Norwegian broadcasting did – this was as much a conscious decision as choosing a European film-maker as role model.

Nothing but the best would do. London was, for Jonas Wergeland, what Rome had been for Henrik Ibsen. He found a new aim in life, a standard to live up to. He had his eyes opened to true excellence – a crucial lesson for someone from a country where every mediocre variety-show crooner was hailed as the new Caruso. Jonas also formed a firm belief – one to which he would hold even when many, later, would call him naive: the belief that television could have a democratising effect, that at certain happy moments television could actually rouse people, encourage them to think big. In short, it was in London, through the studies he conducted in a hotel room in the early eighties, that Jonas Wergeland became convinced that it paid to go for quality, even in a commercial context, and that quality did not necessarily preclude entertainment.

So it was no great achievement to simply lie on a bed and watch TV for a whole month at a stretch, jotting down the odd note now and again, more or less sketching out an idea; in fact it was a pleasure. Jonas felt sure that he could train himself to be a TV wizard merely by lying back and moving nothing but his fingertips. People today often complain that they get up from the television with a feeling of emptiness. When Jonas Wergeland got up off that bed in London after staring at the screen for four solid weeks, he did so as a cultivated man. He did not even feel bad about the fact that he had not visited any of the countless museums and galleries around his hotel as he had planned.

The fact is, you see, that Jonas was a bit of an art lover. As a small boy he had often attended exhibitions with his maternal grandmother. Not only did he love looking at the pictures, he delighted just as much in the things Jørgine was liable to say about them, comments which made passers-by turn their heads and stare, dumbfounded, at the elderly lady with the cigar stump wedged in the corner of her mouth. He particularly remembered their wanderings through the National Gallery, best of all their visits to the red room where the light streamed down over magnificent canvases by the so-called National Romantics – not least among them Johann Christian Dahl. Granny could spend half an hour just gazing at the massive painting from Stalheim in Sogn, telling Jonas about how it was painted and what it depicted, and look at those teeny-weeny figures on the road and the goats in the foreground and oh, isn't that sweet, that horse there has a foal, d'you see? As a grown man, whenever Jonas came across that picture in one of its countless reproductions it was not only his grandmother he thought of – J.C. Dahl's painting also brought with it another, even stronger memory, one bound up with the Byrds' exquisitely wistful, biblically-inspired song 'Turn, Turn, Turn'.

Jonas remembered seeing Leonard's back as he walked off towards the antique sculptures, disappearing into the maze of grubby plaster copies, while Jonas himself followed the sound of the strings and soon found himself in the gallery containing the masterpieces of the National Romantic period, among them 'From Stalheim'. But he did not look at Dahl's painting, commanding though it was; he looked at her, Sarah B., he *stared* at her, at her face, her lips, the fingers moving with virtuoso precision over the violin's finger board. She must have sensed his gaze because she turned, sent him a startled glance, then her lips flashed him a quick smile. He could not take his eyes off her, the lovely blue dress, her chignoned hair, her throat, her hands, but most of all her fingers. It was there, in those first few seconds that everything happened; this was the high point, not what would occur in the weeks thereafter. Because he knew how it would go. She would note his interest and when they had finished playing she would come over to him and say: 'I didn't know you were into paintings, are you into music too?' And he would know that this was an invitation, an opening, a fork in the road.

With his eyes riveted on her he listened to the music, heard how the orchestra threw itself into the lively second movement, a waltz, and he knew that he would not speak to her in the schoolyard on Monday, but that they would look at one another differently during break, and that he would walk up to her on Friday, just before they went home and ask if she would like to go to the Film Club with him the following day. And she would say that she would call him. He stood in the National Gallery, in the shadow of J.C. Dahl's painting from Stalheim, one of the icons of his childhood, listening to a rousing waltz – so infectious that he almost felt like taking a twirl around the floor – and foresaw that he would go crazy, waiting for Sarah to call.

Jonas would have the house to himself that Saturday and he would spend the whole day waiting. The waiting would drive him round the bend, and he would realise that he was in love, so much in love that he had to think of something, which is to say: without being aware of it he would think of something, a ploy which would convince her that he was special, that he appreciated music, and not just any old music. When the phone rang he needed to have something really unusual playing on the stereo in the background, so she could hear that he liked this music, which in turn would persuade her that he was the boy for her.

He would know exactly what to play. The reason Jonas knew about Rickenbacker guitars was that, for reasons only his body understood, he had chosen The Byrds as his favourite group. And if there was one thing which epitomised the sound of this – sadly, and undeservedly, somewhat forgotten – American group, it was a twelve-string Rickenbacker. So Jonas would get out all of his Byrds' records and have a good think, because it was, of course, absolutely vital that he pick the right song; and after long and agonising consideration he would finally decide upon bass player Chris Hillman's simple, but catchy 'Have You Seen Her Face' from the consistently excellent album *Younger Than Yesterday*. In choosing this track he would in fact be saying: See, you caught my eye! See, I'm an outsider too, I don't play the same crap as everybody else!

Jonas stood in the red room in the National Gallery and observed how the light fell on Sarah's chignoned hair, how her fingers danced over the violin strings, and he thought of that Saturday when he would start to play the carefully selected Byrds' track. And he would play it again and again because she could call at any minute; he would commence playing it at nine in the morning, and by the time ten o'clock came, still with no phone call from her, he would have played it almost twenty times. He would know that it was crazy, sheer stupidity, and yet at the same time not know it, he would continue to ensure that the strains of 'Have You Seen Her Face' filled the living room, again and again, with him caterwauling along to it, adding his own frantic tones to the harmonies; he could not *stop* playing it, because she had to hear that he was listening, just by chance really, to this song when she called; in other words: that he had the most discriminating taste in music and definitely merited her keen interest. Eleven o'clock would come and go and the same Byrds' track would be sounding from the stereo for something like the fiftieth time – and then, just as he was contemplating giving up, or had decided to play 'Have You Seen Her Face' just one last time, more as a dirge this time, she would call, and even then, at this moment of triumph, he would not be able to help thinking, far at the back of his mind, that the fulfilment of this most heartfelt wish also came as something of a letdown. And without any indication that she could hear a tune distinguished by the sound of a twelve-string Rickenbacker playing loudly, remarkably loudly, in the background, Sarah would arrange to meet him outside the Saga cinema later that day, but still he would be positive that she had been in two minds right up to the second when he picked up the phone, that it was only because he had been playing that song that she had consented to go out with him.

Jonas stood in the National Gallery listening to a string orchestra, noticing how the instruments gleamed like freshly varnished boats, and he thought of how they would see one another several Saturdays in succession. She would go to the Film Club with him and afterwards they would stroll down to Karl Johans gate and say goodbye at the corner of Universitetsgaten, where their ways parted. And it would be on one such Saturday, in late April, when Leonard had gone off home, leaving Jonas alone with Sarah, that she would place her fingers lightly on the back of his neck and draw him towards her and they would kiss for the first time, right there on the corner, in the middle of Karl Johans gate, in the middle of the main thoroughfare in Oslo. Not counting the kiss from Margrete in elementary school, this would be the first serious kiss of Jonas Wergeland's life and yet again he would discover that there was something unique about these first experiences with girls, for while one's first oysters, for instance, or first sip of wine seldom tasted good, Jonas would feel that this kiss, the touch of her lips, exceeded all expectations – which is saying a lot, when one considers his gift for simulation; it would be like experiencing a twelve-string kiss after dreaming of a six-stringer. It would, therefore, be only right and proper that this should take place on Karl Johan, the most public spot in the whole of Norway; and Jonas would be quite giddy with pleasure, the very fact of blatantly kissing in the middle of the main street on a Saturday afternoon, kissing for all to see, rendering it all the more exciting, causing a delicious tingling sensation to ripple from his lips into every muscle and joint in his body, until it seemed to him that he had actually keeled over and was hovering, flat on his back, the way conjurers could make people hang in mid-air, while at the same time standing in the middle of Karl Johan, kissing.

Jonas stood in the National Gallery's red room, next to J.C. Dahl's huge painting from Stalheim, that sweeping vista, and thought of how they would kiss and kiss, greedily, avidly; how Sarah would stand with those longed-for fingers of hers on the nape of his neck before running them through the hair at the back of his head as if she had found some invisible strings on which she could play; and they would stand there intertwined, intent on losing themselves in one another, and he would note the way her nostrils vibrated when she kissed him, just as they did when she was playing the violin, and his tongue would meet hers and he would think to himself that he would never break contact with it, that nothing could drag him away from that mouth, not even the sight of a neighbour, such a notorious gossip as Mrs Five-Times Nielsen; and they would stand there, kissing unrestrainedly, and the days would pass, and the outdoor cafés would open, offering prawn *smørbrød* and foaming glasses of beer, and the long children's parade would pass them by on May 17th, shouting and cheering and waving flags in their faces; but they would carry on kissing, totally engrossed, while summer came in with blaring brass in the small circular bandstand directly opposite and people popped into Studenten for fragrant ice-cream cones; they would stand with their lips pressed together while pigeons landed and shat on the statue of Henrik Wergeland in Studenterlunden and young men came out of Cammermeyer's bookshop carrying copies of *Line* by Axel Jensen; they would kiss and kiss even while Spanish-speaking tourists unfolded maps round about them and different flags were raised on the poles along Karl Johan as heads of state from various countries saw fit to visit the city, and the weeks would pass and they would kiss, feverishly, oblivious to the fact that school had started and schoolchildren were pouring out of Norlis' bookshop armed with new sets of compasses and rulers, and focused-looking law students were once again strolling into lectures in the old University banqueting hall; they would kiss while tempting posters advertising the season's programme were hung up outside the National Theatre and even when autumn drew on and the leaves fell off the lime trees still they would stand there kissing, observed on the last Friday of the month by cabinet ministers driving, discreetly, impotently, past them and up to the Palace in black limousines; they would kiss, shamelessly, insatiably, while people walked by on their way to see American films at Palasseatret, they would kiss, stand there embracing, mouth to mouth, only snatching a breath every now and again, much in the way that whales occasionally rise to the surface, while the Town Hall bells marked each hour with a different folk tune they would remain in this haze, kissing despite the fact that it began to snow, kissing all the harder in fact, to keep warm; and they would stand there, lost to the world, as Christmas approached, with festive decorations in the street and people going into the record shop to buy Bach's *Christmas Oratorio* as a present for especially dear friends, and they would kiss as the New Year fireworks banged and crackled above their heads, they would kiss, unfazed by the decidedly merry diners emerging from Restaurant Blom, reeking of brandy and trying vainly to hail cabs, and they would kiss as folk trudged past with skis over their shoulders, off to catch the tram to Frognerseter, they would go on kissing until spring came, with birds singing and newly-sprung, heart-shaped leaves on the lime trees and ejaculating fountains in Studenterlund, Jonas would stand there for an eternity, kissing Sarah, and perhaps for that very reason this kiss would be as much of a revelation as if she had removed her mask at the very end of an exhausting masquerade and when it was gone so too would the thrill, though Jonas could not have said why or how – if, that is, it was not that the thrill lay in the mask and not in the face, and all at once Jonas realised that he was kissing an illusion, depths which again turned out to be flatness; in any case, Jonas would have to tear himself free and with the kiss thus over he would say a cheerful, but uneasy goodbye.

They would go on seeing one another for some months, would kiss repeatedly over those months, but because what he had found behind the mask was not what he had hoped for there would come a day when he would decide to break it off, and he would be strengthened in his conviction that Sarah, like him, had reached the stage where she wanted to do more than kiss – yet again Jonas would, in other words, find a romance being struck by Melankton's syndrome. Unless, that is, his own fear or, to couch it in more positive terms: his honourable intent, was actually a vicarious motive. For what if all of this merely concealed a horror of losing his independence, a fear of having to consider another human being?

And he would take her back to that corner on Karl Johan, imagining that she would not make a scene with so many people about. But when he said it, said that it was over, breaking it to her as considerately as he could, she would not let him off that easily and she would ask him why, and he would finally come up with the answer for which he had searched on a couple of previous occasions, an answer which, while it might smack of high romance and chivalry, would strike at the heart of the matter; and even though this answer had been drawn from another person's life Jonas would now feel mature enough to use it himself: 'You're not worthy,' he would say and even though he said it gently and was at pains to assure her that someone else would find her worthy, she would simply stand there staring at him in disbelief, and then, still with her eyes fixed on his, she would scream, really howl, so stridently and piercingly that everybody, every single person on or about Karl Johan would look round in alarm, but still she would go on wailing, as unabashed as when they had kissed; a ghastly shriek, like the screech from the highest violin string, with her hands over her ears. Then she would turn on her heel and hurry away, while in his head, like a grim echo, he would hear a verse from 'Have You Seen Her Face'.

She would be off school for a week. This would surprise him. They had gone out together for a few months, they had talked for hours, played music to one another. And now – it would dawn on him that he had not known anything about her, not a blind thing.

Jonas stood in the National Gallery, where he and Leonard were supposed to be investigating the possibilities of being allowed to film in the sculpture gallery, but where instead Tchaikovsky's exquisite music had led him up to the first floor, to the room containing J.C. Dahl's huge painting from Stalheim. He listened to Sarah B. playing the violin, watched her fingers as the orchestra came to the end of 'Serenade in C-major'. There was a burst of applause, loud and heartfelt. One starry-eyed gentleman, clearly a tourist, possibly American, went up to Sarah and presented her with his ring before bowing gallantly and walking out. She got to her feet, smiling, and came over to him, to Jonas, and said: 'I didn't know you were into paintings. Are you into music too?'

Jonas looked from her face to her fingers, from her fingers to her face. She was a closed book. He stood there facing Sarah B. and knew that he would soon be embarking upon an arduous expedition. What should he take with him?

This question, one which was to colour his whole life, stemmed from his summer with Bo Wang Lee and their assiduous endeavours to find the Vegans' hiding place in Lillomarka. Bo Wang Lee lived in the United States, but was spending a month at Solhaug, in the end block of flats, with his Norwegian mother. His father was at home in the States – he was an American, an archaeologist and his surname was Lee. His mother, surname Wang, was in Oslo to complete a course at the university. The flat belonged to Bo's mother's sister. Jonas knew that Miss Wang worked on one of the ships of the Norwegian American Line – that was the sort of fact boys tended to pick up. She was on holiday in Florida with her boyfriend, who also happened to be the man responsible for the model ship which Bo had launched at Badedammen. The flat was sparely furnished and had the air of a place owned by someone who was not at home much. What with all the suitcases and cardboard boxes which Bo and his mother had brought with them, some of the rooms seemed more like ship's cabins to Jonas, an impression which was reinforced when he went to the toilet and found himself sitting looking at two photographs hung on the wall, just at eye level: the MS *Oslofjord* and the MS *Bergensfjord*, two floating palaces. Jonas sometimes thought of that summer with Bo as being like a wonderful cruise through totally uncharted waters.

Since Bo's mother had to get as much work done as possible during their stay in Norway, Bo had the flat pretty much to himself. Jonas caught only fleeting glimpses of his mother, usually laden with books and papers, on her way down to her sister's little yellow Citroën 2CV. But there was always a stack of freshly-made sandwiches waiting for them, usually thick, American-style double sandwiches, with ham and a kind of mayonnaise from a big glass jar that you spread on with a knife.

On one of their first days together, when they were sitting eating out on the balcony, Bo told Jonas about the Vegans. It was no accident that Jonas had run into him up at Badedammen. Bo had been *on reconnaisance*, as he put it. He had been spying out *coordinates*, as he said. He was trying to find a hidden country, an entire forgotten civilisation. He shot a searching glance at Jonas.

Why were they called the Vegans? Jonas asked, mainly out of polite-ness, while licking the last of an unbelievably good sandwich filling from the corners of his mouth – it was the first time he had tasted peanut butter.

Because they were a small colony of beings from a planet near the star Vega, Bo said. They had arrived on Earth some years earlier and had hidden them-selves away here, in the heart of Lillomarka. This was 'top secret' information. Bo had it from a relative who worked for NASA. Again Bo eyed Jonas, as if assessing whether Jonas was worthy of his confidence, before continuing: a special task force within NASA had traced the unknown spaceship's wherea-bouts to Norway, more specifically to a spot slightly to the north-east of the capital. According to Bo's findings – he showed Jonas the map with the two lines forming a cross – the Vegans were located in the area around the little lake. Couldn't they just go and have a look, Jonas suggested. It was not that simple, Bo said. These beings inhabited another dimension. Bo explained the meaning of 'dimension', speaking slowly and solemnly. He described how he imagined this place to be, pulled out the yellow notebook and opened it at an imaginative and highly detailed drawing with, at its centre, a sort of entranceway or passage. Jonas thought it looked a little like Bo's drawings of the Emperor Qin's mausoleum. He had started out smiling, but his smile gradually faded as Bo plied him with so many colourful pieces of information that Jonas actually began to believe *him*.

Although Bo knew where the Vegans were located, there were still a couple of snags. One of these concerned the question of how they were to open up the terrain. 'Open up the terrain?' Jonas repeated. 'You mean we'll have to chop down trees and bushes and stuff?'

'We have to open up the landscape, but not with an axe or a shovel,' Bo said. 'The Vegans' land lies hidden, a bit like the treasure in the story of Ali Baba and the Forty Thieves. We have to find something that will work in the same way as saying Open Sesame.'

Jonas tried to picture a grove of trees suddenly 'opening up', as if a huge trapdoor of heather and moss had been thrown back only to disclose an alien landscape under the ground. Bo's story appealed to Jonas, it accorded with a suspicion he had long harboured: that the world could not possibly be as flat as it appeared to be. That there had to be 'trapdoors'. It had always been a disappointment to Jonas that reality never seemed to match up to his image of it. Consequently he was always on the lookout for a different world. He would have liked to think that it was only a hand's grasp away, as Bo intimated. A tiny twist and everything would be changed.

Bo never did say how he had figured it out, but he had discovered the key that would open up the landscape. A picklock of sorts. They needed eight things: four crystals and four butterflies. Jonas did not know what he found more surprising: the crystals or the butterflies. And yet it fitted, it struck a nice chord inside him. Something hard and something soft. Something dead and something alive.

Bo took the stub of pencil from behind his ear and opened his notebook. If the black pageboy hairstyle made Bo look like Prince Valiant then these, the pencil and the little yellow book, were his sword and his shield. Swiftly and with a sure hand Bo sketched four crystals on a blank page – 'from memory' as he said. What Jonas saw was four differently shaped prisms. 'I know where I can get hold of something like that,' he cried eagerly. Bo nodded, as if he had expected nothing less of Jonas.

That left only the butterflies. Why butterflies, Jonas asked. It had something to do with chemistry, Bo said. Jonas barely knew what chemistry was, could not even guess at a future in schoolmaster Dehli's Indian classroom.

The next week they went butterfly hunting. And not just any specimens of these tiny fluttering creatures would do. Far from it. Bo knew exactly what was needed: a brimstone butterfly, a peacock butterfly, a red admiral and a small tortoiseshell. Again Bo pulled out his notebook and presented a brief rundown of their markings, their flying season, behaviour, the sort of terrain and flowers they preferred – it made Jonas think of the descriptions of wanted criminals, but then Bo showed him the most beautiful, meticulously coloured drawings of all four butterflies in the notebook. Each armed with a net they proceeded to comb the fields around the Ammerud farms and the hillsides along the roads down to the stamp-mill and the quarry; they searched the woods around Monsebråten and, of course, Transylvania. Catching butterflies was not nearly as easy as Jonas had thought. And when they did spot one, on the banks of the stream running down to Grorudsdammen and the ski-jump hill, for instance, it was usually the wrong species. Often, Jonas would simply stand, butterfly net in hand, gazing in wonder at the way some butterflies flew swiftly and purposefully, while others flitted this way and that;

he wondered whether there was a conscious navigational strategy governing the inscrutable routes a butterfly could follow across a meadow; it seemed to him that his thoughts travelled in different directions depending on which type of butterfly his eyes were fixed on. Bo had told him a bit about just how remarkable these little creatures were. They tasted with their feet. Jonas tried to imagine what it would be like to taste with your feet, stick your toes into a bowl of chocolate blancmange and custard. Even stranger, Bo said, was the butterfly's ability to see ultra-violet colour patterns which were invisible to human beings. 'This fact, that they can see something we can't, is very important,' Bo said portentously. 'Do you think somebody could train their eye to see such things?' Jonas asked. 'Ssh, there goes a butterfly,' said Bo, almost as if he did not like this question.

They eventually managed to catch a peacock, a tortoiseshell and an admiral. This last had only just arrived in Norway from the south. Bo popped each insect into its own large glass jar with air holes in the lid. Ranged side by side in this way, they looked like parallel thoughts, Jonas thought. But the brimstone butterfly presented more of a problem; its primary flying season was probably over, Bo said; their only hope was to find a straggler. He studied the yellow notebook, with a worried frown. 'Couldn't we use a Camberwell beauty?' Jonas asked. Bo glowered at him. 'It has to be a *gonepteryx rhamni*, otherwise the whole thing'll be ruined.' It was Bo who taught Jonas never to make compromises.

At last, one day on a hillside just down from the dump behind the garages, Jonas spied a brimstone butterfly, as bright and conspicuous as a yellow Citroën tootling around on the slope. Jonas's heart was pounding, he had never thought a fluttering yellow insect could make him feel so happy, so thrilled. He caught this wonderful creature in his net at the first attempt, and the ground seemed to tremble slightly, as if something were already starting to reveal itself.

In the afternoon they sat out on the balcony with their ham and mayonnaise sandwiches, contemplating the four different butterflies in their respective clear glass jam jars, as if they were looking at the key to some vital code. Bo had placed an orangeade top filled with sugared water in each jar. They observed the way the butterflies unrolled the proboscis which at other times lay coiled like fire hoses under their heads – a real little fakir trick, this. Crouched down in front of the jars, examining the insects' markings – the admiral's reddish-orange bands, the blue spots on the peacock's lower wings – Jonas sensed that they had an inherent potency, that they embodied tremendous forces, that collectively they were, in a way, dynamite. That they could be downright dangerous, were they to come into contact with one another. Bo studied the contents of each jar through a magnifying glass. 'Perfect,' he murmured, taking the pencil stub from behind his ear and scribbling down a sentence in the notebook. That pencil always seemed to Jonas to be sharp, although he never saw Bo sharpen it.

'We'll go tomorrow,' Bo said. 'That leaves just one question. What should we take with us?'

'D'you mean like sandwiches and stuff?'

'I was thinking of something to show the Vegans what we are. Who we are. What we believe in. So they won't turn us away.'

For Jonas, this question was to be of much greater consequence than the expedition itself. Bo made it sound as though they could be killed on the spot if they did not come up with just the right things to take with them. Maybe that was why Bo talked more than usual that evening about his homeland. As they sat on the balcony surveying the holiday-quiet lawns and roads, as they sipped from their mini bottles of Cola through paper straws, Bo spoke, with a stronger American accent, about everything from cars with fins to the delights of candy floss – spun sugar on a stick; of grilled steaks as big as pancakes and machines with popcorn whirling around inside a glass box, and had Jonas ever heard of marshmallows? Bo scooted off and came back with a bag; Jonas sniffed that blissful aroma. Bo described the Chrysler building, waxed eloquent about Disneyland and hummed songs by Elvis, the king of them all. But above all else he told him about American television, which even had programmes in the middle of the day: game shows and quiz programmes and really great series, best of all *Batman*. From then on Jonas always thought it was nice to sit on the toilet at Bo's place and consider what he ought to take with him, while feasting his eyes on the pictures on the wall of the American liners with 'fjord' in their names. In his imagination, these ships were breakaway fjords that had branched outwards.

The thought of Norwegian-American Bo Wang Lee crossed my mind several times during our visit to Fjærland. Although I was actually thinking more of the mass exodus from Norway to America in the nineteenth century. After Ireland, Norway was the one country in Europe which had sent the largest percentage of its population across the sea, and Sogn was one of the areas hardest hit by emigration; between thirty and forty thousand people were said to have left the hamlets and villages around the fjord. I have always been fascinated by the thought of another Sogn in the United States. By the possibility of a 'Lærdal Association' in Iowa. There is more than just one small town in Kansas called Norway, to some extent a whole Norway is contained within the USA. In that vast land there lies a hidden Norway, like an invisible, many-armed fjord. During their first years there, some enthusiasts even dreamt that 'the spirit of Norway' would come to form the backbone of the American nation. The reason such reflections should have been prompted by Fjærland, of all places, was, of course, that Walter Mondale, former vice president of the United States, had made several much publicised visits to the village of Mundal, home of his forebears. He had even had the honour of opening one of the long tunnels not far from where we were docked, just down from the lovely old Hotel Mundal, near the very head of the narrow Fjærlandsfjord which at this time of year had an otherwordly air about it, owing to the way the mineral particles washed down with the glacier water in the rivers refracted the light, lending a mystical green cast to the fjord.

The thought of America also gave me a sense of affinity, stronger than before, with Columbus. My discovery was, however, the result of journeying not outwards, but inwards, deeper and deeper into my native land. I was forever making new discoveries. It was almost too much sometimes. I did not see how we could possibly include even a fraction of all the possible subjects which presented themselves. What about the seals in Nærøyfjord? What about Balzac's strange tale *Séraphîta*, set in a Norwegian fjord? What about Johann Christian Dahl; all the pictures he had painted of places around the fjord: 'View of Fortundalen', 'Winter in Sogn'? What of all the old photographs by Wilse and Knudsen? What about the mass of information we had collected on bird reserves, wilderness museums and nature trails? There were times when I wondered whether we had bitten off more than we could chew, or whether the notion of converting Sognefjord into digital form was, in fact, both blasphemous and insurmountable.

Nevertheless, we endeavoured to make the most of every minute at each stop along the way, noting down thoughts and suggestions for a concept of this, the longest, and most beautiful fjord in the world; in just a few months we had to present the initial outline to our clients. Sometimes it felt as though the abundance of ideas would alter, or break the bounds of the very medium we meant to employ, and this in spite of the fact that it was a totally new medium, an unprecedented fusion of words, pictures, film, sound, architecture and design, of facts and storytelling. Were we already working towards something else, an as yet unconceived medium?

In any case, we had to choose what to take with us, which is to say: decide on the essentials. We tried to evade the issue, but it was brought home to us again and again: some sort of hierarchy was unavoidable. Certain things had to be accorded higher priority than others. A thought occurred to me: this was the all-eclipsing problem of our age, ethically and existentially, a dilemma we did not like to think about. For people today the difficulty lay both on the horizontal and the vertical plane. You could not take in everything, far less immerse yourself in everything. Maybe that was the main challenge of life, apart from meeting the primary needs: choosing what to take with you and which elements of this to concentrate on. For an individual living in the first years of a new millennium, it was more difficult to discard than to accumulate. It was a constant struggle for us. As far as I can remember it was at this stage that we discussed the possibility of restricting the menu to twenty-odd carefully selected headings or 'links', the main attractions, as it were. We knew that many consumers of our product would be short on time; what their senses first encountered was most definitely not immaterial. Every visitor to Sognefjord suffered the same agonies of indecision. You have three days. What should you see, visit? When the brain was seething with such questions as these it was a relief to resort to the saloon and dig your teeth into one of Martin's pizzas with sardines and black olives.

I noticed how my thoughts on the Sognefjord project were increasingly coloured by my interest in Jonas Wergeland. Or perhaps it was the other way round. Ought we to design our product, this service, as a 'biography' of the fjord? Ought I to write about him as if I were describing a place? He was sitting right there on the deck in front of me. At any minute I could go over to him and touch him, talk to him. What I most wanted to do was to hug him, to just sit beside him with my arms around him. More and more often I found myself thinking: if he lay flat out and spread his limbs he would look like a piece of the Norwegian landscape – or, why not: a fjord.

I had taken a particular liking to Fjærland. Not merely because of the almost unbelievable scenery around us: Skeisnipa with the dazzling Flatbreen glacier rearing up at the head of the valley, the green waters of the fjord, the surrounding fields, the roads fringed with dandelions. I believe it may have had more to do with the fact that in this small place one was so aware of branches reaching out into the world. And here I am thinking not so much of the migration as of all the books. Fjærland was full of books. Fjærland was positively awash with books. Inwardly and outwardly. There were bookcases ranged along the roadsides. One could have been forgiven for thinking that the glacier had retreated, leaving behind a moraine of books. Hen-houses and old shops, disused ferry terminals and hotel lounges had all been turned into second-hand bookshops. Byres still complete with pig troughs and slurry channels running down the middle of their floors now held shelves and shelves of books. Fjærland had a name for being Norway's book town. It was part of a network of other book towns – Hay-on-Wye in Wales, Montolieu in France, Bredevoort in Holland; when you walked the streets of tiny Fjærland you were, in a way, also in touch with book towns in Germany and Switzerland, in Canada and America, Australia, Malaysia, South Korea and

Japan. It was a beautiful idea. Almost too beautiful. I kept my fingers crossed as I walked around. Long may Fjærland endure as Norway's book town.

I was particularly taken with the bookcases by the roadsides, crammed with books, surrounded by the humming of bees and the smell of seaweed. It was something like this that we were trying to do: to put information out on the streets, set it down in a landscape; wrap knowledge in an experience; show that our product, this apparently inexhaustible source of learning, was only one small part of the great narrative that was the world. Occasionally I spotted Jonas Wergeland prowling about, looking into second-hand book-shops, albeit circumspectly, as if he were afraid of running into a ghost, one of those spiteful biographies of his person. Might his thoughts have gone to his old neighbour, Karen Mohr, with the library in her bedroom? One morning when the whole eastern side of the fjord and the hillsides were in shadow and the other bathed in golden sunlight, I came across him sitting on the hatch above the companion-way to the for'ard cabin, reading a slim volume he had purchased. This surprised me. He was not a reader. I noticed that the book was *Victoria* by Knut Hamsun. He spent the whole morning sitting there reading it. Reading it while unconsciously running a finger over the cross-shaped scar on his forehead. Now and again he would look up, close his eyes and move his lips, as if he already knew the passage by heart. Once or twice I could have sworn he wiped away a tear. When he did that he looked like a little boy.

Why did he do it?

On our second last day at Fjærland, Kamala Varma came to join us. She had hitched a ride with Jonas's sister Rakel. Benjamin, the brother with Down's syndrome was there too. They had driven up in Rakel's trailer-truck, or at least, there was no trailer attached to the black tractor – or juggernaut as Kamala called it – when it pulled up, rumbling and bulldog-like. Benjamin was bursting with pride, he tooted the horn before jumping out of the massive rig. Later he let me hear the wheezing air brakes and showed me the impres-sive hi-fi system and the bunks in the cab, the fridge and the TV. He babbled on about how wonderful it was to sit so high above all the other traffic – like being on a horse galloping through a flock of sheep. And with ABBA playing full blast. 'The favourite right now being "Gimme, Gimme, Gimme"', Rakel chipped in, rolling her eyes. Usually Benjamin slept in a tent, but he agreed to stay the night at the Hotel Mundal when Jonas promised that he could have the room the queen slept in when she was there. Benjamin straightened his shoulders at the prospect of sleeping in the same bed as a queen. And an American vice president. Not only that but the place was said to be haunted. Benjamin broke into 'Dancing Queen' and walked off with his brother.

I could not help thinking that this was a rather solemn, an almost historic gathering. Here we were, three women, all of whom had written, or were in the process of writing about Jonas Wergeland, telling his story; each coming from our own corner of the world to meet, as it were, at a crossroads. We were like three sisters. And it seemed only fitting that we should rendezvous in a place that was full of books.

Kamala was already enthusing about Fjærland. They had stopped at the Glacier Museum, designed by Sverre Fehn. Straight away she had noticed how the building, lying there on the plain underneath the glaciers, looked like some weird astronomical instrument, of the sort found at Jantar Mantar, the old Indian observatory in Jaipur. Carl and Hanna, who had made several visits to the inspiring Glacier Museum, each time with a feeling of boarding a ship, were gratified to hear her make this comparison. Kamala was even more bowled over by the fjord, or what she had seen of it so far. 'Sognefjord has more pairs of arms than Shiva,' she exclaimed.

While Jonas drove off with Rakel to Boyabreen, the fastest moving glacier in Norway, to let Benjamin see the almost phosphorescent blue light emanating from the glacier face and hear the noises it made – cracks like rifle shots – Kamala strolled around Fjærland with a dumbfounded expression on her face, looking at the book displays; hen-houses, boathouses, cafés offering literature of every description. She spent a long time reverently observing a gull sitting on a nest above the entrance to one of the smallest antiquarian bookshops, an ochre-coloured sheep cot. When she came to the bookcases set out along the roadside she stopped short. Kamala Varma, a woman of Indian descent and herself a writer, stood there gazing at the rows of books against that stunning panorama, the mighty mountains and the glaciers, then she suddenly whispered: '*Māyā*. This is pure *māyā*.'

Although Jonas found it interesting to roam around Fjærland, and even went so far as to buy a novel by Knut Hamsun, he actually had a somewhat fraught relationship with books. One of his nastiest boyhood experiences dated from an encounter with a book and, as one might expect, it involved his big brother. At home, under the telephone table of all places, as if it were a phone book, lay a fat Family Bible. This treasure had lived out at Hvaler, but after Jonas's paternal grandmother died, his grandfather could not bear to have it in the house. In Åse and Haakon Hansen's nigh on bookless home this Bible was something of a museum piece, and the boys used it as a prop in the most bizarre games. The hefty clasps made it look like a chest, a proper little piece of furniture. Only after Daniel had run up against the gravity of life in the long-jump pit did this volume come to serve its rightful purpose: as the revelation of God's word.

It was, though, the illustrations which first captured Daniel's interest. He could spend hours studying Gustav Doré's marvellous pictures, as if he had grown out of the Illustrated Classics and wanted to try something more edifying. He was especially fond of the dramatic etchings depicting the Flood, the tiger on the cliff with its cub in its mouth; or David and Goliath, the blood streaming from the neck of the headless giant. 'Have you read the Bible?' people today ask and back comes the answer: 'No, but I saw the film.' Daniel, on the other hand, would have said: 'No, but I've seen the pictures.' As a grown man, Jonas was inclined to think that his brother's image of God owed more to Gustav Doré than to all the sophistic theological text books he later read.

One day when Daniel was sitting in his room poring over Doré's illustration for the story of Moses breaking the tablets of the law, Jonas walked in and wanted to know what his brother was looking at – grew even more curious when he noticed that his brother was peering at the page through the self-same magnifying glass which he used to burn his name into wooden walls. Jonas asked if he could see. Daniel said no, almost on principle, and the squabble escalated into a regular fist-fight which ended with Daniel – possibly inspired by Moses and the tablets – hitting his brother so hard over the head with the Family Bible, that little piece of furniture with the metal clasps, that Jonas was actually knocked out cold. The doctor was sent for, this being in the great days when family doctors still made house calls – in the Hansen family's case a GP who drove up in a jeep like the ones used by the emergency services, for all the world as if Grorud was a jungle, or a highway littered with broken-down vehicles. After examining the patient and looking at the sizeable bump on his tender scalp, he said he believed that Jonas was suffering from concussion. The doctor ordered a day in bed under careful observation. On his way out he cast a glance at the Family Bible, which had been presented as evidence, and shook his head eloquently. Daniel was all innocence, standing there with an affectedly pious expression on his face. Sometimes, if Jonas happened to be in a church where Daniel was preaching, he would see that same look on his brother's face, up there in the pulpit.

Jonas developed an early mistrust of books. And although he was obliged, over the years, to plough his way through a lot of textbooks, he regarded the fame he eventually won by announcing programmes on a flat screen as proof that his childhood suspicions had been well-founded. The way Jonas Wergeland saw it, books could not be the path to making a name for oneself. In this he would prove to be sadly mistaken, although it would take him many years under lock and key to discover this.

Nonetheless, there came a day when Jonas Wergeland picked up a book and almost lost his life. How could that be? Not only that, but it was a novel, and Jonas *knew* that there was nothing worse than fiction. His bright sister Rakel disappeared into a world of her own at an early age; for years she drifted around Grorud like a local version of Don Quixote on his deluded wanderings, all thanks to the tales of the *Arabian Nights*. Later she became a truck-driving samaritan after reading a book by Albert Schweitzer. Something told Jonas that the covers of a book could harbour a bewitching power, that the contents could paralyze you, quick as a flash, like the strike of a cobra. Books too, like women, ought to bear a sign saying 'Danger. High Voltage.' *All* books ought to be fitted with hefty clasps and a solid padlock.

This suspicion was borne out by Viktor Harlem, Jonas's best friend in high school, who told him how he had become hooked on literature. He actually used the word 'hooked', as if it were a drug addiction. Viktor had been in eighth grade at the time and had to make a herbarium for school. In order to press the flowers he borrowed the thickest book from his mother's not exactly extensive library and some weeks later, as he was removing one of the flowers, his eye happened to fall on the page and he started to read. And that was that. 'It was a germander speedwell that led me to Leo Tolstoy,' Viktor said. And from there, thought, Jonas, it was no great leap to Ezra Pound and *The Cantos*, and a life as a vegetable in an institution, or perhaps one should say: a pressed flower in a herbarium.

Even as a child, Jonas understood that the words in books, particularly works of fiction, could be addictive, and read therefore only as much as was absolutely necessary. He did, of course, have to look at those volumes used in school, but even these he merely skimmed, with all his mental defences raised. He knew that at any minute he might be carried off to some Lambaréné, that a slightly unfortunate choice of book could result in him selling up on the spur of the moment and going off to Calcutta to help the poor. But since the works on the school syllabus were usually ruined for ever by one zealous teacher or another, Jonas escaped unscathed.

He never forgot, though, the lesson which Daniel had thumped into him: books *were* a weapon. They were dangerous. And like wolves, they were at their most dangerous in packs – as he discovered when a shelf full of books came crashing down on him in Karen Mohr's bedroom. Only rarely did Jonas venture into a bookshop or a library – it was almost as if he half-expected that at any moment the bookshelves would come tumbling down on his head again, and bury him, or that the books themselves, seeing that he was alone, would attack him and tear him to shreds. The unease which Jonas felt in a well-stocked bookshop was not unlike Tippi Hedren's dread of the crows and gulls perched on tree branches and railings all around her in Alfred Hitchcock's horror film *The Birds*.

And yet – one day, of his own free will, Jonas picked up a book. Why? Because he was in love. And because he wanted to kill a fly.

This was in the days between Christmas and New Year, barely a year after Jonas, now a young man, had met Margrete again. They were spending the holiday somewhere on the outskirts of Jotunheimen, in a cottage owned by Margrete's parents. Jonas had been working for a short time as an announcer with NRK, he was just beginning to notice the first signs of his growing fame. Beyond the rough log walls it was bitterly cold, more than twenty below zero. They went only for short ski trips in the middle of the day, their shadows long in the almost horizontal rays of the low sun. The rest of the time they made love. They made a bed for themselves in front of the fireplace in the living room so that they would at all times have a view of the landscape outside. They lived on love and hot cocoa. Jonas had never felt so contented, so blissful, so inexplicably happy. He was, you might say, laid wide open to new impulses.

Sometimes Margrete would read. On one such occasion Jonas was lying staring into space, limp from lovemaking and intense conversations. All was quiet. No wind. A fly, wakened by the heat in the cottage, began to buzz; it was like the hiss of a snake in Paradise. Jonas glanced round for something to hit it with and his eye lighted on a paltry shelf of dog-eared paperbacks. He pulled out a copy at random and flattened the fly at the first attempt. Without looking up, Margrete murmured from her chair: 'Books are not weapons.'

What was the greatest danger to which Jonas Wergeland was ever exposed? Not an easy one to answer, one would think. He had reefed sail in a gale in the middle of the night. He had ignited fury in an English pub. If anyone had asked Wergeland himself he would, however, have had no hesitation in replying: 'The biggest risk I ever took was to read a book.'

He stood there holding the old paperback, weighing it in his hand. He was feeling a little reckless. He sank down into a chair, opened the book at the first page and began to read. Margrete and he sat each in their chair, with the mountain right in front of them if they raised their eyes: a slope so steep that the snow did not lie there, a normally black rock face to which the freezing cold and the low sun now lent a pinkish cast, a view which seemed almost to belong to another country, another planet. Jonas thought fleetingly of Bo Wang Lee and the Vegans, of the possibility of opening up the terrain. He dropped his eyes to his book again. He did not know that with this seemingly harmless act he had let a wolf out of its cage and that all unknown to him this wolf was now sneaking up on him from behind. For a few fateful seconds Jonas Wergeland forgot all about his ingrained sense of mistrust. He forgot what a profound impact a novel can have on one. He forgot that every work of fiction, even a flimsy paperback, is a Bible, a sacred text, containing layer upon layer of meaning. In opening a book you could be putting your whole view of the world to the test.

He should have remembered, because in junior high they had also had Mr Dehli for a third subject, one which the schoolmaster himself maintained, with all the enthusiasm and inspiring authority at his command – which is saying something – to be the most important subject of them all: Bible studies, or religion, as the students called it. 'Choose religion and you choose everything,' Mr Dehli asserted.

It possibly bears repeating, since teachers of this calibre are the exception: Mr Dehli saw himself not just as a teacher, but also as a guide and mentor. His pupils had to learn facts, but they also had to bear in mind that something bound these facts together. Even in subjects such as Norwegian and history. Mr Dehli dared to bandy that inflammatory word 'meaning'. 'And nowhere is the attempt to establish meaning more apparent than in the religions of the world,' he said. Over a couple of years, Jonas was introduced to the main principles of Islam, Hinduism, Shinto and Buddhism; in other words, he was made aware that there were other philosophies of life besides the Christian one. This may seem obvious, but it was not obvious to Jonas – he belonged, after all, to the last generation in Norway which had to learn Luther's little catechism by heart.

How could so many fail to see it? Page upon page has been written about Jonas Wergeland's years at elementary school and high school. But no one has looked at the two years in between. Nevertheless, it was here in junior high that Jonas's curiosity about the world, not to say life, was truly awakened. It would not be too far from the truth to say that, during this time, Jonas came very close to becoming a Hindu.

Mr Dehli – who did not turn up for classes in a duster coat, but in his best bib and tucker, so to speak – told them even more than usual about Hinduism, possibly because he was especially interested in this religion himself, or because this was the late sixties, when the fascination with all things Eastern was at its height and celebrities were flocking to India to sit at the feet of more or less genuine gurus. All of a sudden it was orange robes, Hare Krishna, sitars and incense at every turn.

It was through Hinduism that Jonas was introduced to Maya. Although this was, of course, not a girl called Maya as Jonas had first thought, but *māyā*, a concept. Mr Dehli, sporting an exceptionally colourful bow tie for the occasion and with a snowy-white silk handkerchief peeking out of his breast pocket, explained to them that there were many different interpretations of *māyā*, but that *māyā*, roughly speaking, was a principle which prevented us from seeing the world as it really was. You mistook something for something else. A coiled rope became a snake. *Māyā* worked mainly in two ways: it could conceal something, or it could present something false. The concept of *māyā*, the great cosmic illusion, may have grown out of an ancient weaving symbol, an image representing creativity. Mr Dehli produced a strip of gauze bandage and covered his eyes with it: 'With my sight thus masked there would be things in the room which I would not notice, on the other hand my eyes could perhaps be confused or deluded into seeing certain other things that are not there. I might, for example, think that Pernille was a statue. Having a little snooze, Pernille?'

Due to our ignorance we apprehended only the material world and not the real world behind it. We could not cope with the idea of infinity and so we created something finite for ourselves: the world. But it was only because we were as if hypnotised that we mistook this mirage for reality. '*Māyā* can be compared to a cloud covering the sun, the moon and the stars,' Mr Dehli said. 'And this cloud is there because our consciousness is not clear enough. There is a veil before our eyes. But not everything is an illusion. There is something behind the cloud. Without it there would be no illusion.'

It occurred to Jonas that Leonard had been on the right track: it all came down to honing the eye. The Hindu view of the world, with its assertion that the power of *māyā* concealed the true nature of existence proved in many ways to be a lifeline for Jonas, a ray of hope. It confirmed his firm belief that there had to be something *behind* the flatness – of both the world and people, including himself – which was a constant vexation to him. Because, if there were several planes, veil upon veil, might they not even form a chamber, create some sort of depth?

The first time Jonas heard his teacher speak of *māyā*, he was reminded of Bo Wang Lee and the Vegans, but later he came to think of another, more infamous episode. Those who are familiar with life at Grorud around that time will not be surprised to hear that this drama centred around a boy by the name of Ivan. Ivan – a problem child, to put it mildly – had long had a crush on the daughter of Arild Pettersen, or Arild the Glazier as he was known, after his business: he was the local Grorud glazier, and most people were acquainted with him through no choice of their own, thanks to accidents great and small. His slogan was: Life is a smash. The best bit, as far as the kids were concerned, was his van, a Volkswagen truck with a flat bed and a rack shaped like an upside-down V on which the plates of glass were carried. One day Ivan took his courage in both hands – in such circumstances even Ivan had to steel himself – and asked Britt, as the object of his affections was called, if she would go out with him, a request which, with the perverse, heartless temerity that girls can display, she flatly rejected. Why didn't he just run on home, cheeky sod – who the hell did he think he was?

Ivan slunk off, but everybody knew that the matter would not end there. This was, after all, Ivan. A bunch of boys dogged Ivan's footsteps at a safe distance for the rest of the day, to act as chroniclers of an event which they knew would become legendary. Suddenly the central character announced: 'I'll bloody well smash her window in, so I will.' Later that evening, just as it was getting dark, Ivan set out, cool as you like, to do the deed – only to find, on reaching the house, that Arild the Glazier's little truck was parked right in front of Britt's ground-floor bedroom, which looked onto the driveway. Ivan was not one to be put off by a little thing like that. 'I'll just have to smash my way through then,' he muttered, loud enough for the others to hear.

He went for a walk round about and returned with his hands and his pockets full of stones. Afterwards the other lads would try to outdo one another with their descriptions of what happened next. Ivan had thrown the first stone with convincing ferocity and a huge pane of glass had shattered and landed in a tinkling heap on the bed of the truck. Ivan hurled another stone, as surely as the first and another pane of glass disintegrated. And so he continued, unleashing a never-ending avalanche of glass. He threw and he threw as the sheets of glass came cascading down one after another. But he never did break through to Britt's window, or, as he saw it: to Britt's heart, *behind* all the sheets of glass. Britt's Dad must have had more panes than usual on the back of the truck that day, layer upon layer of them. Ivan was growing desperate. He was breaking sheets of glass as fast as he could, if only to get her at least to show face, but there seemed to be no end to it – or not, at any rate, until Arild the Glazier himself finally came out and belatedly, but effectively put a stop to the vandalism with a headlock invested with more than mere upset at the shattered window panes.

That, thought Jonas, that is how it must be with *māyā*. An endless succession of windows. We would never be able to break through to the truth. *Māyā* spoke, quite simply of gaping holes in our knowledge. When Jonas pictured the world as being flat, this was exactly what he was getting at. Everyone was well aware that our view of the world, our view of human nature, would be totally different in a few hundred years, in a thousand years. And yet we believed, surprisingly often at least, that we knew just about everything there was to know. *Māyā* showed us that we knew very little.

Schoolmaster Dehli had another, possibly even better, way of illustrating this. He positioned himself next to the map rack. 'Just as maps are like masks of the world, so the world is merely a mask covering something else, something more real,' he said. Sitting at his desk, Jonas thought of Karen

Mohr's flat, the grey hallway concealing a Provence in the middle of Grorud. Mr Dehli had pulled down all of the maps, about ten altogether. Then he sent them whipping up, one after another, tugging and releasing with superb precision, as if he had had a lot of practice at this. The maps snapped and cracked in a sort of chain reaction, pure pyrotechnics. It made Jonas think of roller-blinds shooting up to disclose an endless succession of different prospects, different worlds, until they, the pupils, were almost shaking in their shoes, half expecting something horrendous to stand revealed at the very back, Reality itself, in all its awfulness or beauty. But at the very back – and this Mr Dehli left as it was – hung an enormous map of the solar system, of the cosmos as it were, and of all the hovering jewels here displayed, the one on which Jonas fixed was the planet Uranus, a shimmering green eye. What a show – perfect, like a conjuring trick rounded off with one final mind-boggling sleight of hand.

There are too few teachers like Mr Dehli. There are too few teachers who pull such original, inventive educational stunts. Who charge their classrooms with electricity and the smell of chalk dust.

Such sessions were not easily forgotten. Not for nothing did three members of this class go on to become religious historians, while two became ministers of the church. And, even more noteworthy perhaps: five ended up in the Oslo Stock Exchange. As for Jonas, in the first instance they would result in the world coming tumbling about his ears.

The Hindu concept of *māyā* occupied a central place in Jonas's memory. It instinctively sprang to mind, for example, when he was lying in a hotel room in London, zapping back and forth between the best television channels in the world. Occasionally he even had the notion that each new channel caused the previous one to disappear, like a map being pulled up – that he disclosed a new world each time he pressed the remote control.

To the question as to how he had learned the ropes of television production, Jonas Wergeland had been known to reply – as if to denote how difficult it had been: 'I swam the English Channel.' By rights he should have said 'the English Channels', because there were four of them; he arrived in London on the very day that Channel 4 was launched, a channel which aimed to be innovative and experimental and to win viewers by appealing to their good taste. So he was lucky enough to catch many of the exceptionally fine programmes scheduled for Channel 4's first weeks on the air, productions which, regardless of genre – soap opera or science documentary, sit-com or arts magazine – oozed intelligence at all levels of production. Even the sports broadcasts were bearable, thanks largely to the civilised British commentators. Jonas felt like a guest in the TV equivalent of a gourmet restaurant.

But he could not stay in that room all the time – although if he had, he would have avoided a rather unpleasant confrontation which left him with a nasty bump on the back of his head and a black eye. Jonas followed the same routine every day. He slept till around twelve, then went out for breakfast, or rather, lunch. Within a very small radius, in the streets around South Kensington tube station, Jonas found restaurants serving food from every corner of the globe – the culinary equivalent, if you like, of the British television which he was studying: around the world in eight minutes. During his weeks there he could choose between French, Italian, Indian, Thai, Chinese and Japanese restaurants. His favourite, he eventually decided, was Daquise, a little Polish dive with dingy walls and oilcloth-covered tables, serving *shashlyk* and *chlodnik* soup, as well as eight different brands of vodka.

On the way back to the hotel he always picked up a good-sized stack of sandwiches from a shop in the arcade next to the station. He ordered a pot of coffee at reception and his working day could begin. He settled back on the bed, with an appetising tuna fish sandwich within easy reach, and switched on the television.

The aforementioned unpleasant incident was something of an intermezzo. It occurred on an evening when, for once, there happened to be a gap between two programmes he wanted to see. Instead of doing a bit of skipping, as he sometimes did, he went for a walk around the neighbourhood and on the way back he was tempted to pop into a pub, The Zetland Arms in Old Brompton Road. He had to stand for a minute just inside the door until his eyes adjusted to the gloom of the interior which, like most English pubs, was all dark mahogany and oriental-style fitted carpets – as if deep down every Briton longed for a return to Victorian times. Jonas meant just to have a quick whisky at the horseshoe bar, but he soon got chatting to an Englishman who invited him over to his table; he had ordered so many pints that Jonas had to help him carry them. Thus Jonas suddenly found himself in the midst of a vociferous group of men around his own age, and as the mood grew even livelier and the conversation turned, quite naturally, to television – as all conversations at that time eventually did – Jonas put in his three-ha'pence worth, commenting on aspects of everything from *Coronation Street* to *The South Bank Show*. His companions were impressed, wanted to know how come a Norwegian, a snowed-in Viking, was so well-informed on such matters. 'I'm writing a thesis on the new British era of world supremacy,' Jonas said. 'Cheers!'

He did in fact feel rather like a researcher as he lay on the bed in his hotel room, combing the two weekly TV magazines. Each day he would find masses of programmes he wanted to see; the pages in both magazines gradually became covered in red circles; many a time there would be a clash between a couple of the delights on offer and he would have to choose; either that or he ended up switching back and forth between two, or even three, programmes – a documentary, a music broadcast, a film made for television – trying to catch the gist of each one.

And as he watched he made notes: a couple of words maybe, a sentence, or some hieroglyphics, a framework, an original idea. After close-down he would make other notes in the margins alongside those he had jotted down earlier in the evening, sketchy associated ideas scrawled in an Outside Left area, a fertile borderline in which the writing became more and more closely packed. Jonas had never written so much at one go. He would lie there, eating a corned-beef or turkey sandwich and writing, scribbling down words that only he could read, in those books with the marbled covers. They were the same as the ones in which Aunt Laura made her almost obscene erotic sketches – male members depicted as the most weird and wonderful creatures – on her travels in the Middle East and Central Asia in search of new rugs for her collection. Jonas believed that he filled his four books, collectively referred to by him as 'the golden notebook', with what might be called 'bed art'. However that may be, he certainly regarded them, together with the eight copies of the *TV Times* and *Radio Times* from that month, covered in red circles and marginalia, as lecture notes from the greatest university he ever attended. Later in his career he would still take those fat notebooks out every now and again, looking for tips or inspiration. Those four books were for him what the little yellow notebook was for Bo Wang Lee.

Jonas was, in other words, well qualified to air his views on British television at that table in The Zetland Arms, raucously toasting with his effusive, open-handed drinking cronies, and as if to boost the spirit of camaraderie still further – after his fourth pint – he declared *Not the Nine O'Clock News* to be the funniest thing ever shown on a television screen. Several of the guys round the table began to clap, while others broke into a chorus of 'We are the champions', and it may have been this, or possibly a desire to pursue his winning line in witty repartee that prompted Jonas to declare, a little too loudly, that that wasn't always the case, though, was it? That the English were the champions, that is. Well, nobody could say – he plucked an example out of thin air – that Captain Scott had done all that well; Jonas laughed, but this time he laughed alone, and conscious though he was of the sudden, not to say ominous, hush that had fallen over the table, still he continued to hold forth, all undaunted, on that prize idiot, Captain Robert Scott, who had actually gone so far as to take ponies, *ponies* God help us, to the South Pole, and not only that, but – would you believe it – *motor-driven* vehicles, I'm sorry guys, but I can't see any good reason to sing 'We are the champions' for Robert Scott. Here's to Roald Amundsen!"

One burly character rose to his feet with demonstrative nonchalance, hoiked Jonas out of his seat on the sofa – as if deeming it cowardly to hit a man when he was sitting down – then slammed his fist smack into Jonas's eye, the obvious target for his indignation. Jonas toppled backwards, smashing his head into the large ornamental mirror above the sofa, and slid to the floor in a shower of broken glass. And even as his legs gave way he had time to think that it was not only him, but also the image of a hero that had been shattered; it dawned on him that there were other ways of looking at Roald Amundsen than the one which had been instilled in him at school. A hero in one land could be a villain in another. The point might be to come first, but not at any price.

Jonas was ejected from the premises as roundly as an undesirable individual being kicked out onto the street in a Hollywood movie. 'Goodnight, Mr Amundsen,' they roared after him. 'The South Pole's that way.' Jonas huddled on the pavement, the back of his head and his eye throbbing with pain; he knew, though, that they had not hurt him badly, they had contented themselves with teaching him a lesson.

And Jonas accepted it as such, although his drinking cronies would probably have been surprised to discover how he took it to heart. He had never been all that interested in Roald Amundsen. He was now, though. He was really keen to know more about a fellow-countryman who could still, so long after his death, make people's blood boil. At the airport he did something unusual: he bought a book, a relatively new book about the race between Scott and Amundsen – written by an Englishman at that.

Jonas knew nothing of these ructions, or of his off-the-cuff book purchase, that evening at Margrete's cottage somewhere on the outskirts of Jotunheimen, then too in polar conditions as it happened, looking out each time he raised his eyes from the book he was reading onto a vast, snow-covered landscape. Nor did he realise that he could well be exposing himself to something far worse than the risk of a black eye.

Almost a year had already passed since he had run into Margrete again, but their unexpected reunion was still fresh in his memory. Suddenly there she had been, at the tram stop, and he had had the impression of maps, worlds, flying up to reveal something quite different at the very back. Her. He realised that all the other girls had been *māyā*. Jonas sat in the cottage, in a chair next to Margrete, still in the first flush of love. The room smelled of woodfires and cocoa. He was filled with an indescribable sense of well-being. He glanced fondly at her. As far as he could see she was reading a novel called *The Golden Notebook*.

Why did he do it?

Jonas had often been surprised by the way Margrete read. She always kept one hand flat on the page, as if constantly searching for a deeper meaning; as if she imagined that there was some sort of Braille underneath the visible print. If, that is, she was not trying to hold on to the story, much as a gecko clings to the ceiling with its feet. She had the same look on her face when she read as when she was hunting for something, a pair of stockings, mushrooms in the forest: intent, on the lookout. The stillness of Margrete with a book in her hand was a stillness full of movement. It was not hard to see how she became involved, with all of her being, in what was going on in the pages of the book. And this despite her intelligence, Jonas always thought to himself, as if reading novels and having a high IQ were mutually exclusive. She was also liable to say things which to Jonas came worryingly close to sounding simple-minded. 'Marguerite Duras changed my soul for ever,' she said once. Was that possible? Could one be changed by a book? And one's *soul*? Margrete was also prone to sentimentality when she read. It was not unusual for Jonas to find her crying over a book. On one occasion he had asked what the matter was. It was Berthe, she said. Berthe who? he asked. It turned out it was Emma Bovary's daughter, who had had to go to work in a cotton mill; she was only a peripheral character, but to Margrete she was the whole key to Flaubert's novel. It may have been wrong to call it sentimentality. It had more to do with her gift for empathy. Now and again Jonas discerned a link between this ability to identify, even with fictional characters, and her skills as a doctor.

In any case, Jonas understood that Margrete regarded reading as an experience on a par with other experiences in life. Books, for her, had to do not with escape, but with a zest for life. Which may be why she read everywhere, even in the kitchen. Where other women had a shelf of cookery books close to the cooker, Margrete had a little library of novels. This was where she kept her favourite books, volumes which she was quite liable to suddenly dip into in the middle of making dinner, to read a particular passage; and these readings seemed almost to inspire her cooking, or her appetite, as much as any cookbook.

When Jonas thought back on those first months after he started seeing Margrete again, he could see – if he was honest – that he had been more shaken by the discovery that she was a reader than by other, possibly more questionable aspects of her character. He noticed how Margrete became someone else when she opened a book, that she slipped away from the girl he thought he had come to know; she became a person with whom he feared he would never be able to make contact. As if to prove him right in this she frequently sat like a mermaid, with her legs drawn up underneath her, when she was reading. As if she truly was in another element, in the deep, in an ocean of words. Seeing her sitting like that, as now, at the cottage on the outskirts of Jotunheim, with a rock face outside the window turned pink by a temperature of twenty below, Jonas was reminded of the film *Blow-Up*; it struck him that he would never be able to discover what this picture of a woman reading held in the way of secrets. He could enlarge it all he liked, but it would do no good.

Jonas sat there, enjoying the smell, the *sound*, of burning logs, the sight of a rosy rock face, and reading an old paperback, not knowing that he was playing hazard with his life. The first pages were rather heavy going, but he soon became totally absorbed. It never occurred to him that it was an unusual book, he had read very few novels, so he had nothing with which to compare it. He did not wonder at the measured pulse of the opening lines, at the odd way in which the one character's pages-long reflections were inserted between brief, banal remarks about the weather that fell every few seconds. Jonas simply enjoyed it, he had a pleasant sense of two parallel phenomena moving at different speeds. Jonas was in a cottage on the outskirts of Jotunheim and for once he was reading a book. Outside it was more than twenty below, but he was sitting beside a roaring fire. He was in love, he was happy with his new job as an announcer with NRK, he was in a good mood, he was open, he read page after page with a faint smile on his lips, he entertained no expectations of this novel, he simply read it, word by word, conscious of nothing but a profound sense of well-being. When he looked up – first glancing at Margrete in her mermaid position in the chair next to his, then out at the pink rock face before him – time stood still. He emerged from a maelstrom into stillness. The events described in the book were totally undramatic, and yet when he looked up, his heart was *pounding*, as if he had been in a state of unbearable suspense. For a second he had the feeling that the rock face before him could open up at any moment, in response to some magic password, like Open Sesame.

He read on, page after page in which a description of various doings was interlaced with a stream of thoughts. He got caught up in his own associations, lost himself completely in his own memories, dreams, what might almost have been perceptions. Every sentence, every word seemed to lead him down a sidetrack and from there down offshoots from this sidetrack. He began to discern the central theme: the transience of all things. That and the eternality of the smallest daily task. Millions of years as opposed to a second. Now and then he had to laugh at a particular formulation. 'The very stone one kicks with one's boot will outlast Shakespeare,' he read at one point. Jonas was filled with a colossal intensity; he sat quite still, but on another level he was firing on all cylinders. By chance he happened to look up again. Two hours had passed. For some time he had had a definite sense, in his mind, of being by the sea; he thought he could hear the waves, the swell. He flinched at the sight of the motionless pink rock face, the freezing winter panorama. The landscape had not opened up, but *he* had.

And which book was this? It was *To the Lighthouse*. He read on, conscious of how the author, Virginia Woolf, made him think about thinking, how she could almost catch a thought before it was born. At last, a kindred spirit, his heart exulted; someone who succeeded in showing how thousands of thoughts criss-crossed in one's mind in the course of a day. Someone who made thought the protagonist. Jonas was bursting with excitement and delight. He did not think that Margrete had read this book. But then he came to a passage which she had marked, he recognised her handwriting in the margin, or a youthful version of it. On the next page he was pulled up short by a metaphor to the effect that in the heart and mind of a woman there could stand tablets bearing sacred inscriptions, like treasures in the tombs of kings. Then came a question which Jonas had also asked himself: was there some art known to love or cunning, by which to push through to those sacred chambers? In the margin he saw a 'Yes!' in Margrete's girlish hand. Again Jonas's heart began to pound palpably.

He carried on reading, even more engrossed, if that were possible. Little did he know that he was risking his life. He had the feeling that he was not looking down at a book, but down into a brain, a body, a landscape far, far greater, deeper, wider than the scene, Jotunheim, which lay before him when he raised his eyes. Jonas felt the world's flatness threatening, thanks to a measly book, to give way to hitherto unseen depths. Later he was to believe that he had, for a couple of endless seconds, been only a hair's breadth away from discovering the true nature of life; it was so clear and concrete that he could almost have reached out and touched it, and said: 'Here it is!'

Then something happened. He came to a new chapter, totally different. Time sped past, year after year and people departed. All of a sudden things were happening with bewilderingly rapidity and this transmitted itself to his thoughts, they were jammed nose to tail, causing pile-ups. He felt as though he had been sucked into a corridor and God knew what awaited him at the other end. And then – it was like being brutally robbed – the central character died, in a parenthesis, for God's sake, wise Mrs Ramsey, this was too much, how could the author let her die like that, just by the bye; and then a few pages further on Prue, the eldest daughter, died – this, too, by the bye. When Jonas came to the part where the son Andrew died as well, in yet another bloody parenthesis, he had to stop. He could not take it. That these people to whom, though he did not know why, he had begun to feel attached, should die just by the bye, while that blasted abstract time flowed callously onward, filling page after page.

He had to stop. He could not breathe. The insight was too much to bear. He was in imminent danger of being concussed again. He was being hunted by some monster that he could only escape if he closed the book. Jonas slammed it shut, in desperation almost, smack in the face, so it seemed, of something – something deadly. He remembered how as a boy he had run away from Daniel and only just managed, we're talking millimetres here, to lock the door against him and his murderous rage. The faint smile still played around Jonas's lips, as if his body had not yet caught up with his horror-stricken mind. But then: he realised that he was terrified. It was as though a whole pack of wolves had crept up on him unawares and were all suddenly breathing down his neck. Jonas stared out of the window at the rock face, the wintry Norwegian landscape. He was covered in goosebumps. He had almost lost his life. His old life. Had he finished it, that book would have changed his life. He knew it. And he did not want a novel changing his life.

He had closed *To the Lighthouse*. In the middle of the chapter entitled 'Time Passes'. He pressed a palm against each cover, as if to stop it from falling open again. It actually took some effort. The bang made Margrete look round, a question on her face. He made the excuse of a sudden headache. 'I'll read the rest some other time,' he said, trying to smile. But he knew he would never pick it up again. He knew that he had come close to making a fatal blunder. He swore to himself that he would never open another novel.

And yet, even though he had put the book down, something had happened. He noticed it later that evening when he got up, still trembling slightly, to light a candle on the dining table. As he struck the match and his hand edged towards the wick, it occurred to him that all life could be contained in that movement, that a person could write hundreds of pages about this simple action and what was going on in his mind at that moment. He *had* been changed. Not much, but a bit. He was marked for life. Why do you have a scar over your eyebrow? I got it in a fight with Virginia Woolf.

He had read a novel about a woman who knew how to appreciate the perfection of the moment – small everyday miracles. To be able to say, merely of the light on the sea: It is enough! And if he thought about it: Margrete was the same. But what was to become of his life now? What of the ambitions that drove, or had driven, him?

He thought he knew: when he closed Virginia Woolf's book, he salvaged his faith in his project, or the vestiges of this project. But he also closed the door on his chance of ever understanding Margrete. Who knows, maybe *To the Lighthouse* would have been the very device that would have opened her up, afforded him some insight into her, just as Bo's butterflies and crystals could lay open a stretch of terrain in Lillomarka.

Late that night when Jonas was sitting in the outdoor privy in the dark, peering up at Orion, which seemed remarkably close, it was with a sense of having both lost and won. He sat there on the ice-cold toilet seat, gazing up at the stars and thinking of a distant summer, of a friend who looked like Prince Valiant, and who presaged the existence of people like Margrete.

Bo Wang Lee came, in fact, as a foretoken of just about everything. During that brief summer with Bo, Jonas was confronted with a whole bunch of life's challenges. And possibly the greatest of these took the form of a question. Because, just when he thought that they were all set for the expedition to the Vegans' hiding place, Bo placed his hands on his hips and said: 'That just leaves the most difficult question. What should we take with us?'

To begin with Jonas thought that Bo meant something that would guarantee their safety. He remembered the pass which Kubla Khan had given to Marco Polo, a gold tablet covered in strange characters which said that Marco Polo was a friend of the Great Khan and enjoyed his mighty protection. If the Vegans were as intelligent as Bo believed, then it was no use trying to fool them; you could not go to meet a race from another solar system carrying little mirrors, copper wire or beads in eleven different colours – the sort of gewgaws that Stanley took with him to Africa. 'It has to be something which will show them that we are worthy envoys,' Bo said gravely. He pronounced the word 'worthy' exactly as Jonas would later hear Karen Mohr pronounce it, stretching the vowels and rolling the 'r'.

Bo's mother was studying social anthropology, or ethnography as it was then called – so Bo knew a little bit about what other explorers had taken with them, people from Europe and America, that is, who set out to visit tribes which might never have seen a white man before. It was a fascinating idea – to think that you could be eaten if you brought little bells, but crowned as an honorary chief if you handed out marbles. Bo told of explorers who had, for example, taken salt to the highlands of New Guinea. Others leaned more towards practical items: pocket knives or watches. Liquor had also been a popular gift among some primitive tribes. But they had to bear in mind, Bo said, that things also carried a message. 'What about a record by Jim Reeves?' suggested Jonas, off the top of his head. '"I Love You Because". Then they would know we come in peace.'

What should they take with them? Jonas considered little gifts epitomising Norway – a bar of Freia milk chocolate or a box of Globoid aspirins, a can of sardines from Bjelland. Too local, maybe. What about a kaleidoscope? One of his father's metronomes, a pyramid with its own hypnotic, in-built pulse? He could always ask Wolfgang Michaelsen if he could borrow one of his Märklin locomotives. The forthcoming expedition induced Jonas to ransack his surroundings and his life as he had never done before. Did he have in his possession anything good enough to merit a place in his rucksack when he set off into the woods to meet the Vegans? What on Earth was at all worth collecting?

There was something Aunt Laura had once told him. During the Renaissance, palaces were sometimes built with a small, windowless room at their centre, a chamber which did not even appear on the architect's drawings of the building. This was known as the *studiolo* or *guarda-roba*. In this the prince kept the most widely diverse objects, all of which had just one thing in common: they inspired wonder. Here one might find rarities from the animal and plant kingdoms together with a whole gallimaufry of other things, all with nothing to connect them except whatever the viewer himself could detect. The German princes called this room a *Wunderkammer*. Jonas had always thought that Uncle Lauritz must have had just such an inner chamber to which he could withdraw in order to meditate. All he needed were two inexhaustible objects: a box of Duke Ellington records and a tiny portrait of a woman.

The day before their departure Jonas at last found the article which he would take with him: Rakel's slide rule, with its movable Perspex panel and a centre section which could be pushed out and in. He was always left speechless by the sight of this, a device which could help you to work out difficult maths problems. In his mind he saw himself, Jonas W. Hansen standing face to face with a being the like of which no man had ever seen, in a small clearing in the woods, with the sunlight slanting through the trees; saw how he, Jonas, held out the slide rule, pi signs and all, whereafter the alien accepted this gift and immediately made a gesture which said that he, she, it understood everything – in other words, that he, Jonas, standing there bathed in the slanting sunlight, had somehow saved the Earth by finding the one thing which carried the right message: here you are, our civilisation in a nutshell.

He was surprised to see what Bo had chosen. A book. A book! What sort of thing was that to bring? *Huckleberry Finn*. Why this one? Jonas asked. Because it was the best book Bo had ever read. 'One hundred per cent wisdom,' Bo said. 'Pure, compressed power. Mightier than an atom bomb.'

They began to get ready for the next day, packing their things into two small rucksacks. 'Have you got the crystals?' Bo asked. He had not yet seen them. Jonas pulled out the handkerchiefs containing the four prisms he had collected from his grandmother. She had had no hesitation in lending them to him once he had told her what it was for. 'The Vegans – I see,' she had said. 'Ah yes, it's always best to stay on the right side of them.'

Where had he got them, Bo wanted to know, holding first one, then another prism up to the light like a master jeweller.

It was a secret, Jonas said. Why did they need the crystals anyway?

Because they contained the whole world, Bo told him.

Jonas said nothing, he knew Bo was right. Jonas had seen for himself some of the pictures a prism could contain. A yellow cabinet. A palace ball with hundreds of guests. The question of 'keys', of what to take with one, was possibly the same as asking: how small a piece of the world do you need in order to see the whole world? That was why Bo had brought a book.

His friend was sitting in one of the rooms in his aunt's flat which reminded Jonas of a ship's cabin and almost made him believe that if he looked out of the window he would see the entrance to New York harbour. Bo was studying the map of Lillomarka and looking up various entries in the yellow notebook. Jonas noticed that more lines had been drawn on the map. Some contour lines of equal elevation had been coloured in. 'Tomorrow it is, then,' Bo said happily. 'Tomorrow we're off to find the Vegans.'

Jonas had always been fascinated by maps. Despite their indisputable two-dimensionality they made him feel that the world could not be flat after all. Not because of the swirling lines denoting elevation and gradient, but because they appealed so strongly to his imagination. He never forgot the pleasure of his first atlas, the thrill of discovering that Norway and Sweden together looked like a lion, while Norway on its own resembled a fish. Little did he know that an imaginative way with maps could also lead to the world coming tumbling about your ears.

Mr Dehli shared Jonas's weakness for maps; he frequently employed them in his lessons and not only as a means of illustrating one of the most enigmatic words in Sanskrit – *māyā*. The huge expanses of paper which could be pulled down to cover the wall behind the teacher's lectern seemed charged with a singular magic. This was partly due to the fact that the maps in junior high were newer than their more tattered and faded counterparts in elementary school. In any case, it was a real treat to see Mr Dehli – while telling them, say, about Xerxes and the ancient kingdom of Persia – send his pointer dancing across a map of Asia half the size of the wall, printed in colours so bright and clear that the topographical features seemed to take on three dimensions and bulge right out into the room. Learning was suddenly brought to life, a connection established between it and the real world. They were halfway into the wonderful reddish-brown massifs of the Zagros Mountains when the bell rang.

The classroom itself altered character completely depending upon which map he had pulled down. The atmosphere in the room was different when savannah-covered Africa hung down over the board than when South America's rugged Andean spine dominated the field of vision. Sometimes Jonas thought that the maps made the front of the class with the dais and lectern look more like the stage in a theatre. And the sheets of paper hanging rolled up, one behind the other, on that marvellous rack were prospective sets or backdrops. 'Today we're going to talk about the Nile,' Mr Dehli said, loosening his bow tie; and even though it was winter and the classroom was cold, once the wall behind the schoolmaster had been covered by the Middle East and Egypt with their warm green and yellow hues, Jonas was hard put not to remove his jersey. He was transported back to his childhood, to when he had been the owner of an elegant, aromatic cigarette tin with a picture on the lid of the sphinx, the pyramids and Simon Arzt in a red fez.

Many of Mr Dehli's teaching *tours de forces* involved maps or globes. By turning the world upside down he taught them the meaning of the word 'perspective'. On one occasion he actually cut an old map of the world in two, right up the middle of the Atlantic Ocean. 'Why should the Atlantic always been in the centre?' he asked. 'Let's stick it together again with the Pacific in the middle.' The effect was remarkable. Suddenly Norway was right out on the periphery, up in the far corner – though, to Jonas's satisfaction, still in a possible Outside Left position. 'What if so-called Western supremacy was no more than a parenthesis in history?' Mr Dehli said, thereby anticipating those prophecies made towards the end of the millennium to the effect that the balance of economic power would shift to the east. During another lesson he held up a globe at a particular angle: 'What do you see?' They were looking straight at the Pacific Ocean. They could just make out the edges of the continents around the rim of the circle. Jonas had had a globe of the world for years, but had never realised that it could be viewed from such an angle. 'Nothing but sea,' Mr. Dehli said. 'Has it ever occurred to you that seventy-five per cent of the Earth's surface is covered in water?' This was during a history lesson, on Vasco da Gama. Mr Dehli then went on to tell them about the great voyages of discovery and the background to them, about sailing ships and navigation. You never forgot it. It seemed to Jonas that this was the whole point of lessons: to teach them how to navigate. Through life.

Mr Dehli's use of maps to illustrate *māyā* had its sequel in a Christmas show put on by the pupils in the classroom. It was actually during this same show that Leonard – or Leonardo, rather – despite restless rumblings from his classmates, showed his first 8 mm cine film, a bleak drama in which Jonas and Pernille played a boy and a girl in black polo-neck sweaters, standing back to back in an open field with a huge bulldozer in the background.

Jonas was a much bigger hit on his own and in the flesh. He did an impression of Mr Dehli, wearing a jacket and a bow tie deliberately and hilariously askew. 'Today I am going to tell you about Maya,' he said, getting a laugh right away by playing on his own misapprehension and pronouncing *māyā* like the girl's name. All the maps had been pulled down beforehand – and at the very back hung an affectionate caricature of Mr Dehli himself. Gesticulating wildly and brandishing his pointer Jonas worked up to his big conjuring trick. But just as he was about to tug on the first cord, acutely aware that all eyes were upon him, he suddenly began to feel very self-conscious, was struck by a terrible fit of shyness, with the result that he tugged too hard; he thought the map was stuck, so he yanked as hard as he could, the map rack came away from the wall and the whole kit and caboodle came crashing down on top of him, to the riotous glee of the class. Jonas must have lifted the pointer on instinct, in an attempt to defend himself against this avalanche of countries and continents, because he came round to find himself sitting on the floor like an emperor draped in a many-layered cloak, with the pointer stuck through the map of Asia. 'That was the day when the world came tumbling about my ears,' he was fond of saying.

Mr Dehli showed that he had appreciated this performance by laughing louder than anyone else. 'I think you're going to be a great discoverer,' he said, straightening Jonas's cock-eyed bow tie on the way out. I should perhaps add that the pointer had not pierced the map just anywhere. Jonas had actually run it right through Samarkand. Thus providing, you might say, the perfect illustration of *māyā*. In any case, from that day on, Samarkand stood for him as a reality behind reality, he developed a belief that there was a Samarkand behind Samarkand.

The memory of those maps and his attempt to demonstrate the concept of *māyā* cropped up more than once during the making of his televised portrait of Edvard Munch, a programme which also showed quite clearly how intent Jonas Wergeland was on challenging people's deeper awareness, or the way they *saw* things – what Mr Dehli would have called their philosophy of life. Although *Thinking Big* attracted record-breaking audiences, Wergeland was less interested in viewing figures than in the imprint which the series might leave on people's minds. In this respect he was a true programme-maker; he wished to programme, or reprogramme, the Norwegian people's way of thinking.

Owing to his own unforgettable encounter with the wall decorations in one of Oslo's public buildings – an experience to which we will return – Jonas was seriously tempted to focus on Munch's popular murals for the Oslo University assembly hall, but he eventually came down in favour of an early phase in the artist's life. In the key scene, the young Munch was shown standing in a large circular room with many windows. Viewers saw him walking slowly from one window to the next; gazing, clearly moved, out of each of them in turn, as if looking out onto a bewildering and troubling world. Thereafter he sat down on a bench in the centre of the room, his elbow propped on his thigh and his chin resting on his fist, like Rodin's celebrated sculpture 'The Thinker'. Here was a man at what was arguably the most crucial stage of his life; a man who had just lost his father, a man who had had the benefit of a couple of inspiring sojourns in France, in St Cloud and Nice, a young man who had only just begun to see what he wanted to do in his art, to find his own style. And underpinning the images of this man deep in thought, nothing but the sound of a brush on canvas. To the viewers it must have seemed as though the deep musings, or memories, around which his thoughts revolved had generated the vision or metamorphosis that now occurred, with first one, then another window, one prospect then another – still accompanied only by the rasp of a brush – turning first into a translucent panel, not unlike a transparent map, and then into a painting, until the circular room was seen to be a gallery, its walls hung with works recognisable as Munch's own, canvases covered with lines and colours which – one could tell – Munch had seen in his mind's eye. The world had become art.

Jonas Wergeland had filled the room with over twenty pictures painted by Munch around this time, including a number from the series which Munch would later dub The Frieze of Life. His idea, one which may even have begun to germinate while he was in France, was to create a series of paintings which would present an overall picture of existence, of all the stages of human life. The canvases which formed a circle round Munch showed individuals and landscapes reduced to timeless, placeless images. All inessentials had been omitted. Here were such pictures as 'Night' and 'Evening' – later renamed 'Melancholy'; viewers spotted 'The Sick Girl', 'Puberty' and 'Death in the Sickroom, 'Jealousy' and 'Despair' – Jonas did also include a few pictures painted one or two years later. The camera captured a room which bore little resemblance to other rooms containing nineteenth-century Norwegian art, those in the National Gallery in Oslo, for example, full of works by Tideman and Gude, Fearnley and Dahl. You did not play Tchaikovsky in such a room, Debussy or Stravinsky might have done at a push.

In the next scene, Munch was seen pacing restlessly back and forth, round the walls of the room, continually taking down pictures, switching them about, as if he could not decide which paintings should hang next to one another. He evidently felt that there were hidden links between some, or all, of the works, some inner bond. At long last he appeared to be satisfied, sat down again on the bench in his Thinker position. And once more one had the sense of great mental exertion, the impression that Edvard Munch was endeavouring to think about all the pictures, all of these key experiences, at once. And as if it were a result of this very process of visualisation, of the profound insight thus attained, something happened to the pictures: they began to live and breathe. Each painting turned into a screen filled with moving pictures. The works of art, the flat canvases, came to life, with each film presenting a plot, a drama which corresponded with the subject matter of the picture, before they all faded, in perfect sync, into exactly the same scene: a couple kissing, closely entwined, a man and a woman at one of life's sacred moments. Edvard Munch sat in the circular room, watching as all twenty-odd paintings, or films, became identical, with every scene showing a couple clinging to one another, almost merging into one, in a kiss.

After a prolonged close-up of Munch's anxious features, his eyes, the camera pulled back to reveal a room once more lined with Munch's famous works, the kissing couple turned back into the painting entitled 'The Kiss'. At this point in the programme Jonas Wergeland appeared on screen, in the foreground, in the guise of a reporter and advised in a whisper, before disappearing again just as quietly, that we were in Berlin, the year was 1892 and Edvard Munch had been invited by Verien Berliner Künstler, the Berlin Society of Artists, to exhibit his pictures in the Architektenhaus, in the circular gallery. The exhibition was about to open.

Munch stood up. The soundtrack consisted solely of heartbeats, heavy breathing, the occasional cough. Munch crossed to the nearest paintings. Viewers could now see cords attached to the bottom of each frame. One by one Munch tugged the cords, as if the paintings were roller blinds, and they positively shot up to disclose entirely different pictures underneath. One was given to understand that Munch did the same to every single picture because, when he left the circular room, on the walls hung twenty-odd unrecognisable paintings, glowing ominously and offensively. These pictures had been produced by Jonas's skilled technicians; they were digitally distorted versions of Munch's images; hideous pictures with garish colours and tortuous figures, a long way from the modern idea of a good painting. This was Wergeland's way of showing that we have already forgotten how radical Munch's work once was, how *differently* he painted. He did not observe, he *saw*. To us, those paintings with their smouldering energy had long since become tame calendar fodder, something for the bedroom wall, reproductions to hang in our toilets. It was no longer considered shocking for someone to paint a tree without showing the branches, or a green face, or a countenance with no nose, ears, mouth; for paint to be squirted onto the canvas. With his distorted images, these 'new' Munch pictures, Jonas Wergeland wanted to show just how outlandish the original works must have seemed to his contemporaries, what an outrageously far cry they were from anything else being painted at that time, not least in the German art world, where battle scenes and naturalistic pictures were all the rage. Wergeland may even have wished to imply that somewhere in Norway today there had to be another young Munch – an artist we laughed at. It was ironic, certainly, that so many of those who complained to NRK about this scene resorted to the same sort of invective as was levelled at Munch by critics of his day. These 'new' pictures in Jonas Wergeland's otherwise enthralling programme had to be the work of some 'charlatan painter', they wrote; those painting were nothing but hideous 'daubs', 'feverish hallucinations'.

The scene ended with the doors of the gallery being opened to the Berlin public. Jonas Wergeland presented close-ups of faces streaming past, their features expressing shock, disgust, laughter, fury. The last shot was of the face of a man putting his hands to his head and screaming in horror at what he had seen.

When this programme was shown on British television – one newspaper described it as being every bit as revolutionary in terms of form and colour as Munch's pictures – Jonas Wergeland felt that he had repaid a little of his debt; he knew how much he owed to Great Britain after his course of study in a hotel room in London. In fact, towards the tail end of that 'term', as he liked to call it, Wergeland himself witnessed something which made him want to scream. This too involved seeing, seeing something behind reality – or what, up to this point in his life, he had taken for reality. In London, he would think later, it wasn't just my outer eye that got whacked, but my inner eye too.

One afternoon, before the start of the day's programmes, Jonas took the tube out to White City to take a look at an edifice which held for him the same sacred status as St Paul's Cathedral, and was as closely bound up in his mind with the proud history and culture of Britain as Trafalgar Square or Bloomsbury: the BBC Television Centre at Wood Lane. Jonas stood outside the brick façade, aware that he was looking at a monument to a highly advanced civilisation. The old British Empire might have collapsed, but what he saw before him, or that which it represented, British television, was the seat of a new, modern empire – an invisible dominion. And the might of this empire was founded on such diverse wonders as *The Great War*, *Monty Python's Flying Circus*, *The Six Wives of Henry VIII*, *The Dave Allen Show* and *The Voyage of Charles Darwin*.

Outside, and later inside, this building, his thoughts went to the most groundbreaking piece of television he had ever seen, this too from the BBC stable. Jonas had been at home, nodding off in front of the box, when Dennis Potter's drama series *Pennies From Heaven* was shown on NRK; he had been totally unprepared for it when, only minutes into the first episode, Bob Hoskins, playing a sheet-music salesman who had just been rudely rebuffed by his wife, suddenly pulled back the curtains in his bedroom and burst into song, broke into 'The Clouds Will Soon Roll By', or rather: it was not him who was singing, it was a woman, but Bob Hoskins lip-synched along, as rapturously and sincerely as if the song were emanating from his own head, a thought abruptly transformed into song. It came as such a shock, Jonas had to rub his eyes precisely as he had done when Mr Dehli did conjuring tricks with the maps or showed how a third thought could act as a catalyst. Television was never the same again; Jonas Wergeland always said that it was at that moment, when Bob Hoskins put his heart and soul into 'The Clouds Will Soon Roll By' in a seemingly drab naturalistic setting from thirties' England, that he first felt the urge to make television programmes himself, even though some years were to pass before he finally came to that decision. Potter had shown him that you could do anything on TV. Good television could show you the inside of a head, show how a person was *thinking*. As far as Jonas was concerned, Dennis Potter was the only true genius fostered by television, and indeed one of the greatest artists of the twentieth century, the one against whom Jonas himself most wished to be measured. Just as the Renaissance ushered in a new approach to painting, Dennis Potter proved that flat television images could offer experiences of a hitherto unknown depth. Jonas was especially fascinated by the way he used the old popular songs of the thirties and, in *The Singing Detective*, the forties, as if they were every bit as valid, as fraught with emotion, as hymns or fairy tales. Thanks to his experience with *Rubber Soul*, Jonas had no difficulty in comprehending the sentimental force of these tunes, their ability to convey the inexpressible. The way Jonas Wergeland saw it, it was Dennis Potter who had led him to that hotel bed in London.

Possibly it was because of the exalted frame of mind induced by his visit to the BBC's headquarters that he was caught so much off guard by the sight that awaited him when he got off the train in South Kensington. He was in his usual shop on the corner of the arcade in the old station building, taking receipt of a bag containing two chicken sandwiches and two bacon-and-egg sandwiches for the evening's television marathon, when he started, actually jumped about three feet in the air. Somebody he knew had just walked by outside. His aunt. Aunt Laura. Flamboyantly dressed and looking, from her make-up, as if she had come straight from a stage on which she was playing the lead in an Egyptian romance. And she was not alone, with his aunt was another woman, similarly dressed. Both wore the sort of hats you saw on women at Royal Ascot. Jonas heard them speak to one another in English. They were followed by a man wheeling a goods trolley. Propped up on it was a rug. Jonas had noticed that there was a shop between the two flights of stairs leading down to the platforms. The man lifted the rug into an estate car sitting right outside the arcade; it had British plates and obviously belonged to the woman with his aunt. As if that wasn't enough, Jonas got the definite impression that these two women were more than friends, they were lovers. Jonas was on the point of calling out, but something stopped him.

Standing there in the sandwich shop he wished he could see the pattern on the rug that Aunt Laura had had wheeled out to the car. Something about the cylinder on the trolley reminded him of a piece of paper – a message – in a bottle, he was sure that everything would be explained if he could just unfold it.

He stared after the car as it drove away. It was blue – blue as the tiled domes in a distant city. Jonas stood outside of himself, saw himself standing there with a black-and-blue eye, a souvenir from the Zetland Arms. It was true. He had been his aunt's blue-eyed boy, but he had also been blind. He hailed the man when he came past pushing the empty trolley. 'Excuse me, but do you know that lady, the one who was wearing the bigger hat?' The carpet dealer stopped, eyed him pleasantly, or with genteel courtesy, adjusted his glasses for a better look at Jonas and his shiner. 'Why do you ask?' Jonas hesitated, did not want to say that he was her nephew. 'I just thought I had seen her before. Is she somebody famous?' The man motioned towards his shopfront. 'I couldn't say,' he replied, 'I only know that she's a good customer. She must have bought fifty rugs from me over the past twenty or thirty years. My shop is one of the oldest in England. She orders rugs from particular regions, specific patterns. And I give her a call when I find one.' Before disappearing into the shop, the man told Jonas that the two women had a big old house with a luxuriant garden outside of London. He occasionally had to deliver something to them. The house was full of rugs and antiques. 'Funny thing, though,' the man said, 'they call the place "Samarkand".'

Back at the hotel, Jonas switched on the TV and opened his notebook. He filled a whole page with notes on the first programme he saw, about a trip to Titicaca: the sort of documentary that made you want to race off to the nearest travel agent. And while in his eyes he was on the shores of Lake Titicaca, in his mind two and two slowly flowed together. And did not make five. The Samarkand with which Aunt Laura had presented him was *māyā*. She had never been to Samarkand. She had never been outside of Europe. She had bought her rugs here, in London, every single one of them. London was the world centre for the Oriental rug trade. This, London, was Aunt Laura's Samarkand. That grimy little passage in the arcade next to the station was her bazaar. And why was he surprised? Jonas had always known: Samarkand could be anywhere on Earth. Samarkand was the home of our dreams and longings.

He lay on the bed in a hotel room in London. He closed his eyes, left the programme on Titicaca running, as if it inspired long cruises in his mind. Aunt Laura, this too he realised now, had never been with a man. Not one. All of her sketchbooks – like the one in which he himself was now making notes – in which she had drawn penises in all shapes and forms and in every conceivable state, had been nothing but flights of fancy. Jonas lay on the bed, with a voice in his ears talking about the fauna around Lake Titicaca, and thought about Aunt Laura, and he realised that he was not disappointed. It was not a lie that had led him to Samarkand. It was another kind of truth.

So there could be something to the rumour: although Jonas Wergeland was most certainly in London, one could say that his revelation on the secret of good television came to him in Samarkand. In the Samarkand behind Samarkand.

It often struck Jonas that all of the journeys he made had their beginnings in the expedition into Lillomarka with Bo Wang Lee to find the secret hiding place of the Vegans. On the 'right' day – Bo consulted a complicated diagram in his little yellow notebook and mumbled something about favourable constellations – they set off from home in the afternoon, each with their small rucksack on their back. Jonas was carrying the jam jars containing the brimstone butterfly and the peacock butterfly, two prisms and the slide rule; Bo bore the jars containing the red admiral and the small tortoiseshell, the other two crystals and *Huckleberry Finn*. Jonas's suggestion that they take along a couple of little kids as 'bearers' was rejected. 'You still don't get it, do you,' Bo snapped. 'This is serious.'

The hill up to Badedammen smelled of fresh tarmac, the road might have been resurfaced specially for them. They headed out along the old Bergen road, built at the end of the eighteenth century. Jonas was not sure exactly where they were going, but Bo purposefully proceeded along a blue-flashed path which brought them to the northern end of Romstjern Lake. Shortly afterwards he struck off again, onto a barely visible, unmarked track. Jonas had never been here before. The hillside was a mass of yellow crested cowwheat. The vegetation grew lush and dense all around them; it was like walking through a greenhouse with the sun filtering through green windows in the roof. The scents were remarkably strong, rising from the ground like fragrant gases. Bo stopped. Thought for a moment. The birdsong sounded unnaturally intense, Jonas thought. Only now did he realise how nervous he was. Bo swivelled around, as if he were listening, using all his senses. 'Watch out for that rock!' he cried suddenly, pointing. Jonas jumped as if he were standing next to a landmine. Bo took out his notebook, scribbled something down with the stub of pencil. Nodded. 'This is good,' was all he said and walked on.

They reached a shadier hollow, a little valley through which ran a brook with lovely little waterfalls tumbling over flat rocks; it looked man-made, like something out of a Japanese garden or the like. Jonas saw Bo nod again. His friend with the glossy, black Prince Valiant hair pulled out a pocketknife, pried a piece of bark off a pine tree and showed Jonas the engraved markings on the backside. The look Bo gave him told Jonas these were not marks left by larvae, but an extra-terrestrial form of writing. They followed the brook upstream until they came to a very long, narrow tarn with a steep cliff running all the way down its western side. At their feet water lilies floated on the surface of the water. This had to be Lusevasaen. Spooky, thought Jonas. He had heard rumours of dangerous undercurrents in this tarn, that it was bottomless. He felt like getting away from there as quickly as possible, was half expecting something to burst to the surface and cast a net at them.

Bo sprang over the brook. They entered some sort of primeval forest, began to clamber up a steep slope under tall fir trees, the nethermost branches of which were dry and withered. Bo zigged and zagged as if negotiating an invisible maze. Jonas felt sure that they had to be the first people ever to penetrate this patch of forest. 'We could have done with a machete,' he grunted as they fought their way through the undergrowth. He eyed all the exquisitely shaped toadstools uneasily: what if they were spaceships, spying on them and warning of their arrival? The trees, their branches, blocked out the light, like massive umbrellas rising in tiers. Here and there a fallen tree lay with its vast network of roots in the air. Jonas thought he heard a strange humming sound coming from a gigantic anthill they passed. His face cut through spider's web after spider's web, as if he were breaking one finishing tape after another, or better: ripping through veil after veil. 'Good,' he heard Bo mutter under his breath. 'Absolutely excellent.'

At long last they reached the top, coming out suddenly and breathlessly into the open near the edge of the cliff overlooking Lusevasaen. 'Here,' Bo whispered. 'This is it.' He did not even refer to his notebook.

They were looking out across a small hilltop covered in grass and heather and dotted with large rocks. An archetypical Norwegian country scene, such an ordinary sight as far as Jonas was concerned that it seemed hard to believe that anything alien could lie hidden here. Beyond, on the lip of the cliff, stood a couple of gnarled pines, smaller versions of the trees his grandmother had pointed out to him in Lars Hertervig's paintings in the National Gallery. For a second the view took their breath away. They could see all the way across to the northern end of Østmarka, on the other side of the Grorud Valley. A brilliant observation point for any Vegans who might be around, Jonas thought to himself.

The tarn lay black below them. The air was rather close. Oppressive. The sun still hung in a large patch of blue sky, but big clouds were building up in the west. Bo unwrapped the prisms from their handkerchiefs and set them out in a square, roughly in the centre of the hilltop, then he arranged the four jars containing the insects in such a way that they formed a larger square around the crystals. At a sign, Bo and Jonas each took off one lid then raced to the other two jars and did the same with them. And more or less as one the four butterflies fluttered upwards. Jonas was held utterly spellbound. The four butterflies, all so different in colour and pattern, hovered almost motionless above the heather, forming a square with an area of something like five metres. Jonas was able to take in the four movements and the four crystals at one glance, like eight simultaneous thoughts. It was weird. And beautiful. Four sets of sensitively fluttering butterfly wings – so distinct that he thought he could even make out their tiny, colourful scales – and four smooth, sparkling prisms, like mysterious civilisations nestling in the heather. Jonas realised that this could be a gateway. And then, he could hardly believe it, the brimstone and the peacock, the admiral and the small tortoiseshell began to gravitate towards one another. The insects' square grew smaller, looked set to merge with the square formed by the light-refracting prisms. Because that was the whole idea: all four butterflies had to enter the square defined by the crystals.

Again they held still, or flew in spirals, up and down in the same spot. Jonas was more or less expecting something to manifest itself. He did not know how. Only that something might be revealed, or be *opened up*. Bo, standing there so proud, a prince, a Chinaman, had convinced him of this. In a way it seem quite natural that the insect which represented the divine process of metamorphosis, from larvae to butterfly, should also be capable of transfiguring this ordinary patch of countryside. Jonas was already starting to feel in his rucksack for the slide rule, the object which would persuade the Vegans that he was a worthy envoy.

But just as it looked as though the butterflies were going to flutter into the centre of the square; just as Jonas was thinking that the landscape was starting to vibrate ever so slightly and emit a faint purplish glow, there came a roar; they turned their heads and saw a small plane flying towards them, or under them. Jonas thought it was a model airplane, he was *positive* that it was a model airplane, it must have shot out of an invisible slit in the weir of life, until it dawned on him that the plane was actually some distance away, skimming over the trees on the other side of Lusevasaen, that it was, in other words, a real aircraft, and even at that distance Jonas knew which type it was: a Piper Cub, white with red trim – a big butterfly – identical to the one that Uncle Lauritz had had, but it could not possibly be his uncle, because he had been dead for years. Nevertheless, the plane came wobbling over the tops of the trees, as if it was in trouble; it was flying low, far too low, heading straight for the cliff, the rock face underneath them; then, just as Jonas thought they were about to witness a terrible calamity, the aircraft's nose lifted sharply, bringing it clear of the precipice, it came swooping over the hilltop on which they stood, passed right over their heads, and then it was gone, a sight which would normally have filled them with awe and wonder, but which now only left them panic-stricken, realising as they did that the roar of the plane, the vibrations in the air, could have had an adverse effect on the 'gateway'. And sure enough: the butterflies had come to a halt. As Bo and Jonas looked on helplessly the insects flitted up and down, then darted away from one another, all flying off in different directions. 'Shit!' Bo cried. 'Shit, shit, shit.'

Later, after a long walk home in silence, Bo said. 'Did you see what I saw?'

Jonas nodded, he knew what his friend was referring to. There had been no one at the controls. The cockpit had been empty.

But Bo had observed something else: 'What was an SAS pilot doing in that plane? And a captain, at that. I saw the four gold bands on the sleeve of his uniform jacket quite clearly when he waved.'

Nonetheless, Jonas was disappointed. The experiment with the crystals and the butterflies had failed. Not until they turned the corner into Solhaug, did he begin to suspect that something might, nonetheless, have occurred. The estate seemed unfamiliar, different somehow. When Five-Times Nielsen stepped out of his entry with a carpet beater in his hand, Jonas felt a burning desire to run up to him and present him with the slide rule, as if the Vegans actually dwelt here, in that place in the world which he knew best of all. Jonas shot a glance at Bo. He too seemed different. And at last it dawned on Jonas: it was not the world that had opened up, but him, Jonas. *He* had changed.

Miranda

Why did she do it? I need to write more. About the middle part. About the longest seconds in my life. Evening. Late April. Returning home from a World's Fair. I ask the driver to drop me off at the shopping centre. I want to walk the last bit of the way, I want to savour the smell of spring, I want to pass through pockets of air of varying temperatures. I breathe deep, fill my lungs as after a long dive. I think, I am sure, that I have never been so full of drive, of ideas, of a sheer desire to embrace life. So *present in spirit* – yes, that's it.

I delighted in the fresh coolness on my brow after the heat in Spain; I savoured every sound, every millimetre of the scene, those familiar surroundings, trees with branches on which the leaves were already discernible. Greedily I inhaled the powerful odour of the soil. I walked along with my senses wide open. I caught the scent of bonfires. I heard the smack of a skipping rope. I knew it could not be right, but I had rediscovered my powers of thought, the sparkling exuberance of my childhood. A belief in the impossible. I had the urge to stop by the stream, sink my teeth into the bark of a pussy willow tree from which we used to make flutes. At one spot I actually left my suitcase standing in order to experience again the feel of a coltsfoot stalk against the skin of my finger, came very close, in fact, to prostrating myself – the way people do in ultra-romantic film scenes – and kissing the earth on which, by some cosmic will, I had been allowed to walk. And more than anything: I could not wait to see Margrete again, the mere thought of her face, her eyes, the gold glints in those eyes, sent warm jolts running through me. I was aching to tell her all about Seville, about my new plans; I was longing to hear her tell me what she had been up to, what Kristin had been up to; I was looking forward to sitting on the sofa, nuzzling her neck, listening to her talk, maybe while she peeled an orange in that ingenious way of hers, popping a wedge into my mouth and making some wry comment in response to my breathless description of a World's Fair on the theme of 'The Age of Discovery', featuring life-size replicas of everything from Columbus's ships to space shuttles. For Margrete, the woman I loved, the great discoveries began much closer to home, for example with an orange wedge in the mouth. 'And feel this,' she might say, guiding my hand roguishly to her shoulder. 'This isn't a collar-bone, it's a clavicle – a "key-bone". Go on, feel it.'

The spring was in my blood, I was all set to unfold. My head was full of colossal, and possibly dangerous, notions, Wagnerian ideas. I had regained my faith in a Project X. Once again I was going to be a mover in the deep, someone who could make people all over the country snap their chairs into the upright position before swivelling them round, as one, like tiny cogs in a gigantic mechanism, to face a screen which gave them, the whole national machine, a fresh injection of energy. For a few giddy seconds on the plane, with impressions of a hectic World's Fair buzzing around in my head, I had had the feeling that I could make something no one had ever seen before; a television production which would represent a new synthesis of all knowledge and all art forms.

There was an explanation for my elation: several times in the course of the past year Margrete had criticised me. Tactfully, it's true. I had brooded more on this than I cared to admit. I also knew what it was that she found hardest to forgive: I had succumbed to the temptation to become a TV host. I had been seduced by empty flattery. I had presented two of the light entertainment department's main offerings, on Friday evenings one autumn and on Saturdays in another. A huge hit. Pages and pages about me in every weekly and weekend supplement going. But Margrete was right, it was mindless. And, what was worse, pointless. She reminded me of the *Thinking Big* series. One evening she pretty much forced me to watch the programme on Kirsten Flagstad again. By the end she was in tears. I asked her why. 'Can't you see how good it is?' she said. 'So why are you crying?' I asked. 'I'm crying because it lifts me up,' she said.

I had thought a lot about this. Which is why I felt such eagerness now, as I tramped up the gravel driveway to the house, drinking in air suffused with spring. Margrete had asked me not to go. She had seemed somehow listless when I left. 'I need you to hold me,' she had said. But I had to go. She would forget, forgive me, when I came home inspired – *inspirited* – my head full of great plans. I had not, as she said, degenerated as a programme-maker. In this buoyant frame of mind, with a sense of being on the threshold of something totally new, I opened the living-room door and found her dead. And the world turned upside down.

I sit on deck, writing, as the *Voyager* glides along the peaceful green fjord. We pass few other craft. Mainly ferries and shuttle boats, the odd cruise ship, its loudspeakers blaring tinny facts across the water in three languages. Carl is sitting across from me. Just at this minute he is showing his brass figure of Ganesh to Kamala. It's such a comical sight: this crop-headed, broad-shouldered bodyguard type holding out, tenderly almost, an object which is all but lost in his huge hand. It is shiny where his fingers have been rubbing at it in his pocket. I cannot hear what they are saying, but I think Kamala is telling him a story about the elephant-headed god, possibly something from *The Mahabharata*. Carl is all ears. Captivated. Everyone is captivated by Kamala. At one planning session the OAK Quartet were discussing the possibility of setting up 'sites' for users to visit like so-called 'avatars'. With a little smile, and almost as a digression, Kamala treated them to a brief lecture on avatars in Hindu philosophy. That gave them food for thought.

Rakel is up aft with skipper Hanna. Benjamin is in the well, manning the tiller. He is wearing Kristin's black beret and an expression worthy of Ghengis Khan himself.

A little while ago I experienced again that sensation of everything being turned upside down. We had just cast off, Fjærland was slipping away to stern. I was lying on the foredeck, peering over the bow. The smooth surface of the water reflected the surrounding scenery as perfectly as a mirror: the steep mountainsides bounding the narrow fjord, the snow on their tops, the sky and the clouds. I had an uncannily strong sense of being on an interface, of balancing on a knife-edge between two worlds, one real and one reversed. I thought: this feeling is the perfect encapsulation of my view of life. An existence characterised as much by artificiality as by reality. Then, all of a sudden, everything spun around. I had an utterly lifelike sensation of the world revolving. The next moment I had no idea where I was, in the real or in the reflected world. I had to shut my eyes, lay there just listening to the rush of the bow cutting through the water. When I opened my eyes I was once more lying safely in between, right on the interface.

Through the skylight I can see Kristin and Martin, still hard at work in the saloon. Their project keeps putting out new shoots. I have to smile at their almost ferocious zeal. And at the contrast in their appearances: it is like seeing a guerrilla leader deep in conversation with a Silicon Valley hacker disguised as a thief from Marrakesh. I can tell that she is in love with him.

Who is she? I have picked up snatches of locker-room stories that made my hair stand on end with worry. She has had her dark times, I think. But she has come through them. I do not know how.

The hardest part about being in prison was to know that I was missing out on the last stages of Kristin's adolescence, the fact of not being there to experience her hundred and one ways of slamming a door. Her experiments with black nail polish. There was not much of that sort of thing when she came to see me. In short, I missed being able to take an active daily part in her upbringing.

Otherwise it soon became quite easy to keep up with her doings on the outside. I could read all about them in the newspapers. I am not thinking here of her television career. When she was only fifteen and still living with her grandmother, my mother, she won the Golden Mouse award for the best Norwegian homepage on the Internet, but it was through her music that the media first latched on to her. She became the lead singer with a band playing advanced techno. I could never make anything of it; let's just say her music was a far cry from *Rubber Soul*. After her spell as a talk-show host and the whole TV circus thing, she joined a new young advertising agency and had a hand in several landmark campaigns, including one in which she painted a red nose on Che Guevara, thus inflaming the ulcers of the old '68 generation – not to mention the Hitler moustache she stuck on the face of the peace-loving Mahatma Ghandi.

And it may well be the same people who are now fighting to give her work, competing for the unique expertise possessed by the OAK Quartet, a company working on the borderline between the multinational software and hardware corporations and Norwegian culture. One of the big television channels has already tried to buy the company. It doesn't surprise me. Anyone can see that the OAK Quartet is on its way up, that it is starting to make its mark on the international scene. Which is actually no more surprising than the fact of a Norwegian firm of architects designing the new library in Alexandria.

More and more I can see what a clever idea it was to do their research for the Sognefjord project from a boat. This compels them to think of navigation on all levels, and not merely in an electronic space. I note the assurance with which they work their way along the fjord. How confidently, but unassumingly, they gain their bearings in the world. I believe this is how they envisage the product which they are developing – as a navigational tool for people who are curious. Not only about Sognefjord, but about things in general. They are working on a kind of astrolabe or a sextant which could, in principle, be employed within any sphere of existence.

One day, while we were sitting in the saloon eating curried pirogs, made by Martin and Kamala amid much hilarity, I told them, at Kristin's request, about the Voyager mission, which is to say: the two space probes launched in 1977. I knew more about Voyager 2 which, having sailed past Jupiter, Saturn, Uranus and Neptune – a tremendous navigational feat, this – had now left our solar system and was heading out into the far reaches of space. Although my astrophysics studies were only a blind, right from the start I had been fascinated by this project. In the primitive, but warm light of a paraffin lamp I told the crew on board their Norwegian sister ship some of the new things

273

we had learned about the outer planets, thanks to the Voyager probes – like the fact that Io, one of the moons of Jupiter, was volcanically active, or that Saturn had thousands of separate rings, the particles of which were held in place by 'shepherd moons'. And then there was the unbelievably complex and varied surface of Miranda, one of Uranus's moons. I could tell that my audience was astonished, although they had obviously heard of this before. Carl who, as well as Ganesh, always kept a little yellow notebook and a stub of pencil in his pocket, came over to me later, wanting to know more, particularly about the 'message' disc carried by both Voyager probes.

I told him what I knew. I never tire of thinking of this concept: a sort of gramophone record attached to each spaceship, containing greetings to any eventual extra-terrestrial civilisations. The people who made this had asked themselves the same questions as Bo Wang Lee had done: 'What should we take with us?' What should we present? And which of all the Earth's sounds should we select? They had ended up with 118 pictures, all of which, in different ways, said something about mankind and its culture; these included diagrams of the DNA structure and of the human sex organs, but there too were photographs of fungi in a forest, a dancer in Bali and a classroom in Japan. Somewhere far beyond Pluto's orbit there also drifted greetings in almost sixty different languages. 'You could say that the Voyager disc is a World's Fair shot into space,' I said to Carl. 'But first and foremost – obviously – it's a message to mankind itself.'

The middle part. My homecoming from a World's Fair. It is all there in those minutes. I remember how I paused outside the house. I stood there looking at, admiring, the bricks of the walls, the extension in Grorud granite; I feasted my eyes on the crocuses in the flower beds, the bare branches of the apple trees in the garden. I positively revelled in my own good fortune. For a second I could not believe that this was my home, this welcoming house, the warmth of the light beyond the gauzy white curtains covering the living-room window – all that was lacking was for her shadow to go gliding past.

I knew how I would find Margrete when I entered the living room. She would be writing letters. She almost always wrote letters in the evening, when she was not reading. And when she had finished a book she wrote letters non-stop. For her these two things went hand in hand, reading and writing. She used expensive pens and the finest quality writing paper; when we were out travelling she was always on the lookout for pretty envelopes and unusual paper. I often watched her on the sly when she was writing. Her face took on a different expression then, as if she were doing something requiring deep concentration. 'I'm weaving,' she would say. She said the same thing when she was reading: 'I'm weaving.' I had no idea what she put in her letters, mostly everyday stuff I guessed: quotes from books she had read, a verse of a poem. And she wrote in a hand which must have given the receiver as much pleasure as the actual contents.'Attractive handwriting is as important for a woman as beauty,' she said once. It must have been an honour to receive a letter from Margrete. She wrote to her friends abroad on tissue-thin paper. Sometimes, if I was there, she would hold the paper up in front of her eyes. And I saw her face as if through a veil of script.

There was one evening when she had hung lots of Chinese lanterns around the terrace. We had had guests, they had just left and she was stretching out in a mahogany chair. The coloured lanterns made the house, made Grorud, look as if it lay under other skies. I thought of something, fetched a thick sheet of paper which I kept at the back of a cupboard. It was a large Chinese character, written – or painted – by Bo Wang Lee as a farewell present. I showed it to Margrete. 'This means friendship, right?' She considered it for some time. 'This is the character for love,' she said, her face bathed in the glow of the paper lanterns. 'Don't be silly,' I said. 'The person who wrote this said it was the sign for friendship.' She looked up at me, with a smile in her eyes. 'That's as may be,' she said, 'but this says "love".' She explained the intricate character to me, even showed me how the Chinese word for heart – four exquisite strokes, like chambers – lay in the middle of it, like a word within the word. 'Love without heart is no love at all,' she murmured, more to herself. Then she looked at me again. 'Maybe there was something about the person who wrote this that you didn't understand,' Margrete said. She was right, of course. There was a lot I had not understood about Bo Wang Lee.

I opened the gate at the bottom of the drive with my heart hammering – like a man in love, I thought. I walked slowly up to the front door, with waves of warmer air wafting towards me, caressing my brow. I knew Kristin was at her grandmother's, that we, Margrete and I, had the weekend to ourselves. To this day I can recall the distinctive sound of gravel under my shoes, a sound I have always liked and which, on this fragrant spring evening, felt especially good, as if each little stone were scrunching expectantly, welcoming me home.

And then, I open the door, step inside, put down my suitcase, walk into the living room – and there she is, Margrete, this precious person, lying dead in the middle of the room, shot, and not just shot, but shot through the heart.

What was my first impulse? I know no one will believe me, but my first impulse was to get out, fast, and shut the door behind me. Fast. I thought I had come to the wrong place. Not the wrong house, but the wrong reality.

One autumn, when I was a student and working on my Titanic Project X, I accepted an invitation – a rare exception, this – to a party. I do not know whether it was because I was tired, had eaten too little or been working too much, but that evening I had a very weird experience, one which I interpreted nonetheless as a sign that I was on the right track, that there really was something lying behind, beyond, just waiting for me. I did not know the people who were holding the party, presumably medical students or pharmacy undergrads: the pure alcohol was flowing freely, mixed with everything imaginable, from juice to the most sickly-sweet essences. There seemed to be about a hundred rooms in the flat, all painted white and almost bare of furniture. And in the background, throughout, the lazy sound of Billie Holiday singing. At one point, pretty late on, I set off down one of the long corridors. I was looking for the guys I had come with. I opened a door and stepped inside. And – I swear to God – I found myself in the Forum Romanum; which is to say: I had entered it at the corner closest to the Temple of Vespasian, and not only that, but I was in Roman times, people walked past dressed in togas and everything, although it might not have been Roman times, because there were other things there too, ultra-modern looking objects which were strange to me, I had no idea what they were. I have always regretted that I did not attempt to speak to someone, to ask, but I got such a fright that, more or less on instinct, I fled back out of the door, slamming it shut behind me, and hurried off down the corridor. Once I had calmed down I went back and opened the door again. Behind it now was a large, white-painted room and a couple having it off on a mattress in the corner, next to a Ludwig drum kit. I opened the other doors round about, but found only white rooms, sparsely furnished, and partygoers with glasses in their hands, standing around, flirting or discussing Schopenhauer. I know it sounds crazy, but it was not a dream, nor was it a hallucination.

After having stood – for I don't know how long – outside, I opened the living-room door again. So great was my belief, or my hope, or my horror, that I fully expected another sight to meet my eyes: she would be sitting there, pen in hand, she would turn to me, smiling. But she was still lying on the floor, shot through the heart, just as dead. In my dressing gown. For ages I stood there, looking down at her, as if there was a tissue-thin sheet of paper lying on her face, covered in the loveliest handwriting. A letter to me.

We have reached Balestrand. We are moored right alongside the aquarium, at the mouth of the little Esefjord, surrounded by towering peaks: Vindreken, Tjuatoten, and in the middle Keipen – the 'Rowlock' – with its characteristic notched peak, with Gulleplet Crag in front of it. It is a breathtaking sight, even for a Norwegian used to such landscapes. Fruit trees in bloom at the feet of these sculpted, snow-capped massifs. I can well understand why the artists of the nineteenth century reached frantically for their brushes the moment they set eyes on this scene.

There was a letter waiting for me at the hotel reception desk. From Viktor Harlem, a friend from high school, now a name known to all of Norway. He knew I was coming here. It was nothing really, just a hello and a line from *The Cantos* by Ezra Pound: 'And then went down to the ship …' The others collected the company's mail, forwarded to the local post office. I had noticed that they received amusing – and creative, also in their outward appearance – missives from all over the world. Benjamin immediately started clamouring for the stamps. The OAK Quartet think nothing of being in close contact with individuals, groups, with similar interests, in other countries. Without even being aware of it, Kristin and her friends tend to think in terms of categories which transcend national boundaries. In sailing the fjord they are also sailing all over the world. I like to think that they are in the process of founding a county within a virtual space, populated by 'Sogn folk' from every corner of the globe.

Kamala and I had decided to book in to Kvikne's Hotel for the days when we were docked at Balestrand. Kamala wanted to stay in the old house, a grand and graceful, wooden, Swiss-style building overlooking the fjord. The manager gave us one of his best rooms, high up and with its own balcony. I thought at first this was for my sake. Then I realised it was for Kamala's.

The most obliging manager also allowed Benjamin to pitch his well-used, twelve-man army tent on the lawn next to the hotel, just across from the little islet of Lausholmen. We gave him a hand. Benjamin is a nomad. As soon as his tent is up he is home. Benjamin. There's a whole book right there. I often think about how mad I was when he was born. I was so upset that I spent years after that fuming with rage in a basement we called the Red Room. I pretended to be incensed by everything and everybody, when I was really only angry at myself. I abhorred my thoughtless act of sabotage, that imperceptible slit in a diaphragm. I was to blame for his birth. Sometimes it occurs to me that Benjamin is my deepest motivation. Once, when he visited me in prison he left behind a note. It said: 'Thank you because I'm alive.' It could be read in several different ways. Today that note forms the core of my being.

A group of Japanese tourists were taking pictures of Kristin. Someone at the hotel had told them she was a celebrity in Norway. No one recognises me any more. I am merely a secretary. And a name, a minor name on the title page of a love story.

When the Japanese caught sight of Kamala there was almost a riot. They were all shouting and screaming and pointing. They could not believe that it really was Kamala Varma, a world-famous personality, right here in their midst.

I am sitting on the balcony. Benjamin, a restless specimen of the species Homo Ludens, is out swimming, jumping off the diving board on Lausholmen even though it is drizzling with rain. The view is even more spectacular in grey weather. Low shreds of cloud melt into one another or drift apart in fits and starts, like stage curtains opening or closing. Suddenly one of the mountains will heave into sight, mighty and distinct, almost like a separate planet, before its peak is enveloped again; or Vik, on the other side of the fjord, lies bathed in sunlight for a few minutes, while the countryside round about is dark and rain-drenched. I feel as though I am beholding several landscapes, like an increasingly hazy succession of veils. Suddenly Sognefjord has a Chinese look about it. I like it better this way. In fine weather all of the National Romantic aspects stand out so starkly, so unequivocally.

Some places have an impact that cannot be put into words. Margrete did right to take me to Xi'an. I am sure that certain spots spark off specific thoughts better than others. Were anyone to ask me, I would say that Sognefjord was the best place to start for anyone wishing to understand Norway. Our nation's mentality. It is said that the sense of recognition engendered by a tree is so powerful because it is a reflection of 'the inner tree'. Might not the same apply to a fjord. Do not all Norwegians have a fjord inside them?

Is it strange, I wonder, that I think so little about my years in prison? In many ways I found prison life as such, both the physical surroundings and the practicalities, the least difficult part of it all. I had no problem with the locked doors, the interrogations; with having to strip to my skin, with the knowledge of being under surveillance. I did not need to resign myself to my new life. I was already resigned to it. The other inmates very soon dubbed me The Monk. An apt nickname. I never spoke and wished only to be alone. The way I saw it I had entered a monastery. There were days when I did nothing in my free time except sit and repeat a mantra to myself, a word which encompassed everything I did not understand: 'Purusasukta.' I had finally found the perfect hiding place. I felt like the man in the print Margrete bought for me in Xi'an, a picture which I had hung up and often contemplated: a tiny, solitary figure in a vast and rugged vertical landscape full of blank patches.

After some years I began to think of my cell as the first cell, to imagine that I was back at the start, that everything was beginning anew, *could* begin anew. It was up to me to fertilise this cell, to generate life again.

For the first time since Project X I was reading – the first time, that is, not counting my readings to Viktor from *The Cantos* by Ezra Pound. I read a tattered copy of *Victoria* twenty times and more. I also read a bundle of books which I had come across as a teenager, books my mother had inherited and which I secretly sold off to antiquarian bookshops, having first noted down a quote from each one. From the library I borrowed the standard classics of the nineteenth century, books by Alexander von Humboldt, Søren Kierkegaard, William Morris. I didn't understand it all. I understood a little. But I read them all resolutely, from cover to cover: Johann Wolfgang von Goethe, Ralph Waldo Emerson, Karl Marx, Oscar Wilde. It was a kind of penance, an act of contrition. As if I wished to atone for my ignorance. I waded my way through the whole of *The History of Philosophy* by G.W.F. Hegel from which, prior to this, I could cite only one sentence – taken from the introduction, at that: 'We may affirm absolutely that nothing great in the world has been accomplished without passion.'

Despite the efforts made to shield me, I did of course get to hear of a lot of the vicious, spiteful things that were written about me. That was tough. Then Kamala's book appeared, and after it the strange biography for which Rakel was responsible. These marked a turning point. And were of invaluable help. To listen to, to read, my story as it was told by these two, by people who wished me well. I might not be alive today were it not for their accounts. And Kristin. Her visits. Her hands holding me. I was encouraged to survive by the knowledge that I was loved.

I am also quite certain that I began to write as a direct consequence of the two aforementioned books. And even though my manuscript was an embarrassingly cack-handed affair, circling evasively around a dark centre, it did serve a purpose. In the evenings, before I got rid of those sheaves of paper, I would run my eye over all the lines of letters. I was reminded of a long thread. For many years I had believed that I could not possibly have any more unfolding to do. This was not true. All the writing had helped me to evolve even further. I was not the person I had been when I started writing.

I had borrowed an old IBM typewriter with a golf ball. At the time when I was writing, I was forever taking the golf ball off and placing it on the desk in front of me. It looked like a miniature globe, its surface covered in letters. Maybe that is how the Earth looks from space, I thought: like a symbol-bedecked sphere.

It is a relief to be on board the *Voyager*, not only because of the crew's optimism, their young minds, but because they are working on a project with which I have such a lot of sympathy – a combination, no less, of the world's two greatest industries: travel and entertainment. Life on board is not exactly as I had imagined it. Granted, they do play computer games on laptops, but they are just as likely to be found playing chess on an actual board. They know as much about the Nimzo-Indian opening as they do about Myst. They are comfortable with everything from an old Commodore 64 computer to antiquarian books, from rococo balls and foxtrots to rave parties and trip hop music. They visit Net cafés, swathed in Palestinian *keffiyehs*.

I can see, of course, that they also have their problems to contend with, individually and as a group – oh yes, there can be friction on board! – but right now, at the stage I am at, I am much more interested in their positive than their negative sides. Hanna, for example – who, with her Korean features, sometimes reminds me of Bo Wang Lee – is also a qualified architect. She has worked on what was, at that time, the busiest building site in Europe, Berlin's Potsdamer Platz, and is still liable to refer to things she learned there, theories on town planning, when discussing the OAK Quartet's own ideas. The other evening the four of them suddenly got onto the subject of the world's biggest dam-building project, the Three Gorges Dam in China. Carl had actually been there and seen the work in progress. I cannot believe how much they have managed to do in such a short space of time.

And then there is their music. Not by chance have they called themselves a quartet. They can sing just about anything in perfect four-part harmony. Martin plays a whole range of instruments, from the mouth organ to the didgeridoo, the long pipe traditional to the Australian aborigines. He can also play Joni Mitchell's songs, including the tricky 'Song for Sharon' from *Hejira* with the capo in just the right position and the guitar tuned exactly as the writer herself has it. I mean, not even I can do that, and I've listened to my fair share of Joni Mitchell – I, who did, after all, insert an F sharp/A sharp chord on the piano at the beginning of the fifth bar of 'Gentle Jesus meek and mild', a harmonic transition which, if I am lucky, is the only thing likely to get me into heaven.

It is evening. I am sitting on the balcony of our hotel room with a whisky. The weather has cleared up. I look across to the other side of the fjord. I was over that way once, to the west of Vik, west of Arnafjord. I saw something there, a man with his head in a woman's lap, a sight I will never forget.

It is still light. The air is balmy. It is the sort of evening that causes me to remember. Takes me back to the inescapable centre of my life. To the living room and Margrete's body. A dead wife clad in my own dressing gown. The spring evening outside the windows; a yellow, then a reddish glow on the horizon. I stood there staring. For how long I do not know. I realised that, unconsciously, I had been holding my breath. For more than a minute. For much more than a minute. As if I was diving for her, hunting for a pale glint of gold in the mud, that flash of gold which sometimes flickered in her eyes. I think I was making a last, desperate effort to save Margrete's life. If, that is, it was not – again – my own.

Then, as if it were the only natural thing to do, I sat down next to her. I lifted Margrete's head onto my lap. For a long time I sat like this, sat with her head in my lap. It reminded me of something. Reminded me very much of something else. I had once seen two people sitting exactly like this, in a wild and desolate landscape, a man and a woman on an almost luminously green grassy bank by a lake. The man had been lying with his head in the woman's lap. The water was like glass, mirroring the encircling mountains. It could have been a happy scene, set in an almost impossibly beautiful landscape. Then all at once the woman began to sing, with a large orchestra behind her, and the whole scene altered character due to the deep solemnity of the music. The woman sang, she sang in German, she sang 'Mild und leise' from the end of the third and final scene in the third and final act of Richard Wagner's revolutionary opera *Tristan and Isolde*; sang out of great pain, great love, great sorrow. Her lover, the man whose head lay in her lap, was dead, and she too was close to death. She sat there, surrounded on all sides by tall cliffs, looking almost as though she were shut inside an enormous cauldron which, because of the singing, the music behind it, seemed to be full of seething passions.

I did not see it when we were filming the scene. Only afterwards, when I was looking at it on the screen, that shot, the posing, was I struck by how much it reminded me of an episode from my youth: Margrete with my head in her lap, in her garden at Grorud.

No other programme in the *Thinking Big* series was as easy to make as the one on Kirsten Flagstad. It made itself. Right from the start I knew that I had to avoid depicting her as she appears in a well-known film clip, kitted out with chainmail and wingéd helmet and spear, her hair fluttering in the breeze from a wind machine as she sings 'Hojotoho! Hojotoho!' from *The Valkyrie*, the sort of set-up which, magnificent voice or no, only served to confirm all of the prejudices which so many Norwegians had about opera. I wanted to break this pattern by filming in the outdoors, to bring opera to life, you might say. Not until later did I realise that I had built the whole programme around one of the biggest operatic clichés of all: a person singing as they die.

I had no difficulty in deciding which incident from Flagstad's life to high-light. It had to be her stupendous breakthrough at the Metropolitan Opera House in New York in February 1935, performances which turned her into an international star overnight. And since she could be said to have made two debuts, I chose the second one, made four days after the first, when she sang

Isolde – which was also the part she was to sing more than any other in her career. The audience is reported to have been in ecstasies; they had apparently stormed the stage at the end of the second act. And it truly *was* a sensation. For the first time, a Met audience heard the voice which, some said, Wagner must have heard in his subconscious when he wrote the opera: possibly the most dramatic soprano of all time – the Voice of the Century as she was also called. The way I saw it, I was not making a programme about Kirsten Flagstad the woman, but about her lungs. About breathing. Because that was the secret: to be capable of turning air into resonance, into music. Into images. When you heard Flagstad sing, you thought of rivers of gold and floods of light.

I had listened to this opera again and again and was in no doubt that I had to concentrate on the ending, the 'love-death'. When I mooted the possibility of shooting outdoors, of finding a dramatic natural setting, one of the cameramen, who hailed from Vik in Sogn, suggested filming the scene in what he called 'Sognefjord's best kept secret' – to which, sadly, more than a million Norwegians were now to be made privy – namely Finnabotn at the head of Finnafjord. And when we arrived there by boat I knew with every fibre of my being that this was the place. Something about the landscape at Finnabotn told me this was the chance of a lifetime. One almost felt that the scenery alone could have engendered that all-embracing, yet uncompromising, love.

The scene opened with a still from the actual occurrence, the 1935 performance of *Tristan and Isolde*, Act III, at the New York Met, with Kirsten Flagstad as Isolde and Lauritz Melchior as Tristan, a picture which I held, flickering, on screen while I narrated the events leading up to this moment. Playing in the background – a recurring motif throughout the programme, this – was the famous prelude, a piece of music which, from the first fateful, ominously atonal bars warned of a stable core, the music's very centre of gravity, which had become distinctly shaky, just as life does when love comes along. Then – let there be light! – I had the dead image of Flagstad and Melchior in their typical opera costumes and extravagant make-up, fade into living film, full colour, and a couple, ordinary people, in the same pose as Flagstad and Melchior on the stage, only here they were lying on a green hillside by the lake in everyday clothes, clothes that made one think of young people, teenagers even. And gradually the prelude gave way to the music from Act III and the woman on the grassy bank lip-synched rapturously to Flagstad's voice, as it sounded in a superb recording from 1953 conducted by Wilhelm Furtwängler: a voice full of light, velvet and molten gold.

A couple: a woman with a man's head in her lap. Only when I was going through the rough footage for the programme did it strike me that this scene could have been drawn straight from my own life. One day I dived into

Svartjern and found a gold bracelet and not long afterwards I found myself lying on a luminously green lawn with my head in Margrete's lap, while opera music streamed into the garden next door from an open window. She had given me freshly pressed orange juice and I was enchanted. I lay with my head in her lap, revelling in those minutes, not knowing that this would be the happiest moment of my entire life.

She, Kirstin Flagstad, or rather, the actress playing Flagstad, or the actress who played all those who have ever had a broken heart or known what it is to lose someone you love, sang 'Mild und leise', and as she, Flagstad, this unhappy woman, sang the camera began to pull up, suddenly showing the scene from the air, revealing more and more of the surrounding scenery, the wild and truly spectacular landscape of which the grassy bank by the water was a part. Soon, as the sound of the music and the singing intensified, one saw that these two, the woman with the man's head in her lap – Isolde with the dead Tristan, Isolde, who was herself about to die, and her dead lover – were not sitting in a crater, by a lake bounded by plunging cliffs, as first thought; as the camera pulled even further up it became apparent that the couple were lying on a grassy slope at the head of a fjord, at Finnabotn which, some kilometres further on, near Finden's Garth, ran into a narrow sound before opening out into Finnafjord itself which, in turn, ran into Sognefjord with all its many other arms. Even for me it was a stunning prospect; the view of Finnabotn with, barely visible, a couple of dots, two people, two lovers, dying. And then they were gone, as if transformed into music, or to landscape: a fjord, encircled by snow-covered mountains, which was also a part of the great fjord, all its branches. The beauty and the drama of Flagstad's voice accorded perfectly with the beauty and the drama of the scenery. The two became one.

The first time I saw television – probably an episode of *Robin Hood* on a Saturday at Wolfgang Michaelsen's house in the early sixties – I went up and placed my hands flat against the screen. I felt the prickle of the static, but I was disappointed that nothing happened. The picture, the world inside the box, remained flat. Kristin and the OAK Quartet work with a medium that has overcome this flatness. When I touch the screen something happens. Their screen, that interface with its appetising signposting, gives me the feeling of something leading one endlessly further and further in. When I study their intricate structure map, I cannot help thinking of *māyā*.

I really was not sure about it when I booked the helicopter for the shoot; I was afraid the whole thing might end up being a bit too Hollywoodish, or too much like a music video. But the end result exceeded all expectations. It took the helicopter a little over ten minutes to climb to 12,000 feet, but by speeding up the film we managed to get it to fit exactly with the final three minutes of 'Mild und leise', the point of view rising as the music intensified, soaring upwards, until both the viewpoint and the music reached their peak with '*in des Welt-Atems wehendem All*'. The fabulous thing about it was the way the point of view, the shot, the helicopter spiralled upwards. When I ran through the final cut of the scene I was so moved that I could not speak. The shot of that scene and that landscape from a certain height told us that those two people did not die, there was no way they could die. They were not shut in, they were on a fjord. In their love-death lay the opening of something new.

I struck lucky with that programme. A commentary in one newspaper said that I had cut through the whole debate as to where the new opera house should be situated. I had shown that the opera lay *here*, in the heart of the rugged Norwegian countryside. Norway *was* opera.

Once when she was telling a story from *The Mahabharata*, Kamala mentioned one of the weapons which Drona the master gave to the hero Arjuna; an *astra* which could hold all the warriors on a battlefield spellbound by the illusions it created. 'That's pretty much what you did with your television programmes,' she said to me.

One writer pointed out that, seen from above, this landscape, with the arms of the fjord reaching deep into the country, looked not unlike a network of nerve fibres, and as such could lead one to think, or imagine, that one was inside the brain, in the area relating to hearing, the enjoyment of sounds – or indeed, why not: inside the nervous system of love itself. I have heard that this place, the grassy bank running down to the water at the head of Finna-fjord, has become a sacred spot of sorts for lovers. Quite a number of bridal couples have reportedly gone there after their weddings.

There would come a day when it would dawn on me that with this scene I had not only unwittingly reflected one of the happiest moments in my life, but that I had also prefigured the unhappiest. For a moment, as I sat there on the floor of Villa Wergeland, with Margrete's lifeless head in my lap, I had a feeling of stepping outside of myself, of being lifted up; of seeing myself and Margrete on the living-room floor from a great height. A picture of dead love.

For a long, long time I sat there with her head in my lap, looking round about me. Looking at all the blood. Outside the sky was red, lit up, so it seemed by a huge flare. For one bewildered second I had the idea that she had been shot by some incensed viewer. Or rather: I hoped. But I had known straight away. She had shot herself. Right before I got home. And something told me that her mind had been perfectly clear when she chose to curl her finger around the trigger. That she had not been consumed by the darkness. That she may merely have seen the darkness approaching. And that she had done it not because of me, but – however inconceivable it seemed – for my *sake*. Shot herself in the heart. In her innermost chambers. Those four strokes at the centre of the Chinese character for love. Distraught though I was, behind it all there was a feeling of anger. You simply did not do something like this. Something so brutal. Why not pills? She was a doctor, for Christ's sake. She could have cut her wrists, the way other women do. But this was Margrete. And I knew nothing about her. It was almost as if she wanted to show me that I had not understood a single thing.

Why did she do it?

I cursed my stupidity; to think that, in a fit of paranoia and worry about our safety, I had shown her that bloody gun, which I kept in the cupboard in my workshop. I had even had it primed and loaded. I had received threats after a programme on immigrants – I may even have been a little bit proud of this, proud that – after all those tame light-entertainment shows – I had once again made a programme with the ability to shock, something with a touch of dangerous originality. I let her hold the gun, an old Luger, a relic of an enigmatic grandfather. I showed her, solemnly almost, ceremoniously, how to release the safety catch. She had muttered something about *Hedda Gabler*. Smiled. I eyed the gun lying there on the living-room floor, with its remaining bullets. Gently I removed her head from my lap. I picked up the pistol. It seemed suddenly heavier. I put it to my head. I beheld her, with the gun muzzle pressed against my temple. It was almost as though I saw her – her beauty – for the first time.

I had had this same thought that time when I ran into her again, while I was studying architecture. Suddenly, one day, there she was. She had left me on a winter day in the rain and now, on a spring day years later, there she was again, in that same soft rain, as if she had only gone behind a waterfall and now calmly stepped out again.

I stood for a long time staring in disbelief at the more mature, but just as unmistakeable face, there, right in front of me, in a web of water. I was overcome by a sense of touching wonderful depths. Meeting Margrete again, being faced with that rather diffident smile, was like seeing a whole lot of tangled threads gather themselves into one solid, conclusive knot, like receiving a sign that everything had a purpose. I remembered the stories of people who lost gold rings only to find them twelve years later, inside a potato, or a fish.

It's hard to describe the sort of first impression Margrete could make. Once, for example, when she was eighteen, she was on a plane: as the daughter of a diplomat she travelled a lot and usually first class. Someone came over and placed a hand on her shoulder – a young man, the heir to the throne of a small but wealthy country in the East. He asked her to marry him. Right out of the blue, but most formally. She knew right away that he was not just flirting with her, he was offering her the life of a princess. Such was the effect the sight of Margrete had on some people.

Including me. I stood in the soft spring rain, trying to take it in. The unusual orange coat. Her 'Persian' beauty. Her eyes. Those black pupils in irises shot with gold. She stood there glowing, shining, at me. I remembered what my old neighbour, Karen Mohr, had once said: 'Someone looks at you – and everything changes.' When Margrete fixed her eyes on me, it felt as though I had not been seen in a very long time. As if I had been invisible for years. I stood there before her and I was discovered.

I had, of course, always cherished a hope of meeting her again, quite by accident like this, at a tram stop. I had dreamt of this scene a thousand times. And even though, deep down, I knew the chances of it happening were very slim, one thought was always there: I swore that I would not fall in love. And not only that – as if it were the twin of the hope of seeing her again, I toyed with the notion of revenge. Even when I ran into her again on that spring day and could hardly believe it, my luck, this merciful turn of events, for a fleeting moment I did also consider paying her back for the pain she had caused me in seventh grade.

The spring after the break-up outside the Golden Elephant restaurant was the most miserable of my life. It's easy to joke about it today, but when you're in seventh grade and you're unhappy, there is no end to how miserable you can be. When summer came I went into hiding on Hvaler, I camped out at Smalsund, in the very south of the island, could not face being at the house with everybody else; they left me alone, understood that I was upset, merely made sure that I had everything I needed, some food and, most important of all: batteries. I was a castaway. I lay out on the rocks, just me and a couple of mink which soon got used to me; I simply lay there, flat out, stupefied by sunshine and the sparkling sea, listening to the waves, the water lapping and splashing right at my feet, for all the world as if the elements shared my grief, were sobbing with me. I was a real 'nowhere man, sitting in his nowhere land'. The holidays were almost over and I had worn *Rubber Soul* thin, playing it on a battery-driven Bambino record player. That LP had spun round and round all summer long, like a black sun next to my head, and was now as bent out of shape as I felt in my mind. I had long since memorised every song on it, but still listened intently for something in the background hiss, *behind* the music, like one of those indefatigable, ever-hopeful scientists who listens out for radio signals from outer space. I lay there and I knew: I had to do something.

It was August, the nights were already starting to draw in. I was sitting by the Pilot Lookout on its hilltop, gazing at the lights out at sea. I often sat by this little shed. Maybe because I too was in sore need of a pilot. Maybe because it contained an advanced short-wave radio. Through the wall I could hear calls in lots of different languages. This put me in touch, in a way, with the wide world, with that place far overseas where *she* was. One day in the spring I had even taken the bus out to Fornebu Airport, just to be able to hear the flights being called over the tannoy.

I scanned the sea, gazed at the Koster Islands on the horizon. How was I going to get her back? Because that was obviously what I wanted. I wished that somehow, possibly by means of telepathy, she would be overcome with remorse, with love for me. Or – a common thought, this, at such self-pitying moments – that she would *see* me, on a monitor, sitting here next to a pilot lookout, next to a radio, benumbed, yearning. What I wanted was for her, wherever she was, to get on a plane and fly to Norway, move back, live with relatives or whatever. Just as long as she came back. 'Do something,' I told myself. 'You have to do something.'

I grasped the iron railing and pulled myself to my feet. And then it hit me, as such thoughts have a way of hitting an adolescent, that I could get her back, on one condition: I would have to swim across the strait I saw before me, an ocean in miniature; I would have to swim across Sekken, one of the most exposed and daunting stretches of open sea along the whole coastline. Only by doing this could I, in some mysterious – but in my mind completely logical – way, win her love again. Awaken her. Wherever she was, whatever she was doing.

I had never swum such a long distance at one go. It was a risky venture. But I was in no doubt. I ran back to the tent, cast a glance at the battered cover of *Rubber Soul,* from which the four members of the Beatles gazed up at me approvingly. I changed into swimming trunks, strode down to the beach, slipped through the seaweed and out into the dark, almost lukewarm water. I swam with quick, impatient strokes across to Gyltholmen, walked up to the cairn and stood there for a moment considering the broad band of sea at my feet. The nearest, dark islets on the Swedish side were a long way off. In another continent so it seemed. The continent of hope. During the war this last stretch had spelled life or death for many refugees. I clambered down to the rocks and did something close to a racing dive, shallow and flat, as if

I were in a hurry. The weather was with me. A few clouds. A light breeze. A gentle swell. No current to speak of. I swam. I swam without thinking. Or at least, I thought in the way that leaves no trace. I tried to conserve energy, to simply drift across. Soon I was level with Sekkefluene, those insidious skerries. A light flashed on a post to starboard. Many a boat had gone down just here. Wrecks lurked in the darkness below me.

I swam on, and as I began to flag my thoughts became clearer. Each stroke was like throwing myself at her, into her arms. I bobbed up and down in the swell and my thoughts seemed to me to rise and fall in the same way. I tried not to think about it, but thought about it anyway, behind my other thoughts: the deeps underneath me. The unknown. There was a reason why Margrete had left me, one which I had never known. Which I ought to have known. I had disappointed her in some way. I was swimming more slowly. I was exhausted. My arms were aching. My legs were turning numb. I was more than halfway there. For a channel swimmer this stretch of water would probably be a piece of cake. For me, a thirteen-year-old, it was far too long. But only the impossible could bring Margrete back. These tiny currents, I thought, generated by the action of my limbs, will be transmitted through the water, rather like whale song, and come to a sea where she is swimming at this very moment, at another hour, and she will instantly comprehend the message, my desperate plea. The thought struck me: in swimming here I was doing what I had always wanted to do: work in depth. Seen from far enough away, I might have been a spermatozoon on my way to impregnate someone.

The clouds to the south parted. A moon appeared. An unnaturally big, almost full moon. All of a sudden I was swimming through a band of molten gold. The water around me had acquired an odd purplish cast, becoming almost phosphorescent. And yet: I was freezing. I was utterly worn out. Heavy. The temptation: to just let myself sink. So easy. Done with everything. Why should I go on swimming? Go on living? The thought flashed through my mind: was I actually trying to kill myself?

I had a vision. Or maybe it really happened. I looked back and saw that my path through the water, across Sekken, formed a broad inverted S; and that this path was lined on either side with buildings, grand palaces ranged side by side, all of them different and yet almost identical. I distinctly heard a voice say: 'Make it new,' before I sank, before I died.

I drowned. Died. I came to my senses on the white sand of a beach in Sweden, on the islet I had been swimming towards. Whatever had happened, I had done it. I had made it to another country. I was dead, but I was alive. I lay on my stomach on the beach, cold, but hopeful. I felt like Robinson

Crusoe, a man about to embark upon a new life. Build everything up from nothing.

I never told anyone about that swim. The next morning I was back in Norway, I hitched a ride on a Swedish boat which had been anchored in a bay just along from the beach where I was washed ashore. It's an odd thing. For some years I was famous for being on television. But no one knows anything about my greatest achievements. That I fell over a cliff and lived. That I swam across an unswimmable body of water. That I came *this* close to devising a new categorisation of all human knowledge. My most remarkable experiences and thoughts have remained my secret.

That morning, as I took down my tent for the summer, I realised only that I was on the threshold of a new life. One without Margrete.

The thought of my pain, that swim, the idea that she was part of another life, all of these things melted away at the sight of her: Margrete, standing right in front of me in a bright orange coat at a tram stop in Oslo. A glowing spot on a grey rainy day. The thought of revenge, of giving her the cold shoulder, lasted exactly two seconds. I stood there dumbstruck, beholding her through the raindrops, feeling as though a crystal chandelier had slowly been lowered from the heavens and down over my head. I saw Margrete, only Margrete, through all those crystal droplets, thousands of Margretes all around me, filling every part of me, right down to the smallest optic nerve.

'Jonas?' I heard her say, as if she had not bumped into me quite by chance, but had tracked me down to my most secret hiding place after years of searching.

For a moment I thought that I had actually managed to swim her back to me, but that it had just taken longer than I had expected. Again I felt the blue flame which was ignited inside me that day when I saw her at Svartjern, summer-bronzed in a bikini. I stood – with a blissful look on my face, I think – staring after the tram I should have taken, but which was now pulling away. I knew that my life had been radically changed. I suddenly came to think of that amazing day when the Swedes changed from driving on the left to driving on the right. I remembered a newspaper photograph showing a city street in which the cars were in the act of crossing from one side of the white line to the other. That is how it was for me on that spring day, on seeing Margrete again. A deep-reaching change in my life, a switch, as it were, from one side to another.

The first weeks of our relationship, our new relationship I should perhaps say, had about them an air of tentative inquiry. Often we would just sit in two chairs facing one another and talk. We had a lot to talk about. To ask about.

And yet there were times when we simply fell silent and sat there, looking at one another. I had a suspicion that she was testing my endurance – as if we were actually sitting naked, right opposite one another, delaying something. Or that she wished to display a certain gravity, to enhance the pleasure of what we both knew was to come.

During those first months I found myself constantly amazed by all the things she was liable to do or say, from her way of frying an egg to her comments on the Norwegian royal family. A simple yawn could be turned by Margrete Boeck into a not uninteresting work of art. I came home one afternoon from the course in architecture which I had, mentally at least, already dropped out of – long before this I had met my Silapulapu – to find her folding sheets of paper into all sorts of different shapes. Origami, she called it. She had been writing letters, but had suddenly fallen to brushing up her skills in something she had once learned, a Japanese art. It struck me that these shapes could also be letters of a sort. I thought of the letter I had waited for, the letter I never received. Maybe this was it now. She sat there making birds, animals. Fold me, I thought, full of longing. Bend me into an angel, I thought when, as if reading my mind, she took me by the hand and led me into the bedroom.

The house in Ullevål Garden City was all ruby-red walls and gilded frames, brocade sofas and curios from every corner of the world, but nothing made a deeper impression on me than a small collection of butterflies hanging on the wall in one of the small rooms we passed through on the way to the bedroom. Margrete had caught them as a little girl. A brimstone butterfly, a peacock, an admiral and a small tortoiseshell. A constellation with the power to open. I thought to myself: this here, she, was that hidden country.

And then it came, my first experience of sex. It would be safe to say that I was a late developer. And in bed with her, in the midst of that overwhelming experience, I knew that I had made the right choice. Although it had never been hard for me to turn down other girls. In every case I was soon convinced that they could never be the focus of all my attention. Only Margrete could be that. And yet my first experience of sex, making love with Margrete, exceeded all expectations, all conceptions, all possible metaphors. It was out of this world. Margrete led me into a white bedroom watched over by an unknown golden god; laid me down on white bedlinen and guided me into the erotic landscape; she folded herself tenderly around me, folded herself in as many different ways as she could fold a sheet of paper. And in folding herself around me, she unfolded me, transformed me into something other than I was. She actually loved me into new shapes.

When I came to, something had happened to my respiration. I was breathing more freely. It was as if, without being aware of it, I had been suffering from an attack of asthma which had now stopped.

Afterwards she lay and held me in her arms. There was nothing she liked better than to lie quietly with her arms around me. It is said that we discover who we really are in moments of stress. I discovered my true self in a totally undramatic situation, as I lay there in Margrete's arms. It was also on such a day, with Margrete's arms wrapped round me – and suffused with what I had once called spirit, but which I now called love – that I felt something being set in motion, a process, a stream of thought which flowed out some years later into the decision to make my own television programmes. Although at the time I did not know where it would lead. I merely lay there praying silently that she would never let me go.

Why did she do it?

I have long suspected: I cannot answer this because I have not come up with the right question. The whole thing bears a troubling resemblance to another painfully complicated search, a process with a long story behind it. I do know when it began, though: on a visit to Karen Mohr, my reserved and taciturn neighbour, who had decorated her living room like a Pernod-scented Provence and her bedroom like a dim library. One day she asked me to fetch a book by Stendahl, a request which led to me being caught under a veritable avalanche of books. This gave Karen Mohr the excuse for some major renovation work and on my next visit she proudly showed me into a bedroom in which the bookshelves, now repaired, were completely bare. All the books were strewn around the floor. I was invited to stay for a ham omelette, but Karen Mohr apologised for the fact that she would have to go to the shop first. In the meantime there was no reason why I couldn't start to put the books back on the shelves, she said.

'How,' I asked.

'Use your imagination,' she said, and off she went.

I knew I couldn't just stick them on the shelves any old way. She expected more of me. I regarded the mess on the floor. Books that had stood next to one another were now scattered all over the place. I stared despondently at the bookshelves, a bare tree waiting for branches and foliage. I was eleven years old. For the first time I had to try to set the world to rights.

Although it was tempting to do something decorative – at one point I did consider going by the colours of the spines, or by whether they were tall or short, fat or thin – I soon came to the conclusion that I would have to put works on the same subject together. Karen Mohr had a lot of books about painters, about art, so I started putting these on the bottom shelves. Then I stopped, uncertain. Why not on the middle shelf? Or ought I to reserve that for the books Karen Mohr liked best. But which books did she like best?

I was a little giddy at the thought of being in her bedroom. It smelled not of books, but of lady. The bed was spread with a soft patchwork quilt. Without thinking, I buried my face in it and inhaled the scent, as if I needed some pepping up.

I picked up the first book. In my mind I pictured a scheme based on the matrix of the bookcases. Poetry could go in the section next to fiction. And all the books on disease – she had a lot of these – could be placed alongside the countless works with the word 'love' in their titles. I tried my best to keep this provisional arrangement in mind while slowly – as I came upon books on subjects I had not thought of – expanding my system. I soon ran into difficulties. Where, for example, was I to put the big illustrated book on football? Under sport? But she had no other books on sports or games. Under art maybe, or dance? What about politics? Wasn't it right that in South America football could degenerate into a war? Why didn't I simply put it next to the books on religion? There were several sections into which I would have liked to set it, but I could only put it in one place. I kept having to move books off the shelves which I had initially chosen for them, it was like one big jigsaw puzzle in which the pieces could fit into any number of spaces.

My confused, but soon zealous, endeavours may also have been connected to the fact that this happened just after I had collided with Margrete's bike at the school gate so hard that we both landed on the pavement. As I gathered up the books that had fallen out of my satchel, my eyes met hers for the first time. She *looked* at me. I was conscious to the very tips of my toes of being *seen*. Already here, in this fragrant bedroom, I had an inkling that if I was to have the slightest chance of understanding anything of this new addition to my life, a wonder that went by the name of Margrete Boeck, then I would have to get these stupid books into some kind of order.

Luckily Karen Mohr was not gone for too long. Before she started making the ham omelette she inspected my work. I really had not got very far, the shelves looked more like something out of a shop in a country suffering from a severe shortage of goods. She laughed when she saw that I had set her lavish volumes on Provence next to the innumerable works on monasteries and convents and the cloistered life. 'Not bad,' she said. 'But what about this one?' She picked a book off the floor, *The Little Prince* by Antoine de Saint-Exupéry. I recognised the name, remembered Rakel telling me about his flying and his mysterious disappearance at the time when Uncle Lauritz, the SAS pilot, died. I promptly suggested that we put it on the shelf where I had arranged the works on more technical subjects. It was about flying after all, wasn't it? Or space travel? 'I think probably it should go with my other French novels,' she said. 'But you're right, I could slot it in somewhere else, maybe alongside the books on cosmology.' She explained what cosmology was. I never forgot that. Or her fingers, which suddenly, almost unconsciously, stroked my hair. I would remember that hour among the bare bookshelves, up to my knees in books, at the most diverse moments in my life. I kept trying to dredge up again the openness and inquisitiveness and wonder that had moved me to put Dostoyevsky's *The Idiot* in with the medical books and *The Divine Comedy* by Dante next to the Bible. When I picked up a book in Danish entitled *Totem og tabu*, by Sigmund Freud, I placed it – since Karen had, unfortunately, no books on Red Indians – on the shelf containing the detective novels.

Although I did not know it, in Karen Mohr's library, which smelled not of books, but of seductive perfume, I had come up against a problem which would dog me for a long time to come: the numerous parallel associations triggered in my mind by the titles and the lists of contents of the books on the floor did not lend themselves to the simple, primitive shelving system with which I was faced. It was simply too rigid. But while Karen Mohr was search- ing for Stendahl's book on love, I perceived – inspired yet again, I think, by the thought of the new girl at school, Margrete Boeck – the rudiments of a brilliant system, nothing less than the roots of a new tree of knowledge. As if in a deep trance I stood there, thinking to myself that this meant I would have to take the two biographies on Bach and slot them in among the books on oriental rugs, and shift the volumes on the Second World War over to the reference books on wild animals; and *then* – in a flash it came to me – the cookery books would have to go in the section on architecture. I pursued this line of thought until everything went black, as if I was about to pass out.

'Time for a ham omelette,' Karen Mohr said. She must have been able to tell from my white face that I had had enough for one day. Nonetheless she picked out a book.'This is for you,' she said.'It's about Marco Polo and Venice. Maybe you'll go there some day.' I accepted it warily. Just at that moment I had no great interest in owning books.

Karen Mohr must have sensed my silent protest, my misgivings in the face of all her bookshelves, although she said no more about it, not for a long time. I did not know that she also had access to another library, that Karen Mohr had the key to the greatest book collection in Oslo and that I would soon find myself standing, somewhat apprehensively, before it.

I made two good friends in high school, Viktor Harlem and Axel Stranger. Both were in my class at Oslo Cathedral School. Since – not unusually in that hormonally unstable phase in life – we aspired to the wisdom inherent in all forms of heresy, we called ourselves The Three Heretics. One spring Viktor suggested – nay, more or less demanded – that we should go on a study trip to Venice. 'Why Venice of all places?' Axel asked, instantly betraying his qualms about such a venture.

'Because it's a car-free city?' I suggested – this was not long after our legendary demonstration in the Town Hall Square.

'Because the greatest iconoclast of them all lives there,' Viktor announced cryptically. Later, after having seen George Lucas's fabulous masterpiece, one of the colossi of twentieth-century film history, the *Star Wars* trilogy, I always felt that the Venice trip had been a journey to a watery planet; that, convinced as we were of our status as true Jedi knights, we had set out on a mission to find Yoda, the sage of sages, himself.

Axel's doubts about Venice were soon replaced by an enthusiasm which ought to have been a warning to us. He announced, with a rather too fervent light in his eyes, that this would be the most important journey of his life. And he was to be proved right. Axel, who pretty much lived in the Central Lending Department at the Deichman Library, had read a disturbingly large number of the world's books and, galvanised by this passion, he now proceeded to reel off to us all the things he was planning to do in Venice. And it was no small list. He meant to visit the Casetta delle Rose, home to the poet Gabriele d'Annunzio during the First World War; he longed he said, or chanted, to hear the water lapping against the Ca'Rezzonico, where Robert Browning lived for the last years of his life; Axel wanted to breathe the air of the Palazzo Capello, which had provided architectonic inspiration for Henry James when he was writing *The Aspern Papers*; he wished to run his hands over the walls of the Hotel Danieli, which had housed such guests as Balzac and Dickens; Axel had a feverish look about him as he spoke of his resolve to take in the seaside hotels on the Lido, where Gustav von Aschenbach had languished in Thomas Mann's masterly novella *Death in Venice*, before ordering the same drinks as Hemingway in Harry's Bar, then devoutly settling himself in the Caffè Quadri, where Proust had passed his first evening in the city on the lagoon, if – that is – Axel did not actually set out to track down the objects which had triggered such a string of memories in Proust's universe: two uneven marble tiles in the Baptistery of St Mark's. Axel all but swore to swim in the canals like Lord Byron. His list of things to do grew longer and longer, all of it plotted into a very tight schedule. It didn't stop there, though. He also took to speaking a sort of *novelese*. He confessed with half-shut eyes that he could hardly wait to see the domes and crooked campanile of his dreams rising out of the waves. 'I'll push back the shutters in my hotel room to see the golden angel on the top of St Mark's flaming in the sunlight!' he sighed rapturously.

Axel Stranger was pale with excitement. So what happened? When we – The Three Heretics – got to Fornebu Airport, with the prospect of a long May weekend ahead of us, he fainted. The thought that he would soon be treading the very tiles on which Marcel Proust had once set foot, was too much for him. In short, his expectations were too great. As the woman at the check-in desk handed him his ticket, Axel collapsed onto the airport floor. And when he came round he was so weak and dizzy that he declared himself unfit to travel. He insisted, though, that we should go anyway, without him.

I thought to myself, but did not say out loud: reading too many books is bad for you.

And yet – although he never got beyond check-in – Axel always maintained that that journey was the most significant of his entire life. He never went to Venice, but when Viktor and I got back after the long weekend, Axel informed us that he had been writing like a madman. In four days he had written two hundred pages, in a sort of helpless trance, 'rowing through the dark canals of the imagination in a gleaming black gondola'. He claimed it was the thought of the city on the lagoon, all his mental images of Venice that had driven him to it. Triumphantly he showed us the manuscript. It was roundly and soundly rejected, it is true, but from that day on Axel Stranger wanted only to write. And five years later he made his literary debut with Norway's finest publishing house, with the idiosyncratic and artistically ingenious novella *The Lion in Venice*.

'That trip to Venice changed my life,' he always said.

A trip can be short and yet unforgettable. When I was thirteen – heartbroken as I was, I now worked to a new time reckoning: year one After Margrete – Karen Mohr took me to her mysterious workplace in the city. As usual she was dressed in a grey suit which somehow did not look drab. 'Sober grey,' my mother was wont to say. Something about Karen Mohr made me feel that grey had to be the most interesting colour of all. We got off the bus from Grorud at a stop in Møllergata and a very short stroll down the street brought us to a palatial building in the Hammersborg area, on the same square as the main fire station – an open space graced with fountains, which had not as yet been covered over. In my childhood memory, with the monumental wall in front and the long, slanting flights of steps leading up to it, it looks like the Potala Palace in Lhasa. This was the Deichman Library, Oslo's main public library. 'Some bedroom,' she said.

Minutes later we were standing in the Central Lending and Reference

Department, next to a black pillar like something out of a temple, with the vast hall before us. The light falling through the glass in the ceiling brought out a dull golden sheen in the rows of brown leather spines in the tall galleries on either side. 'Carl Deichman's book collection,' Karen Mohr murmured reverently, pointing. To begin with I felt somewhat daunted. Or at least, I had the uneasy feeling that all of the bookcases round about me testified to some tragic event, an unnatural segmentation. These rows of book spines had as little to do with life as a head of beef carved up and frozen, reduced to packs in a cabinet with labels saying 'sirloin' or 'fillet'.

Karen Mohr worked in a room off the main hall which also housed the Technical Department. She ran the section entitled Foreign Fiction, which is to say she was in charge of English and French literature. 'Although it's the French that's closest to my heart,' she whispered.

Karen Mohr gave me a tour, most notably of the fascinating, labyrinthine depositories downstairs: floor below floor, all packed with books. Karen Mohr clearly knew exactly what each shelf contained. I observed her surreptitiously, her enthusiasm, her pride. For some reason I got it into my head that the whole of the Deichman Library, and this vast, hidden library in particular, was bound up with her experience by the Mediterranean, a conversation, an offer from a charismatic painter. In a way, this really *was* an extension of her bedroom. I gazed respectfully round about me, and yet I could not help thinking that even this mammoth attempt to organise thousands of books had to be a far simpler task than that of putting a person's thoughts and motives, dreams and longings in order – be it merely those from a meeting lasting only a few minutes. I was not thinking just of Karen Mohr and Provence. I was also thinking of myself. Because I knew that even the labyrinth of the depositories, all those walls of books, could not contain an explanation of what I felt after Margrete, the glow in her eyes, disappeared out of my life.

The tour ended at the 'catalogue', two huge filing cabinets in the middle of the main hall, under Axel Revold's fresco. 'As you may have guessed, you need a system in order to find what you're looking for,' Karen Mohr said softly, motioning to her surroundings. 'It's not quite as easy to get your bearings here as it is in my bedroom.' She explained that I could search for titles by alphabetical order, by author, title or subject, and that the numbers on the little cards told you where the books were in the library – rather like coordinates.

I opened a drawer and fingered the cards impatiently. 'Okay, so if I want to find out what it looks like in Iran, should I go to the shelf where the books have a 915 on the spine?' There was a reason for my interest in Iran. Margrete, who had so inexplicably broken up with me, was now in Teheran. She might as well have been on asteroid B 612. Nonetheless I had a masochistic urge to see the landscape she now inhabited.

Karen Mohr nodded, clearly impressed, and led me over to the shelves where, sure enough, I found books containing pictures of both Iran and Teheran. While I was leafing through these, feeling quite sick and dizzy, Karen Mohr told me for the first time about the system according to which all the books in the Deichman library were arranged, devised by a man called Melvil Dewey. She asked me to think of the library as being split up into ten rooms, nine of them containing specialised libraries and the first of them a more general library. Each of these ten libraries was then split up into ten smaller libraries. And so on. Roughly speaking, Dewey had divided all human knowledge into ten categories and thousands of subcategories. History fell into the so-called 900 class which we were now standing next to.

I do not know what it was – maybe an aversion to the pictures of Teheran, the thought of Margrete – that prompted me to protest. 'But this is geography,' I said.

'I know,' she said, sounding almost embarrassed. 'It's rather odd. Geography doesn't have a main category to itself, instead it comes under history.'

Even at this point it seemed obvious to me that this system couldn't possibly be much use. I think I must still have had Margrete in mind when I mulishly asked where one would put a work on diamonds.

You had to take a look at the book, Karen Mohr told me, surprised at my contentiousness. It was not always as easy as you might think. It might be that it should go under 'Economic geology', in the main category Natural Sciences and Mathematics, or possibly under 'Mining' in Technology (applied sciences), or even under 'Carving and carvings', in the the Arts. 'Which is to say, either under 553, 622 or 736,' she said with a smile. Karen Mohr knew her Dewey.

I looked at the users browsing through the shelves and the library staff pushing trolleys full of books. I made so bold as to ask: was Love one of the ten main categories?

Karen Mohr stood there clad in sober grey; she gave a long pause, then shook her head. Without looking at me she stroked my hair.

We returned to the Foreign Fiction section and Karen Mohr's secluded desk, which was strewn with English and French magazines and newspapers. I managed to find Saint-Exupéry and *The Little Prince* on a nearby shelf all on my own. And what if I wanted to learn French, where would I find books about that? They were in a totally different section, Karen said. The 400 class, Philology, was out in the Central Lending and Reference Department. She gave me an almost apologetic look, as if she could tell how exasperated I was by a system that did not permit things which were so closely connected to sit next to one another.

But my scepticism went even deeper. I had a suspicion that some things must have been left out of this stupid system completely, that this guy Dewey could not possibly have allowed for everything. I was willing to bet, for example, that not one of his thousands of sections covered heartbreak. I was actually feeling pretty annoyed with Mr Meivil Dewey. And what about all the new branches of knowledge which were continually springing up, on the outside left as it were, right out on the sideline. And anyway, anything could be divided into ten, for heaven's sake. I flinched, as if in horror at the thought. Something told me that a different arrangement of these books could have a great and unimagined ripple effect. It was not merely a matter, here, of books, but of the fundamental thoughts and ideas of mankind. I really was inside a Potala Palace with a thousand rooms, a house dedicated to a religion, an attempt to come to terms with the universe. The faces of the librarians seemed to me to take on a special radiance, and I suddenly saw that they could easily be lamas in disguise.

On our way out, I stopped by the black pillars and looked back. I surveyed the Central Lending and Reference Department, ran an eye over the walls, the books ranged side by side all around that vast chamber. It looked enormously impressive and complicated, but still I knew it was too simple. It was – I thought of Karen Mohr's own words – not *worthy*. This room, this arrangement of books, did not reflect the way people thought. I knew it: this room spoke of too much order. The whole library was an illusion, what my teacher in junior high would call *māyā*. I would go so far as to say that even at this early juncture, and even though I did not consider myself fully evolved, I understood that a voyage of discovery, one of Magellanic proportions, lay waiting for me here. My life's project. A unique opportunity to work in depth.

On the bus home I asked Karen if it wasn't a bit boring being a librarian. She looked at me and winked. 'Don't forget,' she said, 'Casanova worked as a librarian in later life, and he was a great seducer.'

The seeds of my Project X were sown there in the Central Lending and Reference Department of the Deichman Library and would shoot and grow into a jungle which I would manage to hack my way out of only with great difficulty. When I met Margrete again, I had just been dealt the deathblow by Silapulapu, and was about to abandon the whole enterprise. My whole body was smarting from this defeat, but just being with her made the pain go away. She gave me a different perspective on things. Or, as she replied once when I asked her whether she thought there was life on Mars: 'Is there life on Earth?'

The first year was taken up with making love. Every time she lowered herself onto me I had to laugh at the thought of my over-ambitious Project X. No man could ask for anything more than to lie as I did now, enfolded by such a woman. Because Margrete showed me that what I had always hoped for was true, she showed me that the human act of love allowed room for expansion, that it did not consist solely of urges and irrational emotions, of slobbering and grunting, with the possible little addition of tricks picked up from hordes of superficial manuals. Margrete showed me that there ran a path from sex life to life. It may sound strange, but when having sex with her I had a constant sense of being a worker in depth. Making love to Margrete was like being part of an infinitely ramified network. I would never reach higher or deeper in life.

Sometimes, when I was lying, spent, on top of the white sheets, she would get out her stethoscope with a grin and sound me. 'I do believe you are suffering from a very bad case of love, Mr Wergeland,' she would say. I thought she was listening to my pounding, sex-satiated heart. But no. She told me that she was listening to my lungs. 'The lungs, not the heart, are the organ of love,' she said.

The months after we were reunited were full of surprises, but nothing surprised me as much as the riches contained in those silent caresses, that fact that those lips on lips, that *pleasure*, contained so much insight. She could run her finger tenderly and inquisitively over the double scar above my eyebrow and the world would open up before my eyes. It struck me that I, whose aim all my life, or half of it at least, had been to think an original thought, should perhaps have striven instead to experience an original feeling. That feeling and thinking were perhaps comparable. For as I lay beside her, snuggled in to her, holding and being held, I realised that these caresses were every bit as rich and meaningful – and profound – as the thoughts put forward by Plato in his dialogue on love. In that white room, in bed, with Margrete's arms around me, I glimpsed a corrective to the great goal of my life. Then I pushed it from me.

Sometimes when I came home in the evening she would be sitting there in my dressing gown. When I asked her why, she would reply: 'Because I miss you.'

When we were not making love – although this, too, was a part of the love-making – we lay cuddled up together, with our hair sticking in sweat-soaked curls to the backs of our necks. We could lie in bed all day, coiled up together in a sort of circle, playing the second movements of our favourite symphonies and telling each other things. After I had told her about the advent calendars

from my childhood that I remembered best, the three-dimensional ones particularly; and about skimming downhill so fast in a toboggan with a steering
wheel that sparks flew from the runners, and about the entrance exam for
the School of Architecture, she told me about the songs on the red, blue and
yellow Donald Duck records, which she knew by heart; about the taste of her
first strip of Wrigley's spearmint gum, and about the year when she picked
oranges on a kibbutz in Israel. While there, she had also visited the Roman
ruins at Baalbek in the Lebanon. She described this as the greatest trip she
had ever made. Baalbek was akin to other such complexes at Angkor Wat and
Karnak, Borobodur and Persepolis – all of them structures which seemed
to have been built by a race other than mankind. In passing she happened
to mention when she had been there, and I realised that at that exact same
point I had been sitting in Samarkand. I lay on the bed, gazing at the golden
statuette in the corner of the white bedroom and thought of a stone I had
once thrown into Badedammen, of the rings that had spread out and, at an
unforgettable moment, ran into other rings.

'Why do you want to be with me?' I asked one day when she was lying with
her arms around me, hooting with laughter. It was dusk and the light was
fading outside the windows. She grew serious: 'Because you need someone
to hold you.'

'Oh, and why so?' I teased.

Her face remained serious. 'Because otherwise you would fall apart,' she
said, with eyes which, in the twilight, revealed a depth, a glow which almost
made me feel uneasy.

She did not ask me. Maybe she simply took it for granted that I would
have said the same.

I do not know about other people, but to me this was both confusing
and shocking. To encounter someone, a woman, who claimed that to put
your arms round someone could be purpose enough in life. Not to hold your
breath, but to hold a person.

I said: 'Okay. You have my permission to hold me.'

It was on this evening, in my twenty-sixth year, in a white bedroom in
Ullevål Garden City, that I fought shy of my life's epiphany.

As luck would have it, I had just joined NRK TV as an announcer. The
way I saw it, I was done with all projects. My ambitions had been shipwrecked
and I took the unexpected response from viewers as a sign that they could see
this; they showed the same sympathy towards me as they would have done
to a castaway. But something was brewing. New processes had been set in
motion and – strangely enough, considering that she was the catalyst – my
attention was drawn away from her.

When did I receive the first hint that something was wrong?

We're talking hindsight, I know, but I remember one time when we went to a Beethoven recital by a famous string quartet in the University Assembly Hall in Oslo. In the brief pause that followed the Cavatina in Opus 130, that extremely emotional adagio movement which wavers between *tristesse* and hope, as the audience held its breath, waiting for the 'Grosse Fugue' to begin, Margrete suddenly leapt to her feet and started clapping wildly and enthusiastically and shouting 'Bravo!' There she stood, under Munch's sun, all alone and clapping, heedless of the sore breach of etiquette she was committing and the scandalised looks levelled at this person who dared to applaud in the middle of a piece, in front of such world-renowned and no doubt blasé musicians.

After the recital the ensemble's cellist came over to us. Without a word he handed her the bouquet of roses which had been presented to him.

One afternoon, after we had been making love for what seemed like three days in a row, Margrete lay stroking my chest. One of her long fingers traced intricate patterns on the skin over my ribs. We all had a glowing spot inside is, she told me; and this glowing spot was a weaver. It wove into being a small, imperceptible lung. When we departed this life, this alone would remain, and go on breathing for us, saving us from death, even after we were dead. And this lung was our story. It has since occurred to me that Margrete's secret organ must, in that case, contain the following image: that of a woman standing up in a packed assembly hall, under Munch's sun, applauding all alone.

Why did she do it?

On that fateful, maelstrom-like April evening, as I sat looking at her body and put the muzzle of the pistol to my temple, I noticed that one hand, her fingers, seemed to be pointing to her lungs. Was that it? Was this, the Assembly Hall incident, Margrete's story? Did it also tell why she had done it? For what if that misplaced applause was related to this sight before me, a shot in the heart. What if her shouts of 'Bravo' were as much a cry of protest as an impulsive, barefaced show of enthusiasm. She simply could not bear to hear the 'Grosse Fugue'. I bent over the dead body and touched a fingertip with one of my own. I seem to recall feeling the pain in my chest already then, the nasty twinge of discomfort which would plague me for a long time, also in prison.

From the graze on her brow and the smear of blood on the door jamb I guessed that she must have hit her head off the wall, that she might even have spent a long time kneeling there, banging her head against the brick wall before going to get the gun. I had never understood: the molten gold in

Margrete's eyes was the result of the darkness within her. It was a light which had been constantly on the point of going out, which fought against a blackness. That was why they had been so beautiful. I had only seen the glow, not the darkness surrounding it.

A lot happened during those hours. I was confused, I was devastated by grief, but my mind was also uncannily clear, almost as if I had taken some sort of thought stimulant. I put on gloves and wiped the weapon clean. I also wiped the powder residue off her wrist. I was bewildered, I was shattered, but I was alert and businesslike when it came to removing all signs which could point to Margrete having shot herself. And when it came to leaving clues which would, in due course, point to me. I took the Luger's old wrappings, the oilcloth and ammunition box from the cupboard in my workshop and hid them so well that it would take the police a long time to find them. I also took into account my older brother's possible qualms of conscience – he knew about the gun. I was distraught, but at the same time so dazzlingly clear-sighted that the police investigators found only what I wanted them to find, and only at the stages at which I wished them to find them. My own version of what had happened, why I had done it – and it would be a long time before I told it – also took form, almost without my being aware of it, during those hours. It was watertight. Utterly consistent. Perfect, on both the emotional and the rational plane. Just so you know: getting convicted of murder is not as easy as people think.

It is morning at Balestrand. Kamala is asleep. I sit on the balcony of the hotel room looking out on the broad expanse of the fjord. I savour the light, I cannot recall seeing light like this anywhere else in the world. On the lawn below, Benjamin is lying outside his tent gazing up at the drifting clouds, when, that is, he is not shooting glances at the dragons on the spire of the English Church. It is a grand sight: the big, round tent, like a Mongolian *ger*, and him lying there with a blade of grass in his mouth. The other guests must be quite taken aback when they look out of their windows and see this: Benjamin, in Karakorum, Ghengis Khan's old capital, an utterly content individual on a boundless plain. I remember when Dad came home from the hospital and told us that we had a brother who was Mongoloid. I thought he was talking about Globoids, the aspirins. Dad certainly looked as if he had a headache. He told us all about the chromosomes, and how Benjamin had one x too many, as it were. In my universe, Benjamin stands as the first representative of the so-called Generation X. He may not be capable of appreciating irony, nonetheless he has lived his life inside inverted commas.

I think about our expeditions into Lillomarka together. All the camping out. All the stories. I have wondered: could I have been trying to hide him. And myself. He found me, though. Benjamin was the first person to show me that I had imagination, that I could do something with the worlds I dreamed up, outside of my own head. Together we established a position on the sideline, an Outer Mongolia which was also an Outer Norway, an outside left. Thinking back to Harastølen and the refugees: I know why I am so obsessed with this fear of foreigners. It is because of Benjamin. If Benjamin has taught me anything it is tolerance. He broadened my view – the first, possibly, to do so – of what a human being is, and can be.

Rakel comes walking towards him. Benjamin points eagerly at something in the sky. Rakel sits down, puts an arm round him. She is another one – a hugger, a holder. They sit for a while, peering up at the clouds, chatting, then they start to pack up. They are going to catch a boat back to Fjærland then drive home in the truck. With a stop at a riding camp along the way. Benjamin is very happy with Rakel and her husband. Rakel tells me they are going to write a book together, the three of them. About trailer-trucks, long-distance lorry driving. Benjamin has already come up with a title: *The Golden Horde*.

Yesterday I went for a stroll along the road by the beach, past Belehaugene, the two ancient barrows, to take a look at the storybook villas built here a century ago by the artists: half *stabbur*, half stave church. Then I raised my eyes, only – and again: why was I surprised – to find myself still more entranced by the fjord, the mountains. I almost caught myself humming 'Beauteous is the Land'. And once more I had to ask myself: Is this really Norway? If any Norwegian should become too blasé, start to hate their country, then they should take a trip to Balestrand, or sail between the unbelievably high mountains around the green fjord running up to Fjærland, expose themselves to the silver threads of the waterfalls and glimpses of wild side valleys. I know opinions differ on this – I know it took the Romantic movement to change people's ideas about the countryside and what it had to offer – but if you ask me, there is no doubt: Norway's great asset is its scenery. I have made caustic remarks about it, I have scoffed at it, but on reflection it seems perfectly understandable that it should have been *Song of Norway*, that regular holiday brochure of a film, which prompted Kamala to come to this country. In other words, I have the splendour of the Norwegian fjords to thank for the fact that, in a roundabout way, she eventually found me.

Its scenery is Norway's most valuable commodity. Sognefjord is our Grand Canyon, our Guilin and our Machu Picchu all rolled into one. That is why the product, the service which the OAK Quartet is designing is so important. Often it crosses my mind that this could be Norway's only hope:

to translate what Sognefjord represents, our greatest natural asset, into form, into thought, into software.

One afternoon Kamala and I took part in one of the planning sessions on board the *Voyager*. Before the meeting, Martin, that never-resting wizard with copper pans and spices, served up a whole *rijsttafel* of delicious little dishes. They had put up the boom tent to give a bit of shade; it was hot, not a cloud in the sky. The way they talked, their enthusiasm, reminded me of the fun I used to have as a small boy, walking along the beach and popping whatever took my fancy into a bucket: shells, stones, feathers, bits of metal. They do the same thing with information.

Each day they gather on deck to discuss new possibilities arising from what they have seen, explored, studied, heard. And tasted. They are mapping out this part of Norway in a way I would never have believed possible. At each new stop along Sognefjord they search for what Carl who, having an American mother does not baulk at using English terms, calls the place's 'webness', its ability to interconnect with other places, through its hidden 'links'. They mix together all manner of subjects: history, folklore, economics, geography, language, geology. Sometimes I find this work touchingly reminiscent of the television series I once made, but it reminds me even more of my Titanic Project X. They are in the process of doing what I could not: creating a network in which every point of intersection is the centre.

At this particular meeting I surprised them all by suggesting that their main entry on Balestrand should focus on its tourist industry, this place having been one of the main travel hubs in Norway ever since the nineteenth century. They could present an outline of its colourful history, with the German Kaiser and all; I tried to make them see how great it would look with a little cavalcade of the town's more exotic and somewhat eccentric visitors, from King Chulalongkorn of Siam and Queen Wilhelmina of the Netherlands to Egyptian princes and Indian maharajahs. I got quite carried away, suggested that they might also weave in an item on the many old and atmospheric wooden hotels along Sognefjord. They could even insert a link to a page on souvenirs, on which they could show how the rugs and baskets of the old days had evolved into glass polar bears, wooden trolls and pewter Viking ships. And whatever they did – my voice almost cracked with excitement – they must not forget the cruise ships, those 'floating hotels' which were such a common sight on the fjord, in the first half of the twentieth century particularly. I launched into a rapturous and detailed description of the *Stella Polaris*, sang the praises of the picture of the *Stella Polaris* on Esefjord. Could anyone conceive of a prouder, more evocative sight for a

Norwegian – that scenery, coupled with what was arguably the loveliest, the most elegant Norwegian cruise ship of all time, a vessel which might have been designed by Jules Verne for use as a spaceship? I went on talking long into the lovely May night. The others gaped at me – staggered, but also to some degree hooked. Kamala glanced across at me, smiling, as if she were asking: Who are you?

That same evening, still on the subject of travel mementoes, I told them about the disc which the Voyager probes carried with them into space and which could, to some extent, be regarded as a collection of souvenirs from Earth. This disc held, for instance, photographs of the Taj Mahal, the UN building, the Great Wall of China and Monument Valley. Its project was really not that different from the one on which Kristin and her friends were working. Only on a larger scale. While the OAK Quartet was presenting Sognefjord, the Voyager disc was designed to present Tellus herself, including the species which goes under the name *Homo sapiens*.

A thought crossed my mind. I hunted through Hanna's choice collection of CDs, found Beethoven's string quartet no. 13, opus 130, the emotive Cavatina movement. They were clearly mystified. Until I told them that this movement, together with over eighty minutes' worth of other music – including Bach and Mozart, but also Chuck Berry, Louis Armstrong, songs by the Navajo Indians and the court gamelan of Java – had all been recorded onto a gold-plated copper disc which had been hurled out into the cosmos – a sort of high-tech message in a bottle.

The purposeful mood which prevails on board, transmits itself to my writing. My urge to write. I have written a lot. I have been writing by hand, as Margrete did. I have managed fine without my old IBM typewriter with its globe-like printing element. Possibly because I am on a boat, a small sphere in itself, covered in symbols. The landscape, the fjord itself, also fire my imagination. Several times on this trip I have fancied that I am on a journey through Margrete. Through her complex mind. The shape of the fjord resembles that of my memories. Just as when deep inside the smallest arm I am still conscious of the main fjord, so too in the deepest branches of my recollection I never lose sight of the middle part: those hours when everything happened, that evening when I came home from a World's Fair and found her dead.

I knew I had to hold off calling the police. I had to think, I had to come up with a plan, I had to collect my thoughts, I needed time to take a look around, make my own examination of the scene. I staggered about, stumbled from room to room, thinking, searching; searching, at first, as if in my sleep, and then, after a while, wide awake. It is no exaggeration to say that I found things on my nocturnal wanderings that changed my life. I found, for example, her pearl necklace.

A picture comes back to me. She is standing facing me, looking straight into my eyes while her fingers play with the string of pearls around her neck. I know this must have been a fateful situation. This too I know: she might be alive today if I had loved her more. Scientists believe they have proof that animals are sometimes encouraged to stay alive by some sense that they are loved. It took me many years to discover the real reason – the one behind the ostensible, banal explanation with which I had long comforted myself – for why Margrete's condition deteriorated so drastically after my trip to Lisbon: only *then* did she see that she was not loved. Lisbon, what happened there, was the famous last straw, the weight in the balance.

The cracks had been appearing in our marriage long before that, though. As many people know from bitter experience, the extraordinary can very quickly become commonplace. During our first months together, and indeed our first years, I did not think I would ever cease to be amazed by Margrete. My head was in a spin, I was walking on air, I was deliriously happy. I am thinking not least, again, of the physical side – and this despite my unrealistic, essentially Utopian, expectations. My notions of sex were associated, after all, with some sort of mechanical world in which the best one could hope for was an intricate meshing of gear-wheels. Margrete took me into an erotic universe involving causes and effects that far outdistanced this, with connections beyond my comprehension. If I close my eyes and think of that first year, all I can see is a white bedroom and a golden idol, and how in bed she led me through room after room, throwing open door after door and showing me new wings within myself. In my euphoria, in my delight at being unwrapped, I did not see that I was living with a woman who had already unfolded, who was more fully evolved than I was.

Nonetheless, I was so truly enthralled by her presence in the moment, by the intensity with which she savoured the smallest everyday tasks: pouring peppercorns into the mill, cleaning a window, arranging flowers at a particular angle in their vase. Or making a bark boat. Most of all, I loved the way she could get me to converse. After we moved into the house in Grorud we would often go for walks around Steinbruvannet talking, as we walked, about everything and anything. Or telling each other things. Here, too – almost as if it were part of our conversation – she would often fashion bark boats and set them in the water, eager as a little child to see how long the frail craft would float before capsizing. All the same: human beings are capable of adapting, in the most amazing fashion, not only to the most appalling conditions, but also to the most intoxicatingly wonderful circumstances. After some months I no longer responded with the same gratitude to Margrete's refreshing manner, after a couple of years I accepted it as natural, after ten years I took it for granted.

I sometimes thought that we were too unalike, that we represented two different worlds: one of fluttering butterfly wings, one of hard crystals. We, or I, never understood that together, by pure virtue of this, we could have opened up something immense.

But still: why did she do it? When did I spot the first signs of the darkness which took up residence within her. It is with profound shame that I have to confess: I never noticed a thing.

Once or twice, on those rare occasions when her behaviour did disturb me, I may well have asked whether anything was the matter. But she never answered me. I *thought* she had not answered. One evening, when we were in bed, she suddenly said: 'What if the house was on fire and we had to get out and you could only take one thing with you. What would it be?' I did not know, but then I remembered Bo Wang Lee. '*Huckleberry Finn*,' I said. She laughed. 'Why not *Victoria*?' she asked.

She had answered me. I just wasn't listening.

In my defence I should say: she was so different. More than anything, the fact that she was a reader and hence a writer was to me symbolic of something alien, sinister even. She read, she wielded a pen, rather than talk. If she sometimes acted strangely, seemed a bit moody, I took it as just another mark of her eccentricity. She occasionally had bouts of what I would have called depression, but her work as a doctor seemed explanation enough for this. I was always popping into the clinic where she worked at that time, and even I could be depressed by those polished floors and impersonal sofa arrangements, not to mention the hangdog patients with their embarrassing STDs.

She had always done strange things. She was quite capable of getting up and walking out of the cinema in the middle of a film, having suddenly got the notion for onion soup, she simply *had to have* onion soup. I had learned to accept this. In the early days I could spend hours talking about such foibles; I wanted to get to the bottom of the motives behind her weird actions and ideas. But I soon got used to her ways. I ought perhaps to have sensed, however, that something had happened, an acceleration of sorts, just after I got back from Lisbon and the fatal episode at the Belém Tower, distracted though I was by relief at the fact that my plans for a television series were to be realised after all. She was especially tight-lipped, irritable. Hostile, I would say. But – and I never forgot that she had once wanted to be an actress – she never said why.

One day I was at the piano, playing some hymns from the Norwegian Choral Songbook, trying out new chords, the way Viktor did with the jazz standards. Margrete had been known to accuse me of murdering these songs, she said my playing hurt her ears. She did not understand that this was the music of my childhood, a tribute to my father – as well as a means of contemplating Viktor's pointless fate: a gifted pianist one day, a vegetable slumped in front of a television set the next. But on this occasion, as I sat there, wistfully picking out new harmonies in 'Here comes a faithful goatherd', instead of making one of her usual disapproving remarks, she actually slapped me in the face, utterly without warning. 'Blasphemy,' she said – I think she must have been referring to the word 'faithful' – in a voice seething with anger, one which told me I should probably think myself lucky that she had done no more than hit me. A bruise blossomed on my cheekbone. There were jokes at work about 'Margrete's dreaded left hook'. Still, though, I regarded this as no more than a crazy but harmless outburst, something I might even get round to teasing her about later.

But I should have known. And in my memory I keep returning to those endless minutes when she stood there considering me and fiddling with the string of pearls around her neck. The light in Margrete's golden-brown eyes kept changing as she talked; they seemed to undergo modulations, in the same way as a piece of music. They shifted from gold to lead when she said: 'Tell me about Lisbon.'

This conversation took place in the latter half of the eighties. I was in the midst of work on the *Thinking Big* series. We had just come home from an operetta-like party and sat for a while in the living room instead of going straight to bed. The babysitter had gone. Kristin was asleep. We had been visiting Margrete's parents, who were back in Norway that autumn. There had been plenty to talk about. I had gradually grown more comfortable with the ambassador, despite his somewhat domineering manner, fostered by numerous long and not exactly enviable sojourns in countries with, to say the least of it, undemocratic regimes. I had, however, a serious problem with Margrete's mother. I was in the mood for talking. Margrete did not seem to feel like it. I kept her up, trotted out all of the comments I had come up with in the car on the way home, mainly on the subject of her mother, a character whom I found downright scary with her submissive shadow existence. She was always in the background, with a drink and a cigarette in the same hand, as if she needed the other for holding on to something, in case she should collapse. I had a lot to say about Mrs Boeck and the possible alcoholism which she hid behind a collection of anonymous Chanel suits, and I wanted to say it all now, not discuss Lisbon with Margrete. And on the subject of alcohol, I was also all set to poke fun at the ambassador's tedious chat about drinks and how to mix a perfect dry martini. 'I know how to make over two hundred different cocktails,' he boasted, pointing with boyish pride to his ridiculous array of drink mixing equipment, 'but I'm still not sure about the exact ratio of gin to vermouth in a dry martini. Ask me about a Between the Sheets, though. Or a Clover Club. Go on, just ask me!'

Back in our own house, Margrete had risen. She stood in the middle of the room in a short, black dress with spaghetti straps, her arms and shoulders bare. She fiddled absent-mindedly with her necklace; she liked pearls, she had several necklaces made from different sorts of pearls. She was wearing glasses. She wore them for watching television, in the cinema and – as this evening – for driving. They were of indeterminate design, fifties-style maybe. She had had them for as long as I had known her. And yet they always seemed fashionable, signalling, in some way, that here was an outsider. The same went for the slightly tousled hairdo, which gave her a rather impish look, an air of nonchalant elegance. Her whole appearance was, in fact, anachronistic, which is probably why everyone found her so alluring.

I could see that something was bothering her, but at the same time I did not see it, I was too wrapped up in myself, my stockpile of opinions, my interest in a mother-in-law who was clearly teetering on the brink of a nervous breakdown, but concealed it by standing in the background with her drink and a ciggie in one hand, whispering to some other lady about the outrageous amounts of money they made out of the Foreign Ministry's countless overseas allowances, while in the foreground, Ambassador Boeck held forth on the perfect dry martini as if he were talking about complicated matters of foreign policy. It was a speech I had heard at least ten times already; because, of course, the correct ratio was neither three nor four parts gin to one part dry vermouth, but a balance so delicate, according to Mr Boeck's cosmic theories – presented with a perfectly straight face – that I could not help thinking of pi, that mathematical quantity with an infinite number of figures after the point. Margrete was still fiddling with the string of pearls. Then, out of nowhere, came that modulation in her eyes: 'Tell me about Lisbon,' she said.

There have been moments when I have felt that the films of Michelangelo Antonioni have destroyed my ability to love. To communicate properly. It could be that I became so beguiled by that universe, and at such an impressionable stage in life, that I was left ingrained with the belief that it was impossible to gain insight into another person. Sitting there in the living room, held transfixed by a string of pearls, I felt as though I were back in one of Leonard Knutzen's films, standing in an empty field, my back to a girl, with a bloody great bulldozer plonked inexplicably between us.

I was just back from Lisbon, from a trip I believed had saved my career. Everything had been at stake, and I had won. Margrete had not asked, but she asked now, did not want to talk about her decidedly rocky mother; had no wish to discuss her father's priceless theories regarding the optimal dry martini, instead she asked about Lisbon: 'Did you *discover* anything there?' she said. A world of meaning in that one word 'discover'. There was something about her voice, a trace of doubt, of suspicion – I couldn't quite tell.

Lisbon was the last thing I wanted to talk about. I made some offhand remark in reply before returning to her mother's remarkable consumption of alcohol: 'I'd be a bloody alcoholic too, I'm sure, after thirty years of the *corps diplomatique* and their stultifying, ivory-tower existence.'

I saw Margrete flinch. She said: 'Sometimes when you talk it makes me feel the way I did at school when somebody scraped a fingernail across the blackboard.' Pause. Again those eyes, the irises shifting colour: 'Didn't you meet a woman?' Now and again, a look would come into Margrete's eye that betrayed her profession: a dissecting gaze.

I said nothing. For a long time. I sat back in the sofa in a room which I had decorated along with the lovely woman standing right in front of me, and as I sat there it struck me that I was doing the opposite of what I wanted to do with my life. I was not unfolding, I was curling in on myself. At long last, prompted by the primitive impulse which says that the best form of defence is attack, I said: 'Are you jealous. Don't tell me that you – *you* – are jealous?'

She may not have been. She was not the type to want to own me, to own anything. Still she stood there fingering the string of pearls, a present from her mother and father for her birthday some weeks earlier and outrageously expensive, no doubt. It had been bought in Japan, a string of pearls with just a temporary clasp, so that she could put it around her neck right away, see how it looked. Her father had asked her to have it restrung at a jeweller's in Oslo. She had not yet done so, but had wanted to wear it to the party, to please her mother and father. She fingered it like a rosary. As if she were praying, incessantly, entreating me to tell her. I would forgive you everything if only you would tell me, her lips said.

What could I say, I wondered. But I could not think of anything to say. And I could not tell her the truth. I stared at one particular pearl. It did not borrow light, it shed light. I could not breathe, I lacked spirit, that was why I found it so hard to communicate. I stared at the woman before me, I hardly recognised her. The short, black dress with the spaghetti straps, the quaint spectacles, no longer suggested a sexy woman, but a young girl. The collar-bones, which Margrete called key-bones, so sharply defined, spoke of an ominous slenderness, vulnerability. She had her whole hand curled round the necklace now, as if it were an anchor chain that was saving her from being swept away. Away from me, away from this house. Sometimes she seemed so helpless, so flagrantly helpless, that it did not so much confuse as annoy me.

Then there was this other thing. This too a mystery, but in quite the opposite way, you might say. One day, some years into our relationship, and almost by accident, I learned that she was already a respected expert in her field, derma-venereology. She had had several groundbreaking articles published in leading medical journals. Why had she not told me? Or: why had I not got her to tell me? I am no stranger to the thought that I may have viewed her specialty as a threat of some kind, that I was in some way afraid of catching something.

She was a tallboy. I could open the drawers and commit their contents to memory, only to find when I opened them again that they contained something quite different. She, Margrete, was Project X. She always had been. Now, in the instant before it happened, I saw this more clearly than ever.

We were still discussing my trip. She standing, me sitting. The room seemed darker, as if all the light had been sucked into the pearls she wore around her neck. She was worrying so hard at the necklace that one would have thought it felt to her like a detestable dog collar. All at once the skin of her face seemed to craze over. I explained that the trip to Lisbon had been absolutely necessary, a case of to be or not to be. Exactly, she said. But for whom? And then she asked a question which led me to suspect that she might, after all, know everything: 'What was it you called those women at NRK who sleep their way up the ladder – "telly tarts", wasn't that it?' She fixed her eyes on a point on my forehead, just over my eyebrow, as if seeing there not a scar, but a dirty blemish. A semen stain.

And when I did not come up with an answer, or would not give an answer, *could* not give an answer, the string of her necklace snapped, apparently without her being anywhere near it, as if supernatural powers were at work. Pearls sprayed everywhere, a precious, white shower falling to the floor.

During a long period of the life that now lies behind me I felt – for reasons beyond my comprehension – the urge to seek out a worthy mission. How should one spend one's days? Searching for pearls to thread onto a string? Or should one quite simply create new conditions, seek out another sort of string?

When I joined NRK Television and embarked upon what those who like to exaggerate have described as one of the most influential careers in postwar Norway, no one knew that as far as I was concerned I was in retirement. My real working life was already at an end. My Project X. As far as I was concerned, the rest of my life was going to be a real dawdle, involving no great hazards. I began my job as an announcer. I might just as well have begun work as a lighthouse keeper.

In memory my Project X is long since reduced to two activities – plus the echo of some contrapuntal wonders from Bach's *Die Kunst der Fuge*. One of these involved crouching down between two gooseberry bushes in a garden, gazing at a cross spider. The other entailed sitting in state atop a great portal between life and learning, at a desk piled high with books on the cosmos. As a sideline I am sure I could have written a treatise on *Araneus diadematus*. At the very least I should have foreseen the discovery of Pluto's moon.

I would be twenty before I found my calling – and I have no hesitation in using such a highfalutin word. I had had an idea that I would wind up at the Institute of Theoretical Astrophysics right from that day at school when a succession of maps whipped up, one after the other, to reveal a stunning poster of the solar system at the very back, like Truth itself. But I did not opt for astrophysics in order to study the cosmos, I wanted only to use the subject, and the reading room that went with it, as a base camp in an expedition to other, I was about to say higher, objectives. I was occasionally heard to say to fellow students: 'I'm drawing up a new map of the universe.'

It was at this point that all the thoughts that had been running around in my head since the day when I sat amid an avalanche of books, looking at the bare bookshelves in Karen Mohr's bedroom and waiting for a ham omelette, crystallised into the obvious mission, the Project. In a flash I knew: this is what I was born for. As a child I had always liked the standard adult question: 'What are you going to be when you grow up.' Because this told me that I was going to be *something*. Not just *be*. Several times already – with a certainty that I did not dare to reveal – I had had the feeling that I was a wonder, but only now did I feel myself to be fully evolved; it was a long time since I had had the sensation of dying, only to live on as a broader person. I was ready. I could almost hear a voice saying: 'The hour has come.'

I am not so much of a fool that I cannot laugh at it now. Nonetheless, this phase in my life deserves to be described as it was: utterly serious and totally devoid of self-irony. I knew I did not have all the time in the world. Blame my impatience, if you will, on an exceptional teacher from my high school years, a man who may have been a notorious sceptic and atheist, but who, after a terrible disaster at sea in which he lost all of his closest family, became a deeply religious person – which is not to say that he became a sad, old misery guts on that score. He always wore a beret, like a painter. I often thought that he and my neighbour Karen Mohr would have made a good match. 'Teaching is the greatest of all the arts,' he said. During those years I did not go to school, I sat at the feet of a guru. 'Use your head today, tomorrow it may be too late,' he said in every second class. 'Right now, you have no preconceived opinions. And only now, for all too short a time, do you have the necessary measure of naivety.' According to our astute schoolmaster, no one had an original thought after they turned twenty-five. By then one was set. Almost all significant discoveries, particularly within science, were made by relatively young people. Just look at Newton!

All at once the Project was tantalisingly clear to me. I would discover a new way of thinking, a way which lay dormant within us. I would break down the bars behind which human cognition had been confined by the existing categories. I have to restrain myself here – I can see that the more I say, the more overheated and nebulous and crazy it will sound. Let me put it this way: it was a task worthy of Atlas himself, it was an attempt to lift something colossal, to form the basis for a higher heaven. And yet to me it seemed an imperative and manifestly rational task.

Looking back on it, it is easy to see what I was fighting against: Melvil Dewey's classification system. Because even though it was only a tool for organising books in a library, to me it was the crowning example of a mode of thought which had paralyzed our potential for evolving as human beings. Ever since my visit to Deichman's Potala Palace with Karen Mohr, clad in sober grey, I had been unhappy about Melvil Dewey's method of arranging a large collection of books. His system, with its ten main classes had cemented notions of the importance of the different branches of knowledge and of the relationship between them. I was reminded of my own bafflement and lack of vision that time when Granny dragged out all those small boxes full of crystal droplets. Who would ever have thought that together they would form a glittering chandelier?

Dewey's system belonged, moreover, to another world, not to a life in which people's thoughts and ideas were forever changing, in which fields of knowledge expanded in the same way as the universe did. I never forgot the class – a Norwegian class, at that, earmarked for a review of adverbial clauses – in which our unconventional junior-high teacher told us about the explosion of life forms traceable in the Cambrian system. I had a strong sense of living in a new and revolutionary Cambria, in an epoch when everything was gathering speed, when new scientific discoveries were piling up all around us. Dewey's system was based on a simple, single-celled form of life, so to speak. But now new hybrids were bursting forth, fabulous unguessed-at branches of learning.

What interested me, more than the libraries and the classification system as such, was the organisation of human knowledge. I wanted to promote a different understanding of the collective power of all the arts and sciences; I meant to draw up a new map, on a new projection, with different names for all the regions; I wished to create a springboard for unforeseen discoveries. In glimpses I saw, with a shudder of apprehension almost, the Project's aim: a new unity. New connections between the various parts of the whole. The chance of a new kind of dialogue. If mankind was to unfold, then our knowledge would also have to be unfolded. Maybe Project X was born on that day in my childhood when I unwrapped a beautiful map of the world from what everybody thought was a filthy, crumpled wad of cloth.

This task instinctively appealed to me. It was all about depth. I wanted to be a person who worked in depth. I often thought of another of the many keen assertions made by our master in junior high: no one now had the energy to care about the big picture, he said, standing in front of a blackboard covered in circles and dotted lines. Any expert today who claimed to know more than one per mil of the existing knowledge in his field was bluffing. And if you were not even anywhere close to knowing your own discipline, how were you supposed to understand the relationship between your subject and other subjects? The sciences in our day were incapable of communicating with one another, our teacher said. And this was catastrophic. Most fruitful theories sprang from the wedding of two ideas from two unrelated fields. He was right. At my best moments I felt a kinship with Thor Heyerdahl.

My life has been a balancing act between the hope of being a wonder, and the fear that I was a fool. I remember how sometimes in maths tests I could juggle quite brilliantly with abstract quantities, while at others I could make the most unforgivably stupid mistakes, could hardly add two and two together.

I once asked Margrete why she had kept those four butterflies, the ones she had caught as a child, hanging in a frame on the wall. 'I like butterflies,' she said. 'And I'm interested in them from a medical point of view, too. They have the most amazing immune system. It has us stumped. We can inject them with cholera or typhus bacteria. But they don't get sick.' I tended to think of Margrete in much the same way. She was a doctor, there was no way she could ever get sick.

Luckily, my choice of life project went well with a need for concealment which had not lessened with the years. As an astrophysics student I had access to the big reading room on the top floor of the Physics Building, a lofty, bright, square room. Here, in the yeasty atmosphere generated by the deep concentration of countless students, I could wrestle with my Atlas project, well-hidden, but at the same time situated on a vital axis. Beneath me lay the entrance to the campus, a portal through which thousands passed every day. And from the terrace outside the reading room I could drink in the inspiring view of the city and the fjord.

This was the most unsociable, most reclusive phase of my life. And possibly the only time when I actually did some hard work. I can shake my head at it now, but I cannot deny that I was very content. I had a tiny flat in Hegdehaugsveien, but spent most of my time in the reading room surrounded, for appearances' sake, by astrophysics textbooks, while reading other works entirely and jotting down, or occasionally sketching out, thoughts and ideas on sheets of paper which gradually grew into a pile as bulky and fanciful as an old Family Bible.

My frame of reference was the Dewey Decimal System, and in order to know what exactly I was protesting against and wished to improve upon I learned the names of the ten main classes, the hundred subdivisions and the thousands of sections or subjects by heart. I can still remember a lot of them, 786: Keyboard Instruments, 787: Stringed Instruments, 788: Wind Instruments. Or 597: Fish, 598: Birds, 599: Mammals. To begin with, I put a lot of effort into tossing these topics around in my head, to see if they might fall into other constellations, with other names. Since, on paper, I was studying astronomy I thought of the stars, thought to myself that this was like drawing new lines between those points of light, creating different signs from those which had been employed ever since the days of the Ancient Greeks. Why 295: Zoroastrianism, 296: Judaism, 297: Islam? Why not invent a new group in which string instruments, birds and Zoroastrianism were put together.

For the first time, during these years, I felt motivated to read. Or rather: I browsed, frantically skimming page after page, hoping to spot ideas, hints, clues which would help me with my project. I scrutinised the other classification systems, from Francis Bacon's and Henry Evelyn Bliss's to that devised by the far-sighted mathematician Dr S. R. Ranganathan, before expanding my studies to include every endeavour to organise the world of thoughts and things. I delved with a will into the zoological and botanical systems – in particular Carl von Linné's twenty-four classes, as well as his optimistic breakdown into genus and species and the resultant two-part Latin name. I pored over medical books on anatomy, I studied the periodic table, I struggled until

I was blue in the face to grasp the reasoning behind the twenty-eight magnificent volumes of Diderot et al.'s great French Encyclopedia, I even looked at various books on mazes in all their historical forms.

I sat in the reading room – I saw myself as being in a kind of academic outside-left position – enlightening myself on the infinite variety of human knowledge: biology, economics, meteorology. I read and read, leafed through book after book. By bringing all my mental powers to bear, I eventually decided what I considered to be the main branches of learning, the fundamental categories – I gave them new names, instead of such long-winded appellations as philosophy and natural science – then I split these up into smaller sections and – this was the hardest part – devised a sequence for these main and secondary disciplines which might disclose new inter-category relationships.

I sat on the top of the Physics Building, a gateway to the seat of learning in Oslo, a little cathedral, thanks to Per Krohg's frescoes in the entrance hall, but I was studying neither physics nor astrophysics, I was reorganising all the world's knowledge. I sat in the reading room, month after month, in that yeasty atmosphere, trying out idea after idea. I created divisions according to an evolutionary system, based on how things appeared to have emerged in the course of time. I arranged the main classes in the order in which they ought to be studied by someone seeking to be educated. I created systems which progressed from the general to the specific. I tried another sequence which ran from the specific to the general. In one experiment I began with the minor groups and subjects, not the main classes, then drew these groups together to form a bigger picture; attempted, you might even say, to get them to merge together of their own accord, working from the bottom upwards. I tried everything: for a long time, in one of my drafts Ant was a main class, in another I had two categories entitled The Actually Human and The Covertly Human.

It's odd. I have always believed that these were the years when I thought least about Margrete. I see now that I must have been thinking about her all the time. That she may have been the motive behind the whole Project. That this was another swim across an impossibly wide body of water.

One weekend I stumbled upon a fresh source of inspiration. I was on a visit to my parents at the house in Grorud, and when I went out into the garden on the Sunday morning to look at the apple trees I saw the sun glinting off some silken threads strung between two gooseberry bushes. I bent down to look, and there was a cross spider. It had just finished attaching the first frame threads of a web. What with the cross on the spider's back, I could not help feeling that it would be as good as a church service just to sit here in the grass for an hour, observing with creeping fascination how the creature slung its wonderful wheel-web between the branches.

The snag with Dewey's way of thinking was its disastrous one-dimensionality. The main classes and their subdivisions formed one long, vertical chain. My observation of the spider's web inspired me to experiment with a new scheme in which the groups would also be ranged side by side in rows. Such a set-up might well reveal totally new, horizontal links between the subjects. A hitherto unseen interplay between, let's say, biology, economics and meteorology.

I knew it was impossible, but ideally every book in a library would be placed in such a way that it abutted on every other book. It was something of this sort that I had dreamt of as I struggled to organise the books on Karen Mohr's shelves. Each book should have connecting lines running in several directions. What I was looking for was a network, not a classification system. A similar notion had been running through my mind as I stood in the vast Central Lending and Reference Department in the Deichman Library. When you walked over to a shelf and pulled out a book, a string of others ought to be pulled out along with it. Sitting in the garden in Grorud, gazing at the spider's web, I pictured myself taking *Peer Gynt* off its shelf in the Central Lending and Reference Department, and how, in so doing, I caused a number of other works to fall out, including some from other sections: a travel guide to Egypt, Norwegian folk tales, music by Edvard Grieg, the history of the National Theatre, a biography of Ibsen, a history of language, poems by Lord Byron, a lavishly illustrated book on the island of Ischia in the Bay of Naples.

In the reading room on the top of the Physics Building I did occasionally leaf through my astronomy books – more for fun, really. I was particularly taken with a little-supported theory that there might be a tenth planet, lying beyond Pluto, dubbed Planet X. So it came about that I named my own search – or research as I cockily referred to it – Project X. Although it is possible that in adopting this letter I was also saying something else: I did not know what my project actually entailed. And thanks to my ill-fated encounter with Silapulapu, I am still none the wiser.

When the reading room closed I carried on working back at the flat in Hegdehaugsveien, to the accompaniment – morning and evening for many years – of Bach on the stereo, as if I were trying to deduce the spirit with which he bound his notes together; a spirit, a sort of glue almost, which I thought might be of help to my own 'Kunst der Fuge'. I had eventually come up with forty-six main classes and a whole host of subdivisions, some of them denoted only by Greek letters. I had covered large sheets of paper with writing and these I spread out all over the living-room floor. Time and again I was heartened by the astonishing correspondences that came to light when I read across or down or diagonally. But just as often, even with Bach's fugues playing in the background, I saw only impenetrable constellations. Although they may simply have seemed that way due to my own limitations.

At the weekends, summer and autumn, I went out to Grorud where I would spend the mornings in the garden, looking at the cross spiders building their wonderful silken wheels among the bushes. For some weeks I was also able to stuff myself with gooseberries which, with their sharp, complex flavour – the tough, hairy skin and the soft flesh that was both sweet and sour – spurred me on in my hunt for subjects rich in contrast. When the dew was lying and the sun shining, the webs looked like little galaxies, spirals of glittering stars. I wanted to spy out the secret of their construction technique. The first stage of the process in particular appeared to be crucial, the way in which the spider attached the anchor threads, bridges of a sort, often with the aid of the wind, before commencing on the actual framework. It was these foundation threads which varied most from web to web. The radii, the spokes of the wheel, were always spun from the centre outwards. The construction of the capture spiral followed this same pattern, with strands radiating out from the centre and sticky threads running inwards again. Finally – and this really intrigued me – the centre was destroyed and respun. I never tired of lying there in the grass, watching those fragile, shimmering works of wonder take shape before my eyes.

Back at the flat I covered huge sheets of paper with more and more writing, big and small, with connecting lines, fine as silken threads, running this way and that, speaking of a form of order which also had to allow room for disorder. It got to the point where the living-room floor looked like something far more complicated than a spider's web. I felt as though I was on the verge of a spectacular breakthrough. That it was only a matter of time before a veil would be ripped aside and a claustrophobic grey hallway would have to give way to a light, bright, free Provence. And I *was* on the scent of something important. Before long I had transformed my flat into a sailing ship and my project into a voyage worthy of Magellan himself.

I've been thinking – maybe everyone has their secret Project X, something that drives them, moves them to push themselves beyond their limits. Viktor Harlem, for one, wrestled with just such a mind-boggling idea. And whatever one might think about this vision, or utopian concept, so robust was it that one long weekend in May it brought us – Viktor and me – to Venice.

Axel, who had fainted at the airport and had to stay behind in Oslo, was a dark Adonis with whom I lost touch after high school. Viktor, on the other hand, is as present in my mind to this day as he was back then. It is hard to describe the young Viktor Harlem, the brains behind The Three Heretics, but when I close my eyes what I see is a shining face, a face glowing with an almost uncanny intensity, rather as if a hundred-watt bulb had been screwed into a head that was only designed to take sixty watts.

Although I was quite clear on the purpose of our visit, when the time came to complete the final stage of our mission I began to falter. As Viktor stepped aboard the *traghetto* which was all ready to push off from the stop outside the Hotel Gritti Palace, I tried to explain to him that I was not coming, that I did not want to leave, could not face leaving, the Grand Canal, that waterway lined on either side by such mesmerising buildings, the sound of the water grinding away at the age-old stone. Why didn't we find ourselves a table on the hotel terrace, overlooking the canal; order some cake – some *tiramisù* – and coffee, I asked. Please, I said. What I did not say was that I no longer had any faith in my friend's audacious plan. I was trying, as gently as I could, to save Viktor from making a terrible fool of himself.

And what did Viktor have in mind. Viktor meant to pay a call on the poet Ezra Pound, a very old man now, and supposedly still living in Venice. Back in the flat in Seilduksgata in Grünerløkka, when Viktor first mooted the idea of looking up Pound, for a moment I thought he was talking about the British currency, that we were off to find a whole pile of money. Which was not too far off the mark: to Viktor, Pound was as good as a treasure chest.

We were staying in an out-of-the-way hotel, in a dim room dominated by a lagoon-like mirror, with enigmatic stucco decorations on the ceiling. The hotel's one notable feature was a portrait of Armauer Hansen, hanging on the wall of the lobby. 'My great-grandfather was a doctor too,' the hotel manager told us. 'He met the later so famous Norwegian when the latter visited Venice in 1870 on a travel scholarship, then too in May as it happens.' Viktor promptly took this as a good omen. 'We're on the trail of something much more important than the discovery of the leprosy bacillus,' he confidently announced to the manager. For my own part, I interpreted the sight of Armauer Hansen's countenance more as a warning of the city's contagiousness.

After two days I was actually feeling rather weak. I had spent most of my time on board a *vaporetto*; I had travelled up and down the Grand Canal at least twenty times, for much the same reason as one sees a film again and again: to savour scenes that have gradually become familiar and to keep on discovering new details. I could not get enough of it, almost had to rub my eyes as I tried to take in the sight of the rows of Byzantine and Gothic buildings to either side of me; façades redolent of the Renaissance and neo-classicism, walls which altered colour with the light and whose reflections created a rippling fairy tale down in the canal. The fronts of these palazzos *were* Vivaldi's music. I leaned over the rail of the boat, staring, staring with lovestruck, avidly curious eyes. I had planned to see other sights in Venice, but I never got beyond the Grand Canal. I never visited the Doge's Palace, nor the Accademia and – no one will believe it, I know – I did not so much as set foot on the pigeon beset square of St Mark. The Grand Canal was all I needed and more; this lazy, inverted 'S' of water winding between rows of palazzos, with each façade that hove into view more evocative than the one before: Palazzo Dario, Palazzo Barbarigo, Palazzo Loredan. I felt as though I was sailing along a spine in my own imagination, a backbone made up of identical and yet widely differing vertebrae. I was struck by an intriguing and unnerving suspicion: if I were to enter any one of these buildings along the canal – Palazzo Garzoni, Palazzo Grimani, Palazzo Bembo – inside it I would find another Grand Canal, equally spellbinding, which would hold me there for the rest of my life.

Just before the *traghetto* left the little jetty, I joined Viktor on board anyway. Something in his face made me do it. All of a sudden he looked worried. As if he realised that everything was at stake here, his whole life project.

When we stepped ashore on the other side of the canal, he seemed even more uncertain. He led the way up the labyrinthine street, in the opposite direction from the Church of Santa Maria della Salute, and turned left at the first bridge, onto the Fondamenta di ca'Bala. 'What if he's not at home?' Viktor muttered, stopping short. 'Come on, let's go back.'

I had to take charge. 'Of course he'll be at home, where's he going to go? He's as old as the hills, for God's sake.'

Viktor was an avid fan, to put it mildly, of that motley literary bazaar which went by the title of *The Cantos*: a fragmented poetic work touching upon just about everything between heaven and earth. At the flat in Seilduks-gata in Oslo, Viktor kept having to build more shelves to hold the books which were supposed to help him pursue more of the strands in Ezra Pound's vast tapestry of words. *The Cantos* were for Viktor what Provence was for Karen Mohr: an experience which craved a lifetime. Viktor wanted to achieve a thorough understanding of Pound's work, but he understood very little of it. Then he had the idea of going to Venice. He was devoutly convinced that all would be revealed if only he could meet the poet himself. 'Devoutly' being the right word here. Viktor had the same motive for seeking out Pound as some people have for wishing to meet God. It was much like having the chance to ask about the meaning of life.

In spite of all this, or perhaps precisely because of it, Viktor walked more and more slowly along the side of the narrow canal. The street scene was what any holiday brochure would describe as 'picturesque', with just the right number of cats, flower boxes on the walls, little bridges and elegant motor-boats with hulls of gleaming varnished mahogany. Suddenly Viktor turned left again, looking both quite certain and utterly lost, as if he were wavering between a sense of having been here before and of finding himself on some distant, watery planet. We were standing in the calle Querini, a narrow, paved cul-de-sac, outside a deep-pink or terracotta-coloured house. Viktor goggled at the lion's head knocker on the dark-green door. His courage failed him. I basically had to half-carry him back to the canal. Viktor pulled a bottle of aquavit out of his satchel: 'Maybe we should just drink it ourselves.'

I said nothing. We simply stood there, leaning against the railing along the canalside, staring down the cul-de-sac at the pink house front, as if we both knew that all would be revealed if only we waited long enough, stared hard enough. Then the bells of Santa Maria della Salute began to chime. It might have been the cue for a revelation: the green door opened and around it came a head, a lion's head larger than that on the door knocker; an old man walking with a stick and accompanied by a white-haired woman. They came hirpling towards us. Something happened to Viktor. He woke up, or woke up and all but fainted away. Pound appeared to have the same effect on him as Venice had on Axel – the reality was just too much for him. I nudged him in the ribs and as he pulled himself together I heard a panic-stricken: 'What do we do?' And I, to whom this man meant nothing, said: 'Ask him. That's why we're here, isn't it?' As far as I was concerned this was an interesting dilemma. You meet God. You are allowed one, possibly two, questions. What should you ask?

The woman and the old man were now level with us. Viktor took the plunge, he held up his hand, stopped the couple. They did not seem sur-prised, nor particularly well-disposed. Pound was wearing a broad-brimmed brown hat. His hair stuck out from underneath it. The maze of wrinkles on his face was like script, the marks of many lives. I remarked on his eyes, blue but with a sort of mist over them. Viktor approached Ezra Pound. Pro-duced a book, 'every heretic's bible' as he put it, the latest, expanded edition of *The Cantos*. The writer squinted at Viktor for some time before accepting the proffered pen and signing his name, along with a couple of words, on the title page. As he took the book back Viktor handed the bottle of aquavit to the poet, as a thank-you – or, why not: an offering – pointing as he did so to the ship on the label and reciting the first line from 'every heretic's bible': 'And then went down to the ship ...'

Pound peered curiously at Viktor as he handed the bottle to his companion. Viktor's worshipful expression did not appear to make much of an impression on him.

'A masterpiece,' Viktor said, or sighed almost. 'I hope you don't mind my asking, but which canto do you consider to be the most important.' Viktor stood there, waiting for the magic word, the key that would lay the work wide open instead of, as now, being only slightly ajar. This was no formative trip, but something far more ambitious: a mission in search of the answer to all things, the ultimate truth. I was reminded of my own feelings on that day in my childhood when I was introduced to Uncle Melankton.

Pound stood as if in a dream, his mind somewhere else behind those misty blue eyes. 'I was wrong,' he said, motioning towards the book. He went on standing there, gazing into space, shook his head slowly while the fingers of one hand scratched the knuckles of the other. 'Those poems don't make sense,' he said, 'they were written by a moron.' 'But, but, but …' I could see that Viktor was totally thrown. 'But it's … a masterpiece,' he said again.

'It's a botch,' Ezra Pound said. 'Stupid and ignorant. I knew too little about so many things.'

And with that the ancient left us, walked off slowly along the canalside with the white-haired woman. Viktor just stood there with his mouth opening and shutting, as if he were choking on a sentence. I told him to relax, Pound was probably just feeling a bit down, I said. I followed the woman and the old man with my eyes until they disappeared into a restaurant. 'Cici' it said on the sign. And all at once I realised that I had come face to face with myself, a wonder who knew, nonetheless, that he was a fool.

Viktor was left with a faraway look in his eyes. Or maybe he was lost in one of those whirlpool visions Pound was always on about. Viktor stared into mid-air, at the point where the poet's head had been. Aghast, I thought at first, but after he had been standing like this for some minutes it dawned on me that he was actually awestruck. 'What heresy,' he gasped. 'To condemn your own life's work.' Viktor kissed the book. I had a nodding acquaintance with *Hamlet*, and to me Viktor looked exactly like Ophelia at the moment when she started to lose her marbles.

We wandered back to the hotel. Viktor was acting like an absolute lunatic. Hooting with laughter one minute, cursing and swearing the next. Shaking his head and slamming his fist into walls along our way. 'Jesus!' he exclaimed every few minutes. 'Je-sus!' In the hotel room he slumped down into a shabby armchair among all the other heavy, cherry-wood furniture, with a look in his eyes that could have won him a part as the occupant of a deckchair on the beach in the film of *Death in Venice*, which Visconti had just finished making. He opened the bottle of grappa we had bought. 'Holy shit,' he said after the first swig. 'They wouldn't win any prizes for this. I should have kept the aquavit.'

Barely a year later, in Lillehammer, Viktor Harlem received a blow on the head from a block of ice which left him staring into space in an institution for twenty-odd years. The look in his eyes the same as in Venice: faraway. Or rather, the light in his face was extinguished, as if a light bulb had gone out. I always had the feeling that his head would tinkle if I shook it. Despite Viktor's affected wonder at Ezra Pound's self-denigrating statement, it often occurred to me that it was actually in Venice that he was dealt the blow to the head that put him out of action for so many years. That he had been hit, not by a block of ice, but by a book. It was as if he needed twenty years to digest the shock of his guru describing his life project – a superhuman feat and the object of Viktor's unstinting admiration – as a complete and utter failure. Each time I visited Viktor at the institution I was met by the eyes of someone who did not consider it worthwhile being fully conscious in such a meaningless world.

After all those years, he would one day get up and perform an achievement which would leave a lasting impression, but I knew nothing of this in Venice. To be honest I had worries enough of my own. In all probability I had been more thrown by the meeting with Ezra Pound than Viktor, at that point anyway. I needed room to breathe. I needed to be alone with my fear. It seemed clearer to me than ever: I could wind up a fool. Despite the knowledge of the powers pulsating within me.

Having deposited Viktor at the hotel with the bottle of grappa, I hopped onto the first *vaporetto* to come sailing along the Grand Canal. I had to take my mind off things, I had to find solace. I gazed at the buildings slowly slipping past, seeming to pile up in my memory. And suddenly I discerned a secret, mutual affinity between them, an all but invisible similarity, even between façades lying far apart; and at one spot, near the Rialto Bridge, it struck me that if I looked a little closer I would see that all of the house fronts were in fact the same façade. They were all part of an endeavour to say something about the perfect façade. Just as Cézanne painted the same mountain again and again. Palazzo Dario, Palazzo Barbarigo, Palazzo Loredan. Variations on the same possibility. I leaned over the rail of the *vaporetto*, trying to memorise each frontage – Palazzo Garzoni, Palazzo Grimani, Palazzo Bembo – so that in my mind I might be able to lay them one on top of the other, veil upon veil as it were, to create the underlying, ideal, façade, the palace in the depths, behind, beneath everything.

I am not sure, but sometimes I am inclined to see a connection between the television series *Thinking Big* and the ranks of façades along the Grand Canal. At the time I regarded the canal more as a long strand and the palazzos as almost identical pearls. Something I could collect, something which, by mere accumulation, could save me from ending up as a fool.

I had laughed at Viktor's discourses on *The Cantos*, Ezra Pound's megalomaniac attempt to construct a different sort of unity out of fragments. But some years later, by which time Viktor – I almost envied him – had found an impenetrable hiding place in an institution, there I was myself, striving to draw up a new map of human knowledge, a Project X which probably had more in common with the American bard's euphoric songs than I liked to think.

My study of – I might almost say: worship of – the cross spider's wheel web had inspired me also to try working breadthwise and from here it was only a short step to a more spatial perspective. I left my seat in the reading room and took instead to roaming around the campus. By studying the relationship of the university buildings to one another, which departments occupied which floors, I hoped I might discover something about the relative order of the various disciplines. Why were the buildings housing Sociology and Physics situated so far apart? And why did Philosophy occupy the floor *above* Theology in the Niels Treschow building?

It may well have been these strolls around the campus which prompted me to move base to the College of Architecture. Because my aim was not to become an architect; I was still looking for some means of organising all human knowledge – something better than the stunting 534: Sound and related vibrations, 535: Light and paraphotic phenomena, 536: Heat and thermodynamics; what I sought was a set-up which would make the most of the potential stored within the knowledge common to all of us, hence enabling us to take a cognitive leap forward. The first months there seemed especially promising. I had been spurred to apply the principles of floor-planning to my work. I grouped the sheets of paper I had spread out on the floor of the living room in Hegdehaugsveien as if the main classes and the subdivisions listed on them were rooms in a large house, or private and public premises in a metropolis.

This soon had to give way, however, to a more ambitious plan – this too architectonically inspired – in which I tried to find a dimension of depth in the connecting tissue of the arts and sciences. I tore up the sheets of paper on the floor. I started working with larger sheets, progressed from miniatures to massive canvases, so to speak. The living room was now full of transparent plastic tablecloths suspended from the ceiling, closely covered with subject headings. It looked rather like a lot of bookcases sitting one behind another, the only difference being that these you could see through, see all the way to the very back. Sometimes I had the impression that I was once more on a *vaporetto* on the Grand Canal; I felt as though I was gliding past a succession of transparent, almost identical palazzo façades. On the first sheets I had listed the more concrete main classes and subjects; the further back you went the more abstract they became. Each heading had, therefore, possible links running in countless directions. I suddenly perceived, for example – with the taste of gooseberries in my mouth, as it happens – that there might be a connection between palaeontology's interest in fossilised dinosaur bones and modern neurology's theories regarding the reptilian layer of the brain. Often, when I was standing looking at these transparent tablecloths, contemplating the groups of subjects hanging in layers, one behind the other, I felt something close to a new state of mind, as though my vision and my thoughts were now in tune with an awareness I had always possessed.

What Margrete liked better than anything else was to walk around the garden, barefoot and without an umbrella, when it rained in the summer. She was the sort of person who could set such store by a fine dinner service that she would stroke it with her fingers. Sometimes she would kiss me just to enjoy the sound of a kiss. That was the best sound in the world, she said: the sound of a kiss. I never made any allowance for such knowledge, such wisdom, when I was struggling with my Project X.

I have never been all that interested in the so-called explorers, all except one: Fernão de Magalhães, or Ferdinand Magellan as he was known to us in school. True he was killed in the Philippines, so he never made it back to his starting point in Spain himself, but it was his initiative and vision which brought about the first circumnavigation of the Earth. No one combined strength of will with cosmographic perception and nautical know-how the way Magellan did. The others hit upon a bit of land here and there, but it was Magellan who tied a string around it all, binding all of the individual discoveries together, threading the pearls neatly onto a strand so that they formed a circle. There could no longer be any doubt: the world was round.

There were times when I thought of my Project X as a Magellanic voyage. Like Magellan I wanted to find other routes, new straits to sail through. I dreamed, not least, of an outcome every bit as deep-reaching as his: a completely new view of the world. Magellan showed the people of his day that the world was bigger than they thought.

I soon came to look upon the plastic tablecloths filling the living room as sails, especially when I aired the room and the sheets flapped gently in the draught. I was not in Hegdehaugsveien at all, I was on board my *Victoria*, the only one of Magellan's ships to make it home. Magellan sailed round the Earth. I wished to sail round, to encircle reality. When I read those layers upon layers of words, I felt a breeze blowing inside me, or rather, I felt as if something were being opened up, as if I were about to acquire more of that profound insight of which, all my life, I had known myself to possess only a subset. Meanwhile, the work, the thinking, was taking its toll on me. It is said that while crossing the Pacific Magellan's men lived on worm-eaten biscuits and dirty, foul-smelling water, before they took to eating rats and sawdust, and chewing hide ripped off the timbers. During the Pacific Ocean phase of the Project I led an equally spartan, if not quite so drastic existence. Leonard's Italian cuisine was a thing of the past. If I did get round to eating anything, I tended to fall back on Spaghetti à la Capri, which I did not even bother to warm, just spooned straight from the tin. It reminded me of my childhood, when the only provisions we needed for a walk in the forest was a stock cube to lick.

The actual crossing of 'il Pacifico', a totally unknown area, was Magellan's greatest achievement. They thought it would only take a few days to sail from the New World, America, to the Moluccas, the centre of the oriental spice trade, instead it took almost four months. Magellan could almost be said to have discovered the Pacific, its vast scale. I too wanted to find something like that: an unknown, or underestimated sea. In selecting the main classes for my new system I gave priority to those subjects pertaining to the mind or things immaterial. I aimed to disentangle a hidden, as yet unrealised, meaning from the world. Fold out reality. A few of today's particle physicists maintain that we can have no conception of the greater part of the universe simply because it is comprised of a form of matter so essentially different from anything we can imagine. I know it sounds strange, not to say crazy, but I believe that during the most transparent phases of my Project I was on the track of something like that.

Once, I was waiting for Margrete outside a cinema. She took a taxi from work. I observed her through the dark, tinted window as she was paying the driver. I could only just make out her face. The thought struck me that she was trapped inside a black crystal. That I would never be able to break through to her.

The longer I stayed in that room, among those transparent panels covered in writing, the more the feeling I had had ever since studying the spider's web was confirmed – a hunch which was reinforced by the notion of circumnavigating the world: I ought to arrange the subjects in a circle. Like a wheel.

I reorganised the room. This time I hung the sheets in concentric rings. And the first time I sat down on a chair in the centre and scanned the headings of the subjects and the classes surrounding me, receding layers of script, words forming sentences of sorts, spokes radiating to an outer rim, I sensed what a tremendous boost this gave to my thinking. Everything seemed to explode. I saw patterns of breathtaking beauty. I glimpsed concepts, totally new sciences, with names as yet unuttered by any human being. I caught flashes of solutions in which everything interlocked – not by dint of thousands of tiny gear-wheels, but with all the categories mixed up in such a way that gear-wheels meshed with butterfly wings and crystals, the whole thing encircled by elementary particles. I was thrilled, but I was also startled. The plastic tablecloths seemed to glow. For some time I felt that I was on the threshold of a breakthrough which would have incalculable consequences, that I was all set to make a magnificent contribution to civilisation. There I was: friendless, gaunt, dead-beat, but I truly *had* created a chandelier of knowledge, three-dimensional, something that could be considered from all sides, with every piece hanging in its rightful place in relation to the others, not packed in boxes and tucked away singly on shelves. At my most audacious moments I felt I was on the scent of something comparable in importance to the alphabet, something which would enable us to form new concepts; an instrument by which mankind could steer, one which could give progress a hefty, and most timely, nudge.

During those first weeks, when we spent more time in bed than out of it, I told Margrete about my endeavours, about the project which I had, by then, abandoned. She got a big laugh out of my descriptions of this, laughed heartily and sincerely, as if it really was a priceless joke. But she caressed me too, as if to console me; she ran a finger wonderingly over the double scar I have over one eyebrow: 'Hey ... you've got an "X" on your forehead,' she whispered. That was all she said, but I ought to have known what she meant.

And then I met my Silapulapu. Silapulapu was the chief of the natives who killed Magellan on the little island of Mactan. On the threshold of his great triumph, almost at the very moment of victory, Magellan was run through by spears. And that is pretty much what happened to me.

I woke one morning with an awful sinking feeling in my stomach and a bitter taste in my mouth. I leapt out of bed and ran, stark naked, straight into the centre of my circle. It was all just a blur. I stared at the transparent plastic sheets covered in writing, only once again to see nothing but chaos. I tried to regain my clarity of vision, but everything was just grey. *Māyā*, I murmured under my breath. Everything was *māyā*. I spent the whole day wandering around in a daze, staring, reading, thinking. My eyes hurt, my head hurt, I felt sick from exhaustion, from hunger, from lack of sleep. I was still naked when I climbed into bed that night.

I ought probably to repudiate my grotesque project, make fun of it. And yet I have to admit that I look back on those years with something akin to respect. It may have been a ridiculous venture, but it was beautiful. And who knows, maybe, for a second or two, I actually was only millimetres away from a Pacific Ocean discovery.

I stuck at it, almost in spite of myself, for another few weeks, hung up still more closely-written plastic sheets at different points around the circles. All in vain. Nor was my base at the College of Architecture of any use to me now, my studies of the construction and design of some of the world's most audacious buildings: the Guggenheim Museum in New York, the Opera House in Sydney, the Parliament Buildings in Brasilia. I had an idea that the problem lay in the number of main classes. I would have to prune them, single out those which I felt might function in the same way as the spider's anchor points for the first foundation threads. I thought of Francis Bacon who had managed with just three categories: Memory, Imagination, Reason.

Eventually, almost dropping with exhaustion and possibly inspired by Uncle Melankton's attempt to reduce the Encyclopedia Brittanica to a single word, I managed to gather everything under two headings: Matter and Mind. Then: Living and Dead. And finally just one: Storytelling. This single main class could thereafter be split up into subdivisions consisting of bigger and bigger lies.

I gave up. It was – and I say this even when looking at it with today's eyes – the greatest defeat of my life. Or the second greatest. My only comfort was that my shipwreck had been a private affair. No one ever learned of it. I held my peace and went to work in television. I suppose I could say: with Story-telling. Lies. When they showed me the studio, the little cubicle from which I was to do my announcing, in my extraordinary naivety I thought to myself: this could be the perfect hiding place. I did not know that television was a medium within which a fool could be taken for a wonder.

I had one little ray of hope, though. On that day when I found *Le petit prince* by Saint-Exupéry on the Deichman's well-organised shelves, Karen Mohr opened the book and read a sentence aloud to me in exquisite French and then translated it: 'It is only with the heart that once can see rightly; what is essential is invisible to the eye.' I did not think about it at the time, but I thought about it when I abandoned my Project X: maybe it was not my eyes, nor even my brain that I should be training, concentrating on, if I was to discover something new, but my heart.

I reached this insight at about the same time that I met Margrete again. All of the subject headings in the world, all of Melvil Dewey's thousands of sections, flowed smoothly into one: Love. And who knows, perhaps it was those crazy hypotheses which gave wind to Margrete's sails and caused her to set course for Norway once more. She certainly told me that for a long time she had considered settling down somewhere else. But then she had been overcome by an uncontrollable and inexplicable urge to go home.

And now, ten years later, I was standing facing this same woman. And yet even after ten years and thousands of experiences of love I could not understand why she should suddenly seem so hostile; why, towards the end of a confused conversation, she should have worried so much at the necklace that the string snapped.

Pearls sprayed everywhere, went tumbling to the floor. The sound triggered a memory from my childhood: I had knocked a bag of peas out of the cupboard as I tried to sneak a handful of raisins. They made an incredibly complex sound, those peas. A *māyā* sound if ever there was one, layer upon layer of the same sound, in different nuances of tone. I can still recall the sight of it too, how *slowly* the pearls, which had suddenly acquired an even deeper sheen, fell through the dim lamplight in the living room, as if they were not falling, but drifting, floating downwards. I noticed how Margrete seemed to be trying to follow each individual pearl with her eyes, the course of each one, at the same time. As if her eyes were doing the splits. And since I was watching her more than the pearls, I saw how she, too, positively fell apart and tumbled to the floor, shattering into pieces that rolled off in all directions. She muttered something which I only grasped after she had muttered it several times: 'My life's thread has snapped.'

Then she simply walked out. Or at least, she turned in the doorway and said goodnight. She paid no mind to the pearls, it was as if they were now worthless, a currency which had fallen disastrously in value after a terrible crash – of a moral, not an economic, nature.

I felt I ought to pick them up. I crawled around the parquet floor on my hands and knees. I knew there were forty-six pearls; an increasingly tipsy Mrs Boeck had announced this fact often enough at the party earlier that evening. I hunted for all I was worth and when I counted them an hour later, in the middle of the night, I had forty-five. I have always had a suspicion that the missing pearl, that particular pearl, held a secret. Or that it was not a pearl I had lost, but Margrete.

Over the following days she never asked about the pearls. She seemed apathetic. Almost as if she were doped up. The black discs of her pupils put me in mind of a solar eclipse. She complained of headaches. And the nights were different. I would wake to find her lying sobbing. One night she screamed out loud, shook the bed-head like a child. As if she thought I was not there, that I had left her. Gently I got her to lie down again, speaking soothingly to her. Her head looked so small in the big bed, against the white bed linen. It reminded me of the minuscule portrait on the white wall in Uncle Lauritz's flat. I had had the same thought then as now: love was a massive map on which there was just one big white patch, an undiscovered land – all except for one small face.

I returned the pearls to her one Sunday morning, at breakfast. Everything seemed normal enough – the orange juice which she had squeezed herself, English marmalade and two exquisite flowers in a vase on the table. We were alone. I had had the necklace restrung, with knots between the pearls. And I had bought a new Akoya pearl, identical to the others. Margrete took the necklace and counted the pearls. Or no, she did not count them, she ran them through her fingers as she was saying something to me. She smiled. And then she began to cry. For joy, I thought. 'This one's new,' was all she said, her fingers around one pearl, the third from the loop side of the clasp. The jeweller had shown me where he had put the pearl I had bought. 'One of the original pearls is gone,' she said.

She could tell by feel that it was a different pearl. She could *see* with her hands. She could sense that I had been with another woman in Lisbon. She could run her fingers over me, over my penis and know right away that it was no longer the same. This was an intelligence beyond my ken. Margrete could not only read books, she could read the temperature of the skin, the light in the eyes, the taste of the lips, the body's secretions.

I confessed. Or rather, I merely said: 'You're right, something did happen in Lisbon.' She put up a hand, a stop sign: 'I know,' she said. 'I know.' And yet, if she knew, why was it that only after this did I sometimes catch a new look in her eyes. Not jealousy. Her eyes told me that she was hurt. Humiliated. Or forsaken, lonely. That look said she knew she was not loved. That was what destroyed her. She became more and more quiet after that.

Can you kill a person by neglecting to think about them?

Sometimes I can delude myself into believing that I gave up on love back at the point when I abandoned Project X. After all, if I stopped believing it was possible to arrive at a unified whole, then I also stopped believing in love.

Not long after this evening I found a scalpel in our bed. I was making the bed, and there, between the two single mattresses, lay a scalpel, a chillingly sharp surgical instrument, a lethal weapon in the hands of an expert. Like a sword laid between us. When I asked her about it she made light of it, she must have dropped it, was all she said, she used it to cut the pages of the occasional Danish book. I couldn't help wondering, though. She was a doctor. I felt scared. Slept with my hands under the duvet.

The next few weeks were marked by Margrete's baffling behaviour: fits of rage, emotional outbursts over the slightest thing, bouts of weeping. She cried so much that she made me feel as if I had thrown sulphuric acid in her face, her features were so altered, the flesh looked ready to slip right off the bones. Then came a period when she simply seemed lost, sad. Engulfed by darkness. Occasionally I would find her sitting dead still in a chair, with unhappiness written all over her. She looked as though she was trying to do a very easy jigsaw puzzle, one with only six or seven big pieces, but could not even manage that much. 'Buck up,' I told her one day, quite sharply. If only I had known.

Now and again, when I tried to talk to her, to get through to her, I was reminded of when I was a teenager, hunkered down in front of the radio, fingers delicately searching out the music stations on the medium waveband. Still I did not seriously begin to worry about her until near the end of this phase, which culminated during a Christmas holiday when she seemed apathetic. Blank, I would say. It was clearly all she could do just to exist. She shuffled around her own house as if she did not even know that this was where she lived. I did not realise how bad things were, though, until there were no longer flowers on the breakfast table, no freshly ground coffee, no orange juice which she had squeezed herself. The gold glint in her eyes was gone. I could not help thinking of granite. She seemed hard through and through. Not *like* stone. She *was* stone.

Even so, and I am not trying to defend myself here: she did not stay off work and I never saw any sign of Kristin being affected by it.

Could I have done more? I told myself there was nothing I *could* do. With hindsight I would say I could not be *bothered* doing anything. And anyway, I had had my alibi well thought-out long before this: I was so busy; I was working day and night on my masterpiece, my big television series.

I could not even say for certain how many months – years? – this thing that I called her 'problem' lasted. And then, although I did not actually notice the transition, she was, to all intents and purposes, her old self again, recognisable for that vibrant, reckless beauty. I believed, I *wanted* to believe, that everything was okay. Things between us were still a little strained, that was all. War cleanses, as Karl Marx said, but when at last she kissed me again, I felt as though there was a pane of glass between our lips. As if I was already in a prison and she was there to see me, in one of those visiting rooms you see in American films.

Most dreadful of all: her virtual absence of sexual appetite and non-existent orgasms moved me, at one point, to accuse her of having taken a lover. Margrete took me to Xi'an in China. It was like a second honeymoon. For some months I hoped that everything was going to be the same as before, including our love life. But then we lapsed back into our old ruts, circles that never touched.

One night I came upon her standing in the dark kitchen with the fridge door wide open, her face lit by the stark light from inside. I thought she must be feeling peckish, looking for something to eat, but she just stood there like that; stood there for five minutes, ten minutes, stood with her face coloured by that white light, in the way too big T-shirt she wore as a nightie, gazing into the fridge. She reminded me of a pearl. Exquisite, but impenetrable to the eye, hiding its nature under layer upon layer of opacity. In the end I had to speak to her. She did not wake up, but turned slowly to face me. Leaned against me. Her face was cold in the hollow of my throat.

I thought I tried. I did ask her now and again. Asked what was wrong. Asked if there was anything I could do. Questions I had been honing for a long time. She did not answer. Or, again: I *thought* she did not answer. I felt as though we were back in the old situation outside the Golden Elephant, in seventh grade. 'Idiot,' she had answered back then. She seemed to be saying the same thing to me now: 'You're an idiot,' she said wordlessly. 'You're an ignoramus.'

There you have it, my life in a nutshell: I was a wonder who contented himself with being an idiot.

One reason why I chose to study astrophysics while I was working on Project X was that it allowed me to work with the largest possible scale, with a perspective in which the word billion kept cropping up and mankind was an incidental glimmer of light in an atom on the outskirts of a grain of sand called the Milky Way. Nevertheless, at one weary moment when, to distract my thoughts, I opened my textbook for A101, the foundation course in astronomy, I found that the first chapter dealt with the Earth. Maybe Margrete was right. Maybe there was no greater Magellanic prospect than that of embracing another human being.

Very occasionally I could still be woken in the night by her crying. I would reach out a hand to her. I knew it was no use. But now and again, even so, I would catch myself holding my breath, as if my body, independent of my brain, was making a last attempt to save her.

One night she said: 'Why do you lie with your back to me?'

I said: 'You don't hold me.'

Love and time. In my mind I sometimes picture love as being like those charts in the ophthalmologist's office on which the letters get smaller and smaller, harder and harder to read, no matter how good your eyesight is. Until at last there is nothing but meaningless symbols.

As if to show me that she regarded my arrangement with the knots as a contemptible joke, false security, she never wore that string of pearls again. The evening when I came home from Seville and found her dead I could not help thinking that she had done it at last: broken the thread, the strand of her own life. I had not understood a single thing.

I looked down at her, lying there in the middle of the room, surrounded by walls lined with bookshelves. I could practically see plastic tablecloths covered in writing fluttering, ring upon ring, around me. This, Margrete dead on the floor was a true reorganisation of all knowledge. I saw now what I had lacked in my Project X: a person at the centre. A person who was someone other than myself.

After this I stumbled about a house in which Margrete's blood was congealing all around her. I was sure I was going to come unstuck. When I finally raised the alarm and the police arrived, I collapsed. They looked after me. I was taken to hospital, but the very next afternoon I presented myself at Grønland police station to make my statement. I did not say too much, I did not say too little. I told them how I had found her, why I had not picked up the phone right away, and every now and again – very carefully and with a clear-sightedness so cold-blooded that I have to wonder where it came from – I fed them the details which, in due course, would inevitably point back to me.

I had managed to do everything I needed to do before I called the police. I knew the house would be sealed off. If there were any incontrovertible clues pointing to Margrete's own hand and not to mine, I had to find them.

Wearing thin gloves, I embarked upon a methodical, not to say surgical, examination of the house, room by room. I was grief-stricken, in turmoil, but I was also filled with another emotion, one that surprised me: curiosity. I went over my own house like a detective. I looked, listened, turned things this way and that, half purposeful, half stupefied. Her scent, that indescribable scent, still hung in every room. Even in prison, years afterwards, that scent could reach me, in spring especially, a breath on the air, as if the whole world were suddenly exuding the odour of Margrete.

I staggered around the house. Searching. And I found things. A string of pearls fraught with memories. Books in Sanskrit. But first and foremost I discovered how she had managed to conceal how things stood with her. A systematic search of her things eventually turned up an empty box for the sort of pills she must have swallowed by the score over the past few years. It was dated six months earlier. It was a drug I knew of, one of the most popular anti-depressants on the market. She had prescribed it for herself. I had to admire her ingenuity. All tracks covered. Not a single colleague informed. She had never had a nervous breakdown. Her women friends had had no idea, or not, at any rate, of how serious it was, there were plenty of them who would have warned me had they known. I had noticed that there were spells when she spent a lot of time in bed, but I simply assumed it was the job that wore her out, she needed to sleep. As I say, only once did I really feel worried, in the days after the Lisbon episode. Then suddenly she was back to normal. That must have been when she started treating herself.

I knew I had to get rid of the box. I do not know why, but I ate the label bearing the words 'Ad usum proprium' and, underneath this, her name. Then I disposed of the box in a watertight manner.

I will never be able to describe those terrible days. But amid all the commotion, while the newspapers were floating theory after theory, each one more sensational than the one before; while they were reporting what people felt, thought, said, I was simply happy that I did not appear to have forgotten anything. The police investigators found only what I wanted them to find. And so I waited. Waited patiently for the police to do what they had to do. Waited for the net which I myself had spun – a web worthy of a cross spider – to slowly tighten around me.

At the very end of my Project X period, during the days when everything suddenly went black, I took a shower one evening, in the hope that this might help clear my thoughts. Afterwards I went back into the living room, still wet and naked, to take one last, desperate look at my circles of headings covering all the world's knowledge; and because it was still nothing but a haze of words floating on transparent plastic panels, desperation got the better of me. I felt so frustrated that I started tearing at the sheet closest to me, almost as if I refused to give in without one last fight. The sheet came loose and as it did so I slipped, grabbed for something to hold onto and succeeded only in dragging a whole lot of other plastic panels down with me. I crashed to the floor, embroiled in layers of transparent plastic covered in writing. I was encased in a cocoon spun from my own bewildering, abstract attempts to classify the world. I was so mad that I actually burst out laughing.

When I managed to disentangle myself I found that the writing had transferred itself to my damp body. My skin was covered in black fragments, obscure symbols, like an intricate tattoo. For two days I just lay in bed moping.

Not all that long after this episode I was lying in another, a new, world, next to Margrete in the bed in Ullevål Garden City. When she ran her fingers over my body, her fingertips seeming to read the last traces of lettering on my skin, it also felt as though she was stroking a defeat off me, as if she were unravelling me from that cocoon, setting me free.

She stroked my back and I wanted nothing more than to be able to lie there, for ever, next to a woman who caressed my skin with her fingers. Margrete inscribed other, unseen symbols on my body, inscribed new patterns on my skin with a fingernail. She had a sensitivity of touch which I told myself must derive from her work as a doctor. I, who had been driven by that possibly quite ridiculous ambition: to make a mark, work in depth, to leave behind me an inscription that would last for ever – I lay there beside a woman, wanting nothing but to have marks left on me, and they did not need to be any deeper than the almost invisible patterns made by a fingernail on the board of my back.

I found something else on that night I spent in the house with Margrete and her shot-blasted heart. On a bookshelf. Which was only logical, really. I had always been fascinated by the challenge which a bookshelf represented.

At some point I came to the bookcases in the living room, bookcases which held Margrete's novels, bookcases I never looked at; to me they were just so much wallpaper, a pattern I was used to. It was a paradox, of course, a thought which sometimes gave me pause, but which I would promptly dismiss: that I, who had almost driven myself crazy, battling with classification systems, with the question of how to organise all the world's books and knowledge, had read so little.

Was this my real sin? That I did not read?

I do not know what had brought me there, but I must have had an intuition that somewhere in this particular wall there was a secret door, and as I stood there pondering, muttering the occasional title under my breath, like a mantra, I spied a narrow spine, right in front of me, at eye level and when I stepped up and pulled out this book I saw that it was the little novel which Margrete had given me in sixth grade, as a thank-you for diving down and finding her mother's gold bracelet: *Victoria* by Knut Hamsun. I vaguely remembered having packed it with the rest of my belongings each time I moved, it being one of the few books I owned. I also remembered putting it on this shelf when we moved into Villa Wergeland. And I had duly forgotten it, never so much as noticed it among the spines of all Margrete's other novels, whose numbers grew steadily over the years, as if the shelves caused the books to multiply of their own accord. This, I thought; this is the pearl I never found.

And then, when I opened the book for the first time since receiving it, I discovered a number of flimsy sheets of paper tucked in between the pages. And discovered truly is the word – I should perhaps call this the great discovery of my life. Because, on the first of these tissue-thin sheets, which I recognised right away as the same writing paper that Margrete used for letters to friends abroad, I read my own name; it was a letter, a letter from Margrete, written in her uncommonly beautiful hand, a string of words which I would come to know by heart. I glanced at the other sheets of paper. More letters. All to me. Twenty-odd epistles. And when I read that first letter, after only the first few lines – that was when I cracked. I collapsed, quite literally, in a heap, clutching that little love story, as if it was the one tiny twig which could save me, and I felt the pressure behind my eyes, the ache in my throat, and I burst into tears, I wept as I had never wept before, wept for the first time since arriving home, as if this discovery was actually more shocking than the discovery of her dead body; I wept for so long that I lost all track of time. I did not deserve to live. Of all the blind men walking the Earth, I was the blindest.

'15.10.87. How well I remember your heart-rending "Why?" outside the Golden Elephant, and time and again since then you have asked me why I broke up with you so abruptly and so heartlessly that winter when we were in seventh grade. To answer you: it was not, of course, because I was leaving the country. I broke it off because I realised that you had never opened the book I gave you. I decided that you were not worthy. Even back then I loved to read, probably more than other kids of my age, and this story, *Victoria*, had made an indelible impression on me. I wanted to give you my most prized possession. I knew that not many boys read fiction, but I thought you would give it a try. For my sake. I also believed that this book might tell you something about me, and maybe also about the love we felt for one another – if one can talk in terms of love at such a young age. It might even, I thought, give you some warning of the obstacles that might lie in our path. I took it for granted that you would at least look at it, and at the notes I had written in the margins, partly for your benefit, your eyes. I was *sure* you were that curious. About me. I cannot tell you how shocked I was when I asked you a question at the ice rink – and knew from your reply that not once, in over a year, had you so much as opened that book. I simply could not understand it. A girl gives a novel, a love story, the best thing she can think of, to a boy and he does not even open it. Such an insult – such insensitivity – I couldn't bear it. I asked myself: Can I possibly go out with a boy like that? You know what the answer was. Just at that moment I was positive that I would never speak to you or see you again.'

On the first page of the novel was a dedication: 'To Jonas'. I also came upon the little notes in the margins, written in a legible, girlish hand. This book had been there all along. Right under my nose. I noticed that all of the letters dated from the last few years and that the first had been written shortly after my fateful decision in Lisbon. I had been so annoyed by the fact that she had not answered the questions I asked her, but she *had* answered them. And it was so like her not to be able to say it, or not to *want* to say it, but to put it in writing. The answers were here, in blue and white, right in front of me. In a place so obvious that I had not seen them. I remembered this same phenomenon from Hunt the Thimble. Things were always hardest to find when they were staring you in the face.

A week later, when the police were finished examining the scene and I was able to move back into the house, the first thing I did was to go to the bookcase and take out *Victoria*. I could tell that nothing here had been touched. Even the forensic team, for all their thoroughness, had not found the letters. It was meagre comfort.

My self-loathing has never been greater than during the months following these discoveries. Why had I not been able to persuade Margrete that life was worth living? Why did she not tell me she was in torment? Because she knew I would not understand? Did not *want* to understand? What made her stop taking the pills? I ate my heart out; ate my heart out, day after day.

And yet: I knew. I had always had some inkling of it. But she had really seemed to be in good form, especially just after the *Thinking Big* series was screened, and so I lulled myself into the illusion that I had closed a circle, succeeded in becoming a lifesaver, realised my childhood dream through my work in television. When she died I knew that I had failed in everything, even my television series.

The guilt was almost too much to bear. When at long last, towards the end of the court case, I felt that the time was right to confess, I meant it with all of my heart when I said: 'Then I aimed the gun at my wife and executed her.'

That evening, that night, in the living room, bending over Margrete, with a slim volume in my hands, I knew that only one thing could save me. A word was running around inside my head, a word which had haunted me for a long time and which I had first encountered, or actually felt on my person, as if the word were actually physical, once when I was kneeling on a soft hassock at the altar rail in Grorud Church. I was in the same position as I had assumed during my confirmation the year before. Dad had gone, had asked me to latch the door behind me. I was alone. I was – what? I was devastated.

Then that word crossed my mind. A word I remembered. A word I had contemplated more than once, but had never dared to utter. I spoke this word. Kneeling at the altar in Grorud Church I said it out loud. For the first time in my life. And instantly … I do not know whether I heard the rush of wings. I do not know whether I sensed the presence of some divine being. I do not know whether I really *saw* one of the angels depicted on the fresco behind the altar. I only know that a sighing filled my head and my body. I only know that a breeze blew inside me. I only know that I thought of wings. And that something embraced me. Held me.

I let myself out of the church. Christmas was just around the corner. The air was thick with snowflakes, so light that they danced, swirled upwards. They looked not so much like snow as a dense swarm of tiny white butterflies. I felt as light, as full of dance, as those lovely flakes.

I knew everything would be alright. I was breathing differently. I knew I would meet Laila. And meet her I did, down at the shopping centre. She was standing outside the ironmonger's, looking in the window, bareheaded and wearing a thick, white woollen sweater. I called out and for the first time in ages she turned to face me. Snowflakes lay like white flowers on her hair. I had been going to say something, but when she looked round I realised that I did not need to say anything; something in my voice when I called her name may have told her everything anyway. What mattered was that she looked round. After so many wretched weeks she turned to me and smiled. The old smile. 'Hey, Jonas, come and see this fabulous crystal bowl, you can see rainbows in it.' I knew this was an invitation. Nothing had been forgotten. But we could start afresh. She tilted her face to the snowflakes, caught some on her tongue. Even though we were in the middle of the centre and even though Laila was Laila, I walked right up to her, put my arm round her and whispered something in her ear. It sounded, I hoped, like 'Thanks.' I went into the shop and bought the bowl for her. Not for the past, but for the future. 'A Christmas present,' I said. She gave me a hug. She was happy. Stood there with snowflakes, little stars, in her long hair, beaming. When Laila was happy no one was as happy as her.

It all began earlier that autumn. Laila was 'a bit different' as Mrs Five-Times Nilsen put it. I always had the feeling that she must have experienced something which other people rarely experienced. She was a couple of years older than me and lived in a rather seedy-looking Swiss-style villa up the road from the housing estate where I grew up. There were panes of coloured glass in the windows surrounding the veranda, but some of them were broken. For some reason I suspected Laila of having done this herself.

Laila was pretty. Pretty in a wild sort of way. And very well-developed, as they said. 'She looks tarty,' Wolfgang Michaelsen whispered. But I thought there was something exotic about her. She went barefoot all summer. To the boys, particularly those in the throes of puberty, she was the object of masturbatory fantasies and of contempt. Laila's name cropped up regularly in sentences scrawled on walls and the sides of substations. There was something about her blatant sexuality, her lack of self-consciousness which was both appealing and daunting. I did not know why, but she had always liked me, often sought my company, would happily fall in beside me if we happened to meet. I liked her too. When she looked at me she really *looked* at me. She looked at me in a way which filled me with wonder.

One day, one autumn day, I asked her if she would like to come to the church with me. I asked her on the spur of the moment. We could listen to my dad playing the organ, I said, and she could see the new stained-glass windows, how lovely they were when the light shone through them. Once inside the church, however, I realised that I had lured her there under false pretences. I pointed hastily at the coloured panes of glass, like larger versions of the windows around her veranda at home. We all but sidled round the walls of the church and I drew her into the sacristy. I think she knew what was going to happen. Or what I was expecting that she would permit to happen.

We were in a room reserved for 'sacred objects'. The church silver was kept in a big safe in the corner. Even in here the organ music could be heard quite clearly. I do not know whether I had actually planned it, but now that we were alone, seeing her standing right there in front of me, I was seized with a powerful urge to see her naked. Or, to see *it*. My head felt light, my breathing was weak. It was like an attack of some sort. Maybe she really was feebleminded, and now her feebleness had been transmitted to my brain, my lungs. Something took control of me, something that spoke, asked her brusquely to take off her clothes. 'Only if you promise not to touch,' she said, did not seem frightened, did not seem unwilling. I nodded. Something inside me nodded. 'Just look,' she repeated. I nodded. My whole body was one throbbing pulse. 'Hurry up,' I heard a husky, unrecognisable voice say. She hurried up and suddenly there she stood, stark naked. I asked her to position herself up against the door leading to the pulpit, with her arms outstretched. It sounded like a command. She had hair under her arms, masses of hair under her arms – along with the black frizz between her legs these tufts of hair formed a triangle. Next to the door hung a crucifix. On the other wall hung pictures of former vicars. The thought that somebody might walk in, unlikely though it was, rendered the situation even more titillating.

She slid down onto the floor, as if she were a bit embarrassed. I was surprised by how much hair there was around her crotch, a real bush. I asked her to spread her legs. No, she said. Gone was her usual saucy air. Please, I said. Or did it come out as a command? Husky-voiced. She complied, but with her eyes lowered. So it was here, in a church sacristy, that I saw a cunt, for the first time. I say cunt, because I was thinking of Uncle Melankton. Until now the closest I had come to this mystery had been when Daniel showed me something which he claimed was a wisp of Anne Beate Corneliussen's pubic hair. But here I was, looking at the female genitals in all their glory and prosaic majesty. And despite the fact that we boys had discussed all the ins and outs of this subject, and despite all the relatively innocent 'dirty pictures' which we had pored over, I was quite taken aback by the sight that met my eyes when Laila spread her legs for me, opening a safe, so to speak, and presenting the sacred objects.

Later I learned that John Ruskin, the famous aesthete, recoiled in horror when he discovered that the female pudenda were covered in hair, something for which the statues of antiquity had not prepared him. I was not that naive. But still I had to swallow, almost gagging, not because of the luxuriant growth of hair, rather like a swatch of shag pile, but at what lay underneath. Daniel, who had once seen a Swedish porn mag with pictures of a woman showing 'the lot', called it the Inlying Valleys. That triangle of hair was simply there to distract the attention from something far more interesting. And startling. The thought that came into my mind was of something *raw*. Raw meat. It looked as though she had a hundred grams of rare roast beef stuffed up inside that crack. I was filled with the same warring emotions as a squeamish medical student before his first dissection. It looked both enticing and repulsive. I had not expected there to be such long fissures. A great gorge with lots of side crevasses. I was panting with impatience, desperate to explore it. I firmly believe that for a few seconds there I saw before me a Samarkand, a place I had always dreamt of going.

I had promised not to touch her, but I could not control myself. My body felt swollen with desire. My head swam, as if this crack I beheld truly was the mouth of an abyss. I heard organ music playing in the church, but it seemed to fade away as I stuck my finger inside her, tried to stick a finger in, forced it in; she did not stop me, my body was numb, my mouth dry, I began to slide my finger, my hand, back and forth, unrestrainedly, knew I was hurting her but could not stop myself. Everything went black. I was brought to my senses by her stopping me. Firmly. I did not get it. According to the rumours, she had done it with everything from smoked sausages to gearsticks.

She sat before me, her back against the door to the pulpit. Still staring at the floor. I could hear the organ music again. And that she was crying.

A couple of days later the awful news reached my ears: someone had broken the stained-glass windows in the church. Thrown stones at them. It is hard to describe the shock and horror aroused by this. In local terms it was like the crime of the century. Who had done it? Who *could* have done such a despicable thing? By Grorud standards this was an act of vandalism on a par with that committed in Rome some years later, when a man knocked the arm off the Madonna in Michelangelo's *Pietà* with a hammer. Ivan, who was for a long time a suspect, had an alibi. No one knew who had done it. But I knew. You might even say I did it myself.

Over the following weeks I tried everything to get Laila to talk to me again. None of it did any good. Sorry, I whispered, every time I came within earshot of her. But Laila would have nothing to do with me. Not only that, but she looked so woebegone, dejected. People remarked on it. What's wrong with Laila, they said. Laila who was always so blithe and cheery. If I tried walking alongside her, she would stop, turn her back on me, or run away. That was the worst part: the way she turned her face away. That she would no longer look at me. Look at me as no one else looked at me.

Only one thing could help me. Or, why not: save me. So I waited. Waited to be forgiven, although I did not deserve it. I waited, hoping she would be magnanimous. That she would look at me again.

And at long last it happened, just before Christmas, but only after I had had a foretaste of it in the church, on my knees in that chamber next door to the sacristy, as I said a word out loud. When I embraced Laila in the snow outside the ironmonger's, it was like an echo of an embrace I myself had felt.

As I knelt at the altar rail, in the minutes preceding my decision to utter that word, I thought of a milestone in my life, an incident which had occurred at Solhaug some years earlier. We had been playing rounders, a simplified version of baseball, on the flag green. One of the boys on the estate, Rikard, was a brilliant hitter. It was the same story again and again: when everybody else had struck out and desperation was setting in, Rikard would step up and save the day with a real cracker of a hit, one which allowed them all to run right round before the other team could get to the ball.

One Saturday afternoon something quite remarkable happened. I was fielding, standing ready by the flagpole, from which the handsome estate pennant fluttered lazily in the breeze, so I had a front-row seat, as it were, for the events that unfolded. The whole batting team was hopping up and down on the line as usual, waiting for Rikard, the last man in, to hit a sixer and get them out of trouble. Rikard strode up to the wicket armed with his dreaded bat. In woodwork, while the rest of us were toiling over stupid herons with beaks that were forever snapping off, Rikard was surehandedly turning a baseball bat that would have elicited appreciative nods from any craftsman. It was a particularly long, heavy bat, perfect for getting some extra spin on the ball. Rikard hit the ball, gave it such a phenomenal whack that it let out a deep sigh – a tennis-ball orgasm, a gasp at being hit so perfectly, at being launched into such a ballistic dream of a trajectory. It was the sort of strike known in baseball as a 'home run', the sort of strike that sent the ball flying right out of the park, or smashing into floodlights in a shower of sparks, the sort of strike that brought the crowd leaping to their feet with a roar.

There was only one thing wrong with this hit. It went too far. Because, down at the garages – where he spent pretty much all of his free time – Major Otto Ness was polishing his pride and joy, a black Opel Captain purchased the year before. The care which Major Ness lavished on his car foreshadowed, in fact, the worship of material possessions which the whole of Norwegian society was moving towards, a development which, in just a couple of decades, would take them from tree-planting and community parties to each man polishing his own car and scowling enviously at his neighbours. The Major had just completed the day's beauty treatment, and was surveying his car with the same look of satisfaction he would have given a gleaming army boot. Major Ness – known to us, despite his spit-and-polish exterior, as Major Mess – was on the short side, to say the least of it: a right little runt. It was so funny to see him driving home with his head, or at least his uniform cap, barely visible, and his hands clutching, not to say straining at, the steering wheel, like a major trying with great difficulty to control his captain. No less comical was the sight of him walking alongside his wife, who was a head taller than her officer. But his vehicle, the Opel, was most definitely among the top brass of Solhaug's relatively modest fleet of cars – in the Major's own eyes it raised him to the rank of estate general; it made up for an outsize nag of a wife and a disappointing career in which he had ended up behind a desk, and not behind the guns. That car was his battleship, his tank, his command centre, from which he could rule the world. So, as far as he was concerned it was an open insult, a pure act of aggression, when a tennis ball, hit by Rikard, bounced defiantly on the ground once before thumping, not all that hard, but quite audibly, off the bonnet of Major Ness's Opel Captain. With a magnifying glass one might have been able to spot a tiny mark. But in the Major's world this was tantamount to vandalism of the worst sort, a downright declaration of war, in fact.

Major Ness reacted as he was wont to do. In a voice which was surprisingly loud and clear for such a puny little body he demanded to know who had hit that ball. And since he made it sound like a command, Rikard trailed all the long way across the green and down to the garages, where Major Ness pointed first at the ball, then at the car and thereafter, as if it were the natural conclusion, gave Rikard a belt round the ear, *smack*, which I heard all the way up by the flagpole – a 'home run' of a slap, you might say.

The Major had, however, committed one tactical error. His indignation had blinded him to everything else around him. But he had been seen. From above. From one of the second-floor balconies in the block of flats overlooking the flag green Rikard's father, Mr Bastesen, had been a spectator – or perhaps one should say acted as umpire – to the whole thing. In a remarkably short space of time Rikard's dad was out of the house and heading across the green towards the garages, and he did not come alone: on his way he picked up his son's legendary baseball bat, decorated in time-honoured fashion with a branding iron in the Grorud School woodwork room. On his face, one of the blackest looks I can ever recall seeing. I would not call it anger. I would call it *wrath*.

Mr Bastesen was definitely not a man to be meddled with. Not only was he the caretaker at Solhaug, a person with whom it was best to stay on good terms, he was also a big, burly character who – we knew – lifted weights in the shed where the estate's communal tools and equipment were kept. To us kids he was a fearsome figure, especially when marching back and forth across the greens behind a roaring lawnmower with tractor wheels. Or in the spring when he put out signs saying 'Do not walk on the grass!' On the other hand, like a beneficent god he was also quite liable to let us play in the sprinklers on hot summer days. There was some talk of a background in petty crime, whispers of jail sentences and a dodgy past as a bouncer at one of Oslo's shadiest nightspots. And now here he was, large and menacing, descending – on tractor wheels, you might say – upon the garages, with one hand curled around a sturdy baseball bat which could beat the living daylights out of anything, no question, and everybody could see that he was positively seething with wrath over a crime of a far more serious nature than walking on the grass. I could not help thinking that Major Ness really was in a major mess now.

We who witnessed this episode, the boys at least, knew what was going to happen next. Justice, it was called. You could say that our hearts sang in our breasts when we saw Mr Bastesen striding purposefully across the green with the heavy baseball bat, duly decorated, already half raised. Justice was to be done and no one could say a thing against it, because such was the law, among boys at any rate, and despite all our Sunday School lessons. An eye for an eye, a tooth for a tooth. Simple and straightforward. When Roar pinched Guggen's bike, crashed it and smashed his new wing mirror, Guggen's big brother went straight over and smashed the headlight on Roar's bike. That was how it worked.

But everybody also knew that, for all the rumours, Mr Bastesen would never dream of hurting anyone, and certainly not a little runt like Major Ness, who was now basically shaking in his shoes; in the hand he held out, a wisp of cotton waste, like a gift, an olive branch. Or was he perhaps offering Mr Bastesen the divine pleasure of polishing an Opel Captain for a few minutes? He seemed to me to cave in on himself, to shrink still further. But Mr Bastesen was making straight for the car, the Major's pride and joy, his black pearl, and Major Ness must have realised that Bastesen, a man of no education – and quite possibly no cultivation – would not think twice about bashing in the bodywork of this status symbol, this car which, to the Major, was proof that he was not, after all, a complete failure.

The Major, who must have been envisaging the worst of all possible nightmares, a wrecked Captain, did the only thing he could think of, thus going totally against the grain of everything he had striven for in his profession: he went down on his knees – a rare sight for a child, that: a grown man kneeling in the dirt. And as if that wasn't enough, way up beside the flagpole I heard the Major stammer: 'Mercy.' That was all, just one little word, and yet so hard for him to spit out: 'Mercy.'

And it worked. Mr Bastesen stopped short, with the baseball bat already hovering in mid-air, so to speak, ready to deliver the first devastating blow to the Opel's bonnet, a car-wrecker's 'home run'. He stopped, lowered the baseball bat, eyed both the Major and the car, the car again, and the Major again, and then he said, as he flicked a speck of dust off the hood: 'Okay. But don't you ever hit a kid again. I'm just telling you.'

I knew that I was witnessing something momentous. It took some time to penetrate with me. You could get out of being punished for doing something bad, a punishment which you fully deserved, if someone showed you mercy. This was a new and abhorrent concept. That such a thing was possible. That the laws of cause and effect could be broken. That what everyone expected to happen, did not.

And it was this word – bright, clear, lone – which kept rising to the surface, amid all the other chaotic thoughts in my head as I stood over Margrete on the evening when I found her dead. And I remember that I knelt on the floor, right next to her body and muttered it. Or tried to, vainly at first. The word seemed to offer physical resistance. I had to clear my throat again and again, brace myself before, finally, bringing myself to say it: 'Mercy,' I murmured. Again and again: 'Mercy. Mercy. Mercy.' And as soon as I said it I felt an ache in my chest again, as if the word were puncturing something inside me. To begin with I thought this pain might have been caused by the label which I had swallowed, the piece of paper with her name on it, but it felt more like a sort of pressure, as if something were growing inside me. I looked at the four butterflies which Margrete had caught as a child and which she had brought with her from Ullevål Garden City and hung in their frame on our living-room wall. I think – no, I know, that it was here, on my knees beside a dead wife, that my full potential began to unfold. Only then, during those seconds, did I begin to transcend my own boundaries.

The only right thing to do was to go to prison. There are few things of which I have been more certain. I was guilty. Had I had eyes, been able to talk, to listen, Margrete would not be dead.

You have no say in things in prison. You suffer a lot of indignities in prison. But none of this could compare with my overriding problem: myself. My own thoughts. In the early days I was also troubled by this discomfort in my chest. Like powerful growing pains. I thought it was my heart. That I was going to die. It took a while for it to dawn on me that it was my lungs.

What did I do in prison? I skipped. Occasionally I juggled with oranges. And I felt shame. Year after year, I felt shame. To me, prison was like being made to go and stand in the corner.

Sometimes I also think of those years behind bars as one long swim across dark, dark deeps, and I have the distinct impression that at one point I died. On the day that I walked out of prison I felt the way I had when I woke up on that beach in Sweden, after drowning in Sekken.

I assume that Kristin is writing, and will soon be finished, a book about me. She has asked me a lot of questions during this trip. I've noticed that after one of our conversations she settles herself in the saloon with her computer, reads through something, makes changes, inserts details. I have been happy to answer her questions. I have tried to tell the truth. But I know it will be as much of a lie as all the rest.

I am considering giving everything I have written on board the *Voyager* to Kristin. A lot of it was not included in my 'big' manuscript, which she was allowed to look at before I destroyed it. I am thinking, here, of the part about Margrete. I have a suspicion, though, that even as a child Kristin was aware of Margrete's problem, that she knew Margrete better than I did. Margrete's death came as a shock to everyone – apart from Kristin. She understood why her mother did not want to live any more. She would not believe that I had killed her. That much at least I gathered from the love and tenderness she showed me when she visited me in prison. I can never thank her enough for the fact that she did not say anything. Although she could not possibly have known my reasons. Or maybe she did, but kept quiet for my sake.

I know I should have sat down with her, told her everything. We should have talked it through. She was old enough by then. I could not do it. But she'll learn about it now anyway. I am slowly starting to see that all of this may well have been written for her. The irony is not lost on me. I am doing exactly what I accused Margrete of doing. I am writing instead of talking.

It is our last evening at Balestrand. Soon night. I am in bed. Kamala is sitting on the balcony with the door open. All is quiet. Only the lapping of the waves, the odd gull crying. I have lain here for a long while, pretending to be making notes, but all the time watching her. Admiring her. The evening is warm. Kamala is drinking in, insatiably so it seems, the panorama before her: looking across to Vik, to Vangsnes with its huge statue of Fridtjov the Brave, to Fimreite and the ferry landing at Hella. Every now and again she gazes up at the sky, as if in wonder at a light that never lets up.

Why did I survive?

I need to say something about Kamala. I need to say something about this woman who came into my life when it should all have been over. She found me. I had hidden myself away, I thought I had hidden myself too well, but she found me. I could not have cared less, was not the slightest bit interested. Nonetheless I responded to the prison chaplain's request. He had asked if I would like to have a visitor, an anthropologist who originally hailed from India; and when she stepped into my cell I felt exactly the way I used to do as a child when we played hide-and-seek in the dark and someone shone a beam of light on me and cried: 'I've found him, I've found Jonas!' When I looked in her eyes and she said my name I took my first step out of the darkness, away from the thought of death. The five 'a's in her name made it feel like making a fresh start, like learning a different alphabet – Kamala Varma. During her visit she told me that she had just spent some time in Vega, outside Brønnoysund in Nordland. She had been doing a little anthropological study there. I could hardly believe it: she had met, she had written about, the Vegans.

Kamala is an exceptional individual. A woman of the *ksatriya*, or warrior, caste, brought up in the Delhi area, educated at Columbia University, New York, working at the University of Oslo. Her only real teething troubles in becoming a 'Norwegian' had been a couple of hard winters and a problem with the Norwegian 'u' sound. And of course – this was the seventies, after all – a dearth of vegetables, other than potatoes, carrots and cabbage, which was, for a foreigner, hard to credit.

After the first, almost inconceivably wonderful phase, came the break-up. I could not imagine what she saw in me, could not believe the love that had grown. I took fright. Actually took fright. She was gradually turning into Margrete, taking her place. Not least when she started telling stories from *The Mahabharata*. I had heard Margrete tell quite a few of those same stories. I had not asked Kamala to talk about *The Mahabharata*. It was too hard. The whole thing reminded me so much of Margrete. I broke it off. I said, I forced myself to say, that I did not want to see her any more. It was a stupid decision. This was just at the time when the first spiteful books about me were published amid a storm of publicity. I could not help but hear about them, even the most defamatory details reached my ears on the inside. Again the thought of suicide presented itself.

Then, out of the blue, came Kamala's book on me. Or perhaps I should say 'defence'. I read it. I wanted to get in touch, but did not. Then yet another book appeared, this time written by a professor, with Rakel's help. I made up my mind to live. I asked to see Kamala Varma again. And when I met her, while out on a day pass, I was so overcome by emotion that I had to sit down on a bench. I saw that, although her skin was darker, she looked like Margrete. I saw that she very nearly *was* Margrete. It was not Kamala, but Margrete, whom I saw walking towards me. This time I did not take fright. I thought: This – this is mercy.

Kamala understood. She waited. She was there for me when I got out. I knew what it was: Love reborn.

I am a secretary. I am Kamala's secretary. And I am a name at the beginning of a love story. I have done the one thing I have always dreamt of doing: I am hidden, while at the same time working in depth.

I observe her from the bed. She is sitting on the balcony in the bright night, simply gazing out across the fjord, at the approach lights atop Fimreiteåsen and Bleia, the shimmering snow-covered mountain beyond, between Lærdalsfjord and Aurlandsfjord. She is sitting several metres away from me. She has her back to me. And yet I have the strongest feeling that she is holding me in her arms.

It is only a few months since I saw her in a sari for the first time – on one of those rare occasions when she found reason to wear such a garment. And yet, at home, when I undressed her, I was never in any doubt that her naked body was even more beautiful than that long swathe of fabric with its lovely colours and marvellous patterns. When we made love, quietly, slowly, the sari lay over us like a tent. It struck me that we were two nomads whose paths had chanced to cross. Sometimes when I whisper her name, those three 'a's, it sounds like 'Samarkand'.

I must have dozed off. I was woken by her switching on the bedside lamp. She was bending over me, looking down into my face. 'I just wanted to see whether you might surrender your secret when you were asleep,' she said.

There is a well-known adage which says that love bears everything, believes everything, hopes in everything, endures everything. To this should be added: Love changes everything.

Neptune

The most important story has not yet been told. That of the emergence of a genius. How could one man enthral so many thousands, almost inspire an entire nation to change direction. How could anyone come up with an idea as exceptional as that conceived by Jonas Wergeland.

That seminal work of art *Thinking Big*, a feat unparalleled in the history of modern Norwegian thought, has faded from the minds of the Norwegian people. It is a puzzle, and more than a little depressing, but it is nonetheless a fact. Not that the programmes have been forgotten – clips from them are still doing the rounds. There is always a chance, in any gathering, of someone mentioning a scene in which Henrik Ibsen wanders around inside his own brain; or, while out skiing with friends, referring to a programme in which Fridtjof Nansen stood and wept. Jonas Wergeland had a gift for creating scenes as unforgettable as a riff, a phrase you simply cannot get out of your head – but people no longer remember the import of that series, that voyage of discovery, if you like. The great majority have forgotten how much his programmes affected them, *inspired* them, you might say; how, when they switched off the television, they had a powerful urge to talk to someone about what they had seen. A great many of them said the same thing: they felt like doing something. It is no exaggeration to say that, for a whole year, a couple of million Norwegians were on the verge of changing their outlook on life. Changing themselves.

Why did he do it? Or how?

A lot happened to Norwegian television during Jonas Wergeland's time in prison. On the plus side possibly just one thing: the appearance of the first Negro television host. 'Negro' has to be the correct term here, since, even though they believed themselves to be living in a multicultural society, people said to themselves: Gosh, a Negro on NRK – much as the sight of an African in Oslo in the fifties made people turn their heads with a: Gosh, a Negro on Karl Johans gate. Other than that, it was the decline in standards which struck one, the increasingly desperate attempts to win viewers. And the monotony of it, a so-called diversity which, in actual fact, meant almost identical programmes on hundreds of channels, a diversity the essence of which was repetition. In the battle for viewers – read: money – all the television companies were offering the same product.

Jonas Wergeland foresaw this development even before the advent of his own glory days. On his return from Montevideo in the mid-eighties he gave a lecture at the NRK studios. Hardly anyone attended it. The organisers of the evening seminar – all honour to their names – wrote it off as a total flop. But since then that meeting has acquired a legendary status equal to that of the inaugural meetings of political parties which altered the course of history. And if everyone who boasts of having been in attendance truly had been there, the NRK headquarters would not have been big enough to hold them all.

What did he talk about? After a complete, and somewhat sardonic, rundown of the previous week's broadcasts on NRK TV, he concluded by saying: 'Television is a marvellous invention. Is this really the best we can do with it?' The remainder of the lecture was devoted to a ruthless critique of his own work, as good as a confession, some said. Wergeland confined himself strictly to his own productions when it came to citing examples of unoriginality. From the platform he made a vow that from now on he was going to make programmes unlike anything ever made before. It might not be going too far to say that Jonas Wergeland wished to be a Negro on the Norwegian television scene; he wanted to come from the outside and show Norwegians strange things about their own country which they had never noticed. He wanted to turn the viewers into *see-ers*.

What happened in Montevideo?

In Montevideo Jonas Wergeland was down for the count. An observer would have doubted whether he was capable of conceiving any ideas at all. Because in Montevideo, in the far-off country of Uruguay, Jonas Wergeland spent most of his time slumped in a deckchair, all alone on a vast, deserted beach, staring out to sea, or rather the Rio de la Plata. On the other hand, it should come as no surprise to anyone that a Norwegian should have had the great revelation of his life while lounging in a deckchair, considering that Norwegians have grown up, so to speak, in chairs designed to allow one to recline at one's ease. That deckchair was, for Jonas, what the bathtub had been for Archimedes.

This was in October. Behind him Jonas had several years as a programme-maker. Fired by his unorthodox studies in London he had produced shows which, while they may have had a certain zest and were technically superb – his colleagues were full of praise for him – lacked the magic ingredient which could pin a large proportion of the population to their seats as well as making them think, feel, that they had seen something unique and hence important, something which concerned them personally. Jonas himself knew exactly what was missing: an original idea. Not little ideas for single programmes, but a vision, a unifying concept. He needed a rest. And so it was that in that most burnt-out phase of his life he went out into the world, going pretty much wherever the wind took him, and eventually ended up in Uruguay, in Montevideo. It may have been something about the name – a combination of letters containing the verb 'to see' – which drew him. He needed a lookout point. And yet he could never have imagined that this point would turn out to be a person. That it would be a woman, and that her name would be Ana.

He booked in to the Hotel Carrasco, an old and somewhat dilapidated establishment near the road running along the waterfront, the Rambla Naciones Unidas, a palm-lined avenue which wound its way along the coast, past seven white beaches, into the centre of the city. Surrounded by well-tended gardens and pine trees, the hotel still retained traces of the grandeur it had enjoyed in a not too distant past thanks to its casino. Jonas felt at home there right away, he liked the faint air of decadence: the flaking Baroque exterior, the sleepy ballrooms, the cracked marble tiles in the bathroom. It suited his mood. I'm not a tourist, he told himself, I'm a patient in a sanatorium.

In Montevideo the summer season ran from December to the middle of March. Out of season you had the beach to yourself, even though the weather was as warm as a Norwegian summer. It suited Jonas perfectly: a city where you could lounge in a red deckchair, under a blue-striped parasol, on a beach that went on for miles. Just him and the wind, just him and the sun, just him and the waves. He relished this solitude. He did not so much as read a newspaper, simply lay there, lay there with a vague ache in his chest. For Jonas, difficulty in thinking had always been associated with the feeling of having something wrong with his lungs, of not being able to breathe properly. Had he not known better, he would have thought he had TB. I ought to go for an X-ray, he thought listlessly. Just to be on the safe side.

He sat motionless in a deckchair, gazing out across the water, thinking about what he should take with him, or thinking without being conscious of thinking. He may not even have been thinking at all. He may have been almost in a state of coma, not unlike that inhabited by Viktor Harlem. When Jonas visited Viktor at the institution, he would catch himself staring in fascination at the face of his friend as he sat there in a Stressless chair angled towards the television whether it was on or not. Jonas had always, even after the accident, regarded Viktor as a kindred spirit.

Day after day, Jonas lay in a comfortable deckchair thinking, or dozing, on a long white beach. Maybe this was the Norwegian's lot: to be a holiday-maker in the world. An observer by the sea. Nevertheless, it must have been this enervating passivity which at one point caused him to remember another time, a time of activism, a period when he had actually been a rebel. Truth to tell, when Jonas Wergeland was taken into police custody in the wake of

Margrete's death, it was not his first run-in with the powers that be; he had also been carted off to the police station once before – the old headquarters at Møllergata 19 on that occasion – and even though this happened at the beginning of a decade characterised by manifold forms of rebellious unrest, I think it is safe to say that this was the first and last time on which a court ever fined a teenager clad in a Nehru jacket and brandishing a placard inscribed with a fiery slogan in Marathi, a language spoken a fairly long way away from Oslo, namely in the Bombay region.

Not all that many demonstrations from Norway's idyllic post-war period will be remembered. The Mardøla protest is one. And the campaign against the hydro-electric power station at Alta, of course, not least for the Lapps who pitched their tents and staged a hunger strike outside the Norwegian Parliament, and still more for the occupation by outraged Lapp women of Prime Minister – and former Minister for the Environment – Gro Harlem Brundtland's office. Another incident which is sure to stand the test of time is the demonstration staged by Jonas Wergeland and his two friends from high school. This also marked Jonas's first appearance on television: a brief clip which has fortunately been preserved, and deservedly so; this was an event of great symbolic value, one which said a lot about modern Norway.

The brains behind it was, as always, Viktor Harlem. If he had had to choose between his two chums, Jonas would probably have come down in favour of the restless Pound devotee who had drawn inspiration from the lush, green Hedmark countryside around the Løiten distillery until his parents divorced. Viktor – with his eternal black polo necks, eager baby face and fine hair – was a born rebel and freethinker. Jonas always felt a little distanced from Axel Stranger, who came from a well-to-do home on the west side of Oslo and was more of a silk-tie, patent-leather shoe sort of rebel, a rather arrogant revolutionary with a Frogner drawl, a managing-director father, three dinner suits in his wardrobe and a maid who presented him every morning with the world's most elaborate and delectable packed lunch, complete with parsley sprig. In a way, that in itself was an act of rebellion, to even dare to open it at school, in front of his gawping classmates.

The chums – non-conformists to the core – called themselves The Three Heretics, and they met regularly in a flat in Grunerløkka which Viktor had more or less to himself. Here, in a room lined with shelves laden with books about and by Ezra Pound, they could sit undisturbed, finding fault with everything and everyone and boosting their energy levels every so often with swigs of a lethal, greenish variant of absinthe, obtained through Viktor's boyhood friends from the more anarchic corners of Hedmark. The Three Heretics cherished the principles of marginalism – or, in Jonas's parlance: the outside left. According to Viktor, one should never look for a centre or a core, in people or in life. 'Out on the edge, that's where life is,' he declared, raising his glass. 'In the centre there's nothing but red-hot chaos. Look at the Earth!'

In everyone's life there is a time like this, a glorious phase – rather like a long recess – when God is dead and everything is allowed. During their high-school years The Three Heretics were almost always to be found in Viktor's flat in Seilduksgata, dismantling – or, to use a word that would later come into vogue: deconstructing – all of the prevailing schools of thought and leaving the pieces scattered about in all their pathetic absurdity. And now and again they even got off their backsides and went out to put their heretical theories into practice. These acts were invariably memorable; all their woolly ramblings seemed to give the trio added incentive, a barricade-storming urgency – or maybe one should say a bad conscience. On one occasion, though, they bit off more than they could chew: when they tried to break down an invention which was definitely here to stay; or, to put it more plainly: when they set out to reconstruct the traffic system.

Viktor's arch-enemy was the car. 'The automobile is the number one false god of our day,' he said, 'the golden calf that everybody dances around.' It really pained Viktor to observe the devotion with which people washed their vehicles, as if it were some sort of liturgy; or the way in which Norwegians meekly accepted the fact of the several hundred souls sacrificed each year on the altar of the car – on a world scale road accidents cost twice as many lives each year as war. If one wanted to point to something that was quite clearly all wrong, but which no one seemed able, or cared, to do anything about, then the car was the perfect example. Everyone was well aware of the enormous damage done by the motor car to the environment as well as to life and limb, everyone agreed that public transport was better, but no one drove less or took the tram more often. The war against the motor car was, it goes without saying, the most hopeless of all causes in the latter half of the twentieth century, but Viktor seemed to thrive on it; it was, in many ways, an exemplary act of iconoclasm. This was how Jonas remembered Viktor best: a shining baby face chanting the refrain 'Car-free city centres!', unfazed by the ill-concealed yawns this always drew from those listening.

From the moment they met, Jonas knew that Viktor was girding himself for a decisive strike against the automobile and above all against what he called road traffic's - of the cities. Their target was chosen with care. Was there one spot in Oslo which illustrated the whole society's lack of resolve and want of co-ordinated planning and also told an outsider pretty much everything about the Norwegian cultural mentality? Yes, there was: Rådhus-plassen – the Town Hall Square – not for nothing the natural last stop on the Norwegian version of the Monopoly board, as well as the most expensive property.

Since a lot of people have already forgotten, I'm sure, that there was a time when all Norwegian shops closed at five p.m. and there were no newspapers on Sundays, it seems necessary to remind readers of how Oslo's Town Hall Square looked at the time when Viktor Harlem planned to put a spoke in as many wheels as possible. Some have most likely forgotten the dominant presence of a huge and fully operational shipyard right next door to the Town Hall, and the minor, cartoon-style detail of the never-ending goods train escorted by a man with a red flag and a whistle, which caused traffic jams every single day as it chugged slowly across the square. A few may even have managed to suppress the worst memory of all: that for decades the fjord was separated from the town by a six-lane carriageway cutting right across this charming part of the city. To Viktor Harlem, the Town Hall Square epitomised the very worst of all civic stupidity. What, he demanded to know, was the absolute height of lunacy? They build the city's finest building on the city's finest site. And then what do they do? After filling the mid-section of the area between the harbour and the Town Hall with splendid fountains and lovely sculptures, they filled the remaining space with cars. They built a grand square, then dumped a whole load of rubbish in it.

Right from the start the authorities had, of course, been considering plans to channel traffic through a tunnel running under the square. And did anything come of it? The way Viktor saw it, this said *everything* about Norway. After all, how was it that in a country where bridges were built to just about any island with more than ten people living on it, though with little or no economic benefit, and where tunnels of record-breaking length were blown through mountains here, there and everywhere in next to no time, and to hell with the cost – how was it that such a country was incapable of building something as glaringly essential as a tunnel to bypass this magnificent square, Norway's face to the world. We said no to Europe, but for thirty years we allowed a European E-road, the main artery from the south carrying tens of thousands of cars every day, to run right through the capital's front room.

Like hurricanes, demonstrations ought to be given a name, and the heretical triumvirate called their protest against Norwegian inertia after the artist responsible for the sculptures in the exhaust-choked middle of the square. The 'Emil Lie Demonstration' got under way in the middle of the rush hour one September evening in the early seventies, and created an unheard-of commotion. And who knows, perhaps Jonas Wergeland had a premonition of his future as the creator of the television series *Thinking Big* – a man who endeavoured to take as distanced a view as possible of his native land – as he screamed furiously in Anglo-Indian, while being sternly marched off by the police, that they had no bloody right to lay hands on a *māyā* shaman like Vinoo Sabarmati, the world-famous film director from Bombay.

Jonas ought possibly to have had an even earlier premonition of his future career in television, thanks to something he experienced with his grandmother when he was eight, an incident which might also explain why Jonas Wergeland did not think twice about laying his life on the line in the defence of a mere square in the city centre.

Until that day, Jonas had always regarded his maternal grandmother as a pretty ordinary granny. There were aspects to her character which were a mystery to him, it's true, like the fact that she was quite liable to pay a lot of money for paintings which nobody wanted, or that she was sometimes wont to mumble incomprehensible sentences in English while making the V-sign with her fingers, but for the most part, as far as Jonas was concerned, she was an indomitable farmer's wife who had moved from Gardermoen to the city, where she now sat in a throne-like armchair, attending to her main occupation: being a grandmother. To Jonas, Jørgine Wergeland was like a fireplace, a source of warmth, a person whom he liked being around. It was enough just to *be* with her. When he stepped through the door of the cigar-scented flat in Oscars gate he also slipped into a particular mood; it was like entering another world, another century, a sensation which was reinforced by the glitter and the faint tinkling of the fabulous crystal chandelier.

It was a Saturday evening, late on. Jonas was spending the night at his grandmother's, and one of the great fringe benefits of staying at Granny's was that you were allowed to stay up outrageously late. He had been supping bananas with cream and sugar when he happened, just by the way really, to ask his grandmother whether she didn't get a bit bored in the evenings when she was on her own. Why didn't she get a television? This was just around the time when television-viewing was becoming an everyday thing.

His grandmother's response surprised him. She disappeared into the hall as if she were deeply offended. Jonas heard the murmur of her talking on the telephone, thought maybe she was sending for his parents. Then she reappeared and ordered him to put on his outdoor things. She was already wearing a hat which made Jonas think of something live, an animal or a bird. 'I'm going to show you something better than television,' was all she said. At moments like this Jonas could see that his mother was right. Once, when there had been a picture of Winston Churchill in the newspaper she had laughingly pointed out to him that it could easily have been a picture of his Granny's face.

How could anyone have missed seeing it? Over the past couple of decades, few lives have been subjected to as much scrutiny as Jonas Wergeland's and yet no one has ever mentioned the occurrence which represents the foundation stone, as it were, of this edifice of stories.

It was the tail end of April, the sort of spring night that made you lift your chin and sniff the air like an animal. Granny cut through the palace gardens and down towards the city centre. Jonas had no idea where they were going, a state of ignorance which he took a moment to savour just before they reached the junction of Karl Johans gate and Universitetsgaten, a crossroads which, for him, had always been the very best spot in all Oslo. He had never forgotten the first time he had stood there, as a five-year-old, on the corner next to the Studenten ice-cream parlour with his grandmother; how she had pointed up the street towards the University and the Palace, then across to the National Theatre, while telling him, the child, what he was looking at, what these buildings contained, before letting her eager finger travel down to Fridtjof Nansens plass, then the Parliament building and finally, still patiently describing and explaining, turning his face the other way, back towards the National Gallery, thus completing the circle. From this spot, with one sweep of the eye one could take in the finest and most eminent buildings in Oslo, this was the capital's bull's eye. Every child should have the chance to stand with a grandmother at the junction of two main streets and have pointed out to them the central axes of their city as well, you might say, as the central axes of their lives. For Jonas this was as fundamental a lesson as learning the points of the compass – or looking down four arms of a fjord at the same time.

Jonas did not know what to think though, when his grandmother skirted the little bandstand where in summer they listened to bands from Sagene or Kampen, and headed down towards Fridtjof Nansens plass, was even more puzzled when they crossed the square and climbed the slope leading to the Town Hall itself, which loomed over them like a red-brick mountain. The way the two towers slanted away from one another when he gazed up at them from ground level at such close quarters, made Jonas feel that he was about to enter a giant W. It was dark, late, not a soul in sight. Granny rang the bell next to the main door and a moment later it swung open as if by magic. A burly figure in a pale-blue shirt and navy-blue serge trousers was striding down the hall towards them. His face was stern, like that of a strict teacher, but his expression changed when he saw Jørgine Wergeland. 'Welcome to the Hall of the Mountain King,' he said in a deep voice, signalling to the night watchman in his booth that he would take care of these visitors personally.

'Everyone gone?' Granny asked. The man nodded, sneaking a glance at Jørgine's hat. 'Did you forget it's Saturday evening, or night rather,' he said.

'Even the mayor has gone home.' His tone of voice, his smile, told Jonas that it was not the first time this man had met his grandmother. Nonetheless Jonas realised that he was experiencing something very special. He did not understand why they had been allowed in, still less why this man had greeted his grandmother so respectfully, not to say warmly. So, let it be said – since Jørgine Wergeland's reputation as a sort of war hero in Town Hall circles does not fully explain it – that this took place in a soon distant past and in another Norway. Because one thing is for sure: no one, not even an extraordinary grandmother and her grandchild, would be allowed inside Oslo Town Hall late at night today, however magically beautiful the spring evening.

'This is Einar Moe,' Jonas's grandmother told him. 'He's the head warden here, he has his own flat on the premises.'

'What are we doing here?' Jonas whispered, casting anxious, sidelong glances at the head warden's bushy eyebrows. If Moe had been wearing a string vest he would have looked exactly like Mr Bastesen, Solhaug's formidable caretaker.

'Patience, patience,' his grandmother said. 'Shall we start the tour?' she asked Einar Moe.

And so it was that on an April night in the early sixties, Jonas Wergeland got to see the inside of Oslo Town Hall. Or at least, he did not see it all at once, he saw it a little bit at a time. You see, they did not switch on the lights – Jonas thought it was because the head warden did not want to break the rules, but it might also have been because Granny wanted it that way. However that may be, when they stepped into the central hall – that high, wide space – it was in total darkness, although a little of the glare from the spotlights outside filtered through the windows at the bottom end overlooking the fjord. Jonas could only just make out pictures on the walls. And it was evidently these which his grandmother wished to show him, because Mr Moe pulled out a torch and proceeded to shine it on sections of the paintings; and while Mr Moe wielded his torch like a pointer of light, the two adults took it in turns to tell Jonas what he was seeing. They started with the long picture running under the balcony on the eastern wall, a fresco teeming with life, painted by someone called Alf Rolfsen and depicting the years of the German occupation; Granny described each scene, Mr Moe's circle of light moving in time with her dramatic commentary. Jonas actually felt a little scared and had to hold his grandmother's hand, but at the same time he was quite carried away by the show: it was rather like looking at a darkened stage, with a spotlight illuminating one patch after another. Or perhaps he was thinking of the game he played at Aunt Laura's flat in Tøyen, when he shone a torch on the oriental rugs on the wall and pretended that he was the Caliph Haroun al-Rashid going out to see how things stood in his kingdom – a comparison which was not too far-fetched since if anything were capable of revealing the secrets of the kingdom of Norway it would surely be the decorations in Oslo's Town Hall.

Einar Moe shifted the spotlight to Henrik Sørensen's massive picture on the end wall. This was painted in a different style from the previous one, with gold smouldering in the parts submerged in the gloom. Mr Moe, the head warden, shone the torch on a boy in the bottom right-hand corner while Granny explained how this lad was setting out on a journey which could be followed all the way through the painting, right up to the top left-hand corner where he presented his fairy-tale princess with a crown. Jonas stood with his head thrown back and his eyes glued to the beam of light as it travelled slowly over the gigantic, richly-detailed picture, revealing more and more figures and scenes. All of a sudden he realised what, more than anything else, it reminded him of. It reminded him of what it had been like to leaf through his first ABC book, seeing the letters which he would, in time, learn to put together to form words, a language. Or, even more perhaps: of a reading book.

A thought occurred to Einar Moe, he popped back to the night watch-man's booth and returned with another torch for Jonas. The effect was even better. To begin with they both shone their torches on the same part, so that they were able to see more at one time, but after a while Jonas began to aim his beam at different areas from Moe's. While his grandmother talked about the images caught in the head warden's beam, Jonas could light up a detail some way off, so that it presented a kind of parallel illustration, a wordless, amplifying comment. This frequently proved most effective, as when Moe and his grandmother were peering at a figure in Sørensen's massive picture, and Jonas shone his light on the ornamental design which Alf Rolfsen had painted in muted *al secco* on the side wall over the stairway. This provided an excellent complement, and counterpoint, to Henrik Sørensen's vivid painting, almost like a necessary veil hanging over it.

They ascended the broad, imposing staircase, with Jonas sweeping the torch beam over the wall behind him as they went. Suddenly he caught sight of a sailor stepping ashore with a present in his hands, a string of pearls. A proud and extremely knowledgeable Mr Moe treated them to a little lecture on the different sorts of stone used for the building's floors and walls. To Jonas the Town Hall seemed like a monument constructed out of species of rock from all over Norway. In the Festival Gallery they spent a lot of time perusing, or illuminating, the frescoes by Axel Revold at either end of the room. Many of the fragments which Jonas caught in his torchbeam that night – scenes from the shipping and manufacturing industries, fishing and agriculture, popped into his mind years later in Leonard Knutzen's basement, as he flicked through old issues of *Aktuell* magazine. These were images from a pioneering era, a time of cloth caps and an entire nation working together to build a country; to drag it, one might say, from the Middle Ages into modern society within only a few decades.

People who chanced to walk past along the waterfront at Pipervika may have wondered at the beams of light dancing behind the Town Hall windows. They could not know that inside a small boy was being shown a great big ABC of Norway, that he was being told the history of his fore-fathers through pictures, being ushered around the city's front room by an extraordinary grandmother and a hospitable head warden. Later, when Jonas visited the Vatican, he was to some extent prepared. For although Oslo Town Hall could not boast of Michelangelos or Raphaels it did, nonetheless, have Sørensen and Rolfsen, and if that was not Heaven, it was certainly Earth, Life – it was, in short, a good place to start. As a grown man it occurred to Jonas that some day it would be possible – particularly if the ideas which won their first victory at Anders Lange's meeting in the Saga cinema managed to permeate the whole of Norwegian society – to convert the Town Hall into a mausoleum in which the finest ideals of social democracy would lie buried.

On this tour of the Town Hall, with two torchbeams criss-crossing in the air like huge, bright blades, he was also introduced to people. Some names, like Fridtjof Nansen and Bjørnstjerne Bjørnson, he already knew, others, such as Nordahl Rolfsen and Paal Berg, he had never heard of. Head warden Moe called them 'Norwegian heroes' and Jonas was given to understand that from time to time people came along who would be of crucial significance to the progress of their country. It was a lesson he would always remember, even – later – in a day and age when it became popular to maintain that indi-vidual people could no longer influence history. It struck Jonas, as he walked along between his grandmother and Mr Moe, that he might never do any-thing quite as wonderful as this again: to wander through darkened rooms in a vast building, sweeping a circle of light over evocative pictures on walls and ceiling – suddenly spotting an enchanted princess or jumping at the sight of a three-headed troll with a trio of snarling faces. Saturday night entertainment did not come any better than this; he caught himself missing the bar of milk chocolate he was usually allowed when watching Children's Hour.

Best of all he remembered their visit to one of the rooms adjoining the council chamber. There, in the East Gallery, he found Per Krogh's frescoes, one long painting covering three walls and the ceiling. It was like walking right into, becoming *part of* a picture. Jonas paused in front of a jumble of housing blocks on one wall; he shone the beam on one window after another so it almost looked as if he was lighting up the rooms behind them. In one, an old man was playing the flute. In another a bride was adjusting her finery. All at once he came upon himself. In a room in the Town Hall, in a room in a fresco, he discovered an exact replica of himself. Behind one of the windows he illuminated a small boy was doing his homework, a globe of the world at his elbow.

His grandmother registered his reaction and gave his hand an extra little squeeze. 'I'm in one of these pictures too,' she said, with a slight quiver in her voice. Little did Jonas know that this was absolutely true and that, due to a highly unconventional contribution to the war effort, Jørgine Wergeland genuinely had earned the right to be there.

Some years later, when Jonas gained admission to the Town Hall again, during opening hours this time, in broad daylight, and was able to take in the main hall at one glance, the initial impact almost blew him away. He stood in the middle of the marble floor, in the middle of that huge hall and stared round about him until his neck ached, marvelling at Henrik Sørensen's bright-hued oil painting on the end wall and Alf Rolfsen's vibrant patterns of light and shade on the side walls. After a while, however, he became conscious of a vague sense of disappointment. Nothing could compare with the experience of that spring night when he had gone round the Town Hall with his grandmother and Einar Moe, when he had brought the rooms, the pictures, to light a bit at a time; built them up into a whole by himself – images and associations which in many cases were possibly more fascinating than what he now beheld.

It says something about the strength of this memory that many years later, even beneath a parasol on a deserted beach in Montevideo, he could still call to mind some of those imaginative mosaics. After a long, dreamlike tour of his memory – it might have lasted hours, it might have lasted twenty seconds – it was as if, sitting in that deckchair with his eyes fixed on the waves, he suddenly woke up. He understood what it was, above all, that had been implanted in him that night: an appreciation of a project bordering on the impossible. Even as a boy, equipped only with a torch, he had grasped the magnificence of the concept, the power of the vision behind the decorations in Oslo Town Hall. Was there an idea for television here? To create just such circles of light? Present fragments of a greater whole? Pick out, shed light on, people in a crowd?

His thoughts went to his grandmother. He could have done with a dose of her rabble-rousing spirit as he lounged there in that deckchair on the silver sands, gazing out across the Rio de la Plata as if waiting for an idea to come drifting ashore, in the form of a message in a bottle, without him having to lift a finger. Once, his grandmother had looked deep into his eyes and said:'Jonas, there's too much Hansen in you and not enough Wergeland. You're going to have to find the rebel within you.' She would have been appalled if she could have seen him now, lying flat out on a deserted beach in far-off Uruguay. Or maybe she would have understood: he lay there remembering Bo Wang Lee, he lay there looking for something to take with him. A key concept. Material which could be turned into television programmes. Television that was different. Not Hansen programmes, but Wergeland programmes. Dangerous programmes.

Jonas's grandmother was certainly qualified to talk about rebellion; she had always been something of a disruptive element. When Jonas staged his protest in the Town Hall Square, dared to shake his fist at a superior opponent, he thought not only of those nocturnal childhood wanderings among edifying frescoes, but also, and to as great an extent, of his grandmother – and of another inspiring episode in which she played a leading role.

Thanks to Winston Churchill, Jørgine Wergeland had early on acquired a taste for all things British. She had, therefore, one favourite spot in Oslo, a place she would often take a walk around during the war, to bolster her spirits: the English Quarter on Drammensveien, overlooking Solli plass. This exceedingly tasteful residential area – a jewel in the city's crown – consisted of one long, two-storey building with a three-storey corner building to either side of it. It derived its 'English' epithet from the internal layout of the buildings, mansion flats occupying several floors, and not from its outward appearance which, with its domes and pitched roofs, was more reminiscent of the French neo-Renaissance style. But as far as Jørgine Wergeland was concerned the place was as English as No.10 Downing Street.

Then, in the early sixties, the most outrageous, not to say unbelievable thing happened. What the bombers did not succeed in doing during the war, Oslo District Council decided to do. They proposed to tear down the English Quarter. Now, although Jørgine Wergeland took a murderously dim view of property developers – for reasons which will later become clear – she was not opposed to every form of urban renewal. But this lovely group of buildings was not only laden with personal memories of wartime, it was in itself utterly unique, an architectural gem. The English Quarter was quite simply part of the capital's memory. 'This provincial little town will be left even more devoid of history and bereft of atmosphere if we don't preserve the best from every age,' Jørgine muttered under her breath.

It is astonishing to note, today, how few people protested and how little stir this barbaric and incredibly short-sighted decision caused. When the impercipient members of the city council swanned into the Town Hall in

June 1961 they completely overlooked the elderly, cigar-smoking lady who had made her stand outside and who, besides being absolutely furious that such a decision should be taken in this of all buildings, was holding aloft a placard inscribed with an injunction which every schoolchild had been taught to heed: 'Do not erase!' But the city fathers flouted all the rules of good behaviour and passed the planning bill, thereby also passing sentence of death on the English Quarter.

Some people may, however, recall a photograph published in the one vigilant Oslo newspaper, a picture which they had to smile at over their morning coffee. It was a picture of an elderly lady facing up to a massive demolition crane with her handbag raised, as if she were being subjected to a brutal robbery in broad daylight. Which is not, in fact, too far from the truth. That fateful year – which would also see both the Cuban Missile Crisis and a mining explosion in Nye Ålesund on Svalbard which led, some months later, to the downfall of the Gerhardsen government – also got off to a bad start. On one of the very first afternoons in January a twenty-eight ton, motorised monster rumbled across the pavements on Drammensveien, heading straight for the English Quarter's gracious, but oh, so impermanent façades, and the aforementioned photograph was taken during the half hour when Jørgine Wergeland and her raised handbag managed to prevent the one-ton, cast-iron ball on that mobile crane from smashing into something that was as dear and precious to her as a loved one's face. To her this was a living building, a personal reminder of Winston Churchill, but it did no good. Nor did her words: 'Shoo!' she cried – as if she were addressing some mangy old mutt. 'Shoo! Away with you!' In the course of that afternoon and evening, the greater part of the English Quarter's irreplaceable façades overlooking Drammensveien were reduced to a heap of smoking rubble.

Jonas had cut out and saved this photograph of his grandmother. Although in world terms its significance may have been minimal – this illustration of a righteous, but hopeless struggle, an urban patriot waving her handbag at a giant crane – for him personally it had as much symbolic value as the later picture of the lone student with the shopping bags trying to stop the tanks on Tiananmen Square in Beijing – he, too, seeming to be saying: 'Shoo! Away with you!' It is also worth noting that with this doughty demonstration Jørgine Wergeland pretty much gave the starting signal for all the protest marches which, later in the decade, would pass along this very street, Drammensveien, on their way to the American and Soviet Union embassies.

Even before she found out about the civic vandals and their plans, Jonas's grandmother had proudly shown him round the English Quarter, frequently in connection with a visit to Sol Cigar's aromatic premises further down the street. Jonas thought the façades looked rather like the casing of an organ – greater compliment could no building receive. Each time they stood there on Solli plass and Granny described to him the mansion-style apartments behind the red-brick facing, with library and dining room, butler's pantry, maid's room, study and dressing room, she would finish by saying: 'Remember this.' After it was torn down, Jonas and his grandmother would, therefore, sometimes take a walk over to Lapsetorget, stand with their backs to the West Side Baths and take it in turns to describe those richly adorned buildings which they pictured rising up before them, with all their balconies and cornices, doorways and towers, as if the new Industry and Export House in its seventeen-storey tower block simply did not exist.

Jonas reaped the benefits of this powerful memory when he applied for a place at the College of Architecture. In the so-called home project which constituted the first round in the selection process and determined whether one would go on to the two-day entrance exam at the college, applicants were asked to take a well-known place and produce something which expressed their feelings about it. What Jonas Wergeland did was this: inside a box from which he had removed the two long sides he hung three panels of thin fabric, like gauze. On the first panel he painted the grey façade of the Ind-Ex building. On the fabric in the middle he painted the English Quarter, those matchless, now demolished buildings, reproducing them in minute detail, in a glowing red with yellow cornices and cornerstones. The viewer saw it as a ghostly form showing through the transparent fabric façade of the Ind-Ex building, so luminously clear and distinct that it seemed more real than the drab tower block in front of it. And on the third gauze panel, at the very back, he painted a very small, shimmering white building out of his own head, a house unlike any other. It was only just discernible through the two stretches of fabric in front of it, like a tiny, shining organ deep inside a transparent body. The funny thing was – Jonas himself would notice this eighteen years later – that this imaginary building prefigured, with uncanny exactitude, the façade of Oslo's elegant new courthouse.

Later, one of the college professors would say that it was Jonas's home project he had fallen for. 'It looked almost like an X-ray photograph,' he said. Jonas, for his part, gave his grandmother the credit. Had it not been for her rebellious spirit he would never have got into the College of Architecture.

The foundations of Jørgine Wergeland's heroic concern for the city had, however, been laid long before her attempt to stop a monster with a demolition ball from attacking the English Quarter. Her civic mindedness, not to say passion, reached its peak immediately after the Second World War, when she suddenly came into a fair bit of money, a proper fortune, in fact.

Jørgine Wergeland was, in her own eyes, one of the victors of the war and when she unlocked the door of the flat in Oscars gate again, after a period of involuntary exile in Inkognitogaten, it was with a clear conscience that she lit a cigar and raised her fingers in a V-sign. Unlike Churchill, though, she was not only a wartime leader, but also a person capable of coping with peace. As soon as she acquired the money she instituted a conscientious search for a worthy peacetime project, a venture in which to invest it. Although she never thought of it as 'her' fortune. 'It belongs to the people of Norway, and that's that,' she announced to a somewhat worried Åse Hansen, Jonas's mother.

It did not take Jørgine long to see that she might have had one particular aim in mind all along, and that this might also have been the underlying motivation behind a war effort which almost surprised even Jørgine herself. The fact is, you see, that she had conceived an interest at a very early stage for the new Town Hall in Oslo – right from the time when the proposal was first put forward and an Architecture and Planning competition announced towards the end of the First World War. She followed the successive altera-tions to Arnstein Arneberg's and Magnus Poulsson's winning design as if they were episodes in a thrilling serial, the ending of which no one could predict. She enjoyed – nay, nigh on *adored* – monitoring the gradual meta-morphosis from medieval-inspired fortress, by way of the Gothic style, National Romanticism and Neo-Classicism to four-square Functionalism. She positively cheered when she saw the final drawings, the clean lines of the main form also embodying certain historical elements. What she applauded most of all were the two block-shaped towers which gave the building a Janus-like countenance. Something inside her said: Yes, that's just how it should be. Afterwards it would also occur to her that it made a fine, frank heraldic device for a country which had rendered such equivocal resistance during the war.

When Jørgine travelled into town from the family smallholding at Gard-ermoen on some errand or other, she always made a point of popping down to Pipervika to see how work on the building was progressing, especially once things speeded up in the mid-thirties and the solid mass of reinforced con-crete began to rear upwards in pyramidic majesty. And many's the time during the war when she derived encouragement and comfort from a walk down to the harbour to inspect the Town Hall, which Norway expected would be completed as soon as the bloody Germans had been run into the sea.

So when the war was over it seemed only natural that she should decide to invest her money in this. Or at least: the building was finished, but the artistic decoration of it, an uncommonly grandiose project – certainly for Norway – was far from completion. The war had not only delayed the work, it had also prompted several of the artists to make changes to their original sketches. Henrik Sørensen was now painting the return of the royal family into his vast picture on the end wall, and over at the mural in the East Gallery Per Krohg was in the midst of adding a section depicting Grini prison camp, guarded by huge, armour-plated earwigs.

In the early summer of the year after the war ended, Jørgine attended an exhibition at the Art Society in which Alf Rolfsen, a painter who had already come to her attention and who had, what is more, lost a son in the war, was showing a fresco depicting the occupation. This work was so warmly received and spawned so many letters to the newspapers that Rolfsen was asked to reproduce it as a mural for the east wall of the Town Hall's central hall. What is not commonly known is that Jørgine Wergeland also had a large hand in this. In a letter to the people in charge of the Town Hall decorations she offered to cover the costs of Rolfsen's long picture. Jonas's grandmother understood something which would be lost on Norwegian politicians of the future, even at a time when the country was virtually swimming in capital: that nothing pays off better than investment in the arts. Good art creates lasting meaning, an asset which, in due course, becomes so great that it can no longer be measured in terms of money.

Although she did not know it, Jørgine's offer could not have come at a better time. Because at that very moment a number of the artists working on the largest decorations for the Town Hall happened to be asking for additional funds, due to the increased cost of materials. And this was a problem, since the estimated budget for the project had already been exceeded. Consequently, when Jonas's grandmother was invited up to the office of the person in charge, it was with great pleasure that he accepted her generous gift. Jørgine Wergeland's contribution went into a common fund, but she received a verbal assurance that the lion's share of the money would be earmarked for Alf Rolfsen's large, and as yet uncompleted, painting. So although there are no official documents in which it states in black and white that Jørgine Wergeland paid for this mural – on the donations list issued for the inauguration of the Town Hall in 1950 only her name and the tidy sum she contributed are given – she knew, as did the people in charge of the finances and, not least, Alf Rolfsen himself, that she was the one who had paid for the occupation frieze. This was Jørgine Wergeland's gift to the Norwegian people. The way she saw it, it was also reparation for an act of betrayal, made with German money so to speak.

Staff at the Town Hall soon got used to having an elderly woman with a countenance remarkably similar to that of Winston Churchill popping in to see how the work was coming on and have a chat with the artists, who looked like so many workmen, hard at it on their scaffolding and ladders in hats and spattered overalls, applying paint to the wet plaster. But her keenest interest was reserved, of course, for Alf Rolfsen's thirty-metre long picture of the occupation years and the way it progressed in a mesmerising zig-zag fashion: men hiding in the forest, the air raid in April, the Gestapo forcing entry to houses, the execution of resistance fighters, underground activities, the men of Milorg, the secret military organisation. Life in the prisoner-of-war camps, liberation. Standing there, looking at the fresco, surrounded by the smell of paint and damp plaster, she remembered the war again, almost every single day of it, and in her mind she quoted the words of her favourite statesman: I was all for war. Now I am all for peace.

As often as possible Jørgine took the opportunity to have elevenses with Alf Rolfsen and his friend Aage Storstein. The latter had just been forced to chip off and repaint the whole of the end wall in the Western gallery because the colours were too pale – painting *al fresco* was no joke. They usually had their snack in the Festival Gallery, from where they could look down on the Royal Wharf and the Nesodden ferries and across to the Akers Mek shipyard, which Axel Revold had captured, in somewhat abstract fashion, in the now completed fresco on the end wall of the room in which they sat. They were great times, those, also for the two artists, whose discussions on the pitfalls of painting were all the livelier and wittier for having an audience; they frequently ended up sitting there half-an-hour longer than they ought, Rolfsen with his pipe and Jørgine with a Romeo y Julieta, Winston Churchill's favourite cigar. Alf Rolfsen did most of the talking. Jørgine quickly took a liking to this burly character with the strong face. He was also a wonderful storyteller. Sometimes when they were alone, while he was painting the wall, he would start to tell her, quite unprompted, about his travels: to Athens and the Acropolis, or to Paris where he had met, among others, the Mexican artist Diego Rivera, soon to deck what seemed like acres of his homeland's wall space with vivid colour. 'But there's nothing to beat Rome,' he confided to Jørgine as she stood there savouring the smells of plaster and pipe tobacco. 'I saw the frescos of Michelangelo and Raphael at the Vatican. They gave me a whole new conception of the relationship between images and space.' He climbed down and stepped back a couple of paces. 'What do you think?'

'I think you should make that building in the background look more like Victoria Terrasse,' she said.

It was during these years, on those mid-morning breaks and meanderings among zinc buckets and stepladders, bowls and dishes in these huge studios, that Jørgine Wergeland became an art connoisseur. She was not afraid to put in her own three ha'pence worth now and again either – not only to

Rolfson, for whom she felt a particular responsibility, but even to a gentleman as strong-minded as Henrik Sørensen. 'There's something wrong with
that figure,' she was liable to shout, motioning with her cigar as she passed
underneath the high scaffolding on which he perched like a skyscraper construction worker, working on an oil painting which at that time was reckoned
to be the biggest in the world. And sure enough, Sørensen altered that figure.

Jonas's grandmother was proud of the Town Hall and the works of art it
contained, even though they were not, of course, perfect and had, in some
cases, an inevitable air of national self-congratulation about them. To her,
the Town Hall was not only the city's indisputable defining symbol, but also
a monument to freedom. Just as the Statue of Liberty was the first thing to
greet you when you sailed into New York so, at the head of Oslo fjord, you
were greeted by the Town Hall. The building and its decorations marked the
culmination of an era. The Town Hall in Oslo *contained* Norway up until the
middle of the twentieth century. The very best of the country was reflected in
this building, both inside and out, in terms of materials, art and symbols. If
the whole of Norway were to be destroyed, bombed, but this building were
miraculously to be left standing, it would be possible to reconstruct much
of the land's history right up to the post-war years. Not for nothing did
Jonas, influenced as he was by his grandmother, compare the Town Hall, on
one occasion, to the information disc about the Earth carried on board the
Voyager space probes.

As a way of repaying her, but also because he liked her, Alf Rolfsen used
Jørgine Wergeland as the model for a figure in his occupation frieze. She is
one of the four women at the pump in the far left of the picture. This was
his tribute to her. And no greater tribute could anyone receive: to figure in,
for one's life to be made a part of, a fresco in the country's most magnificent
building. Visitors to the Town Hall today should possibly take a second look
at that picture and spare a thought for Jørgine Wergeland. There are, sadly,
too few people of her cast.

'How did you come by all that money?' Alf Rolfsen once asked her.

'It's a secret,' said Jørgine.

And even to Jonas, her grandchild, this was for a long time a well-kept
mystery. He sat alone with his eyes closed, under a blue and white parasol in
Montevideo and let the memories wash over him as he listened to the waves
breaking on the shore. His thoughts stayed with his grandmother. She might
be a vital clue in his search for material, for a kind of television which no one
before had dared to imagine. And now and again, perhaps precisely because
of the memory of his grandmother's resolute actions, he was seized by such
an acute need to soak up life that he got out of his deckchair and took the

bus that ran past the six other white beaches and all the way into the centre of the city, there to stroll, hands behind his back, down the long main street, the Avenida 18 de Julio; taking in the long string of pavement stalls, taking in the countless squares, taking in curious buildings and bombastic statues of dead generals, taking in the people with maté cups and metal straws in their hands and thermoses of hot water under their arms. Montevideo soothed his nerves. In other capitals he constantly felt guilty about all the things he ought to be doing. Montevideo had no famous sights. And what few museums it had were quite liable to be closed, without any explanation. That was fine by Jonas. This city tuned him into a rare, unknown channel. He sauntered along under the indigo veil formed by flowering jacaranda trees, surveying the life on the street, listening, smelling, waiting. An idea, he would give anything for an idea that would provide outlet for the talent he knew he possessed, a flash of inspiration which would also cure this ache in his chest. Later, Jonas would laugh at his own lack of imagination. He kept waiting for a thought to strike him. Instead he met someone.

He also roamed the higgledy-piggledy maze of narrow lanes and alleys in the old town, behind the cathedral, stopping here and there, and more than once outside the same second-hand bookshop near the Plaza Zabala, possibly because of the Spanish edition of *Kristin Lavransdatter* in the window: a fat, worn and yet somehow distinguished book spine. Jonas found it odd – coming across a fellow countrywoman in such a way. Like spying the back of someone you knew through the window of a restaurant in a strange city. Or, yes: it smacked of the Middle Ages. That was Montevideo, modern, but at the same time old-fashioned in a unique, almost wistful way. In Montevideo he could still come upon horses and carts in the streets, and there were mothballs on sale everywhere – Montevideo *reeked* of mothballs. On his strolls, Jonas spotted just about every make of car he had grown up with and the sight of the trolleybuses made him almost sob with nostalgia. It was the gently rusting boats in the harbour, however, which brought back the strongest memories of the fifties. He was back in his childhood. He was in a sort of forgotten, or better still: hidden backwater. *Anything* could happen here, he thought to himself. Here I can start afresh.

Time. He was conscious, as he sat there day after day in his deckchair in the shade of a blue-striped parasol, with a gentle breeze caressing his face while he gazed out across the water – grey, but with the silvery sheen from which the river took its name, La Plata – of how little he knew about time. Time could stand still, or it could fly by. It could also disappear completely, as if through a hole. As Jonas dozed in the deckchair a memory from 1970 drifted into his mind. He had been paying a quick visit to his grandmother, just dropping off something from home, when she had asked him to do her a favour, or rather, she ordered him to nip down to her regular supplier of cigars. 'Proper Suez Crisis,' she said with her most mournful Churchill expression. 'Stock's run out.' He was commissioned to purchase a box of Karel I – she had been forced to switch to Dutch cigars when the Cuban brands were no longer to be had.

Jonas enjoyed running errands like this, especially to Sol Cigar on Drammensveien, where the air was pervaded with the scent of tobacco and the after-shave lotion of distinguished clients. It was a warm Saturday morning in June. As usual he took the path through the Palace Gardens since a stroll through that soft, rolling landscape, under a green veil of maple and lime, elm and chestnut always seemed to affect his way of thinking. He told himself it was the excess of chlorophyll that rendered him even more reflective. It made him curse his shilly-shallying, his indecisiveness when it came to finding a sphere in which to utilise his baffling gifts. He glowered at the black silhouette, a dwarf running at his heels along the path, an illustration of the fate he dreaded more than any other: to end up as a shadow of himself. Never to have used what he had within him. Maybe it was because he was surrounded by such luxuriant vegetation or because he was on his way to buy cigars, that the thought of Che Guevara suddenly came into his mind. A guerrilla. He was filled with a longing to rebel.

As if his frustration had sharpened his eye, he spotted Pernille S., a girl from his class in junior high. He had not seen her in a year. She was sitting on one of the benches next to the pond. It may also have been something about the way she was dressed, her frock, that had caught his eye. Her clothes were always rather unusual, not the sort of things the other girls wore. She was sitting with a large pad on her lap, sketching, totally absorbed. Her rectangular hippie-style glasses with their red lenses made him feel that she must see the world in a charmed light. As he drew closer, he noticed that irresistible neck of hers, which Leonard had always let the camera linger on when they were filming. 'That is the neck of a woman who can go to great lengths,' he always said.

Jonas sat down next to her, whereupon she closed her sketch pad without a word and laid her head on his shoulder as if in greeting, an affectionate way of saying she was pleased to see him again. She was like that. Subtle and yet spontaneous. He drank in the scent of her long, dark hair. They chatted, caught up on each other's lives. She had not gone to high school, had chosen instead to go to Paris for a while, she had only been back a few weeks. Jonas listened to her soft voice while he watched the ducks swimming on the quiet pond, or rested his eyes on the green cascade of the willow on the island in the middle of the pond. 'It's nice here,' she said, 'almost like paradise.' He thought at first that she was referring to Norway in general, but soon realised that she was talking about the Palace Gardens.

He had seen her in a Garden of Eden once before. While in elementary school she had helped out at the nursery up on Bergensveien on Saturdays, wrapping flowers in old newspapers. He had always liked going there with his mother, it was like entering another climatic zone, a lush, humid, jungle-like atmosphere. One winter's day he and a couple of other lads had gone up there to spy on her. The greenhouse was in itself a sight to see, an ice palace – particularly when a milder spell was followed by a cold snap. As small boys they had broken off the long icicles that hung from the eaves and fenced their way right up to the round table in King Arthur's Camelot. But they were older now, with different interests, lay there with their eyes just peeking over the top of a snowbank, peering through the glass to where, when there were no customers, Pernille danced ballet in the greenhouse: she had one of the little new, portable Tandberg tape recorders in there, the kind in which the reels lay on top of one another – how sexy was that! She played classical music, practised graceful positions and steps amid the tulips which the gardeners managed, by some miracle, to cultivate even in winter: row upon row of budding tulips, like serried ranks of hard-ons. It was a real culture shock to see a girl like Pernille doing *ballet*. Shortly after this they heard that she had actually had a walk-on part in a production of *Swan Lake* at the Royal Norwegian Opera with Rudolf Nureyev as guest soloist. They lay there with their eyes peeping over the bank of snow, not feeling the cold; lay there so long that they almost froze their undercarriages off.

And now here she was, in Paradise again, sitting on a park bench with her ballerina neck inclined towards him as they talked, on and on, as if intent on making up for all the wordless scenes in Leonard's films. When he asked to see what she had been drawing it was only with reluctance that she handed him the pad. Inside were sketches. Of people caught in passing. Rendered in just a few strokes, except for their clothes, which were more carefully drawn, or suggested by a detail here and there, as if she were trying to capture the essence of a person through what they were wearing. Or as if a belt, the cut of a jacket, the pattern of a shirt, could say all there was to be said. 'I'm going to apply to the College of Art and Design,' she said. 'I'm practising.' And Jonas thought: I don't practise enough. I'm not practising anything at all. I'm going to be one of those Norwegians who simply squanders their abundant talent. 'It's kind of strange,' she said with a shy smile. 'I got the urge to work in fashion, with fabric, after Mr Dehli told us about *māyā*. Do you remember? Do you remember Mr Dehli?' He remembered Mr Dehli. Who could forget

Mr Dehli? She was wearing a long, cotton summer frock which she had made herself, the fabric had a pattern of alternating open and closed tulips. Even though she was sitting down he could tell how unusual it was, how it accentuated – not her figure, but her personality, her innate elegance. It was as if she had succeeded in transferring the lines of her irresistible neck to the garment. Jonas had always counted himself among those men who believe a woman is infinitely more interesting clothed than unclothed, and he had noticed right away, from a hundred metres off, how sexy, how attractive she looked, in that dress.

They sat for hours on that bench in the heat of the day, until she suggested that they go back to her place, she was living in the city now. He did not know whether it was something to do with the red lenses of her sunglasses, but he felt that she was eyeing him differently, with more interest than before.

They strolled slowly across the grass in the lovely light under the great, green treetops. He found himself admiring her slender, leggy figure, the grace with which she moved, accentuated by the fact that she was barefoot. She had done a bit of modelling work in Paris, but most of the time she had studied, learned, visited people in the fashion business. He had been right about the frock. Even without a low-cut neckline, without long slits up the sides, it made her look sexy, even more attractive. There was something about the way the fabric fell over her form. The tulips, the pattern of the fabric prompted him to wonder again about his future, whether he was going to open up or close in. Some people never opened up. She strode barefoot across the grass towards Kunstnernes Hus and her scooter. She had kept the red Vespa. Pernille's style might not have been altogether in accord with the dawning feminist movement, but in her own way she was as much of a rebel as anyone.

On the way up to Majorstuen they stopped at a café and stayed there so long that by the time they got to her place it was late in the evening. There was no one else home. She got them something to drink. They talked, played music: the Mamas and the Papas, the Lovin' Spoonful. She showed him her new sewing machine, some heavily embroidered fabrics and a portfolio of drawings in which she had copied patterns from paintings by Gustav Klimt. None of this could have told him, though, that ten years later she would be Norway's answer to Laura Ashley, designing both clothes and furnishings in a romantic, floral style which was, nonetheless, surprisingly modern, urban. At that particular moment, though, he was just a bit puzzled by the searching looks she was giving him; so he asked, more to distract her really, whether they might not have some supper. 'Wait right here,' she said, put on Jefferson Airplane and left the room. A good fifteen minutes later she reappeared carrying a small case. 'We're going out,' was all she said, and gave him another funny look.

'Isn't it a bit late for this,' he yelled, when he was seated once more on the pillion of the red scooter with his nose buried in her hair and her neck. 'It's summer,' she yelled back. 'It's never too late in the summer,' she said as she parked the Vespa outside Kunstnernes Hus and handed him the case. The sky was still light. The air tropically warm. The Oslo night smelled of lilac. She was still barefoot. He took off his shoes too, left them under the scooter seat. They strolled across the warm tarmac. She took his hand. Why had they never gone out together in junior high? She did not lead him through the Palace Gardens, headed instead down Parkveien towards Drammensveien. The air was so heavily scented it was like being in some foreign city. Opposite the prime minister's official residence she stopped and glanced round about. 'Give me a hand,' she said and proceeded to climb over the fence into the Queen's Gardens. The park was closed at night. 'This is against the law, we'll get caught,' he said. She turned and gave him a long, hard look, as if trying to get inside his head, discover what could have possessed him to make such a stupid remark. Again he was thrown into confusion. 'Only if someone sees us,' she said. 'And why should anyone see us?' He shot a glance at the Palace, jokingly muttered something about offences against the Crown as he helped her over, making sure that her dress did not snag on the lance-tipped railings of the cast-iron fence. He passed the case to her before hopping over himself. I've finally made it into the Queen's Chambers, he thought. They stole between the trunks of tall hardwood trees, over grass that felt cool and soft under their feet. Here and there they caught the yellow glimmer of creeping buttercups. She made a beeline for a pond with a fountain splashing in it rather forlornly and pointlessly. Or for them alone. She led the way to the end nearest the Palace, bundled up her skirts and waded into the water, across the narrow channel. He followed, feeling the little round pebbles on the bottom. There was an island in the middle of the pond. An island overgrown with trees and dense vegetation, grass as high as a meadow, a miniature jungle, a place in which to play the guerrilla. They settled themselves under the dominant weeping ash. Its branches hung all the way to the ground, hiding them like a parasol from the guardsmen on sentry duty outside the Palace and down by the stables. Jonas was reminded of the deliciously prickly hidey-holes of his childhood. She spread a travelling rug out on the grass. 'Welcome to the Garden of Eden,' she whispered.

She arranged the contents of the case on the rug: cured ham and melon, a highly seasoned pâté, slices of tomato over which she had sprinkled freshly chopped basil. 'Dig in then,' she said, pouring white wine into two simple kitchen tumblers. 'You said you were hungry, didn't you?' She handed him bread and a bowl of black olives. He ate, drank, noticed that she helped

herself to some soft, white cheese and a stick of celery. Never, not even in the
Red Room, in Leonard's basement, had food tasted so good. So erotic. He
lay there enveloped in the scent of earth and growing things, surrounded by
lilies and Solomon's seal, munching honeydew melon, and watched as this
girl draped in a fabric decorated with open and closed tulips poured a few
drops of Tabasco sauce onto a piece of chicken, as if to demonstrate her sin-
gularity, her audacious taste. Her boldness in general. Directly across from
them, on the top of a small hill they could make out a gazebo. The Palace
rose up behind large, flowering shrubs; they might have been in another
country, another time, at the Versailles of the Sun King. He felt – he groped
for the word – reckless. As if, merely by lying there, enjoying all of this, he was
defying the run-of-the-mill. Committing an act of sabotage even.

He was lying listening to the splashing of the fountain when, right out
of the blue, she gave him a kiss, quick and hot, that left behind a taste of red
pepper, salt, vinegar, a breathtakingly sharp tang on his lips. A violent fluttering in his breast. And an unsated hunger, replete though he was. Hunger for
a body. She drew him down onto the rug, among the little dishes. It was such
a relief, an almost vampiric sensation, to at long last be able to press his lips
against that long neck of hers, run his tongue along the hairline at the nape
of her neck, kiss the skin below her ears for so long that her toes splayed and
little moans issued from her throat. One of his hands slipped underneath
her skirt, worked its way up to her knees, while he went on kissing her, while
she went on emitting barely audible sighs. He slid his hand further up, under
the fabric of her frock, under the pattern of tulips opened and closed, with a
sense of performing a kind of covert unveiling; he stroked the soft, smooth
skin on the inside of her thighs, and this in turn made him feel as though he
was almost suffocating with desire. No fabric in the world could compare
with this texture, not even silk; if anyone ever managed to manufacture a
synthetic material that came anywhere close to this they could make millions.
He reached her panties, gently pulled them down, still without lifting up her
skirt. He ran sensitive fingertips over the grooves left by the knicker elastic on
the soft skin below her waist, as if it were a legible script, a vital prophecy. As
he slid his fingers down and into her crotch, not knowing whether it was the
scent of sexual juices or the aroma of flowers and Tabasco sauce that drifted
past his nose, he noticed that her hand had stiffened into a stagey pose while
her toes were pointed, her ankles extended as in a dance, even though she was
lying on the ground.

With his middle finger he explored the folds of her vagina, as if she were
clothed here, too, and he needed to undress her in order to discover her true
nature. She writhed about, moaned so uninhibitedly that he was afraid one of

the guards might hear. As his finger opened up a path for itself, working from the back forwards, he had the sensation of leafing through a book, so much so that that he could actually read, on page after page, of what the future might hold for them; and when his finger at last glided further up and lighted on the clitoris – a scaled down reflection, a tiny island in a queen's garden – and he concentrated on this branching of the ways, he could tell – also from her reaction, the sudden gasp at the very moment that a light went on in one of the Palace windows – that he had found an answer of sorts, something which seemed to be confirmed by the abrupt and violent shudders that were now running through her, radiating as it were from her vagina to every part of her body. Her balletic pose had to give way to the uncontrolled twitching of her fingers and toes, and her writhing limbs set the plates and glasses tinkling; but these convulsions also seemed to cause a veil, or a last item of clothing to fall away from her, enabling him to see quite plainly that she was not the one – to perceive this as clearly, and with as great a shock, as if, at his wedding, he had lifted up his bride's veil to find that she was not who he expected. With a touch of sadness he was forced to conclude that this girl, Pernille, too was a red herring, designed to distract him from a woman as yet unknown to him.

And so he hesitated. And so he refrained from pulling up her skirt and throwing himself on top of her, even when he felt the gentle press of her hands on his back, like an invitation. He tried to excuse himself to her; he wasn't ready, he said, whispered breathlessly. Used just such a high-flown, rather archaic expression. And for this very reason – because she was a romantic, because she was a different sort of feminist – Pernille understood. Still, though, he was afraid – afraid of this lust, afraid that one day, instead of life, a desire to do the right thing, he would make do with a sex life. It was always there, just under the surface: the fear of suffering the same fate as Melankton. Precisely by not falling upon her he would prove his exceptional character, his rebellious will.

Later Jonas would contemplate the choice he had made in this and in similar situations. Because what if sex was life? And what if the life in which he might attain the 'lofty' goals towards which he strove was the life of the nether regions?

They slept, closely entwined. And they did not wake until late in the morning. If anyone had seen them they certainly had not reported it. They were hardly visible anyway, surrounded as they were by the tall vegetation and screened by the weeping ash's tracery of low branches. Jonas woke up brimful of energy, woke up with a feeling of having been recreating on that tiny island for a year. They waded back across to the Queen's Gardens and carried on out of the gate, which was now open. Jonas said goodbye and ran all the way up to Oscars gate, partly in order to burn off some of his excess energy, but also because he thought his grandmother must be worried sick about him. And annoyed, since it was now Sunday and he would not be able to pick up the desired supply of cigars.

She looked up from her newspaper when he walked in and asked what had taken him so long. 'You've been away more than half an hour,' she said.

'Half an hour?' he repeated.

'Yes. And where are my cigars, young man?'

'What day is it?' Jonas asked.

'Saturday,' his grandmother replied. 'Have you lost your wits completely? Now hurry up and get back down there before the shop closes.'

Time. He lay all alone on a broad expanse of beach in Montevideo. Seen from above, the deckchair and parasol must have looked like a small, stranded vessel. Or a target in the middle of a white desert. He merely lay there staring into space while the days passed; after a while he could not have said whether he had been sitting in that deckchair and hanging around the run-down hotel with the sleepy ballrooms for two years or two weeks. Late one afternoon he got up, however, and took the bus into the city centre where he proceeded to wander aimlessly around the old town. Again he had that strong sense of being on the trail of things past, an age of spurs and stirrups, gaucho knives and ancient pistols. He came to a grimy church, or a chapel more like, sandwiched in between some other buildings. Outside it a couple of bent old women in black shawls were standing talking. Although he could not have said why, he went inside. The church was totally empty. Hushed. Candles burned here and there. He sank down onto a pew, soaked up the atmosphere, savoured the pleasant coolness which eased the pressure he still felt in his chest. A murmuring sound reached his ears, only a murmur, but still it echoed faintly around the cavelike room. He became aware that something was going on behind a curtain in one of the neat, dark little stalls – cabinets of a sort – along one wall. Someone was acknowledging their sins in a confessional. Jonas thought he caught a vague whiff of mothballs. On their knees, confessing. He thought about this. Unconsciously shaking his head because he found it so bafflingly antiquated. Baffling altogether, in fact.

A woman pulled back the black curtain and stepped out. His eyes almost started out of his head. She wore jeans and a college sweatshirt, trainers on her feet. Attractive. Dark, the way women here were. Twenty-ish. Jonas's eyes lingered on her. She stood for a moment, hunting for something in a small leather bag before making for the door. He had been struck by her face. He did not get it: a young woman, on her knees in this dusty church. What had she confessed? He felt like following her, but did not. An old priest emerged from the confessional. Jonas caught a glimpse of the grille through which you spoke, noticed that it showed signs of wear at lip level. All of a sudden he had a powerful urge to call out to the old priest, confess, bend the knee inside that stall, at that grille, divulge everything that was in his heart, pour it all out. 'Father, I'm hiding my light under a bushel.'

He left the church and went back to roaming around, restlessly, aimlessly, and yet on the alert. He wandered along lost in thought, though with no idea what he was thinking about. When he looked up, he found himself in front of the antiquarian bookshop outside which he had stopped several times before, the one with *Kristin Lavransdatter* in the window. Inside he saw the girl from the church. Without stopping to think he opened the door and entered premises which summoned up once more the feeling he had had in the church. He found himself in a blessedly peaceful room. Of another order. A place in which an age-old, almost Ptolemaic view of things prevailed.

With the young woman was an elderly man. Both of them stared blankly at him. By way of explanation, or apology, Jonas pointed to the bulky novel by Sigrid Undset in the window, went so far as to pick it up, flick through it – an edition printed in Barcelona, part of a series of Nobel prize-winners. 'Undset,' he said. And then, in halting Spanish 'I am from the same country.' For some reason it sounded to him as if he was confessing. As if a whole story were contained within those few words. Something happened. The faces of the two others broke, as one, into big smiles. They both started talking, very fast. When they realised that he did not understand they switched to English, or rather: the young woman did the talking. He had to answer a great many eager questions – he could not help but smile at such avid curiosity – and in return he learned that the old man was the owner of the bookshop and the woman, Ana, was his granddaughter. Close to, she was even more attractive, or appealing. She wore amethysts in her ears, bluish-violet like the flowers on the jacaranda trees. Her name sounded like a vow. A sort of prefix. He did not know that she also embodied a golden opportunity – that she could be what Mr Dehli had called a catalyst. She had only popped in to pick up a book, was just leaving. In the doorway she paused, thought for a moment. Had Jonas eaten? Would he like to have lunch with her? Jonas glanced uncertainly at her grandfather, thinking to himself that the people here were a bit old-fashioned, Catholics, such a thing might be frowned upon, but the old man merely nodded, waved his arms at them: Go, go!

As they strolled through the streets of the old town, from the Plaza Zabala down to the harbour, she told him more about herself. She had lived in Europe for many years. Her father had gone into exile with his family for the twelve years of the dictatorship, a time full of fear and terrible brutality.

Thousands had been imprisoned, many were tortured, many more simply vanished. But now the country had a new government, only recently elected. Ana had returned home to study sociology. She lived with her grandparents.

When she stopped to point out an enormous bank building to him they heard the clatter of pots coming from an open window. Unnaturally loud, as if someone was pretty mad about something. This prompted a laughing Ana to tell him about an unusual form of protest practised during the dictatorship. At a prearranged time – or quite spontaneously, following a speech on the radio – crowds of women would pour out into the streets, banging on pots and pans, making an ear-splitting din, as a demonstration against the ruling power. Ana explained proudly how, by refusing to be silent, refusing to cooperate, or quite simply by gossiping, by relaying stories, her grandmother and other women, ordinary housewives, had made the most effective, and indeed the only *possible* protest against the regime. Jonas could see it in his mind's eye, hear it. Very funny, was his first thought, but then he thought again: to tell tales, to go out into the streets and bang on saucepans, that had to be just about the diametric opposite of lazing in a deckchair.

As Ana led him closer and closer to the harbour, towards one of the most crucial – catalytic – incidents in his life, Jonas realised that this was a story he had heard before. Of strong women and weak, corrupt men. He thought of his own grandmother and the German occupation. As with most Norwegians, Jørgine's feelings about the war were somewhat ambivalent. On the one hand it had been her finest hour. On the other, those five years had left their traumatic mark. Once, when Jonas accidentally used the word 'Buchtel' of one of the prisms on the chandelier, he almost got his ears boxed. 'No German in this house!' his grandmother had admonished fiercely.

Had Jørgine Wergeland told her grandchild a little more, he might have learned an important lesson about human beings. She could have taught him that there's no telling how your life will turn out, even though you might already be, let's say, sixty. You might look like a pretty ordinary character, a failure even, with a career that was well and truly over, only for some external circumstance to suddenly turn you into a person of paramount importance to an entire nation, possibly even mark you out as the saviour of civilisation. Seen in that light, one person's long, commonplace life might sometimes simply be a preparation for the momentous deeds of their latter years, once he or she had discovered their true mission.

Up until the Second World War, Jørgine Wergeland had led a normal, happy life with her Oscar, Jonas's grandfather, in a smallholding out at Gardermoen, the old drill ground. When the war came to Norway one of the occupying force's first moves was to extend the airfield at Gardermoen. Jørgine and Oscar lost their farm and Jonas's grandfather dropped dead – he did not get much pleasure out of the compensation paid to them by the Germans. Granny always said that he 'exploded with rage'. And apropos that destiny the outlines of which she was beginning to discern, inspired by a British statesman she added: 'Losing the farm was my Dardanelles, my life's lowest point.'

Jørgine moved into Oslo, and in honour of her husband she took possession of a spacious flat in Oscars gate, behind the Palace. But only a year later, in 1943, to everyone's surprise – and consternation – she married an elderly, childless man and moved into his palatial residence in nearby Inkognitogata. No one could have suspected that Jørgine Wergeland had embarked upon a cunning sabotage operation, an operation she was determined to carry out even if it meant selling her soul to the devil.

Then, in the early autumn of the year the war ended, her second husband died. It was to all appearances a natural death – if a coronary can be considered a natural death. 'It's hardly surprising his heart failed him,' Jørgine remarked conspiratorially to Jonas's mother, 'when you think how black and treacherous it was.' It should perhaps be added that Jørgine had known full well that this man had a bad heart. The last thing she had wanted was to have to spend the rest of her life with him.

The fact was that her new husband was a building contractor. And in the self-same war which had caused Jonas's grandfather to 'explode with rage' this other man had made a mint. Jonas's grandmother had not been idle during the year in which she lived alone in Oscars gate. Like a spy she had infiltrated certain circles and, with great care and a surprising degree of cynicism, selected a person who had made money primarily by building airfields for the Germans. There is no point in naming this man or in listing the airfields in question – the country was swarming with such types, and there were airfields all over the place. But for Jørgine Wergeland, who had lost both smallholding and husband because the Germans decided to cover more of Gardermoen with concrete, it was essential that the man of her choice had been contracted to lay runways. Had she lived, Jørgine Wergeland would, I'm sure, have appreciated the irony of it when the time came to build a new main airport in Norway and Gardermoen once more became a goldmine for building contractors.

Another important vital condition in her choice of husband, or victim, was that he had to be an entrepreneur who had ceased his business activities – bluntly described by Jørgine as his treasonous activities – in good time and had seen the wisdom of one of the rules of mountain safety which everyone in Norway would later know by heart: there's no shame in turning back – although in his case it was more a matter of turning his *coat* back. And to be on the safe side he had even become involved, half-heartedly and very circumspectly, in some underground work. The minute she met him Jørgine noticed that his eyes were set abnormally far apart. He looked a bit like a hammerhead shark. This sinister feature became more marked as the war progressed, as if it took its toll to keep looking two ways at once. Be that as it may, he neatly avoided being arrested or punished when peace was declared, despite government investigations and a bloodthirsty public hue-and-cry against collaborators.

It is tempting, even though it lies outside the scope of this story, to take a closer look at the boom in certain sectors during the war. Disturbingly many Norwegians made a lot of money, just as the whole of Norway today grows richer with every war waged, due to the attendant rise in the price of oil. Much has been written about the astonishingly cooperative line taken by the Norwegian authorities, with the exception of the King and the government, towards the occupying force, more or less from day one. 'The wheels have to be kept turning in the interests of the working people,' was how it was phrased. This cooperation also included tasks of such military importance as the repair and extension of airfields. In the spring and summer of 1940, not one class, not one organisation, not one political party advocated an open policy of sabotage, and so it continued, with surprisingly few exceptions, for some time. This says a lot about Norway. Other countries lost millions of people, to famine, in battle; the citizens of the Soviet Union, not least, fought and died – also for Norway's benefit. And what did Norway do? The somewhat less than heroic answer would be: 'We trod softly.' Poland lost about twenty per cent of its population, Norway three per mil. Not counting the sinking of the *Blücher*, the fight put up by certain divisions in the very earliest phase of the war, not least at Narvik, a few dozen genuine heroes and, of course, the navy, the Norwegian resistance campaign could be said to have been one of the least heroic ever. All military operations were terminated in June 1940, after eight weeks. Later, it also came out that every fifth Norwegian officer had been a member of Quisling's National Unity party. Within just about every branch of trade and industry hands were extended to the Germans. And the gains could on occasion be prodigious. Which makes it all the harder to understand – for a foreigner particularly – how Norway, a country which was subjected to a relatively mild period of occupation, could have carried out such an unreasonably relentless series of judicial purges after the war – as if all the hostility and outrage could finally be vented, five years too late. Despite everything so far written about Norway and the Second World War, it would not be too bold a prediction to state that our contribution to the war effort, our spirit of resistance, will be shown to be even more frayed and pathetic when still more researchers have delved into the events of those five years. Such a statement might be hard for a few people to swallow, but Jørgine Wergeland for one would have declared herself heartily in agreement. 'Our military honour was lost when the dreadnought *Norge* was sunk at the Battle of Narvik,' she said once to Jonas. 'With the battleship *Eidsvold* our ideals too went down.'

In other words, by the time the Germans left the country, Jørgine's second husband had made himself a nice packet. Which no one knew anything about. And better still: he had been shrewd and foresightful enough to stash away his money in an obscure network of bank accounts. It had, in other words, been nicely laundered.

Right from the day when he effected his carefully calculated about-turn, at a time when everyone could see that the Germans' luck was also turning, he was convinced that he would get away with it. He had not, however, reckoned with his wife-to-be; how was he to know that behind a smiling, friendly and indeed apparently loving mask, Jørgine Wergeland viewed him quite simply as another Hitler, a man whom she had resolved to bring down. If he had not suspected anything before, then he should have done when she turned to him as they walked out of the registrar's office, looked him straight in his hammerhead face and uttered her first words as a newly-wed: 'I have nothing to offer but blood, toil, tears and sweat.'

Jørgine Wergeland declared war on her husband, she commenced a campaign of resistance of which no one was ever aware, conducted as it was within the four walls of their home. And she resorted to tactics which were much more ruthless than the clattering of pots and frying pans.

I do not know whether Jonas Wergeland associated Høyanger with demonstrations, with women and saucepans, but I noticed the rapt expression on his face one day when we were strolling along the steamship wharf and he spotted the old Høyang emblem on the door of the metalworks. He was clearly moved by the sight of that name, which had been stamped into the aluminium of so many of his boyhood's saucepans, including the ones on which he had done some cacophonic drumming of his own.

Whitsun was just around the corner. We were tied up at a pontoon dock out by the breakwater, under the southern face of Gråberget, with a great view of the town and Hålandsnipa forming a wall behind it, and of Øyrelva, its foaming white stream snaking down the mountainside on the other side of the fjord. The chimneys at the metalworks no longer spewed out black smoke as they did in the old photographs taken by Olav Knutzen; fluoride-laced smoke that had, in the past, done so much visible damage to the environment. No one now could call the works at Høyanger a 'black cathedral' or a 'dark, satanic mill'. And yet, as we sailed up the fjord I had the strong impression of a meeting between a new age and an old. At first glance the sight of the vast metalworks, the production halls and the towering silos in which the raw material, oxide, was stored, was impressive. But when I thought about it I realised that the *Voyager*, our modest little craft, housed an industry every bit as great. It had struck me before that our boat, with its enormous capacity for storing information and its possibilities for wireless communication with the whole world, represented something bigger, mightier, than all the Hydro Aluminium buildings in this mountain-encircled basin. In terms of potential the *Voyager* was, in fact, an aircraft carrier; theoretically we could sit here, out on the fjord, and generate assets as great as Hydro earned by selling the aluminium made at Høyanger. Sailing there on the fjord, we provided the perfect illustration of the new Norway and the old. A small mobile object approaching something massive and steadfast. And vulnerable. No one, least of all the townsfolk, could tell when the owners of Høyanger's cornerstone industry might see fit to shut down the plant, possibly set up production elsewhere.

Sogn. Again and again I was struck by how extraordinary, how *unique*, this area was. In many ways it was Norway in a nutshell. Until well into the nineties there was not a single state wine monopoly outlet in the Sogn and Fjordane region. And in the whole district there was but one set of traffic lights. Sogn was like a little Switzerland smack in the middle of Norway. Often, when we sailed round a point and one of those little towns hove into view, tucked away at the head of an inlet or the arm of a fjord and ringed by high mountains, I would find myself thinking that there was something unreal about it, that it was a bit like the valley of Tralla La in Carl Barks's story about Uncle Scrooge; a place where everyone was happy. And people in Sogn *were* happy. A host of surveys confirmed, time and again, that the inhabitants of this region were the most content in the whole country. In every set of statistics they came out on top where what mattered was to be top, and came bottom where that was best. They lived longest and were least sick, if you like.

I had wondered whether this might have something to do with the contrasts found around Sognefjord. Did they generate a tension, a salubrious force field which in turn made the people expand? Here in Høyanger, with all its clear reminders of aluminium, that attractive light metal, my thoughts often turned – as if running down an opposite track – to all of the fruit-growing which we had also seen in Sogn. I will never forget the view as we sailed past Leikanger. The whole place, the slopes running up to the heights, shimmered with the pale-pink blossom on tens of thousands of apple trees, shot here and there with sunlight glinting off the sprinkler jets. The climate at Leikanger was so favourable that you could plant an apricot tree against a south-facing wall or even grow grapes. We anchored close enough to shore to be able to enjoy the sight of the gigantic walnut tree in the vicarage garden, standing between the main house and the water. Did the key to Sognefjord perhaps lie hidden here? In the tension between plants and minerals, fruit and aluminium? Amanlis, Summer Red and d'Oullins on the one side, cables, ceiling panels and railway wagons on the other. I would not argue with anyone who dared to say that the healthiness and contentment of the local inhabitants stemmed from a kind of visual alchemy – the blossom-covered branches of an apple tree against a backdrop of silvery aluminium cylinder blocks.

In Høyanger Jonas could easily have passed for a local, by which I mean that he seemed even more content than usual. Possibly because he came upon so many unexpected links with his own life. As when, for example, someone told him about the slug factory which had closed down just before the turn of the millennium and he realised that the material for the tubes containing his favourite sandwich spreads had been made there. At another factory, Fundo's, they produced the wheel rims for the car which he himself drove. Høyanger helped one to understand the world of today. In a small town at the head of a narrow fjord, walled in by steep mountainsides, they manufactured a car part for a factory in another country which also received parts from a dozen other countries. You lived in Høyanger, but were part of a global network.

But there was another reason for Jonas Wergeland's happiness, and that reason was Kamala. I have nothing against that – I least of all. It was the best thing about the whole trip: to see those two, Kamala Varma and Jonas Wergeland, together; to observe how devoted they were to one another. 'How's my secretary getting on?' Kamala might say, wrapping her arms around him. And he would not answer, merely allow himself to be hugged. Even when he was sitting alone on deck, possibly writing something in his big notebook or simply staring up at the rigging, her effect on him was clear to see. His name appeared in print at the very beginning of a love story. Whenever I saw him I could not help thinking: there's a man who is loved. Who simply laps up love. So he can learn to love. Become a lover. That may sound easy, but for Jonas Wergeland it was anything but. It had taken him a lifetime to reach this stage.

I think it must also have been this love which enabled him to view his country in a new and unprejudiced light. 'You have the Ganges,' I heard him say to Kamala – in jest, I grant you – on the way to Høyanger, as we were leaning on the rail, gazing incredulously at Ortnevik across the water, 'but we have Sognefjord. This is our sacred river. And the farms clinging to the mountainsides are our temples.'

With similar pride he showed us the church at Høyanger, designed by no less a person than Arnstein Arneberg, one of the architects behind Oslo Rådhus. The old town gate offered a perfect view of it, in its lovely setting on the other side of the river, on a low hill at the foot of Gråberget's steep rock face. Jonas talked Kamala and I into posing on the bridge, so he could take our picture with the church in the background. It might have had something to do with his closeness to Kamala, but sometimes I had the impression that he was starting to look like an Indian, even in his colouring, that soon he really would look like a film director from Bombay – just as his grandmother's features had, over the years, grown more and more Churchillian. He took a long time over it, snapping picture after picture, until eventually Kamala got fed up, went up to him, took the camera and ordered him to go and stand next to me. That was so like her. Kamala Varma is a woman who prefers to take photographs herself.

This same attitude, or mindset, lay at the root of Wergeland's programme on Liv Ullmann. Jonas's heroes and heroines were not only discoverers, they were to just as great an extent rebels. Few have discerned the salute to the spirit of resistance and defiance which underpins the whole series.

At the heart of the Ullmann programme lay an incident which many Norwegians recall with ambivalent wonder: the actress's dinner with Henry Kissinger in March 1973; a banquet which was duly covered by a couple of Norwegian dailies. Jonas Wergeland concentrated, however, on their brief meeting before the dinner, which was by no means an intimate affair, but a huge party in honour of film director John Ford, held at the Grand Ballroom of the Beverley Hilton Hotel; a function also attended by President Nixon. A lot of Norwegians felt very proud, flattered even, on Liv Ullmann's behalf, that Henry Kissinger himself, long-time professor of political science at Harvard University, now the presidential advisor on national security and soon to become the American Secretary of State – not to mention something of a womaniser and one of the world's most written-about men – had personally asked the Norwegian actress to be his dinner companion. But a lot of Norwegians were also rather shocked, and possibly disappointed, that an artist of Liv Ullmann's weighty calibre should allow herself to be dazzled by something as basic, not to say primitive, as power, and such a dubious sort of power at that; they did not like the thought that she might fall for a man who, while famed for his brilliant analyses of foreign affairs and inspired diplomacy, was equally well-known for his cynical, almost sinister internal intrigues, and was even quoted as having said – the nerve of it! – that power is the ultimate aphrodisiac. Many people found it hard to equate the couple's little tête-à-tête with their image of Liv Ullmann as a demure woman with a natural Nordic allure. She was accused of being naive. The possibility that she might have accepted the invitation with her eyes wide open, that she might be a mature woman with masses of self-confidence and great inner strength was almost automatically discounted. This was the politicised Norway of the seventies, readily inclined to think in terms of headlines such as: 'Sweet, innocent woman seduced by nasty, conservative man.'

As an actress, Liv Ullmann was at the very peak of her career, nominated for an Oscar for her role in *The Emigrants*. But despite her international success, despite all the prizes and honorary degrees bestowed on her from all quarters, despite being the subject of a lead story in *Time* the year before, with her picture on the cover and all, Liv Ullmann's acting was not particularly well appreciated in Norway. In people's minds she was always associated with a certain type of 'heavy', doleful role, with a tremulous expression and a voice which was all too easily parodied.

Jonas Wergeland wanted to shatter the stereotype 'Ullmann myth' which prevailed in Norway. In the programme's key scene the couple, Liv Ullmann and Henry Kissinger, were seen having a glass of white wine in Ullmann's Hollywood hotel suite – there was no sign of the secret service people, nor of the friend who was visiting Liv Ullmann at the time. It was Kissinger, ever the diplomat, who had requested this brief meeting, so that they could have a little chat, just the two of them, before leaving for the society dinner in honour of John Ford. Jonas Wergeland portrayed them as actors in a film. He had Ullmann, or rather: Ella Strand who played Ullmann, dressed, not in the white gown which the actress had actually been wearing, but in a red number with a plunging neckline, the one which she had worn in the unforgettable mirror scene, an almost two-minute long close-up – what a piece of acting, what presence, it was enough to make a cameraman forget all about his camera – from the film *Cries and Whispers* – a film in which, incidentally, Liv Ullmann's radiance and beauty were presented in such timeless and touching fashion that not only Henry Kissinger, but even your ordinary Norwegian had to take his hat off to her.

Then something occurred in this half-unreal film scenario, in which a Norwegian woman, a Norwegian maiden – people forgot that she already had two long-term relationships behind her – sat face to face with the world-spirit, to use a rather Hegelian turn of phrase. What followed, though quiet and undramatic, was in fact, a variation on the final scene from *A Doll's House* – it was no coincidence that Nora was one of Liv Ullmann's great roles – and in order to get this across Wergeland played Ullmann's strongest cards: her face, her sensitive mouth and, above all, her eyes, that look, the secret of which lay not in their blueness, but in the strength of will that shone in them. Liv Ullmann would later write a book entitled *Changing*, an international bestseller and a life-changing read for many people. Jonas Wergeland set out to capture just such a moment of change. A moment marked by the urge to object, to do something other than what is expected. In an earlier version – of which he even did a trial cut – at the turning point of the Kissinger tableau he inserted Ullmann's primal scream from Ingmar Bergman's film *Face to Face*, as a cry of realisation or protest; a brief clip from the scene in which, in the part of Jenny, she stands with her back to a wall and screams, really howls. Instead, though, he opted for the quieter transition, partly because he wanted to break with the unfair Ullmann cliché of a face contorted by psychotic angst and pain. Suddenly, while sitting there in that hotel suite with Kissinger, she lifted her eyes, that expressive face, and looked out of the 'fiction', out of the scene, straight at the cameraman, as if she had caught sight of something extremely important, then she abruptly stood up and walked towards the viewers, giving them to understand that she was taking over the camera, the direction, herself; her voice was heard, giving instructions, as another actress entered the scene, dressed in the same red dress and sat down in her, Liv Ullmann's, place, across from Henry Kissinger. With this switching of roles, Jonas Wergeland also wished to show how detached Ullmann actually was from the whole carry-on – and from the gossip and the ridiculous rumours to which she knew it would give rise. She took, as it happens, the same rather blithe approach to a later dinner held to mark the end of the SALT negotiations, at which she was seated between Kissinger and the Soviet ambassador to Washington. For Ullmann, this function had about it the inescapable air of a superficial, inconsequential party game or a first-night shindig. The way she saw it, Kissinger would have made the perfect tragic figure in a Bergman film. And so at this pivotal moment, in this fictional situation, when Ullmann got to her feet and stepped out of Kissinger's dazzling aura, it was with a cool, little smile for which Jonas found justification in her little known sense of humour and self-irony. And by some inexplicable metamorphosis, the woman on the screen, the slightly younger actress who had taken Ullmann's place, now called to mind Kristin Lavransdatter, while Kissinger suddenly looked like Erlend. A note of *defiance* had crept into the scene, a sense of a secret rendezvous between a woman going against her parents' wishes and an excommunicated man. Viewers were witness to a provocative flouting of convention. A passionate woman who stayed true to her convictions, had faith in her own judgement of right and wrong. A woman who was no longer just a good little girl who listened to what everyone else told her she should do. A woman who was also – no small point this – stronger than the man sitting opposite her.

Jonas Wergeland's aim was to show how, at a certain point in her life, Liv

Ullmann chose to become a woman, a person, who *created* reality – who was no longer content to be a 'fiction', a dream. One might say that she turned her back on worldly splendour. All the glamour of film stardom. She went from being out in front, to being behind. From being written about to writing herself. From acting to action. Liv Ullmann did not deny her past, what she did was to broaden her scope. She was an actress, but now she also became a writer and a human rights activist. It says something for Jonas Wergeland's powers of intuition, that he also – unintentionally it's true – anticipated her next step: her decision to become a film director.

The most laudable aspect of the programme was the way it focused so firmly on Liv Ullmann's intelligence – which was also her biggest handicap as a so-called star, not least in Hollywood. What to do with such an actor, one with such rare gifts, such magical power? There were simply no scripts capable of embracing her, of allowing her to give of her best. As an individual she had too much breadth for the standard, formulaic American film roles.

In Jonas Wergeland's version of events, when she got up and walked away from Henry Kissinger and round to the other side of the camera, Liv Ullmann was choosing to write her own part. To quite literally live up to her name which, in Norwegian, means 'life'. The actress gave way to Liv, the woman. Fiction gave way to Life.

Thanks in large part to Jonas Wergeland, from an early age I regarded Liv Ullmann as an ideal. His programme about her was much in my mind when I left the world of television and made the leap from being seen to seeing. Creating. But right now, in Høyanger, I was going through a frustrated phase, I almost felt like rebelling against our own project. One evening, when Martin was doing his best to console me with one of his sumptuous club sandwiches, I began to delete stuff. Did we really have to say that Trotsky had once stayed at a hotel in Vadheim? What about all the foreign submarines that people claimed to have spotted in the fjord? In Sogndal I had paid a visit to a man who worked in a slaughterhouse. He had shown me a collection of things he had found in cows' stomachs – not just nails and rocks, but an old Norwegian coin, the inner tube from a bike tyre and a gold wristwatch. It was funny, but was it relevant?

More and more often my thoughts returned to that disc which I had heard so much about, and which Jonas Wergeland told us even more about: the disc attached to the Voyager probes which, inconceivably many years from now, might pass other stars and planets. Some day – who knew – it might even be opened and played, analyzed, by beings from some distant galaxy. What would they think, if think was the right word, when they saw the picture of a snail's shell, or the leaf of a strawberry plant? Of a dolphin or a banquet in China? What would they think when they heard, on this disc, the sound of wind and rain, of grasshoppers and frogs? Footsteps, heartbeats, laughter? Or, what could they possibly make of this: the sound of a kiss? I tried to imagine the reaction of an extra-terrestrial being on hearing a voice say in the Indian language Gujarati: 'Greetings from a human being of the Earth. Please contact.'

At night, when darkness eventually fell, I would sometimes go up on deck to look at the sky. I liked to think of those two space probes bound for a utopian destination, of the fact that the message they carried, a gold-plated copper disc, was encased in a protective aluminium cover. Wherever you looked there were connections. Even between Høyanger and a space probe. The first object ever to be sent in the other direction, *out* of our solar system, took aluminium with it.

A couple of nights ago Jonas Wergeland told us, with a look on his face I remembered from the treetop conversations of my childhood, about all the new discoveries which Voyager 2 had made for us – it had, for example, found seven hitherto unknown moons circling the planet Neptune. I could not help wondering, the other morning, as I watched him from a distance, sitting with his arm round Kamala: might I be able to discover new 'moons' circling Jonas Wergeland, a man who has been so minutely charted?

There were lots of signs in Høyanger of the halcyon days of the labour movement. Not for nothing was the main street named after the political activist Marcus Thrane. I noticed the keen interest with which Jonas took in the 'Own Home' district and later the Park area or 'garden city', just down from the old hospital: possibly Høyanger's most unique feature. For all I know it was the architect in him waking up. On Kloumann's allé he ran a close eye over the fine residences built for the town's captains of industry, with their privileged location overlooking the fjord. Suddenly, as if inspired by Arnberg's church and the unexpected link with Oslo Town Hall, he decided he wanted to chart the decoration of public buildings in Høyanger and only a couple of phone calls later we found ourselves inside Valhalla, the old red-brick Youth Club building behind the school, the walls of which were covered with pictures of Viking kings and the homes of New Norwegian poet-chiefs. All at once Jonas Wergeland was a bundle of energy, leading the way to the Town Hall, to the community centre and the bank where, almost hidden away, we found pictures and other works by famous Norwegian artists. In a conference room on the fourth floor of the Town Hall we even managed to track down reproductions of the murals which had once adorned the old People's Palace. Jonas spent a long time poring over these lost paintings of men carrying out different sorts of work in and around Høyanger. 'How could they not preserve that lovely building?' he asked.

My guess is that it was these decorations, along perhaps with some memory of his grandmother, that prompted him to ask me what we had thought of doing as regards Sogn and World War II, Sogn and the Germans. Because Kaiser Wilhelm had not been the only German to visit Sognefjord. There were still plenty of traces of their presence, whether as small bunkers, or as vast fortresses like the one at Lammetun. We had discussed this, of course, particularly in connection with another town very similar to Høyanger – Årdal at the very head of Sognefjord – since there too water-power was used to produce aluminium. Årdal could almost be said to have been a gift from the Germans. The liberated Norwegians got the whole thing on a plate. We had considered various angles, but eventually came to the conclusion that it was not within our remit to criticise Norwegian shortcomings during the Second World War or to discuss how beneficial the war had been for the growth of Norwegian industry. We had to draw the line somewhere.

Jørgine Wergeland, on the other hand, was not one for drawing lines. During the war she organised the home front in the truest sense of that term, although hers was a far more ruthless and dogged campaign of resistance than that waged by that other Home Front, the Norwegian underground movement. On her wedding night, when she locked her hammerhead of a husband out of the bedroom it was with an icy paraphrasing of Churchill's words in response to Britain's signing of the Munich agreement: 'You had the choice between shame and war. You chose shame, but you shall have war.'

Having married her unsuspecting building contractor, Jørgine Wergeland took, as they say, the law into her own hands, and funnily enough her main weapon derived from his underground activities. Shrewd entrepreneur that he was, he had contrived to conceal a radio in a rather unlikely, but practical, place: the lavatory. So Jonas Wergeland was not the only one who owed a debt to British broadcasting. Jørgine spent a lot of time in the toilet – or the English Quarter as she called it – on the pretext of chronic constipation, listening to the BBC's edifying transmissions from London. 'I'm a graduate of the WC school of resistance,' she would tell people, who would have no idea what she was talking about. It became something of a code. 'I'm always running in to listen to WC,' she said to Jonas's mother. Everyone, including her husband, thought she was going off her rocker.

By listening to Winston Churchill's stirring speeches, as well as all the references to them and quotations from them in other broadcasts, Jørgine built up a deadly arsenal for use in her clandestine guerrilla war – although it might perhaps be fairer to call it a private judicial purge, since she knew her husband would never be convicted of financial treason. In addition to a store of pithy Churchillian sayings she was armed most appropriately with several boxes of expensive Romeo y Julieta cigars – a gift, ironically enough, to her non-smoker of a husband from certain affluent business contacts. The man was as dull as they come – despite his hammerhead appearance. Jørgine would later use the same words of him as Churchill had used of Molotov, the Soviet foreign minister: 'I have never seen a human being who more perfectly represented the modern conception of a robot.' During one of the first breakfasts they shared, she lit one of her big Cuban cigars and declared, with a slightly revised version of a quote she had heard many times: 'I shall fight you to the last; I shall fight in the hall, I shall fight in the parlour, I shall fight in the kitchen, I shall fight in the bedroom; I shall never surrender.' A statement which actually brought a frown to the brow of this man, whose sole concern in life up to this point had been to find the shortest way to making a fast buck.

It may sound callous, but as far as Jørgine was concerned it was very simple. She was faced here with the same phenomenon which Churchill had labelled, when Germany invaded the Soviet Union, 'a crime beyond description'. She had lost her Oscar because the Germans came to Gardermoen, and she was going to see to it that someone paid for that; she had no pity for a man who had helped the Germans to extend airfields *and* made a packet in the process. A man, who, by some obscure moral logic, regarded himself as innocent, blameless. During her vengeful hunt for suitable candidates, she had not only made sure that the chosen contractor had a bad heart, but that he was in fact *heartless*. Nonetheless, he was subjected not to bloody confrontations, but to strategic manoeuvres. Early on, Jørgine had committed another of Churchill's sayings to memory: 'Battles are won by slaughter and manoeuvre. The greater the general the more he contributes in manoeuvre, the less he demands in slaughter.' In addition to a two-year long policy of evasive action in the bedroom, Jørgine's campaign consisted primarily of dropping sly little hints, day in, day out, as to her husband's crimes, while at the same time inundating him with camouflaged Churchill quotes memorised in that room, the WC, behind whose locked door she was to be found more and more often, puffing on a fat cigar. She quite simply wore him down, mentally; she made life unbearable for him – or rather: for his heart. He did not recognise the charming, considerate woman he had first met, not even to look at. And it was true: during those years Jørgine Wergeland's face would actually start to *resemble* Churchill's round, plump, but exceedingly strong-willed countenance.

Her husband gave up eventually, or gave up the ghost, the year the war ended; and all of those who were present in the Western crematorium believed that they saw, in Jørgine, a genuinely grieving widow. But what was running through Jørgine's mind were Churchill's words when Britain declared war against Japan: 'When you have to kill a man it costs nothing to be polite.' In any case she was too taken up with Alf Rolfsen's impressive paintings in the chapel. These beautiful frescoes reminded her of the fortune she had inherited, because even after the post-war currency stabilisation she had been left with what was, all things considered, a considerable sum of money. And there in the crematorium, as she ran her eyes over Alf Rolfsen's pictures, it came to her, an idea that had been at the back of her mind for some time: she had to use this blood money for something positive, uplifting; it had to be invested in a building. And she did not have to look far: 'I found Norway's biggest piggy bank,' she would later tell the aforementioned Alf Rolfsen as they sat in the Town Hall's Festival Gallery one day, having their elevenses.

Jørgine moved back to her old home in Oscars gate, as if she were once more together with her first husband, or as if her life during the years in Inkognitogaten had been a top-secret affair, a mission performed incognito. When she left the building contractor's flat which had, for her, been more of a battlefield than a home, she took with her just one thing apart from her husband's bankbook: the magnificent crystal chandelier. Had Jonas known the story behind it, he might better have understood why, when they were cleaning the chandelier, his grandmother so often put on records by Vera Lynn, with songs which Jørgine knew from wartime: hits such as 'White Cliffs of Dover', 'Yours' and 'Wishing'. Like Jonas, his grandmother too gazed up at the chandelier, into the crystal droplets, as if they were screens on which she saw scenes being enacted. But unlike Jonas, Jørgine did not see pictures from the Queen's Chambers, she thought about the war, and about Oscar, Jonas's grandfather. Jonas observed how her eyes filled with tears and she became lost in her own thoughts when Vera Lynn's 'We'll Meet Again' was revolving on the turntable. To Jonas these songs were just boring old evergreens, but to her they clearly represented a link with other universes, a portal to infinite inner landscapes. And later he would come to understand that this music must have had the same sort of sentimental associations for his grandmother as *Rubber Soul* had for him. Simple though they were, those tunes could turn some organ inside you to jelly, to soft rubber. So flexible were Jørgine's thought processes that at such times she was not only capable of calling the Town Hall Oslo's Statue of Liberty, she was just as likely to think of it as her Oscar statuette.

Given all this, it should come as no surprise to anyone that Jonas was willing to risk life and limb in defence of the Town Hall. So when Viktor, the leading light of The Three Heretics, came up with the idea for his 'Emil Lie Demonstration' on, or *for*, the Town Hall Square, expressly to save this splendid Statue of Liberty or 'piggy bank', from a new dictatorship, that of the automobile, he was all for it. The Three Heretics recognised something that should have been obvious to everyone, not least the city fathers: the square in front of the Town Hall was an organic part of the building itself. Defile the square and you defiled the Town Hall too.

One suitably beautiful day in September at the very beginning of the seventies, they went to work, which is to say: out into Rådhusgaten, more or less as the gold hands on the clock tower announced that the time was four p.m. and the bells struck up a folk tune – on this occasion 'The Food Song' from Sunnmøre. A lot of people were going to be hopelessly late for dinner, though, because thousands of cars were soon stuck fast in the centre of Oslo due to a demonstration the aim of which was as simple as it was impossible: 'Dancing on the Town Hall Square!'

If one did not know better one could be forgiven for thinking that this event was the forerunner of the somewhat incongruous carnivals which would be arranged a decade or so later. Viktor had succeeded in mobilising about forty students from the Cathedral School as well as some from the Experimental Grammar School – an even better breeding ground for radicalism and iconoclasm than the Cath., if that were possible, and these now proceeded to march round in a circle extending across the four lanes closest to the Town Hall. They were all dressed and made up to look like caricatures of tourists: Frenchmen in berets, Nigerians in gaily coloured robes, Arabs in long djellabahs, Americans in cowboy hats and Hawaiian shirts, Austrians in lederhosen and Tyrolean hats. Those students posing as Japanese carried cameras and snapped non-stop, their jaws dropping in shock – although, if one were being mean, one could say that they focused on the car number-plates, as if their owners were kerb-crawlers. Some carried placards. 'A disgrace to Norway!' and 'Is this the city's finest plaza?' a couple said in German and English. And in Italian: 'Would anyone run a four-lane expressway over the Piazza Navona?' Jonas was guised as an Indian, in a white, high-collared Nehru jacket and Ghandi cap – an outfit which Pernille had helped him with – and he was conscious of feeling not quite so shy in this unfamiliar attire. 'I am a film director from Bombay and I am here to find locations in Oslo for a film about *māyā*,' he announced fearlessly in his best curry-and-rice English to one irate motorist who was yelling that there would be hell to pay if he wasn't there to pick his wife up from the hairdresser's.

The aim of the demonstration was not the same as at Mardøla: to protect something. The Three Heretics set out to dam the heavy and apparently unstoppable stream of painted bodywork flowing past the Town Hall. And the elliptic circle of flabbergasted tourists, or students rather, in the middle of the road actually did succeed in stopping the cars and causing a massive traffic jam around the square. Despite threatening overtures from a few angry drivers and some incipient scuffling, the demonstrators were reassured each time they glanced up at the façade of the Town Hall, where St Hallvard, the patron saint of the city, stood with his arms raised, blessing their venture for all to see.

Viktor had given a lot of thought to what they could possibly hand out to the nearest cars, something which – in the spirit of Ghandi – would illustrate the demonstration's positive aims, but it was Jonas who came up with the idea. He remembered a picture taken around 1950 by OK – Olav Knutzen, Leonard's father – of an open-air dance, or 'cobblestone ball' as they were called, with people tripping the light fantastic, happy and proud, on the Town Hall Square. Jonas called the *Aktuell* photographer, who instantly allied himself with their cause and ran off a couple of hundred copies of the photograph at his own expense. It is never easy to get those affected by it to understand the point of a demonstration. Several of the first motorists got very hot under the collar and kept tooting their horns aggressively, but others thought it was fun – even more so when they were handed the long forgotten photograph, inscribed with the words: 'The heart of the city needs dancing, not lead.' They realised that they were part of something momentous, that they were making history, so to speak. One or two would also save this picture and frame it in fond memory of that day. They might have been late getting home, but they could see that it truly was a disgrace that the Town Hall Square, of all places, this public space laid out so beautifully in front of the city's foremost landmark, should be overrun by cars. On Pipervika, people had welcomed Fridtjof Hansen back from his inspiring expeditions. Here those same people had hailed their dauntless king after the war. Albert Schweitzer himself had addressed a large crowd on this very spot. The Town Hall Square was the heart of the city, but it was also its lungs, a corner designed to give us a breathing space, oxygen. And the politicians and town planners had turned it into the city's colon.

After a while – though not soon enough to prevent total chaos, with a tailback stretching all the way to Malmøya, several kilometres to the south – the law did of course arrive, four squad cars plus mounted police, to disperse the demonstrators. A number had to be carried away, but Jonas and Viktor were the only ones to put up a fight – Jonas was almost happy to feel an old rage stir inside him again. Both were taken to the police station. In a brief item on the *Evening News* Jonas was seen being carted off, still holding aloft the placard bearing his message written, thanks to the kind offices of the Indo-Iranian Institute, in Marathi: 'Destroy not the Gateway of Norway!' – with a clear allusion to the Gateway of India, Bombay's most famous landmark. The irony of it was not lost on Jonas: the first time he managed to achieve his goal in life, to make his name publicly known, it was in the form of an alias, as Vinoo Sabarmati, a famous film director from Bombay. In due course a newspaper photograph was even said to have reached India, and it is not beyond the bounds of possibility that people there really did take Jonas for a film-maker from Bombay who had accidentally strayed into an unknown corner of the world called Norway, a place overrun by police and cars.

Life is full of mysterious coincidences. Jonas had earlier seen how rings could meet and intersect, and not only in water. Still, though, he was startled to read, in prison, that the Town Hall Square – at long last free of cars again – had been paved with flagstones from India. You could almost be said to be walking on the bedrock of India right in the centre of Oslo. This news brought back rather painful memories of his valiant youthful protest, and also revived a thought which had come to him as he was being led down to the harbour area in Montevideo, in far-off Uruguay, by a young, politically-aware woman called Ana: there has been too little iconoclasm and too much orthodoxy in my life. I need to be more of a rebel.

Together with Ana, whom he had got talking to thanks to a copy of *Kristin Lavransdatter* displayed in a window, Jonas reached the main gathering point in the old town. Here, in the shadow of the Customs House, lay the Mercado del Puerto: no longer a market, but a bustling, noisy collection of restaurants, a score or more under one roof, in something resembling an old railway shed; a ferment of barbecue fumes, accordion music and newspaper vendors with grotesque, piercing voices. It was like a cross between an infernal snack bar and a dark, poky pub with long, long bars. With the ease of familiarity Ana led him around open fires, casting a critical eye over the dripping cuts of meat laid out on sloping grill racks. She found a place, ordered food and drinks for them both. 'This is on me,' she said.

Maybe it had something to do with the atmosphere in the bar, Jonas did not know, but Ana started talking again about Sigrid Undset and *Kristin Lavransdatter*, in fact Jonas had the feeling that this was why she had invited him to lunch. She had read the three books as a teenager, she said, and had been absolutely fascinated by Kristin, or Kristina as she was called in the Spanish translation. Jonas simply could not understand it: how could this dusky beauty with amethysts in her ears, a modern woman, a student of sociology who had actually lived in political exile, be so besotted with what was, as far as he was concerned, a stodgy Norwegian novel about a woman in the Middle Ages. And as if to explain, she began alluding, wide-eyed and animated, to different episodes from these books about Kristin Lavransdatter

— keen, or so it seemed to Jonas, to share them with him, to revive a pleasure they had both had. She mentioned the part when the child Kristin meets the elf-maid, and the incident when her poor little sister, Ulvhild, has her back broken by a falling log, and what did Jonas think of Bentein trying to rape Kristin, and Arne being stabbed and killed, wasn't that awful? Jonas, who had not read one word by Undset, found it all pretty hard to follow, but at the same time he could not help being intrigued by the young woman's anecdotes which tended, because she got so caught up in them, to become little stories in themselves.

Eventually he felt compelled to admit that he did not know the story at all. She clapped her hands in disbelief, then burst into ripples of laughter. Fortunately their lunch appeared just at that moment: a bottle of wine and *chivitos*: a thin slice of steak together with bacon, cheese, tomato, egg and a salad of sliced peppers and onions, all served between two huge chunks of bread and held together by toothpicks. She carried on laughing as they ate, could not help it; she seemed to find it hard to believe: a Norwegian who had not read *Kristin Lavransdatter*. And for this very reason, perhaps, she started once again, with redoubled enthusiasm, to relate episodes from the book, as if anxious to show him what he was missing; there she sat, Jonas thought in amusement, pleading a Norwegian writer's case to a Norwegian. Or maybe she simply got so carried away that once she started she could not stop. In any case, she tried to describe to him how wrapped up she had been in the passionate first meetings between Kristin and Erlend, with what trepidation she had read about them dancing together, about Kristin sleeping in his arms, and of how Erlend had kissed her above the knee, thus 'disarming' her, and could then lay her down in the hay. Jonas listened with interest, in suspense in fact, and although he did have to interrupt now and again to inquire about some detail, and once to protest at Kristin's wilful behaviour, for the most part he remained silent throughout the rest of the young woman's very elaborate narration of everything from the lightning that struck St Olav's Church at Jørundgård and set it on fire to Kristin on her deathbed acknowledging God's plan for her. Jonas sat there like a priest in the confessional, one big, hearkening ear, and saw these scenes form a long fresco in his mind's eye. He found it hard to believe, that he could be here in a foreign country, wreathed in the fumes from barbecue coals and grilled meat, with the sound of an accordion in his ears, listening to a young woman recounting extracts from a book by a Norwegian author with such feeling that from time to time she actually blushed.

'And now,' Jonas asked when she was done, with the last sliver of olive on his fork, 'how do you feel about those books now?'

She smiled almost apologetically. 'Well, obviously I feel differently about them today,' she said. 'I find the sombre, rather humourless, view of life which underlies the whole novel hard to take now.' Ana raised her glass and looked at him, the amethysts in her ears flashing a strange purplish-blue in the glow of the nearby fire. 'But I won't let that spoil what they meant to me when I was young,' she said. 'The experience of reading a story which told me love is a primal force that breaks all laws.'

He was back on the white sands, slumped in his deckchair under the blue-striped parasol, listening to the roar of the breakers. He raised his eyes to the horizon. Suddenly he saw things more clearly. It all came down to a woman. To his relationship with a woman. It was possibly Ana who had given him the clue. As he lay there in his chair, thinking, he realised that in searching for a unifying theme for a groundbreaking television series, he had also been trying to discover the driving force behind this ambition. And this driving force – he flushed with shame, his cheeks burning even though he was alone, even though it was only a thought – was love. All he wanted, deep down, was to come up with the makings of a work of art which would show Margrete just a fraction of what she had meant to him. It was not a matter of performing some great feat in order to prove himself worthy of her love, as he had once rather childishly imagined; it was a matter of a gift, an unreserved tribute, a way of saying thank you for reawakening a half-dead aspiration and thereby also his neglected creativity. He wanted to show her what she had made of him. 'Look,' he wanted to say one day, placing the cassettes containing the programmes before her, 'I could never have done this without you.' Yet again, it was *her* he had been thinking about when he did not know what he was thinking about.

Why did he do it? Where did he get the idea?

Jonas was no longer thinking of nothing. He had come to Montevideo in search of not one viewpoint, but many. He needed to garner different perspectives. He sat in a deckchair, thinking several thoughts at once. First and last and under everything else he was thinking of Margrete, but he also thought about his visit to Oslo Town Hall, about a night when he was taught to think big, when he caught Fridtjof Nansen in the beam of a torch, or Harald Hardråde in a tapestry depicting the Battle of Stamford Bridge. Keeping this thought in mind and, beneath it, the thought of Margrete, he continued also to reflect on his grandmother and the war, her strange, secret insurrection, while at the same pursuing a parallel train of thought along the branch leading to the Town Hall Square and the demonstration staged by The Three Heretics, a demonstration in which he had endeavoured to view a Norwegian phenomenon from the outside, as a foreigner; and this last made him see that he would have to view television in the same way, as if he were a Hindu, an Indian, a film director from Bombay. Jonas Wergeland sat in a deckchair in Montevideo and thought of Margrete and of all those other things and, finally, of his meeting with Ana and how they had got talking merely because he happened to mention the name of a Norwegian writer, and in the midst of this welter of thoughts, in the midst of a scene in which he saw himself sitting in an ever-increasing succession of deckchairs stretching out along the beach, Jonas sensed that he ought to concentrate hardest on that last one, on Sigrid Undset, who could actually be regarded as a word in an international vocabulary. A lot of people in Uruguay had never heard of Norway. But some there knew of Undset. Undset, a Norwegian word you might say, was also a word in Spanish. Instead of saying you came from Norway, you could say you came from Undset.

He had had a sudden, catalytic thought and for one long, intense moment he had the whole of that later so renowned television series clear in his head, in astonishing detail. It all came to him in a flash, unfolding as beautifully as a pack of cards fanning out under a conjuror's hand. In his mind he pictured himself meeting Ana again as he was packing to leave for home. She would ask: 'What are you taking with you?' And he would reply: 'A bunch of stories.'

It was as simple as that. None of the countless intellectual and, in some cases, extremely sophisticated analyses of *Thinking Big* can mask the fundamental flash of insight which gave rise to the series, this milestone in television history: in Montevideo, thanks largely to a young woman named Ana, Jonas Wergeland discovered that he wanted to be a storyteller, someone who gathered his people around a gigantic campfire in the shape of millions of switched-on television sets. 'Look,' he wanted to say. 'Listen. Once upon a time there was …' He would seek out stories, find a couple of dozen Norwegian men and women whose tales were worth telling. And that is what he did. When the series was finally in the can, Jonas Wergeland had not only presented Margrete – in secret – with a gift, he had also erected a public edifice full of frescoes, created an ABC for the nation. He felt genuinely proud and pleased the day he discovered that stills from some of his programmes had been used as illustrations in a school reading book.

Jonas gave himself a push, heaved himself out of the deckchair. The canvas billowed like a sail in the soft breeze. He folded the chair without any bother and carried it back to the hotel. Each step told him that he was a well man. He could tell right away: his lungs felt healed.

The worry about his lungs would resurface one last time, though. In prison. And this time it was really serious. During his first year inside he was constantly aware of an inexplicable pressure inside him, an alarming sensation which tended to intensify just before one of Kamala Varma's visits. One evening in late winter a tightness localised in his chest area prompted him to strip to the waist and stand in front of the mirror in his cell. For a second he had the distinct impression – although it may have been a trick of the light – that his chest had become transparent, stood revealed as a web of tissue. He caught a glimpse of colourful, glistening, criss-crossing threads: it looked as if he was wearing a filigree waistcoat. The next day he had himself examined by the prison doctor. He could find nothing. 'Maybe we should get your lungs checked, just to be on the safe side,' he said and gave Jonas a referral slip. A week later, accompanied by two prison officers, Jonas Wergeland made the journey along slush-covered roads to an X-ray clinic in town.

He realised, as he sat in the waiting room, that he was not at all apprehensive. Instead he felt expectant. Like someone who had spent years at sea and was hoping at long last to sight land. The lady at the reception desk had given him a folder. He sneaked a peek at the form inside, read the words 'Thorax front and side.' Had to be something to do with the chest cavity, he guessed.

An assistant in a white coat showed him to a changing cubicle, then to the X-ray room where he was asked to stand with his chest and shoulders pressed against the image plate. He almost felt a little solemn. He thought of the Voyager probes, which were even now zooming out across the cosmos. Among all the information designed to tell extra-terrestrial beings something about the human race was a picture showing an X-ray of a hand – as if to say: we are so clever that we can see through our own bodies. Out of the corner of his eye, Jonas followed the movements behind the screen, in the control room. The radiologist gave him instructions over a loudspeaker, told him how to stand, told him how to breathe. Jonas had no difficulty in holding his breath. He had always been good at holding his breath. Yet again his thoughts returned to life-saving. Or rather, the thought occurred to him that they were going to take photographs of his spirit. And maybe in a way that is what they were doing. What they were actually saying was: 'Hold your spirit!'

Afterwards, as he stood with the X-ray pictures and the letter for the prison doctor in his hand, he was suddenly filled with curiosity. Ungovernable curiosity. The officers who had brought him here seemed to be in no hurry. One of them was reading a newspaper. The other, who was standing by the door, shot Jonas an inquiring glance. Jonas motioned to them to wait a moment. He hefted the large, brown envelope in his hands, as if he thought the weight of it could tell him something about his future. He took out one of the pictures and held it up to the light, remembering Olav Knutzen, remembering the Red Room, that basement in Grorud. He was staring at his own lungs, a dark and yet transparent image. Did this photograph merit an OK stamp? His ribs looked like a sort of cage. It was almost as if prison life had forged bars inside him too. He recognised all he saw. Apart from one thing – something in his lungs, inside the cage, a very small, pale patch, shaped rather like a butterfly. He felt a chill in the pit of his stomach, soon his whole body was caught in an icy grip.

He was in prison, convicted of murder. One little misdemeanour couldn't hurt. He tore open the letter to the doctor and read the radiologist's notes. The conclusion was given at the bottom in block letters: HILUM-MILD FULLNESS. FURTHER EVALUATION RECOMMENDED.

He went back to the woman behind the glass in reception, said he wished to speak to whoever had written the note about his X-ray. 'I *have* to talk to him,' Jonas said. 'Right away.' The lady at the window was not at all sure. It was against all the rules, Jonas knew. Don't you realise who I am, he almost shouted at her, but bit it back. She would have taken this as a reference, not to his erstwhile television celebrity, but to his notoriety as a murderer. Somewhat startled, she picked up the phone, asked him to take a seat, wait.

The doctor came out. The radiologist. It was a woman. She said it was okay, she could make an exception. She did not say why. She took him into the viewing room. The prison officers waited outside. The walls were lined with light-boxes. On one hung some X-rays. There was a Dictaphone on the table. Jonas caught the scent of a discreet, distinctive, but good perfume. He had the feeling that he could trust, could talk to, a doctor who wore such a perfume. The badge on her coat said that her name was Dr Higgs. Her blonde hair was nonchalantly pinned up. When she hung his X-rays on a light-box he noticed her bracelet, an unusual, broad band of gold, decorated with hieroglyphics of some sort. 'I have to be honest,' she said, looking at a picture of his chest viewed from the front, at the vague suggestion of a shadow with a scalloped outline that reminded Jonas of a butterfly. 'I don't know what that is.'

'Don't doctors always know what things are?' he asked.

He could not understand why she suddenly glanced at him in surprise, while at the same time permitting herself a little smile. Was she thinking of his television programmes or – he had to turn this over in his mind a couple of times before daring to pursue it all the way to its conclusion – was she thinking of Margrete, of the fact that he had been married to a doctor? Had she known Margrete?

'Don't tell me you believe that,' she said. And yet, when she raised her hand and pointed to the paler patch in his lung, the sight of that broad bracelet decorated with obscure symbols made him feel that she must possess a rare brand of knowledge, the wisdom of another civilisation.

Interpreting an X-ray was not always easy, she went on. No matter how experienced you were, sometimes you were faced with something you could not explain. Jonas could not help thinking of the College of Architecture entrance exam, the box with the gauze panels, the little, imaginary building barely discernible at the very back. She had never seen anything like it, she said. With her nail she traced an outline in his lungs. It could be a cyst, a tumour, or something to do with the lymph nodes. She didn't think so, though. To Jonas her bracelet, the gold, seemed to hover in thin air. Whatever the case, it was impossible for her to say right here and now whether it was normal or abnormal.

The room seemed supernaturally white due to all the light-boxes. Jonas studied the photographs of his own chest cavity. There was something about the exquisite, almost topographical, structure of the lung tissue that put him in mind of a map. Of an unknown continent. Maybe it was still possible to discover new countries. Inside oneself. He peered intently at the light-box, at these images which, though flat, had a depth to them. A warm, tremulous thrill ran through him. Chill dread was replaced by impatient suspense. Was there any chance of examining it more closely right away? Dr Higgs said yes, that was possible. Jonas liked her even more for that. She's just as curious as I am, he thought.

He went through the same procedure as before, the only difference being that this time the X-rays were taken in the CT lab, after they had injected a contrast dye into his arm. He had a strong impression of being in the hands of Fate as the CT bed was slowly passed through the hole in the gantry and he positively felt the rays slicing through him. Or no: he was a galaxy. Someone was looking at him through a telescope, searching for an unknown planet.

Dr Higgs took him back to the viewing room. In the light-box, next to the first pictures, there now hung forty different sections of his lungs. It was odd to stand there in those bright surroundings and see his innards exposed in this way, spread out like a transparent fresco on the walls. He knew you would have to be very well-versed in anatomy, in the architecture of the human body, to know what you were looking at. The only thing he could make out in each slice was his spine. He could not help thinking of cuts of meat. It's like seeing yourself carved up, he thought.

He looked back at the first X-rays. Again his eye was drawn to the white, butterfly-shaped patch, just above the heart. Now, though, the sight of those wings or whatever they were, seemed to reassure him. He realised that the tightness in his chest could just as easily be a sign of something good – a feeling of well-being so unfamiliar and so confusing that it had actually caused a panic in his breast.

'I had thought it might be *sarcoidosis*,' Dr Higgs said, her gold bracelet flashing across the pictures as she explained what they showed, something about lymph nodes, something about connective tissue. 'But not according to the CT pictures.' She showed him the same section of the lungs in a number of the CT pictures. In these the patch was darker, but still transparent. 'It almost looks like a little cavity within the cavity of the lung,' she said.

He considered this thought: a chamber within a chamber. A tiny lung inside his lung. He relaxed even more. Maybe, he thought excitedly, the body also had a *guarde-roba*, like the ones in the Renaissance palaces that Aunt Laura had told him about: a secret room full of mysterious objects. Dr Higgs was right: there were many things which medical science had not yet discovered – like the gland that caused your head to reel when your girlfriend came walking towards you. Descartes might well have been on the right track when he located the interaction between body and soul, the source of the spark which rendered man more than a machine, in the so-called pineal gland.

'I don't know what it is,' Dr Higgs said again. 'I've never seen anything like it. It might not be anything serious. No two lungs are exactly alike.' She handed him an envelope. 'Give this report to your doctor. It's up to you to decide, in consultation with him, whether you want to have more tests done.'

Jonas thanked her. Thanked her most sincerely. Even shook her hand. Again his eye was caught by her bracelet. He was about to ask about it, but she beat him to it. 'Yes, you're right,' she said. 'I bought it from your aunt. The finest goldsmith in the country.'

Rings in water, spreading outward, touching other rings, far, far out.

He had already made up his mind. He would not be pursuing the matter. The radiologist might not know what it was, but Jonas did. A new organ. Or the rudiments of a new organ. Inside his body, inside the chest cavity, a third lung was starting to develop. The way he saw it, it might even have been this new, little lung that had saved him when he had come close to dying, committing suicide, in the early days of his imprisonment. Later he was also inclined to give this organ the credit for the fact that he had been open to a new and overwhelming acquaintance: Kamala Varma.

He viewed his life in another light. He had become aware at an early age of his rare gift – the ability to think several thoughts in parallel. Which made it all the more frustrating not to be able to put these skills into practice. Because the extraordinary, the truly amazing things of which he felt himself capable were of a quite different order to the highly acclaimed television series which he had eventually managed to produce. As far as he was concerned all his projects had been failures. Like producing scrap iron when he possessed the formula for making gold. Now, though, he saw that there had been a purpose to these fiascos. All his mental powers, the talent he feared he had abused, had been converted into something physical, corporeal. His incessant cerebral exertions, all his grandiose, unrealised plans had prepared the ground for the growth of this new organ.

During his years in prison, his cell would become many things to Jonas. But if it is true that every person has their Samarkand, a place in which they find the essence of life, a place where one can see what lies *beyond* everything else – then yes, that prison cell was Jonas Wergeland's Samarkand.

Jonas was allowed to take one of the X-ray pictures – the one showing his chest cavity from the front – for his cell. He hung it at the window and would lie gazing at it morning and evening. In a way he had always known it: that inside every person there was an Organ X, or at any rate the potential to form such an organ. We could never stand far enough back from ourselves in time. Even though we knew that mankind was constantly evolving. Time was when we had had gills. There in his cell, Jonas saw his youthful conviction confirmed: there is more life in us than we think. We are unfinished.

One spring evening, with the light fading outside and an all too familiar scent wafting into the room through the open window inside the bars, he lay in bed with his eyes fixed on the large, blue-sheened X-ray of his lungs. Before his eyes it turned into a face, a familiar face, Margrete's face. It may have been a mirage, he did not know, nor did he feel like speculating on it; instead he let his mind wander to a concept which had intrigued him when he was studying architecture, a phenomenon known as a room's 'fifth dimension' that occurred when the external surroundings – adjoining rooms or the natural environment – were brought into the room itself. It must be the same with people, he thought, as he beheld the woman's face delineated on the X-ray photograph. A person's true depth lay not in them, but within someone else. He recalled Karen Mohr's words when, as a boy, he had found the door leading to her bedroom and library and she had spoken of secret doors in more personal terms: 'Our secret chambers lie not within us, but outside of us.' When he saw Margrete's face in that picture of his lungs, he knew that she was his 'fifth dimension'. His centre, his core, lay in Margrete. He ought to have realised this when he found her dead, in his dressing gown. His deepest story dealt not with Jonas Wergeland, but with Margrete Boeck.

He lay in bed, in a prison cell, savouring the spring air wafting through the open window, air which brought with it the scent of her. He looked at the X-ray, at the tiny white, butterfly-shaped patch right next to his heart, at the rudiments of the organ which he would dub the love lung. Because he had felt that pressure in his chest for the first time when Margrete died. She had been the catalyst, it was her who had caused this possible organ to develop. And when he finally understood how much she had loved him it began to grow.

He lay in bed in his cell, gazing at the X-ray picture, in which his lungs seemed to shimmer, or gleam gold, in the waning light from outside. He thought: for the first time in my life I may have discovered something important.

Triton

The end. But as always an ending which, in its answers, contains a new beginning. The rudiments of something as yet unimagined. Other questions. What happened to Bo Wang Lee? Why did Viktor Harlem finally wake up? How could Kamala Varma be world famous? What was Melankton's syndrome? And above all: what happened in Lisbon – or rather: why did he do it?

A fork in the road awaited him in Lisbon, that *Kaba* of every explorer. This much Jonas understood even in the taxi from the airport to his hotel, as he gazed out of the window at the grimy house fronts, the traces of a long-gone empire. There was something underneath, behind that faded beauty, something lay waiting for him. Not a country but another life.

The taxi driver had been eyeing him in the mirror for some time. 'I can tell just by looking at you,' he said out of the blue. 'You're from Scandinavia. You are so pure, so noble, you people.' When Jonas laughed and responded with the word 'Norway' the driver, warming to his subject, began to talk about Gro Harlem Brundtland; he had read about her in the newspaper, something about an environmental report soon to be presented to the UN's secretary-general. 'She's far too done-up, though,' he said with a blend of deference and sarcasm. 'But who knows: maybe there is a dark, dangerous Harlem inside this Brundtland – did you ever wonder about that. Whether there might be a black Harlem in Norway itself? Because that is probably your only hope.'

These words echoed in Jonas's head the next day as he was more or less slinking around Rossio, the city's main square. He was about to embark upon a risky venture. He was on the hunt for someone. His only hope. A woman whom he had managed to track down, but had then lost sight of. It should not be that hard to find her again, though. He was feeling mildly optimistic, smitten by the mood that met him wherever he went. Portugal had just become a member of the EU. The country was seething with new building projects. The future was looking bright, Jonas thought to himself, also for his own project.

He made a show of strolling aimlessly along the pavements around the square, trying to disguise his keen, not to say desperate, scrutiny of the tables in each café he passed and glancing impatiently, almost beseechingly, into the shops, half of which were as beautiful inside as the old Swan Chemist's Shop in Oslo. September was moving into its last week and there were not too many tourists about. He strode down to the bottom end of the square, positioned himself in the centre next to the flower sellers, so close to the big fountain that he could feel the spray from it. He had been lookng round about for quite some time, in growing desperation, when at last he spotted her, Marie H., sitting under a yellow parasol at a pavement café just beyond Café Nicola. It was so typical of her, not to go to a place as obvious as the Nicola, but to the one next door. She did not look much like a tourist either. He hardly recognised her. At NRK, or within any group of men she was known simply as the Battleship, a double-barrelled nickname inspired by her three most striking attributes: long legs, stunning breasts and a pair of flashing eyes. The mere sight of her, especially if she happened to be sitting in a chair opposite you with her legs crossed, called to mind a certain class of battleship with three stepped gun batteries. But her nickname also alluded to her impregnability. Or unattainability. She always wore light-coloured suits, with her dark hair pulled back into a tight bun, as if intent on concealing or neutralising her charms. Here in Lisbon, though, her hair hung loose and she was wearing a short, black waistcoat over a white T-shirt, tight, pale-blue jeans and soft sandals. With her long, wavy hair she could easily have passed for a woman from the Iberian Peninsula.

All at once he was overcome by a terrible fit of shyness. In his mind he was already on his way to the airport, having failed in his mission. But he managed to control his frantic breathing. He reminded himself of what was at stake here: everything. A whole life project.

He pulled out a yellow notebook and began to sketch the fountain. With its distinctive statues and jets of water spraying in two directions it was certainly worth looking at. He was standing directly across from her, on the other side of the street. He sketched assiduously, making sure to stand in profile every now and again. If she looked up she was bound to notice him, a man apart, standing there sketching the fountain. At long last he heard her call out and turned round. Affecting bewilderment. Who did he know here? In Lisbon?

She waved to him. Eagerly. And happily. Or was he mistaken? He crossed the street without closing the notebook. 'What in the world are you doing here?' she asked, genuinely surprised. He felt a flutter of panic, glanced down at the notebook as if at a script. 'I'm making a study of Brazilian soap operas,' he said. It could have been a wisecrack. It could have been true. If anyone in Norway were likely to travel to Portugal simply to watch endless *telenovelas*, then that person was Jonas Wergeland.

She motioned to him to take a seat. 'So tell me,' she said. 'Is it true what they say about you camping out in a hotel room in New York for three months, learning all about American television?'

He dismissed the question with a laugh, wondering as he did so why she had never asked him before – if she really wanted to know. He took stock of her. Her long legs were concealed from view by the yellow tablecloth. The ample breasts and flashing eyes were much in evidence though. An unassailable woman. An unmarried workaholic. Other than that he did not know much about her. No one knew much about her. Some people said she drank too much.

'How did the shoot in England go?' she asked, suddenly all business. 'What was it you were working on there, the Harald Hardråde piece?' She kept an eye on the production schedules then. An eagle eye, most likely.

'I got rid of all the extras,' he said. 'Saved a lot of money that way.' A little hint. She did not rise to it, kept her eyes fixed on a nearby shoeshine boy. She was drinking beer. On her plate lay the tail fins of some grilled prawns. She had been reading a book, *Os Lusíadas*. About voyages of discovery – it had to be: on the blue jacket was a picture of an old map of the world. It was no secret that Marie H. was interested in literature. To say the least. As a young girl, after moving from Nordland to the capital she had published two collections of poems in rapid succession. They had been exceptionally well received and not only because of her raven beauty. But she was no longer writing. This had won her a high and somewhat mythical status in NRK circles.

People streamed past. A good many Africans, or Brazilians maybe. A few cripples. 'You know this square was the scene of the Inquisition's bonfires,' he remarked casually, nodding at her book as if this was what had made him think of it. 'Both people and books were burned here.'

'I know what you're driving at,' she said with a hint of hostility in her voice. And disappointment perhaps. 'You couldn't stand the rejection, could you? But it's a far cry from that to the Inquisition, you know. This is about finance, not heresy.' Still she did not look at him, instead she lifted her eyes to the castle on the hill opposite. Jonas felt his diffidence threatening to immobilise his self-confidence. He thought: she's invincible. A battleship. It's no use.

Who was Marie H.? Marie H. was head of programming and financial controller of the three-ring circus that was NRK TV. She had more say than anyone else within NRK, apart from the Director General. Some people even went so far as to say that she carried more clout than the man at the top.

Jonas felt unnaturally detached from the whole situation, felt as if he were sitting on Triton, Neptune's largest moon. He wondered what to do, had the urge to buy a lottery ticket from the seller stationed just across from them. His future career would be decided in these seconds. The *Thinking Big* series was half completed, but they had run over budget to a record-breaking degree – the word scandal was being whispered in the corridors – and Jonas's boss, the head of department, had put his foot down. They had already spent more than the projected budget for the whole series. Jonas had protested as best he could, he had tried reasoning, he had tried yelling, but this man had simply gone to *his* boss, the head of programming – which is to say, Marie H. – who upheld his decision. She ordered Jonas to cease production right away – or at least after filming the footage needed in order to finish those programmes which were more or less in the can.

Only someone familiar with the essential concept behind the series, its very mainstay in formal terms could understand – if only in a small way – what a disaster, what a *death blow*, this was for Jonas. This concept was a part of his being, so to speak, part of his way of thinking; it dated from a discovery he had made back in the summer when he met Bo Wang Lee or, to put it another way, an imaginative force in full bloom.

Naive though children can be, from the very start Jonas knew there was something special about Bo Wang Lee, apart from the fact that he looked like a Chinese, or a handsome Prince Valiant with his glossy, black pageboy haircut; but he never really had the time to speculate on this. And he received no clues from anyone else, since he was always alone with Bo. Only very occasionally did he catch a glimpse of Bo's mother walking off in the morning with a big bundle of papers under her arm, on her way to the yellow Citröen 2CV and the host of things she had to get done for her university course. Each time an unconscious suspicion began to smoulder inside him Bo was right there with a fresh plan. 'I know what we can do,' he would announce at the first hint of a crease in Jonas's brow. 'Let's go diving for the *Titanic* in Badedammen!' That summer passed in such a whirl, the days filled with sundials and windmills and rockets with parachutes that opened automatically. Or sometimes Bo would simply roll away a rock to reveal a microscopic zoo that would keep them occupied for hours. Experiences and bright ideas accumulated, piling up on top of one another. Suddenly life was overflowing with peanut-butter sandwiches and intrepid cave explorations and hazardous rock climbs with clothes-ropes as their only lifeline and stories of maharajahs who killed themselves by swallowing crushed diamonds. Jonas barely had time to gather his thoughts. Whenever he showed the slightest sign of uncertainty Bo would become a proper firecracker, bursting with ideas. His little yellow notebook was a constant fount of suggestions and sketches for the most amazing activities.

'Bo, I was wondering …' Jonas might start. And before he could say any more Bo would be rooting like a badger in one of the numerous boxes scattered around the flat which he and his mother were borrowing from Bo's aunt and which, because of all the suitcases, not to mention the beguiling pictures of the MS *Bergensfjord* and MS *Oslofjord* in the toilet, made Jonas feel that these weeks of summer were one long and eventful cruise on an Atlantic liner. 'Look,' Bo would cry triumphantly, waving a huge hand in the air, 'I brought my catcher's mitt with me. Want to try it?'

Another time he took the best crystal wine glasses out of his aunt's cabinet, set them on the table and filled them, swiftly but surely, with different amounts of water. All at once he was the leader of an orchestra, playing 'Frère Jacques' by moistening his finger and rubbing the rims of the glasses. Bo's ingenuity never waned. After Jonas had examined the odd-looking oval ball which his chum claimed was used in a weird sport called American football, Bo showed him how to fix a silver ashtray to the bottom of it with some sticky tape and hey presto, they had a brilliant zeppelin with which they could have hours of fun. When, that is, Bo did not spend the morning showing Jonas how Chuck Berry hopped across the stage with his guitar. 'Here, use this carpet-beater as a guitar. It's called the "duck-walk". That's it, well done, bend your knees a bit more!' Or they would go off into the woods and make a campfire. Bo had an inexhaustible supply of marshmallows, soft and sweet, which they threaded onto sticks and held over the hot coals until the outside of the velvety cushion had gone all golden and runny. In Jonas's memory that whole summer with Bo smelled of marshmallows.

And then there was the juggling, an experience which would leave its mark on Jonas for the rest of his life. This particular show took place during the careful preparations for the indisputable high point of those weeks: the expedition to the Vegans' hide-out in Lillomarka. Jonas had happened to ask why they had to plan everything in such detail, do so many things at the same time; work out positions on the map, catch butterflies, get hold of glass prisms, choose things to take with them. And it was then that Bo – they were in the living room at the time – picked up three, then four, then five oranges from a dish and started to juggle with them. Jonas construed this as a practical lesson of sorts: if they were to uncover the hidden country they would need to combine things, keep several balls in the air at one time. He did not realise that what he was witnessing was a rare feat. Anyone can juggle with three balls; juggling with four is far more difficult and takes dedicated practice; juggling with five is a real tour de force, of which only very few are capable. It was all Jonas could do simply to follow the golden pattern that took shape before his eyes: five oranges passing so quickly through Bo's hands and so high up in the air that the effect was quite mesmerising. 'This is what we're going to try to do,' Bo cried, as if he had to raise his voice in order to break through his own wall of concentration. As far as Jonas was concerned this was pure alchemy: Bo had transformed something perfectly ordinary into a ring of gold.

'Here, now you try,' said Bo. He handed Jonas three oranges and proceeded to peel one of the others.

Jonas had a go, tossed the oranges into the air one after another. Made a complete botch of it, of course. 'Try again,' Bo said. 'And look up this time. Focus on a point just under the top of the circle.' Bo taught Jonas the basic techniques while sitting on the sofa, popping wedges of orange into his mouth and laughing at Jonas's hapless efforts, with oranges thudding, and eventually splattering, onto the floor. 'Don't walk forward!' Bo yelled, doubled up with laughter.

'What's the record?' Jonas asked.

Bo handed him the rest of the orange wedges as a consolation prize and took out his yellow notebook. 'Eleven balls,' he said. 'Did you know that scientists today believe that the world has at least eleven dimensions?' He could tell from Jonas's face that he would have to explain again what dimension meant, even though he had already done so when talking about the Vegans' hide-out.

'I bet there are even more,' Jonas said.

'Just as one day somebody will manage to juggle with more than eleven balls,' Bo said, and scribbled down something with the stub of pencil that was always tucked behind his ear.

That summer, Jonas actually did learn to juggle first with three oranges, then with four. He never felt quite the same about this golden fruit again; from then on he could never eat an orange without thinking of Bo Wang Lee. And for the rest of his life he was always able to impress anyone with his little party trick. Even in the midst of a serious discussion he was quite liable to suddenly toss four oranges into the air and thus manage to say something which he could not put into words. The following year, when Jonas met the triplets, the first thing he thought of was a juggling act, felt he was faced with the possibility of an extraordinary experience. All he had to do was to keep three schoolboy crushes in the air at one time.

But the best was yet to come. The day before the expedition into the forest – Jonas had just wrapped the four crystals carefully in four checkered handkerchiefs – they were in the room where Bo slept. Each sat with a mini bottle of Cola, sipping through a paper straw, as if to gather sustenance, while observing the way the four butterflies in the jars on Bo's bedside table mimicked their actions, unrolling their probosces like straws and sipping from the orangeade tops filled with sugared water. In one of the open suitcases in the bare, cabin-like room, Jonas spied a dubious-looking shoebox lying next to a Viewmaster containing pictures from Yellowstone National Park. He reached out for it, but Bo stopped him, as if it were taboo. Or private – because Bo opened the box himself, gently lifted out one object after another. 'It's just some things I've collected,' he said. 'Things to speed up the thought processes.'

Bo's shoebox reminded Jonas of Aunt Laura's story about the Renaissance princes and the curiosities they kept in secret rooms at the heart of their palaces. Bo laid the objects out on the bed. An old pocket watch which no longer worked, but had a nice pattern engraved on the lid; a pencil sharpener shaped like a globe; a chunk of rock with a trilobite embedded in it; a bunch of funny-looking keys; an old-fashioned purse containing three silver dollars – one of them with a bullet hole in it, made by Wild Bill Hickock. Jonas understood that he ought to take note of these things, since they probably said a lot about who Bo Wang Lee was.

As if to encourage Jonas, to give him heart before setting out on their hair-raising expedition in search of the Vegans, Bo began to juggle with first three, then four, and finally all of these objects. The spinning oranges had been a wonderful sight, but this was more wonderful. Much more. 'This is the sort of thing we're going to try to do,' he told Jonas again, speaking as if through a circular portal. Although these things did not actually form a circle, like the sort you see in drawings of jugglers; they criss-crossed in mid-air in what was for Jonas the most mind-boggling fashion, tracing a loop rather like a figure-of-eight on its side. And Jonas stared and stared; he saw how the purse, a trilobite, a pocket-watch, a bundle of keys and a globe of the world seemed to hover in mid-air while at the same time forming a unified whole, what he would later describe as a synthesis. It was a concrete manifestation of something he had experienced before, many times, when thinking about several things at once. And not only several things, but several *different* things. And he was delighted to see that the result, this spellbinding infinity symbol which Bo was weaving with his hands, was something quite other than the sum of its individual parts; that it was a whole new, little world, one which belonged to another sphere or perhaps what Bo called another dimension. Or even Vega, he thought. Why not?

Bo juggled the objects so fast that soon they were nothing but a blur. It reminded him of that chain of Bo's, the one with the words 'I love you' broken up into two incomprehensible sets of symbols on either side of a metal disc. Jonas perceived a great deal at that moment, as he watched a friend – a boy he had become closer to than anyone else in only three weeks – who juggled as brilliantly as any wizard. Jonas sensed that he too might be like that, that he could consist of two – or more – elements, completely dissimilar, incomprehensible elements, which could, somehow or other, be set in motion in such a way that they spun together to form a whole. He also had the feeling that with his juggling act Bo was trying to tell him something else; that with this strange pattern in the air he might even be saying: 'I love you.'

'That … is absolutely phenomenal,' Jonas stammered. He motioned to Bo to keep going while he went to fetch a camera from the living room. Jonas wanted with all his heart to capture this sight, since it was for him as sensational and indeed as unbelievable as a UFO. 'Don't stop,' he said, backing cautiously towards the door. But at these words Bo lost his concentration and everything tumbled to the floor or, fortunately, onto a soft carpet. 'Shit!' Bo said nonetheless. 'Shit, shit, shit!'

At the sight of the objects on the floor and Bo's nimble fingers quickly gathering them up, as if he were anxious to hide something, Jonas felt another niggle of suspicion – he could not have said why – and decided that the time had come: 'Bo, there's something I need to ask you …'

'Have you seen these?' And all of a sudden Bo became a whirlwind, roiling around in another suitcase. 'American comics!' And Jonas forgot all else. For a while.

But he never forgot the revelation he had had when Bo was juggling. So powerful was this lesson that years later Jonas would lay it like a keel under his ambitious television series. And it was the threat to this essential premise which Jonas had in mind as he sat opposite Marie H. – looking, you might say, down the barrels of the guns on a battleship – in a café on the Rossio in Lisbon. He had all twenty-odd programmes planned out in minutest detail, not least the links between them, the wide-ranging network of cross-references. If the NRK management, which is to say: Marie H., ordered him to call a halt now, halfway, it would not only mean that the series as a whole would be ruined, that viewers would miss experiencing the magical effect produced when snippets from all of the programmes were borne in mind at the same time – it would also cause the twelve partially completed programmes to fall out of Jonas's hands. The management did not understand the motivation behind his concept, the truly original, challenging aspect of it. They simply could not grasp the idea of a unified whole. Nor that the potential existed for unimagined wholes. Loose, crazy, tentative, but intriguing schemes. Jonas was afraid that *no one* today appreciated the idea of an alternative whole. But that was what he had to offer – to offer NRK and the viewers. A whole that only art could produce. A whole so valuable that it could not be measured in terms of money. Half the programmes would only give half a whole. It would be like seeing only one side of the disc on Bo Wang Lee's chain. A lot of meaningless symbols spinning in mid-air.

Jonas was exaggerating. He knew that a few of the individual programmes would be good. And it was not as if they could be sure of selling the entire series to every foreign television station that had expressed an interest. But the main endeavour, the possibly quite brilliant concept behind the work would come to nothing. The result would not be revolutionary television, in the sense that it changed lives, changed people, opened them out. No one can blame Jonas Wergeland for feeling frustrated. It *was* tough, it *was* unbearable to think that this magnificent and utterly original project was in danger of being cancelled by blinkered bureaucrats who did nothing but count the money and pore over administrative jigsaw puzzles; people who lacked the ability to see that, strange though it seemed, it was even possible for out-and-out 'individualists' to break onto the scene in Norway, and who were therefore also incapable of cutting the crap, making an exception, *investing*, in order to ensure a fertile environment for such rare individuals. There was – there is no getting away from it – also a *Festung Norwegen* within the arts, a cultural Norway which preferred to remain isolated, in all ways.

Jonas knew, however, that despite her battleship bearing, Marie H. was not an anti-visionary bureaucrat, she was among other things a poet. Therein lay his hope. Only she had the power to quash all the other second-rate and to some extent envious programming controllers. Jonas searched frantically for words, for arguments, that might sway the woman sitting across from him, almost wished he had a bowl of oranges handy; he sat at a café table on the Rossio and knew that he had come to a milestone in his life – whatever the outcome. She did not seem all that interested, did not even look at him, but began to leaf absent-mindedly through her book. For Jonas this was an intolerable situation. Like having to turn back just as one sighted a cape, the sea route to a new continent. He had written a long and impassioned report to Marie H., explained the grand artistic concept, the overall structure and the threads linking the programmes to one another. His appeal was turned down. And as if that wasn't enough, when he looked across the desk in her office at Marienlyst, he noticed that she had also corrected his language, that several sentences were marred by red squiggles. It was like writing an ardent love letter in which you bared your soul, only to have the recipient proceed to correct your spelling.

Jonas looked up at the forest of television aerials rising over the jumble of tiled roofs on the hillside behind the theatre. Not that long ago Norway too had been covered with aerials like that. This sight was a comfort to him, an indication of the many people who were waiting to receive his signals, his series. All the more reason then that the project should not be amputated, left half-done, like so much else in Norway.

'Did you really come all this way to try to make me change my mind?' She glanced up from her book. In her eyes he saw laughter and disbelief.

'I honestly had no idea you were here,' Jonas said. Then said it again. He may have said it once too often. She was still eyeing him doubtfully. 'I'm here on holiday. Or rather, ever since I studied architecture I've wanted to have a look at the weird Manueline architecture. I often visit cities to look at the buildings.'

She picked up his yellow notebook, as if thinking to catch him in a lie. She studied the sketch of the ornate fountain in the square in front of them. He knew it was good. She raised her eyebrows, genuinely impressed. Or as a sign that he had been accepted.

'You'll be going to see the Hieronymite Monastery and the Tower of Belém, then?' she said. 'We could go together if you like?'

He nodded, inwardly exulting, but managing to keep a straight face. She was going out to dinner, had to take a train to Sintra from the Rossio station, just around the corner. She had friends who lived out there among the eucalyptus trees, the ruins of Moorish castles and old palaces. But she would be back the following day. They arranged to meet outside the monastery, fixed a time.

That evening he roamed desultorily through the narrow streets of the Bairro Alto, one of Lisbon's two hills. The strains of commercialised, almost caricatured versions of wistful *fado* songs drifted out of doorways here and there, but could not entice him in. In any case he was not feeling at all melancholy, he felt hopeful. He ran his fingers over the glazed ceramic tiles on the walls of the houses. He liked this proof that by repeating the pattern in one tile you could turn a large flat surface into a work of wonder. While at the same time nullifying the flatness. Now that, *that* was how he envisaged his television series: as a string of almost identical programmes which, when set side by side, would create an optical illusion. A form of infinity. *Māyā*.

He rounded off his stroll with a trip on the old street lifts, the mini Eiffel Towers in the Chiado district. Rode up and down like a kid. He thought about the next day. Things could go up or down. He wondered – possibly because she was a poet – whether there had been a message in the last thing she had said before leaving the café: 'Remember, television is bad for you.'

After a period of youthful scepticism, Jonas had gradually come to accept the more dubious aspects of television. But only after his own television career was at an end did he find conclusive proof, in the strange story of Viktor Harlem, that TV viewing, even when taken to the extreme, was not necessarily the evil which certain prophets of doom made it out to be.

Viktor Harlem was one of those who died young. During the spring term of his third year at high school, as he was poised, so to speak, on the last step of the school stairway, all set to stride out onto what everyone predicted would be a gilt-edged path, Viktor was hit on the head by a block of ice – as improbable as it was heavy – which fell off a roof as he was walking along a street in Lillehammer arm in arm with Jonas and Axel, at about the same moment as, amid gales of laughter, they were pronouncing him outright winner of the contest to see who could sing 'I was Born Under A Wandering Star' in the deepest voice. Viktor was in a coma for a week, but when he regained consciousness he was still not really there. With the minimum of help he was capable of dressing himself, eating or walking about a bit, all in a mechanical, abstracted fashion, but he was, nonetheless, quite helpless. Jonas was afraid that Viktor had finally succeeded in doing what he had striven to do all through high school: to deconstruct everything – the only problem was that he had done it to himself. All of Viktor's individual components were intact, but they weren't connecting, they weren't working as a whole. There was nothing for it but to put him in an institution.

Jonas visited him regularly, even though there seemed little point. Viktor never so much as noticed him. Jonas could not get through to him. His friend seemed to have retreated into himself. It occurred to Jonas – talking of blocks of ice – that Viktor might be the counterpart of certain animals who went into hibernation in order to survive periods of severe cold. Jonas sometimes felt like going up to him and knocking on his skull, asking if there was anyone home. Viktor's case confirmed the truth of a statement with which Jonas would be confronted many times in the course of his life: there are a lot of things for which medical science cannot account. No one could explain, for example, why Viktor did not seem to get any older. Days, years, passed, while Viktor reclined in his armchair, looking as if he was still in his final year at Oslo Cathedral School. Although actually, with his abnormally babyish features he looked even younger.

Every time Jonas visited Viktor at the institution, he would read aloud to him from Ezra Pound's poem, for one thing because there was nothing else to do. He read from an edition of *The Cantos*, the title page of which was inscribed with an all but illegible dedication from the author himself – after some years Jonas succeeded in deciphering the words 'Roaring madness' above Pound's wavery signature. When he eventually closed the book, having decided that he had read enough or because he could not take any more of those unfathomable, lyrical passages, he usually sat for a while quietly staring at the TV screen along with Viktor. The television was always on – Jonas simply turned down the sound when he took out *The Cantos* – and even when Jonas was reading, Viktor would sit there in his Stressless Royal, the flagship of all armchairs, with his eyes riveted on the screen, as if on it he saw illustrated in minutest detail whatever part of Ezra Pound's endless poem Jonas was reading.

To Jonas, Viktor gradually came to represent the average Norwegian, a person who sat unfailingly, day after day, in front of the box. When Jonas started making his own television programmes he told himself that it was these people, countrymen like Viktor, he wanted to reach. Like Henrik Ibsen he did not merely want to make them think big, he wanted to *waken* them. Once his acclaimed television series was finished he had a video recorder installed in Viktor's room and arranged for all the programmes to be taped for his friend. Jonas gave one of the permanent members of staff instructions to play the tapes regularly. 'We have to see to it that he gets some good, solid Norwegian fare, and not just American fast food,' Jonas told the nurse.

This notion of television images as nourishment of a sort had not been plucked entirely out of thin air. Whenever Jonas walked into the room and saw Viktor staring fixedly at the screen he had the feeling that the television set, or possibly the rays from it were keeping Viktor alive. Or that his friend was actually in a large incubator, an idea which Viktor's babyish looks – his fine, blonde locks and big, heavy head – seemed to bear out. And yet Jonas also believed he detected signs of mental activity. It sometimes seemed to Jonas's mind as if, his vegetative appearance notwithstanding, Viktor was staring at the screen in search of help, in search of someone who could save him. As more channels came along and Viktor's only exercise consisted of finger-hopping on the remote control and a bit of wriggling to adjust his Stressless Royal from one comfortable position to another, Jonas noted that Viktor clearly liked some programmes better than others. One could really have been forgiven for thinking that he was looking for, waiting for, a revelation. This observation left Jonas with the disturbing suspicion that Viktor's mind was perfectly sound, but that he did not feel like letting anyone know this. That it was all an act. Or that Viktor was leading a normal life in a parallel world, a perfectly decent life. Jonas was quite prepared to believe that in this other life his friend, who looked so much like a chrysalis sitting there in his Stressless chair, might be a butterfly. However that may be, Jonas continued to visit Viktor regularly – until, that is, he ended up in an institution himself or, to be more exact: in prison.

And this last circumstance would prove to be a turning point. At first Jonas thought it must have been the shot on Bergensveien in Grorud that had roused Viktor, but he was woken, or rather: brought to his senses, some time later by another shot. Jonas only heard about it. One day, when the nurse who made sure that Viktor got to see Jonas Wergeland's programmes regularly looked in to check on him, she found Viktor pointing excitedly at the television screen and uttering the first words anyone had heard him say in more than twenty years: 'Jeeze, who fired that shot?'

What was on the TV? The aforementioned nurse was able to reveal that she had popped in forty-five minutes earlier to put on a video and that, because she remembered it so well herself, she had chosen the episode dealing with Harald Hardråde. She had even stayed to watch a bit of it before having to tear herself away and continue her rounds.

The programme which resulted in Viktor's miraculous shout, opened with a boy shooting with a bow and arrow in a clearing beside a river, and the scene had been composed in a way which told viewers this was an art, that it took years of training to become such a fine archer. The boy moved as if in a dance, with everything – from the moment he drew the arrow out of the quiver until it left the bowstring and the bow was lowered – executed in one smooth, fluid action; it made viewers think of the moves performed in *tai chi*, or the *katas* in karate. Jonas realised later, partly because he had made the sound of the bowstring so pronounced, that he must have been thinking not so much about the glorious games of bows and arrows from his own boyhood – which he had also been fortunate enough to be able to relive with Benjamin – as the Indian epic *The Mahabharata* and the marvellous tales from it told to him by Margrete: of Drona who trained the Pandava brothers in the use of arms; of Arjuna and his bow Gandiva which was so formidable that it was recognisable to his enemies by its sound alone. The whole of that mesmerising opening sequence, indeed the sound of the bowstring alone – part music, part dangerous threat – spoke of a programme about a heroic warrior. And a brutal death.

At the close of the scene one saw what the boy, Harald Sigurdsson, had been shooting at: a huge sheepskin stretched out on a log wall. Drawn on this golden fleece was a rough map of Europe, with each arrow marking a different place, like a guide to one of the most wide-roving and warlike of all wide-roving, warlike Viking lives. The fifteen-year-long voyage which began after the Battle of Stiklestad, would take Harald, half-brother of Olav II, to places known to us today as Novgorod, Jerusalem, Sicily and, above all, Istanbul. One arrow, embedded at York in England, was broken: a token of the prophecy which says that he who lives by the sword shall die by the sword. But also of an ambition unparalleled in the history of Norway.

Indirectly, the programme on Harald Hardråde also served as a reminder of Viking times, an age with which all Norwegians were still secretly in love, which is fair enough when one considers that never since has Norway or any other Scandinavian country left such an indelible stamp on the world. By dint of artful little details, rather like a limning of the biographical account, or a juggling act in the background, Jonas Wergeland managed to say something about the double-edged nature of the Viking culture: bloodthirsty, plundering forays which also acted as cross-fertilising cultural exchanges. Viking raids and trading expeditions rolled into one. One caught glimpses, images neatly and almost imperceptibly inserted, of longships – to the Vikings what the horse had been to the Huns – scabbards, drinking horns, runic inscriptions, amulets in the shape of Thor's hammer and small bronze statuettes of one-eyed Odin. But also there, if one looked carefully, were furs and lumps of amber, gold spurs and silver jewellery, scales and Anglo-Saxon coins, carved wooden caskets and chess pieces made from walrus tusks, parchments covered in writing. Wergeland used a sign from the main street in modern-day York – Micklegate – to illustrate how Nordic words had left an enduring mark on the language and names of England, Ireland and Normandy.

But it was the end of the programme that people remembered best, the original depiction of the Battle of Stamford Bridge. After all, who was Harald Hardråde? Harald Hardråde – or Hardrada – was not only an unscrupulous, power-hungry man, a seasoned and victorious warrior who came home from foreign parts with ships so laden with gold that they listed in the water, he was also the only Norwegian ever to have so much as a little finger in the course of history. When he decided, at the age of fifty, to assert his right to the English throne, he timed it so that Harold Godwinson had to divide his attention between two fronts. Harold, then King of England, was in the south, anxiously awaiting William, later to be called the Conqueror. But when Harald Hardråde and his fellow-conspirator, Tostig Godwinson, Harold's brother, landed in Northumbria the English king was forced to march north to York with all haste. And the bitter and exhausting Battle of Stamford Bridge had only just been won – with Harold losing many of his best warriors, among them some of his indispensable bodyguards – when he received word that William had sailed across the channel and landed in the south. The man who was at that point still King of England had to rush south again, set out on yet another gruelling forced march. Had Harold Godwinson met William and the Normans with a rested and, above all, undepleted army, the Battle of Hastings – although it would have been fought elsewhere and at an earlier date – would in all likelihood have had another outcome. Harold would not have died when that dreadful stray arrow pierced his eye. And the history of Europe would have looked very different.

But it was not so much this, which can never be anything but speculation, albeit interesting speculation – questions are always more important than answers – as the scenes of the battle which stuck in people's minds. Earlier,

Harald Hardråde and Tostig had beaten the armies of the Earls of Northumbria and Mercia at the battle of Fulford Gate, whereupon York surrendered without a fight and accepted Harald as king. On the morning of Monday, 25 September 1066 – one of the most important dates in Norwegian history, right up there with 17 May 1814 and 9 April 1940 – the Norwegians reached Stamford Bridge, about a mile outside of York, either because they were on their way to the town to hold council or to receive hostages from the villages around the bridge, which stood at a spot where many roads met. The question has been raised as to what would have happened had it not rained before the Battle of Waterloo, but one might just as well ask how history would have turned out if the sun had not been shining before the Battle of Stamford Bridge. Because, since the day was uncommonly hot, Harald's and Tostig's men had left their vital coats of mail in the boats, in the over two hundred ships anchored at Riccall, where a third of the seven thousand strong army was gathered.

To begin with at Stamford Bridge all Harald and Tostig could see was a cloud of dust. Then they began to make out the glint of weapons – like a wall of ice in the sunlight, a mirage in the heat – as Harold Godwinson's vast army advanced on the other side of the little River Derwent. Instead of running back to the ships and putting on their chain mail or making a temporary retreat downriver, the Norwegians sent messengers to summon the rest of the army. Then they took up their positions, shield to shield. Rather than run they would all fall together, one on top of the other as Harald had said on a previous occasion, when faced with another apparently superior foe. In the end, after a long, fierce battle, it was Harold Godwinson's cavalry which tipped the scales. Only thirty or so Norwegian ships sailed back across the North Sea. Harald Hardråde had meant to win the whole of England, but all he got, in the words of the English king, was six feet of its soil – or a foot more because he was so tall.

The truly unforgettable thing about the programme was the way that Jonas Wergeland depicted that mighty battle, over ten thousand men clashing in a hellish, bloody melee, with just one person, Harald Hardråde himself. No one knows for sure where the battlefield lay, nor whether the wooden bridge of that time crossed the river at Danes Well or somewhere else. But Jonas Wergeland used the present stone bridge which, with its patina, could easily pass for a thousand-year-old bridge. He specifically wanted to feature the bridge because of the classic Viking legend which told of how a giant, a red-haired berserker, had single-handedly defended the bridge for several hours before being killed by a sneak attack from below – an event which is actually pictured on the sign outside the Swordsman Inn at Stamford Bridge today.

Wergeland decided to have Harald Hardråde take the swordsman's place. Actor Normann Vaage, tall and well-built and blessed still with the agility of his young days as a promising gymnast, was perfect in the part.

In the programme Harald Hardråde, clad in a blue tunic and silvery helmet, was seen standing on the parapet at the centre of the bridge, battling on alone with a fearsome two-handed sword that sang as it cut through the air. Jonas Wergeland shot this stylised spectacle from the bank of the river in order to get the whole bridge in the shot. One saw Harald, the universal warrior, executing a kind of sword dance. His actions were as acrobatic as they were measured and balletic – again: like the moves in the more medita-tive forms of the Asian martial arts. And even though there was no sign of the pennants or the barricades of spears or the rain of arrows or the wall of raised shields or the rocks thrown by slings and catapults, viewers were treated – thanks to the soundtrack, a marvellous recreation of the hideous din of battle, with lots of ringing swords and screams and thundering hooves – to the illusion of a real battle. Nothing like it had ever been seen on televi-sion before. Jonas Wergeland made viewers *see* the horde of adversaries, he had them biting their nails, even though Harald Hardråde was quite alone, hacking and slashing at thin air. The Norwegian king fought in lone majesty on a bridge in England, one which also represented a decisive crossroads in European history, but people at home had a clear, vivid impression of a battle surging nerve-rackingly back and forth, and no one could help but see that Harald Hardråde was a splendid warrior, displaying as he did, with his lithe, supple movements, all the resourcefulness and skill in arms he had developed as commander of the Nordic division of the Varangian guard in Constantino-ple. Harald Hardråde – or Jonas Wergeland, as Kamala Varma once pointed out – seemed to possess one of those *astras* spoken of in *The Mahabharata*: a weapon that can create mighty illusions.

At last, when it actually looked as though Harald Hardråde was gaining ground on the bridge, one of his adversaries, he too invisible, loosed an arrow from his bow. A resounding *twang* was heard, like a symmetrical echo of the programme's opening scene. A fateful sound, a sound louder than everything else. There was a shot of the arrow flashing through the air, heading straight for the viewer, so lifelike and deadly, a bloody great arrowhead about to burst right through the screen. In a thousand homes people ducked, threw them-selves off their chairs. A moment later, from the floor, they saw the arrow embedded in Harald's throat and the sword slipping from his hand.

And it was this same pitiless ending, this grisly shot that caused history to take a different turn, so to speak, which also changed the story of Viktor Harlem. It was the shot that woke him, or so he said. He had clutched at his throat, as if to pull out a hurtful arrow, and suddenly he could talk. 'Well, that was a long trip, I must say,' he exclaimed. 'Where am I? Who are all these old folk? Wow, what a great chair, is it mine?'

Jonas read all about it in his cell a few days later. A medical miracle the papers called it. Sadly, though, all was not as it should be. Viktor had woken up, but he could not remember a thing. Where his head might have been designed by the Creator to take a sixty-watt bulb it now seemed to be running on twenty-five watts. He had no idea who he was, and he could remember nothing of his past. He could, however, remember absolutely everything else. He knew that Habakkuk was a prophet, that Ittoqqortoormiit was a region of Greenland and that the birr was the unit of currency in Ethiopia. He knew that Haydn's mother was Anna Maria Koller and that his wife's name was Maria Anna Keller. He knew that Galileo died in the year that Newton was born. He knew that B.B. King's guitar was called Lucille. Everyone was baffled. Not least the doctors. Jonas alone guessed the truth. Viktor had spent a couple of decades watching television, to begin with only NRK and the two Swedish channels, but also the other channels as they came along. For some reason every single bit of what he had seen – snippets of news broadcasts and documentaries, natural history series, soap operas and music programmes – had lodged inside his brain. He remembered nothing from 'the real world', but everything from twenty years of television-viewing, from an artificial exist-ence spent with his face turned to the television screen. He also had a rapid, rather staccato way of speaking, as if he were zapping between channels in his head.

But Viktor Harlem was to make the headlines again later. It so hap-pened that his awakening occurred around the same time that the Norwe-gian version of the popular American quiz programme *Jeopardy!* was first screened. Viktor, who was now back living with his mother – not that he remembered her, he simply accepted that she was who she said she was – was persuaded to apply for the show and passed the tough and pretty extensive audition with almost daunting bravura. As a contestant he was unbeatable. It was clear that he could answer just about anything, that is to say: answer in the form of a question. He had the most unbelievable fund of knowledge on everything from Ananga Ranga to orang-utans, and could differentiate without blinking between Lee Marvin, Hank Marvin and Hank Williams, not to mention Pasteur and Patorius. After becoming the all-time greatest *Jeopardy!* champion five times in a row, he was accorded the title of Grand Champion, as if he had suddenly joined the upper echelons of some mys-terious brotherhood. Never before had a winner scooped up such breath-takingly large cash prizes or provided such stunning entertainment. Viktor's popularity soon reached such heights, helped along by all the press cover-age, that the TV2 management decided, after consultation with the company which produced *Jeopardy!* for them, to break with the rules of the game just this once, to bow to public demand – with one eye on the advertising revenue, naturally – and invite him back on to the show. With equally fabulous success for Viktor and equally gratifying viewing figures for the channel. Viktor, who had reverted to his black polo necks and who, with his baby face and longish, wispy hair, looked rather like a seven-year-old Einstein, became something of a national hero. His staccato voice was soon to be heard on every talk show and his zap-zapping comments could be read in every newspaper and maga-zine. Jonas followed his friend's *Jeopardy!* escapades from his cell, shaking his head in disbelief. This Viktor was almost the very opposite of the boy he had been when they were knocking back his illicit absinthe in Seilduksgata in Grünerløkka and calling themselves The Three Heretics. The Viktor whom Jonas saw on television had a head bursting with facts, but his mind was a blank. He could answer any question on the most trivial subject, but he did not know who he was.

Viktor was now proclaimed Norway's only Double Grand Champion, but the story does not end there. Once there were enough *Jeopardy!* Grand Cham-pions – twelve in all – a special tournament was held. For weeks beforehand the papers were full of it, with hundreds of column inches devoted to what might have been a showdown between the gods on Olympus. On an Easter weekend in the latter half of the nineties the scene was set for the actual final between the remaining Grand Champions – and a record viewing figure. With Viktor in the last three it seemed certain that everyone was going to get what they were hoping for: a tremendous fight. And a battle it *was* – with Napoleon playing a starring role.

Although Jonas very rarely watched the television in his cell, for obvious reasons he did follow Viktor's bizarre career on *Jeopardy!* with ever-increasing wonder. To Jonas it seemed so ironic: you could be considered an expert on the world without having been consciously present in that world. On the other hand, he had to admit that he enjoyed the programme, and not only because it tended to suggest that the questions were more important than the answers. Like his countrymen Jonas had been fascinated by quiz shows of this sort ever since the first series of *Double Your Money* was broadcast in the early sixties – that same *Double your Money* which had played and would play such a curious part in Viktor Harlem's life.

Before the much publicised Grand Champions Final that Easter, Jonas decided to take a hand in things. Not to spoil anything, but to try, if possible, to shake Viktor awake. Fully awake. Because Jonas knew something known only to a few. Viktor had a complex. Which is to say: a complex of which he had no recall. As a child, in the days when everybody, absolutely everybody, watched the same programmes, especially on Saturday evenings, Viktor had been bullied terribly and had had to watch his father go seriously downhill after the latter, as a contestant on *Double Your Money* answering questions on the multi-faceted subject of Napoleon, had failed to answer one of the last parts of the 10,000-*krone* question. The fateful question was: What was the name of the marshal in command of Napoleon I's Corps at the Battle of Austerlitz? The answer, which his father could not remember due to a mental block as freakish as it was unfair, was of course Jean Baptiste-Jules Bernadotte. In other words, the man later to be known as Karl Johan, the king who lent his name to Oslo's main thoroughfare.

The memory of this gave Jonas an idea. He called the producer of *Jeopardy!*, a former colleague at NRK who now worked for the company responsible for the quiz show. Jonas knew that this man could pull a few strings with the compilers of the questions for the *Jeopardy!* Grand Champions Final with no one being any the wiser. Despite the impropriety of the request, Jonas's former colleague had immediately agreed to help. 'Remember, we're dealing with a sick man here,' Jonas stressed. 'We have to try everything.'

And so it came about that in this extraordinary final between the Grand Champions, in front of a million viewers, in the 'Final Jeopardy!' round in which the answer also had to be written down, Viktor suddenly heard the quizmaster announcing that the subject was Napoleon and the clue was: 'The marshal in command of Napoleon I's Corps at the Battle of Austerlitz.'

Even though Jonas knew the outcome, since the programme was recorded, he sat on the edge of his seat, his eyes glued to the screen, much the way we sometimes watch a suspenseful film again, even though we know how it ends. In his cell, Jonas held his breath as Viktor, in a studio in Nydalen in Oslo, stiffened when this tricky 'answer' was read out, as though, despite its name, only now did he understand that the programme was all about taking risks. For the viewers this was a dramatic moment. They saw Viktor Harlem put his hands to his large, babyish head, as if in pained confusion. This reaction lasted, however, only a matter of seconds and did not prevent him from writing down the question and reading it out, when his turn came, in a soft, tremulous voice: 'Who was Jean-Baptiste-Jules Bernadotte, who later took the name Karl Johan?' Strictly speaking this last part was not necessary, but Viktor had obviously wished to include it. Jonas never did find out whether this was just another fact which he had gleaned from watching the box, or whether it was a memory so traumatic and so powerful that it had broken through the wall from a past which he had forgotten.

Whatever the case, Viktor had outclassed his rivals, and now boasted the title of Supreme Grand Champion. There is also a little coda to the story. Afterwards, at an emotional press conference, Viktor recounted his traumatic childhood experience with his father and *Double Your Money* so movingly that the journalists presented him in their fulsome reports as a hero twice over. His father's bitter defeat had finally been turned to victory.

In due course, Jonas also got to hear what had happened in the contestants' room after the show. Viktor had sat down and started asking questions, delving and probing as if his whole life were suddenly a gigantic game of *Jeopardy!*, the only difference being that now the subject was anything but trivial. Because he had remembered who he was. He had come to his senses in two stages. After the arrowshot in the programme on Harald Hardråde he could only remember what he had seen on TV, which is to say over the past twenty-odd years. But after the Napoleon question he could remember everything about his life from his childhood up to the March day in 1972 when he had been strolling through the streets of Lillehammer with his two chums, Axel Stranger and Jonas W. Hansen; that was why he had put his hands to his head: in some way he had been feeling the pain of the blow from that block of ice, over twenty years delayed. Where were his two chums now? was the first thing he asked. And after that the questions came pouring out. What had happened to poor Krystle in the last episode of *Dynasty*. Why did he look so young? And why had no one given him the latest model of the Stressless Royal, with additional lumbar support and a neck rest that adjusted automatically? Thanks to all his television viewing, Viktor did not suffer from any sort of Rip van Winkle syndrome, he knew what a computer was and how the new Volvo looked. People, including the doctors, still did not know what to think. And they never would.

As far as Viktor's physical condition was concerned time appeared to have stood still. When he woke up he was not pushing forty, he was nineteen. He not only looked nineteen, he also seemed to have the mind of a nineteen-year-old. When Jonas met Viktor in the visiting room at the prison shortly after the Easter holidays he felt as though he was shaking hands with, hugging, Viktor's son. 'You don't have to say anything,' Viktor said, with that hundred-watt bulb back in his head. 'I know it was you who arranged for that question to come up, who else could it have been?' And then, puzzled: 'But what are you doing here, Jonas? You're no murderer? And it's not like a chunk of ice struck *you* on the head.'

'That's my business,' Jonas said, making it clear that he did not wish to talk about it. Although he almost said: 'A block of ice struck at my heart.'

It was a strange, and emotional, reunion. Jonas could not help feeling, possibly because of Viktor's disconcertingly youthful appearance, that it was only a day or so since they had parted in Seilduksgata and that they could simply pick up the threads of a conversation they had broken off twenty-five years earlier. 'Over the past few days I've been reading *The Cantos*,' Viktor said as he was leaving, with his old, familiar hundred-watt enthusiasm. 'And do you know what? I understand it all now. Do you remember Venice? Ezra Pound was so wrong. I've waded through the whole thing again. It *is* a masterpiece. I actually think I have Pound to thank for the fact that I could answer so many questions on *Jeopardy!*'

'I thought the TV might have had something to do with it,' Jonas said cautiously, almost afraid that Viktor might have a relapse.

'Oh, that too of course, but I'm sure I picked up a lot of those nonsensical facts from *The Cantos*,' Viktor answered with a laugh. And added, serious now: 'Pound really has written a work of genius. I think that when you started to read it aloud to me, somewhere in my subconscious I must have connected those extracts with all the books I studied in order to understand Pound's verses – the books I built so many shelves for.' Viktor's baby face was shining, almost as if he felt this longed-for insight into *The Cantos* was worth the price he had paid: twenty years in hibernation – or perhaps one should say of education.

What became of Viktor after that Easter? He received masses of tempting offers, and one of these he accepted. In many ways the most logical one. Viktor did not only wake up, he also began to think big. He decided to help sell the *Norwegian Encyclopedia*. He took a job with its publishers, Kunnskapsforlaget, one of the country's foremost promoters of knowledge – a post in their marketing department created just for him – and was involved in the launching of a new edition of a work which was to reference books what the Stressless Royal was to armchairs. Viktor also signed a lucrative contract in which he gave the publishing house permission to use him in their advertising campaign. He became, quite simply, the public face of Kunnskapsforlaget. 'Learning keeps you young,' Viktor announced from huge posters on walls all over the city where scantily clad models for H&M normally reigned supreme. For some time Viktor Harlem's smiling and indecently youthful Einstein countenance was to be seen everywhere: 'You too can be a champion!' he declared. The campaign was, of course, a stroke of genius. Sales of the encyclopedia broke all records. Seeing Viktor, the *Jeopardy!* king, the Supreme Grand Champion, associated in this way with the *Norwegian Encyclopedia*, people automatically assumed that *this* was why he was so good at answering questions. Or asking them. The majority of Norwegians regarded Viktor as living proof that it paid to own a sixteen-volume encyclopedia. It appeared to be conducive both to a healthy body and a healthy bank balance. So it was in large part thanks to Viktor Harlem that Norway in the nineties had no trouble defending its ranking as one of the top countries in the world when it came to the number of encyclopedias per head of population.

Viktor started visiting Jonas as Jonas had visited him and one day at the prison, when they were chatting about television, Viktor said that he had recently watched the *Thinking Big* series again. He understood now what an impact it must have had on him, how much of it he could remember, even though at the institution he had watched the programmes, regularly, in a very different, abstracted frame of mind. 'I hope you won't be annoyed if I say I like the programme on Harald Hardråde best,' he said to Jonas. 'That arrow didn't just kill Harald Hardråde, it saved my life.'

I could not help thinking of both Viktor Harlem and the aforementioned programme when we were in Eivindvik, in Viking country, where there are traces dating back even further than Harald Hardråde. Outside the church-yard gate stood an ancient stone cross, and on a green hillside nearby we found a similar cross, carved in a slightly different style. Both could have been erected around the time when Christianity came to Norway, by kings such as Håkon the Good, Olav I or Olav II. The ground on which the *Gulatinget*, the first regional moot, was held had also lain somewhere in these parts, possibly in Eivindvik first, then at Flolid, where a stone now marked the site of the moot ground.

From Brekke we had sailed out into the fjord estuary, bore south, then made our way into Eivindvik's nice, sheltered harbour, where we were assigned a berth alongside the local shop. Eivindvik was the perfect place in which to review our findings on Sognefjord and Viking times: with the pictures we had taken and the plethora of notes regarding rune stones and burial mounds – and the battlefields, like the bay off Fimreite where King Sverre won such a decisive battle over King Magnus in 1184. And only a little to the north of here, at Solund, Harald Hardråde had assembled his fleet before the disastrous expedition to England. Carl thought we should insert clips from Jonas Wergeland's television programme into our presentation of Solund. I saw a circle being closed, I saw my two projects being juggled together to form a whole. I saw how, simply by being there, Jonas Wergeland had moved us to take a more radical approach to the OAK Quartet's prod-ucts, to wonder whether it was possible for us to transcend our medium, as he had once expanded the television medium.

From Jonas's own ramblings it was clear that he was more interested in Dean Niels Griis Alstrup Dahl, of whom there were traces at every turn in Eivindvik. I could see why Jonas Wergeland would identify with someone like Dahl: a Prometheus, a popular enlightener in the true sense. Dahl was an individual who wanted to think big, a man who squeezed 'bread from stones', who instilled culture in farmers and fishermen. Jonas said he liked the thought that his mother's family came from around here, most likely from Verkland Farm, not far from Brekke.

Just before we were due to leave I was sitting alone in the saloon on board the *Voyager*, making a note of things to add to my manuscript. It was here in Eivindvik that I decided to write a frame story about the sail along Sognefjord, because I saw that the inclusion of this voyage would make a difference – *all* the difference – to the picture of Jonas Wergeland's life presented in the final draft. Here, too, I realised that by observing him so closely I had come to see myself in a new light. In writing this account I had also changed my own life. I think this must have been what I had in mind all the time. That deep down this was why I had done it. I now knew, what is more, how I felt about Martin.

The previous day I had taken myself off to a bench outside the old church to read through the big notebooks which Jonas Wergeland had come up and handed to me with a smile, just like that, as we were sailing up Prestesundet towards Eivindvik. 'I'd better add my pittance,' he said, 'my contribution to the collective epic.' I sat there, reading the handwritten pages, surrounded by the scent of cherry blossom, and I make no secret of the fact that I was so moved that I frequently had to stop, as my emotions got the better of me. Here, at long last, I had the answer to my question as to why he had done it, why he chose to go to prison. I had known. But I had not known in quite this way. I realised right away that I would have to weave these stories into my own book. With his permission. I would probably have to synchronise our accounts of some events. In other cases the contradictions would be allowed to stand.

But still: even our joint efforts offered no guarantee. It struck me that I might have been writing with a confidence that was quite unwarranted. The true story about Jonas Wergeland might just as easily be the sum of all the untold stories about him. Even at that point, sitting outside the church, I began to have some doubts about his own version of events. What bothered me most were the passages in which he described all his ventures, even his television series, as failures. I could not agree with him. As I rested my eyes on the old vicarage, once the home of Niels Griis Alstrup Dahl himself, a memory surfaced. Things get a bit more personal here, there's no way round it: the truth is, you see, that I not only think, I am quite positive, that Jonas Wergeland once saved me, and possibly even my life.

This incident occurred on a beautiful autumn day, the sort of day that sharpens all the senses, a day so ineluctably clear that you suddenly become sensible to the element air. It was no coincidence that I should have been inspired to conduct my experiment, or seen that it could be done, on such a day.

I was working at the time for an advertising agency, among bright, young things with hip lighters and slick business cards: a milieu in which the right sunglasses counted for more than moral backbone. It had been a hectic week: the Advertising Association's gala dinner and awards ceremony on the Friday followed, on the Saturday, by a party to mark the fifth birthday of our distinctive little agency; a pretty riotous affair at which we fêted ourselves as if we were the very lynchpin of society. The latter do was held at one of the city's rock clubs, one of those dingy venues which make you feel as if you've landed in a disused factory or the hallway to hell. The only decorative element in the vast, totally black hall were the television sets dotted around the room on little trolleys, each one hooked up to a video recorder. On these monitors we had our own ads running non-stop without the sound. I had been responsible for setting this up, it was also up to me to make sure that all the equipment was returned to the suppliers. On the Sunday, after only a few hours of fitful sleep, I went for a walk on my own, and that's when the idea came to me. I don't know why. It may have been the wistfulness encapsulated in such crisp, clear autumn hours, the detachment from life that they bestow. As I watched a maple leaf drifting gently to the ground, the thought settled in my mind, as crisp and clear as the air around me.

I ought to say that this was also a special day in another respect. I had woken that Sunday morning with a feeling of listless melancholy, of body and spirit, which I had long feared was going to engulf me completely. All I wanted was to stay there in bed with the curtains drawn for days. I had just come out of a relationship, so maybe that had something to do with it. Or maybe it was all the partying I had been doing, two bashes as vacuous and frenetic as only such gatherings can be. But even that could not explain it all. I knew my mother had suffered from depression; I had always been scared, terrified, that I might succumb to something similar. In my teens I had sometimes caught glimpses of a darkness that frightened me, but I had never felt anything like this vague numbness, this *weight* which was pressing down on me when I opened my eyes that Sunday. All my senses told me that I was in danger, that at any moment I could be hurled into some indefinable darkness. For the first time it occurred to me that my life might go the same way as my mother's. The thought made my heart pound with dread.

So even as I tried to make the most of this clear autumn day, the keen, invigorating air, inside I felt gloomy and angst-ridden. It is hard to put it into words, but I walked along beneath the flaming yellow leaves on the trees with an uneasy feeling that the world was grey. Grey and flat. It must have been this that rendered me so receptive. An idea that should have occurred to me before was forced to the surface by a semi-conscious sense of desperation, a vague horror that all the colour and depth would drain out of life.

When I got home I got out the tapes of Dad's – or no, I had better maintain, still, the distance I have tried to observe throughout: Jonas Wergeland's – television series. I kept them on the same shelf as Knut Hamsun's collected works, since I happen to believe that this series ranks alongside the great works of Norwegian literature. I drove into the city, back to the club. As soon as I set foot in that vast, empty space and saw the television sets scattered about like basic forms of basalt or black marble I knew I was on the right track.

The smell of the party still hung over the barren, black-painted hall: cigars and booze, the whiff of expensive perfumes mingled with the indeterminate, aromatic odour of the somewhat disappointing food we had had. There were still a few bottles sitting about. The floor was sticky. Purely by chance I was dressed all in black and for a moment I had the feeling that I was merging with the room, that the massive hall was going to swallow me up. I shrugged it off and began to arrange the trolleys holding the TV sets and video recorders in a big circle. I thought of Stonehenge, that enigmatic arrangement of megaliths in England. On reflection, I seem to remember a newspaper photograph from the time when the *Thinking Big* series was first shown on NRK TV: a pensive-looking Jonas Wergeland pictured in his office, like an inventor in his laboratory. My eye had been caught not so much by his facial expression as by the screens in the background, flat panels arranged in a semi-circle. On them one could see large sheets of paper covered in writing, squares with lines running between them. It looked as though he was standing in a many-sided room packed with ideas.

I slotted one tape, one programme from the series, into each video recorder. The machines were all of the same make and hooked up to one another in such a way that I could start them all at the same time with just one remote control. I pressed the button and there I stood, all at once, in the centre of a vast hall, in the centre of a circle of television screens, each showing a programme from Jonas Wergeland's television series. The sets seemed almost to form an electronic membrane around me, as if I were inside a massive, life-giving organ, a breathing entity. Let me put it this way: I would not have missed it for the world. It was like being touched, caressed almost, by something, a quality, which was light-years away from the universe I ordinarily inhabited and by which I was surrounded in this room, in the shape of mementos of a meaningless party: the dregs of wine in plastic cups and the reek of stale smoke, a slip of paper scrawled with headings for a pretentious speech tramped into some sticky gunge on the floor.

I tried to take in as much as I could, but at one point, possibly because I found it so overwhelming and needed to rest my eyes, I stood and watched the programme on Harald Hardråde, the king who had tried to do the unthinkable, to conquer England. I remembered my reaction, one time when the programme was being repeated, to the final scene: the bloody battle of Stamford Bridge represented solely by Harald himself, a king fighting an army which we could not see, yet did see. I had sat up, wide-eyed, thinking to myself that this was him, Jonas Wergeland, it was a self-portrait, an assertion that one man could have the width to populate a whole world. It was also a picture of Jonas Wergeland battling alone with a Titanic task, invisible to all but him; an attempt to achieve the impossible.

I stood in that black, party-fumed club with its dead echoes of here today, gone tomorrow music and inane adverts. I looked. I began to move my eyes from one screen to the next, as if they were different parts of a circular mosaic. The thought occurred to me that if all of the programmes were in the nature of self-portraits then Jonas Wergeland had succeeded in fulfilling an old dream: of living several lives at once. Standing there in that dark, factory-like space I slowly let my eyes travel round, feeling a little dizzy, but also amazed that I could actually manage to watch so many screens at once. It was an enthralling, almost unearthly, experience. At one point it crossed my mind that this must be what it was like to stand with one's head inside a crystal chandelier, inside a circle of light.

I had seen every programme several times over, but never – obviously – at the same time. Suddenly – after twenty minutes or so – my subconscious told me that they were all connected, that if I could just manage to look at all the screens at once I would have the sensation of watching just one programme. I found an office chair on which I could spin round; I rewound the tapes, restarted them all simultaneously. And it was when I sat down on the chair and began slowly to rotate that the revelation came to me. The sum of the images I saw on each screen metamorphosed into a stupendous juggling act; I witnessed the way in which, throughout all these programmes, Jonas Wergeland kept so many images, impressions, in the air at once, as an expert juggler does with balls.

I spun myself round, a warm thrill running through me. These flat screens offered me a peek into wonderful depths, and filled me with an unfailing certainty that reality was round. In this almost vacuum-black hall, in which only hours earlier I had attended a superficial party, heard the stupidest things being said, and made the silliest remarks myself, I was now having my life's epiphany, an insight which filled my every smallest cell. At some point – although I had no sense of time – I developed the strong suspicion that the lines in each programme also fell in a very specific order, such that if I were to join together the pieces of the separate lines I would hear quite different sentences; a sentence ending in one programme would continue, like an elaboration of a statement, in another programme, while in a third programme it might be the music which picked up the thread, or added another dimension to the argument. At other times I had the idea that the whole thing evolved into a dialogue, that the programmes were speaking to one another. To me, in the state I was in and precisely because I was confronted with this incomparable work of art – stories subtly bound together to form a magnificent fresco – in a hall that stank faintly of leftovers and vomit, that reeked of adverts and commercialism and facile kitschiness, the screens, the programmes surrounding me seemed almost to come to life. I sat in a circle of pictures and sound which gradually expanded until it encompassed everything. I remember what I thought. I thought: this is my Samarkand. This black room.

As I spun slowly round and round on my office chair I noticed how the light from the twenty-odd television sets struck me like rays. Like healing rays. I understood, or had some inkling of, what mental planning, what work – and, not least: what an idea – had to lie behind this complex interaction, the thousands of minute links which caused all these programmes to run together to form one cross-referring network. In the end, in his own way, he had succeeded in organising all of human learning in a new way, shown how the most diverse insights could hang together, on an organic tree of knowledge, so to speak. He had proved it to himself; I doubt if he felt the need to prove it to anyone else. I am pretty certain that I am the only person to discover this secret. And this superb self-portrait: how manifold and yet how homogenous is man.

I think it must have been at this point, as I sat in the circle of light, that I realised how little I knew about him. I felt that I was – at long last – discovering him. Discovering who my father was. It may sound high-flown, and I really ought not to be the one to say it, but no one else has seen it: Jonas Wergeland was not – when his career was at its height, I suppose I should say – an important person because he represented the world of his day, as he grew so sick of hearing. He was an exceptional person, one in a billion, because he embodied the *possibilities* of his day, all the unrealised potential. He reflected the future. He showed us, me at least, what mankind could be.

As I went on swirling round and round, as I went on trying to keep my eyes on as many screens as possible, I felt the impending depression loosen its grip. I had a sense of being lifted up. Pulled up. At that moment I was sure that by vouchsafing me a glimpse of his vision, this circle of tales which filled each other out, Jonas Wergeland had saved my life. Saved me from the darkness.

I made up my mind to do something different, start a new kind of company, the OAK Quartet, try to break new ground.

It was morning in Eivindvik. With departure in the air. Kamala and Jonas were travelling on with the *Voyager*; Martin and I were driving back to Oslo. Hanna cheerily announced that they were planning to sail out to Utvær because Jonas was so keen to see the outermost isle, where the Vikings were said to have sharpened their swords before setting out on expeditions into the west. Harald Hardråde too must have gone ashore there on his way across the North Sea to conquer England.

Martin suggested that we wave them off from a spot from which we would be able to see them for as long as possible. The others had found someone who knew the waters around there, they huddled round a sea chart while he showed them a possible course through the scattering of rocks and islets to the west of Ytre Sula. We walked briskly up the slope to Høgefjell, reached the radar dish on the top then carried on across the broad sweep of Kjeringefjell. We parked ourselves on the rise furthest to the west. It was a hot day, we were dressed in just shorts and T-shirts. We sat with the sun on our backs, gazing out to sea. It was the Whit weekend so there were quite a few boats out. Visibility was exceptionally good. We could see the skerries around Gulen, the islands out at Solund and Lihesten's distinctive rocky profile all the way to the north. Below the knoll on which we sat lay the foundations of a lookout hut used during the war. From here you could spot any enemy approaching Sognefjord.

We had not been there many minutes before the *Voyager* came sailing under engine-power through Nyhamarsund, right below us. Martin waved his T-shirt. Hanna and Carl, Kamala and Jonas waved back. The water of the sound was an unreal turquoise due to the algae, shifting to blue at the mouth of the fjord. I settled myself more comfortably while Martin warmed up some mulligatawny soup on the storm cooker, leftovers from the previous evening's farewell dinner on board the *Voyager*. 'I'm terribly sorry, memsahib, I'm afraid it lacks a little pinch of coriander,' he said, and made me laugh. He was actually working on another little project on the side, a booklet he intended to call *Cookbook for Two Nomads and a Primus*. We followed the boat with our eyes as we slurped the highly seasoned soup. We saw the old lifeboat veer west, saw them setting sail – mainsail, foresail, jib – and suddenly, at that distance, the *Voyager* took on the air of a timeless vessel. It was a beautiful sight. And a beautiful thought. One Norwegian, one half-American, one Korean and one Indian. And all of them Norwegian. On their way to Utvær. An Outside Left position, I thought. A new Norway.

I glanced across at Martin, a guy who claimed to come from a little junction in Troms, a guy I liked a lot. He had Norway's most common surname, but he was the most uncommon Norwegian I had ever met. He had climbed just about everything, from the Bonatti Pillar to Ama Dablam, but here he was, sitting next to me at the top of a 1,400-foot hill, looking totally awestruck. He gazed out across the sea. 'I've never seen anything like it,' he said. 'It's like sitting at the world's biggest crossroads.'

We sat quietly, relishing the last spoonfuls of mulligatawny soup and the sight of the boat. A boat laden with questions. I glanced at the ruin below me, the vestiges of the lookout hut. Jonas Wergeland was sailing away from *Festung Norwegen*. I thought fondly of the man on board the lifeboat out there at the mouth of the fjord. I had finished his story, I knew what was needed to complete the final draft. I would have to bring myself to write about the Belém tower. It was only right that this idea should have come to me atop a hill called Kjeringefjell – Old Wife's Fell. It was from women that the most telling stories about Jonas Wergeland had come.

The *Voyager* had a fair wind. As the lifeboat passed the southernmost point of Husøy and bore north, something flashed on the deck, like light off a mirror. I was not sure, but it was my guess that Jonas had got out the sword he had bought, more as a joke really, at Balestrand: a copy of a magnificent Viking sword. I pictured him standing in the stern, brandishing this sword, putting on a little show for Kamala; or maybe he was waving it at us, in farewell. Or signalling that he was cutting himself out of a net – a net which so many people had tried to throw over him, catch him in. One mighty slash and he would be free. Maybe this was only the beginning. Maybe Jonas Wergeland was, in fact, now poised on the starting line, all set to embark on his real career, the great conquests of his life. He just had to stop off at Utvær first, to hone his sword. I suddenly remembered the moment when he gave me his two notebooks. I had not been quite sure whether he had called them his pittance or his pretence. He had been smiling, but the look in his eyes had been quizzical, admonitory: So you think you have me now?

We lay there for a long time – until the *Voyager* was no more than a speck slipping or drifting off into the blue. For a second the vessel looked like a little spaceship heading for a star cluster, heading out across the cosmos.

When the boat vanished from view, the thought flashed through my mind that Jonas Wergeland had 'left the saga' as they said in the old tales; but on second thoughts I am more inclined to say that he sailed out of a minor, local saga and into another, greater one. As the secretary of a world-class story-teller. Lying there on the top of Kjeringefjell I realised that all of my thoughts and my literary efforts were not, in fact, aimed at explaining, through reference to stories from the past, why Jonas Wergeland had become who he was. I was more intent on looking forward, on considering what he *could* become. He would have applauded such a thought: the future, that was the crucial story.

It was also the future he had been thinking of in Lisbon, when he met Marie H., the head of programming, at the Hieronymite Monastery as arranged, having first run into her, accidentally on purpose, on the Rossio the day before. She was dressed differently, in a light, patterned summer dress which revealed that she still had a healthy tan. After almost dutifully surveying the south portal of the chapel, a prime example of Manueline architecture, they walked round the monastery gardens, with Jonas airing his knowledge, perhaps a little too blatantly, as if keen to prove that he was only here for the architecture. He could never be sure, but Marie's suggestion that they visit the Maritime Museum might have been a form of revenge; he meekly followed her to the west wing of the monastery, and through the endless rooms dedicated to the discoveries made around 1500. Wherever he turned his eyes were met by objects testifying to great navigational feats. And yet: right then he could not have cared less about navigation; he wanted to drift with the wind and the waves. He eyed her on the sly: her tanned legs, her partially exposed breasts, her glowing eyes; he tried, vainly, to concentrate on the makeshift sea charts, the compasses, the astrolabes. There's only one way to save my life's work, he told himself. By losing control.

Why did he do it?

'It was from the harbour here that Vasco da Gama set out,' Marie said when they were outside again. 'Belém is where it all began.' How apt, Jonas thought. He too would have to discover a cape, a new strait, if he was to have any future. The next minutes with this woman who had decided to call a halt to his *magnum opus*, a television series the likes of which had never been seen, would decide everything. Whether he would be able to produce an extraordinary work or merely an amputated version, the contours of which would be indiscernible. Jonas felt as though he were standing before a great queen, and that he had to convince her of the possibility that an apparently hazardous expedition could succeed.

Both his eyes and his legs were tired from wandering around the museum; he made no objection whatsoever when, on the way to the Belém Tower, she led him towards a building, a café, and through a door half-hidden by shrubs covered in purple and pink flowers. She seemed to know her way around, made straight for the bar, and that in a place where one was constantly reminded of the importance of navigation. On the walls, alongside the stuffed fish and pictures of old sailing ships, hung all sorts of nautical instruments. But he had no time for them now. He drank too much. Deliberately drank too much. She drank a lot too. Something about her make-up, her black-lined eyes made him think of Maria Callas. Was he reading anything, she asked. Like what, he said. Fiction, she said. He played for time, tried to change the subject. What was his favourite book? she asked. *Victoria*, he said, plucking it out of thin air, a title from a distant memory. She ordered them another drink. He began alluding to his series again, as if the alcohol had given him fresh courage, fresh hope. 'How can you cancel it now, halfway?' he said. 'Doesn't anyone see that without the whole thing you have nothing.'

She did not reply. But there was a look in her eyes. A different look. Less forbidding. And she was looking at him. *Seeing* him, as if sighting him for the first time. She continued to cast burning, sidelong glances at him as they strolled the last bit of the way to the Belém tower, a building so unique that UNESCO had designated it part of our world heritage. Again the thought flashed through his mind, she seems to know her way around. And as if to confirm this she pulled him impatiently round to the other side of the building and pointed to a weathered, sculpted form underneath a watchtower jutting out over the water. 'A rhinoceros?' he said. She nodded vigorously and told him that in olden days there had been a plan to stage a fight near the monastery they had just visited between a rhinoceros and an elephant. Like a fight between you and me, Jonas thought. The two strongest forces within NRK.

How could anyone miss seeing it? Why has no one before described the most important decision, or absence of a decision, in Jonas Wergeland's life?

On the way back to the ramp running across the water to the entrance, she suddenly took his hand, in a way that made him think that at last he was going to discover who she was, the Battleship, this unapproachable, seemingly flinty woman who played around with people's lives. He marched towards the tower, feeling hopeful – but also a little afraid. He had not felt anything quite like this since the summer of the year he was seven when, clad in a freshly-ironed white shirt, he sat in a hot bus trundling along a narrow road lined by golden pine trunks. He would start school that same autumn, but looking back on it he realised that his schooling had begun some weeks earlier. He learned a lesson that summer that would leave its mark on him for life.

It was not a Sunday, but it felt like a holiday all the same. He was going to meet 'Uncle' Melankton, the pride of the family, for the first time. Now, he thought, he was going to be told something about the hidden meaning of life.

And, if he was lucky: about Venus. The name Melankton made him think of something fundamental, a first cause of sorts, in the same way that the word plankton did.

It was June, that month so extravagant with light. As always, they were spending the summer holidays at his father's childhood home on Hvaler, an island at the mouth of Oslo fjord. Herringbone clouds stretched across the sky and the swallows were on the wing until late in the evening. To Jonas, life was just one long, lazy Sunday, full of peaceable bumble bees, motor-boats with flags flying astern and the smell of freshly baked beer bread. It had been an exceptionally hot week, he could not remember ever having seen such low tides; it was a time when things came to view. Some days, when especially large patches of the seabed lay exposed, he half-expected Venus herself to show up. He had detected an unwonted note of anxiety in his mother's voice as they ran off down to the steamship wharf to swim: 'I'm just going to say one thing, boys: watch out for Venus!'

The story of how Melankton had become something of an attraction had been told to him by his father. The way people saw it, Melankton had conducted a successful rebellion against the islanders' limited options – and, what is more, given some intimation of certain hereditary traits in the otherwise unexceptional Hansen family. When just a young lad Melankton had vowed to do something that no one before him had ever done, and instead of becoming a fisherman or a sailor, or something in trade, he had, against all the odds, taken the university entrance exam over at Fredrikstad then gone on to Oslo to study. After that the trail went dead. No one knew what he had read at university, or how he had lived, but one day there he was, back on the steamship wharf, wearing the same – albeit odd-looking – clothes he had had on when he left twenty years earlier. The only luggage he had with him was a big wooden crate and a remarkably battered suitcase.

Melankton Hansen did not say much. He took a job on the pilot boat as if nothing had happened. During the holidays he kept his lip buttoned even tighter than usual, not to shatter the idyll for the summer visitors from the capital, or holidaymakers as the locals, and in due course Jonas too – his father had been born on the island, after all – called them somewhat condescendingly. Because there was nothing the city folks liked better than to be on speaking terms with one of the locals. This carried as much prestige as, later, Norwegian aid workers derived from saying that they knew a Negro. One could, for example, be forgiven for thinking that Mr Wilhelmsen the shipping magnate flew over in his seaplane every Friday evening, then exchanged his suit for an old sweater and jeans with holes in the knees, purely in order to pass the time of day with Melankton Hansen down by the harbour and listen, in the lags in the conversation, to the clip-clip of an oystercatcher skimming the waves at their feet. The holidaymakers loved to be able to come back from the shop in the morning and tell the rest of the family: 'I ran into Melankton. He had a pail full of flat fish, heaped up like pancakes. He netted twenty-odd plaice out at Ekholmsflua.' It was all part of the joys of summer: you wrote postcards to friends in the city about the Simple Life and Getting Back to Basics.

Melankton could not only show the city folk a freshwater spring on a tiny islet, or take them out to a stretch of water where porpoises often popped up like spluttering wheels, he could also teach them the *words*, the essential words, the ones which, when the holidaymakers repeated them, sent shivers of pleasure running down their spines, as if they were not on a small island in the Norwegian skerries, but on a foreign continent where they had managed the prodigious feat of learning the native language. They rocked back and forth on their heels, bursting with pride, when they used the correct terms for different types of boat or reeled off the names of islets or reefs – or better still, a fishing ground, or a skerry which was good for torching crabs. 'Hue,' they repeated to themselves after a conversation with Melankton about the headland across from the steamship wharf. 'Rokka,' they would murmur, almost reverently, with reference to the narrow strait leading to the open sea.

But Melankton was not always able to contain himself, and less and less as the years passed. Occasionally he would let fall a remark which – and on this all the islanders were agreed – betrayed his vast knowledge and experience of life. Stories started to circulate about weird conversations he had had with holidaymakers, of words and phrases such as 'the Pre-Raphaelites', 'Ernest Hemingway' or 'Cartesian philosophy'. One summer visitor, a teacher from Oslo, told the island postmaster that for the first time he now understood the theory of relativity, after having had it explained to him by Melankton Hansen. Some people said that the crate Melankton had brought back to the island with him contained a complete set of the *Encyclopedia Brittanica*, a massive work of reference, and that he had worked his way through this in much the same way as other people read *Gone with the Wind*. Secretly they called him 'the walking encyclopedia'. The islanders were proud of Melankton Hansen. But he was also something of a mystery to them. He looked like someone who had miraculously managed to escape from East Germany to Western Europe and then, having seen all the delights of its countries, had inexplicably and quite voluntarily, returned to the East as if nothing had happened.

Jonas's father had told him how proud he had been of his uncle – his father who, as a boy, would willingly give up anything to go trolling for mackerel with

Melankton. There was nothing to beat sitting in a motor-boat as it chugged gently across a sea which in Haakon Hansen's memory was always calm and shimmering, with half an eye on your lines. Once every fifteen minutes or so his uncle might come out with a word, or a sentence, or a whole little story – about the names of the clouds, about life in the rainforests, about the Hindu belief in *karma* or the big earthquake in Lisbon; fragments which to Haakon – the way he told it to Jonas – went far beyond what any one person could pick up in the way of learning. Not even the mackerel's rainbow-hued sheen could match his uncle's sparse utterances; not even the thought of dinner: crisp, fried mackerel and rhubarb soup.

And yet. There were things which Melankton had seen and done which he never spoke of to anyone – that much even Haakon gathered. 'Something bad happened to Melankton,' people on the island whispered. One of the lads on the pilot boat claimed to have heard Melankton mumbling something about 'a lost ruby'. He had been hurt, folk said. It must have been something to do with a woman. And Jonas's father realised that there might be a grain of truth in these rumours because sometimes Melankton would take a deep breath and let it out again in an eloquent sigh, shaking his head, as if Haakon were not there. Then he would come to himself, fix his eyes on the boy and declare: 'When you get right down to it, lad, there's only one thing to say: "Watch out for Venus!"'

As he bounced up and down on the seat of the old bus in his freshly ironed shirt, on his way to meet Uncle Melankton, Jonas was thinking to himself that now at long last he was going to learn what had happened to this man, the pride of the family and, even more exciting, the story behind a lost ruby.

The thought of Venus, a warning to watch out, may also have crossed his hopeful and mildly inebriated mind as Marie led him into the Belém Tower in Lisbon. But at that particular moment he had no will of his own, and he was curious; it was like waiting for a verdict which he could do nothing to change. She paid for their tickets and led the way to the first floor, an open platform from which they could admire – of all things – a statue of the Virgin Mary. They were alone. It was just before closing time, they had seen people leaving. Again Jonas was conscious of the way her eyes kept flickering across him, as if she were seeing him in a new light, as another person almost. She grabbed his hand and drew him through a narrow doorway, then up the stairs to the bottommost room in the tower itself. She located another opening, a door leading to a dim, tight spiral staircase. She had to let go of his hand and precede him up the stairs. The thin stuff of her dress fluttered like bait in front of his eyes. The smell of her filled his nostrils and reinforced the sense of intoxication. On the steep stairway he could see right up her legs to the edging of her underwear. She wants me to see that, he thought. She climbed quickly, all but running up the smooth, worn stone steps. He followed on her heels, his head spinning, had to put one hand on the rough wall for support, stared at the play of muscle in her legs, at her ankles; he was surprised to discover how lovely and sexy an ankle could be, thought what an underrated part of the female anatomy it was, or perhaps he was thinking about the Achilles tendon, his own Achilles tendon, his weak spot, that he was about to tear it, that something bad was about to happen, which is to say something good, but at the same time bad. They passed through several rooms, met no one, carried on up the stairs until they reached the top; stood there, dazzled by the strong, late-afternoon light. Jonas lifted his face to the refreshing breeze, but his head felt no clearer for it. Again he had the impression, although he could never be sure, that she had been here before. If she had a plan then it had to have been a spur-of-the moment thing, a combination of common sense and madness.

In each corner of the square platform was a small domed watchtower. She pulled him into the one overlooking the river. From it, they could see due west, to the mouth of the Tagus and the ocean stretching out beyond it. He had to turn sideways to get through the door and into the tiny white chamber – there was just room enough for them both. She leaned through the peephole in the wall, leaned far out. Her dress slid up, exposing her thighs, the soft skin; her bottom arched towards him, the pattern on the thin fabric stretched over it making him think of a globe. 'Look,' she said, without turning, as if wanting Jonas to bend over her. He tried, moved in close to her. The sea air wafted past him, but did not dilute the smell of her, a heavy scent of patchouli and perspiration. The sun hung low in the sky straight in front of them. She pointed across the glittering sea. 'This is where they sailed from, the great discoverers,' she said. Her voice rang hollow in the narrow chamber. For some time nothing was said. Then: 'Do you feel a bit … peculiar too?' she asked. Long pause. They both stared at a container ship gliding past. The *Nuova Africa*, a black hulk heading out to sea. He heard her breathing, every sound amplified under the small domed roof. The water sparkled beneath them, before them. His heavy breathing was bound to sound, to her, like panting. Like a rhinoceros. He swallowed and was about to say something when he felt her hand curl round his buttock and draw him closer, right up against her. Aroused though he was he could not help seeing the funny side of it. To be standing inside a work of art, a building on the UNESCO World Heritage List; to be inside a monument to the triumph of civilisation – and to feel like a beast, so horny that the two halves of one's brain have shrunk to two testicles. All thought of his project even, the television series he was trying to save, disappeared,

437

sliding as it were from his brow and down through his body, as if rather than life, rather than anything, he would take sex life. He feared – he *knew* – that he was succumbing to Melankton's syndrome, but he didn't bloody well care; he had long since realised, believed he had long since realised, that for far too many years he had held back in such situations because in his mind he had created a dilemma for himself, one which did not really exist.

Jonas aged seven, in the freshest of freshly ironed white shirts and on his way to meet the family's learned treasure, was blissfully unaware of these future deliberations. Jonas's father was a conscientious man who made a point, every summer, of visiting his surviving relatives on Hvaler. It was a couple of years, however, since he had last seen Melankton Hansen, his uncle having moved into an old folks' home on one of the neighbouring islands. And since Jonas was now old enough he was given the honour of accompanying his father. He knew Haakon was looking forward to introducing him to this unique uncle who would prove to Jonas, once and for all, that they were not descended only from simple, fishy-smelling folk, rough, loose-living machinists or the keepers of general stores with paintbrushes hanging from the ceiling, outdated advertising posters on the walls and a spittoon still set discreetly in the corner. 'In our family, son, we also have some real, live geniuses. Just you wait and see.'

And Jonas, bumping up and down on the bus seat in his white shirt, could hardly wait. Soon he was going to hear words he had never heard, *the* words. He might even – if he were lucky – get to hear more about 'the lost ruby', or about Venus. He had heard the story many times: when Melankton returned from his unknown adventures he moved into one of the little white cottages on the south side of the island, a property which he gradually turned into a star attraction. While his neighbours toiled over dry lawns covered in molehills, Melankton's garden was a riot of exotic blooms and every sort of fruit tree – he was even said to have succeeded in growing apricots. It was like coming to another place, another country, visitors said.

The final proof that something bad had happened to Melankton came on the day that the steamship pulled into the wharf with a very strange object standing in the bow, rather like a figurehead. Jonas's father had also been there that day: Haakon Hansen, soon to leave the island himself to go over to the town, later the capital, and become an organist. It was a naked woman, a divinely beautiful creature holding aloft a pitcher. Melankton stood proudly on the quayside, like a groom waiting for his bride. He told people that it was a statue of Venus, the goddess of love. He meant to put it in a fountain he was planning for his garden. No one dared to say anything, but secretly they shook their heads: Melankton had gone too far this time, this was hubris. And they were right. Very carefully the crew began to hoist the marble statue ashore, having almost bashfully refrained from laying hands on her bare breasts – and just at the moment when she hung suspended between the bow and the wharf, as everyone was secretly admiring the lines of this divine figure, the rope gave way and the statue plunged into the deep with a white, frothing sigh.

From that day on Melankton said not one word to the locals. Whatever they did hear about him they got in dribs and drabs from the summer visitors. But no one forgot that story. Any time children, including those just there on holiday, swam off the wharf, the grown-ups would shout: 'Watch out for Venus!' They were worried that the marble goddess would be sticking out of the blue clay like a white lance, ready to spear anyone who dived too deep, or that she would drag them into the mire if they tried to swim down to her. Despite all the warnings a lot of boys did dive, trying to catch a glimpse of Venus; they may even have been excited by the thought of stroking those smooth breasts, sticking a hand into her pitcher.

Haakon Hansen was in a good mood as he and Jonas rattled along the narrow road in the old bus. Jonas had brought a bag of King of Denmark aniseed balls, which he thought might be just the gift for Uncle Melankton. He knew intuitively, although back then he could not have put it into words, that he was to be offered a glimpse of his own potential. He was about to have his fortune told.

Jonas would never forget that warm summer day and the visit to the old folks' home: the large, white wooden building set amid copper-coloured pines with swaying tops, the blue sky with clouds scudding across it. He and his father walked along a path, over a soft carpet of pine needles, surrounded by the scent of resin and salt water. He was going to meet the family genius, the 'walking encyclopedia'.

A nurse in a pristine white uniform showed them up the worn stairs to a room in which they found Uncle Melankton sitting by the window in a mouldering spindleback chair; a room with flaking paintwork, a room that stank of piss and sweet, half-rotten bananas. 'Someone to see you, Melankton,' she cried, as if talking to a child. Jonas noticed that the room was completely bare except for a bed and a chair. Not a picture. Not a book. The old man was wearing a shirt that had once been white, but which was now almost yellow, and most definitely not freshly ironed. He was looking out at the garden. He's dreaming of apricots, Jonas thought. He sees Venus standing in the middle of a fountain, encircled by laden apricot trees.

'Hello, Uncle Melankton,' Haakon Hansen said a little too cheerily and rather uncertainly. Even at that point he must have known.

Slowly the old man turned round. Jonas had been expecting a countenance that spoke of matchless sagacity, but this face looked blank. Still, though, Jonas was sure that Uncle Melankton had an amazing memory, that he could come out with nuggets of nigh on divine wisdom at any minute. His face was bathed in sunlight and the furrowed skin had the same warm cast to it and the same deep criss-crosses as smooth, weathered rocks by the sea at the end of a quiet, sunny day. Jonas stood there in his white Sunday-best shirt, hair neatly combed, waiting for some pearls of wisdom, for something close to the essence of life itself to be revealed.

'Cunt,' said Uncle Melankton-

For a few seconds there was total silence.

'Uncle, it's me, Haakon,' Jonas's father said patiently. 'We brought you some grapes and a bag of aniseed balls.'

'Cunt, cunt, cunt,' babbled old Melankton, with a trickle of drool running from the corner of his mouth.

'Totally senile,' Jonas's father murmured softly, half to himself, half to Jonas. 'Totally gaga.'

Jonas liked the fact that his father did not seem embarrassed, and did not try to smooth things over. Although he could not have said why, he felt an immediate sympathy for this family member. He opened the bag of aniseed drops and slipped a couple into Melankton's hand. The old man promptly popped them into his mouth and a blissful expression spread across his face, as if he suddenly remembered that he had once shaken the hands of kings or dallied with beautiful women in distant harbours. Haakon Hansen sat down heavily on the bed and lifted Jonas onto his knee. They sat there for a while, as if they had to stay for a set length of time so as not to offend convention's invisible timekeeper. They sat there with Uncle Melankton, the pride of the family, as he rocked back and forth in his chair, muttering 'Cunt, cunt,' every now and again, sucked on another sweet and stared out of the window at the clouds sailing swiftly, like Flying Dutchmen, across the sky, above pine-tree tops which, with a little stretch of the imagination, could be likened to luxuriant pussy hair.

Jonas did not know what to think. He was not disappointed, though. Some profound truth about life *had* been revealed. Later it would occur to him that this man's words had given him his first sight of mankind's strange ability, for good or ill, to simplify complex concepts. It was a phenomenon he would later encounter again and again, in the most unexpected areas of life: the *Encyclopedia Brittanica* boiled down to one word.

As they were leaving, Uncle Melankton winked at Jonas and stuck out his tongue, on which an aniseed drop lay moist and glistening – almost as if his words had taken the shape of a sparkling, polished ruby.

In time, this experience would give rise in Jonas to a certain anxiety. He became wary where girls were concerned. It might even be that part of the reason Jonas was so slow in making his sexual debut lay in his boyhood meeting with Melankton Hansen. Senile old man or no, Jonas could not help interpreting that slavering 'cunt, cunt' of his great-uncle's as an explanation of sorts for his return to the island at the mouth of the fjord, for why his gifts were never allowed to burst into full bloom. The path from cultivating one's genius to cultivating one's genitalia could be appallingly short. For a long time, Melankton represented for Jonas the living embodiment of a dilemma, the question of either-or. Not until he met Margrete again was Jonas able to see, thanks to her, that the one did not necessarily exclude the other. By then he had for years been labouring under a sad misapprehension, been afraid that he would go the same way as Melankton: that the yearning for life would be forced to give way to the yearning for sex life.

But now – he had been cured, believed himself to have been cured, ages ago of such stupid ideas. The Jonas who stood in that small corner tower in Belém had long since dismissed any possibility of suffering the same fate as Melankton; of setting the highest goals for oneself, of meaning to do something that no one else had ever done, only to have to settle for less. Right now, though, he had only one thought in his head, the one which has, down through the ages, formed a common bond between most men: a constantly churning 'cunt, cunt'. He had had a hard-on for some time. Marie felt it, but did not turn round, still seemed totally absorbed in scanning the bend of the river and the sea below. And then, with one foot – he had to admire her technique – she flipped shut the two narrow, red flaps which served as a door, while at the same time lifting up her skirt, positively offering herself to him, and not only that – offering the confirmation of a possibility to which he had closed his eyes for far too long: he could bring his grand and noble project to fruition while at the same time satisfying his basest desires. The enticing backside before him could be viewed as a globe, and the crack in it as a strait into which he could sail. All at once she seemed more impatient than him, as if she did not wish to give him time to think; she started fumbling for the zip on his fly, an unmistakable sign which gave him the courage to carry out this operation himself, to take out his swollen member, pull down her panties and then, almost without having to push at all, let his erect penis be piloted into her, up inside her, by the slippery fluids which were already present in abundance. And he knew, although he would not admit it to himself, that he had reached his goal, that this had always been his goal. This was why he had left Oslo so quickly, barely stopping to pack, when he heard that she was here. Margrete had been furious, it had not fitted in with her work schedule at all, but he had not listened to her, simply had to jump on a plane, knew it was his only chance. He found out which hotel she was staying at and on the very first morning he stationed himself a little way off, to watch the entrance. He hardly recognised her, though, when she came swinging through the door in her almost frivolously girlish outfit. He had lost sight of her down in the maze-like gridwork of Baixa when she walked out of a stationer's in the Rua do Ouro, but had spotted her again, thank heavens, outside the café on the Rossio. He may, for one resolute moment, have thought that he could actually manage to talk her round, but deep down he had always known that it would end here, with him driving into her from behind like a – yes, exactly what they called women who slept their way to the top in NRK: a telly tart.

He heard the waves breaking against the bank behind the tower, heard seagulls crying. He saw himself from the outside, saw himself standing there like a panting rhino, a primeval, galloping beast. He stared at the shining sea. Discovered nothing. Only that intense light. I was dazzled, he told himself, as if memorising something to use later in his defence, an answer to the question as to why he did it. And all the time she just stood there, seemingly unfazed, gazing out across the Tagus and the countryside on either side of the river, and perhaps it was the fact that he could not see the look on her face, had no way of knowing what she was thinking, which worked him up to such pitch that he knew he was going to come at any minute, that for once he would not be able to control himself and that this was the aim: not to control oneself, but simply to succumb to a fateful moment of ecstasy in which all else was forgotten; surrender to the madness, a madness much worse than banging one's head off a wall, because there can be seconds when your life is turned upside down, when you do something that can never be altered, something which will have the greatest conceivable consequences. And behind this thought again he knew that he would never be able to blame it on a fit of madness, because underneath the frenzied, and to some extent, false excitement, lay a cynical, crystal-clear and quite deliberate plan.

He climaxed, so violently that it seemed to come all the way from his toes, but as he came, in a complete daze and yet one hundred per cent aware of what he was doing, she pulled away from him, held onto his penis with one hand and let his semen spill into the other. Afterwards his thoughts would keep returning to this action; he could not help marvelling at how, by some instinct, she had had the presence of mind, or sensitivity of muscle to detect the final engorgement preceding his first convulsions, and had managed to draw away in time. And he never forgot how, in full view of him, she slung the semen she had caught in the palm of her hand out over the river, in a sowing action, and how, still bent over her, he was sure he saw the drops of sperm fall through the air, glittering, truly sparkling in the light before striking the water far below, like a shower of pearls. He thought: that's a life being tossed out there, the life I really ought to have chosen.

Afterwards – he did not remember much of what happened afterwards – she had turned and looked at him. She put a semen-drenched finger to the scar on his forehead, the wound from that time when he had been thinking too much during a skipping game, as if wondering what it was, or as if she were saying: Now you're marked for life. And he could not help thinking that what he considered the badge of his nobility, the proof that it was possible to think parallel thoughts, was now smeared with semen. Then she had quickly tidied herself up, opened the door of the tower and smiled – a smile that was neither accusing nor rueful; a smile which said that she would neither belittle nor make too much of what had happened. And, whether because of that smile or what, he saw that this, this act, even though it was not all that immoral, and even though it was the sort of thing that millions of people did every day without blinking and without it having any serious repercussions – that in his, Jonas Wergeland's, case this was the one thing in life he should not have done. He knew that from the instant his semen touched the palm of her hand, or from the second the drops of sperm hit the water below, his life was spilt, ruined, as strangely and inexorably as tearing a tendon – only a tiny tendon but still enough to make one collapse in absolute agony. I'm going to fertilise the whole world, he thought, but I am dead.

They walked down the stairs and took a taxi into town, drove past the vast Comércio Square down on the waterfront, before ending up at a small restaurant, a *tasca*, in Alfama, not far from the cathedral. He remembered very little of that meal. The food was probably excellent. The wine too. He stared at a building on the other side of the street, faced with glazed tiles so begrimed that the pattern on them could only just be made out, like another world, behind the dirt. He sat as if in a trance. Remembered only that she appeared to be having a nice time, that she revealed a charming – surprisingly charming – side of herself, that there was a smell of grilled sardines, that darkness fell outside, that the tile-covered building front took on a deeper and deeper glow; lots of small, identical tiles combining to produce a mesmerising effect, rather the way kiss upon kiss can do. He had a vague idea that they had talked about many things, that someone had sung, possibly the proprietrix, and that she, Marie, had suddenly got up and said she had to go. But before she left, this he remembered quite clearly, she had leaned over him and whispered in his ear, as if it were a big secret, that he shouldn't worry any more about his series, it would be okay. 'We'll figure something out,' she whispered, as if she really cared. 'We might be able to dip into the DG's kitty.' Then she made her way out, waving to their hosts, flashing him a smile, one of those rare smiles that sticks in the memory. 'See you in Oslo,' she said from the door. 'And go easy on those Brazilian soap operas. Take a ride on a tram-car instead.'

He completed his television series. And it was good – some said brilliant. A substantial additional injection of funds made it possible for the remaining programmes to be made. He would be hailed as an artist who did not prostitute himself – this was the very word used in several reviews. He had read them and hung his head. But still he could not rid himself of the thought that Marie H. had done it out of genuine sympathy for his project. That the incident at the Belém Tower was neither here nor there as far she was concerned.

He was left sitting dejectedly in a *tasca* in Alfama, staring at the fish bones on his plate with no memory of having eaten fish. There was just one thought racing around his head: of Margrete. Daniel had been right. The soul did lie in the seed. To anyone else this would have been a mere bagatelle. Only he perceived the true gravity of it. Because he was married to an extraordinary woman, there was no telling how she would react to a 'bagatelle'. At some point she would ask him what he had done in Lisbon. She would spot right away, however well he washed himself, that he had come back with a smear of semen on his forehead. He knew even then, as he sat in that *tasca* in Alfama, that one day he would stand over Margrete's dead body and ask himself why she had done it. And he knew that he would be forced to answer: Because I didn't think about her here in Lisbon. Or rather: for the first time, with this act, he had given open expression to his lack of empathy, his unforgivable blindness. He knew what Margrete was like, that he ought to have considered the labyrinthine turnings of her mind, but he pretended not to know.

He had been confronted with his exceptional blindness back in the summer he spent with Bo Wang Lee. He was never quite sure when he discovered it – the truth about Bo, that is. Or whether he had actually known right from the start, but had simply chosen to ignore it. Bo was more than he seemed. More than a Chinese even.

It may have started with the little electronic organ in one of the rooms in Bo's aunt's flat. Bo said his aunt was keeping it for her boyfriend, who also worked with the Norwegian American Line. Bo had been given strict instructions not to touch it, but he thought he could at least demonstrate the hypnotically pulsating rhythm box. Simply by pressing a few buttons Bo conjured up the sensuous rhythms of the rumba, the samba, the cha-cha-cha. Jonas thought it was pretty smart. But it was more than smart to Bo, he turned up the sound and began to dance, and Jonas saw, to his amazement, horror almost, that Bo knew the basic steps, and not only that: something weird had happened to his body, there was something a little too graceful and supple – voluptuous – about it as he swayed around the floor with an invisible Latin American partner, sending Jonas a strangely enigmatic, zig-zag smile, as if he were feeling both proud and a bit sheepish.

Even more thought-provoking, though, was what happened when Jonas showed Bo one of Daniel's ballpoint pens, purchased in Strömstad. On it was a lady in a black bathing-suit and when you turned the pen upside down the bathing-suit slid off. Jonas thought it was kind of sexy. But when he looked at Bo, expecting to be complimented on the stripper in his pen, he saw that Bo was not the least bit impressed. If anything, he looked as if he was disappointed that Jonas should fall for something so appallingly cheap and vulgar.

There had been more of such incidents, but they had been evenly dispersed and only later was Jonas able to view them all together as one long clue to something he should have noticed right away. If, that is, he had not, in fact, seen it but – busy as they were with their games – had chosen not to see it.

Tucked away in one of the many cardboard boxes which testified to the fact that Bo and his mother were nomads, residing only temporarily in the flat at Solhaug, was a calligraphy set. Often when Jonas rang Bo's doorbell in the morning his friend would be sitting writing with elegant pens and real ink which contrasted sharply with the rude pen which Jonas had shown him. Jonas simply did not get it – a boy who just sat there writing. Who liked to write. Not only liked it – Bo loved it, Jonas could tell from the rapt expression look on his face. Bo's father, the archaeologist who was so interested in China and the Emperor Qin Shi Huangdi, had taught him some of the Chinese characters which he knew. One day when Jonas arrived earlier than usual, Bo went straight back to a large, white sheet of paper and carried on writing, or drawing I suppose one should say, with a brush and ink as black as his Prince Valiant hair. Jonas stood and watched. They had arranged to go fishing up at Breisjøen – 'to catch the biggest swordfish in the world,' as Bo said – but Jonas could not bring himself to disturb his friend, so absorbed was he, sitting at his aunt's desk writing, or drawing. The sheet of paper bristled with weird brushstrokes; Jonas thought it looked like an octopus, with tentacles going all ways. 'What's that?' he whispered, afraid of breaking Bo's concentration. 'The Chinese sign for friendship,' Bo said. 'These four strokes in the middle, like four chambers, stand for "heart".'

Jonas thought it looked difficult. As difficult as true friendship, Bo said. Writing and reality went hand in hand.

Bo picked up a new sheet of paper, wrote the word again. Slowly but surely, better than his previous attempt. This time the character looked more like a woman doing a pirouette with arms outstretched. Jonas stood looking over Bo's shoulder, watching as the brush was drawn, moist and black, over the white paper, seeing the lovely, damp pattern which took shape. He marvelled at the movements, it was like a dance, except that it was executed with a brush. 'Why are you doing it again?' Jonas asked. Bo looked more like a Chinese than ever before. 'Because I'm practising friendship, or something that's more than friendship,' Bo said and suddenly glanced up at him with a penetrating look in his eye that Jonas had never seen before. 'Here, you can have it,' he said and handed the paper to Jonas.

So Jonas was prepared, and yet not, when they were playing up at Badedammen one day, just before Bo was due to go back to America. The day was sultry; they got caught in a sudden hail shower. 'Somebody's getting married in heaven,' Bo cried delightedly and did a pirouette with arms outstretched. Jonas knew where they could take shelter, he ran ahead to a small tunnel through which the stream from Steinbruvannet was channelled underneath the road and down to Badedammen. They could barely stand upright in the square concrete pipe, but at least they didn't get their feet wet – the stream only ran down the very centre of the pipe. They were in a secret chamber.

Outside the hail hammered down. Jonas listened to the lovely, pattering sound mingling with the purling of the stream. Big, white pearls sprayed down and bounced away. Within a couple of minutes the stream was almost white. 'A farewell present from me,' Bo said with a smile, fiddling with the chain around his neck.

Jonas was not sure whether it was this hail shower which caused some sort of membrane to burst. At any rate this was when it happened. A moment which branded itself into him. The hail abruptly stopped and the sun came out, bathing everything in a golden light. They heard the loud drone of an engine. Across the patch of sky visible from the tunnel mouth glided a light plane, white with red stripes, like a giant butterfly. At that same moment Jonas became aware that something was happening to Bo. Jonas stood there and watched a person unfold. Bo turned slowly to face him and was someone else. One turn and everything had changed. He was she. And she put her arms around him and hugged him, embraced him in the true sense of the word, wrapped her arms around him, and Jonas felt embarrassed and pleased and confused and happy all at once, as if lots of conflicting emotions were being juggled about inside him and kept in the air at the same time.

'I'll never forget you,' Bo said, she said, close against him and smelling of marshmallows.

Jonas felt a lump in his throat and a pressure behind his eyes, but he bit his lip, swallowed again and again.

'I love you,' she said, in such a way and such a tone that ever afterwards, when Jonas heard those words uttered, in a song, in a film, or even in a soap opera, he would remember that moment.

Jonas was lost for words. Outside the hailstones were melting in the sun, sparkling like tiny crystals. He wanted to stay there holding, being held by, this girl for the rest of his life. He wanted her to juggle him into a unified whole. And when she finally let go of him, and he let go of her, he knew that from then on he would always be looking for a girl like Bo. And maybe that was why he had to wait so long. Because girls like Bo, who practised writing the sign for love while pretending that it was the sign for friendship, did not exactly grow on trees. Who knows, Jonas thought, they could be as rare on Earth as Vegans.

Margrete was, however, just such a girl. And she too went away and left him. But he waited. He did not know that he was waiting, but he waited patiently till she returned. After Margrete died he met Kamala Varma.

One day towards the close of the millennium, while Jonas Wergeland was still in prison, Kamala Varma walked into the office of her talented and experienced agent in Holland Park Avenue in London and laid the manuscript of her new novel on his desk. 'You won't regret having put your faith in me,' she said.

As the book's title – *The Tree of Love* – suggested, it was a love story. Kamala Varma had been writing for a long time; as she said later in interviews, she had always written. She enjoyed great international respect as a social-anthropologist, but she had also published a couple of novels which had been well received in the English-speaking world; for, although she was a Norwegian citizen and had even written a controversial biographical novel in almost flawless Norwegian – and that despite the Hindi of her childhood – English was her natural first language. But nothing in these earlier works of fiction could have prepared anyone, not even her clever agent, for the impact of the story she had now delivered.

The British publishers knew a good thing when they saw it; they could tell right away that this was something special. Bidding for the rights was unusually fast and furious and the publisher who won the auction – to everyone's satisfaction the same house which had published her previous books – had not thrown away its money. Unlike Harald Hardråde, Kamala Varma really did conquer England and thereafter the rest of the world. When the novel came out it was instantly welcomed by ecstatic, nigh on infatuated reviewers and readers who had apparently been waiting for, not to say yearning for, such a story for decades. Within just two years *The Tree of Love* had been translated into over forty languages. Suddenly everybody wanted a piece of Kamala Varma: the press, television, this body and that, and all of them at the same time. She was interviewed everywhere, she was invited to appear eve-rywhere, she was discussed everywhere. There was a period when her name cropped up in every corner of the information society, from Hammerfest to Santiago de Chile.

That Kamala Varma survived that first wave of hysteria, the huge spate of publicity which can inundate and all but drown anyone who achieves inter-national success, was due not so much to her own level-headedness as to the book itself. Because *The Tree of Love* was – in the words of one reviewer – the sort of story which no one could explain. 'It is a book that strikes straight at the heart of everyone who opens it,' he wrote, 'a story which sinks in and lodges inside the reader like a vital organ.' Not long ago an American liter-ary critic declared that *The Tree of Love* had done as much for our view of love as Charles Darwin's *Origin of the Species* did for our view of mankind. And that may be true. Because readers of Kamala Varma's novel would like to believe that love can evolve, that love is not necessarily the same today as it was four thousand years ago. That it encompasses hitherto unknown pos-sibilities. So too with the heart, Kamala Varma said: the human heart also undergoes change.

Overnight Kamala Varma became a world-famous woman. And a rich woman. Even in Norway, that fortress of a country which had tried for so long to kick her out, she gained recognition. People would turn and stare blatantly at her in the smallest, most out-of-the-way places, and not merely because of her colour now. Around the time when Jonas was released from prison, Kamala started writing a new novel – one that went beyond *Victoria*, she told Jonas – while still travelling all over the world, promoting new trans-lations of *The Tree of Love*.

What did all this have to do with Jonas Wergeland? It had a great deal to do with Jonas Wergeland, even though Kamala Varma's love story was not about him in any way. You see, *The Tree of Love*, a work praised to the skies by people all over the world, was dedicated to Jonas Wergeland. At the bottom of one of the very first, perfectly white pages of the original, English edition were the words: 'For Jonas W.' That was all: 'For Jonas W.'

It took him a while to get round to asking her about it, it was almost as if he did not dare. One evening they were sitting by the fire in Kamala's flat in Russell Square in London, not far from where Virginia Woolf had lived. Neither of them had spoken for some minutes. Then he asked: 'Why did you do it?'

She had stroked the cross-shaped scar on his forehead with her finger and stared at him, as if surprised that he could not guess. 'Because it was meeting you, your otherness, that put the idea into my head,' she said.

Jonas thought about this again and again. What an honour. To have one's name appear as the first words, as a prelude to, a story which had been printed in millions of copies, a book which would be read by young people sitting on park benches who would turn their faces to the sky every now and again and make sacred vows to themselves. A book which men would buy and quote from at difficult moments, as they knelt before their wives. A book which old folk would read and weep over, because they realised that the insight which this novel had given them and which they had rejoiced over in their youth had been no more than a seed, one which had since sprouted and grown into a mighty tree inside them.

When Jonas got out of prison he became Kamala's secretary. He took care of the mass of paperwork associated with her books. She would have preferred to give him another title. 'You're not my secretary,' she said, 'you're my reader.' But Jonas insisted on being allowed to call himself a 'secretary' – a word which, in its original sense, meant a person entrusted with a secret, a private seal, and that was exactly what he wanted to be.

Jonas often took out *The Tree of Love* and ran a finger over his name printed on that page, as if he could not believe it was true. When everything was over, all that would be left of him would be this little dedication in a romantic novel. People would always wonder who 'Jonas W.' was – some people would even take the trouble to find out. He, Jonas Wergeland, who had held a whole nation in the palm of his hand, who had once ranked second only to the king, would wind up as a footnote, so to speak, in a love story. What a paradox. All his travails with television – only to be remembered because of a book.

The first time Jonas opened *The Tree of Love*, in prison, and saw those letters on the expanse of white at the very front of the novel, he found it hard to read what they said. The letters seemed to him to be shining, his name seemed to be shining. He sat with the book in his hands and knew that he had made the greatest discovery of his life, a discovery which redefined everything, truly expanded him, made him a new person.

So far I have not understood a thing, he thought. I need to go back to the very beginning.

Jan Kjærstad

The Seducer

Winner of the Nordic Prize for Literature 2001
Translated from the Norwegian by Barbara J. Haveland

Jonas Wergeland is a successful TV documentary producer and also something of God's gift to women, with balls of gold, as one newspaper puts it. One day he returns from the World's Fair in Seville and discovers his wife dead on the living-room floor. What follows is a quest to find the killer but more than that is a playful look at how our hero has arrived at this particular juncture in a life full of twists and turns.

This post-modernist Norwegian novel, an international bestseller and winner of Scandinavia's top literary award, the Nordic Prize, will have you on the edge of your seat, as Jan Kjærstad weaves his magic wand. Prepare to be seduced.

'An enormously accomplished and compelling novel by one of Scandinavia's outstanding contemporary writers. Barbara J. Haveland and Arcadia Books have performed a great service by giving us Kjærstad in English at last' – Paul Auster

'An irresistibly playful romp, by turns mischievous, manipulative, intellectual and bluntly sensual… hugely satisfying' – Ali Smith, *Books of the Year, TLS*

Price £8.99
ISBN: 19781905147014

Jan Kjærstad

The Conqueror

Translated from the Norwegian by Barbara J. Haveland

In the second volume of the trilogy about Jonas Wergeland, Jan Kjærstad's narrative enmeshes the reader even more closely not only in the life of one man, but also in that of an entire nation and its culture in the latter half of the twentieth century.

Jonas Wergeland has been convicted of the murder of his wife Margrete. What brought Norway's darling to this end? A professor has been set the task of writing the biography of the once celebrated, now notorious, television personality; in doing so he hopes to solve the riddle of Jonas Wergeland's success and downfall. But the sheer volume of material on his subject is so daunting that the professor finds himself completely bogged down, at a loss as to how to proceed, until the evening when a mysterious stranger knocks on his door, and offers to tell him stories which will help him unravel the strands of Wergeland's life.

'Go on, try something different – this brick of a book is witty, savage, elegant and strange – and comes from Norway's leading writer' – *The Times*

'One of the most important novels you'll read this year' – *Sunday Herald*

Price £8.99
ISBN: 9781905147380